Archie in MERMAID SERVICE!

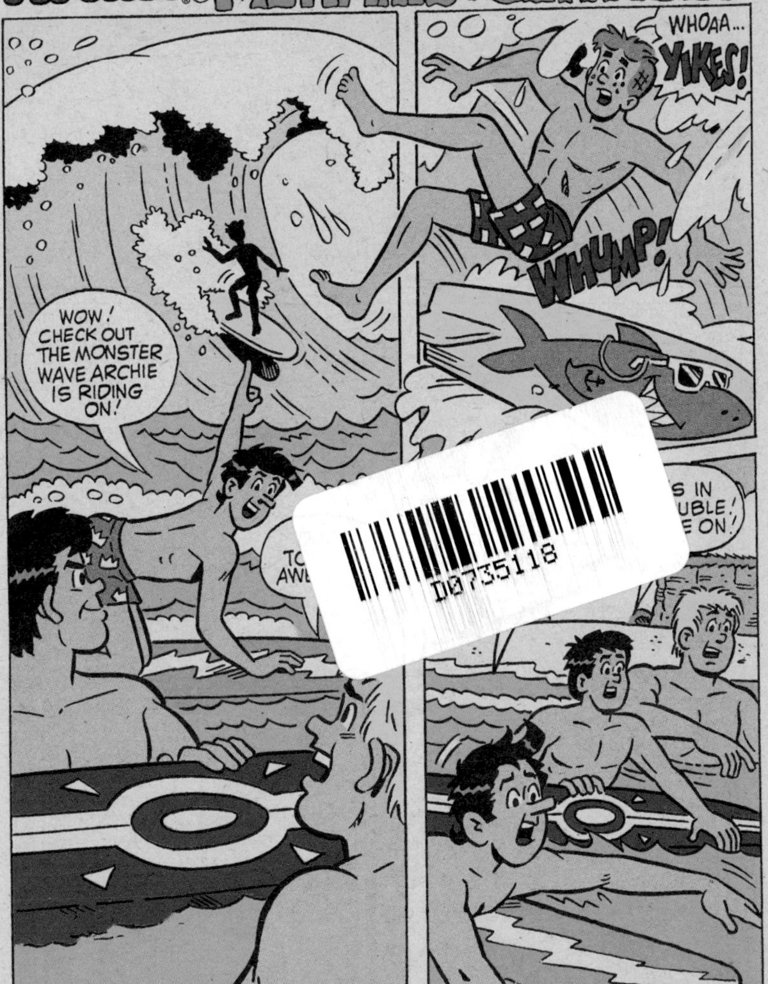
WOW! CHECK OUT THE MONSTER WAVE ARCHIE IS RIDING ON!
WHOAA... YIKES!
WHUMP!

Script & Pencils: **Bill Golliher** Inks: **Rudy Lapick** Letters: **Bill Yoshida** Colors: **Barry Grossman**
Editor-In-Chief: **Victor Gorelick** President: **Mike Pellerito** Publisher: **Jon Goldwater**

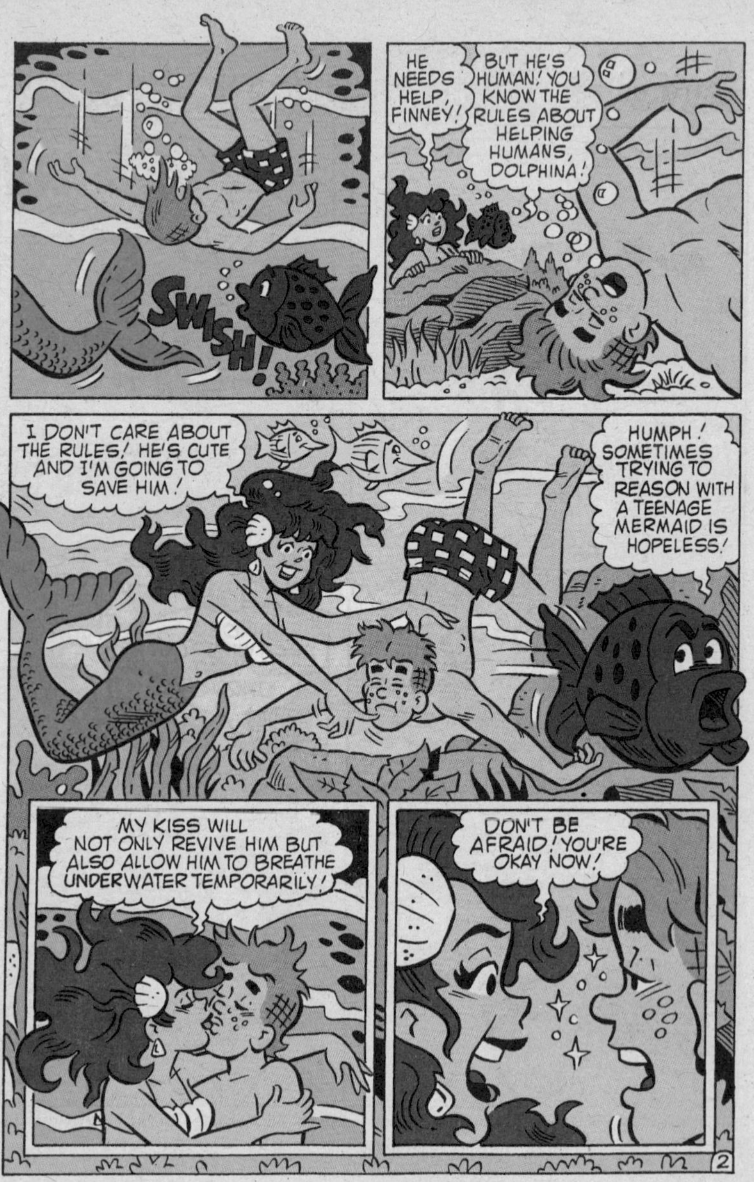
SWISH!
HE NEEDS HELP, FINNEY!
BUT HE'S HUMAN! YOU KNOW THE RULES ABOUT HELPING HUMANS, DOLPHINA!
I DON'T CARE ABOUT THE RULES! HE'S CUTE AND I'M GOING TO SAVE HIM!
HUMPH! SOMETIMES TRYING TO REASON WITH A TEENAGE MERMAID IS HOPELESS!
MY KISS WILL NOT ONLY REVIVE HIM BUT ALSO ALLOW HIM TO BREATHE UNDERWATER TEMPORARILY!
DON'T BE AFRAID! YOU'RE OKAY NOW!
2

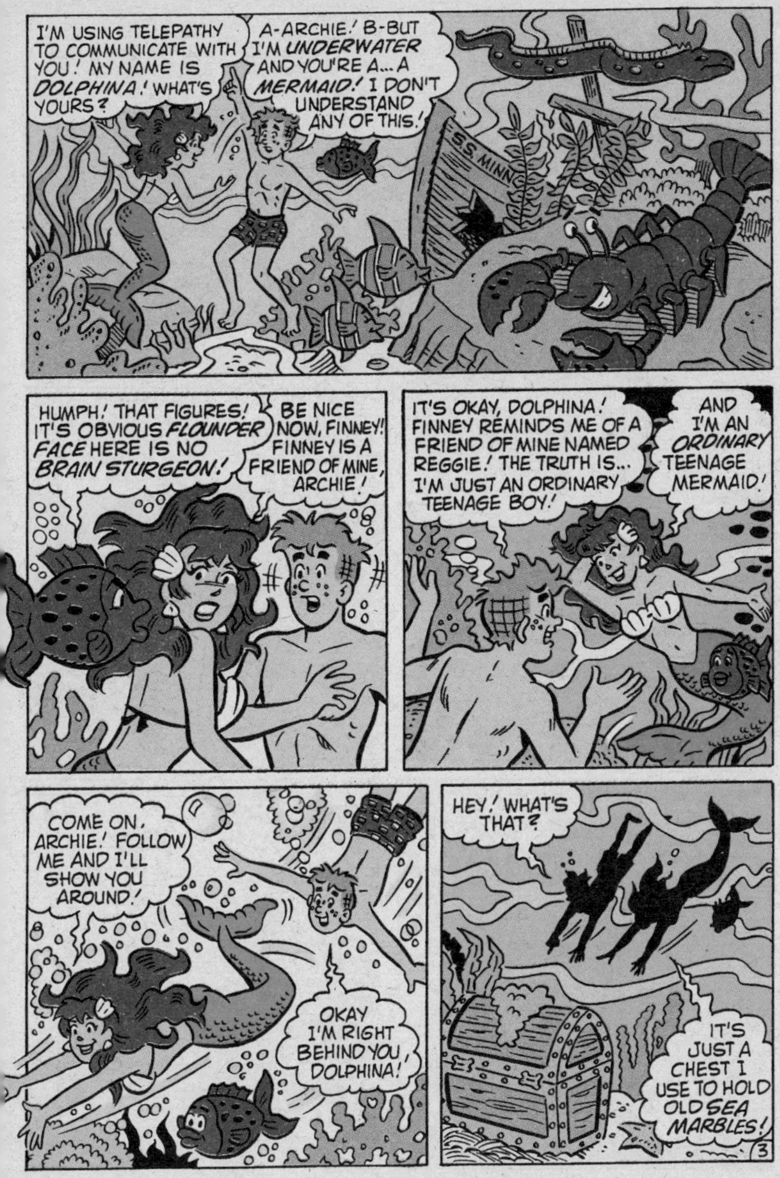
I'M USING TELEPATHY TO COMMUNICATE WITH YOU! MY NAME IS DOLPHINA! WHAT'S YOURS?
A-ARCHIE! B-BUT I'M UNDERWATER AND YOU'RE A... A MERMAID! I DON'T UNDERSTAND ANY OF THIS!
S.S. MINN
HUMPH! THAT FIGURES! IT'S OBVIOUS FLOUNDER FACE HERE IS NO BRAIN STURGEON!
BE NICE NOW, FINNEY! FINNEY IS A FRIEND OF MINE, ARCHIE!
IT'S OKAY, DOLPHINA! FINNEY REMINDS ME OF A FRIEND OF MINE NAMED REGGIE! THE TRUTH IS... I'M JUST AN ORDINARY TEENAGE BOY!
AND I'M AN ORDINARY TEENAGE MERMAID!
COME ON, ARCHIE! FOLLOW ME AND I'LL SHOW YOU AROUND!
OKAY I'M RIGHT BEHIND YOU, DOLPHINA!
HEY! WHAT'S THAT?
IT'S JUST A CHEST I USE TO HOLD OLD SEA MARBLES!
3

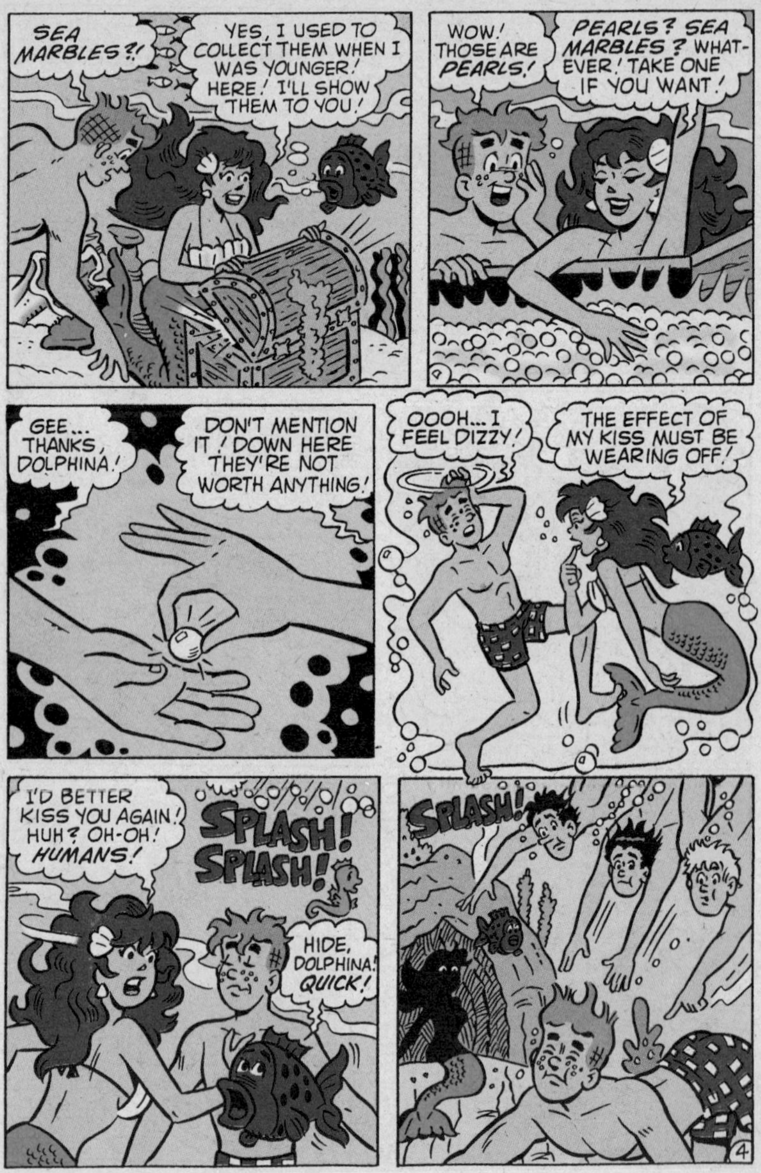
SEA MARBLES?!
YES, I USED TO COLLECT THEM WHEN I WAS YOUNGER! HERE! I'LL SHOW THEM TO YOU!
WOW! THOSE ARE PEARLS!
PEARLS? SEA MARBLES? WHATEVER! TAKE ONE IF YOU WANT!
GEE... THANKS, DOLPHINA!
DON'T MENTION IT! DOWN HERE THEY'RE NOT WORTH ANYTHING!
OOOH... I FEEL DIZZY!
THE EFFECT OF MY KISS MUST BE WEARING OFF!
I'D BETTER KISS YOU AGAIN! HUH? OH-OH! HUMANS!
SPLASH! SPLASH!
HIDE, DOLPHINA! QUICK!
SPLASH!
4

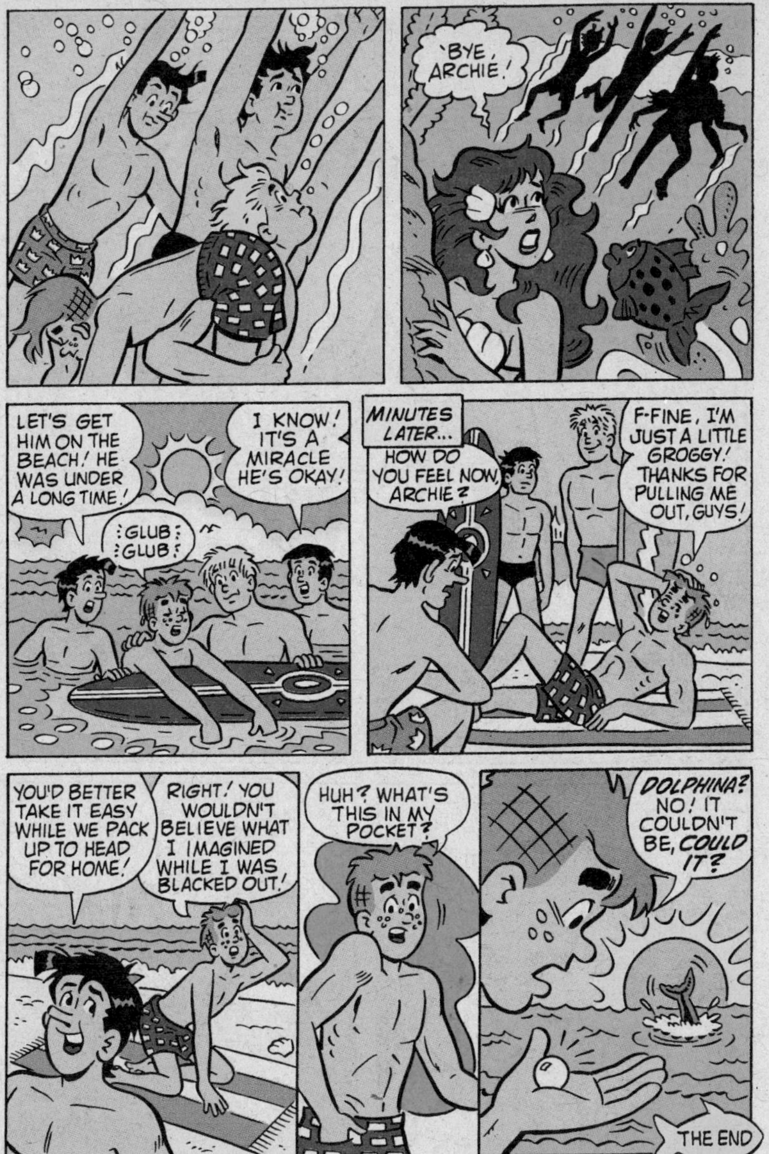

'BYE, ARCHIE!
LET'S GET HIM ON THE BEACH! HE WAS UNDER A LONG TIME!
I KNOW! IT'S A MIRACLE HE'S OKAY!
GLUB GLUB
MINUTES LATER...
HOW DO YOU FEEL NOW, ARCHIE?
F-FINE, I'M JUST A LITTLE GROGGY! THANKS FOR PULLING ME OUT, GUYS!
YOU'D BETTER TAKE IT EASY WHILE WE PACK UP TO HEAD FOR HOME!
RIGHT! YOU WOULDN'T BELIEVE WHAT I IMAGINED WHILE I WAS BLACKED OUT!
HUH? WHAT'S THIS IN MY POCKET?
DOLPHINA? NO! IT COULDN'T BE, COULD IT?
THE END

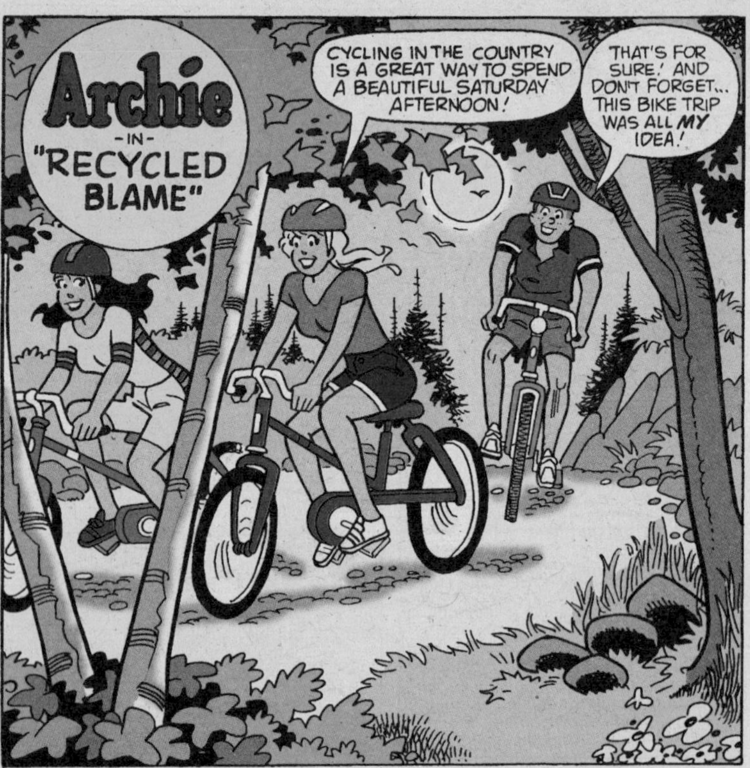
Archie
-IN-
"RECYCLED BLAME"
CYCLING IN THE COUNTRY IS A GREAT WAY TO SPEND A BEAUTIFUL SATURDAY AFTERNOON!
THAT'S FOR SURE! AND DON'T FORGET... THIS BIKE TRIP WAS ALL *MY* IDEA!

Script: George Gladir / Pencils: Stan Goldberg / Inks: Bob Smith / Letters: Bill Yoshida / Colors: Barry Grossman

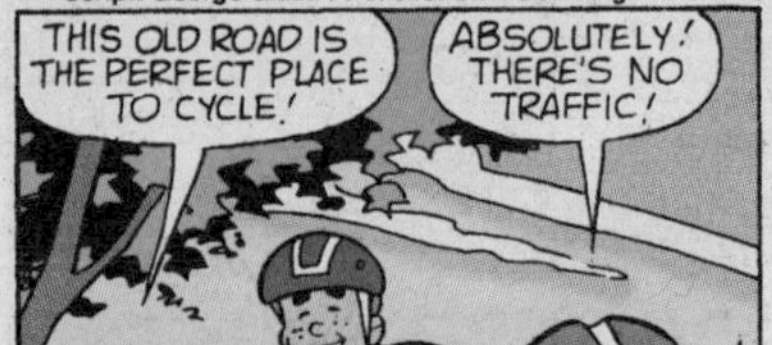
THIS OLD ROAD IS THE PERFECT PLACE TO CYCLE!
ABSOLUTELY! THERE'S NO TRAFFIC!

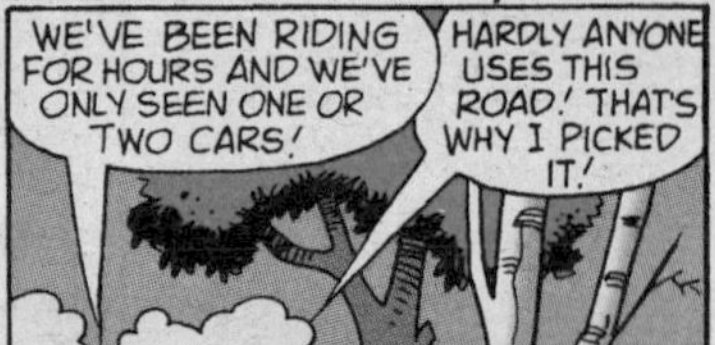
WE'VE BEEN RIDING FOR HOURS AND WE'VE ONLY SEEN ONE OR TWO CARS!
HARDLY ANYONE USES THIS ROAD! THAT'S WHY I PICKED IT!

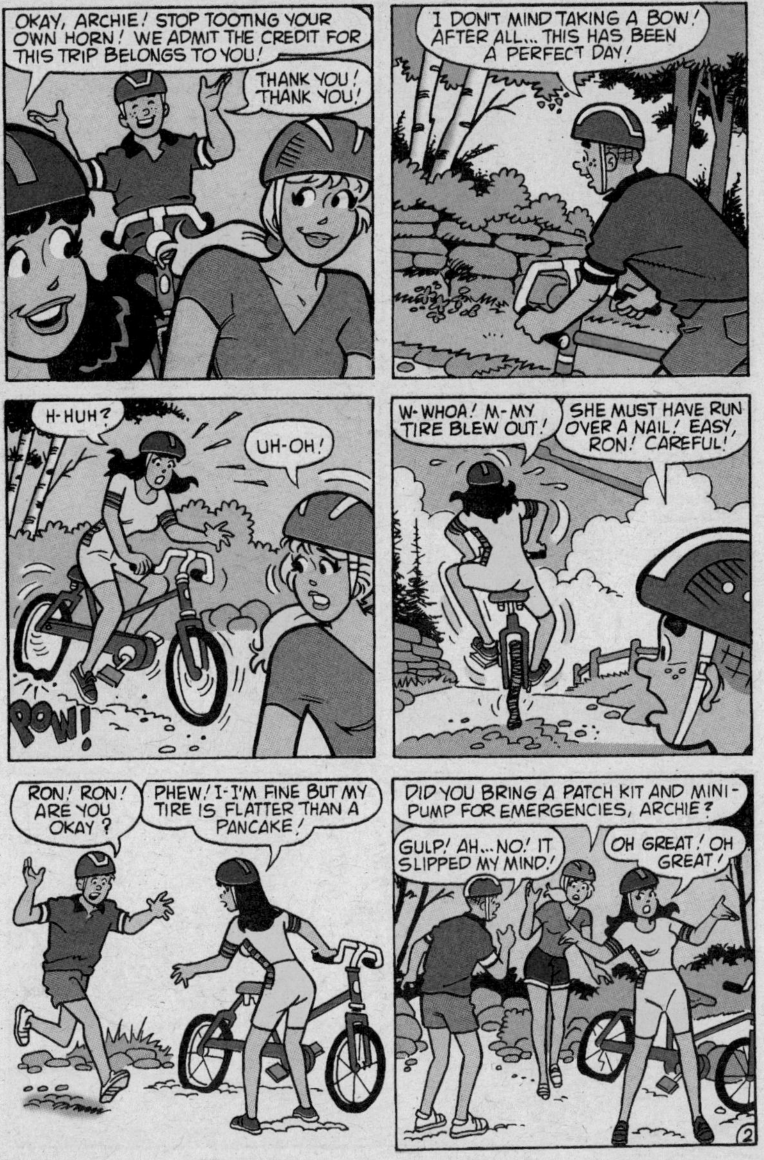

OKAY, ARCHIE! STOP TOOTING YOUR OWN HORN! WE ADMIT THE CREDIT FOR THIS TRIP BELONGS TO YOU!
THANK YOU! THANK YOU!
I DON'T MIND TAKING A BOW! AFTER ALL... THIS HAS BEEN A PERFECT DAY!
H-HUH?
UH-OH!
POW!
W-WHOA! M-MY TIRE BLEW OUT!
SHE MUST HAVE RUN OVER A NAIL! EASY, RON! CAREFUL!
RON! RON! ARE YOU OKAY?
PHEW! I-I'M FINE BUT MY TIRE IS FLATTER THAN A PANCAKE!
DID YOU BRING A PATCH KIT AND MINI-PUMP FOR EMERGENCIES, ARCHIE?
GULP! AH... NO! IT SLIPPED MY MIND!
OH GREAT! OH GREAT!
2

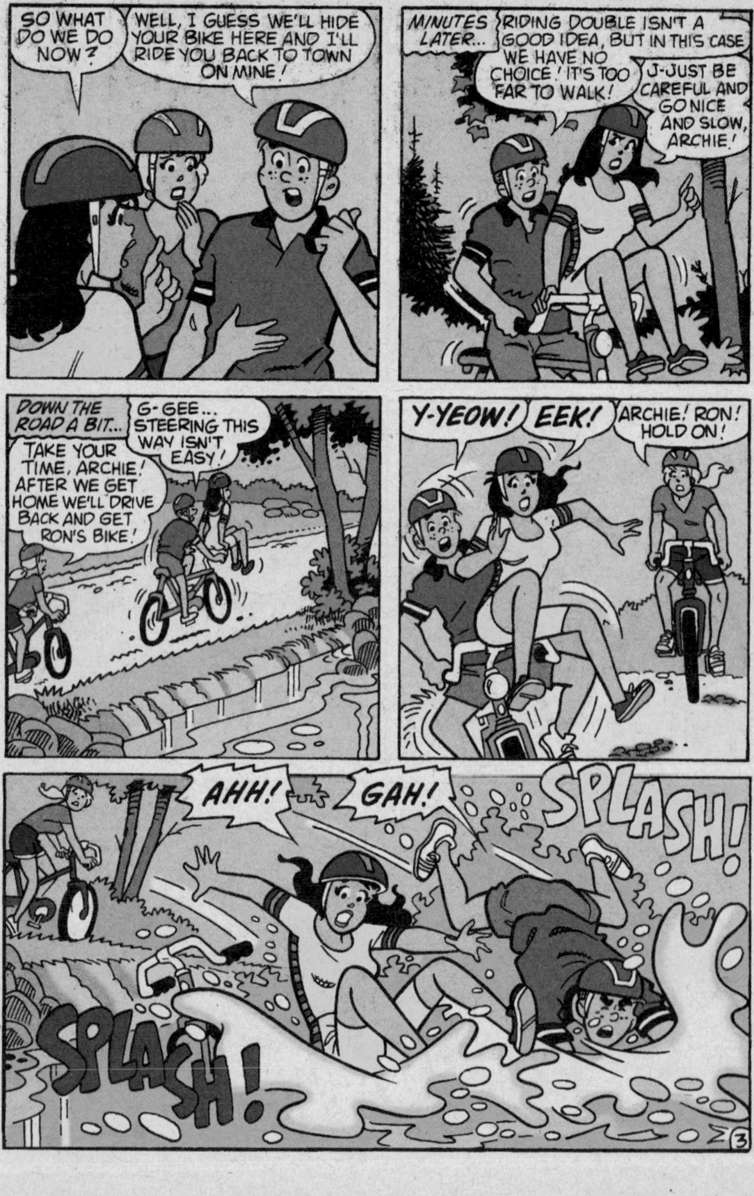
SO WHAT DO WE DO NOW?
WELL, I GUESS WE'LL HIDE YOUR BIKE HERE AND I'LL RIDE YOU BACK TO TOWN ON MINE!
MINUTES LATER...
RIDING DOUBLE ISN'T A GOOD IDEA, BUT IN THIS CASE WE HAVE NO CHOICE! IT'S TOO FAR TO WALK!
J-JUST BE CAREFUL AND GO NICE AND SLOW, ARCHIE!
DOWN THE ROAD A BIT...
G-GEE... STEERING THIS WAY ISN'T EASY!
TAKE YOUR TIME, ARCHIE! AFTER WE GET HOME WE'LL DRIVE BACK AND GET RON'S BIKE!
Y-YEOW!
EEK!
ARCHIE! RON! HOLD ON!
AHH!
GAH!
SPLASH!
SPLASH!
3

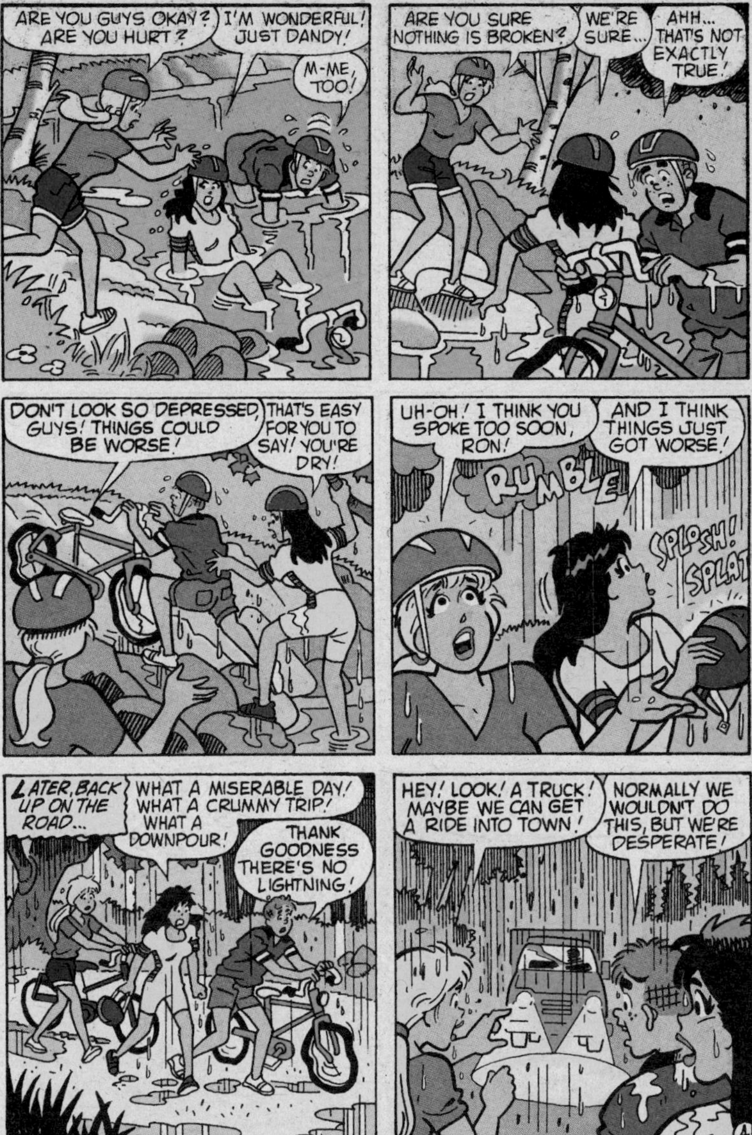
ARE YOU GUYS OKAY? ARE YOU HURT?
I'M WONDERFUL! JUST DANDY!
M-ME, TOO!
ARE YOU SURE NOTHING IS BROKEN?
WE'RE SURE...
AHH... THAT'S NOT EXACTLY TRUE!
DON'T LOOK SO DEPRESSED, GUYS! THINGS COULD BE WORSE!
THAT'S EASY FOR YOU TO SAY! YOU'RE DRY!
UH-OH! I THINK YOU SPOKE TOO SOON, RON!
AND I THINK THINGS JUST GOT WORSE!
RUMBLE
SPLOSH!
SPLAT
LATER, BACK UP ON THE ROAD...
WHAT A MISERABLE DAY! WHAT A CRUMMY TRIP! WHAT A DOWNPOUR!
THANK GOODNESS THERE'S NO LIGHTNING!
HEY! LOOK! A TRUCK! MAYBE WE CAN GET A RIDE INTO TOWN!
NORMALLY WE WOULDN'T DO THIS, BUT WE'RE DESPERATE!
4

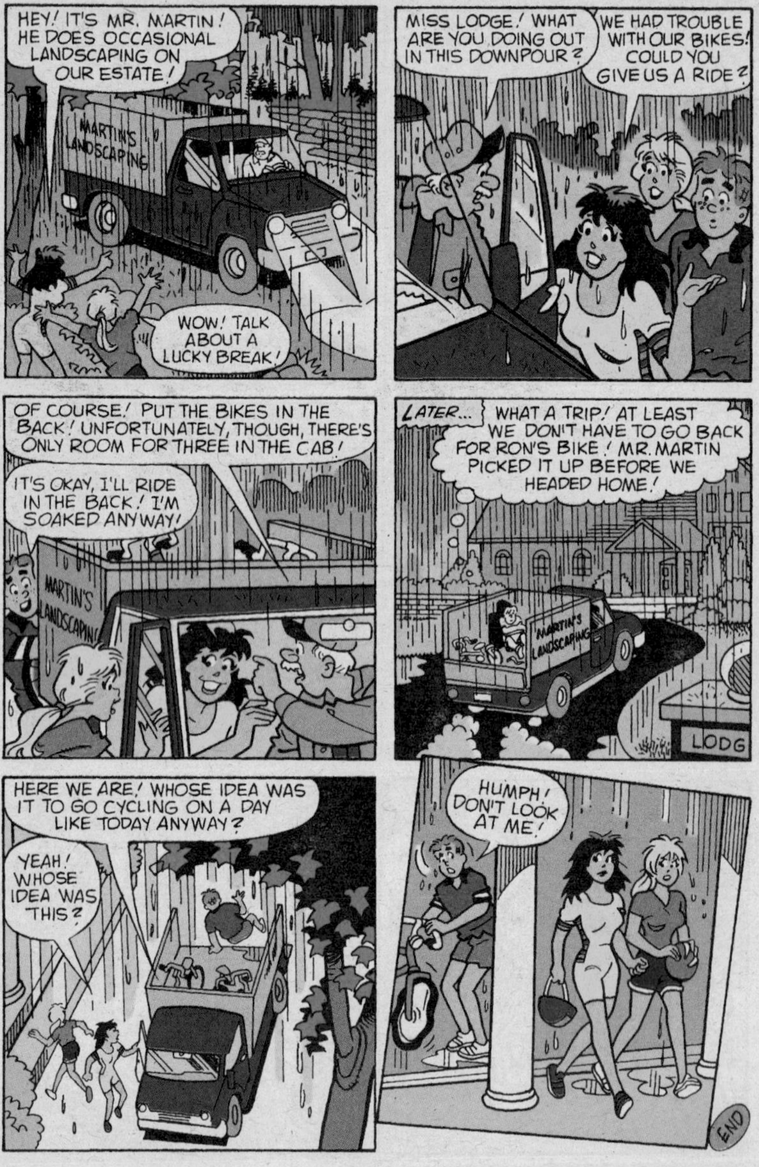
HEY! IT'S MR. MARTIN! HE DOES OCCASIONAL LANDSCAPING ON OUR ESTATE!
MARTIN'S LANDSCAPING
WOW! TALK ABOUT A LUCKY BREAK!
MISS LODGE! WHAT ARE YOU DOING OUT IN THIS DOWNPOUR?
WE HAD TROUBLE WITH OUR BIKES! COULD YOU GIVE US A RIDE?
OF COURSE! PUT THE BIKES IN THE BACK! UNFORTUNATELY, THOUGH, THERE'S ONLY ROOM FOR THREE IN THE CAB!
IT'S OKAY, I'LL RIDE IN THE BACK! I'M SOAKED ANYWAY!
MARTIN'S LANDSCAPIN
LATER...
WHAT A TRIP! AT LEAST WE DON'T HAVE TO GO BACK FOR RON'S BIKE! MR. MARTIN PICKED IT UP BEFORE WE HEADED HOME!
MARTIN'S LANDSCAPING
LODG
HERE WE ARE! WHOSE IDEA WAS IT TO GO CYCLING ON A DAY LIKE TODAY ANYWAY?
YEAH! WHOSE IDEA WAS THIS?
HUMPH! DON'T LOOK AT ME!
END

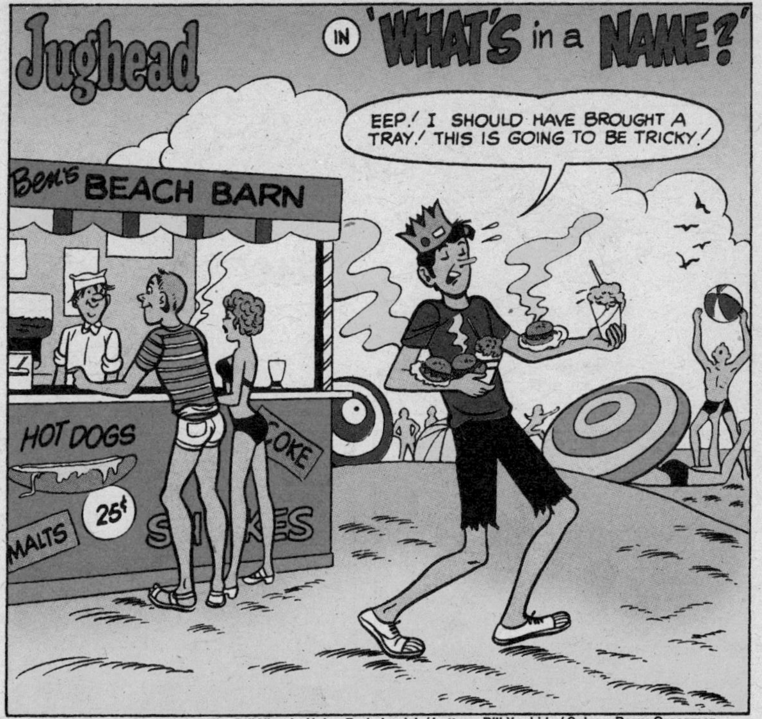
Jughead
IN 'WHAT'S in a NAME?'
EEP! I SHOULD HAVE BROUGHT A TRAY! THIS IS GOING TO BE TRICKY!
Ben's BEACH BARN
HOT DOGS
25¢
MALTS
COKE

Script: George Gladir / Pencils: Bill Vigoda / Inks: Rudy Lapick / Letters: Bill Yoshida / Colors: Barry Grossman

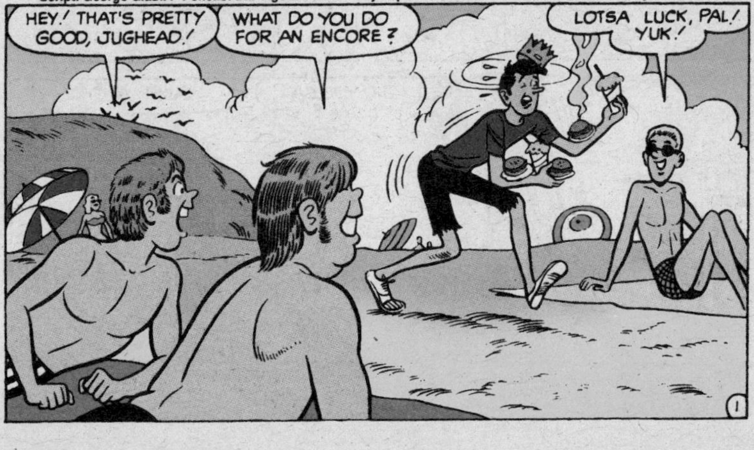
HEY! THAT'S PRETTY GOOD, JUGHEAD!
WHAT DO YOU DO FOR AN ENCORE?
LOTSA LUCK, PAL! YUK!

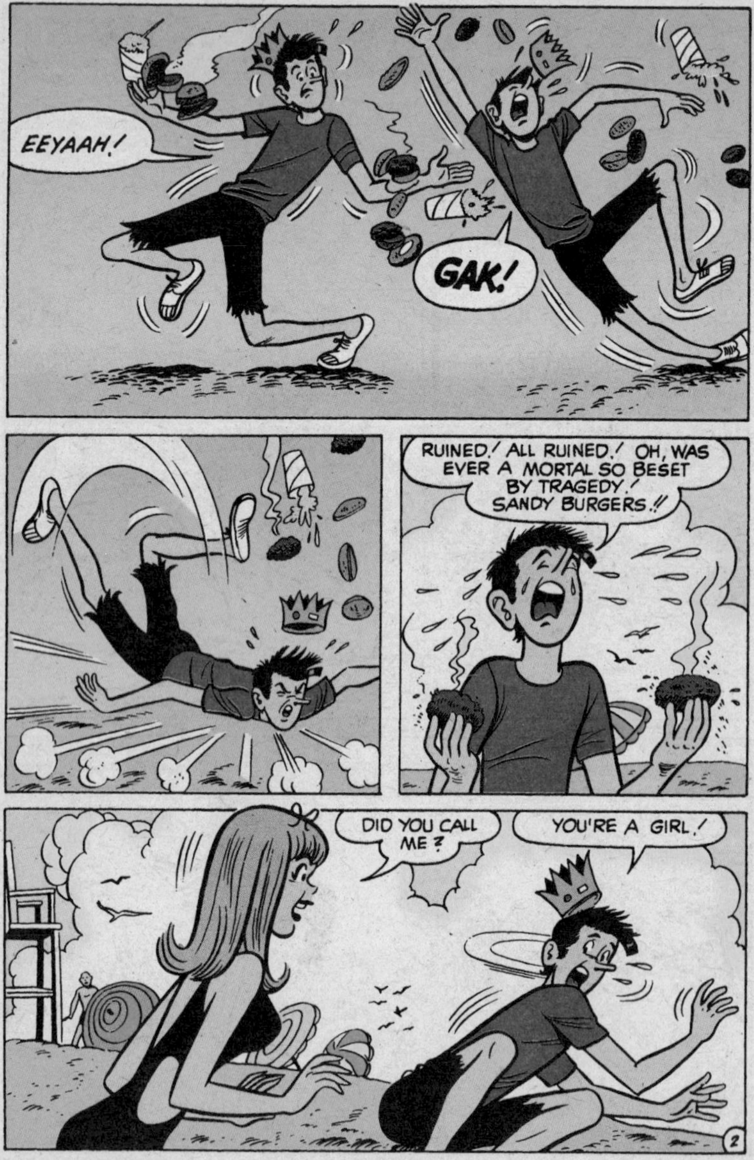
EEYAAH!
GAK!
RUINED! ALL RUINED! OH, WAS EVER A MORTAL SO BESET BY TRAGEDY! SANDY BURGERS!!
DID YOU CALL ME?
YOU'RE A GIRL!
2

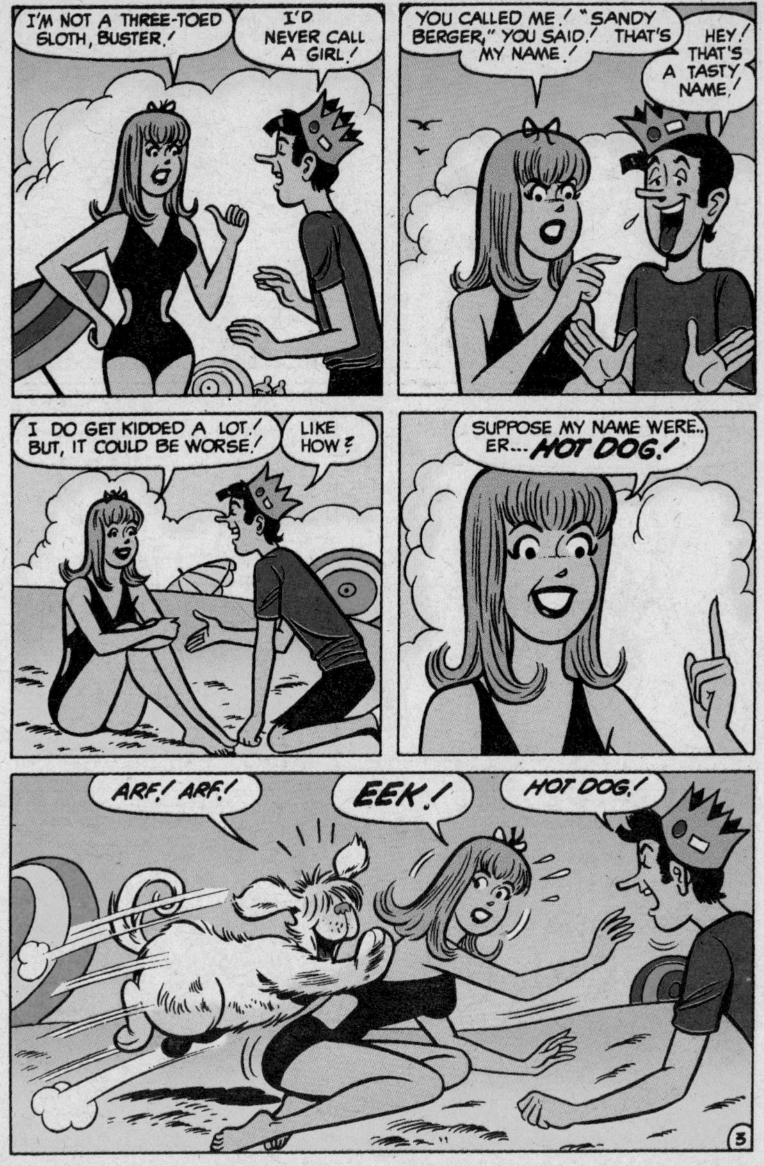

I'M NOT A THREE-TOED SLOTH, BUSTER!
I'D NEVER CALL A GIRL!
YOU CALLED ME! "SANDY BERGER," YOU SAID! THAT'S MY NAME!
HEY! THAT'S A TASTY NAME!
I DO GET KIDDED A LOT! BUT, IT COULD BE WORSE!
LIKE HOW?
SUPPOSE MY NAME WERE.. ER... HOT DOG!
ARF! ARF!
EEK!
HOT DOG!
3

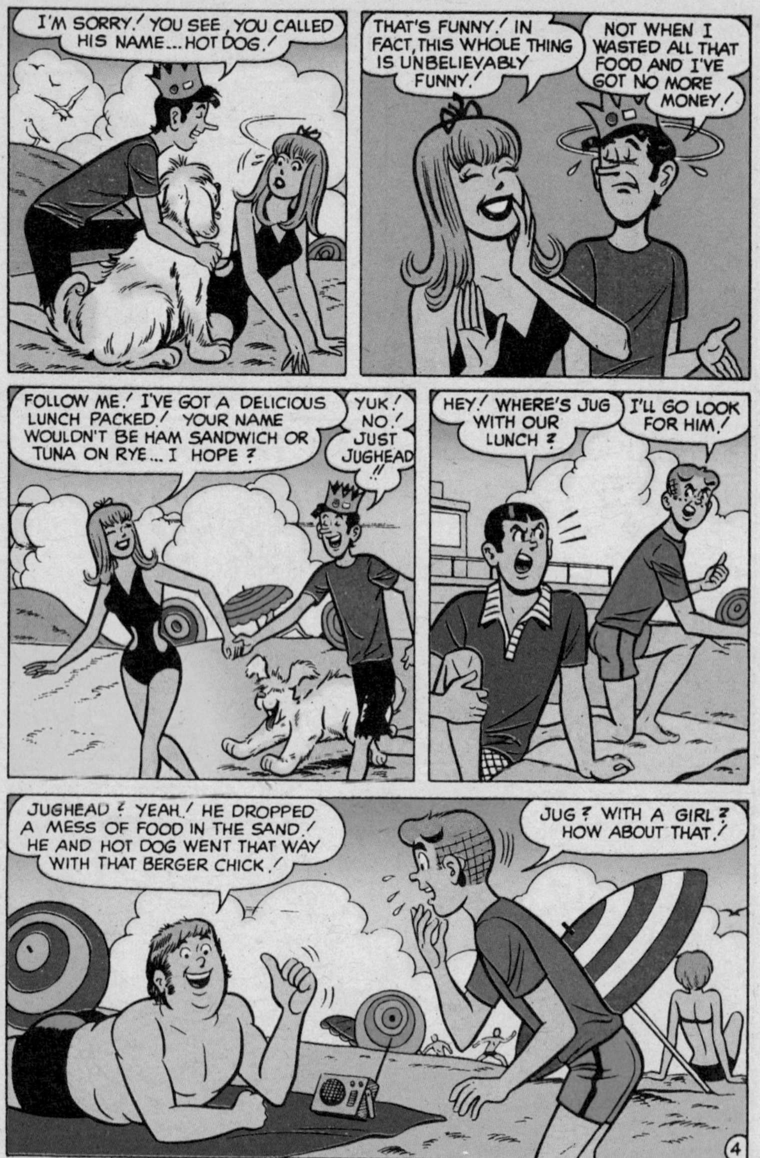
I'M SORRY! YOU SEE, YOU CALLED HIS NAME... HOT DOG!
THAT'S FUNNY! IN FACT, THIS WHOLE THING IS UNBELIEVABLY FUNNY!
NOT WHEN I WASTED ALL THAT FOOD AND I'VE GOT NO MORE MONEY!
FOLLOW ME! I'VE GOT A DELICIOUS LUNCH PACKED! YOUR NAME WOULDN'T BE HAM SANDWICH OR TUNA ON RYE... I HOPE?
YUK! NO! JUST JUGHEAD!!
HEY! WHERE'S JUG WITH OUR LUNCH?
I'LL GO LOOK FOR HIM!
JUGHEAD? YEAH! HE DROPPED A MESS OF FOOD IN THE SAND! HE AND HOT DOG WENT THAT WAY WITH THAT BERGER CHICK!
JUG? WITH A GIRL? HOW ABOUT THAT!
4

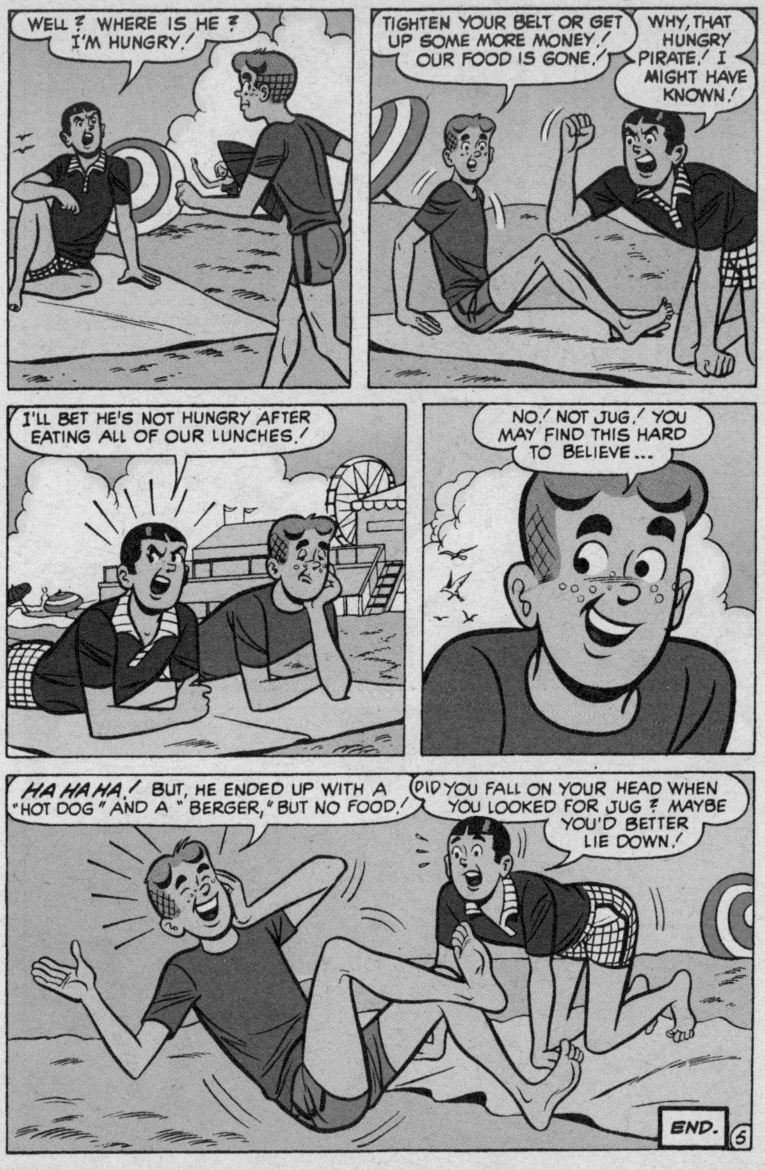
WELL? WHERE IS HE? I'M HUNGRY!
TIGHTEN YOUR BELT OR GET UP SOME MORE MONEY! OUR FOOD IS GONE!
WHY, THAT HUNGRY PIRATE! I MIGHT HAVE KNOWN!
I'LL BET HE'S NOT HUNGRY AFTER EATING ALL OF OUR LUNCHES!
NO! NOT JUG! YOU MAY FIND THIS HARD TO BELIEVE...
HA HA HA! BUT, HE ENDED UP WITH A "HOT DOG" AND A "BERGER," BUT NO FOOD!
DID YOU FALL ON YOUR HEAD WHEN YOU LOOKED FOR JUG? MAYBE YOU'D BETTER LIE DOWN!
END.
5

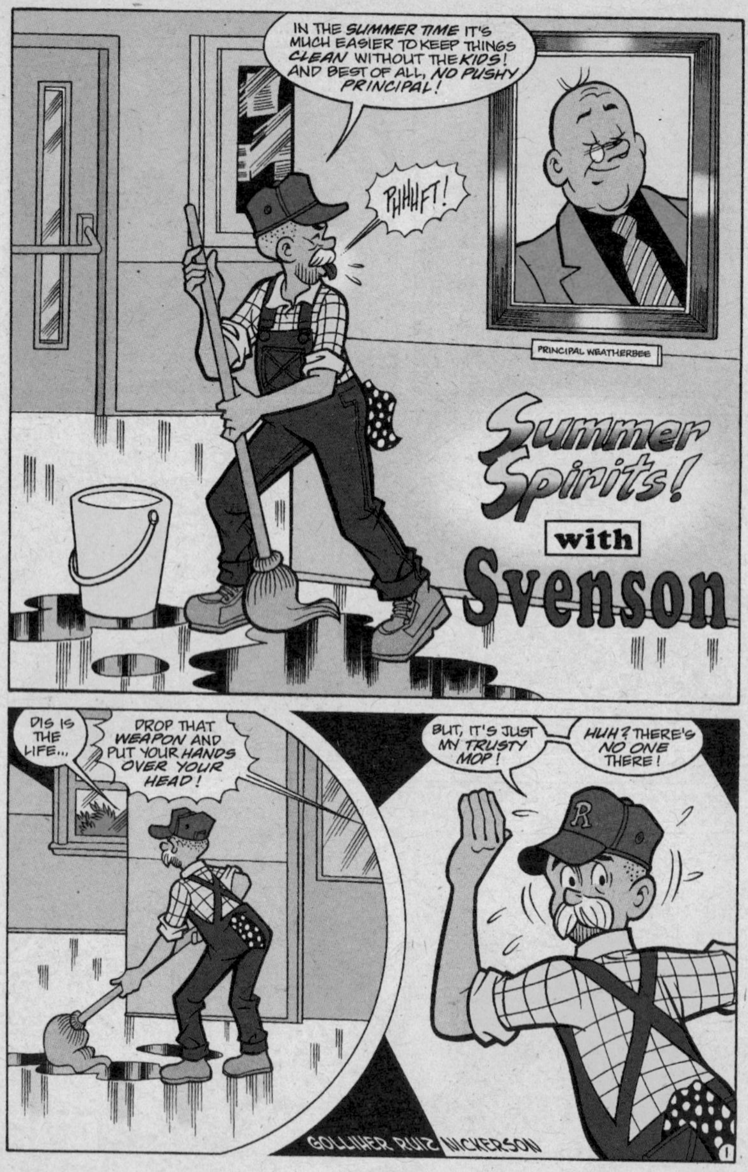
IN THE SUMMER TIME IT'S MUCH EASIER TO KEEP THINGS CLEAN WITHOUT THE KIDS! AND BEST OF ALL, NO PUSHY PRINCIPAL!
PHHHFT!
PRINCIPAL WEATHERBEE
Summer Spirits! with Svenson
DIS IS THE LIFE...
DROP THAT WEAPON AND PUT YOUR HANDS OVER YOUR HEAD!
BUT, IT'S JUST MY TRUSTY MOP!
HUH? THERE'S NO ONE THERE!
GOLLIHER RUIZ NICKERSON
1

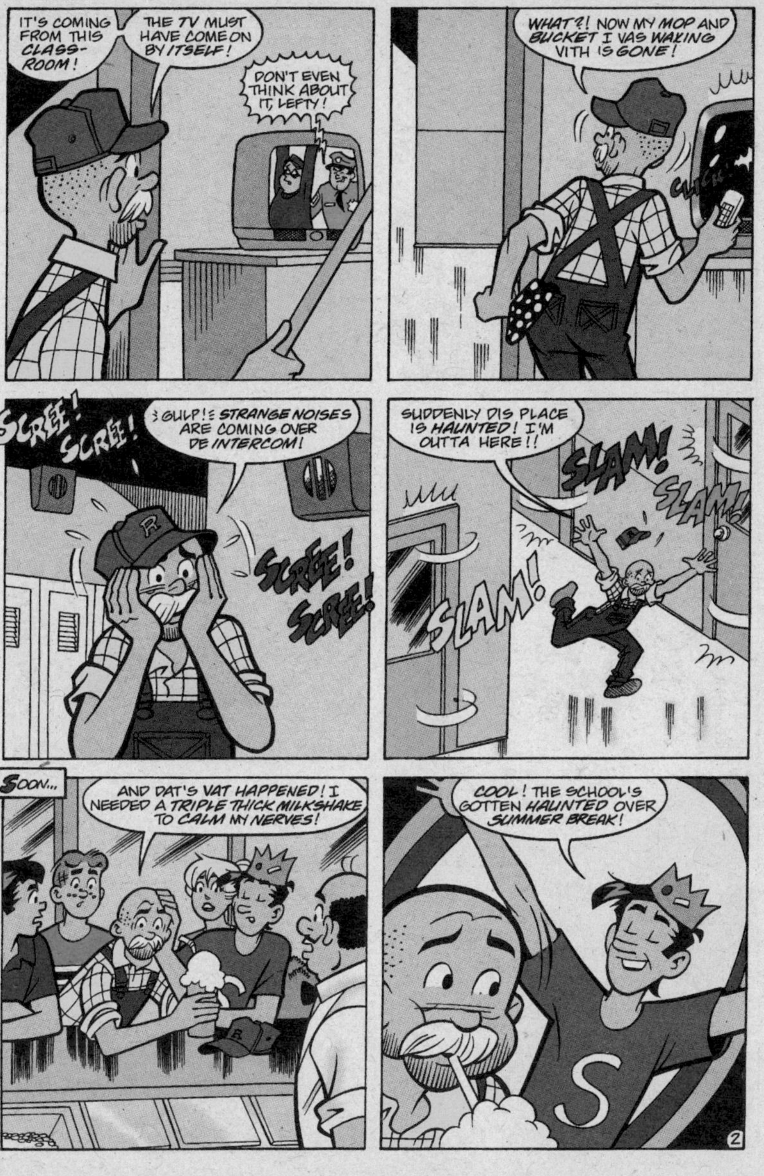
IT'S COMING FROM THIS CLASS-ROOM!
THE TV MUST HAVE COME ON BY ITSELF!
DON'T EVEN THINK ABOUT IT, LEFTY!
WHAT?! NOW MY MOP AND BUCKET I VAS WAKING VITH IS GONE!
SCREE! SCREE!
GULP! STRANGE NOISES ARE COMING OVER DE INTERCOM!
SCREE! SCREE!
SUDDENLY DIS PLACE IS HAUNTED! I'M OUTTA HERE!!
SLAM! SLAM! SLAM!
SOON...
AND DAT'S VAT HAPPENED! I NEEDED A TRIPLE THICK MILKSHAKE TO CALM MY NERVES!
COOL! THE SCHOOL'S GOTTEN HAUNTED OVER SUMMER BREAK!
2

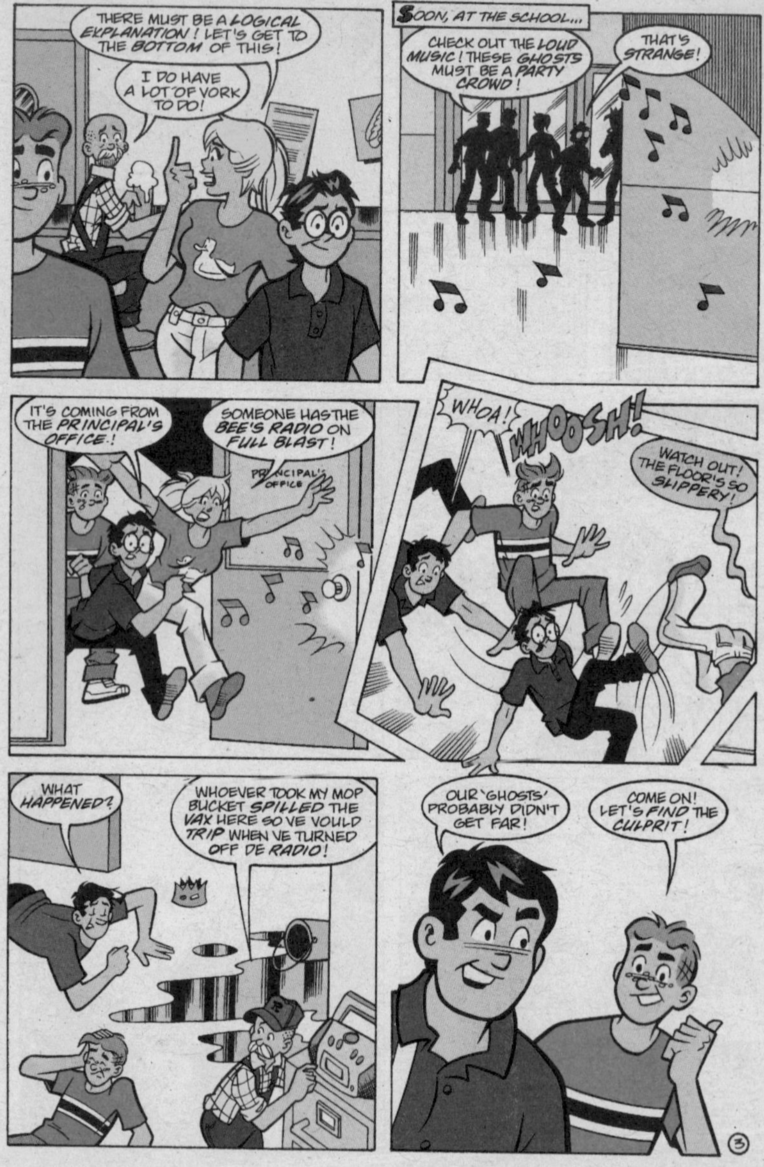
THERE MUST BE A LOGICAL EXPLANATION! LET'S GET TO THE BOTTOM OF THIS!
I DO HAVE A LOT OF VORK TO DO!
SOON, AT THE SCHOOL...
CHECK OUT THE LOUD MUSIC! THESE GHOSTS MUST BE A PARTY CROWD!
THAT'S STRANGE!
IT'S COMING FROM THE PRINCIPAL'S OFFICE!
SOMEONE HAS THE BEE'S RADIO ON FULL BLAST!
PRINCIPAL'S OFFICE
WHOA!
WHOOSH!
WATCH OUT! THE FLOOR'S SO SLIPPERY!
WHAT HAPPENED?
WHOEVER TOOK MY MOP BUCKET SPILLED THE VAX HERE SO VE VOULD TRIP WHEN VE TURNED OFF DE RADIO!
OUR 'GHOSTS' PROBABLY DIDN'T GET FAR!
COME ON! LET'S FIND THE CULPRIT!

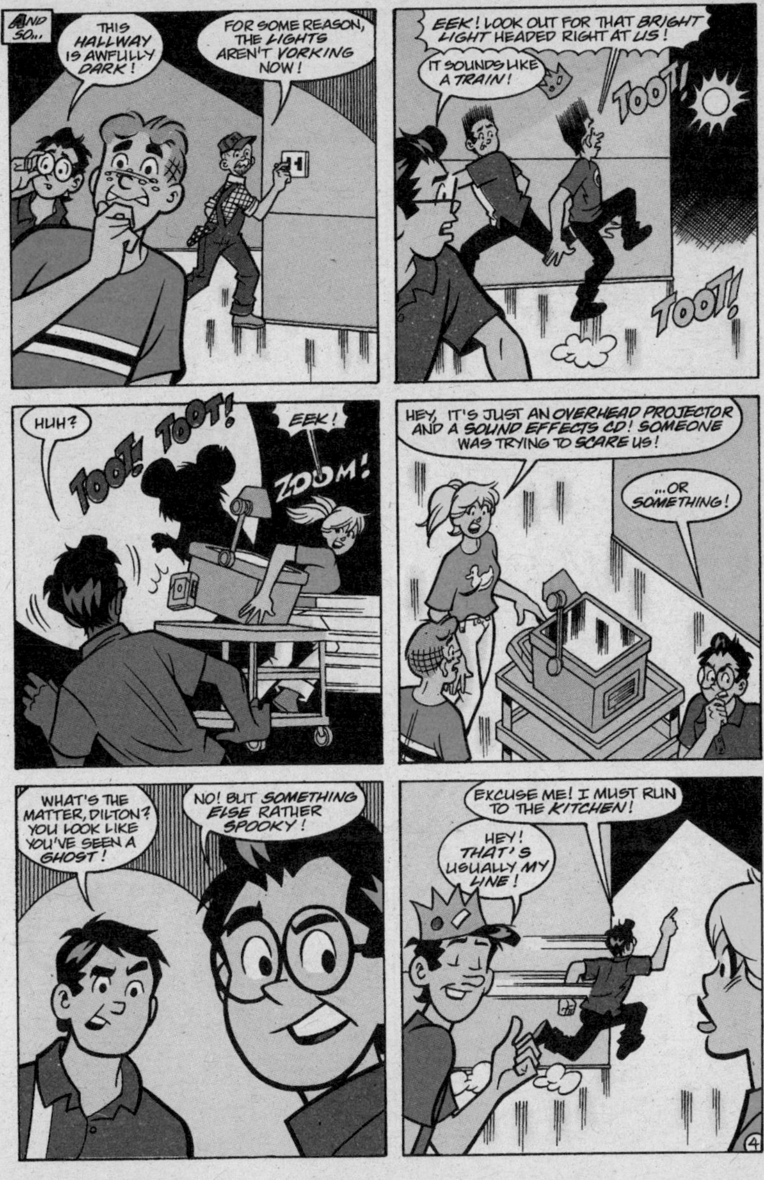
AND SO...
THIS HALLWAY IS AWFULLY DARK!
FOR SOME REASON, THE LIGHTS AREN'T VORKING NOW!
EEK! LOOK OUT FOR THAT BRIGHT LIGHT HEADED RIGHT AT US!
IT SOUNDS LIKE A TRAIN!
TOOT!
TOOT!
HUH?
TOOT! TOOT!
EEK!
ZOOM!
HEY, IT'S JUST AN OVERHEAD PROJECTOR AND A SOUND EFFECTS CD! SOMEONE WAS TRYING TO SCARE US!
...OR SOMETHING!
WHAT'S THE MATTER, DILTON? YOU LOOK LIKE YOU'VE SEEN A GHOST!
NO! BUT SOMETHING ELSE RATHER SPOOKY!
EXCUSE ME! I MUST RUN TO THE KITCHEN!
HEY! THAT'S USUALLY MY LINE!
4

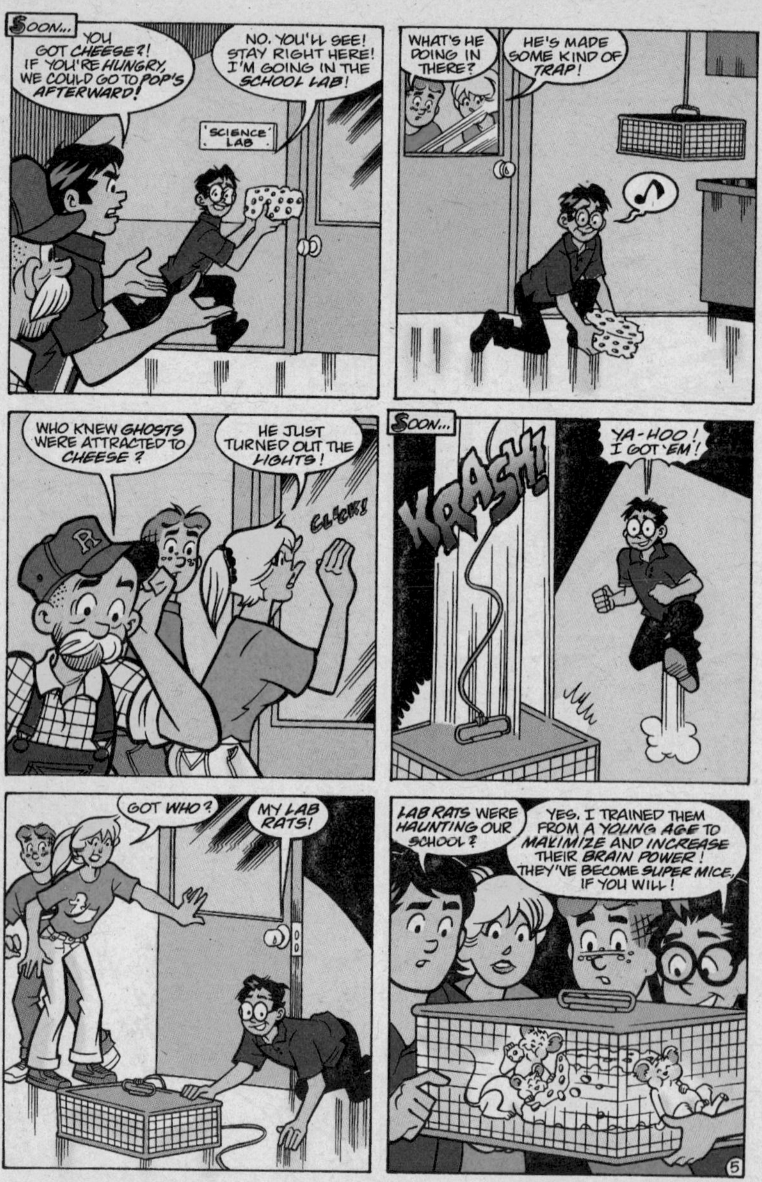
SOON...
YOU GOT CHEESE?! IF YOU'RE HUNGRY, WE COULD GO TO POP'S AFTERWARD!
NO. YOU'LL SEE! STAY RIGHT HERE! I'M GOING IN THE SCHOOL LAB!
SCIENCE LAB
WHAT'S HE DOING IN THERE?
HE'S MADE SOME KIND OF TRAP!
WHO KNEW GHOSTS WERE ATTRACTED TO CHEESE?
HE JUST TURNED OUT THE LIGHTS!
CLICK!
SOON...
KRASH!
YA-HOO! I GOT 'EM!
GOT WHO?
MY LAB RATS!
LAB RATS WERE HAUNTING OUR SCHOOL?
YES. I TRAINED THEM FROM A YOUNG AGE TO MAXIMIZE AND INCREASE THEIR BRAIN POWER! THEY'VE BECOME SUPER MICE, IF YOU WILL!

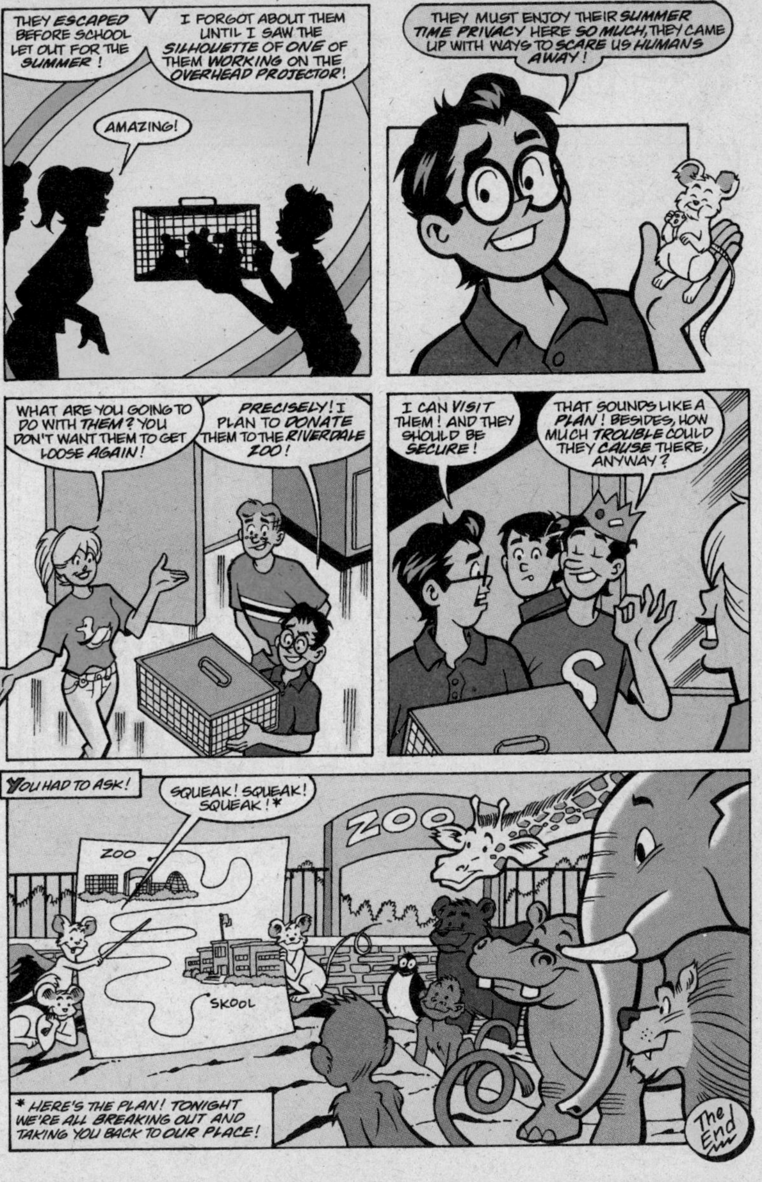
THEY ESCAPED BEFORE SCHOOL LET OUT FOR THE SUMMER!
I FORGOT ABOUT THEM UNTIL I SAW THE SILHOUETTE OF ONE OF THEM WORKING ON THE OVERHEAD PROJECTOR!
AMAZING!
THEY MUST ENJOY THEIR SUMMER TIME PRIVACY HERE SO MUCH, THEY CAME UP WITH WAYS TO SCARE US HUMANS AWAY!
WHAT ARE YOU GOING TO DO WITH THEM? YOU DON'T WANT THEM TO GET LOOSE AGAIN!
PRECISELY! I PLAN TO DONATE THEM TO THE RIVERDALE ZOO!
I CAN VISIT THEM! AND THEY SHOULD BE SECURE!
THAT SOUNDS LIKE A PLAN! BESIDES, HOW MUCH TROUBLE COULD THEY CAUSE THERE, ANYWAY?
YOU HAD TO ASK!
SQUEAK! SQUEAK! SQUEAK!*
ZOO
ZOO
SKOOL
* HERE'S THE PLAN! TONIGHT WE'RE ALL BREAKING OUT AND TAKING YOU BACK TO OUR PLACE!
The End

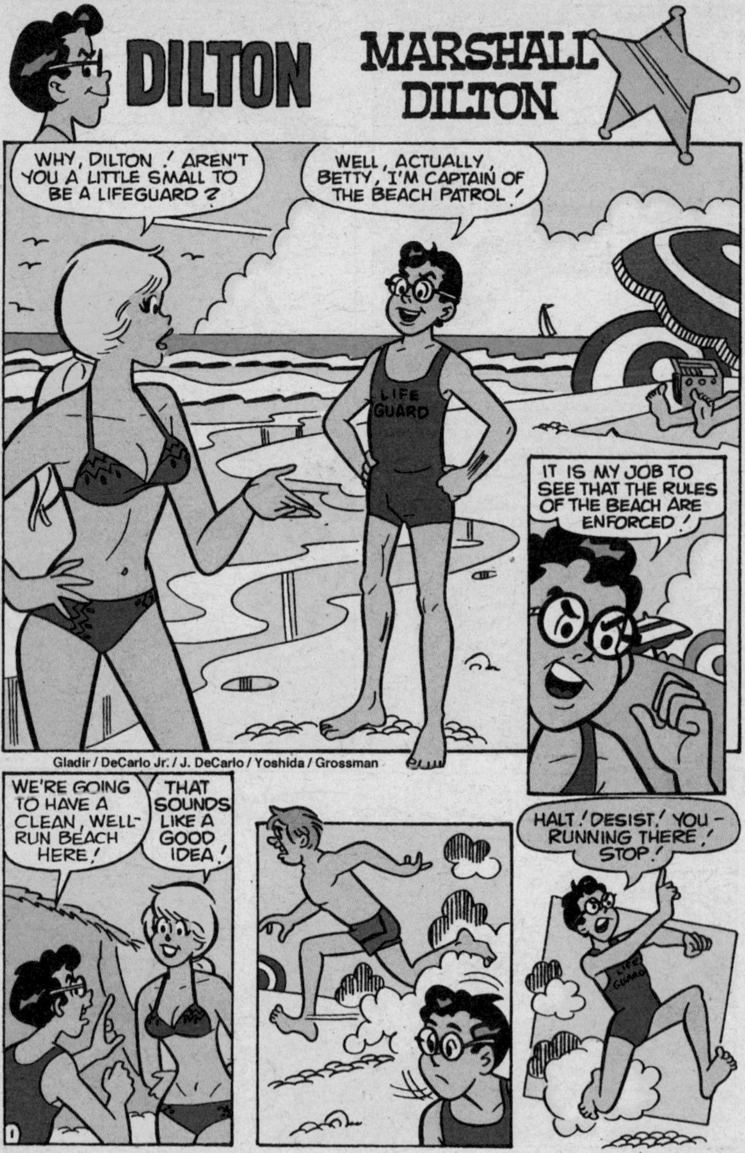
DILTON
MARSHALL DILTON
WHY, DILTON! AREN'T YOU A LITTLE SMALL TO BE A LIFEGUARD?
WELL, ACTUALLY, BETTY, I'M CAPTAIN OF THE BEACH PATROL!
LIFE GUARD
IT IS MY JOB TO SEE THAT THE RULES OF THE BEACH ARE ENFORCED!
Gladir / DeCarlo Jr. / J. DeCarlo / Yoshida / Grossman
WE'RE GOING TO HAVE A CLEAN, WELL-RUN BEACH HERE!
THAT SOUNDS LIKE A GOOD IDEA!
1
HALT! DESIST! YOU - RUNNING THERE! STOP!
LIFE GUARD

YOU TALKIN' TO ME, LITTLE GUY?

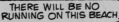

THERE WILL BE NO RUNNING ON THIS BEACH!

NO RUNNING? ARE YOU CRAZY?

NOT ALLOWING RUNNING ON A BEACH IS LIKE NOT ALLOWING BALL PLAYING IN A GYM!

I'M NOT IN CHARGE OF A GYM!

A BEACH IS FOR FUN AND FROLIC! IT'S FOR THE PURSUIT OF PLEASURE!

FROM NOW ON, YOU'LL PURSUE IT AT A WALK!

IF I SEE YOU RUNNING, I'LL HAVE YOU BANISHED FROM THE BEACH!

HAH! YOU AND WHAT ARMY?

DOES THAT ANSWER YOUR QUESTION?

EEP!

GRRRR!

2

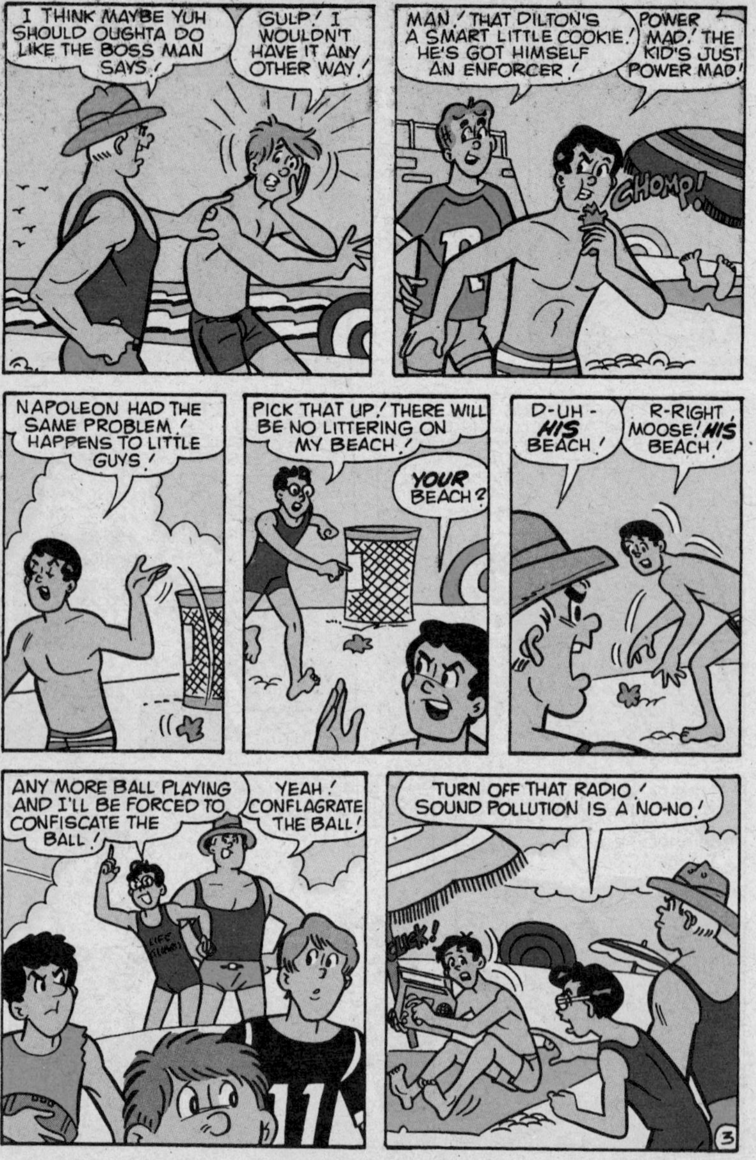
I THINK MAYBE YUH SHOULD OUGHTA DO LIKE THE BOSS MAN SAYS!
GULP! I WOULDN'T HAVE IT ANY OTHER WAY!
MAN! THAT DILTON'S A SMART LITTLE COOKIE! HE'S GOT HIMSELF AN ENFORCER!
POWER MAD! THE KID'S JUST POWER MAD!
CHOMP!
NAPOLEON HAD THE SAME PROBLEM! HAPPENS TO LITTLE GUYS!
PICK THAT UP! THERE WILL BE NO LITTERING ON MY BEACH!
YOUR BEACH?
D-UH - HIS BEACH!
R-RIGHT, MOOSE! HIS BEACH!
ANY MORE BALL PLAYING AND I'LL BE FORCED TO CONFISCATE THE BALL!
YEAH! CONFLAGRATE THE BALL!
TURN OFF THAT RADIO! SOUND POLLUTION IS A NO-NO!
CLICK!
3

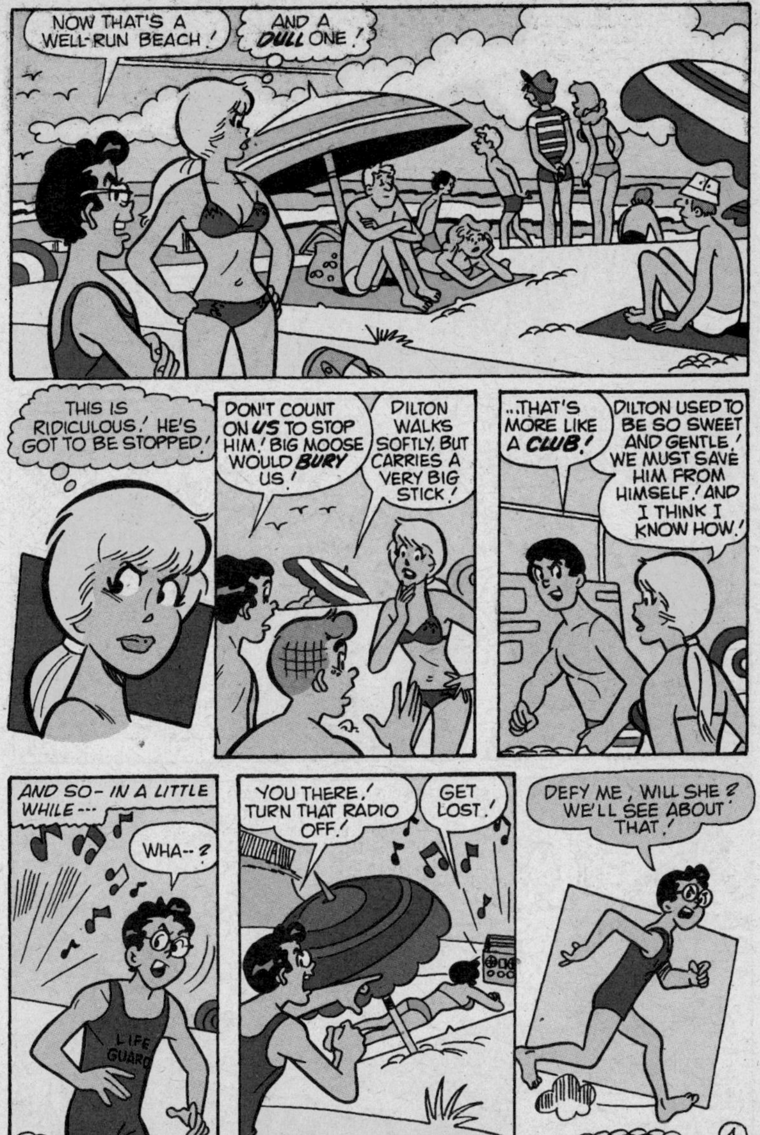
NOW THAT'S A WELL-RUN BEACH!
AND A DULL ONE!
THIS IS RIDICULOUS! HE'S GOT TO BE STOPPED!
DON'T COUNT ON US TO STOP HIM! BIG MOOSE WOULD BURY US!
DILTON WALKS SOFTLY, BUT CARRIES A VERY BIG STICK!
...THAT'S MORE LIKE A CLUB!
DILTON USED TO BE SO SWEET AND GENTLE! WE MUST SAVE HIM FROM HIMSELF! AND I THINK I KNOW HOW!
AND SO- IN A LITTLE WHILE---
WHA--?
LIFE GUARD
YOU THERE! TURN THAT RADIO OFF!
GET LOST!
DEFY ME, WILL SHE? WE'LL SEE ABOUT THAT!

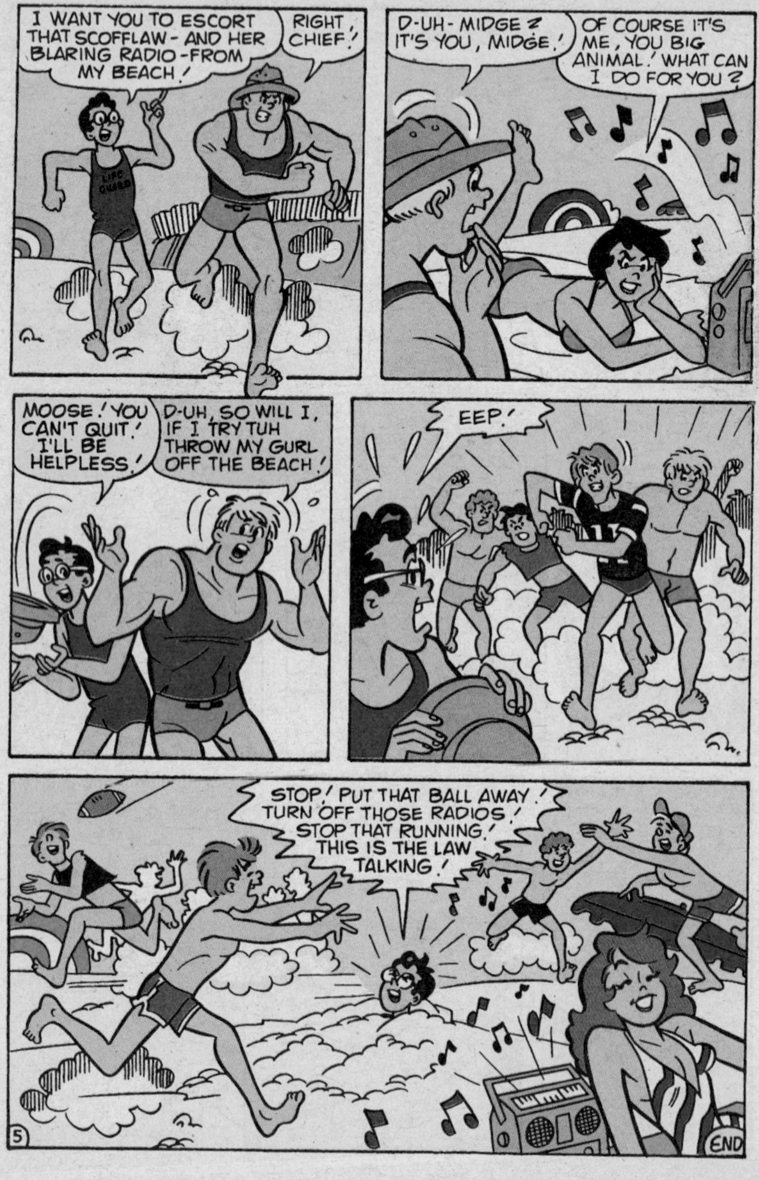
I WANT YOU TO ESCORT THAT SCOFFLAW - AND HER BLARING RADIO - FROM MY BEACH!
RIGHT, CHIEF!
LIFE GUARD
D-UH - MIDGE? IT'S YOU, MIDGE!
OF COURSE IT'S ME, YOU BIG ANIMAL! WHAT CAN I DO FOR YOU?
MOOSE! YOU CAN'T QUIT! I'LL BE HELPLESS!
D-UH, SO WILL I, IF I TRY TUH THROW MY GURL OFF THE BEACH!
EEP!
STOP! PUT THAT BALL AWAY! TURN OFF THOSE RADIOS! STOP THAT RUNNING! THIS IS THE LAW TALKING!
5
END

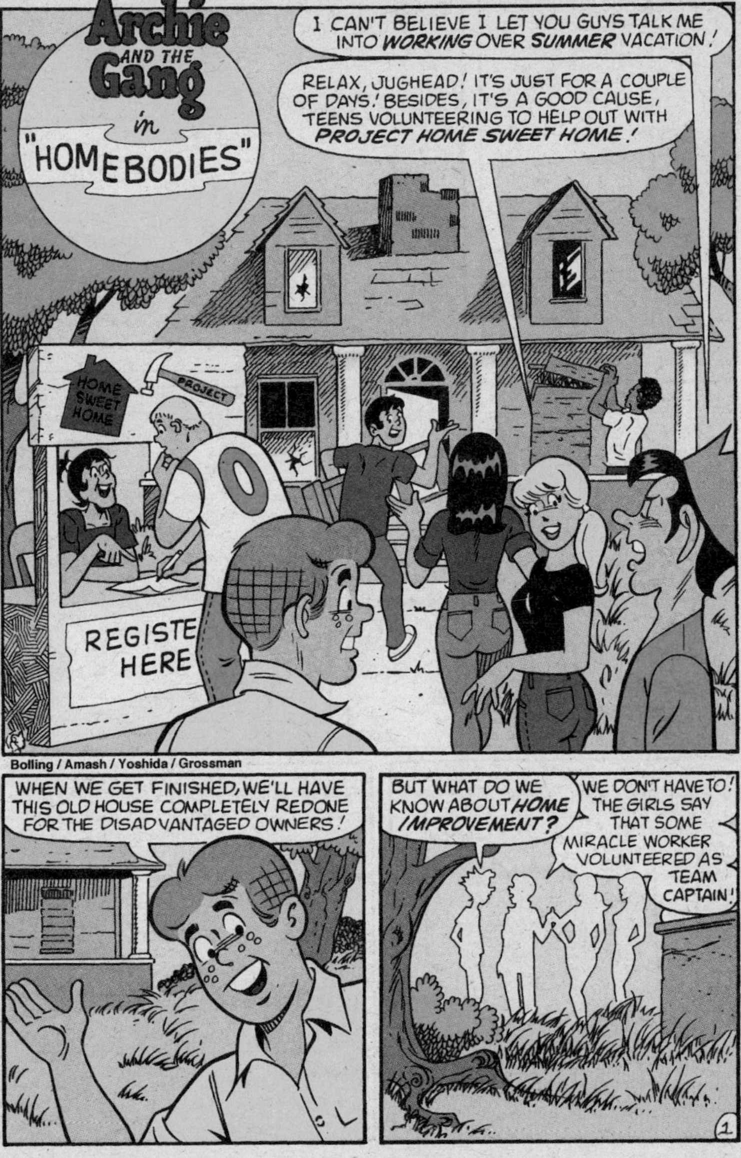
Archie AND THE Gang in
"HOMEBODIES"
I CAN'T BELIEVE I LET YOU GUYS TALK ME INTO WORKING OVER SUMMER VACATION!
RELAX, JUGHEAD! IT'S JUST FOR A COUPLE OF DAYS! BESIDES, IT'S A GOOD CAUSE, TEENS VOLUNTEERING TO HELP OUT WITH PROJECT HOME SWEET HOME!
HOME SWEET HOME
PROJECT
REGISTE HERE
Bolling / Amash / Yoshida / Grossman
WHEN WE GET FINISHED, WE'LL HAVE THIS OLD HOUSE COMPLETELY REDONE FOR THE DISADVANTAGED OWNERS!
BUT WHAT DO WE KNOW ABOUT HOME IMPROVEMENT?
WE DON'T HAVE TO! THE GIRLS SAY THAT SOME MIRACLE WORKER VOLUNTEERED AS TEAM CAPTAIN!
1

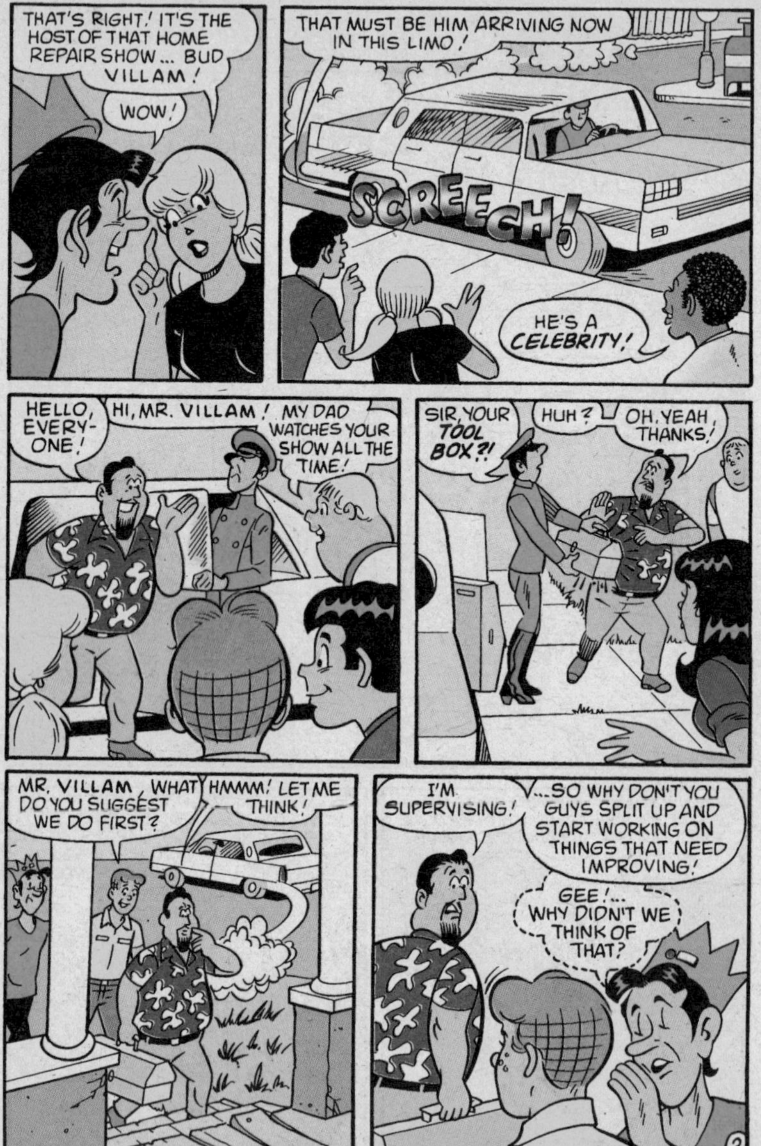
THAT'S RIGHT! IT'S THE HOST OF THAT HOME REPAIR SHOW ... BUD VILLAM!
WOW!
THAT MUST BE HIM ARRIVING NOW IN THIS LIMO!
SCREECH!
HE'S A CELEBRITY!
HELLO, EVERY-ONE!
HI, MR. VILLAM! MY DAD WATCHES YOUR SHOW ALL THE TIME!
SIR, YOUR TOOL BOX?!
HUH?
OH, YEAH, THANKS!
MR. VILLAM, WHAT DO YOU SUGGEST WE DO FIRST?
HMMM! LET ME THINK!
I'M SUPERVISING!
...SO WHY DON'T YOU GUYS SPLIT UP AND START WORKING ON THINGS THAT NEED IMPROVING!
GEE!... WHY DIDN'T WE THINK OF THAT?
2

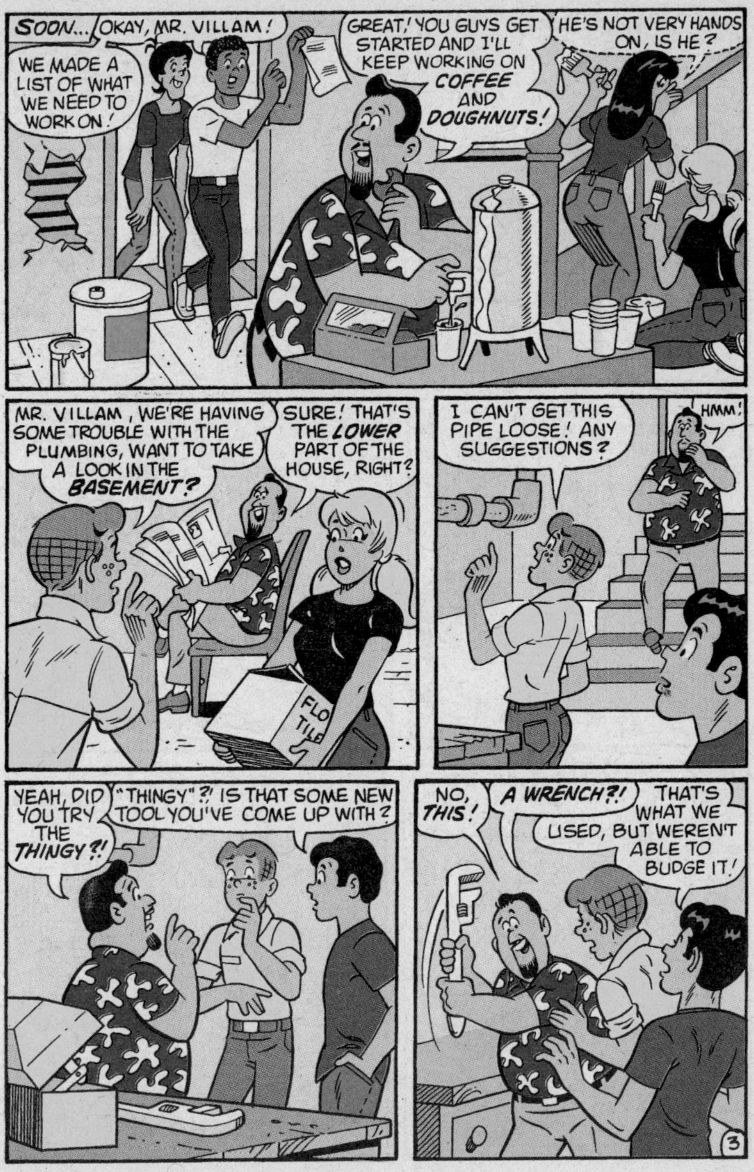
SOON...
OKAY, MR. VILLAM!
WE MADE A LIST OF WHAT WE NEED TO WORK ON!
GREAT! YOU GUYS GET STARTED AND I'LL KEEP WORKING ON COFFEE AND DOUGHNUTS!
HE'S NOT VERY HANDS ON, IS HE?
MR. VILLAM, WE'RE HAVING SOME TROUBLE WITH THE PLUMBING, WANT TO TAKE A LOOK IN THE BASEMENT?
SURE! THAT'S THE LOWER PART OF THE HOUSE, RIGHT?
FLO TILE
I CAN'T GET THIS PIPE LOOSE! ANY SUGGESTIONS?
HMM!
YEAH, DID YOU TRY THE THINGY?!
"THINGY"?! IS THAT SOME NEW TOOL YOU'VE COME UP WITH?
NO, THIS!
A WRENCH?!
THAT'S WHAT WE USED, BUT WEREN'T ABLE TO BUDGE IT!

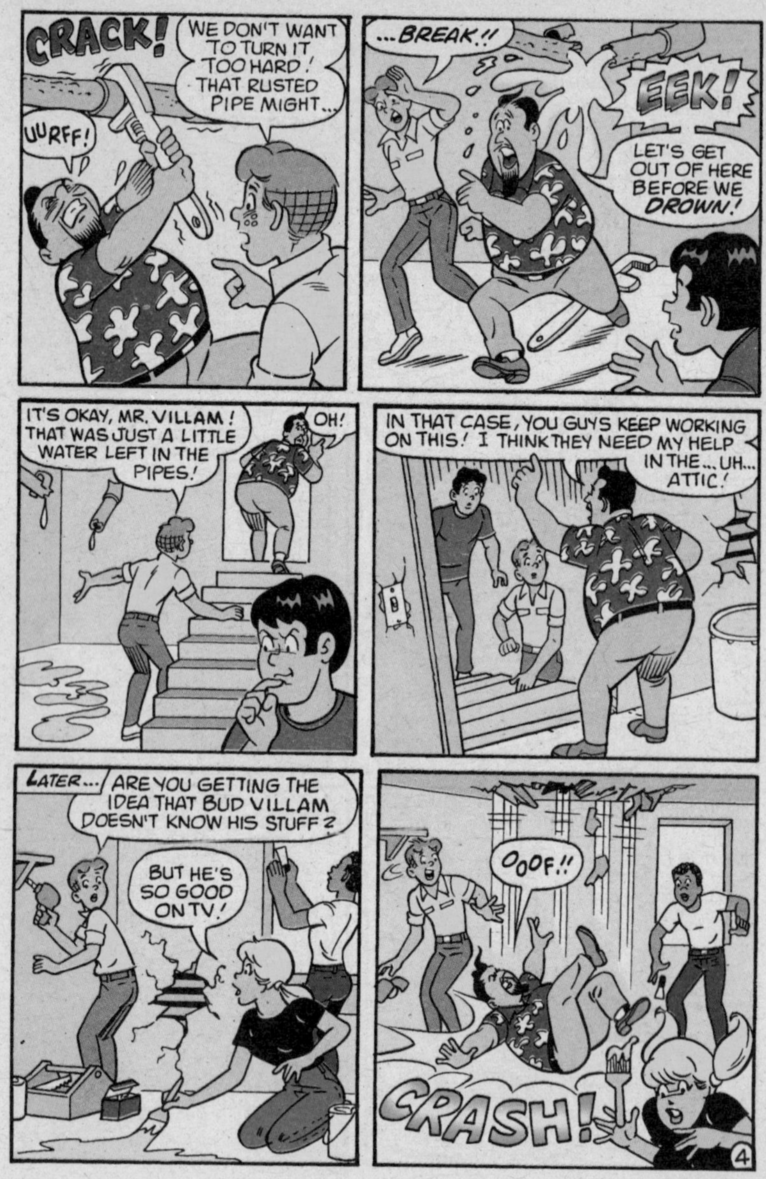

CRACK!
WE DON'T WANT TO TURN IT TOO HARD! THAT RUSTED PIPE MIGHT...
UURFF!
...BREAK.!!
EEK!
LET'S GET OUT OF HERE BEFORE WE DROWN!
IT'S OKAY, MR. VILLAM! THAT WAS JUST A LITTLE WATER LEFT IN THE PIPES!
OH!
IN THAT CASE, YOU GUYS KEEP WORKING ON THIS! I THINK THEY NEED MY HELP IN THE... UH... ATTIC!
LATER...
ARE YOU GETTING THE IDEA THAT BUD VILLAM DOESN'T KNOW HIS STUFF?
BUT HE'S SO GOOD ON TV!
OOOF!!
CRASH!
4

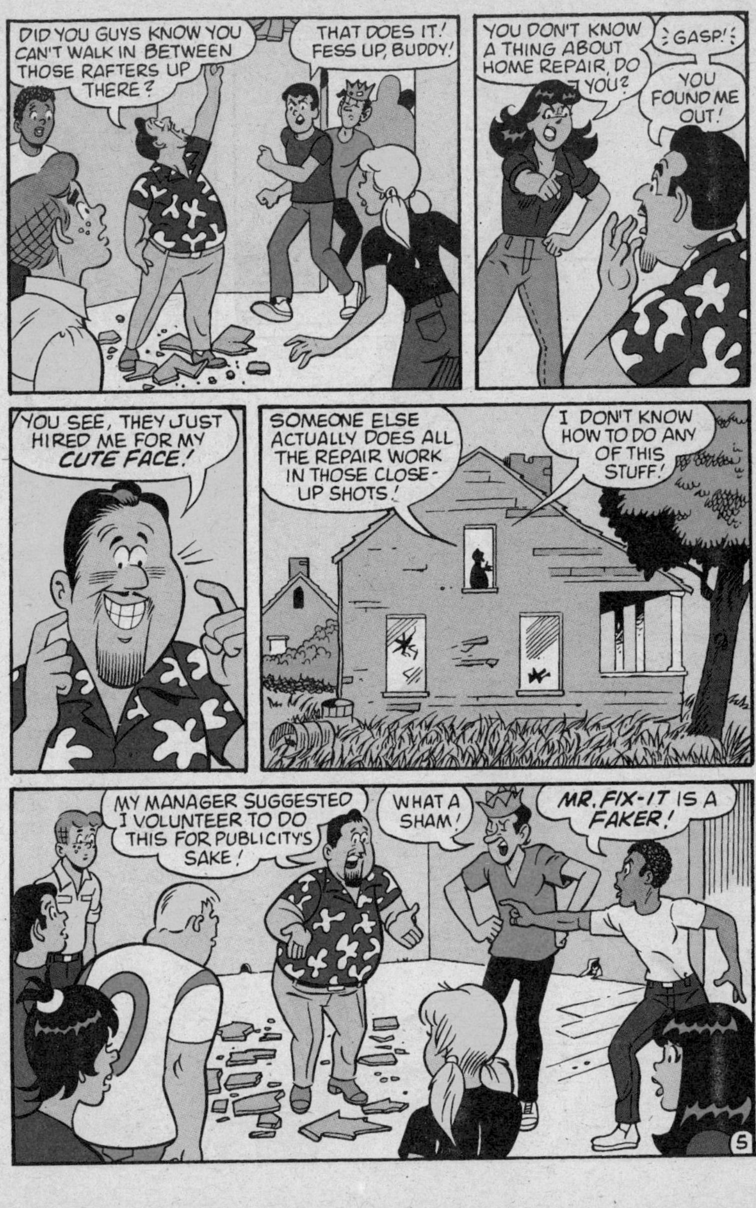
DID YOU GUYS KNOW YOU CAN'T WALK IN BETWEEN THOSE RAFTERS UP THERE?
THAT DOES IT! FESS UP, BUDDY!
YOU DON'T KNOW A THING ABOUT HOME REPAIR, DO YOU?
GASP!
YOU FOUND ME OUT!
YOU SEE, THEY JUST HIRED ME FOR MY *CUTE FACE*!
SOMEONE ELSE ACTUALLY DOES ALL THE REPAIR WORK IN THOSE CLOSE-UP SHOTS!
I DON'T KNOW HOW TO DO ANY OF THIS STUFF!
MY MANAGER SUGGESTED I VOLUNTEER TO DO THIS FOR PUBLICITY'S SAKE!
WHAT A SHAM!
MR. FIX-IT IS A *FAKER*!
5

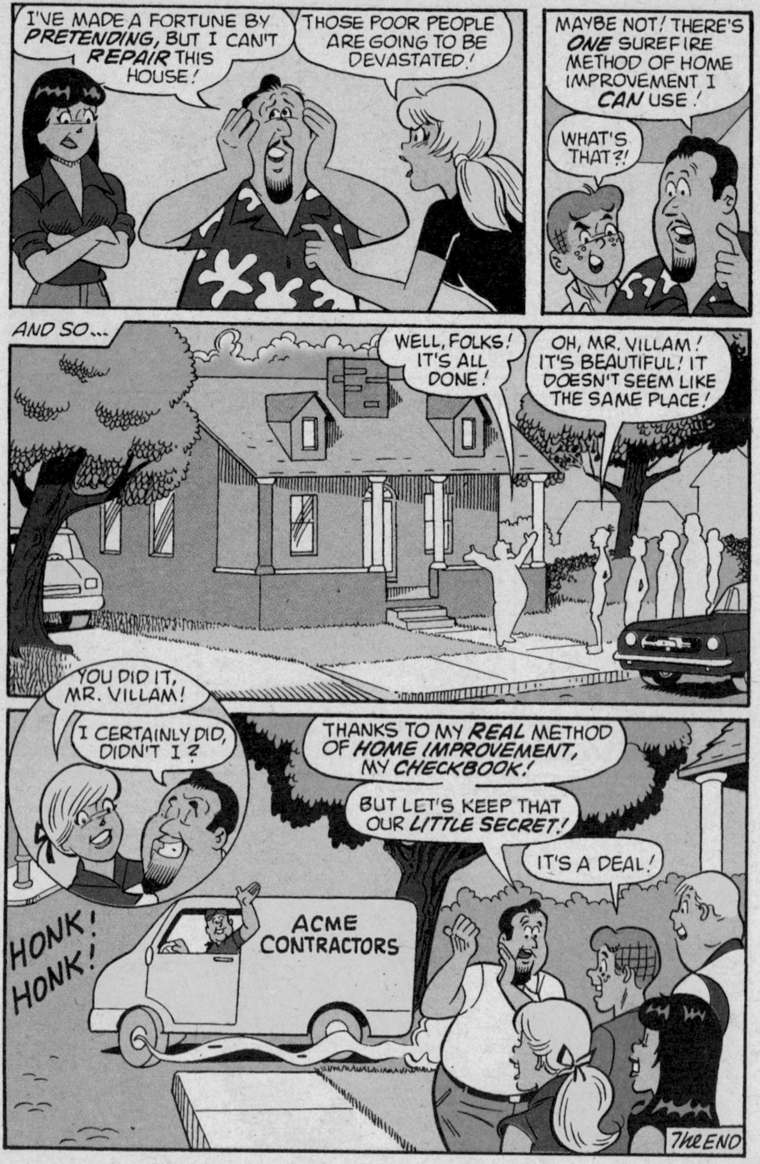
I'VE MADE A FORTUNE BY *PRETENDING*, BUT I CAN'T *REPAIR* THIS HOUSE!
THOSE POOR PEOPLE ARE GOING TO BE DEVASTATED!
MAYBE NOT! THERE'S *ONE* SUREFIRE METHOD OF HOME IMPROVEMENT I *CAN* USE!
WHAT'S THAT?!
AND SO...
WELL, FOLKS! IT'S ALL DONE!
OH, MR. VILLAM! IT'S BEAUTIFUL! IT DOESN'T SEEM LIKE THE SAME PLACE!
YOU DID IT, MR. VILLAM!
I CERTAINLY DID, DIDN'T I?
THANKS TO MY *REAL* METHOD OF *HOME IMPROVEMENT*, MY *CHECKBOOK*!
BUT LET'S KEEP THAT OUR *LITTLE SECRET*!
IT'S A DEAL!
HONK! HONK!
ACME CONTRACTORS
The END

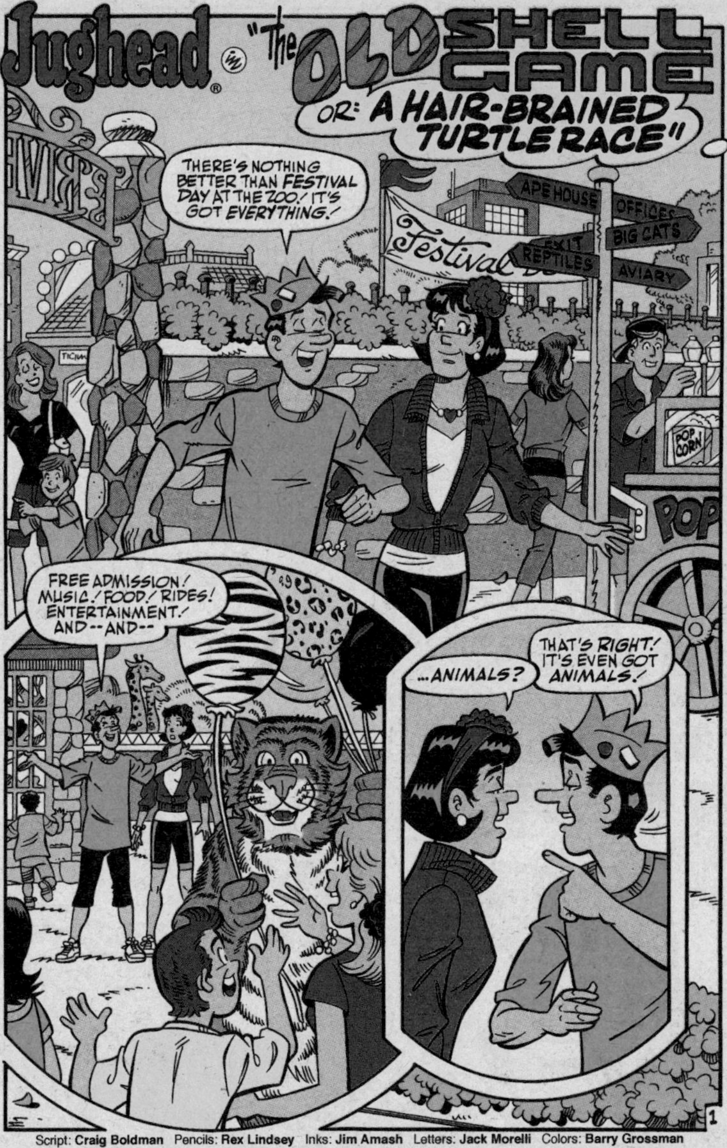
Jughead in "The OLD SHELL GAME
OR: A HAIR-BRAINED TURTLE RACE"
THERE'S NOTHING BETTER THAN FESTIVAL DAY AT THE ZOO! IT'S GOT EVERYTHING!
Festival
APE HOUSE
OFFICES
BIG CATS
EXIT
REPTILES
AVIARY
POP CORN
POP
FREE ADMISSION! MUSIC! FOOD! RIDES! ENTERTAINMENT! AND--AND--
...ANIMALS?
THAT'S RIGHT! IT'S EVEN GOT ANIMALS!
1

Script: **Craig Boldman** Pencils: **Rex Lindsey** Inks: **Jim Amash** Letters: **Jack Morelli** Colors: **Barry Grossman**
Editor-In-Chief: **Victor Gorelick** President: **Mike Pellerito** Publisher: **Jon Goldwater**

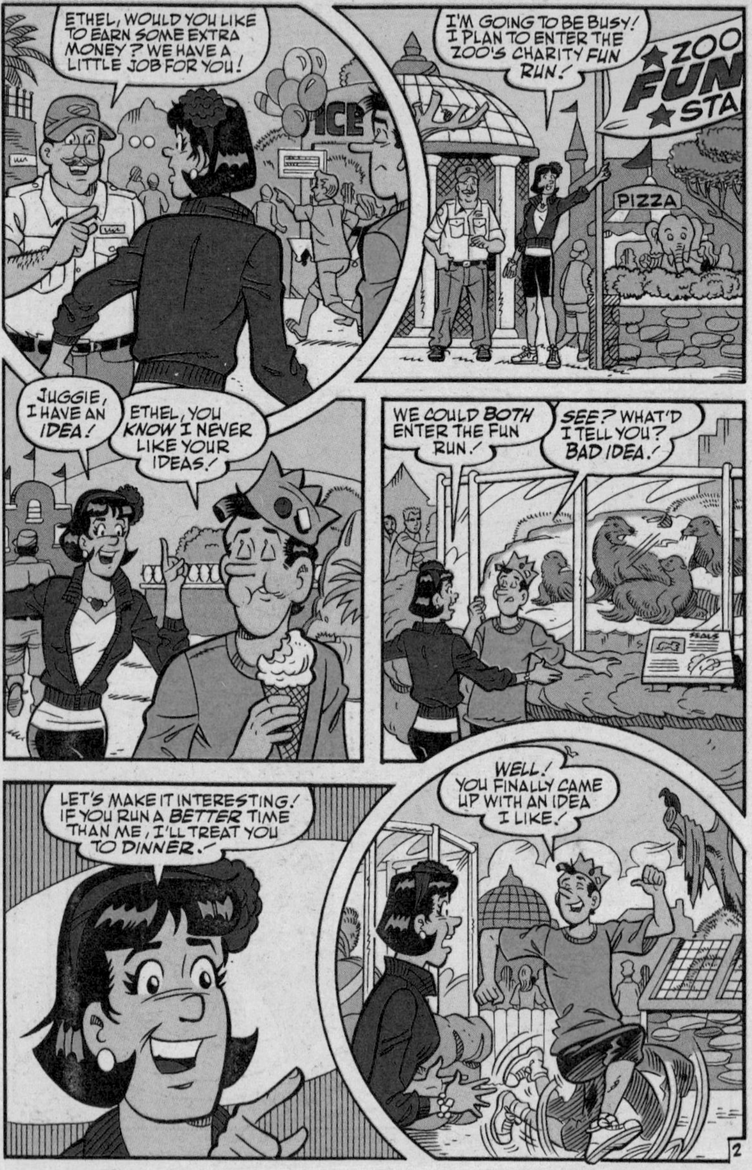

ETHEL, WOULD YOU LIKE TO EARN SOME EXTRA MONEY? WE HAVE A LITTLE JOB FOR YOU!
ICE
I'M GOING TO BE BUSY! I PLAN TO ENTER THE ZOO'S CHARITY FUN RUN!
ZOO FUN STA
PIZZA
JUGGIE, I HAVE AN IDEA!
ETHEL, YOU KNOW I NEVER LIKE YOUR IDEAS!
WE COULD BOTH ENTER THE FUN RUN!
SEE? WHAT'D I TELL YOU? BAD IDEA!
SEALS
LET'S MAKE IT INTERESTING! IF YOU RUN A BETTER TIME THAN ME, I'LL TREAT YOU TO DINNER!
WELL! YOU FINALLY CAME UP WITH AN IDEA I LIKE!
2

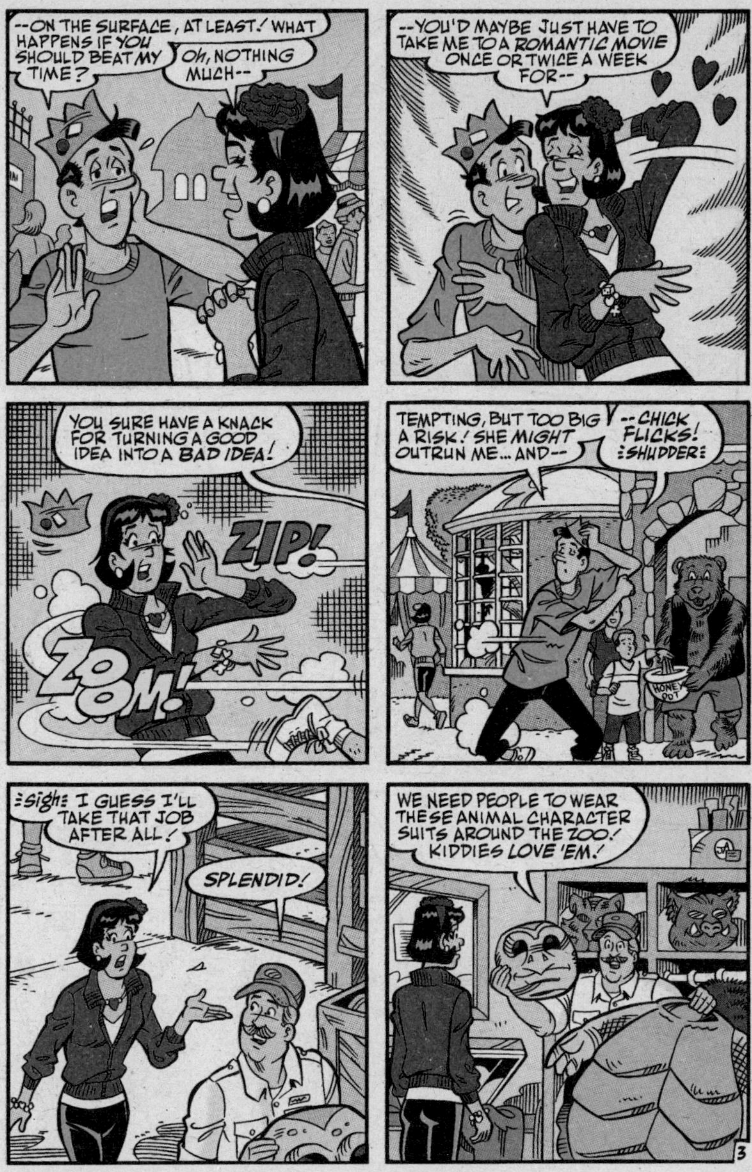
--ON THE SURFACE, AT LEAST! WHAT HAPPENS IF YOU SHOULD BEAT MY TIME?
Oh, NOTHING MUCH--
--YOU'D MAYBE JUST HAVE TO TAKE ME TO A ROMANTIC MOVIE ONCE OR TWICE A WEEK FOR--
YOU SURE HAVE A KNACK FOR TURNING A GOOD IDEA INTO A BAD IDEA!
ZIP!
ZOOM!
TEMPTING, BUT TOO BIG A RISK! SHE MIGHT OUTRUN ME... AND--
--CHICK FLICKS! :SHUDDER:
HONEY POT
:sigh: I GUESS I'LL TAKE THAT JOB AFTER ALL!
SPLENDID!
WE NEED PEOPLE TO WEAR THESE ANIMAL CHARACTER SUITS AROUND THE ZOO! KIDDIES LOVE 'EM!
3

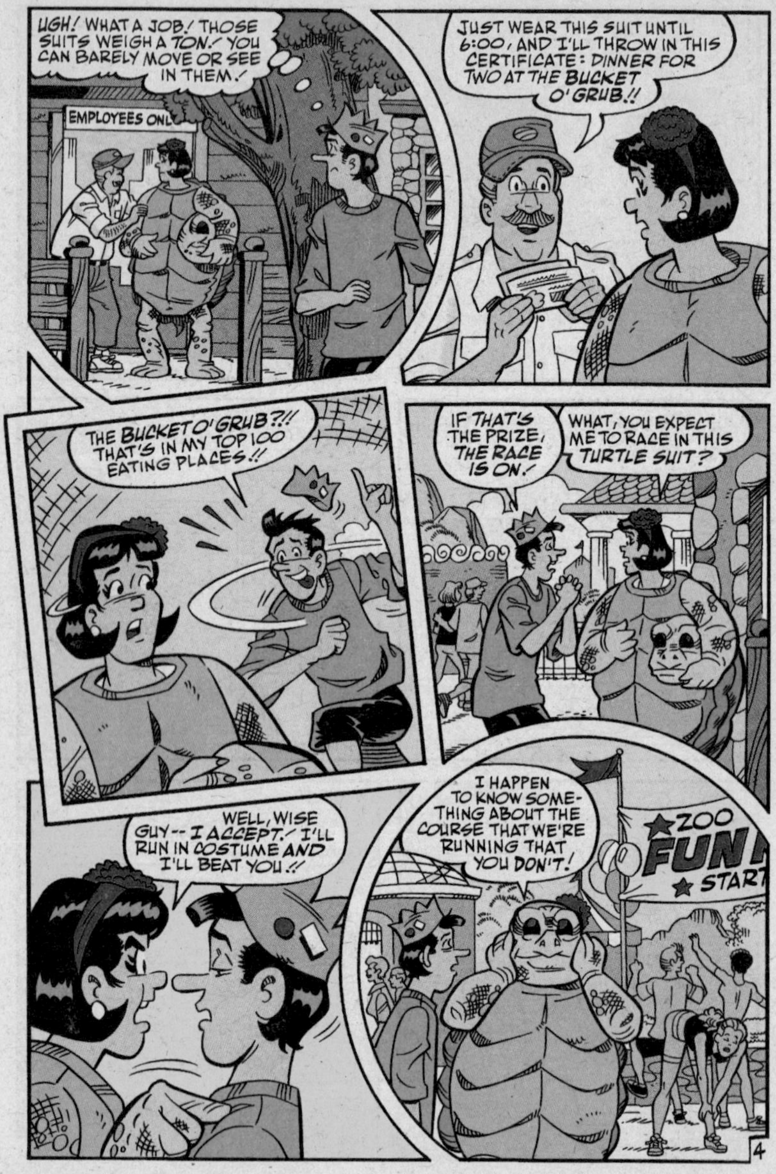
UGH! WHAT A JOB! THOSE SUITS WEIGH A TON! YOU CAN BARELY MOVE OR SEE IN THEM!
EMPLOYEES ONL
JUST WEAR THIS SUIT UNTIL 6:00, AND I'LL THROW IN THIS CERTIFICATE: DINNER FOR TWO AT THE BUCKET O' GRUB!!
THE BUCKET O' GRUB?!! THAT'S IN MY TOP 100 EATING PLACES!!
IF THAT'S THE PRIZE, THE RACE IS ON!
WHAT, YOU EXPECT ME TO RACE IN THIS TURTLE SUIT?
WELL, WISE GUY -- I ACCEPT! I'LL RUN IN COSTUME AND I'LL BEAT YOU!!
I HAPPEN TO KNOW SOMETHING ABOUT THE COURSE THAT WE'RE RUNNING THAT YOU DON'T!
ZOO FUN
START

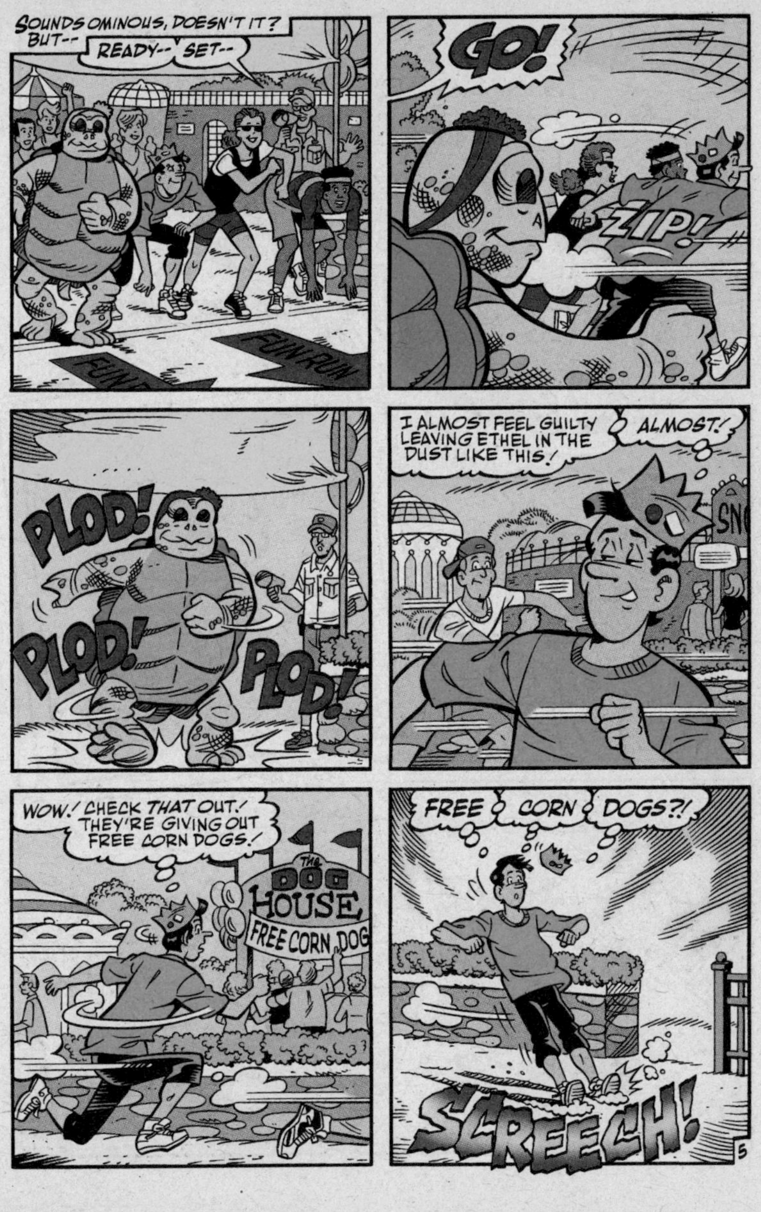
SOUNDS OMINOUS, DOESN'T IT? BUT--
READY--
SET--
FUN RUN
GO!
ZIP!
PLOD!
PLOD!
PLOD!
I ALMOST FEEL GUILTY LEAVING ETHEL IN THE DUST LIKE THIS!
ALMOST!
WOW! CHECK THAT OUT! THEY'RE GIVING OUT FREE CORN DOGS!
THE DOG HOUSE
FREE CORN DOG
FREE
CORN
DOGS?!
SCREECH!

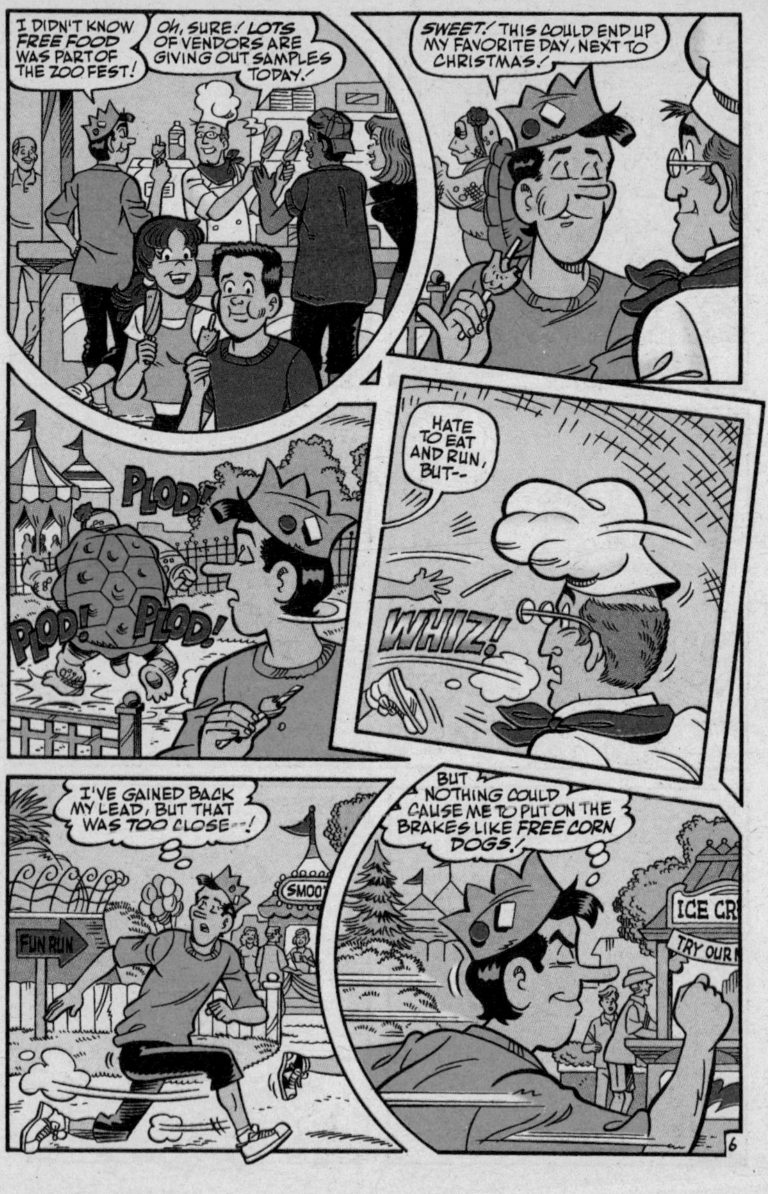
I DIDN'T KNOW FREE FOOD WAS PART OF THE ZOO FEST!
Oh, SURE! LOTS OF VENDORS ARE GIVING OUT SAMPLES TODAY!
SWEET! THIS COULD END UP MY FAVORITE DAY, NEXT TO CHRISTMAS!
PLOD!
PLOD!
PLOD!
HATE TO EAT AND RUN, BUT--
WHIZ!
I'VE GAINED BACK MY LEAD, BUT THAT WAS TOO CLOSE--!
FUN RUN
SMOO
BUT NOTHING COULD CAUSE ME TO PUT ON THE BRAKES LIKE FREE CORN DOGS!
ICE CR
TRY OUR

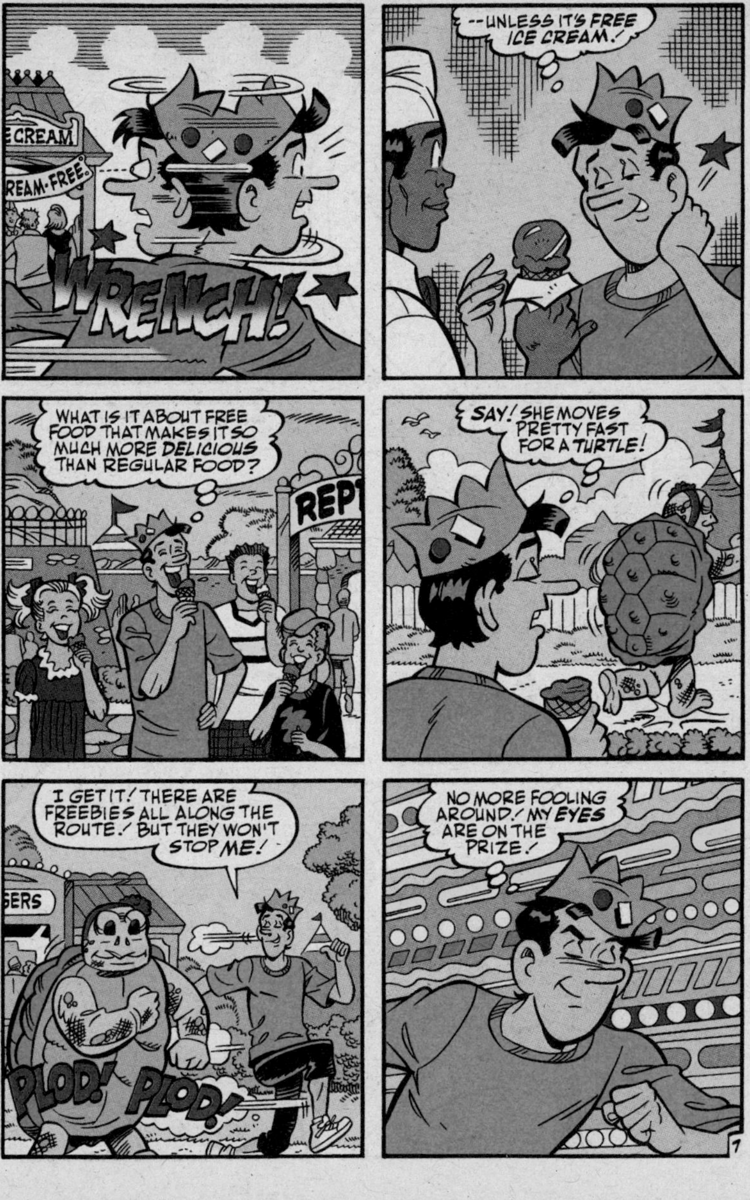
ECREAM
REAM-FREE
WRENCH!
--UNLESS IT'S FREE ICE CREAM!
WHAT IS IT ABOUT FREE FOOD THAT MAKES IT SO MUCH MORE DELICIOUS THAN REGULAR FOOD?
REP
SAY! SHE MOVES PRETTY FAST FOR A TURTLE!
I GET IT! THERE ARE FREEBIES ALL ALONG THE ROUTE! BUT THEY WON'T STOP ME!
SERS
PLOD! PLOD!
NO MORE FOOLING AROUND! MY EYES ARE ON THE PRIZE!

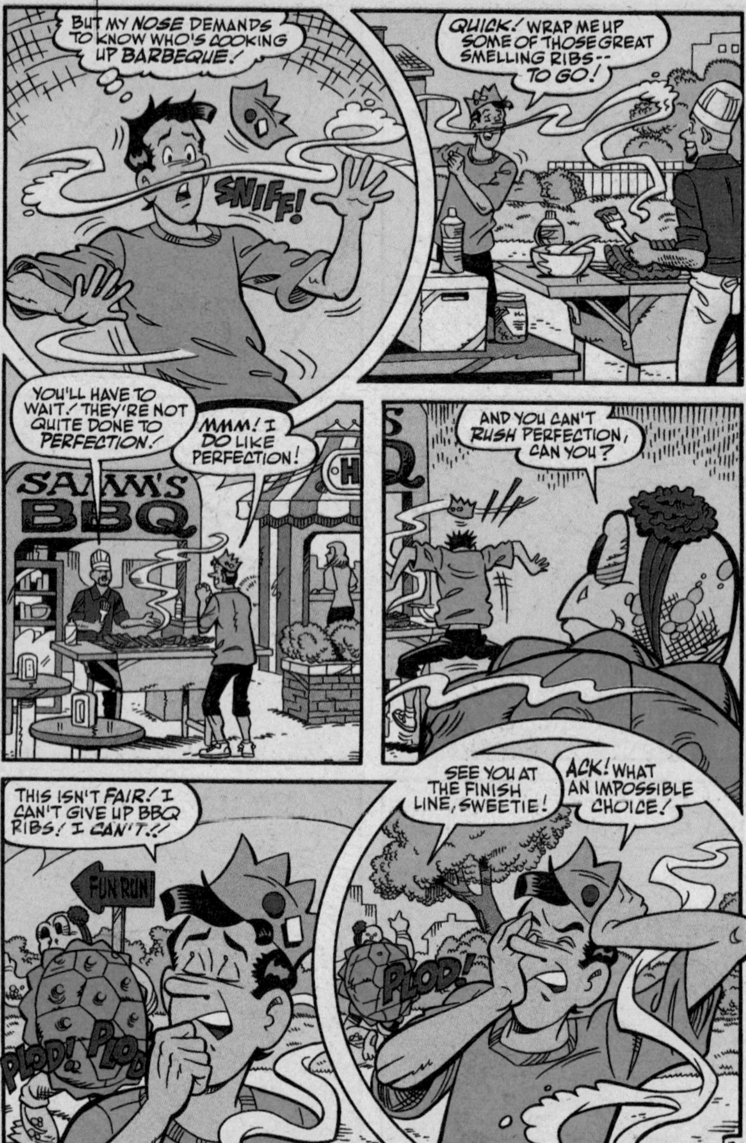
BUT MY NOSE DEMANDS TO KNOW WHO'S COOKING UP BARBEQUE!
SNIFF!
QUICK! WRAP ME UP SOME OF THOSE GREAT SMELLING RIBS-- TO GO!
YOU'LL HAVE TO WAIT! THEY'RE NOT QUITE DONE TO PERFECTION!
MMM! I DO LIKE PERFECTION!
SAM'S BBQ
AND YOU CAN'T RUSH PERFECTION, CAN YOU?
THIS ISN'T FAIR! I CAN'T GIVE UP BBQ RIBS! I CAN'T!!
FUN RUN
PLOD! PLOD!
SEE YOU AT THE FINISH LINE, SWEETIE!
ACK! WHAT AN IMPOSSIBLE CHOICE!
PLOD!

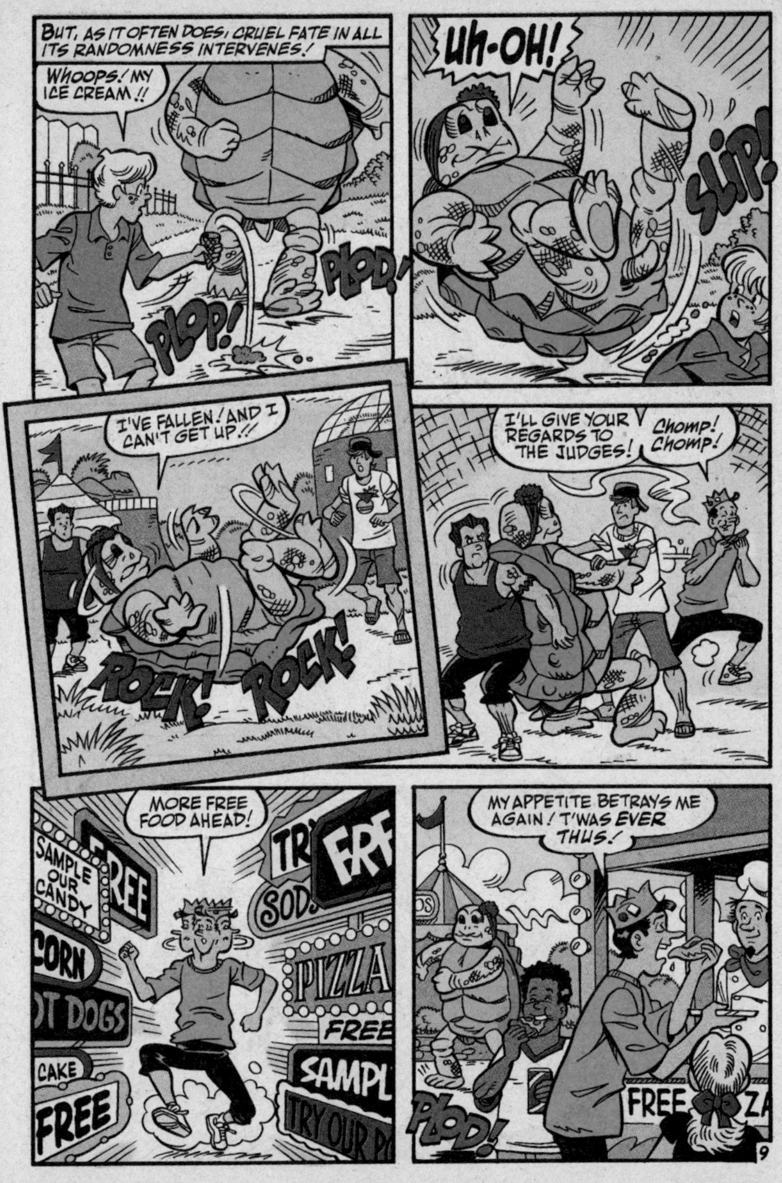

BUT, AS IT OFTEN DOES, CRUEL FATE IN ALL ITS RANDOMNESS INTERVENES!
WHOOPS! MY ICE CREAM!!
PLOP!
PLOD!
UH-OH!
SLIP!
I'VE FALLEN! AND I CAN'T GET UP!!
ROCK! ROCK!
I'LL GIVE YOUR REGARDS TO THE JUDGES!
CHOMP! CHOMP!
MORE FREE FOOD AHEAD!
SAMPLE OUR CANDY
FREE
CORN
OT DOGS
CAKE
FREE
TR
FRE
SOD
PIZZA
FREE
SAMPL
TRY OUR P
MY APPETITE BETRAYS ME AGAIN! T'WAS EVER THUS!
FREE
ZA
PLOD!

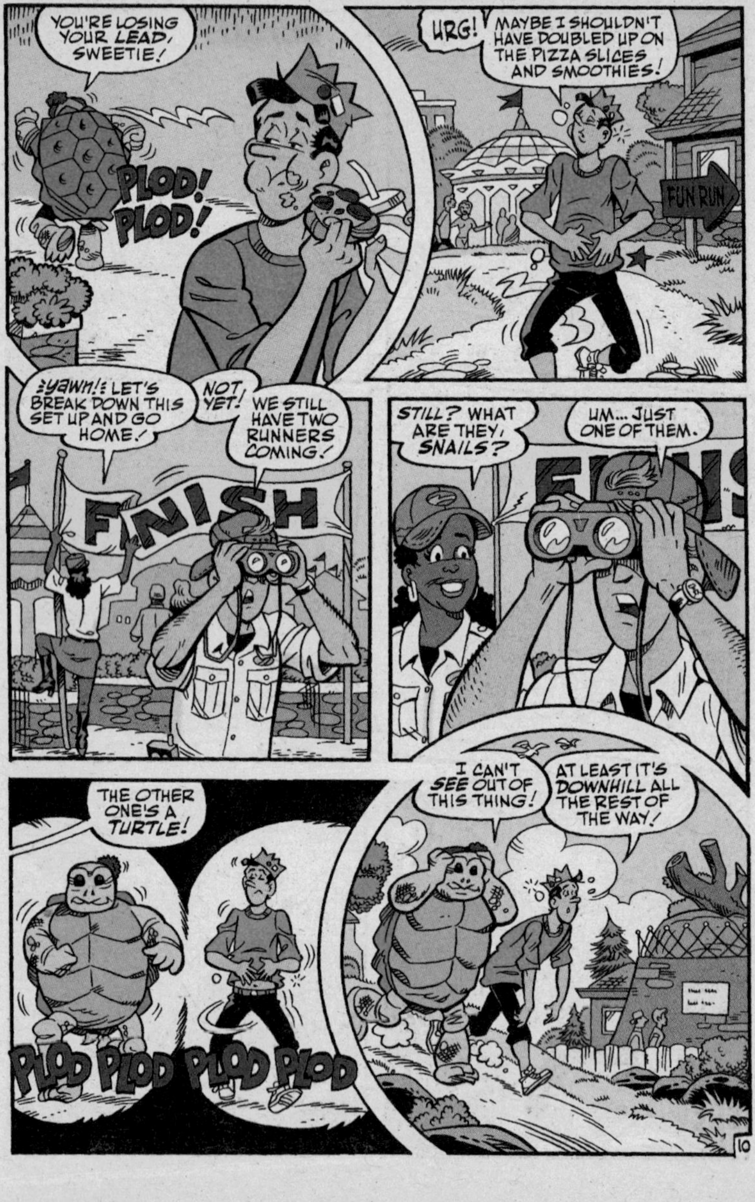
YOU'RE LOSING YOUR LEAD, SWEETIE!
PLOD! PLOD!
URG!
MAYBE I SHOULDN'T HAVE DOUBLED UP ON THE PIZZA SLICES AND SMOOTHIES!
FUN RUN
:YAWN!: LET'S BREAK DOWN THIS SET UP AND GO HOME!
NOT YET!
WE STILL HAVE TWO RUNNERS COMING!
FINISH
STILL? WHAT ARE THEY, SNAILS?
UM... JUST ONE OF THEM.
THE OTHER ONE'S A TURTLE!
PLOD PLOD PLOD PLOD
I CAN'T SEE OUT OF THIS THING!
AT LEAST IT'S DOWNHILL ALL THE REST OF THE WAY!

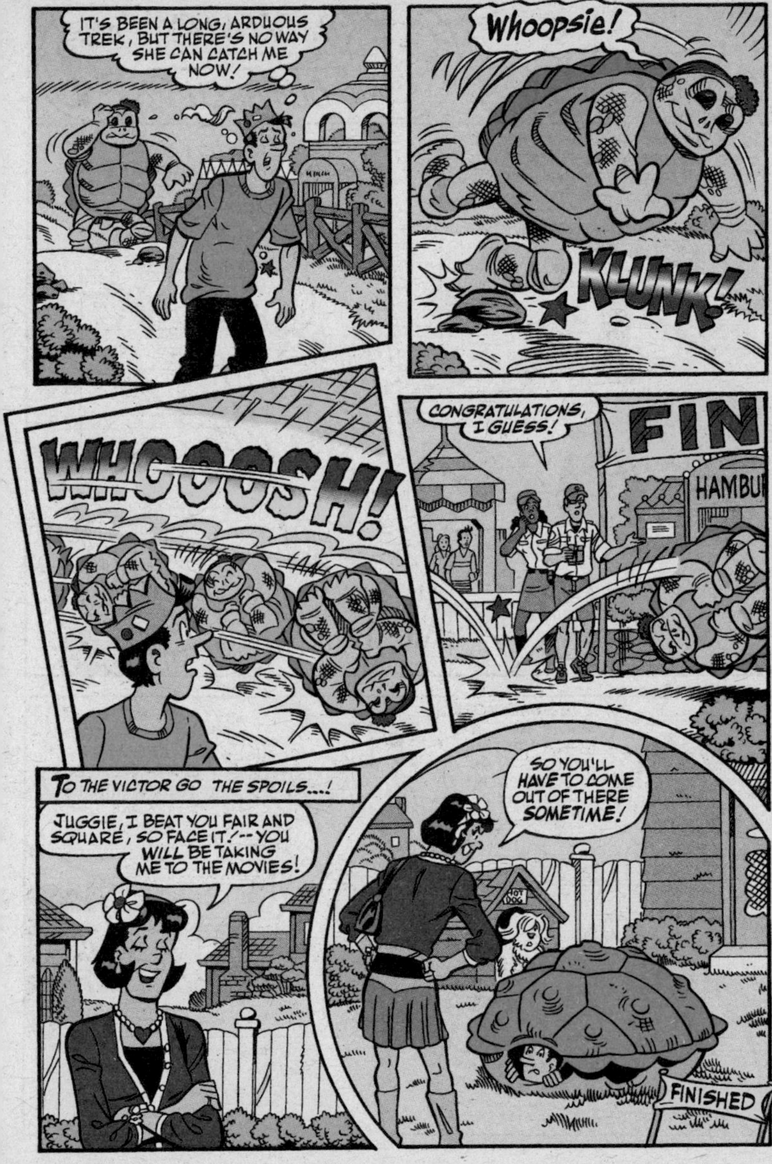
IT'S BEEN A LONG, ARDUOUS TREK, BUT THERE'S NO WAY SHE CAN CATCH ME NOW!
Whoopsie!
KLUNK!
WHOOOOSH!
CONGRATULATIONS, I GUESS!
FIN
HAMBU
TO THE VICTOR GO THE SPOILS...!
JUGGIE, I BEAT YOU FAIR AND SQUARE, SO FACE IT! -- YOU WILL BE TAKING ME TO THE MOVIES!
SO YOU'LL HAVE TO COME OUT OF THERE SOMETIME!
HOT DOG
FINISHED

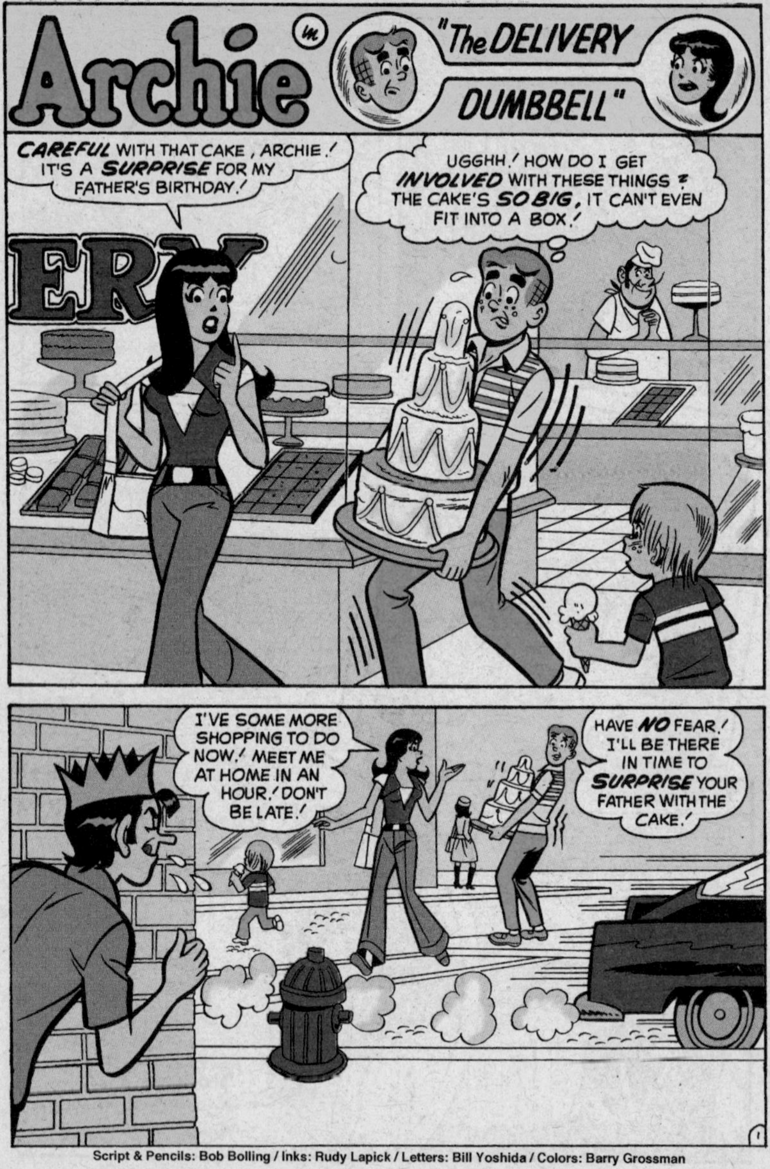
Archie in
"The DELIVERY DUMBBELL"
CAREFUL WITH THAT CAKE, ARCHIE.! IT'S A SURPRISE FOR MY FATHER'S BIRTHDAY.!
UGGHH.! HOW DO I GET INVOLVED WITH THESE THINGS ? THE CAKE'S SO BIG, IT CAN'T EVEN FIT INTO A BOX.!
I'VE SOME MORE SHOPPING TO DO NOW.! MEET ME AT HOME IN AN HOUR.! DON'T BE LATE.!
HAVE NO FEAR.! I'LL BE THERE IN TIME TO SURPRISE YOUR FATHER WITH THE CAKE.!
1

Script & Pencils: Bob Bolling / Inks: Rudy Lapick / Letters: Bill Yoshida / Colors: Barry Grossman

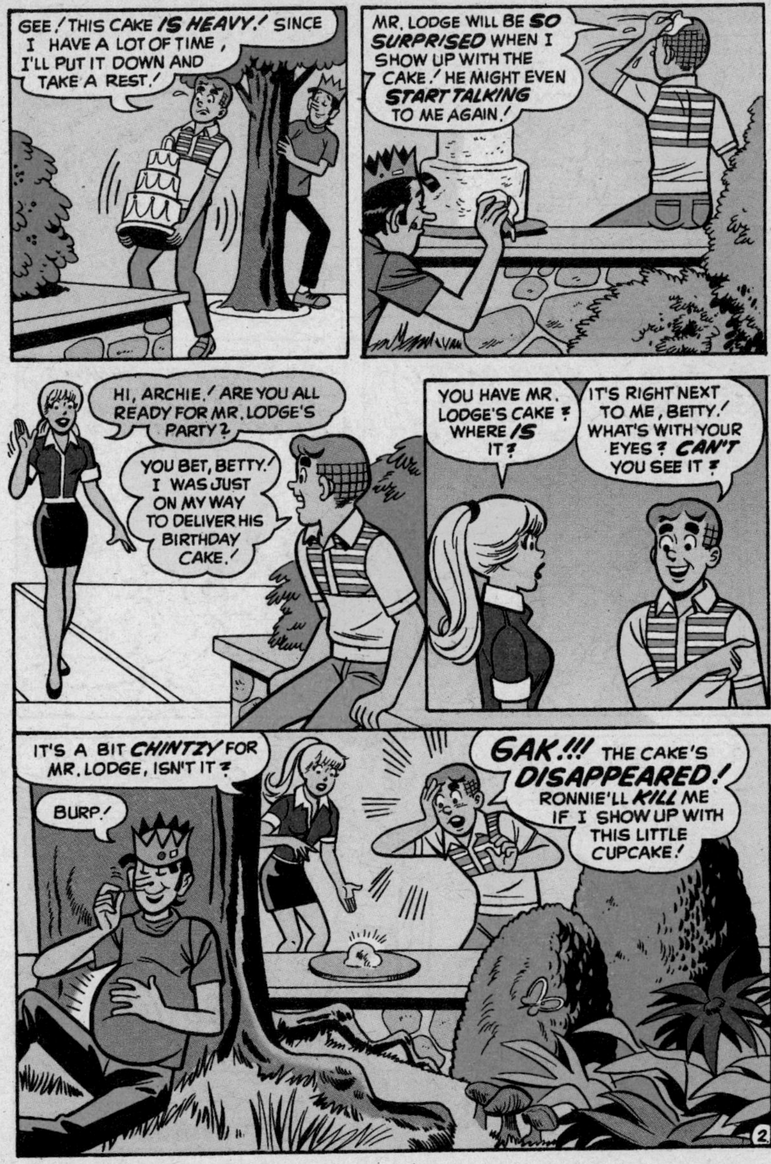
GEE! THIS CAKE IS HEAVY! SINCE I HAVE A LOT OF TIME, I'LL PUT IT DOWN AND TAKE A REST!
MR. LODGE WILL BE SO SURPRISED WHEN I SHOW UP WITH THE CAKE! HE MIGHT EVEN START TALKING TO ME AGAIN!
HI, ARCHIE! ARE YOU ALL READY FOR MR. LODGE'S PARTY?
YOU BET, BETTY! I WAS JUST ON MY WAY TO DELIVER HIS BIRTHDAY CAKE!
YOU HAVE MR. LODGE'S CAKE? WHERE IS IT?
IT'S RIGHT NEXT TO ME, BETTY! WHAT'S WITH YOUR EYES? CAN'T YOU SEE IT?
IT'S A BIT CHINTZY FOR MR. LODGE, ISN'T IT?
BURP!
GAK!!! THE CAKE'S DISAPPEARED! RONNIE'LL KILL ME IF I SHOW UP WITH THIS LITTLE CUPCAKE!
2

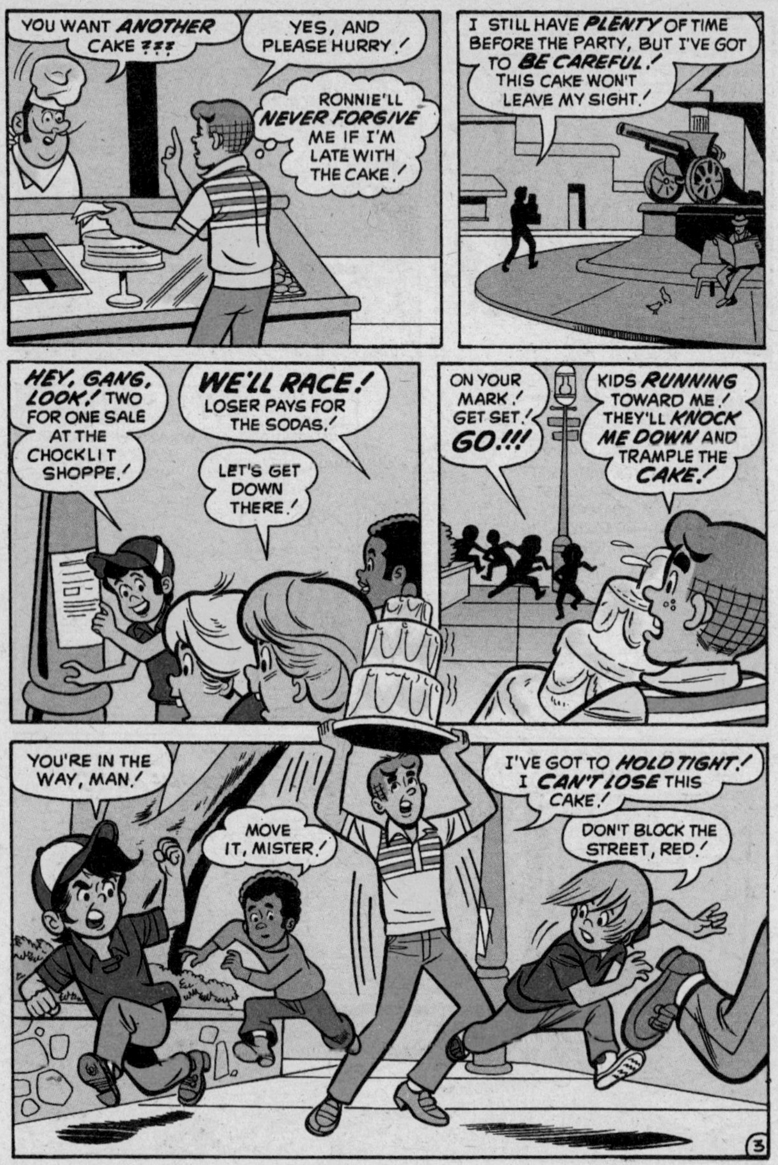

YOU WANT ANOTHER CAKE ???
YES, AND PLEASE HURRY!
RONNIE'LL NEVER FORGIVE ME IF I'M LATE WITH THE CAKE!
I STILL HAVE PLENTY OF TIME BEFORE THE PARTY, BUT I'VE GOT TO BE CAREFUL! THIS CAKE WON'T LEAVE MY SIGHT!
HEY, GANG, LOOK! TWO FOR ONE SALE AT THE CHOCKLIT SHOPPE!
WE'LL RACE! LOSER PAYS FOR THE SODAS!
LET'S GET DOWN THERE!
ON YOUR MARK! GET SET! GO!!!
KIDS RUNNING TOWARD ME! THEY'LL KNOCK ME DOWN AND TRAMPLE THE CAKE!
YOU'RE IN THE WAY, MAN!
MOVE IT, MISTER!
I'VE GOT TO HOLD TIGHT! I CAN'T LOSE THIS CAKE!
DON'T BLOCK THE STREET, RED!

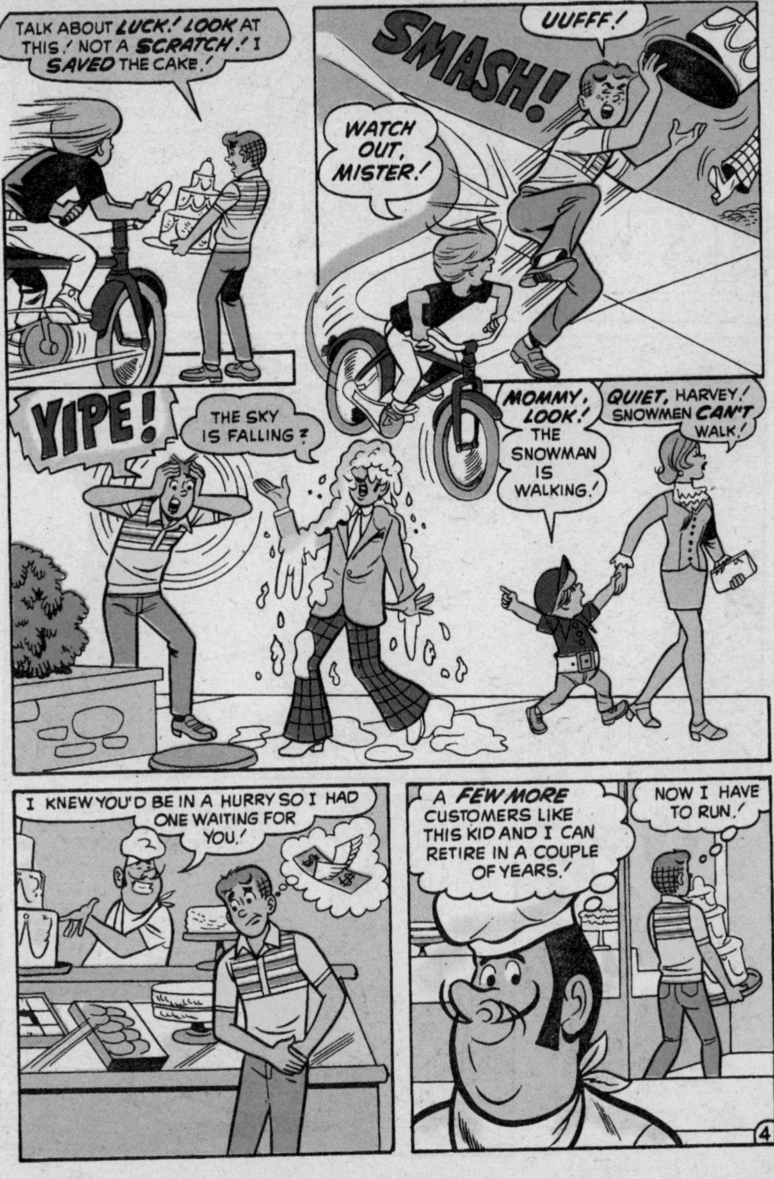

TALK ABOUT LUCK! LOOK AT THIS! NOT A SCRATCH! I SAVED THE CAKE!
SMASH!
UUFFF!
WATCH OUT, MISTER!
YIPE!
THE SKY IS FALLING?
MOMMY, LOOK! THE SNOWMAN IS WALKING!
QUIET, HARVEY! SNOWMEN CAN'T WALK!
I KNEW YOU'D BE IN A HURRY SO I HAD ONE WAITING FOR YOU!
A FEW MORE CUSTOMERS LIKE THIS KID AND I CAN RETIRE IN A COUPLE OF YEARS!
NOW I HAVE TO RUN!
4

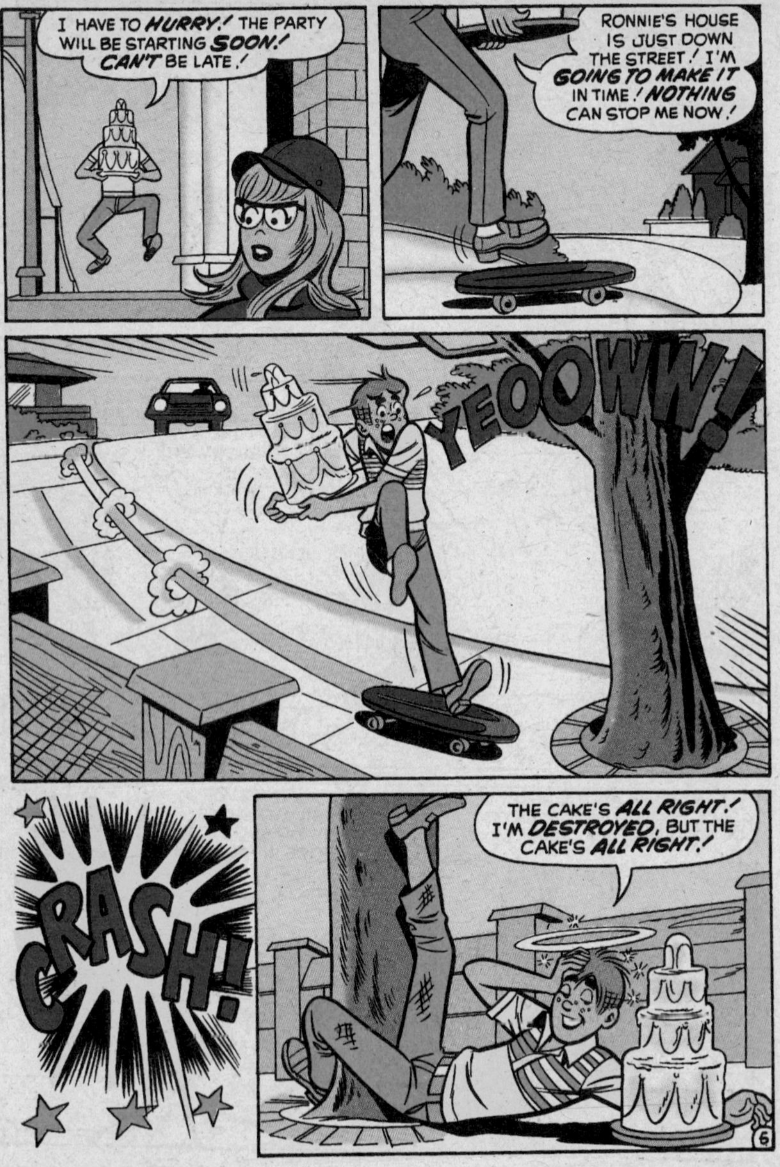
I HAVE TO HURRY! THE PARTY WILL BE STARTING SOON! CAN'T BE LATE!
RONNIE'S HOUSE IS JUST DOWN THE STREET! I'M GOING TO MAKE IT IN TIME! NOTHING CAN STOP ME NOW!
YEOOWW!!
CRASH!!
THE CAKE'S ALL RIGHT! I'M DESTROYED, BUT THE CAKE'S ALL RIGHT!
6

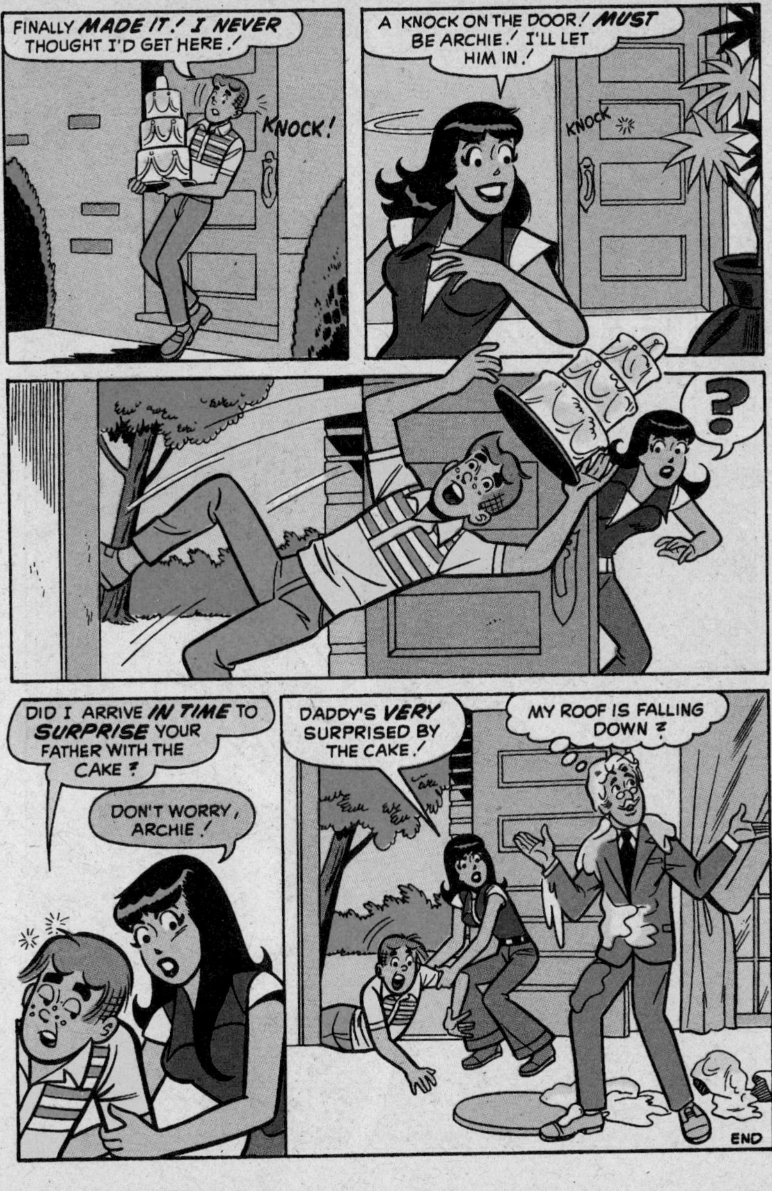
FINALLY MADE IT! I NEVER THOUGHT I'D GET HERE!
KNOCK!
A KNOCK ON THE DOOR! MUST BE ARCHIE! I'LL LET HIM IN!
KNOCK
?
DID I ARRIVE IN TIME TO SURPRISE YOUR FATHER WITH THE CAKE?
DON'T WORRY, ARCHIE!
DADDY'S VERY SURPRISED BY THE CAKE!
MY ROOF IS FALLING DOWN?
END

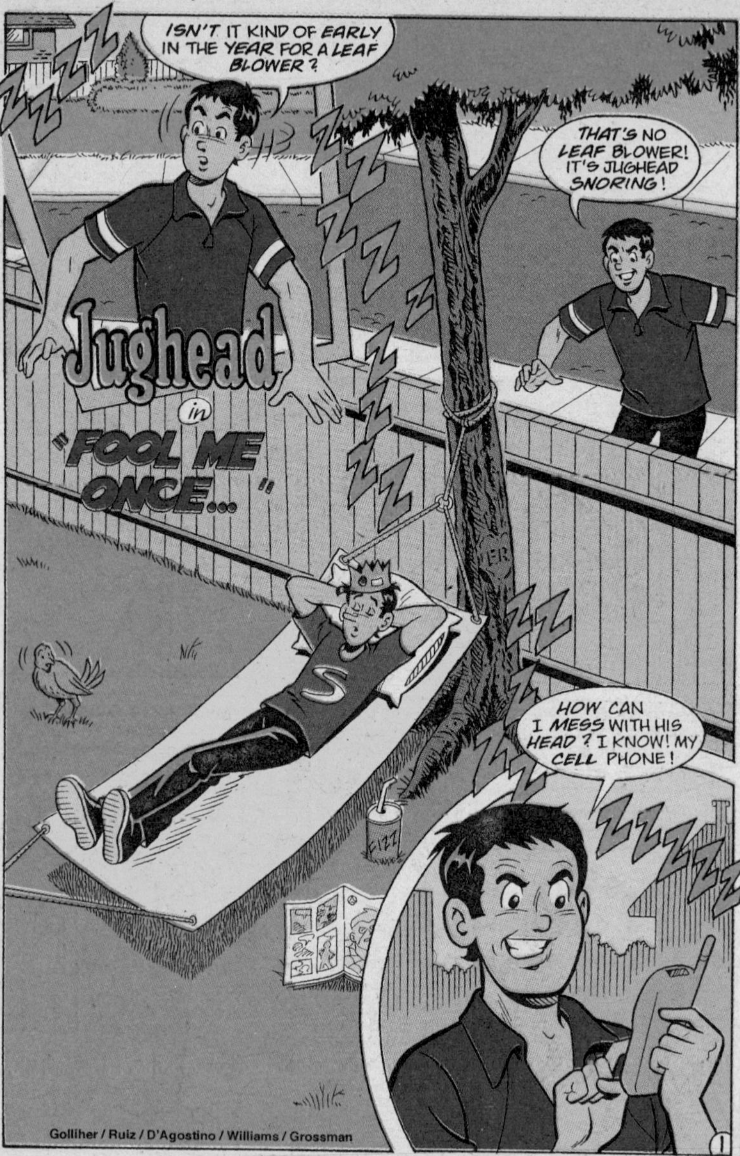
ZZZZZ
ISN'T IT KIND OF EARLY IN THE YEAR FOR A LEAF BLOWER?
THAT'S NO LEAF BLOWER! IT'S JUGHEAD SNORING!
Jughead
in
"FOOL ME ONCE..."
HOW CAN I MESS WITH HIS HEAD? I KNOW! MY CELL PHONE!
FIZZ
Golliher / Ruiz / D'Agostino / Williams / Grossman

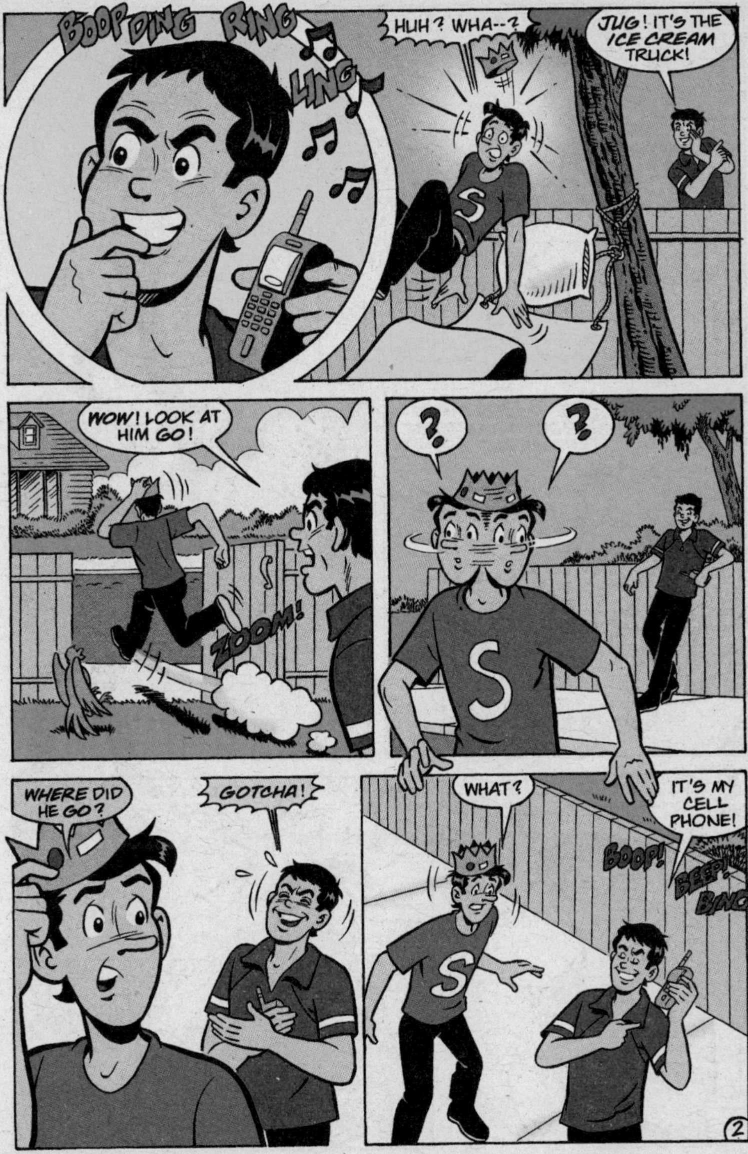
BOOP DING RING
LING
HUH? WHA--?
JUG! IT'S THE ICE CREAM TRUCK!
WOW! LOOK AT HIM GO!
ZOOM!
?
?
WHERE DID HE GO?
GOTCHA!
WHAT?
IT'S MY CELL PHONE!
BOOP! BEEP! BING!
2

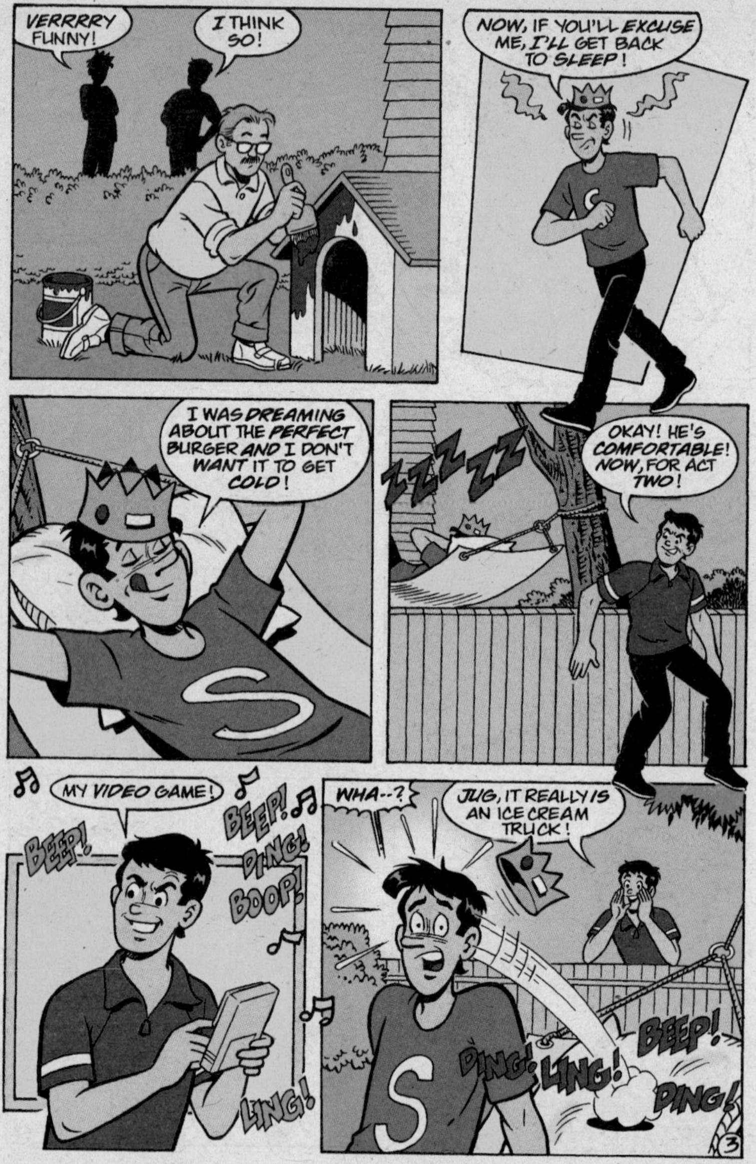

VERRRRY FUNNY!
I THINK SO!
NOW, IF YOU'LL EXCUSE ME, I'LL GET BACK TO SLEEP!
I WAS DREAMING ABOUT THE PERFECT BURGER AND I DON'T WANT IT TO GET COLD!
ZZZZZ
OKAY! HE'S COMFORTABLE! NOW, FOR ACT TWO!
MY VIDEO GAME!
BEEP!
BEEP!
DING!
BOOP!
LING!
WHA--?
JUG, IT REALLY IS AN ICE CREAM TRUCK!
DING!
LING!
BEEP!
DING!

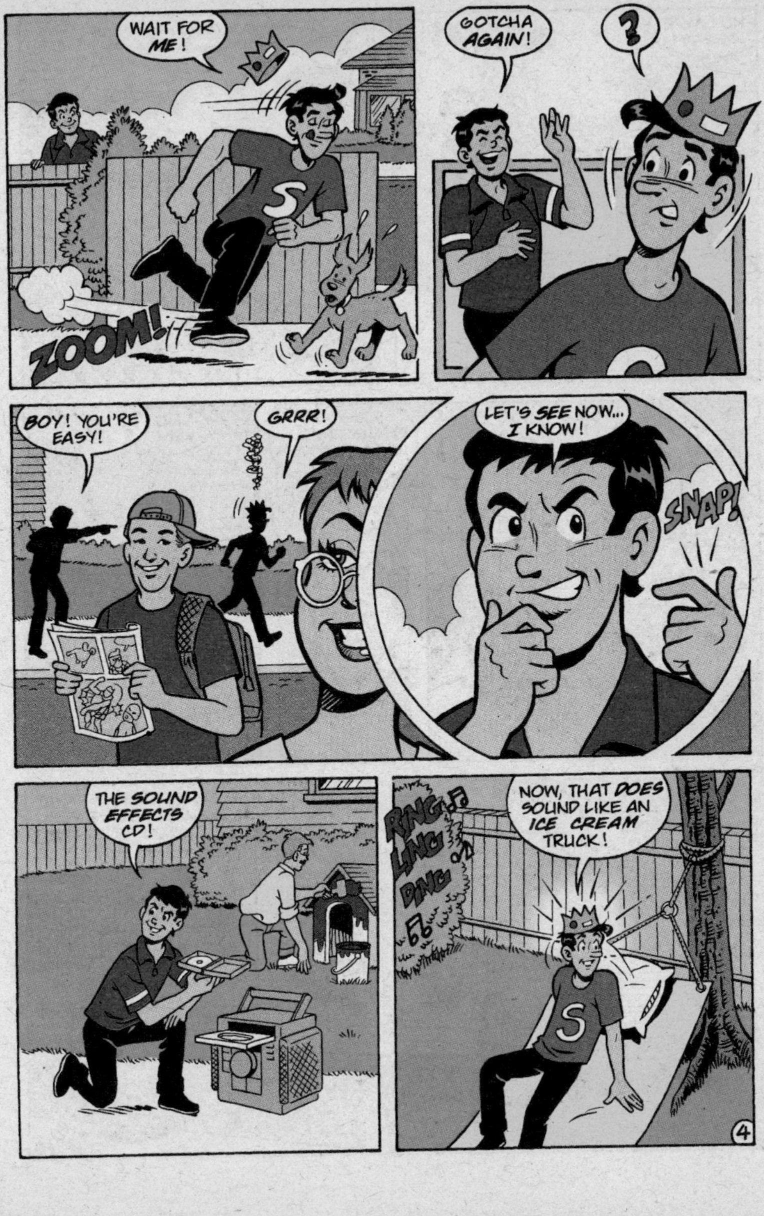
WAIT FOR ME!
ZOOM!
GOTCHA AGAIN!
?
BOY! YOU'RE EASY!
GRRR!
LET'S SEE NOW... I KNOW!
SNAP!
THE SOUND EFFECTS CD!
RING LING DING
NOW, THAT DOES SOUND LIKE AN ICE CREAM TRUCK!
4

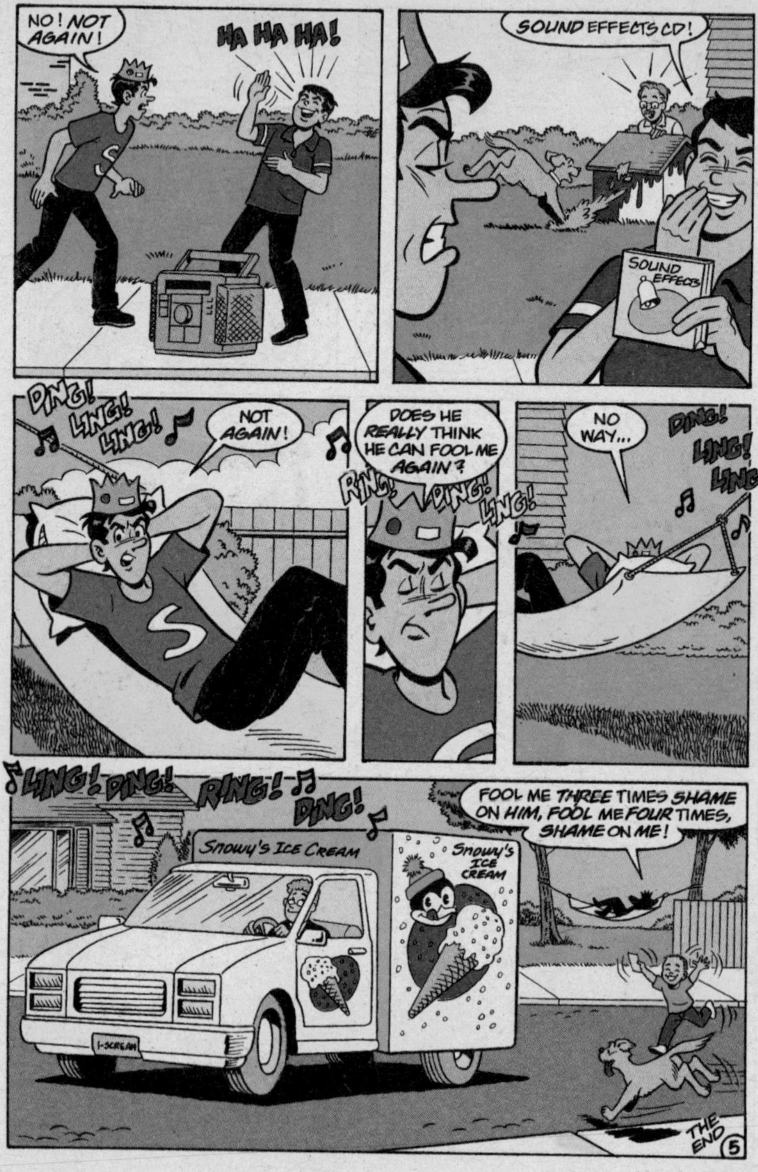
NO! NOT AGAIN!
HA HA HA!
SOUND EFFECTS CD!
SOUND EFFECTS
DING! LING! LING!
NOT AGAIN!
DOES HE REALLY THINK HE CAN FOOL ME AGAIN?
RING! DING! LING!
NO WAY...
DING! LING! LING!
LING! DING! RING! DING!
FOOL ME THREE TIMES SHAME ON HIM, FOOL ME FOUR TIMES, SHAME ON ME!
SNOWY'S ICE CREAM
SNOWY'S ICE CREAM
I-SCREAM
THE END

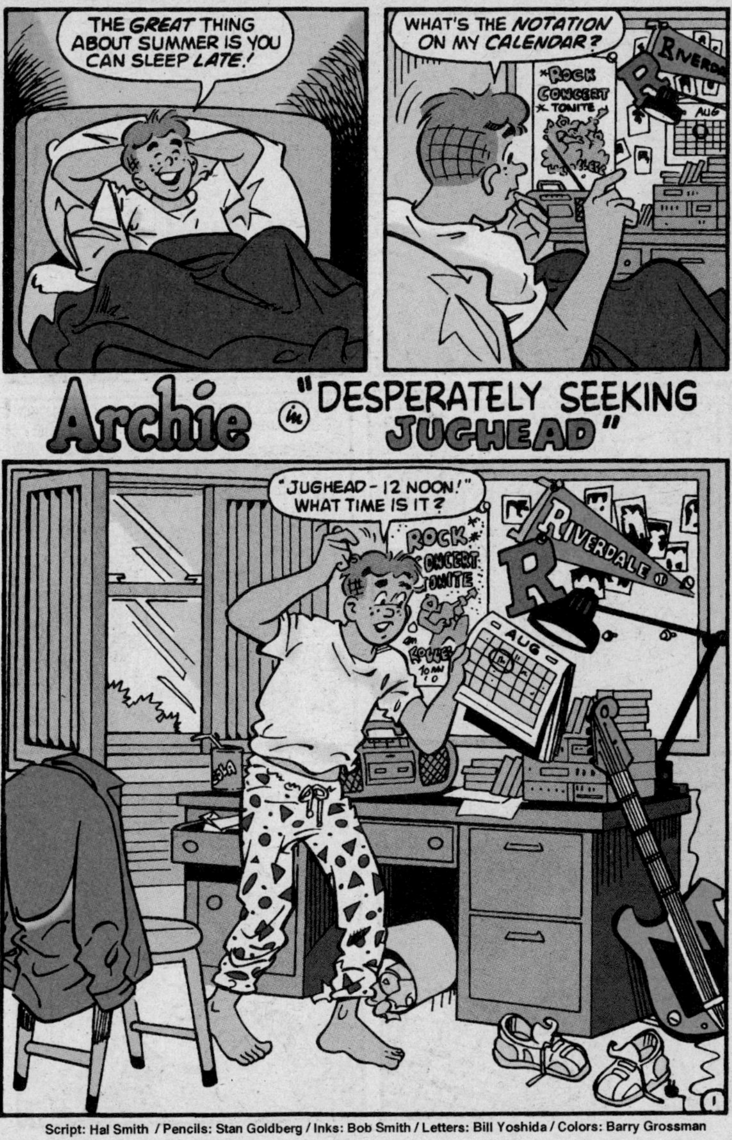
THE GREAT THING ABOUT SUMMER IS YOU CAN SLEEP LATE!
WHAT'S THE NOTATION ON MY CALENDAR?
ROCK CONCERT TONITE
RIVERDALE
AUG
Archie in "DESPERATELY SEEKING JUGHEAD"
"JUGHEAD - 12 NOON!" WHAT TIME IS IT?
ROCK CONCERT TONITE
RIVERDALE
AUG
1

Script: Hal Smith / Pencils: Stan Goldberg / Inks: Bob Smith / Letters: Bill Yoshida / Colors: Barry Grossman

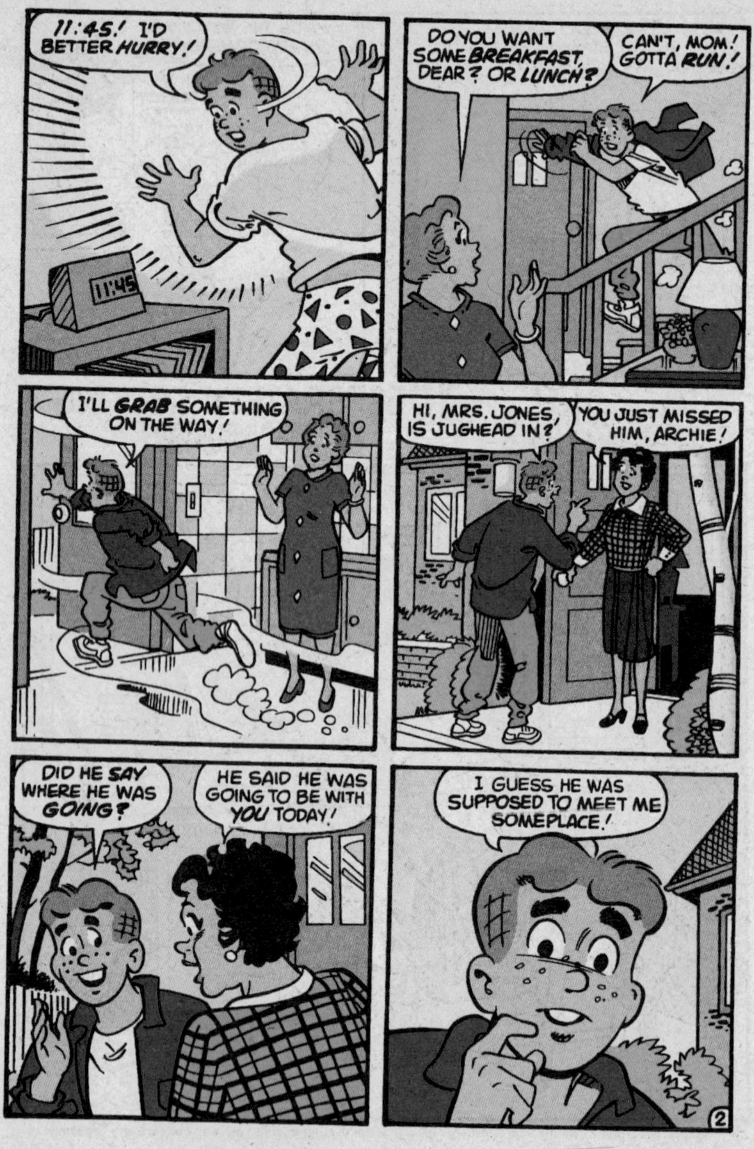
11:45! I'D BETTER HURRY!
11:45
DO YOU WANT SOME BREAKFAST, DEAR? OR LUNCH?
CAN'T, MOM! GOTTA RUN!
I'LL GRAB SOMETHING ON THE WAY!
HI, MRS. JONES, IS JUGHEAD IN?
YOU JUST MISSED HIM, ARCHIE!
DID HE SAY WHERE HE WAS GOING?
HE SAID HE WAS GOING TO BE WITH YOU TODAY!
I GUESS HE WAS SUPPOSED TO MEET ME SOMEPLACE!
2

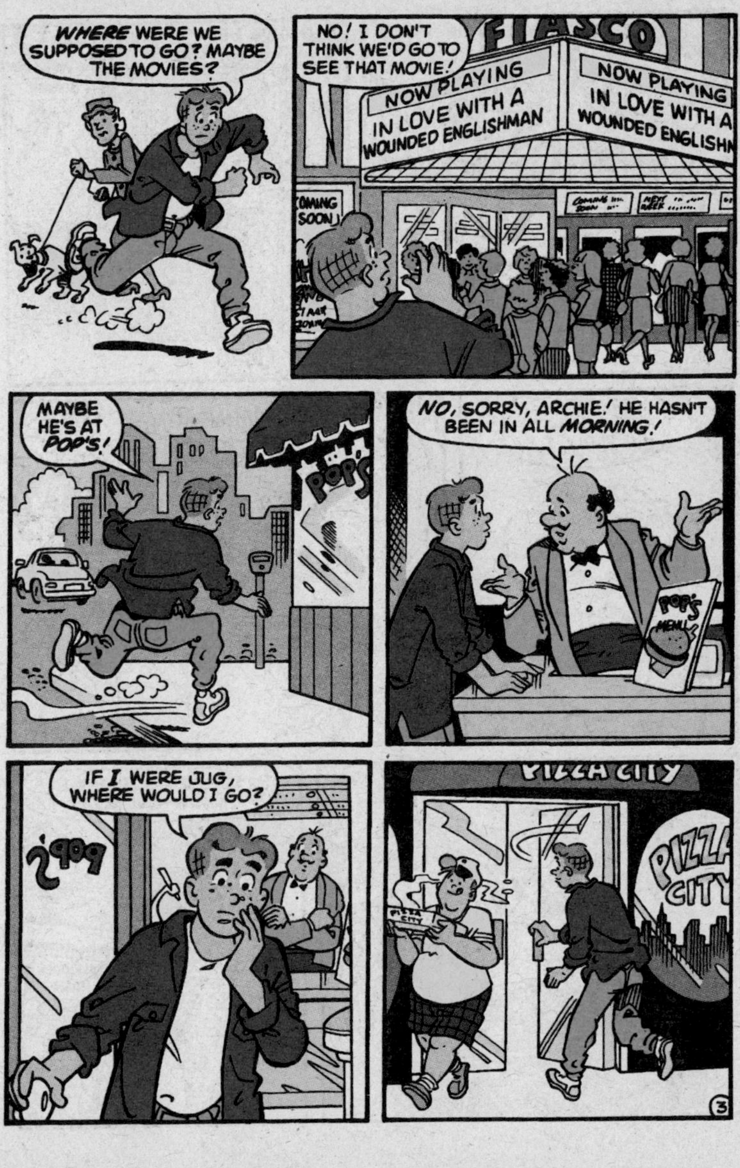
WHERE WERE WE SUPPOSED TO GO? MAYBE THE MOVIES?
NO! I DON'T THINK WE'D GO TO SEE THAT MOVIE!
FIASCO
NOW PLAYING IN LOVE WITH A WOUNDED ENGLISHMAN
NOW PLAYING IN LOVE WITH A WOUNDED ENGLISHM
COMING SOON
MAYBE HE'S AT POP'S!
POP'S
NO, SORRY, ARCHIE! HE HASN'T BEEN IN ALL MORNING!
POP'S MENU
IF I WERE JUG, WHERE WOULD I GO?
POP'S
PIZZA CITY
PIZZA CITY
PIZZA CITY
3

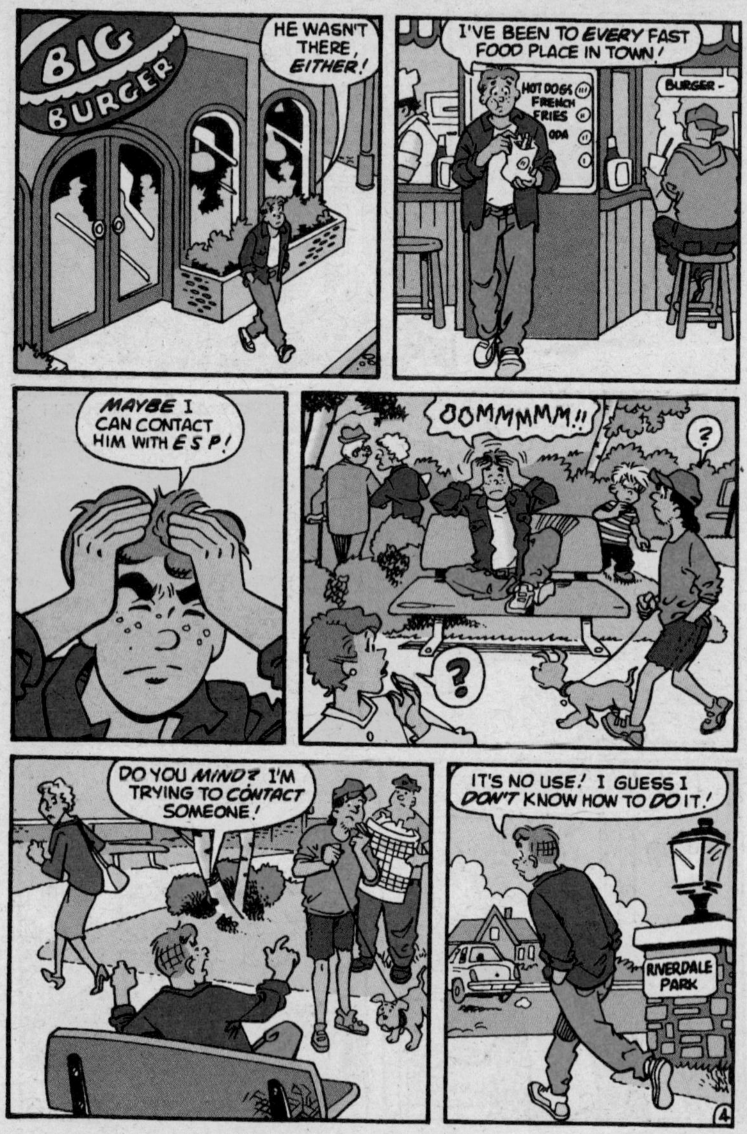
BIG BURGER
HE WASN'T THERE, EITHER!
I'VE BEEN TO EVERY FAST FOOD PLACE IN TOWN!
HOT DOGS
FRENCH FRIES
BURGER-
MAYBE I CAN CONTACT HIM WITH E S P!
OOMMMMM!!
?
?
DO YOU MIND? I'M TRYING TO CONTACT SOMEONE!
IT'S NO USE! I GUESS I DON'T KNOW HOW TO DO IT!
RIVERDALE PARK
4

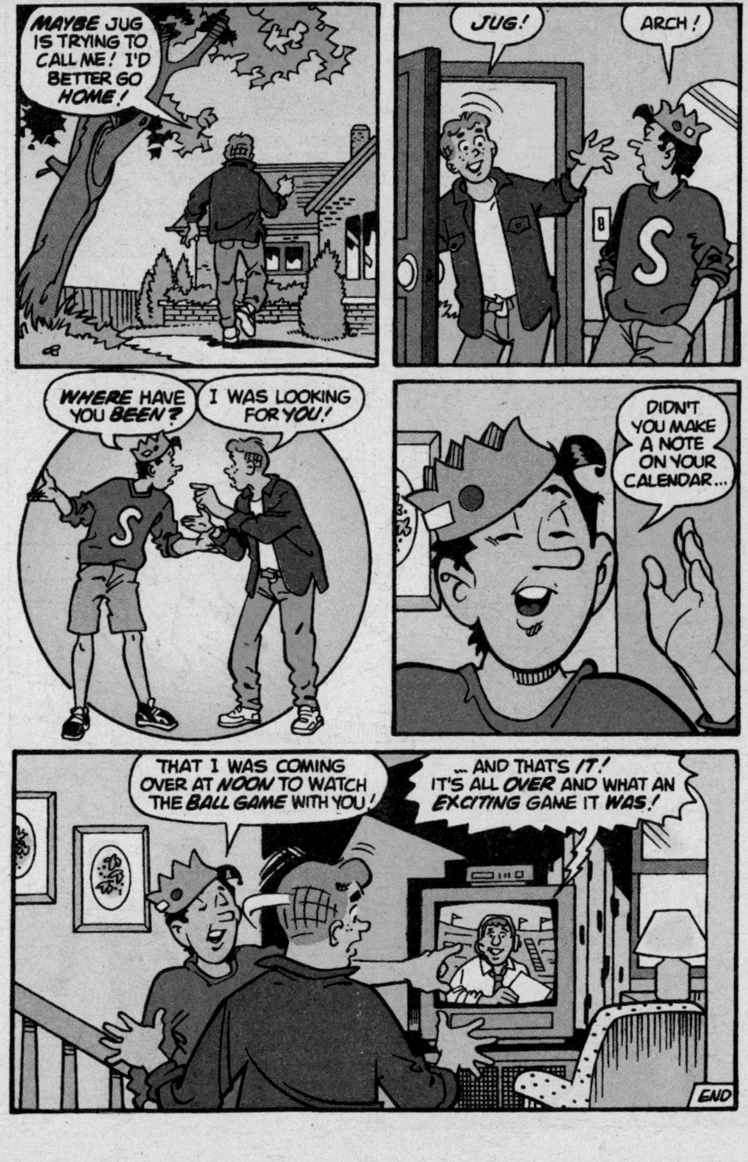
MAYBE JUG IS TRYING TO CALL ME! I'D BETTER GO HOME!
JUG!
ARCH!
WHERE HAVE YOU BEEN?
I WAS LOOKING FOR YOU!
DIDN'T YOU MAKE A NOTE ON YOUR CALENDAR...
THAT I WAS COMING OVER AT NOON TO WATCH THE BALL GAME WITH YOU!
... AND THAT'S IT! IT'S ALL OVER AND WHAT AN EXCITING GAME IT WAS!
END

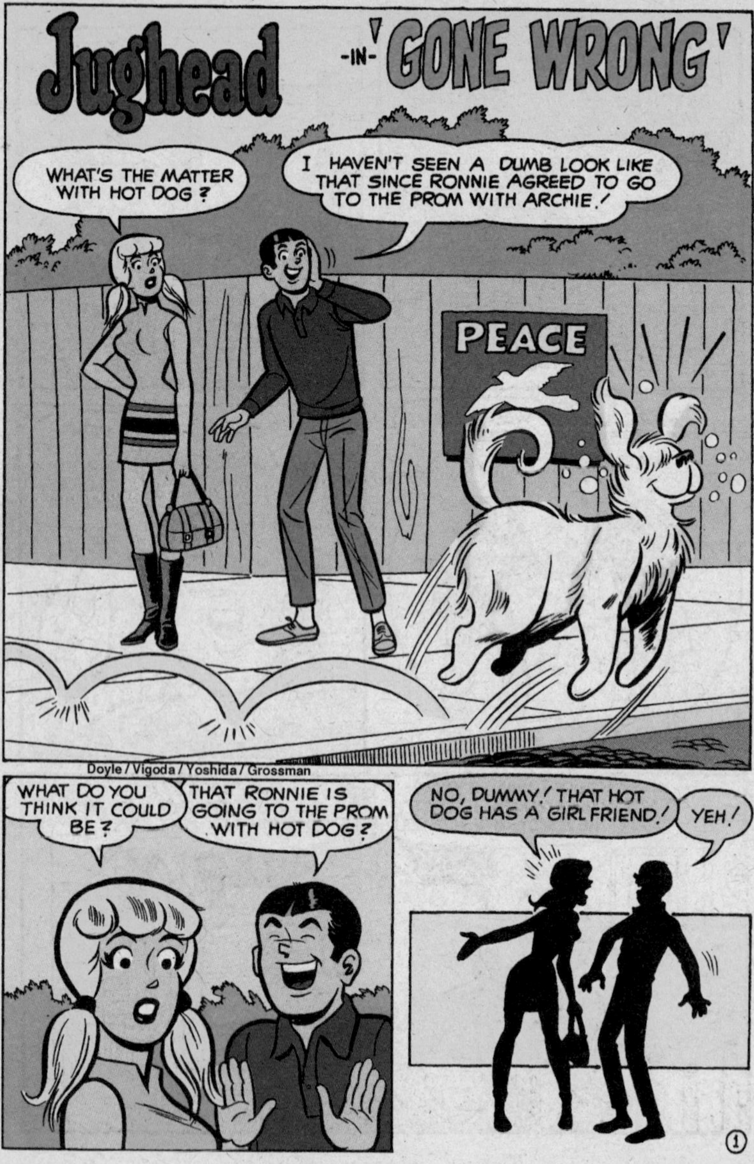
Jughead -IN- 'GONE WRONG'
WHAT'S THE MATTER WITH HOT DOG ?
I HAVEN'T SEEN A DUMB LOOK LIKE THAT SINCE RONNIE AGREED TO GO TO THE PROM WITH ARCHIE !
PEACE
Doyle / Vigoda / Yoshida / Grossman
WHAT DO YOU THINK IT COULD BE ?
THAT RONNIE IS GOING TO THE PROM WITH HOT DOG ?
NO, DUMMY ! THAT HOT DOG HAS A GIRL FRIEND !
YEH !

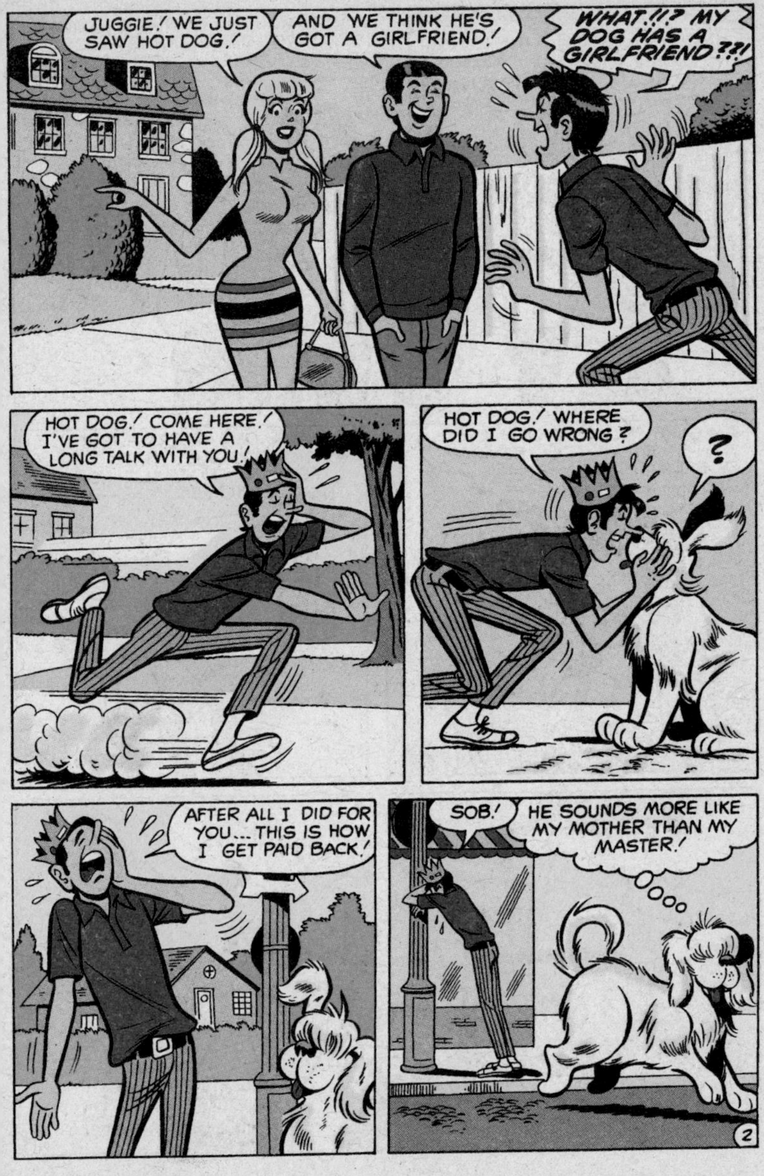
JUGGIE! WE JUST SAW HOT DOG!
AND WE THINK HE'S GOT A GIRLFRIEND!
WHAT!!? MY DOG HAS A GIRLFRIEND??!
HOT DOG! COME HERE! I'VE GOT TO HAVE A LONG TALK WITH YOU!
HOT DOG! WHERE DID I GO WRONG?
?
AFTER ALL I DID FOR YOU... THIS IS HOW I GET PAID BACK!
SOB!
HE SOUNDS MORE LIKE MY MOTHER THAN MY MASTER!
2

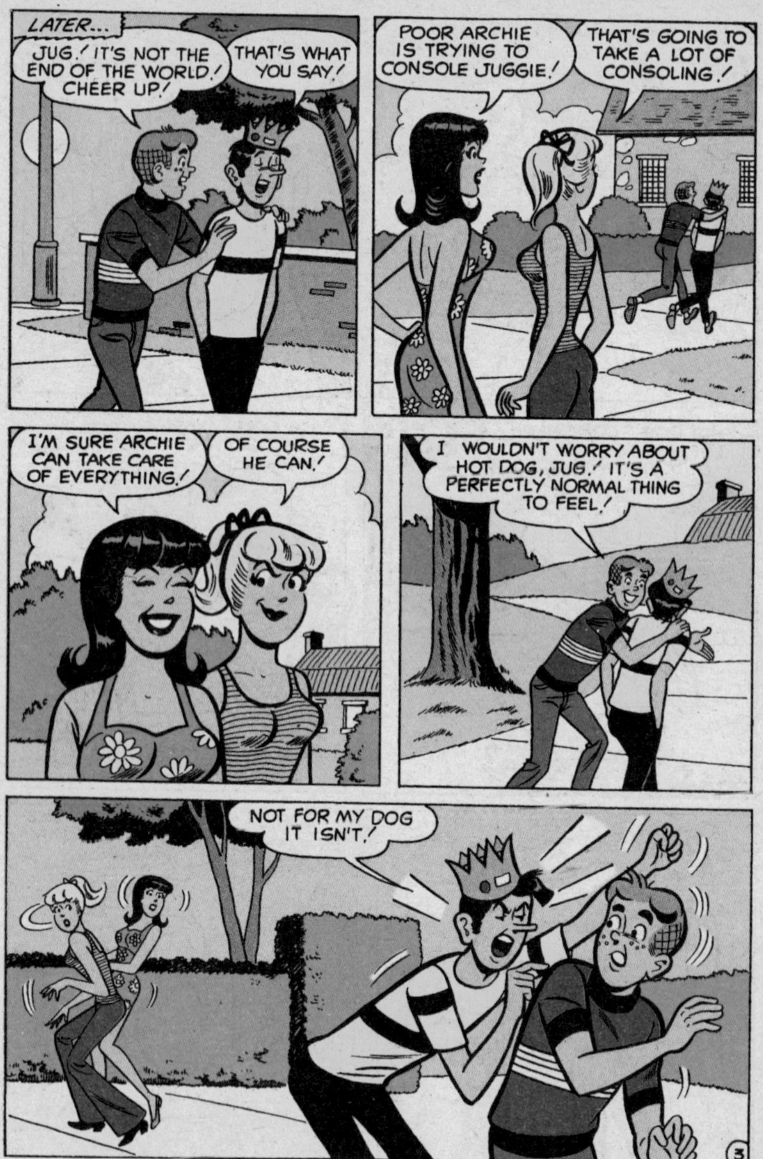
LATER...
JUG! IT'S NOT THE END OF THE WORLD! CHEER UP!
THAT'S WHAT YOU SAY!
POOR ARCHIE IS TRYING TO CONSOLE JUGGIE!
THAT'S GOING TO TAKE A LOT OF CONSOLING!
I'M SURE ARCHIE CAN TAKE CARE OF EVERYTHING!
OF COURSE HE CAN!
I WOULDN'T WORRY ABOUT HOT DOG, JUG! IT'S A PERFECTLY NORMAL THING TO FEEL!
NOT FOR MY DOG IT ISN'T!

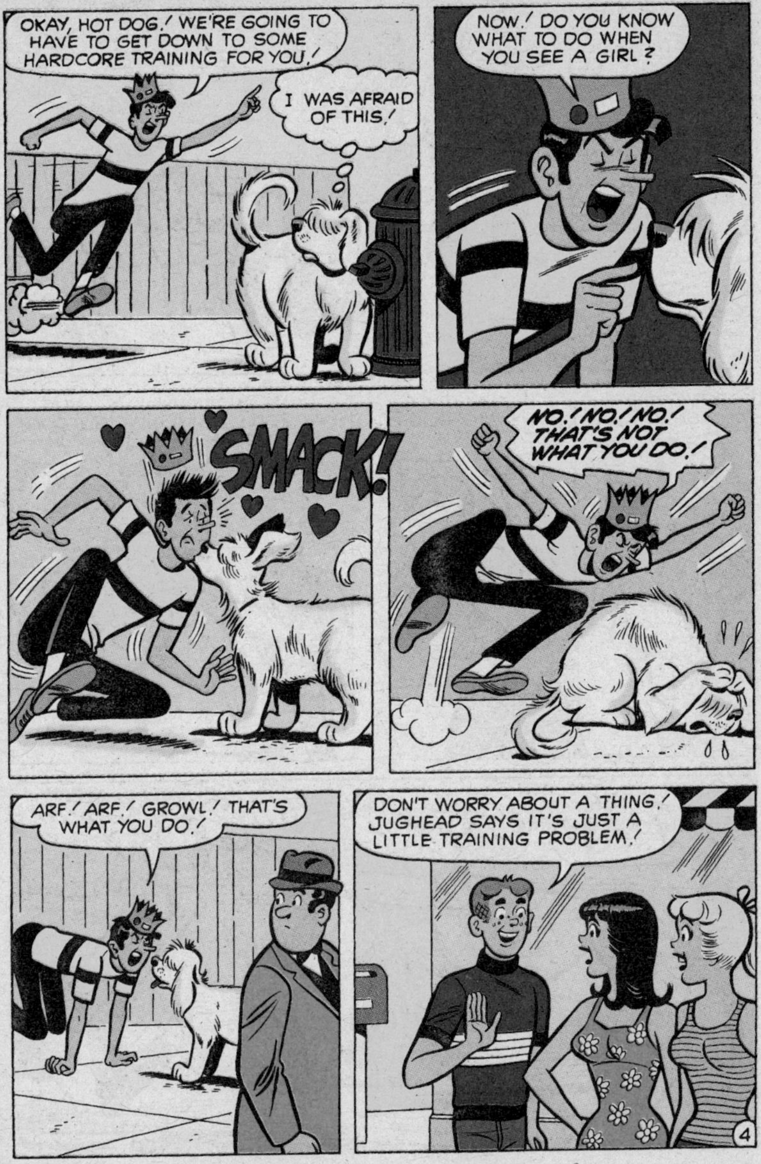
OKAY, HOT DOG! WE'RE GOING TO HAVE TO GET DOWN TO SOME HARDCORE TRAINING FOR YOU!
I WAS AFRAID OF THIS!
NOW! DO YOU KNOW WHAT TO DO WHEN YOU SEE A GIRL?
SMACK!
NO! NO! NO! THAT'S NOT WHAT YOU DO!
ARF! ARF! GROWL! THAT'S WHAT YOU DO!
DON'T WORRY ABOUT A THING! JUGHEAD SAYS IT'S JUST A LITTLE TRAINING PROBLEM!
4

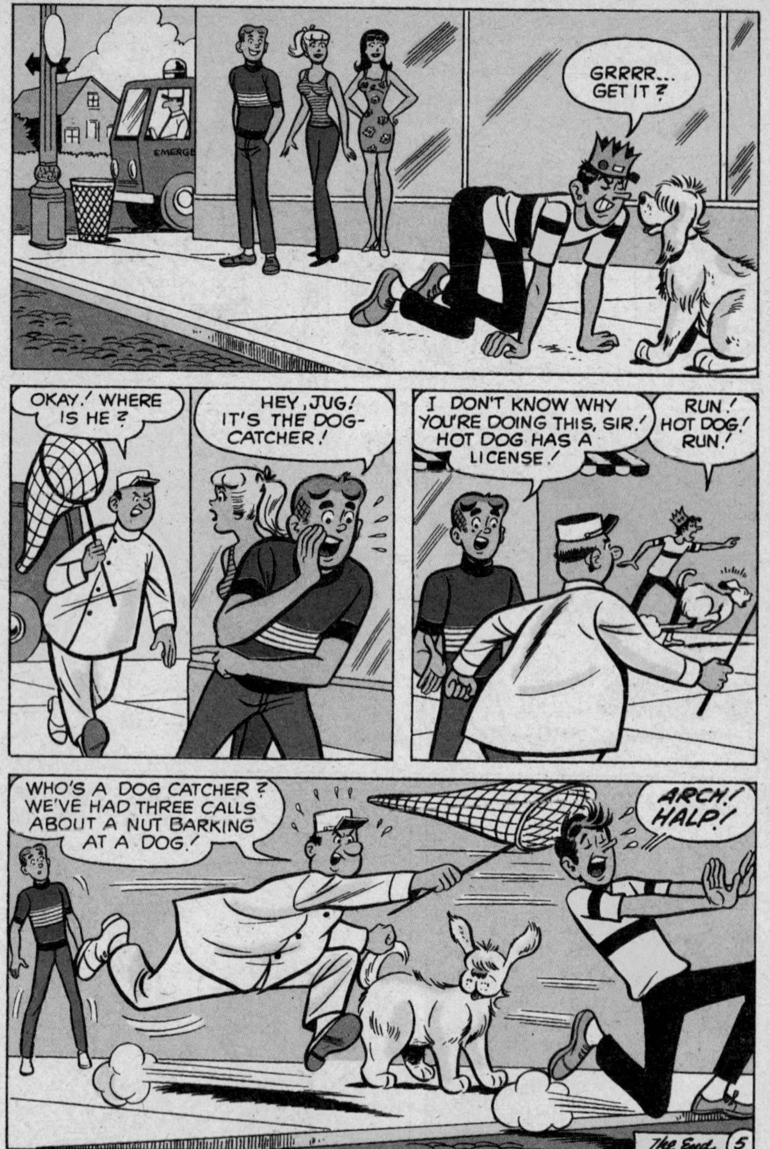
EMERGE
GRRRR... GET IT ?
OKAY! WHERE IS HE ?
HEY, JUG! IT'S THE DOG-CATCHER!
I DON'T KNOW WHY YOU'RE DOING THIS, SIR! HOT DOG HAS A LICENSE!
RUN! HOT DOG! RUN!
WHO'S A DOG CATCHER ? WE'VE HAD THREE CALLS ABOUT A NUT BARKING AT A DOG!
ARCH! HALP!
The End

Betty and Veronica in The LIST!

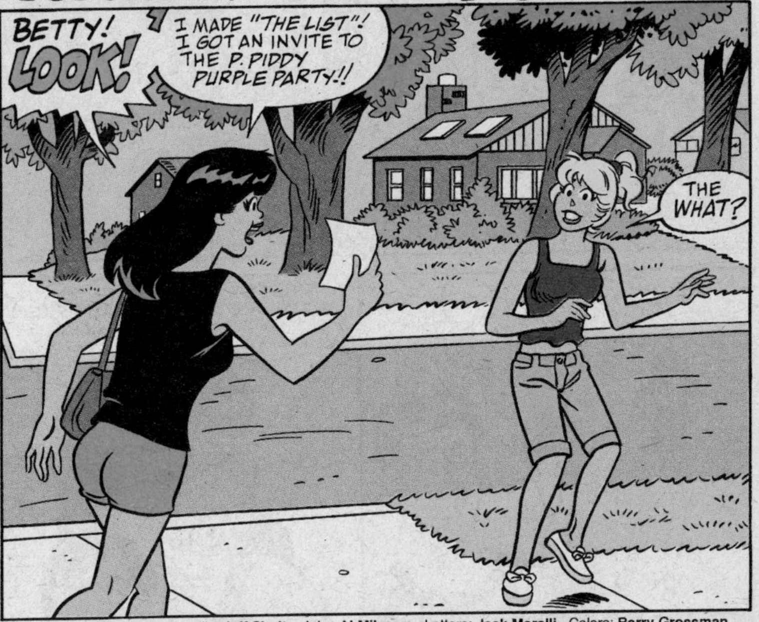

BETTY! LOOK!
I MADE "THE LIST"! I GOT AN INVITE TO THE P. PIDDY PURPLE PARTY!!
THE WHAT?

Script: **Barbara Slate** Pencils: **Jeff Shultz** Inks: **Al Milgrom** Letters: **Jack Morelli** Colors: **Barry Grossman**
Editor-In-Chief: **Victor Gorelick** President: **Mike Pellerito** Publisher: **Jon Goldwater**

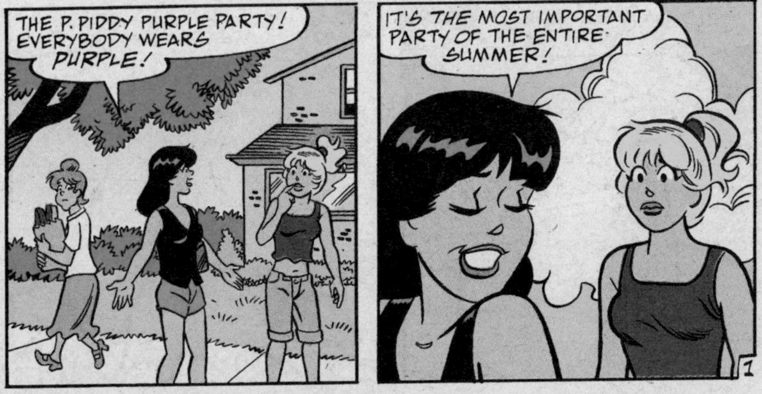

THE P. PIDDY PURPLE PARTY! EVERYBODY WEARS PURPLE!
IT'S THE MOST IMPORTANT PARTY OF THE ENTIRE SUMMER!

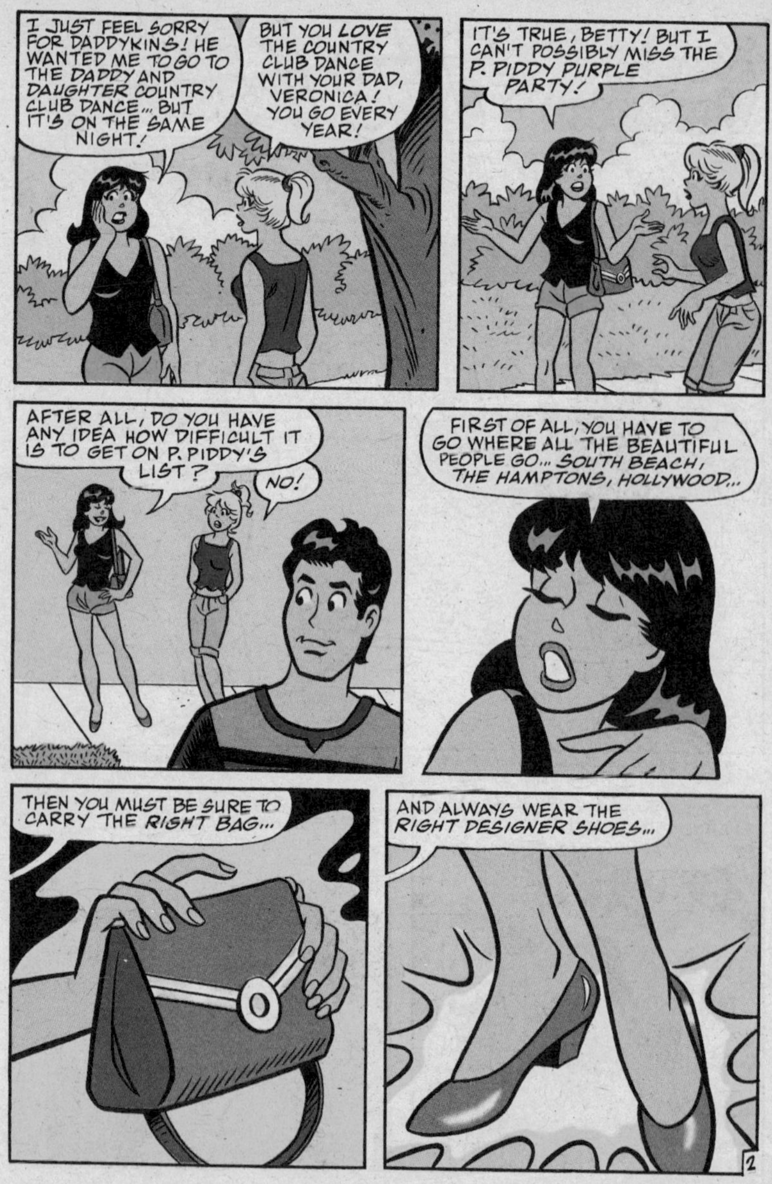
I JUST FEEL SORRY FOR DADDYKINS! HE WANTED ME TO GO TO THE DADDY AND DAUGHTER COUNTRY CLUB DANCE... BUT IT'S ON THE SAME NIGHT!
BUT YOU LOVE THE COUNTRY CLUB DANCE WITH YOUR DAD, VERONICA! YOU GO EVERY YEAR!
IT'S TRUE, BETTY! BUT I CAN'T POSSIBLY MISS THE P. PIDDY PURPLE PARTY!
AFTER ALL, DO YOU HAVE ANY IDEA HOW DIFFICULT IT IS TO GET ON P. PIDDY'S LIST?
NO!
FIRST OF ALL, YOU HAVE TO GO WHERE ALL THE BEAUTIFUL PEOPLE GO... SOUTH BEACH, THE HAMPTONS, HOLLYWOOD...
THEN YOU MUST BE SURE TO CARRY THE RIGHT BAG...
AND ALWAYS WEAR THE RIGHT DESIGNER SHOES...
2

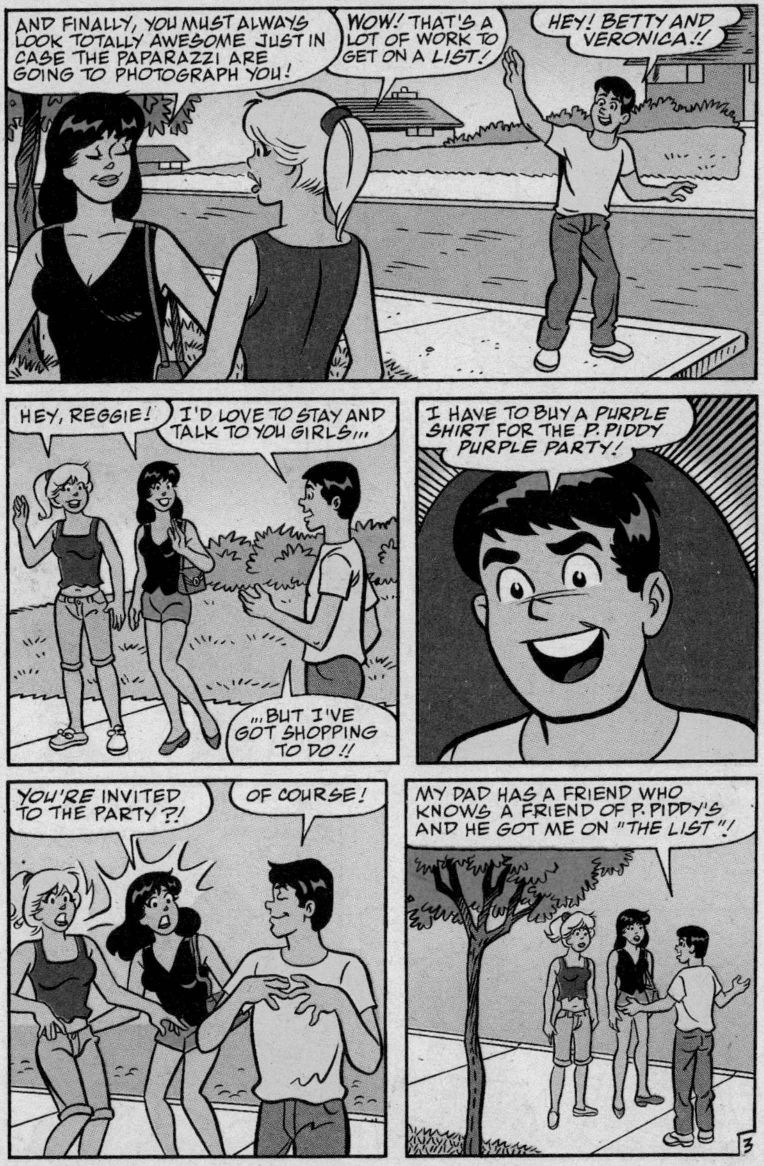

AND FINALLY, YOU MUST ALWAYS LOOK TOTALLY AWESOME JUST IN CASE THE PAPARAZZI ARE GOING TO PHOTOGRAPH YOU!
WOW! THAT'S A LOT OF WORK TO GET ON A LIST!
HEY! BETTY AND VERONICA!!
HEY, REGGIE!
I'D LOVE TO STAY AND TALK TO YOU GIRLS...
...BUT I'VE GOT SHOPPING TO DO!!
I HAVE TO BUY A PURPLE SHIRT FOR THE P. PIDDY PURPLE PARTY!
YOU'RE INVITED TO THE PARTY?!
OF COURSE!
MY DAD HAS A FRIEND WHO KNOWS A FRIEND OF P. PIDDY'S AND HE GOT ME ON "THE LIST"!
3

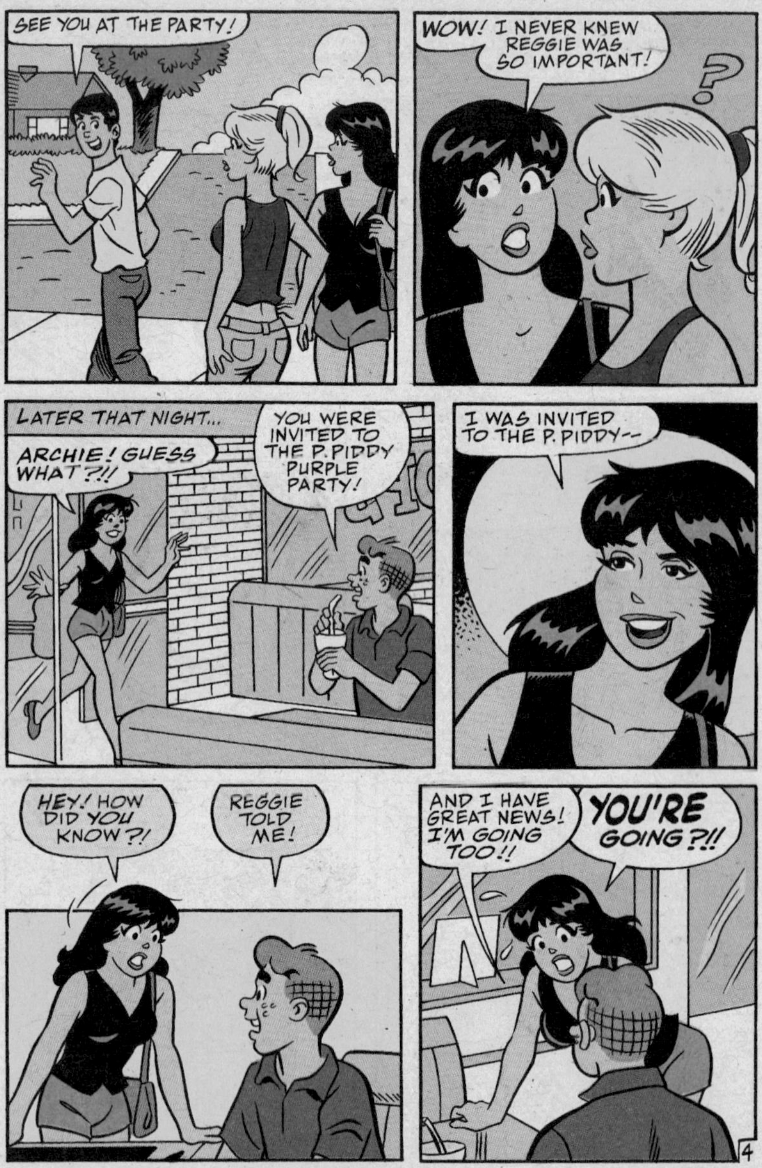
SEE YOU AT THE PARTY!
WOW! I NEVER KNEW REGGIE WAS SO IMPORTANT!
?
LATER THAT NIGHT...
ARCHIE! GUESS WHAT?!!
YOU WERE INVITED TO THE P. PIDDY PURPLE PARTY!
I WAS INVITED TO THE P. PIDDY--
HEY! HOW DID YOU KNOW?!
REGGIE TOLD ME!
AND I HAVE GREAT NEWS! I'M GOING TOO!!
YOU'RE GOING?!!

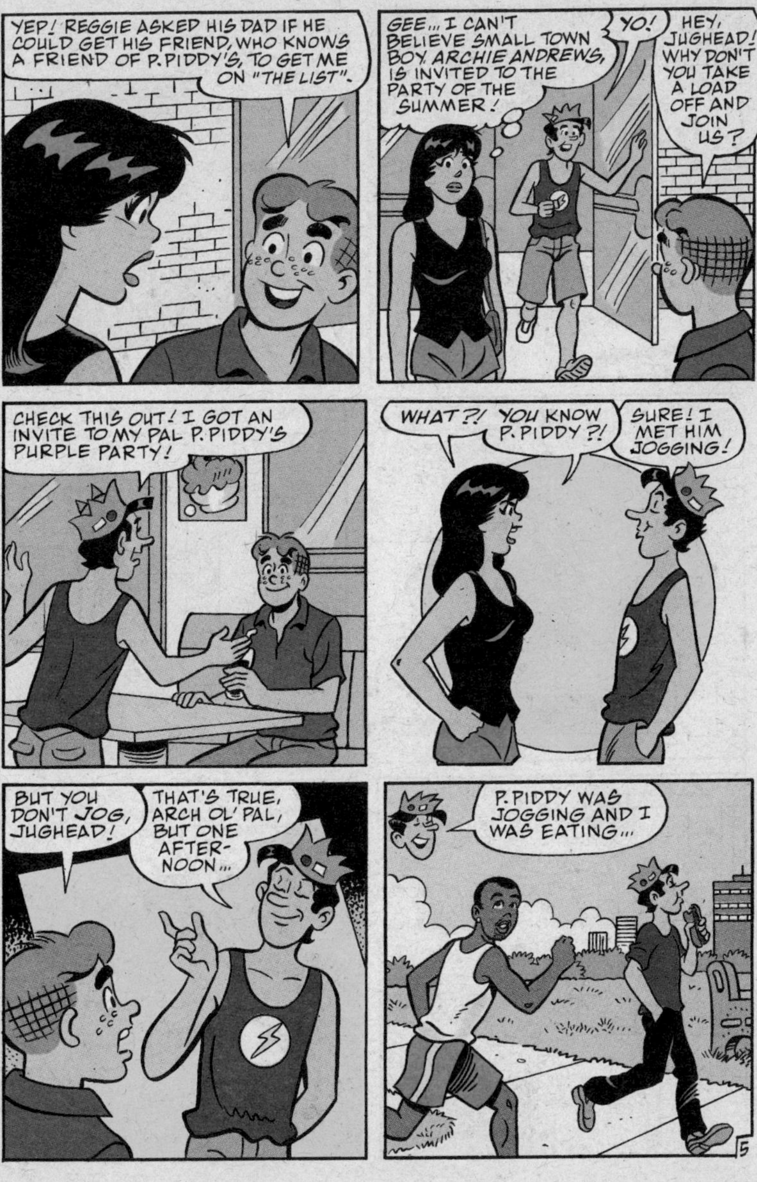

YEP! REGGIE ASKED HIS DAD IF HE COULD GET HIS FRIEND, WHO KNOWS A FRIEND OF P. PIDDY'S, TO GET ME ON "THE LIST".
GEE... I CAN'T BELIEVE SMALL TOWN BOY ARCHIE ANDREWS, IS INVITED TO THE PARTY OF THE SUMMER!
YO!
HEY, JUGHEAD! WHY DON'T YOU TAKE A LOAD OFF AND JOIN US?
CHECK THIS OUT! I GOT AN INVITE TO MY PAL P. PIDDY'S PURPLE PARTY!
WHAT?! YOU KNOW P. PIDDY?!
SURE! I MET HIM JOGGING!
BUT YOU DON'T JOG, JUGHEAD!
THAT'S TRUE, ARCH OL' PAL, BUT ONE AFTER-NOON...
P. PIDDY WAS JOGGING AND I WAS EATING...
5

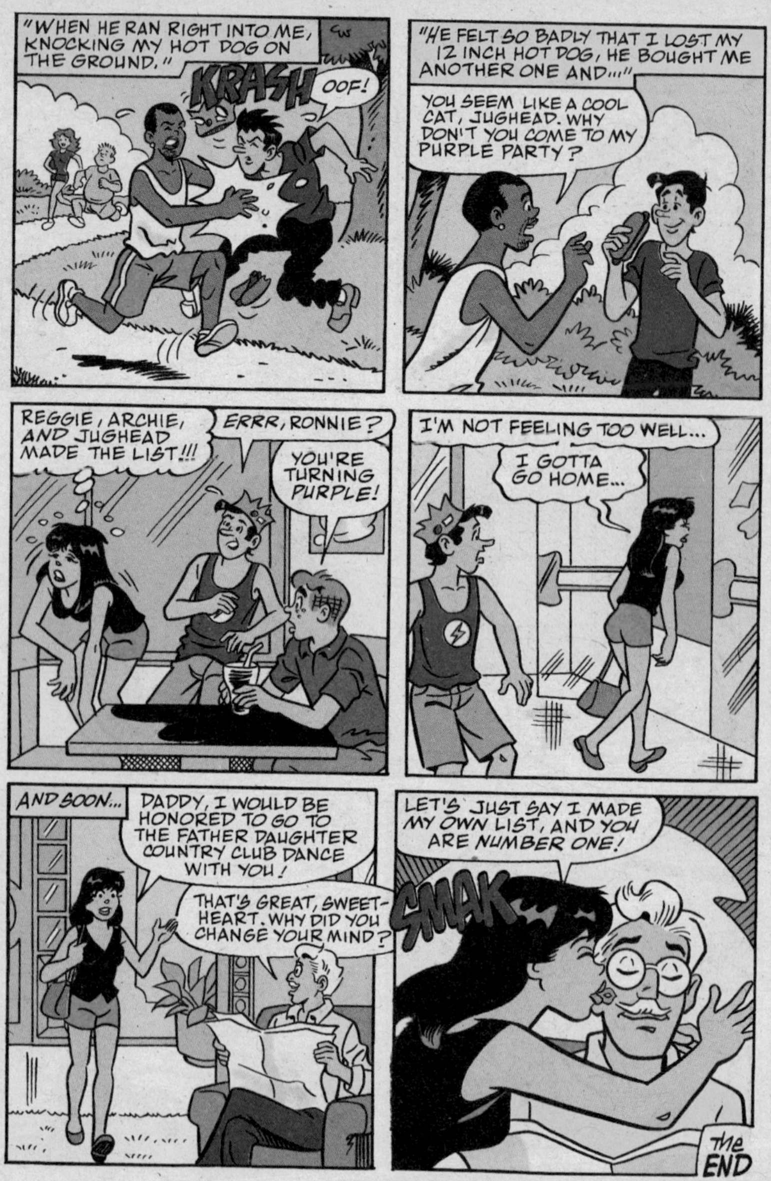
"WHEN HE RAN RIGHT INTO ME, KNOCKING MY HOT DOG ON THE GROUND."
KRASH
OOF!
"HE FELT SO BADLY THAT I LOST MY 12 INCH HOT DOG, HE BOUGHT ME ANOTHER ONE AND..."
YOU SEEM LIKE A COOL CAT, JUGHEAD. WHY DON'T YOU COME TO MY PURPLE PARTY?
REGGIE, ARCHIE, AND JUGHEAD MADE THE LIST!!!
ERRR, RONNIE?
YOU'RE TURNING PURPLE!
I'M NOT FEELING TOO WELL...
I GOTTA GO HOME...
AND SOON...
DADDY, I WOULD BE HONORED TO GO TO THE FATHER DAUGHTER COUNTRY CLUB DANCE WITH YOU!
THAT'S GREAT, SWEET-HEART. WHY DID YOU CHANGE YOUR MIND?
LET'S JUST SAY I MADE MY OWN LIST, AND YOU ARE NUMBER ONE!
SMAK
THE END

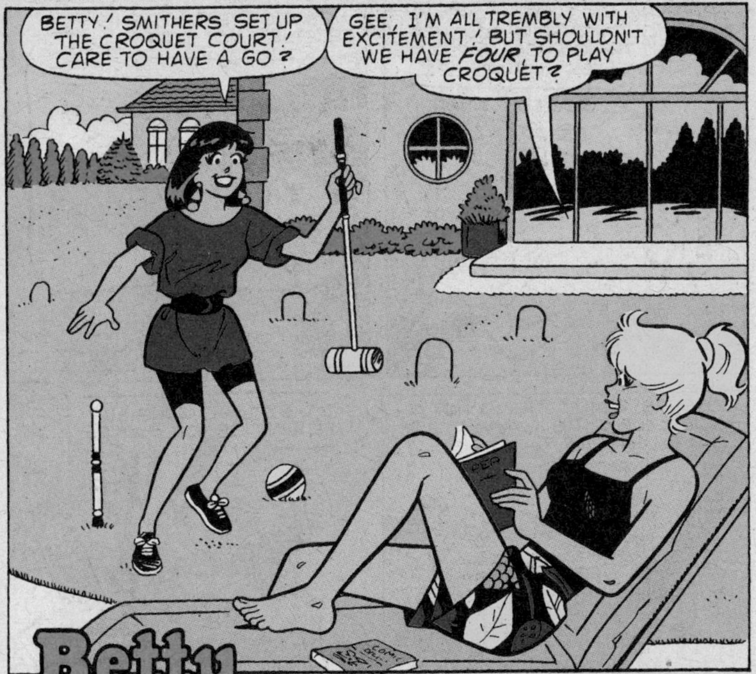
BETTY! SMITHERS SET UP THE CROQUET COURT! CARE TO HAVE A GO?
GEE, I'M ALL TREMBLY WITH EXCITEMENT! BUT SHOULDN'T WE HAVE *FOUR* TO PLAY CROQUET?
PEP

Betty and Veronica (IN) "IT'S A WICKET WORLD"

Script: George Gladir / Pencils: Dan DeCarlo / Inks: Alison Flood / Letters: Bill Yoshida / Colors: Barry Grossman

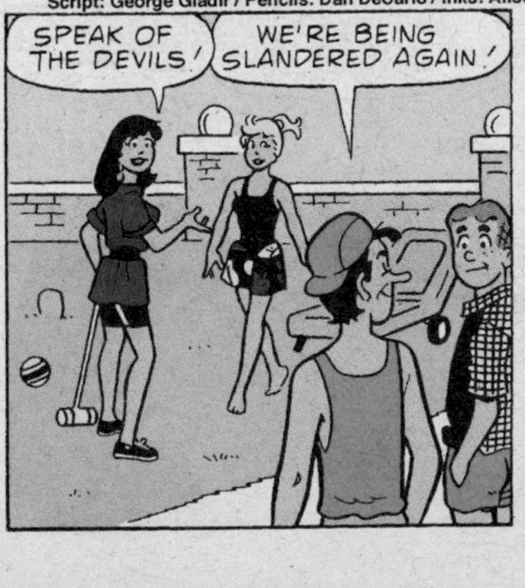
SPEAK OF THE DEVILS!
WE'RE BEING SLANDERED AGAIN!

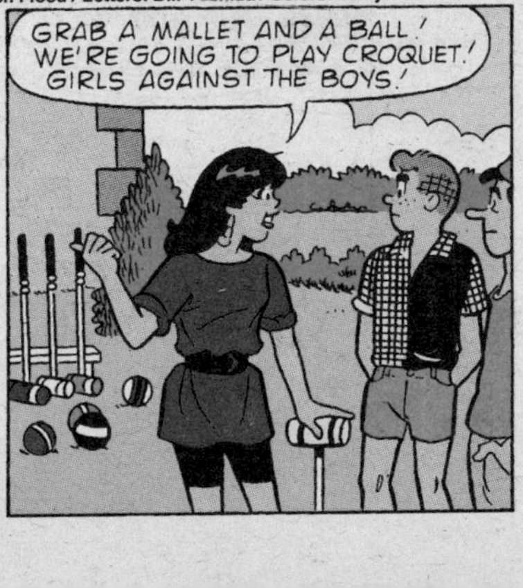
GRAB A MALLET AND A BALL! WE'RE GOING TO PLAY CROQUET! GIRLS AGAINST THE BOYS!

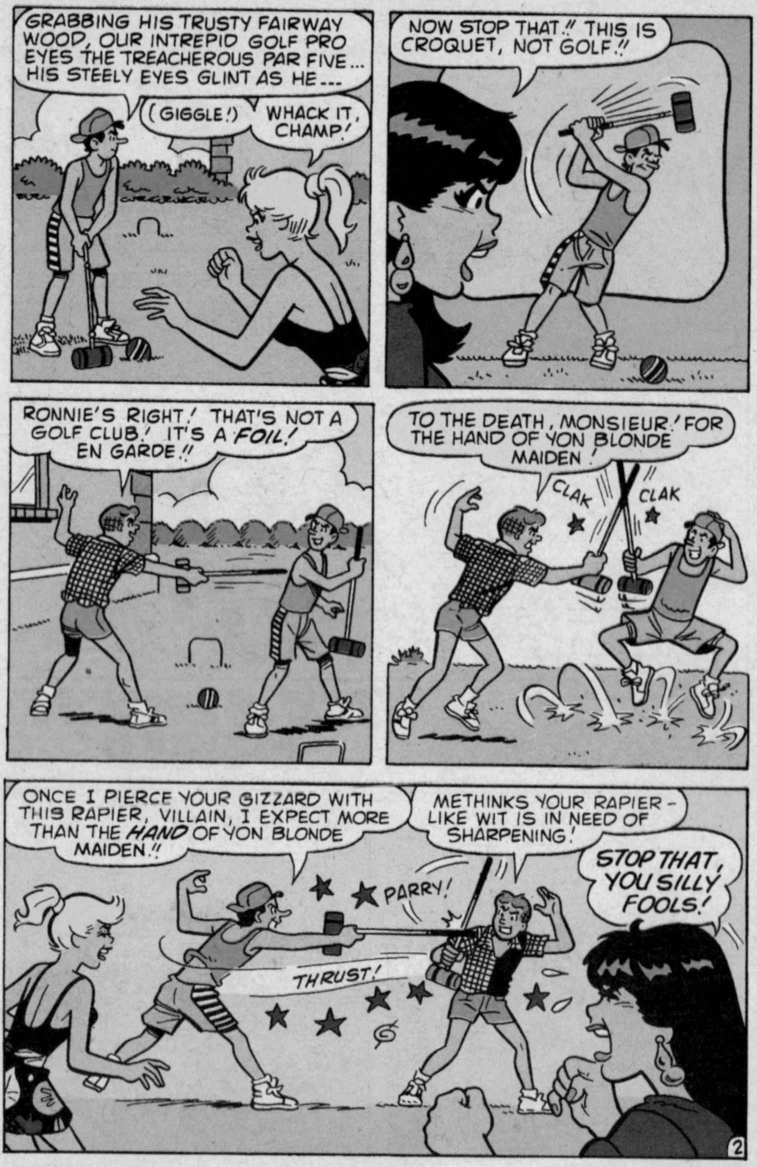
GRABBING HIS TRUSTY FAIRWAY WOOD, OUR INTREPID GOLF PRO EYES THE TREACHEROUS PAR FIVE... HIS STEELY EYES GLINT AS HE---
(GIGGLE!)
WHACK IT, CHAMP!
NOW STOP THAT!! THIS IS CROQUET, NOT GOLF!!
RONNIE'S RIGHT! THAT'S NOT A GOLF CLUB! IT'S A FOIL! EN GARDE!!
TO THE DEATH, MONSIEUR! FOR THE HAND OF YON BLONDE MAIDEN!
CLAK
CLAK
ONCE I PIERCE YOUR GIZZARD WITH THIS RAPIER, VILLAIN, I EXPECT MORE THAN THE HAND OF YON BLONDE MAIDEN!!
METHINKS YOUR RAPIER-LIKE WIT IS IN NEED OF SHARPENING!
STOP THAT, YOU SILLY FOOLS!
PARRY!
THRUST!
2

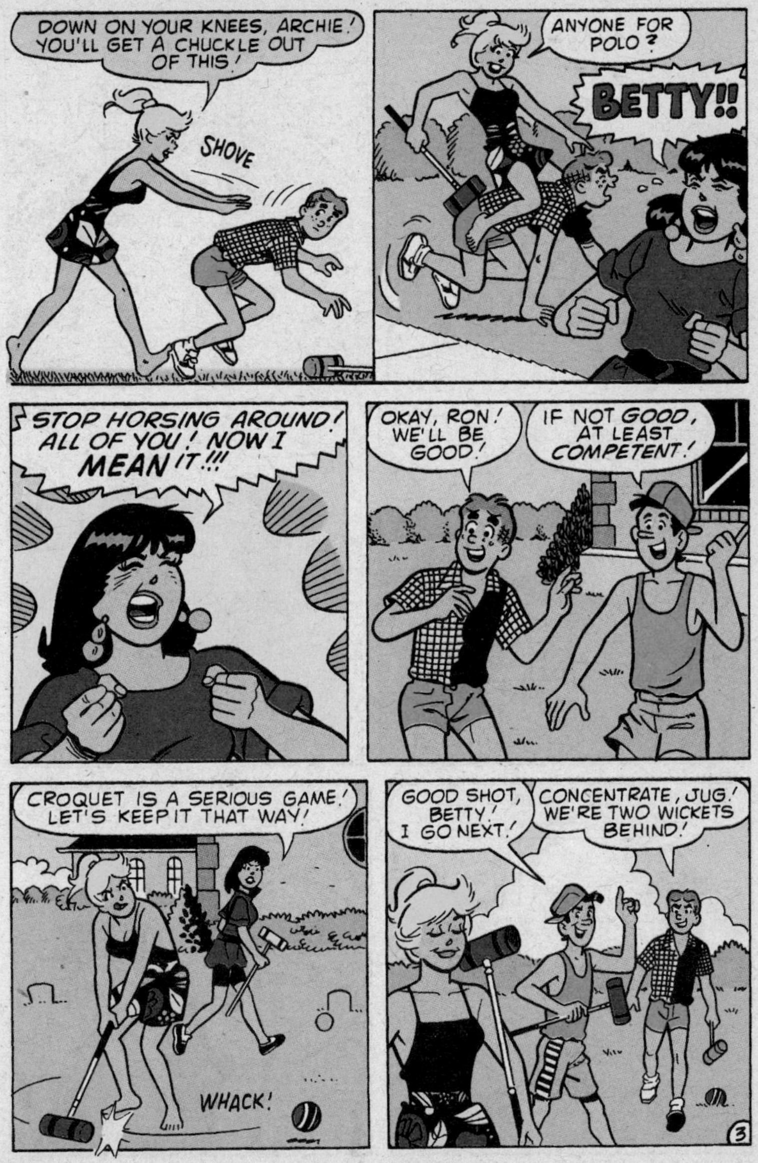
DOWN ON YOUR KNEES, ARCHIE! YOU'LL GET A CHUCKLE OUT OF THIS!
SHOVE
ANYONE FOR POLO?
BETTY!!
STOP HORSING AROUND! ALL OF YOU! NOW I MEAN IT!!!
OKAY, RON! WE'LL BE GOOD!
IF NOT GOOD, AT LEAST COMPETENT!
CROQUET IS A SERIOUS GAME! LET'S KEEP IT THAT WAY!
WHACK!
GOOD SHOT, BETTY! I GO NEXT!
CONCENTRATE, JUG! WE'RE TWO WICKETS BEHIND!
3

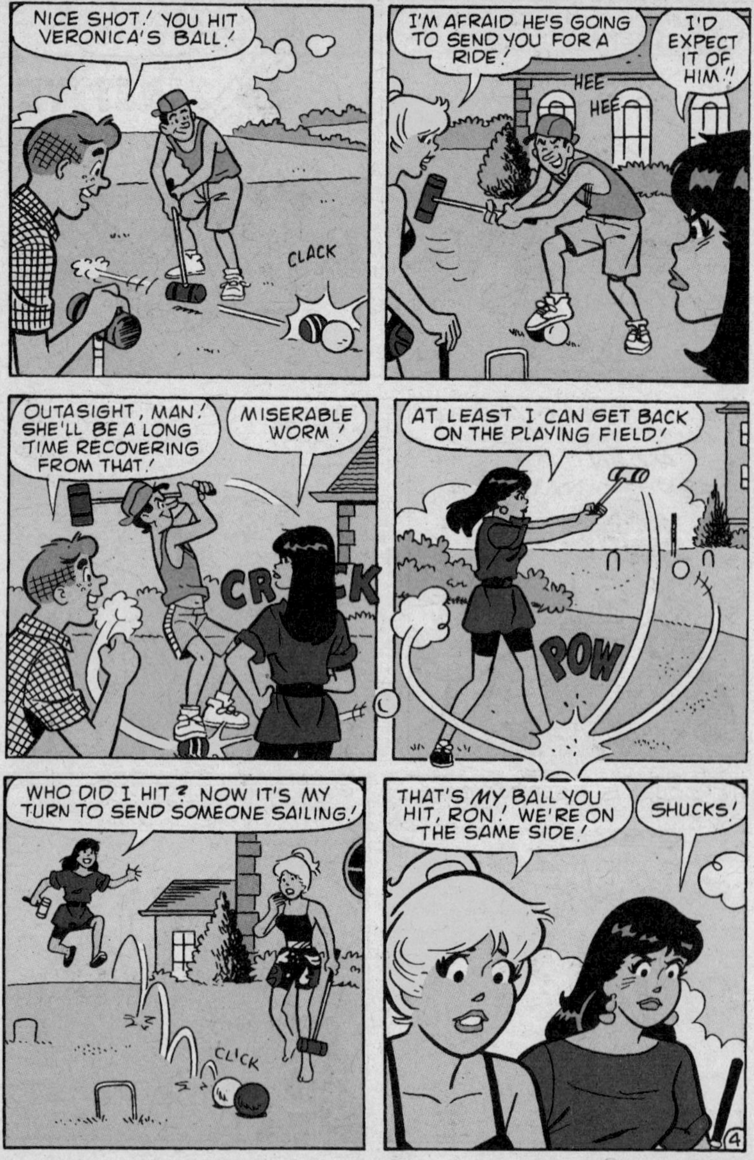
NICE SHOT! YOU HIT VERONICA'S BALL!
CLACK
I'M AFRAID HE'S GOING TO SEND YOU FOR A RIDE!
I'D EXPECT IT OF HIM!!
HEE HEE
OUTASIGHT, MAN! SHE'LL BE A LONG TIME RECOVERING FROM THAT!
MISERABLE WORM!
AT LEAST I CAN GET BACK ON THE PLAYING FIELD!
POW
WHO DID I HIT? NOW IT'S MY TURN TO SEND SOMEONE SAILING!
CLICK
THAT'S MY BALL YOU HIT, RON! WE'RE ON THE SAME SIDE!
SHUCKS!
4

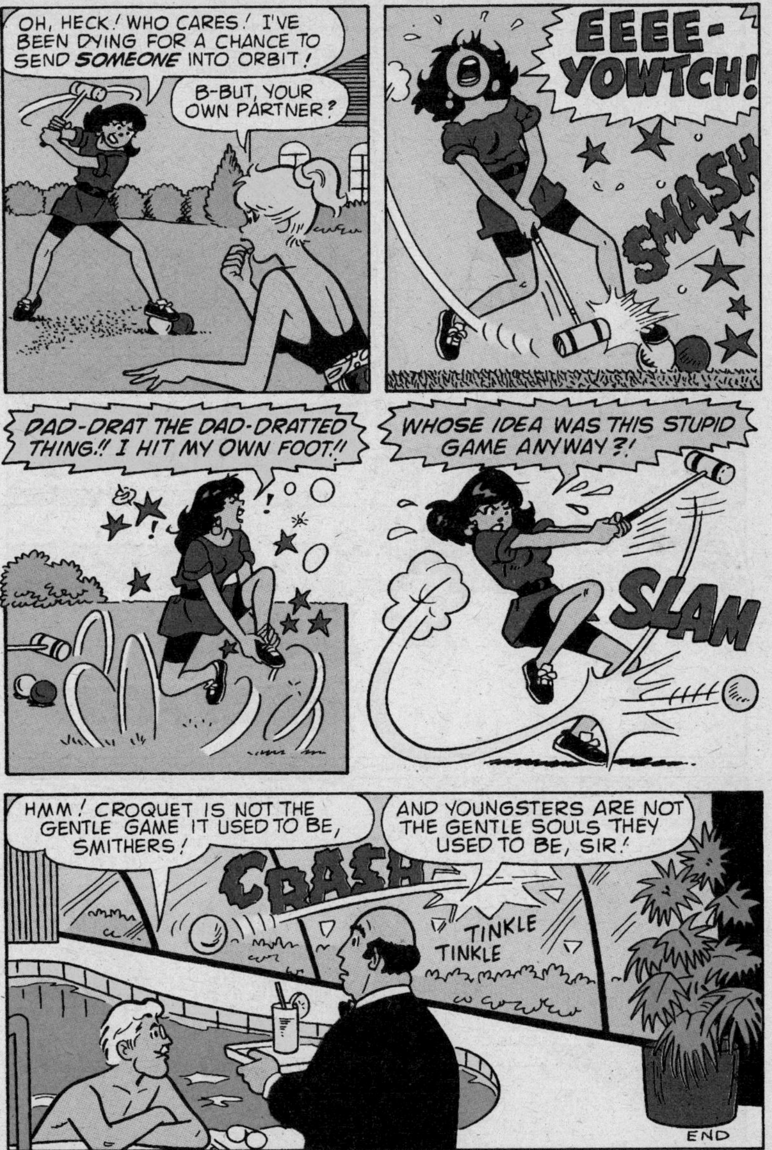

OH, HECK! WHO CARES! I'VE BEEN DYING FOR A CHANCE TO SEND SOMEONE INTO ORBIT!
B-BUT, YOUR OWN PARTNER?
EEEE-YOWTCH!
SHASH
DAD-DRAT THE DAD-DRATTED THING!! I HIT MY OWN FOOT!!
WHOSE IDEA WAS THIS STUPID GAME ANYWAY?!
SLAM
HMM! CROQUET IS NOT THE GENTLE GAME IT USED TO BE, SMITHERS!
AND YOUNGSTERS ARE NOT THE GENTLE SOULS THEY USED TO BE, SIR!
CRASH
TINKLE
TINKLE
END

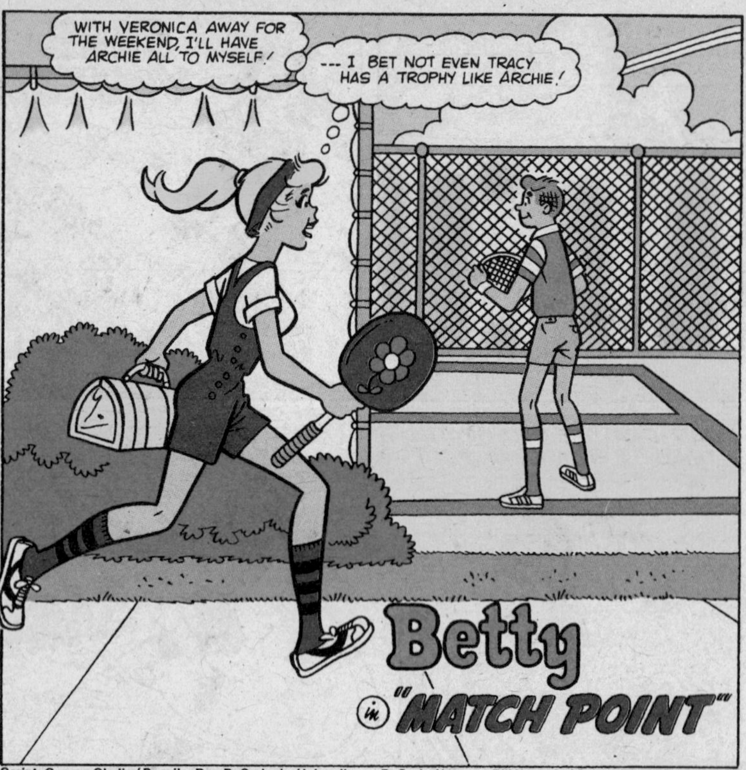
WITH VERONICA AWAY FOR THE WEEKEND, I'LL HAVE ARCHIE ALL TO MYSELF!
--- I BET NOT EVEN TRACY HAS A TROPHY LIKE ARCHIE!
Betty
in "MATCH POINT"

Script: George Gladir / Pencils: Dan DeCarlo Jr. / Inks: Jimmy DeCarlo / Letters: Bill Yoshida / Colors: Barry Grossman

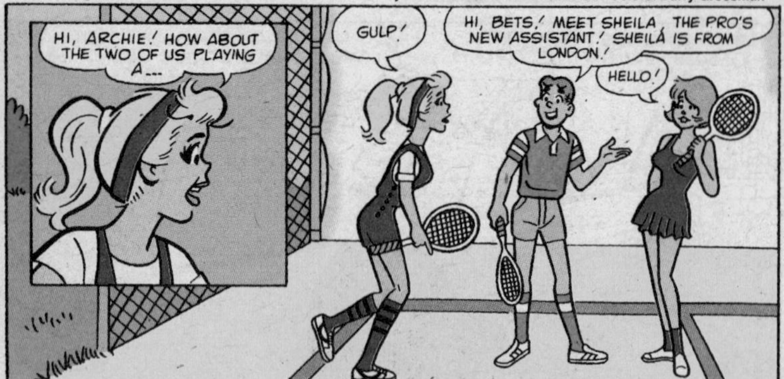
HI, ARCHIE! HOW ABOUT THE TWO OF US PLAYING A---
GULP!
HI, BETS! MEET SHEILA, THE PRO'S NEW ASSISTANT! SHEILA IS FROM LONDON!
HELLO!

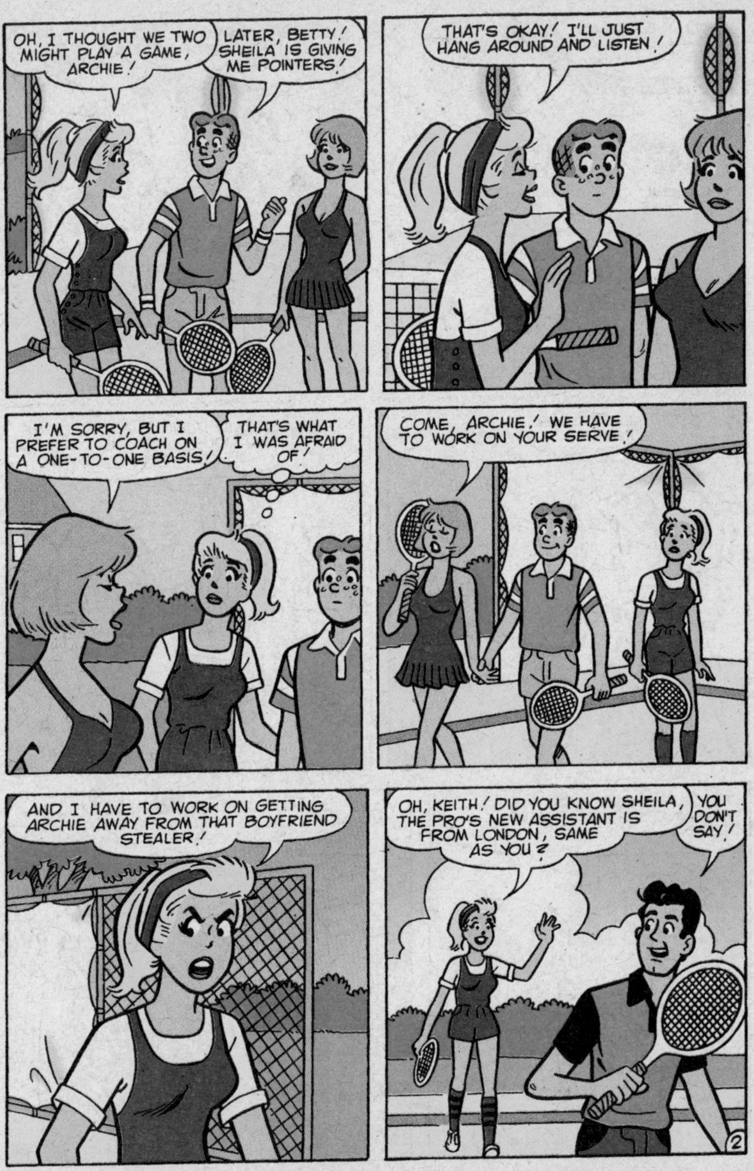
OH, I THOUGHT WE TWO MIGHT PLAY A GAME, ARCHIE!
LATER, BETTY! SHEILA IS GIVING ME POINTERS!
THAT'S OKAY! I'LL JUST HANG AROUND AND LISTEN!
I'M SORRY, BUT I PREFER TO COACH ON A ONE-TO-ONE BASIS!
THAT'S WHAT I WAS AFRAID OF!
COME, ARCHIE! WE HAVE TO WORK ON YOUR SERVE!
AND I HAVE TO WORK ON GETTING ARCHIE AWAY FROM THAT BOYFRIEND STEALER!
OH, KEITH! DID YOU KNOW SHEILA, THE PRO'S NEW ASSISTANT IS FROM LONDON, SAME AS YOU?
YOU DON'T SAY!
2

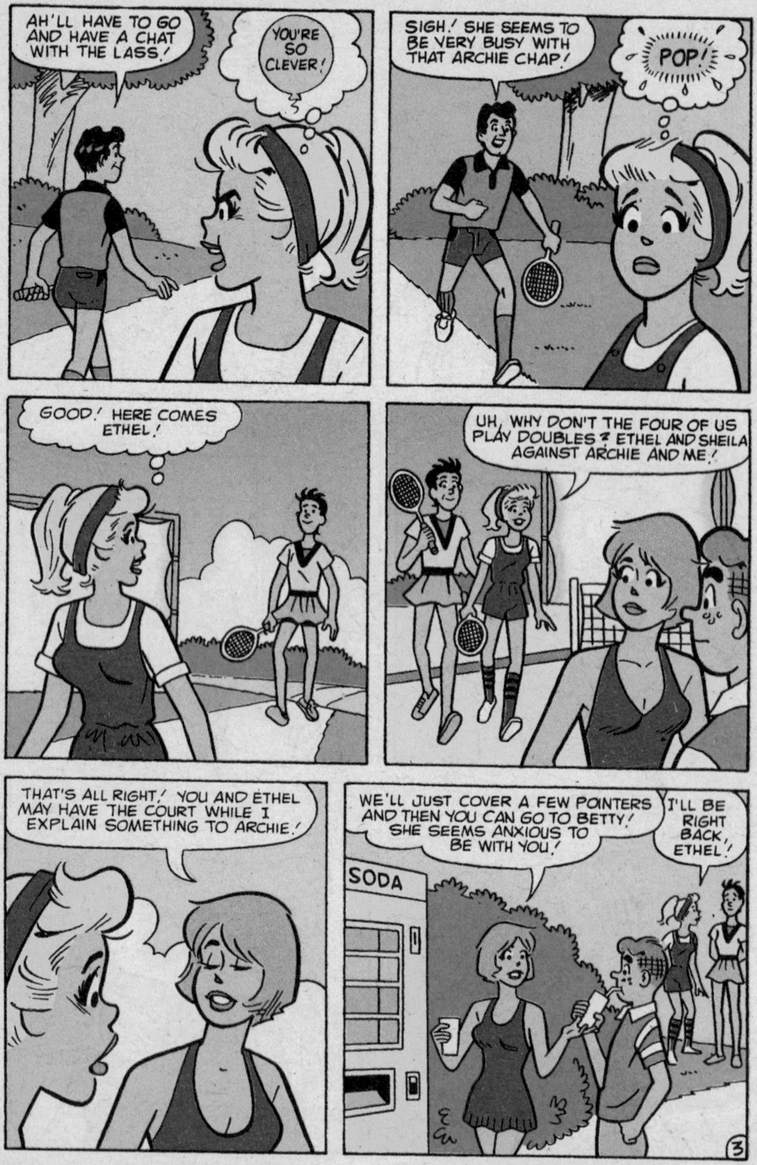
AH'LL HAVE TO GO AND HAVE A CHAT WITH THE LASS!
YOU'RE SO CLEVER!
SIGH! SHE SEEMS TO BE VERY BUSY WITH THAT ARCHIE CHAP!
POP!
GOOD! HERE COMES ETHEL!
UH, WHY DON'T THE FOUR OF US PLAY DOUBLES? ETHEL AND SHEILA AGAINST ARCHIE AND ME!
THAT'S ALL RIGHT! YOU AND ETHEL MAY HAVE THE COURT WHILE I EXPLAIN SOMETHING TO ARCHIE!
WE'LL JUST COVER A FEW POINTERS AND THEN YOU CAN GO TO BETTY! SHE SEEMS ANXIOUS TO BE WITH YOU!
I'LL BE RIGHT BACK, ETHEL!
SODA
3

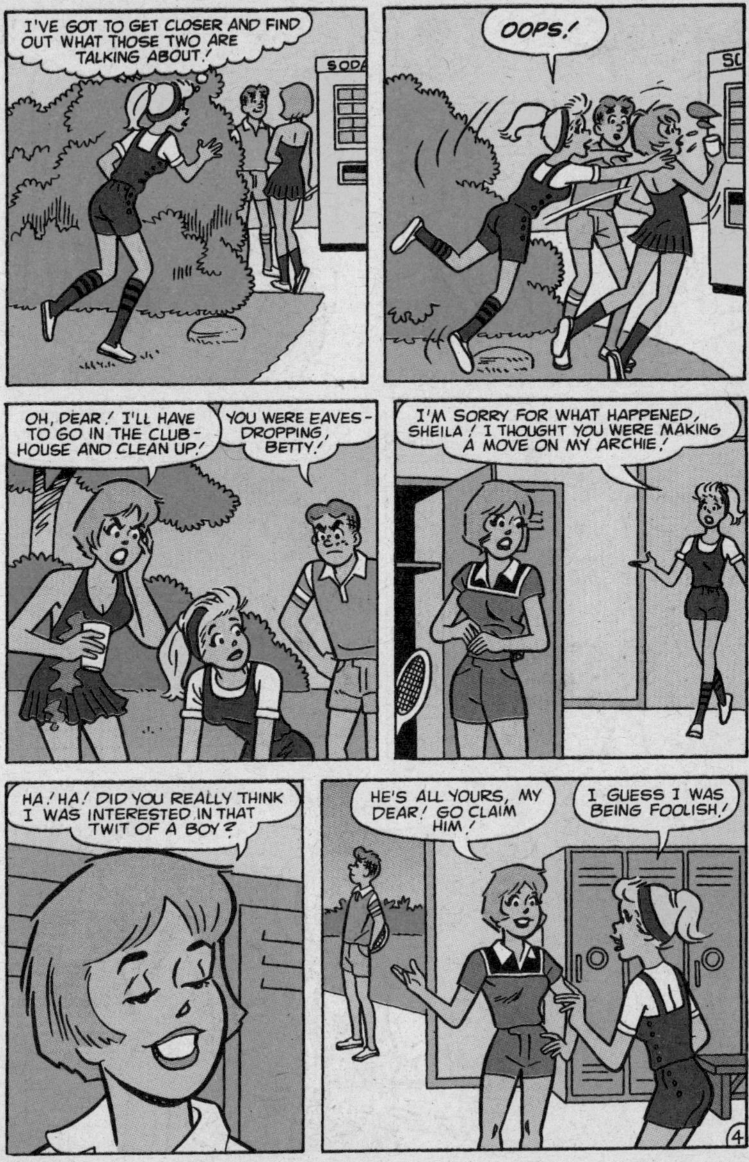

I'VE GOT TO GET CLOSER AND FIND OUT WHAT THOSE TWO ARE TALKING ABOUT!
SODA
OOPS!
OH, DEAR! I'LL HAVE TO GO IN THE CLUB-HOUSE AND CLEAN UP!
YOU WERE EAVES-DROPPING, BETTY!
I'M SORRY FOR WHAT HAPPENED, SHEILA! I THOUGHT YOU WERE MAKING A MOVE ON MY ARCHIE!
HA! HA! DID YOU REALLY THINK I WAS INTERESTED IN THAT TWIT OF A BOY?
HE'S ALL YOURS, MY DEAR! GO CLAIM HIM!
I GUESS I WAS BEING FOOLISH!
4

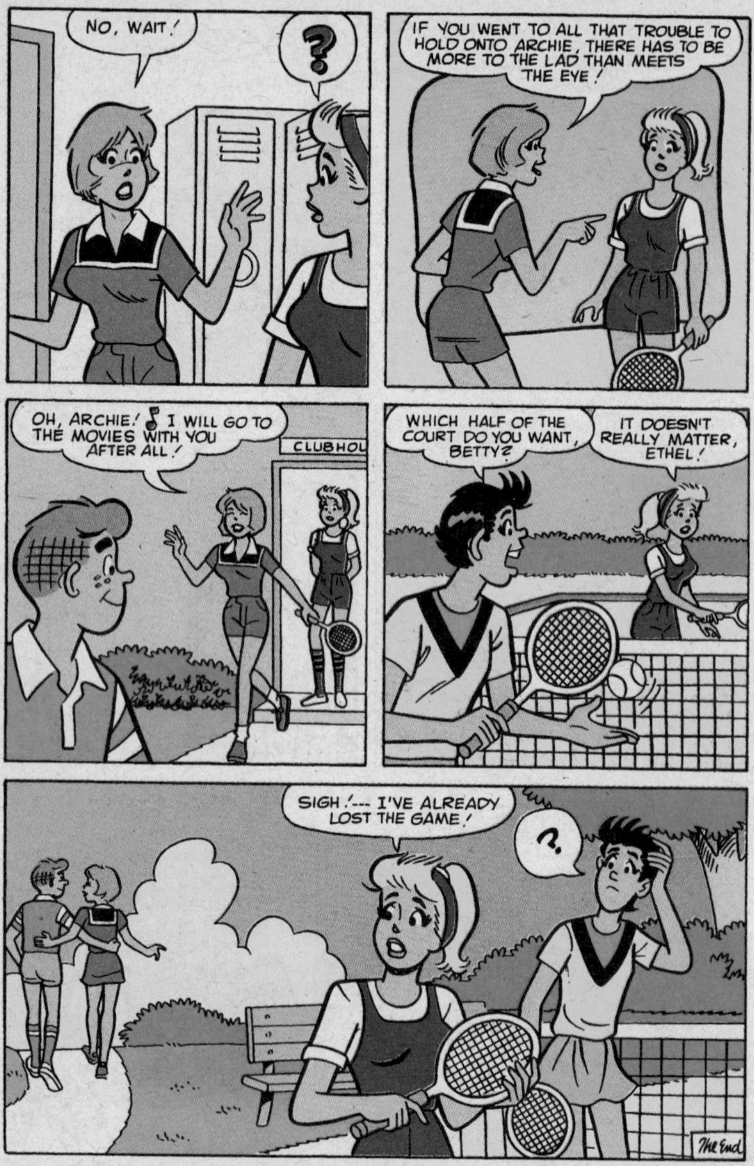
NO, WAIT!
?
IF YOU WENT TO ALL THAT TROUBLE TO HOLD ONTO ARCHIE, THERE HAS TO BE MORE TO THE LAD THAN MEETS THE EYE!
OH, ARCHIE! I WILL GO TO THE MOVIES WITH YOU AFTER ALL!
CLUBHOU
WHICH HALF OF THE COURT DO YOU WANT, BETTY?
IT DOESN'T REALLY MATTER, ETHEL!
SIGH!--- I'VE ALREADY LOST THE GAME!
?
The End

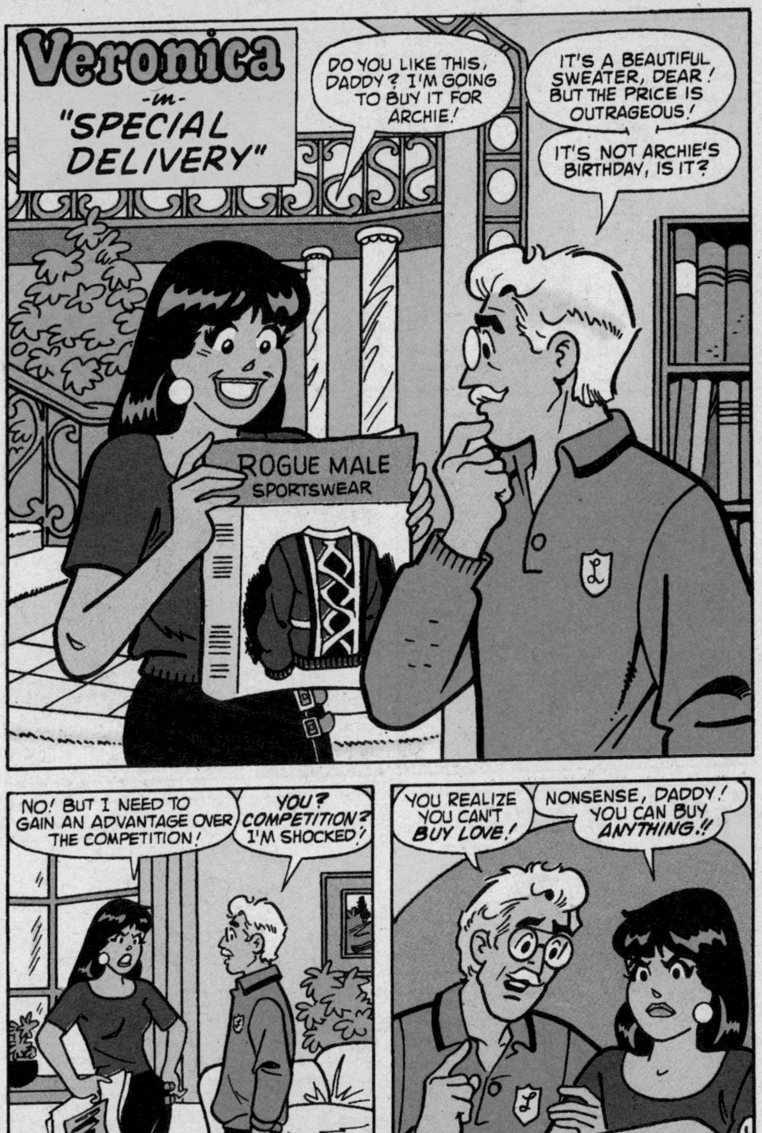
Veronica
-in-
"SPECIAL DELIVERY"
DO YOU LIKE THIS, DADDY? I'M GOING TO BUY IT FOR ARCHIE!
IT'S A BEAUTIFUL SWEATER, DEAR! BUT THE PRICE IS OUTRAGEOUS!
IT'S NOT ARCHIE'S BIRTHDAY, IS IT?
ROGUE MALE SPORTSWEAR
NO! BUT I NEED TO GAIN AN ADVANTAGE OVER THE COMPETITION!
YOU? COMPETITION? I'M SHOCKED!
YOU REALIZE YOU CAN'T BUY LOVE!
NONSENSE, DADDY! YOU CAN BUY ANYTHING!!
1

Script: Frank Doyle / Pencils: Dan DeCarlo / Inks: Henry Scarpelli / Letters: Bill Yoshida / Colors: Barry Grossman

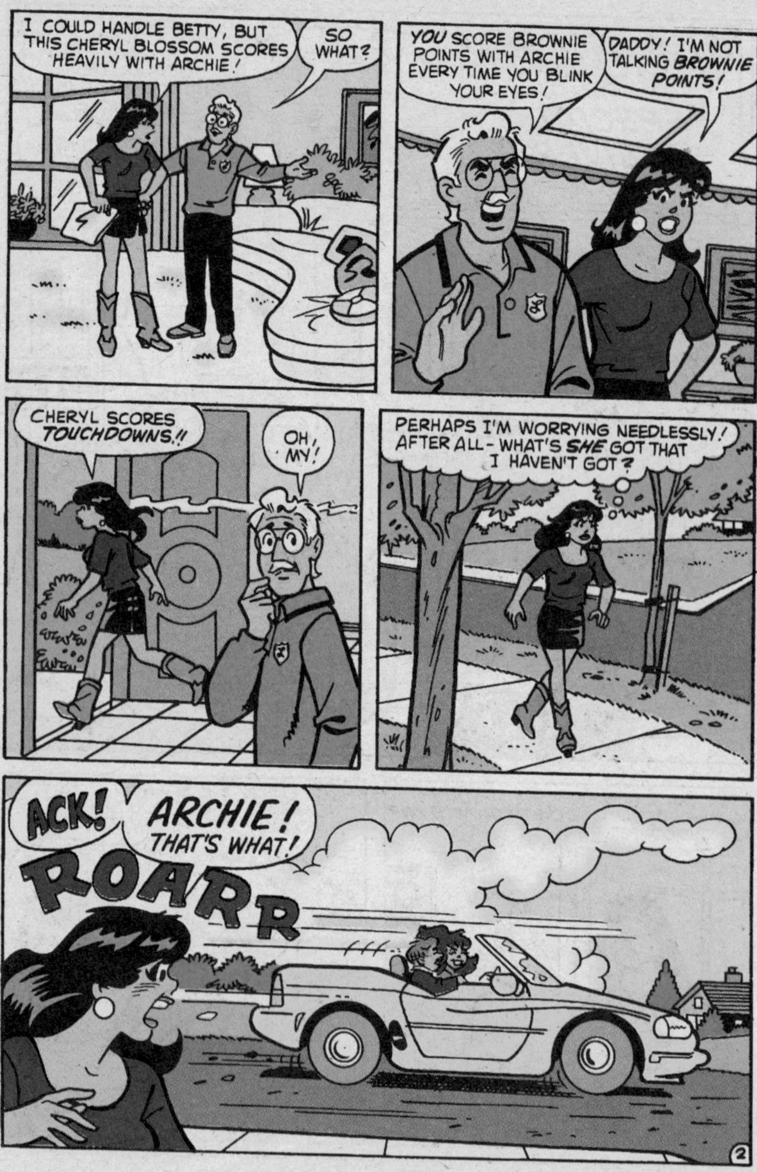
I COULD HANDLE BETTY, BUT THIS CHERYL BLOSSOM SCORES HEAVILY WITH ARCHIE!
SO WHAT?
YOU SCORE BROWNIE POINTS WITH ARCHIE EVERY TIME YOU BLINK YOUR EYES!
DADDY! I'M NOT TALKING BROWNIE POINTS!
CHERYL SCORES TOUCHDOWNS!!
OH, MY!
PERHAPS I'M WORRYING NEEDLESSLY! AFTER ALL - WHAT'S SHE GOT THAT I HAVEN'T GOT?
ACK!
ARCHIE! THAT'S WHAT!
ROARR
2

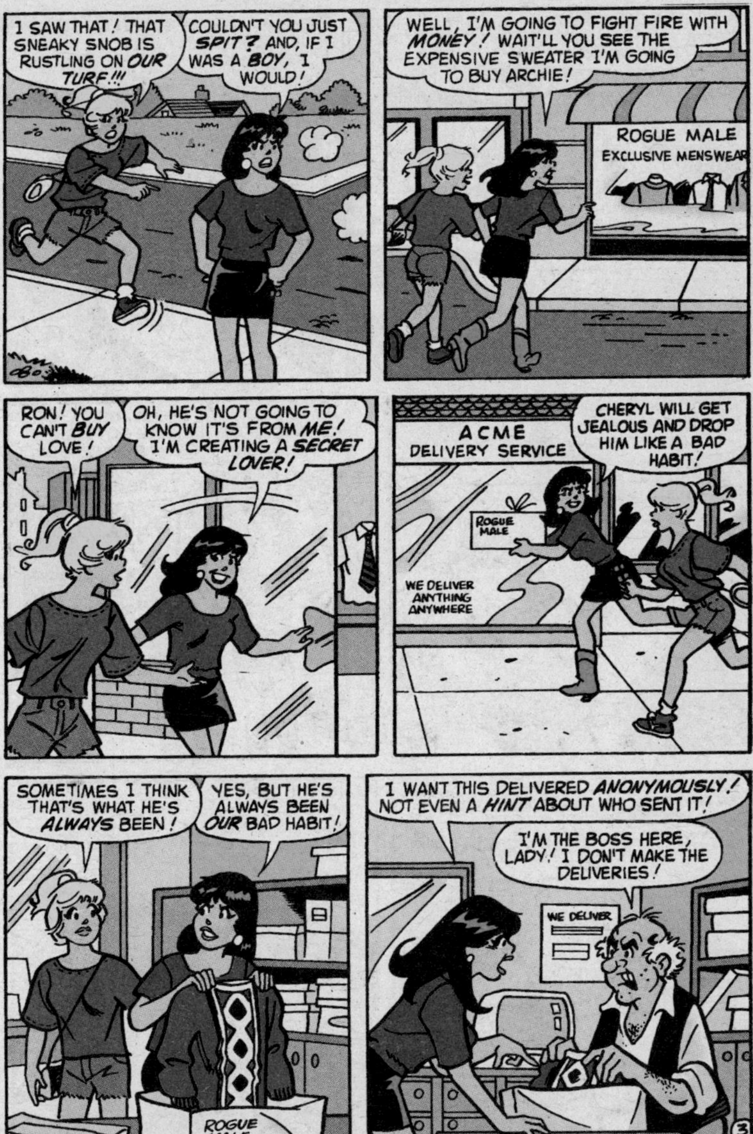
I SAW THAT! THAT SNEAKY SNOB IS RUSTLING ON OUR TURF!!!
COULDN'T YOU JUST SPIT? AND, IF I WAS A BOY, I WOULD!
WELL, I'M GOING TO FIGHT FIRE WITH MONEY! WAIT'LL YOU SEE THE EXPENSIVE SWEATER I'M GOING TO BUY ARCHIE!
ROGUE MALE
EXCLUSIVE MENSWEAR
RON! YOU CAN'T BUY LOVE!
OH, HE'S NOT GOING TO KNOW IT'S FROM ME! I'M CREATING A SECRET LOVER!
ACME
DELIVERY SERVICE
CHERYL WILL GET JEALOUS AND DROP HIM LIKE A BAD HABIT!
ROGUE MALE
WE DELIVER ANYTHING ANYWHERE
SOMETIMES I THINK THAT'S WHAT HE'S ALWAYS BEEN!
YES, BUT HE'S ALWAYS BEEN OUR BAD HABIT!
ROGUE MALE
I WANT THIS DELIVERED ANONYMOUSLY! NOT EVEN A HINT ABOUT WHO SENT IT!
I'M THE BOSS HERE, LADY! I DON'T MAKE THE DELIVERIES!
WE DELIVER
3

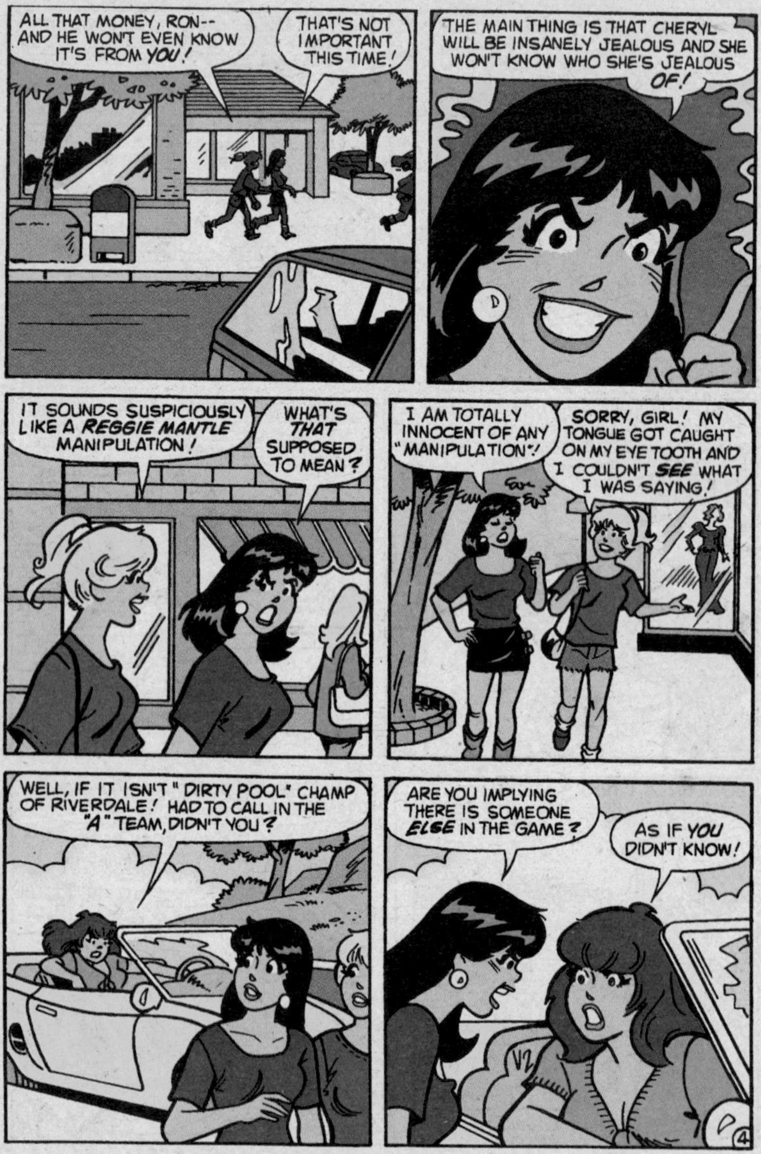

ALL THAT MONEY, RON-- AND HE WON'T EVEN KNOW IT'S FROM *YOU*!
THAT'S NOT IMPORTANT THIS TIME!
THE MAIN THING IS THAT CHERYL WILL BE INSANELY JEALOUS AND SHE WON'T KNOW WHO SHE'S JEALOUS *OF*!
IT SOUNDS SUSPICIOUSLY LIKE A *REGGIE MANTLE* MANIPULATION!
WHAT'S *THAT* SUPPOSED TO MEAN?
I AM TOTALLY INNOCENT OF ANY "MANIPULATION"!
SORRY, GIRL! MY TONGUE GOT CAUGHT ON MY EYE TOOTH AND I COULDN'T *SEE* WHAT I WAS SAYING!
WELL, IF IT ISN'T "DIRTY POOL" CHAMP OF RIVERDALE! HAD TO CALL IN THE "*A*" TEAM, DIDN'T YOU?
ARE YOU IMPLYING THERE IS SOMEONE *ELSE* IN THE GAME?
AS IF *YOU* DIDN'T KNOW!
4

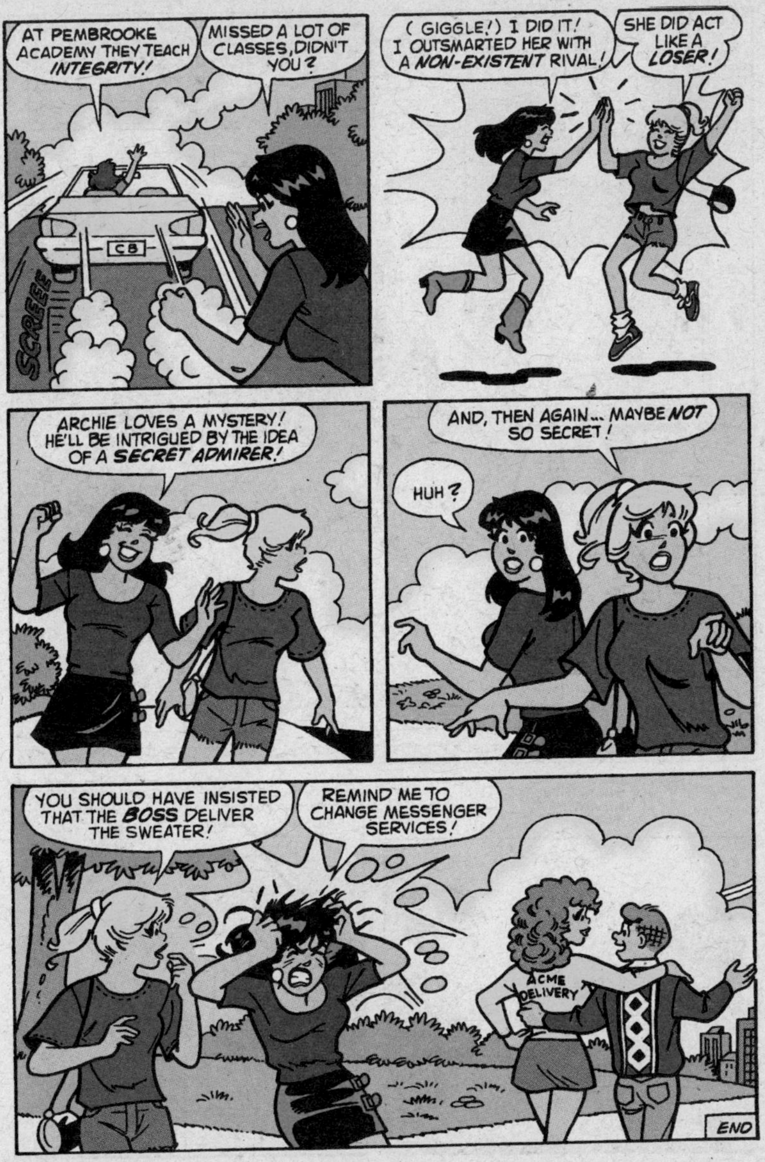
AT PEMBROOKE ACADEMY THEY TEACH INTEGRITY!
MISSED A LOT OF CLASSES, DIDN'T YOU?
CB
SCREEE
(GIGGLE!) I DID IT! I OUTSMARTED HER WITH A NON-EXISTENT RIVAL!
SHE DID ACT LIKE A LOSER!
ARCHIE LOVES A MYSTERY! HE'LL BE INTRIGUED BY THE IDEA OF A SECRET ADMIRER!
AND, THEN AGAIN... MAYBE NOT SO SECRET!
HUH?
YOU SHOULD HAVE INSISTED THAT THE BOSS DELIVER THE SWEATER!
REMIND ME TO CHANGE MESSENGER SERVICES!
ACME DELIVERY
END

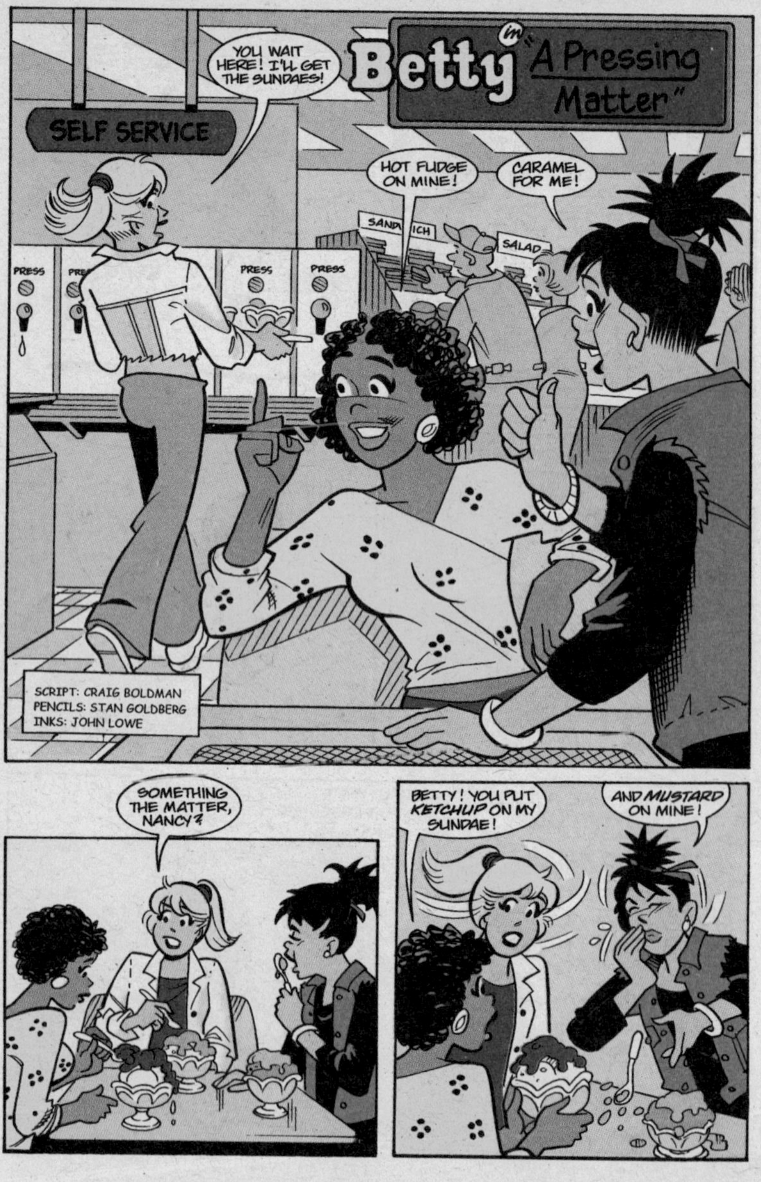

YOU WAIT HERE! I'LL GET THE SUNDAES!
Betty in "A Pressing Matter"
SELF SERVICE
HOT FUDGE ON MINE!
CARAMEL FOR ME!
SANDWICH
SALAD
PRESS
PRESS
PRESS
SCRIPT: CRAIG BOLDMAN
PENCILS: STAN GOLDBERG
INKS: JOHN LOWE
SOMETHING THE MATTER, NANCY?
BETTY! YOU PUT KETCHUP ON MY SUNDAE!
AND MUSTARD ON MINE!

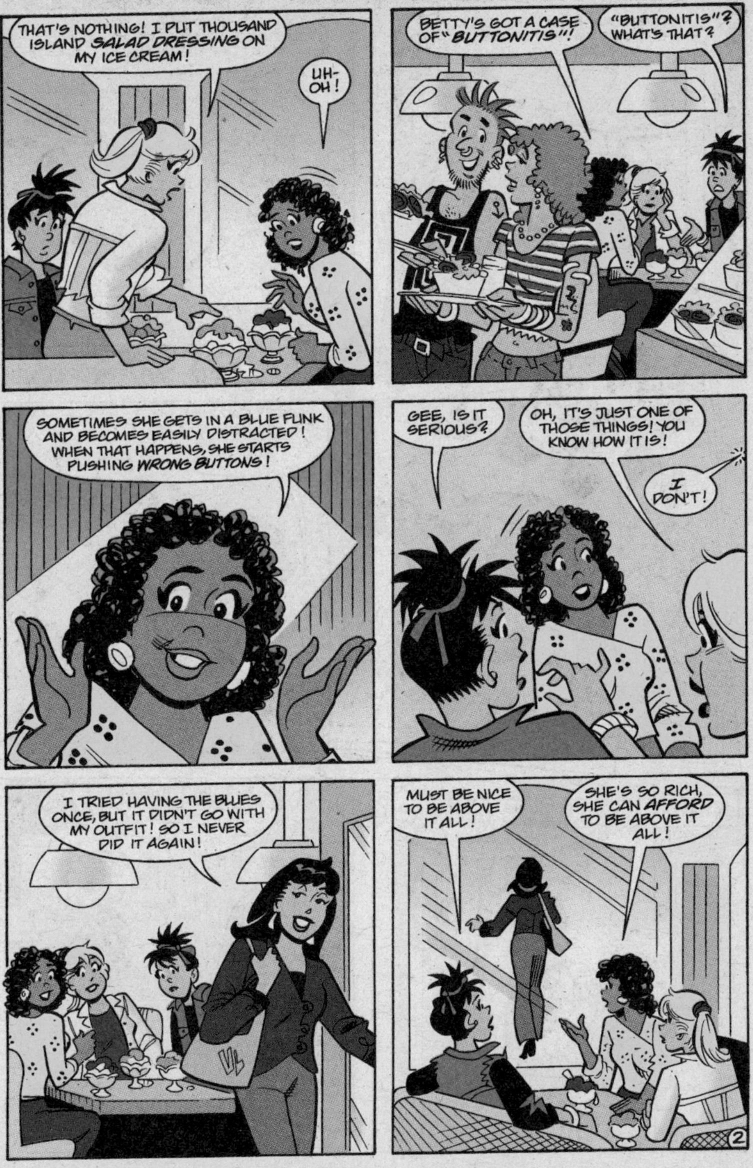
THAT'S NOTHING! I PUT THOUSAND ISLAND SALAD DRESSING ON MY ICE CREAM!
UH-OH!
BETTY'S GOT A CASE OF "BUTTONITIS"!
"BUTTONITIS"? WHAT'S THAT?
SOMETIMES SHE GETS IN A BLUE FUNK AND BECOMES EASILY DISTRACTED! WHEN THAT HAPPENS, SHE STARTS PUSHING WRONG BUTTONS!
GEE, IS IT SERIOUS?
OH, IT'S JUST ONE OF THOSE THINGS! YOU KNOW HOW IT IS!
I DON'T!
I TRIED HAVING THE BLUES ONCE, BUT IT DIDN'T GO WITH MY OUTFIT! SO I NEVER DID IT AGAIN!
MUST BE NICE TO BE ABOVE IT ALL!
SHE'S SO RICH, SHE CAN AFFORD TO BE ABOVE IT ALL!

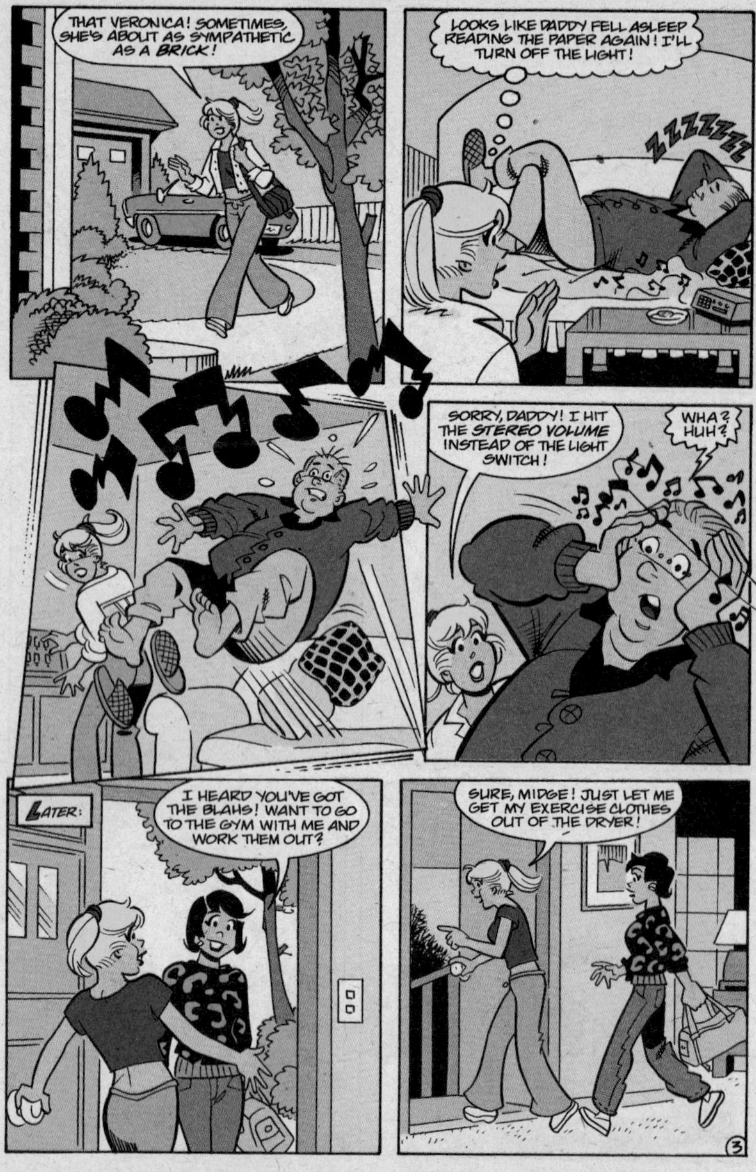

THAT VERONICA! SOMETIMES, SHE'S ABOUT AS SYMPATHETIC AS A BRICK!
LOOKS LIKE DADDY FELL ASLEEP READING THE PAPER AGAIN! I'LL TURN OFF THE LIGHT!
ZZZZZZZZ
SORRY, DADDY! I HIT THE STEREO VOLUME INSTEAD OF THE LIGHT SWITCH!
WHA? HUH?
LATER:
I HEARD YOU'VE GOT THE BLAHS! WANT TO GO TO THE GYM WITH ME AND WORK THEM OUT?
SURE, MIDGE! JUST LET ME GET MY EXERCISE CLOTHES OUT OF THE DRYER!

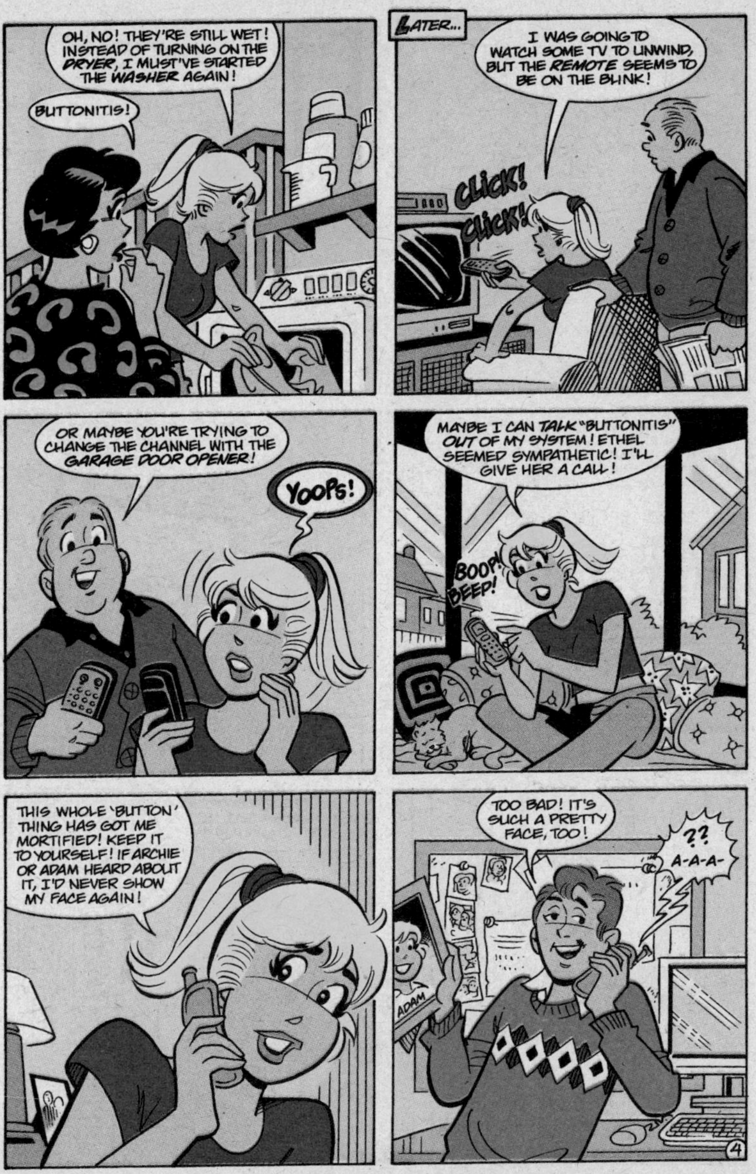
OH, NO! THEY'RE STILL WET! INSTEAD OF TURNING ON THE *DRYER*, I MUST'VE STARTED THE *WASHER* AGAIN!
BUTTONITIS!
LATER...
I WAS GOING TO WATCH SOME TV TO UNWIND, BUT THE *REMOTE* SEEMS TO BE ON THE BLINK!
CLICK!
CLICK!
OR MAYBE YOU'RE TRYING TO CHANGE THE CHANNEL WITH THE *GARAGE DOOR OPENER*!
YOOPS!
MAYBE I CAN *TALK* "BUTTONITIS" *OUT* OF MY SYSTEM! ETHEL SEEMED SYMPATHETIC! I'LL GIVE HER A CALL!
BOOP!
BEEP!
THIS WHOLE 'BUTTON' THING HAS GOT ME MORTIFIED! KEEP IT TO YOURSELF! IF ARCHIE OR ADAM HEARD ABOUT IT, I'D NEVER SHOW MY FACE AGAIN!
TOO BAD! IT'S SUCH A PRETTY FACE, TOO!
??
A-A-A-
ADAM

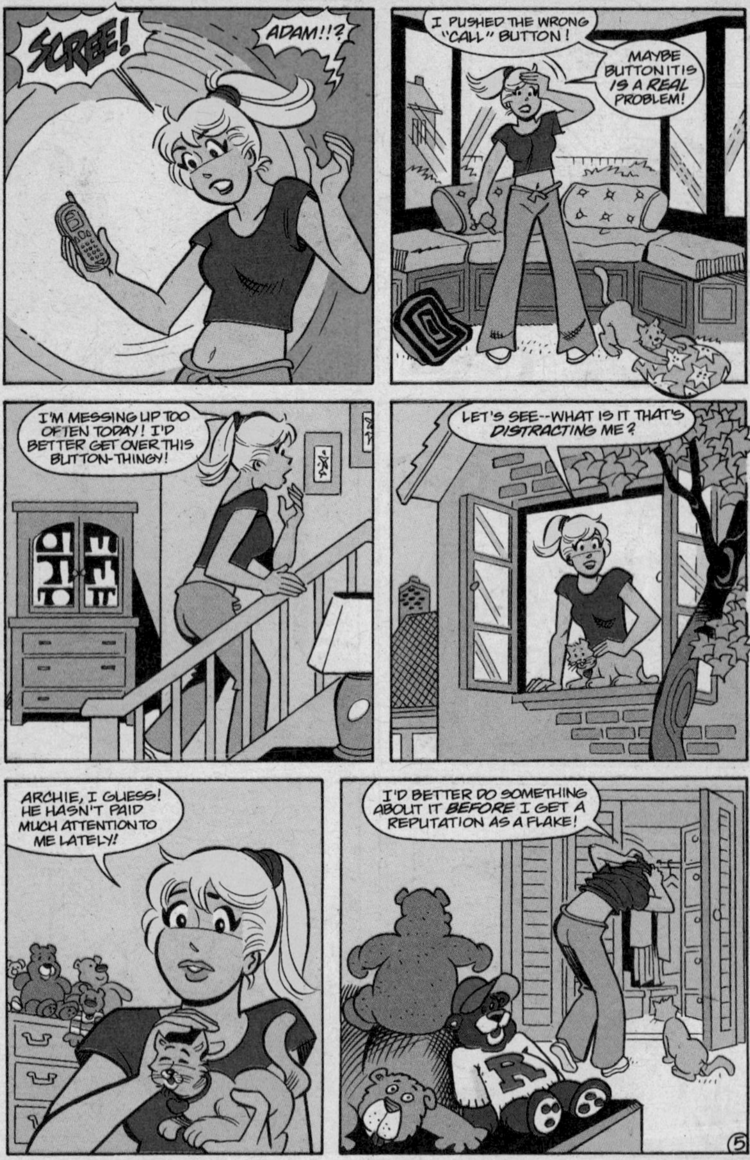
SCREEE!
ADAM!!?
I PUSHED THE WRONG "CALL" BUTTON!
MAYBE BUTTONITIS IS A REAL PROBLEM!
I'M MESSING UP TOO OFTEN TODAY! I'D BETTER GET OVER THIS BUTTON-THINGY!
LET'S SEE--WHAT IS IT THAT'S DISTRACTING ME?
ARCHIE, I GUESS! HE HASN'T PAID MUCH ATTENTION TO ME LATELY!
I'D BETTER DO SOMETHING ABOUT IT BEFORE I GET A REPUTATION AS A FLAKE!

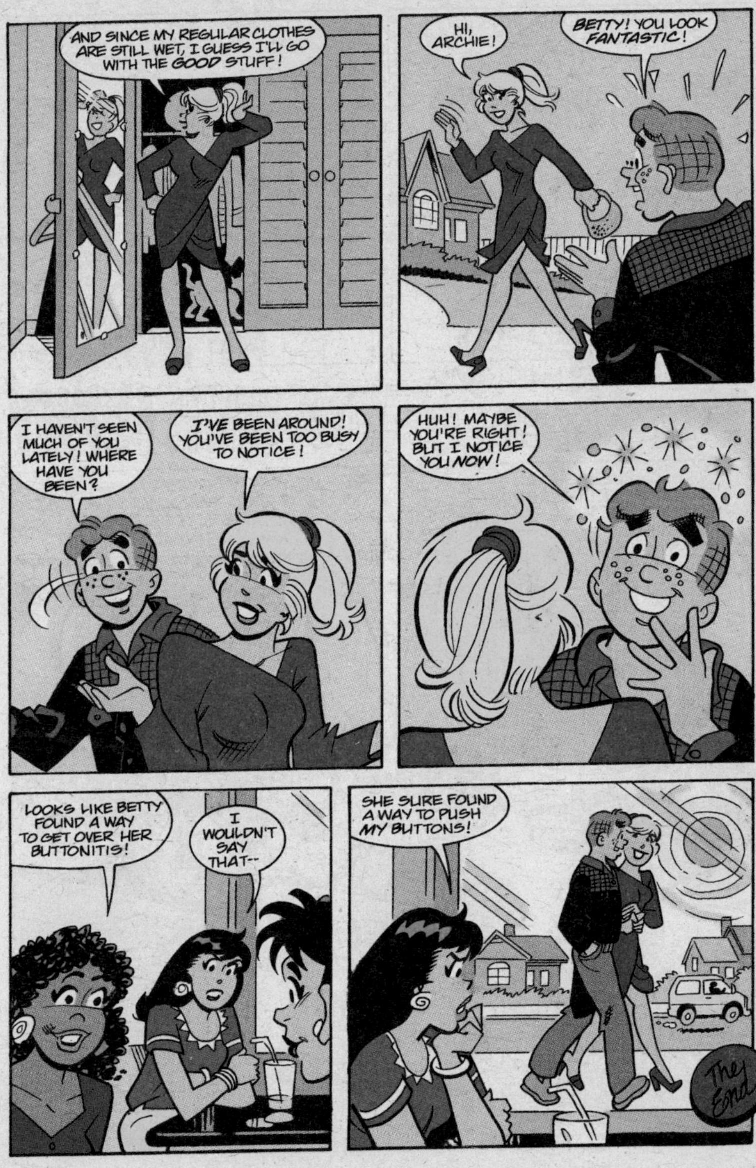
AND SINCE MY REGULAR CLOTHES ARE STILL WET, I GUESS I'LL GO WITH THE GOOD STUFF!
HI, ARCHIE!
BETTY! YOU LOOK FANTASTIC!
I HAVEN'T SEEN MUCH OF YOU LATELY! WHERE HAVE YOU BEEN?
I'VE BEEN AROUND! YOU'VE BEEN TOO BUSY TO NOTICE!
HUH! MAYBE YOU'RE RIGHT! BUT I NOTICE YOU NOW!
LOOKS LIKE BETTY FOUND A WAY TO GET OVER HER BUTTONITIS!
I WOULDN'T SAY THAT--
SHE SURE FOUND A WAY TO PUSH MY BUTTONS!
The End

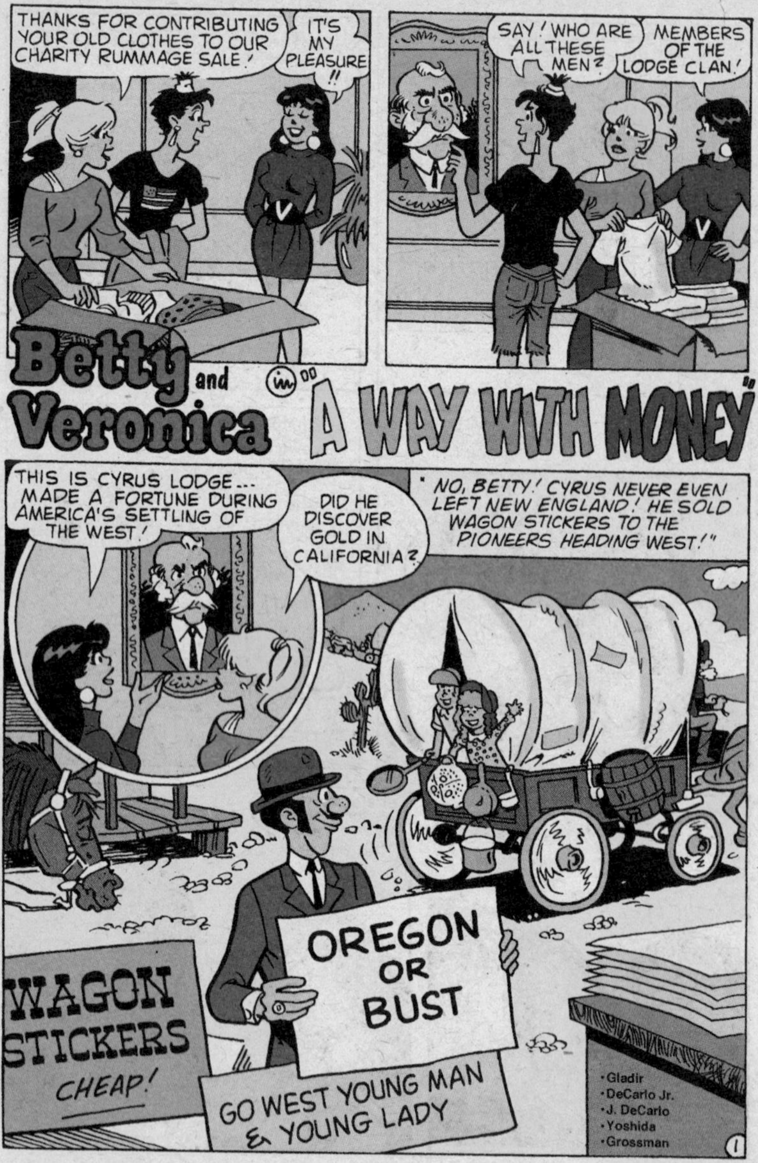
THANKS FOR CONTRIBUTING YOUR OLD CLOTHES TO OUR CHARITY RUMMAGE SALE!
IT'S MY PLEASURE!!
SAY! WHO ARE ALL THESE MEN?
MEMBERS OF THE LODGE CLAN!
Betty and Veronica
"A WAY WITH MONEY"
THIS IS CYRUS LODGE... MADE A FORTUNE DURING AMERICA'S SETTLING OF THE WEST!
DID HE DISCOVER GOLD IN CALIFORNIA?
"NO, BETTY! CYRUS NEVER EVEN LEFT NEW ENGLAND! HE SOLD WAGON STICKERS TO THE PIONEERS HEADING WEST!"
OREGON OR BUST
WAGON STICKERS CHEAP!
GO WEST YOUNG MAN & YOUNG LADY
•Gladir
•DeCarlo Jr.
•J. DeCarlo
•Yoshida
•Grossman
1

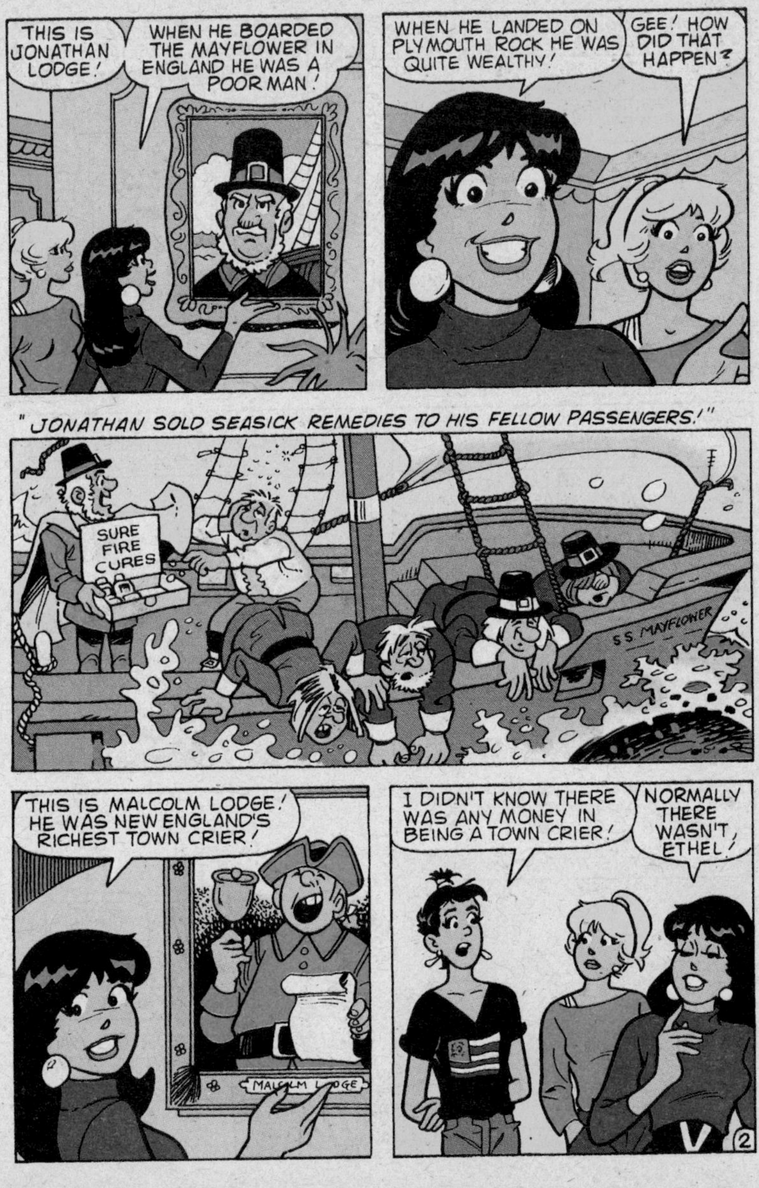
THIS IS JONATHAN LODGE!
WHEN HE BOARDED THE MAYFLOWER IN ENGLAND HE WAS A POOR MAN!
WHEN HE LANDED ON PLYMOUTH ROCK HE WAS QUITE WEALTHY!
GEE! HOW DID THAT HAPPEN?
"JONATHAN SOLD SEASICK REMEDIES TO HIS FELLOW PASSENGERS!"
SURE FIRE CURES
S.S. MAYFLOWER
THIS IS MALCOLM LODGE! HE WAS NEW ENGLAND'S RICHEST TOWN CRIER!
I DIDN'T KNOW THERE WAS ANY MONEY IN BEING A TOWN CRIER!
NORMALLY THERE WASN'T, ETHEL!
2

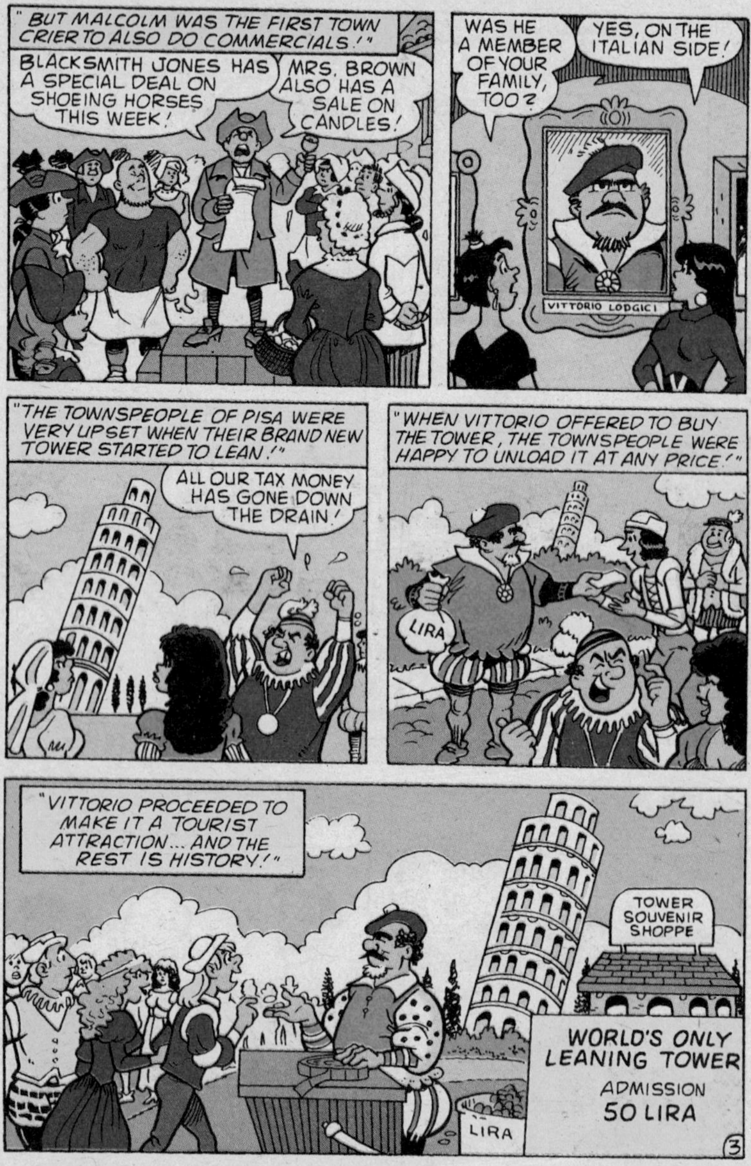
"BUT MALCOLM WAS THE FIRST TOWN CRIER TO ALSO DO COMMERCIALS!"
BLACKSMITH JONES HAS A SPECIAL DEAL ON SHOEING HORSES THIS WEEK!
MRS. BROWN ALSO HAS A SALE ON CANDLES!
WAS HE A MEMBER OF YOUR FAMILY, TOO?
YES, ON THE ITALIAN SIDE!
VITTORIO LODGICI
"THE TOWNSPEOPLE OF PISA WERE VERY UPSET WHEN THEIR BRAND NEW TOWER STARTED TO LEAN!"
ALL OUR TAX MONEY HAS GONE DOWN THE DRAIN!
"WHEN VITTORIO OFFERED TO BUY THE TOWER, THE TOWNSPEOPLE WERE HAPPY TO UNLOAD IT AT ANY PRICE!"
LIRA
"VITTORIO PROCEEDED TO MAKE IT A TOURIST ATTRACTION... AND THE REST IS HISTORY!"
TOWER SOUVENIR SHOPPE
WORLD'S ONLY LEANING TOWER
ADMISSION 50 LIRA
LIRA
3

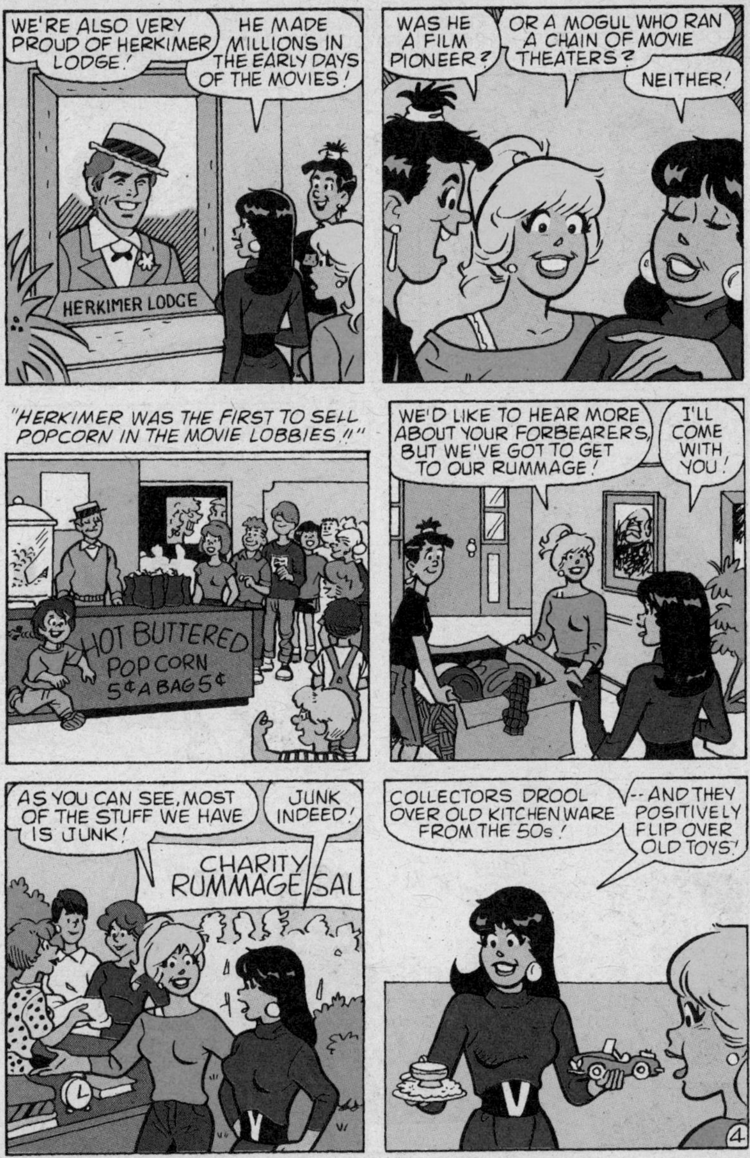

WE'RE ALSO VERY PROUD OF HERKIMER LODGE!
HE MADE MILLIONS IN THE EARLY DAYS OF THE MOVIES!
HERKIMER LODGE
WAS HE A FILM PIONEER?
OR A MOGUL WHO RAN A CHAIN OF MOVIE THEATERS?
NEITHER!
"HERKIMER WAS THE FIRST TO SELL POPCORN IN THE MOVIE LOBBIES!!"
HOT BUTTERED POP CORN 5¢ A BAG 5¢
WE'D LIKE TO HEAR MORE ABOUT YOUR FORBEARERS, BUT WE'VE GOT TO GET TO OUR RUMMAGE!
I'LL COME WITH YOU!
AS YOU CAN SEE, MOST OF THE STUFF WE HAVE IS JUNK!
JUNK INDEED!
CHARITY RUMMAGE SAL
COLLECTORS DROOL OVER OLD KITCHENWARE FROM THE 50s!
--AND THEY POSITIVELY FLIP OVER OLD TOYS!
V
4

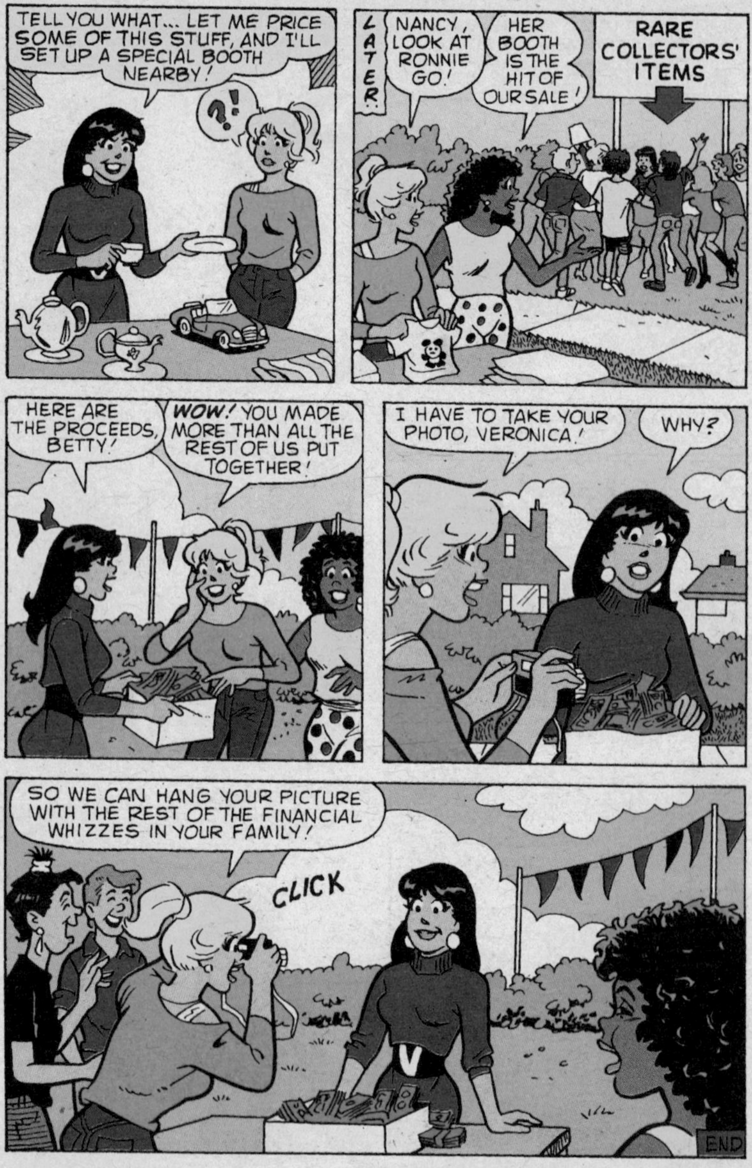
TELL YOU WHAT... LET ME PRICE SOME OF THIS STUFF, AND I'LL SET UP A SPECIAL BOOTH NEARBY!
?!
LATER
NANCY, LOOK AT RONNIE GO!
HER BOOTH IS THE HIT OF OUR SALE!
RARE COLLECTORS' ITEMS
HERE ARE THE PROCEEDS, BETTY!
WOW! YOU MADE MORE THAN ALL THE REST OF US PUT TOGETHER!
I HAVE TO TAKE YOUR PHOTO, VERONICA!
WHY?
SO WE CAN HANG YOUR PICTURE WITH THE REST OF THE FINANCIAL WHIZZES IN YOUR FAMILY!
CLICK
END

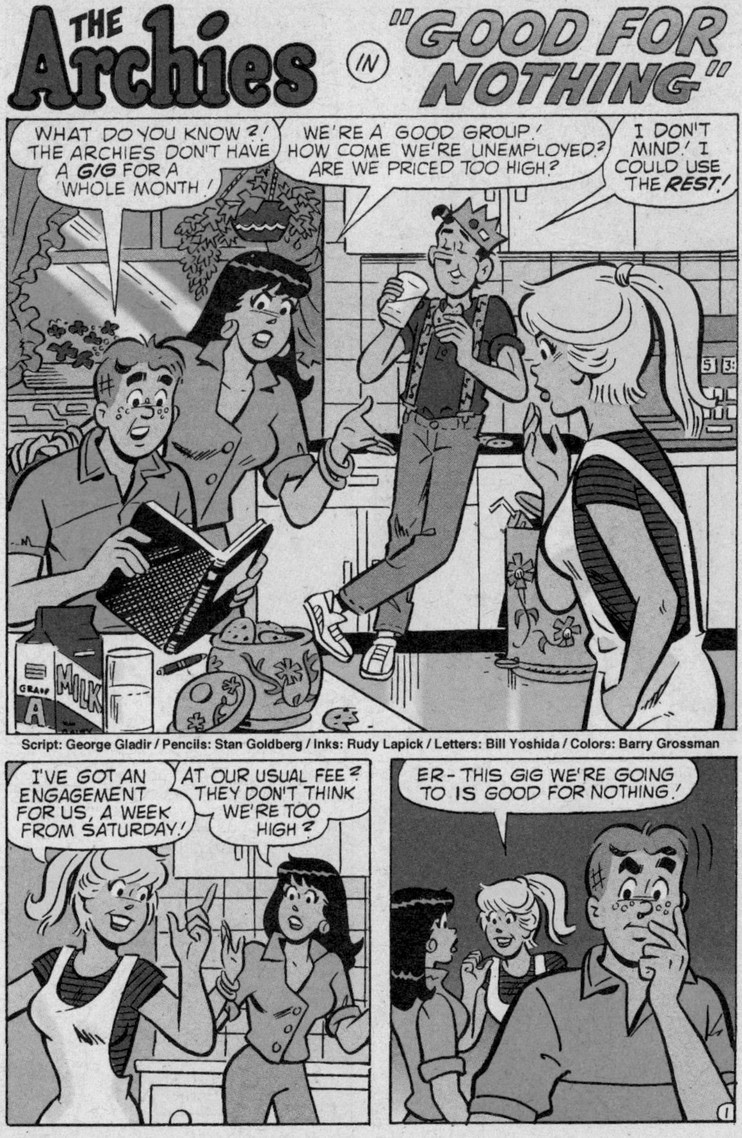
THE Archies IN "GOOD FOR NOTHING"
WHAT DO YOU KNOW?! THE ARCHIES DON'T HAVE A GIG FOR A WHOLE MONTH!
WE'RE A GOOD GROUP! HOW COME WE'RE UNEMPLOYED? ARE WE PRICED TOO HIGH?
I DON'T MIND! I COULD USE THE REST!
MILK
Script: George Gladir / Pencils: Stan Goldberg / Inks: Rudy Lapick / Letters: Bill Yoshida / Colors: Barry Grossman
I'VE GOT AN ENGAGEMENT FOR US, A WEEK FROM SATURDAY!
AT OUR USUAL FEE? THEY DON'T THINK WE'RE TOO HIGH?
ER- THIS GIG WE'RE GOING TO IS GOOD FOR NOTHING!
1

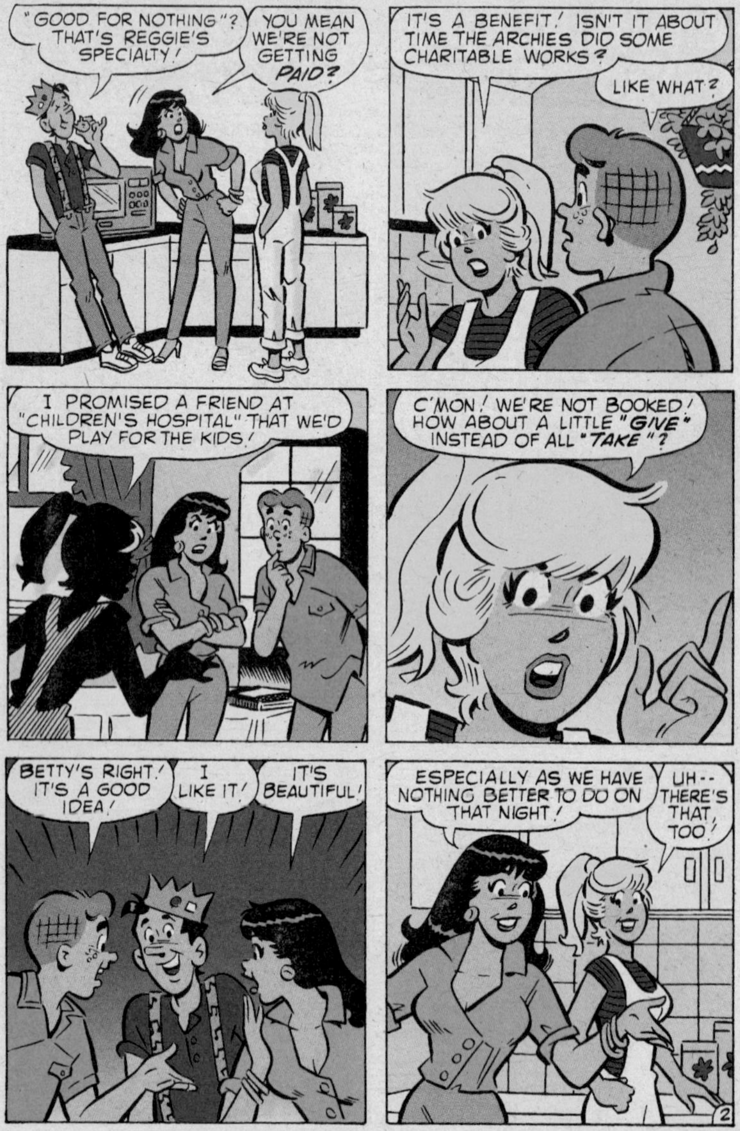
"GOOD FOR NOTHING"? THAT'S REGGIE'S SPECIALTY!
YOU MEAN WE'RE NOT GETTING PAID?
IT'S A BENEFIT! ISN'T IT ABOUT TIME THE ARCHIES DID SOME CHARITABLE WORKS?
LIKE WHAT?
I PROMISED A FRIEND AT "CHILDREN'S HOSPITAL" THAT WE'D PLAY FOR THE KIDS!
C'MON! WE'RE NOT BOOKED! HOW ABOUT A LITTLE "GIVE" INSTEAD OF ALL "TAKE"?
BETTY'S RIGHT! IT'S A GOOD IDEA!
I LIKE IT!
IT'S BEAUTIFUL!
ESPECIALLY AS WE HAVE NOTHING BETTER TO DO ON THAT NIGHT!
UH-- THERE'S THAT, TOO!
2

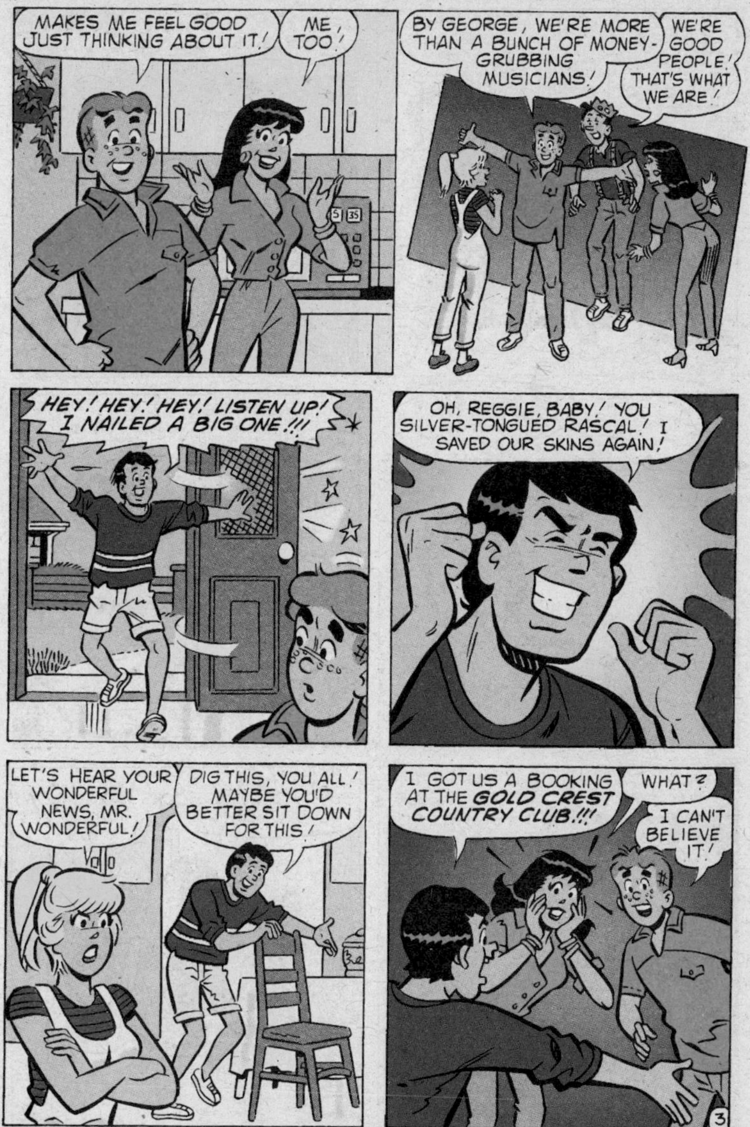
MAKES ME FEEL GOOD JUST THINKING ABOUT IT!
ME, TOO!
BY GEORGE, WE'RE MORE THAN A BUNCH OF MONEY-GRUBBING MUSICIANS!
WE'RE GOOD PEOPLE! THAT'S WHAT WE ARE!
HEY! HEY! HEY! LISTEN UP! I NAILED A BIG ONE!!!
OH, REGGIE, BABY! YOU SILVER-TONGUED RASCAL! I SAVED OUR SKINS AGAIN!
LET'S HEAR YOUR WONDERFUL NEWS, MR. WONDERFUL!
DIG THIS, YOU ALL! MAYBE YOU'D BETTER SIT DOWN FOR THIS!
I GOT US A BOOKING AT THE GOLD CREST COUNTRY CLUB!!!
WHAT?
I CAN'T BELIEVE IT!
3

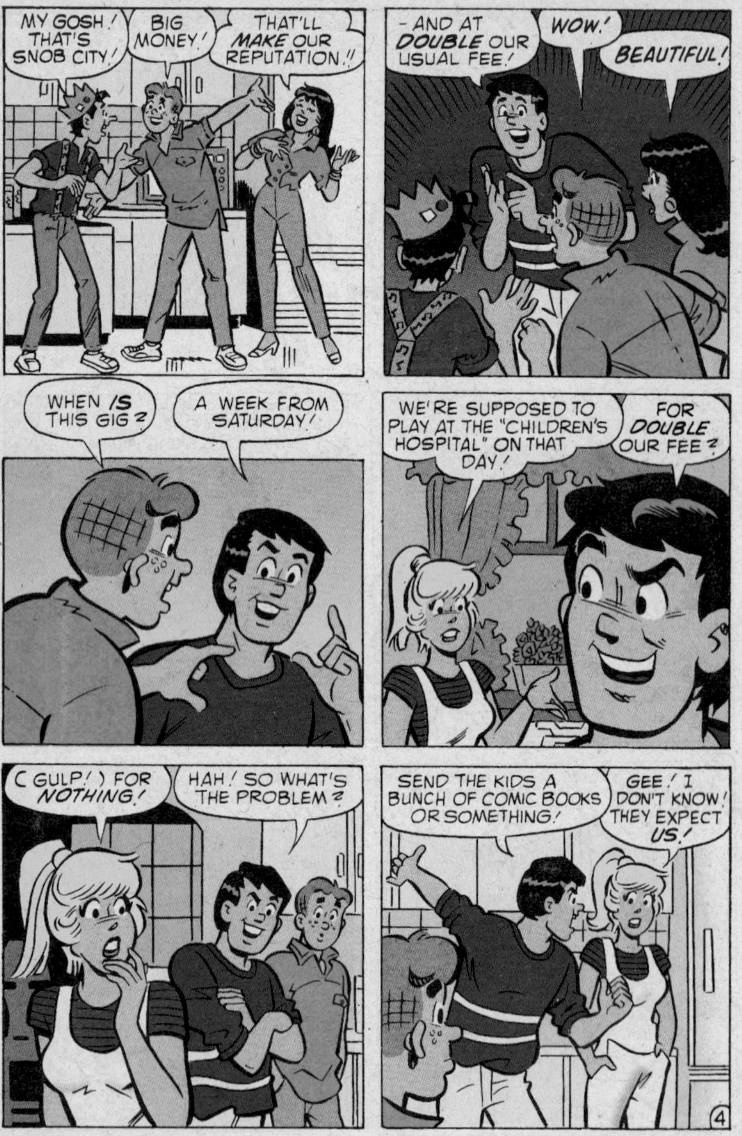
MY GOSH! THAT'S SNOB CITY!
BIG MONEY!
THAT'LL MAKE OUR REPUTATION!!
- AND AT DOUBLE OUR USUAL FEE!
WOW!
BEAUTIFUL!
WHEN IS THIS GIG?
A WEEK FROM SATURDAY!
WE'RE SUPPOSED TO PLAY AT THE "CHILDREN'S HOSPITAL" ON THAT DAY!
FOR DOUBLE OUR FEE?
(GULP!) FOR NOTHING!
HAH! SO WHAT'S THE PROBLEM?
SEND THE KIDS A BUNCH OF COMIC BOOKS OR SOMETHING!
GEE! I DON'T KNOW! THEY EXPECT US!
4

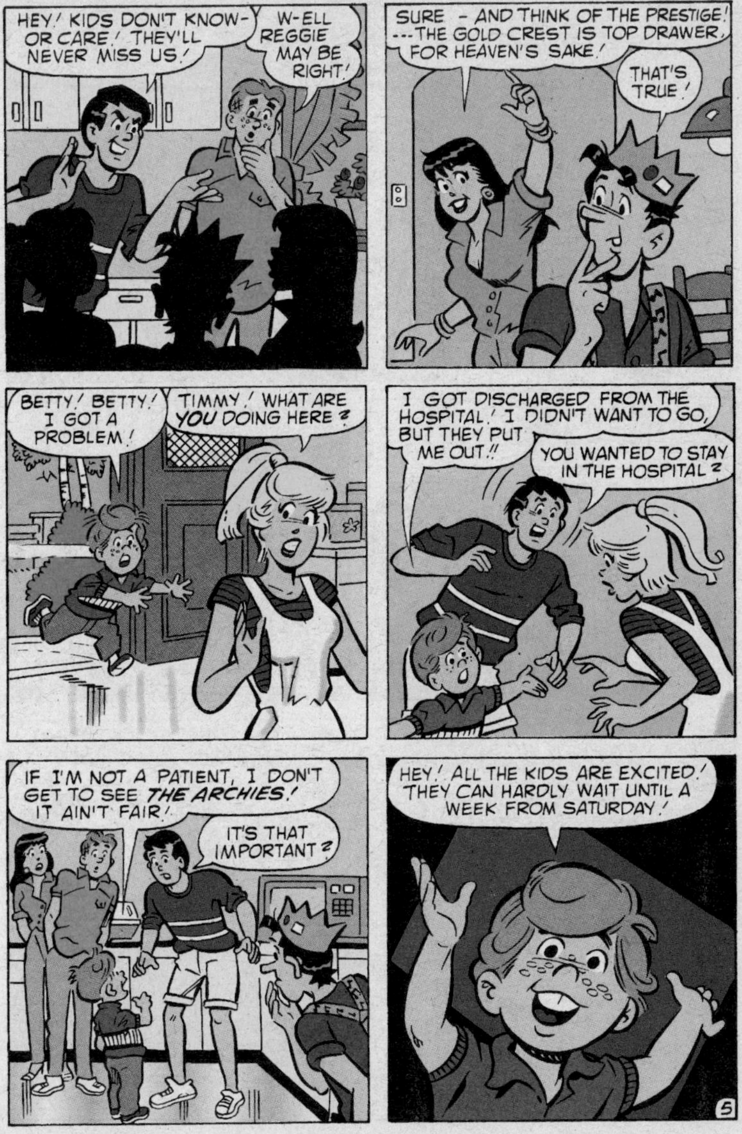
HEY! KIDS DON'T KNOW-- OR CARE! THEY'LL NEVER MISS US!
W-ELL REGGIE MAY BE RIGHT!
SURE - AND THINK OF THE PRESTIGE! ---THE GOLD CREST IS TOP DRAWER, FOR HEAVEN'S SAKE!
THAT'S TRUE!
BETTY! BETTY! I GOT A PROBLEM!
TIMMY! WHAT ARE YOU DOING HERE?
I GOT DISCHARGED FROM THE HOSPITAL! I DIDN'T WANT TO GO, BUT THEY PUT ME OUT!!
YOU WANTED TO STAY IN THE HOSPITAL?
IF I'M NOT A PATIENT, I DON'T GET TO SEE THE ARCHIES! IT AIN'T FAIR!
IT'S THAT IMPORTANT?
HEY! ALL THE KIDS ARE EXCITED! THEY CAN HARDLY WAIT UNTIL A WEEK FROM SATURDAY!
5

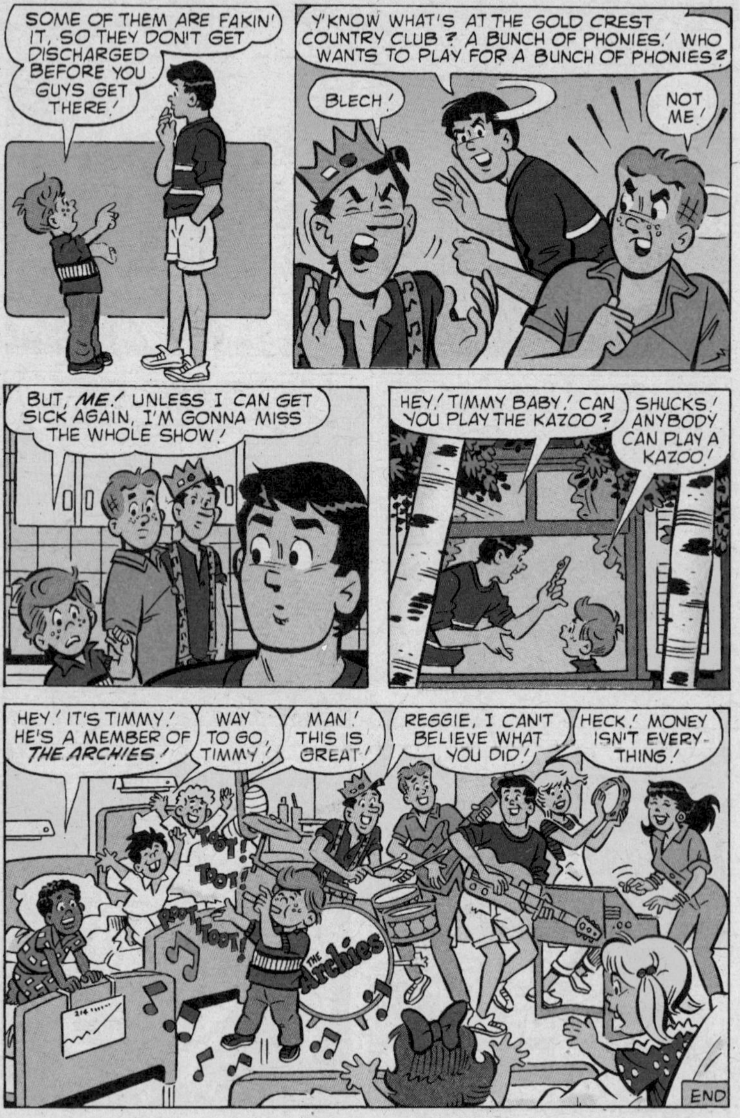

SOME OF THEM ARE FAKIN' IT, SO THEY DON'T GET DISCHARGED BEFORE YOU GUYS GET THERE!
Y'KNOW WHAT'S AT THE GOLD CREST COUNTRY CLUB? A BUNCH OF PHONIES! WHO WANTS TO PLAY FOR A BUNCH OF PHONIES?
BLECH!
NOT ME!
BUT, ME! UNLESS I CAN GET SICK AGAIN, I'M GONNA MISS THE WHOLE SHOW!
HEY! TIMMY BABY! CAN YOU PLAY THE KAZOO?
SHUCKS! ANYBODY CAN PLAY A KAZOO!
HEY! IT'S TIMMY! HE'S A MEMBER OF THE ARCHIES!
WAY TO GO, TIMMY!
MAN! THIS IS GREAT!
REGGIE, I CAN'T BELIEVE WHAT YOU DID!
HECK! MONEY ISN'T EVERYTHING!
TOOT! TOOT! TOOT-TOOT!
THE Archies
END

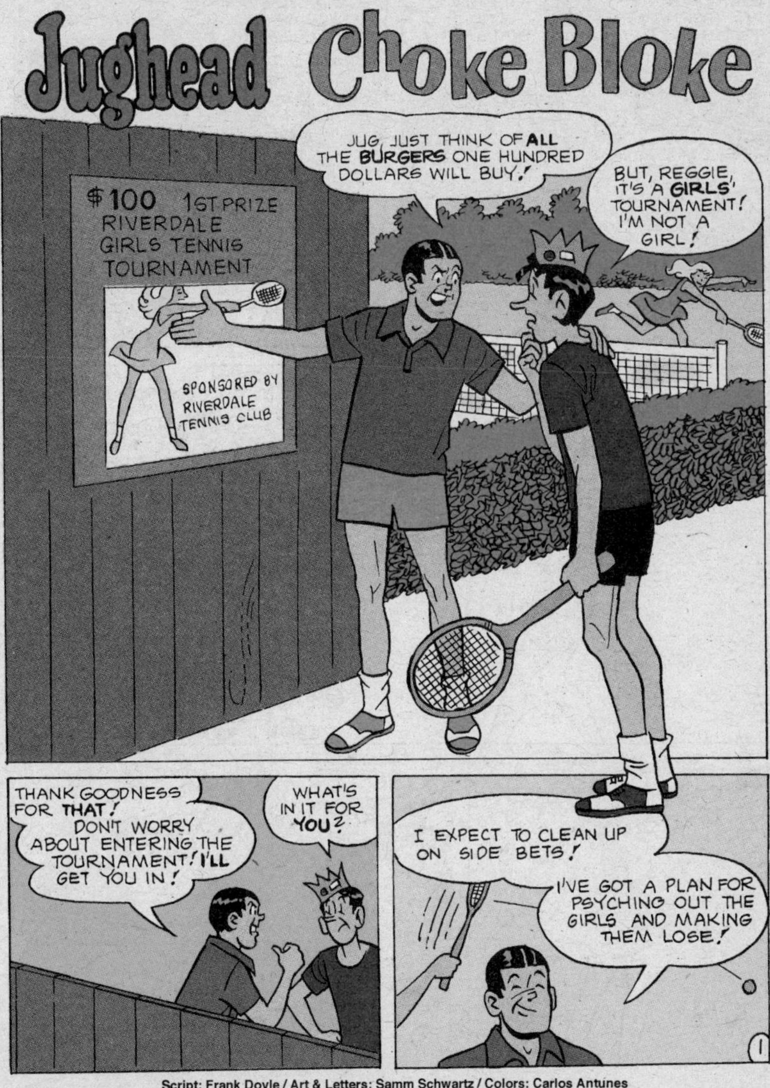
Jughead
Choke Bloke
$100 1ST PRIZE
RIVERDALE
GIRLS TENNIS
TOURNAMENT
SPONSORED BY
RIVERDALE
TENNIS CLUB
JUG, JUST THINK OF ALL THE BURGERS ONE HUNDRED DOLLARS WILL BUY!
BUT, REGGIE, IT'S A GIRLS' TOURNAMENT! I'M NOT A GIRL!
THANK GOODNESS FOR THAT! DON'T WORRY ABOUT ENTERING THE TOURNAMENT! I'LL GET YOU IN!
WHAT'S IN IT FOR YOU?
I EXPECT TO CLEAN UP ON SIDE BETS!
I'VE GOT A PLAN FOR PSYCHING OUT THE GIRLS AND MAKING THEM LOSE!
1

Script: Frank Doyle / Art & Letters: Samm Schwartz / Colors: Carlos Antunes

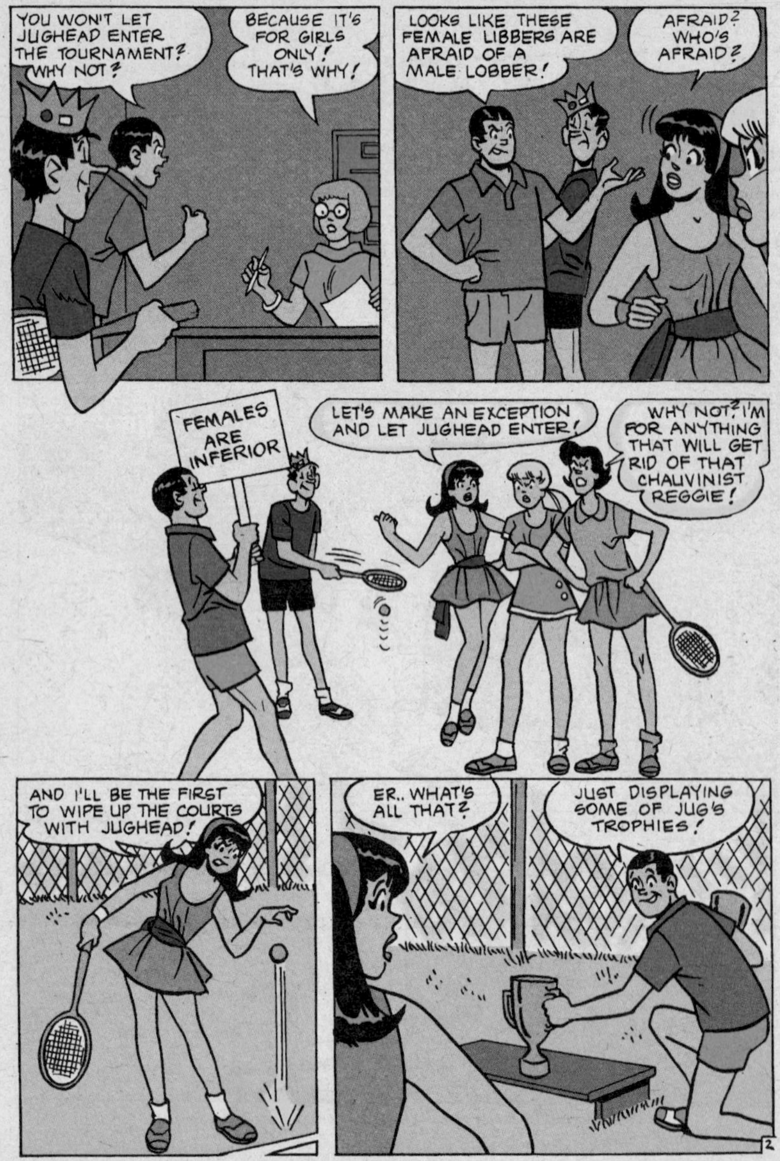
YOU WON'T LET JUGHEAD ENTER THE TOURNAMENT? WHY NOT?
BECAUSE IT'S FOR GIRLS ONLY! THAT'S WHY!
LOOKS LIKE THESE FEMALE LIBBERS ARE AFRAID OF A MALE LOBBER!
AFRAID? WHO'S AFRAID?
FEMALES ARE INFERIOR
LET'S MAKE AN EXCEPTION AND LET JUGHEAD ENTER!
WHY NOT? I'M FOR ANYTHING THAT WILL GET RID OF THAT CHAUVINIST REGGIE!
AND I'LL BE THE FIRST TO WIPE UP THE COURTS WITH JUGHEAD!
ER.. WHAT'S ALL THAT?
JUST DISPLAYING SOME OF JUG'S TROPHIES!
2

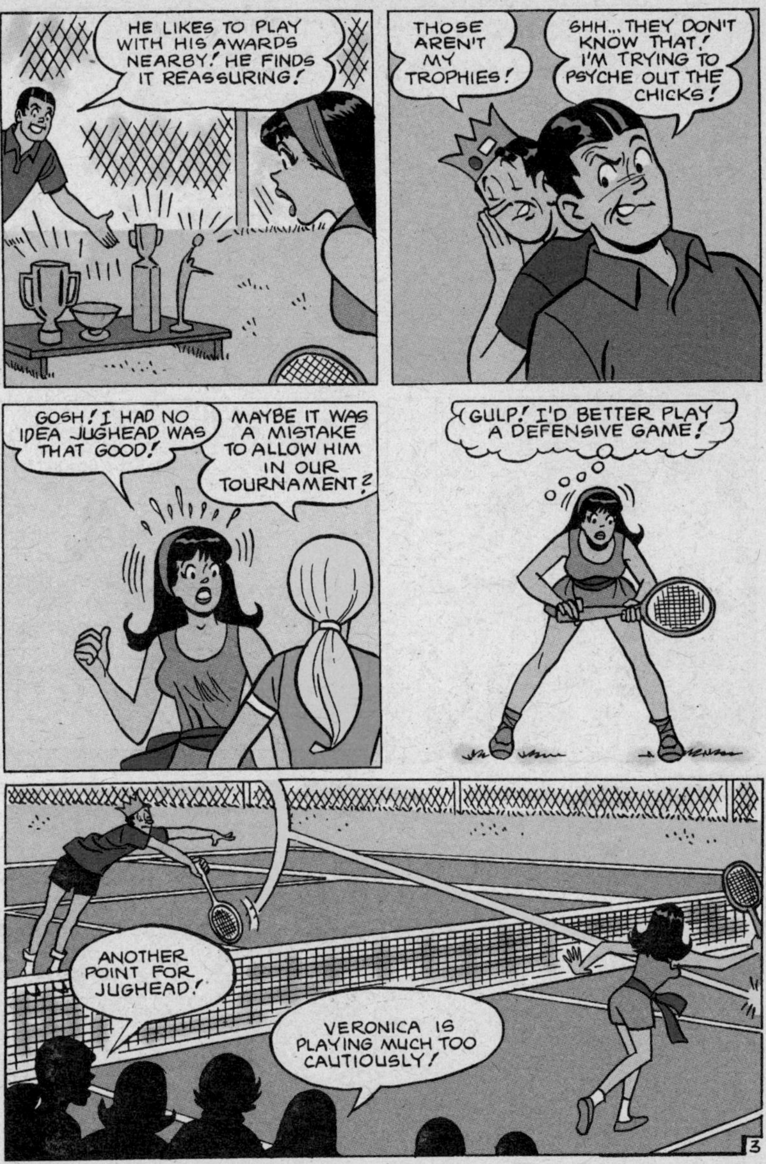
HE LIKES TO PLAY WITH HIS AWARDS NEARBY! HE FINDS IT REASSURING!
THOSE AREN'T MY TROPHIES!
SHH... THEY DON'T KNOW THAT! I'M TRYING TO PSYCHE OUT THE CHICKS!
GOSH! I HAD NO IDEA JUGHEAD WAS THAT GOOD!
MAYBE IT WAS A MISTAKE TO ALLOW HIM IN OUR TOURNAMENT?
GULP! I'D BETTER PLAY A DEFENSIVE GAME!
ANOTHER POINT FOR JUGHEAD!
VERONICA IS PLAYING MUCH TOO CAUTIOUSLY!
3

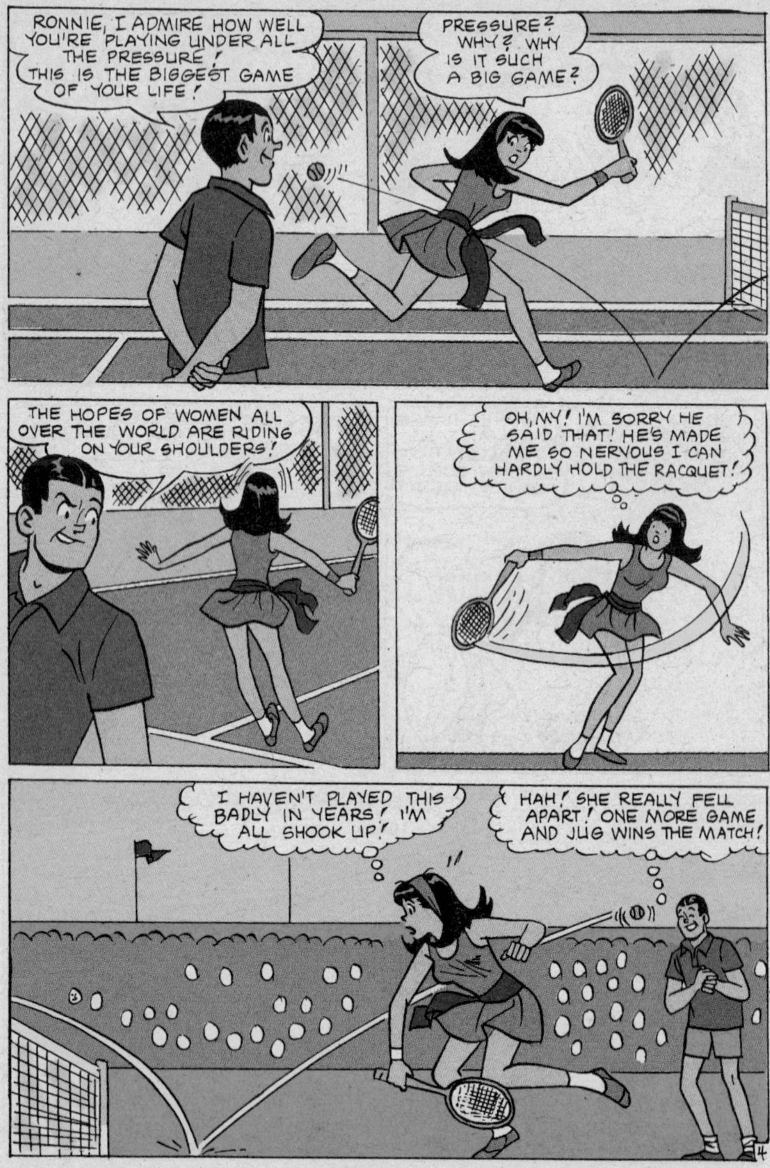

RONNIE, I ADMIRE HOW WELL YOU'RE PLAYING UNDER ALL THE PRESSURE! THIS IS THE BIGGEST GAME OF YOUR LIFE!
PRESSURE? WHY? WHY IS IT SUCH A BIG GAME?
THE HOPES OF WOMEN ALL OVER THE WORLD ARE RIDING ON YOUR SHOULDERS!
OH, MY! I'M SORRY HE SAID THAT! HE'S MADE ME SO NERVOUS I CAN HARDLY HOLD THE RACQUET!
I HAVEN'T PLAYED THIS BADLY IN YEARS! I'M ALL SHOOK UP!
HAH! SHE REALLY FELL APART! ONE MORE GAME AND JUG WINS THE MATCH!
4

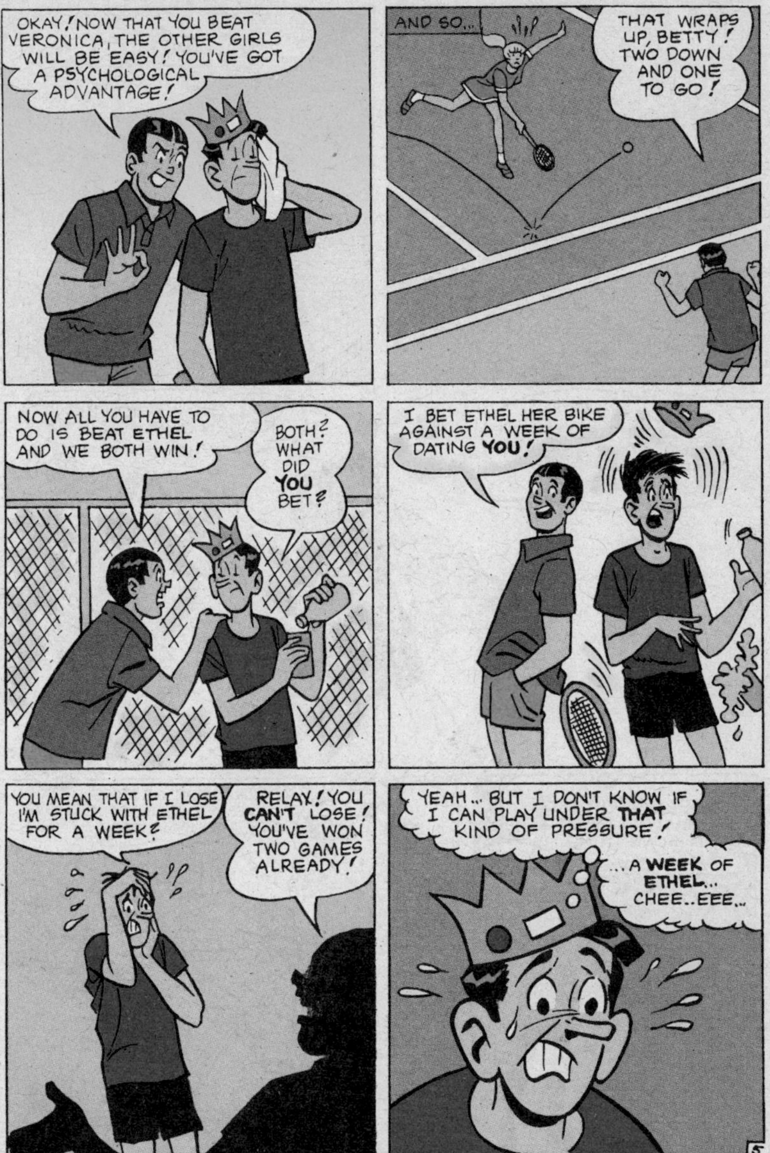

OKAY! NOW THAT YOU BEAT VERONICA, THE OTHER GIRLS WILL BE EASY! YOU'VE GOT A PSYCHOLOGICAL ADVANTAGE!
AND SO...
THAT WRAPS UP, BETTY! TWO DOWN AND ONE TO GO!
NOW ALL YOU HAVE TO DO IS BEAT ETHEL AND WE BOTH WIN!
BOTH? WHAT DID YOU BET?
I BET ETHEL HER BIKE AGAINST A WEEK OF DATING YOU!
YOU MEAN THAT IF I LOSE I'M STUCK WITH ETHEL FOR A WEEK?
RELAX! YOU CAN'T LOSE! YOU'VE WON TWO GAMES ALREADY!
YEAH... BUT I DON'T KNOW IF I CAN PLAY UNDER THAT KIND OF PRESSURE!
...A WEEK OF ETHEL... CHEE..EEE...
5

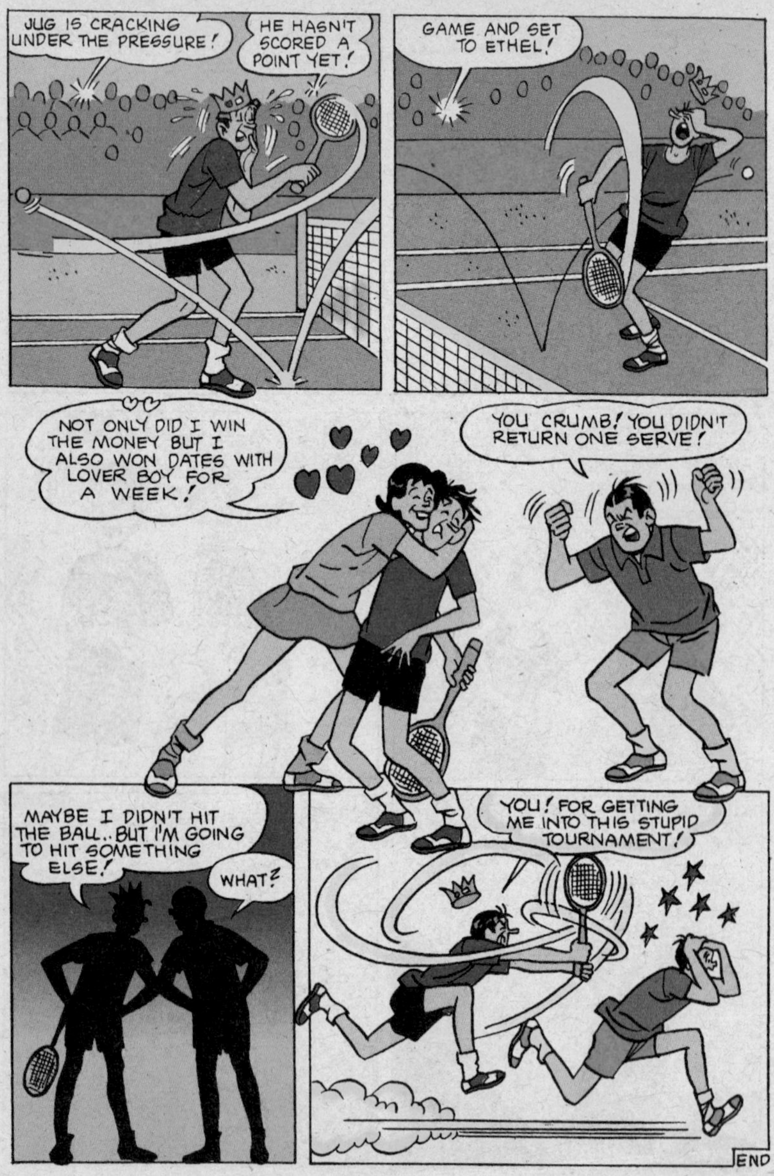
JUG IS CRACKING UNDER THE PRESSURE!
HE HASN'T SCORED A POINT YET!
GAME AND SET TO ETHEL!
NOT ONLY DID I WIN THE MONEY BUT I ALSO WON DATES WITH LOVER BOY FOR A WEEK!
YOU CRUMB! YOU DIDN'T RETURN ONE SERVE!
MAYBE I DIDN'T HIT THE BALL.. BUT I'M GOING TO HIT SOMETHING ELSE!
WHAT?
YOU! FOR GETTING ME INTO THIS STUPID TOURNAMENT!
END

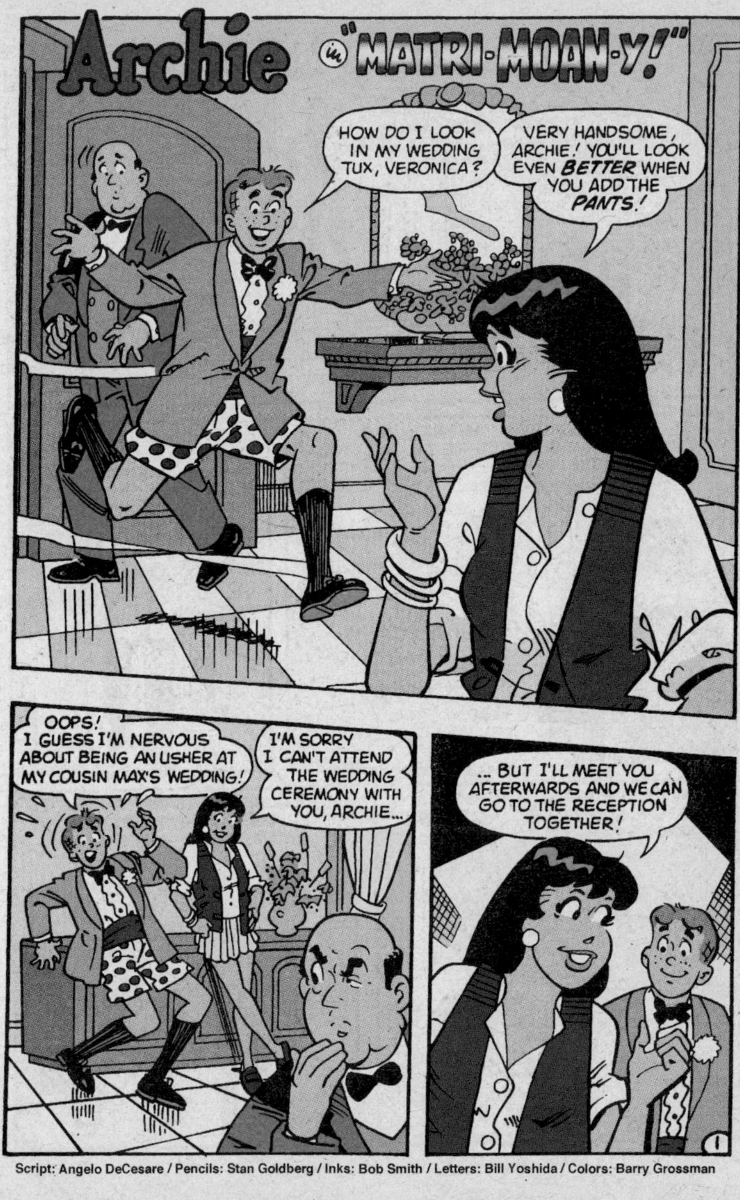
Archie
in "MATRI-MOAN-y!"
HOW DO I LOOK IN MY WEDDING TUX, VERONICA?
VERY HANDSOME, ARCHIE! YOU'LL LOOK EVEN BETTER WHEN YOU ADD THE PANTS!
OOPS! I GUESS I'M NERVOUS ABOUT BEING AN USHER AT MY COUSIN MAX'S WEDDING!
I'M SORRY I CAN'T ATTEND THE WEDDING CEREMONY WITH YOU, ARCHIE...
... BUT I'LL MEET YOU AFTERWARDS AND WE CAN GO TO THE RECEPTION TOGETHER!
1

Script: Angelo DeCesare / Pencils: Stan Goldberg / Inks: Bob Smith / Letters: Bill Yoshida / Colors: Barry Grossman

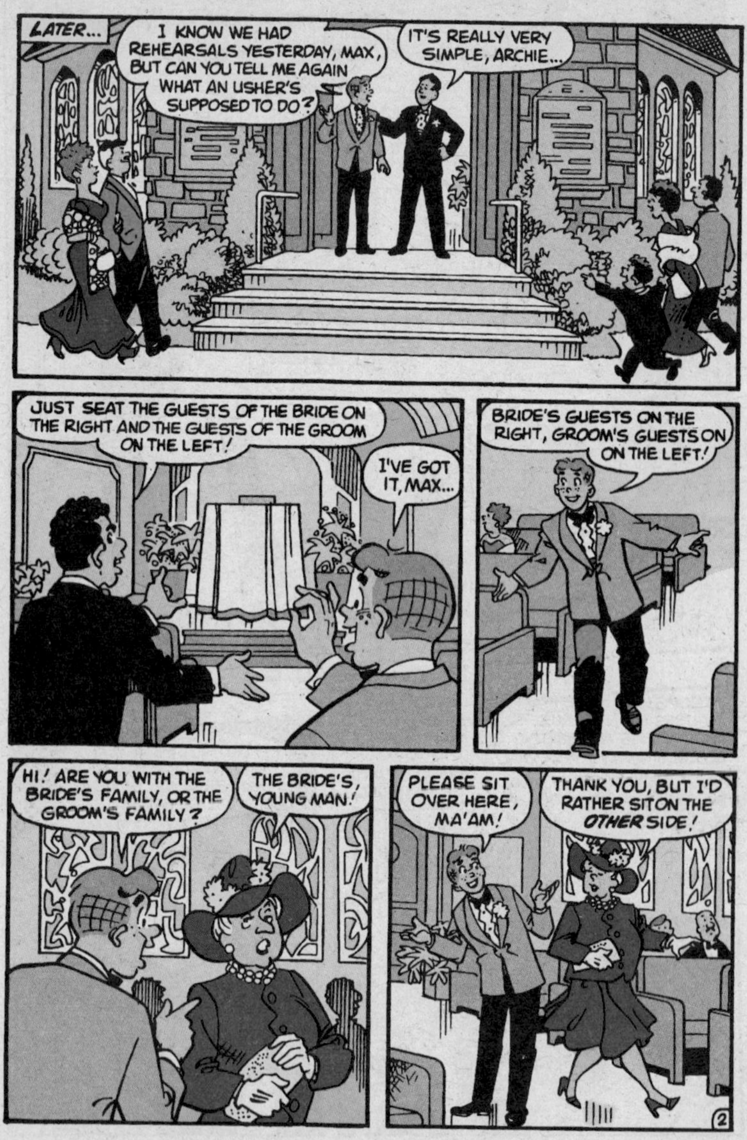
LATER...
I KNOW WE HAD REHEARSALS YESTERDAY, MAX, BUT CAN YOU TELL ME AGAIN WHAT AN USHER'S SUPPOSED TO DO?
IT'S REALLY VERY SIMPLE, ARCHIE...
JUST SEAT THE GUESTS OF THE BRIDE ON THE RIGHT AND THE GUESTS OF THE GROOM ON THE LEFT!
I'VE GOT IT, MAX...
BRIDE'S GUESTS ON THE RIGHT, GROOM'S GUESTS ON ON THE LEFT!
HI! ARE YOU WITH THE BRIDE'S FAMILY, OR THE GROOM'S FAMILY?
THE BRIDE'S, YOUNG MAN!
PLEASE SIT OVER HERE, MA'AM!
THANK YOU, BUT I'D RATHER SIT ON THE OTHER SIDE!
2

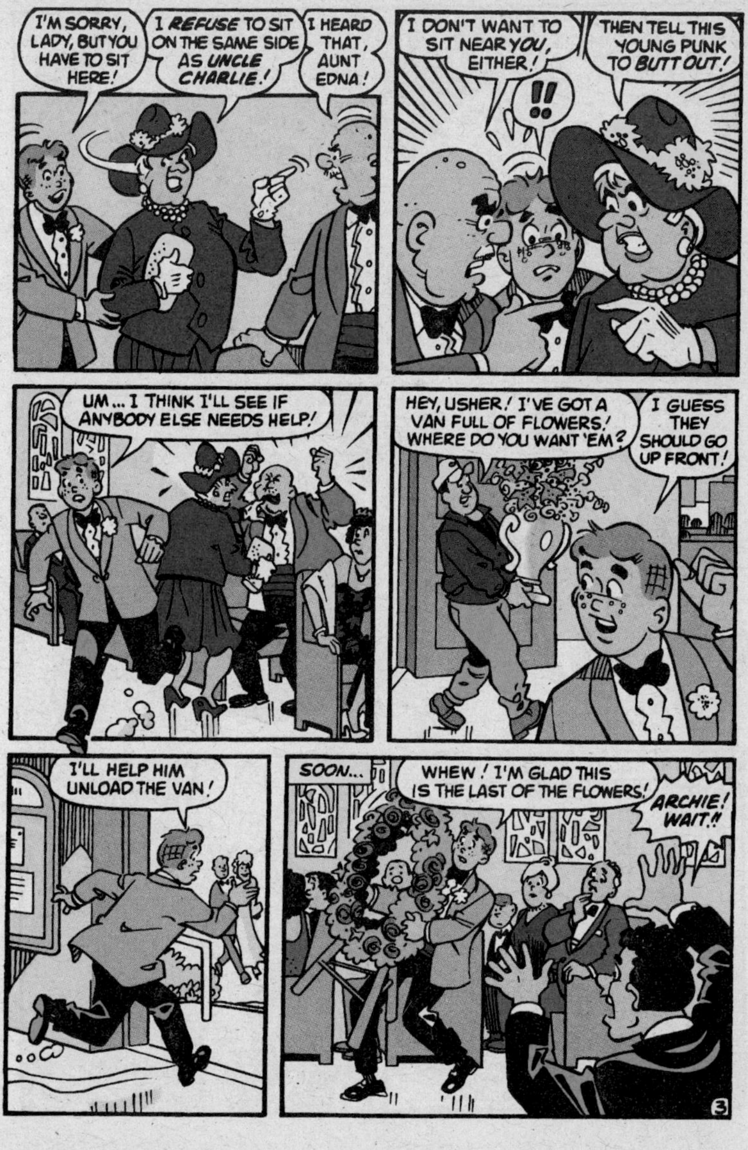
I'M SORRY, LADY, BUT YOU HAVE TO SIT HERE!
I REFUSE TO SIT ON THE SAME SIDE AS UNCLE CHARLIE!
I HEARD THAT, AUNT EDNA!
I DON'T WANT TO SIT NEAR YOU, EITHER!
!!
THEN TELL THIS YOUNG PUNK TO BUTT OUT!
UM ... I THINK I'LL SEE IF ANYBODY ELSE NEEDS HELP!
HEY, USHER! I'VE GOT A VAN FULL OF FLOWERS! WHERE DO YOU WANT 'EM?
I GUESS THEY SHOULD GO UP FRONT!
I'LL HELP HIM UNLOAD THE VAN!
SOON...
WHEW! I'M GLAD THIS IS THE LAST OF THE FLOWERS!
ARCHIE! WAIT!!
3

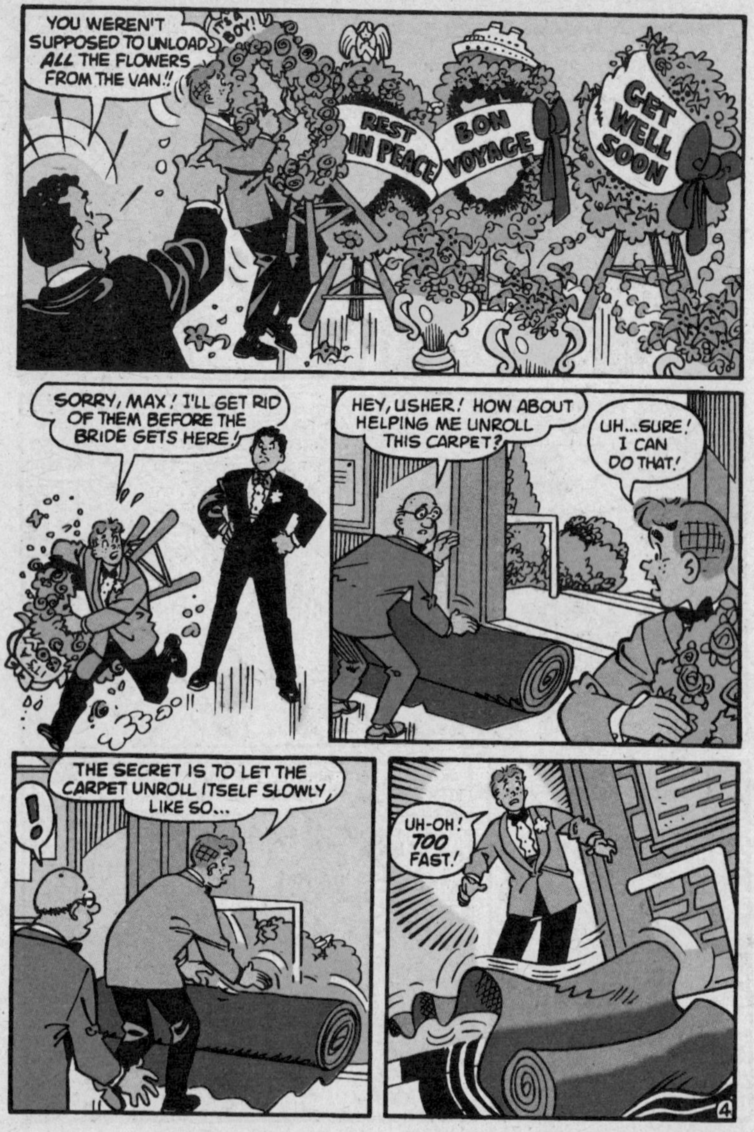

YOU WEREN'T SUPPOSED TO UNLOAD ALL THE FLOWERS FROM THE VAN!!
IT'S A BOY!
REST IN PEACE
BON VOYAGE
GET WELL SOON
SORRY, MAX! I'LL GET RID OF THEM BEFORE THE BRIDE GETS HERE!
HEY, USHER! HOW ABOUT HELPING ME UNROLL THIS CARPET?
UH...SURE! I CAN DO THAT!
THE SECRET IS TO LET THE CARPET UNROLL ITSELF SLOWLY, LIKE SO...
!
UH-OH! TOO FAST!
4

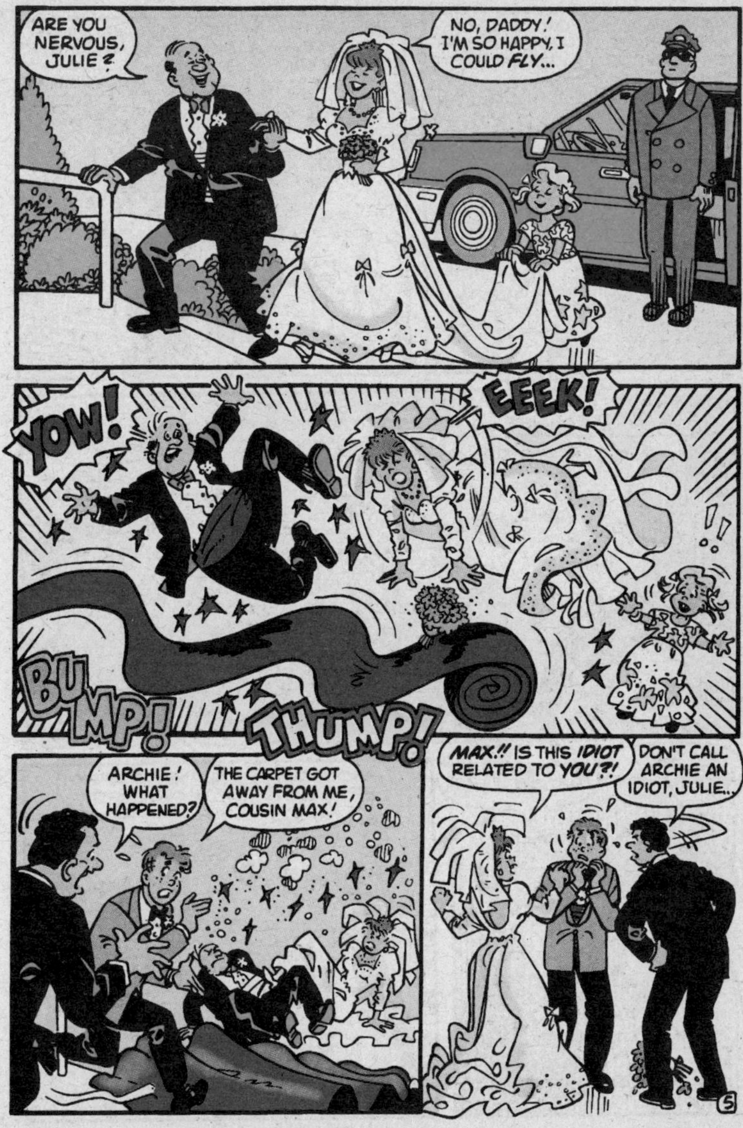
ARE YOU NERVOUS, JULIE?
NO, DADDY! I'M SO HAPPY, I COULD FLY...
YOW!
EEEK!
BUMP!
THUMP!
ARCHIE! WHAT HAPPENED?
THE CARPET GOT AWAY FROM ME, COUSIN MAX!
MAX!! IS THIS IDIOT RELATED TO YOU?!
DON'T CALL ARCHIE AN IDIOT, JULIE...
5

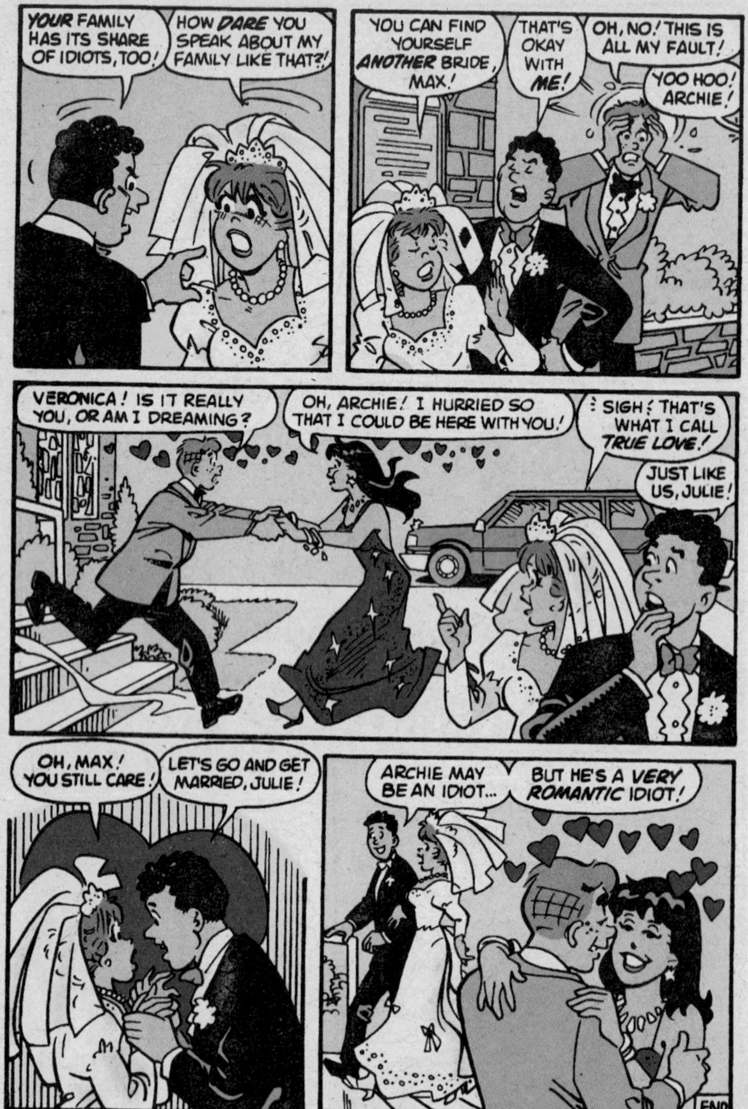
YOUR FAMILY HAS ITS SHARE OF IDIOTS, TOO!
HOW DARE YOU SPEAK ABOUT MY FAMILY LIKE THAT?!
YOU CAN FIND YOURSELF ANOTHER BRIDE, MAX!
THAT'S OKAY WITH ME!
OH, NO! THIS IS ALL MY FAULT!
YOO HOO! ARCHIE!
VERONICA! IS IT REALLY YOU, OR AM I DREAMING?
OH, ARCHIE! I HURRIED SO THAT I COULD BE HERE WITH YOU!
SIGH! THAT'S WHAT I CALL TRUE LOVE!
JUST LIKE US, JULIE!
OH, MAX! YOU STILL CARE!
LET'S GO AND GET MARRIED, JULIE!
ARCHIE MAY BE AN IDIOT...
BUT HE'S A VERY ROMANTIC IDIOT!
END

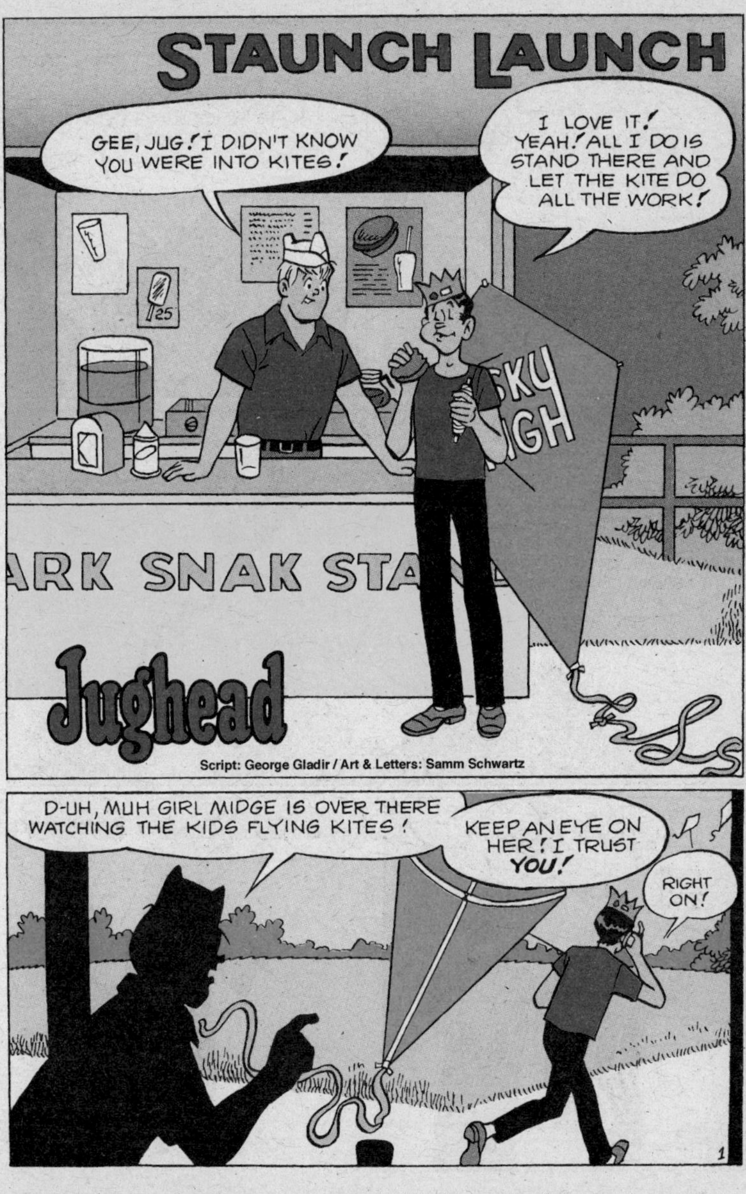
STAUNCH LAUNCH
GEE, JUG! I DIDN'T KNOW YOU WERE INTO KITES!
I LOVE IT! YEAH! ALL I DO IS STAND THERE AND LET THE KITE DO ALL THE WORK!
25
SKY HIGH
ARK SNAK STA
Jughead
Script: George Gladir / Art & Letters: Samm Schwartz
D-UH, MUH GIRL MIDGE IS OVER THERE WATCHING THE KIDS FLYING KITES!
KEEP AN EYE ON HER! I TRUST YOU!
RIGHT ON!
1

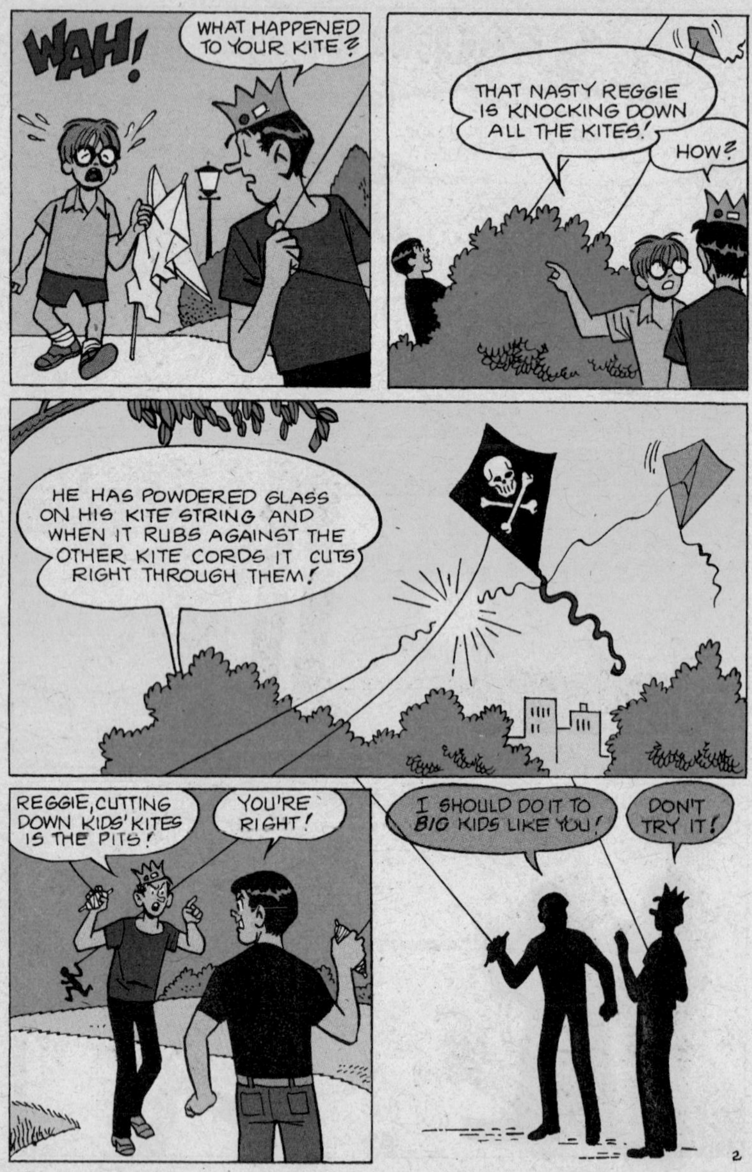
WAH!
WHAT HAPPENED TO YOUR KITE?
THAT NASTY REGGIE IS KNOCKING DOWN ALL THE KITES!
HOW?
HE HAS POWDERED GLASS ON HIS KITE STRING AND WHEN IT RUBS AGAINST THE OTHER KITE CORDS IT CUTS RIGHT THROUGH THEM!
REGGIE, CUTTING DOWN KIDS' KITES IS THE PITS!
YOU'RE RIGHT!
I SHOULD DO IT TO *BIG* KIDS LIKE YOU!
DON'T TRY IT!

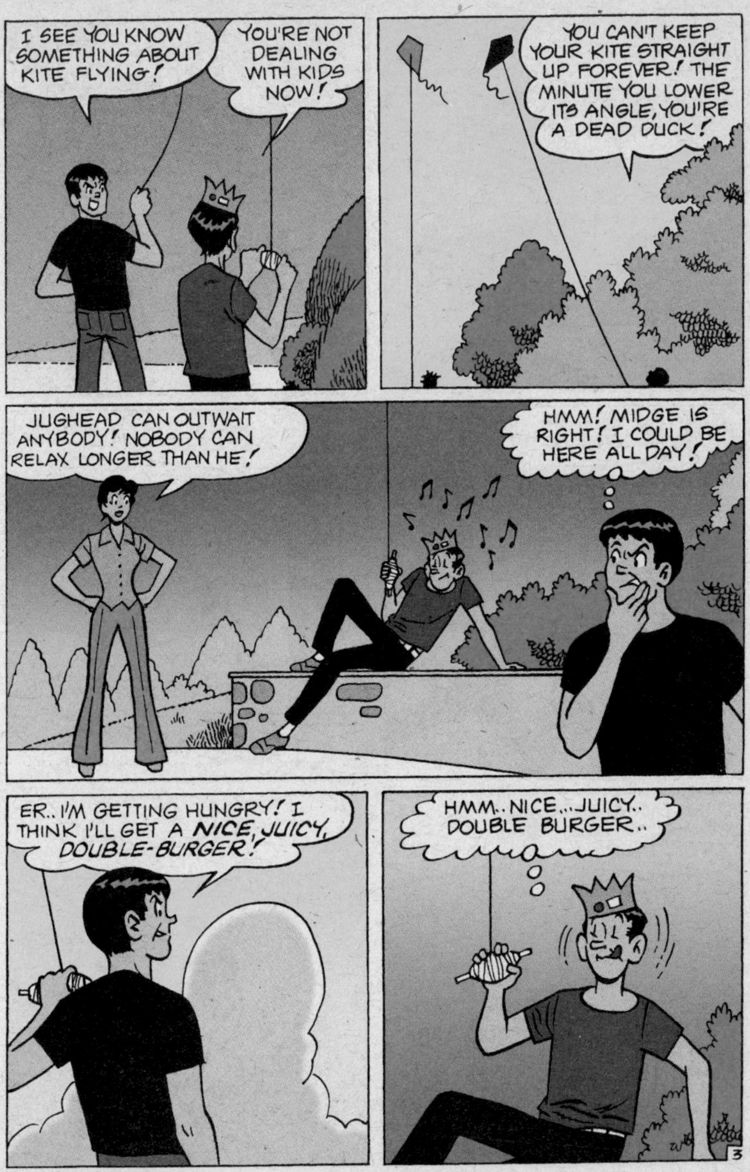

I SEE YOU KNOW SOMETHING ABOUT KITE FLYING!
YOU'RE NOT DEALING WITH KIDS NOW!
YOU CAN'T KEEP YOUR KITE STRAIGHT UP FOREVER! THE MINUTE YOU LOWER ITS ANGLE, YOU'RE A DEAD DUCK!
JUGHEAD CAN OUTWAIT ANYBODY! NOBODY CAN RELAX LONGER THAN HE!
HMM! MIDGE IS RIGHT! I COULD BE HERE ALL DAY!
ER.. I'M GETTING HUNGRY! I THINK I'LL GET A NICE, JUICY, DOUBLE-BURGER!
HMM.. NICE... JUICY.. DOUBLE BURGER..
3

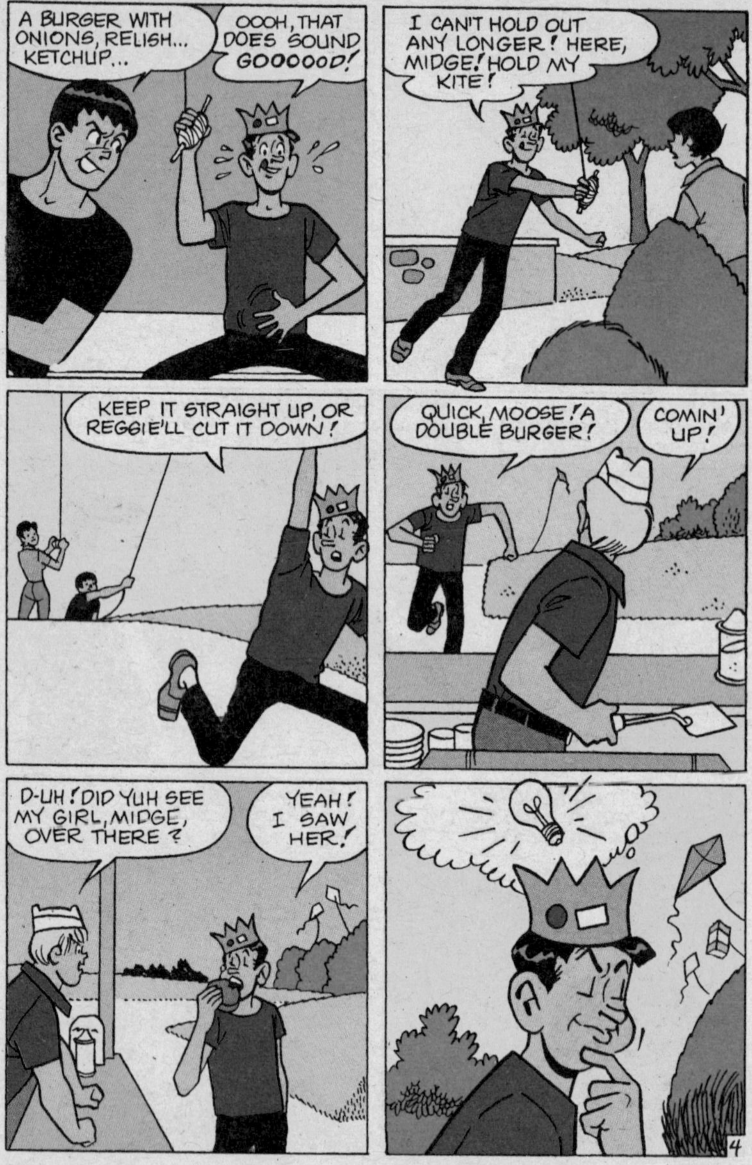
A BURGER WITH ONIONS, RELISH... KETCHUP...
OOOH, THAT DOES SOUND GOOOOOOD!
I CAN'T HOLD OUT ANY LONGER! HERE, MIDGE! HOLD MY KITE!
KEEP IT STRAIGHT UP, OR REGGIE'LL CUT IT DOWN!
QUICK, MOOSE! A DOUBLE BURGER!
COMIN' UP!
D-UH! DID YUH SEE MY GIRL, MIDGE, OVER THERE ?
YEAH! I SAW HER!

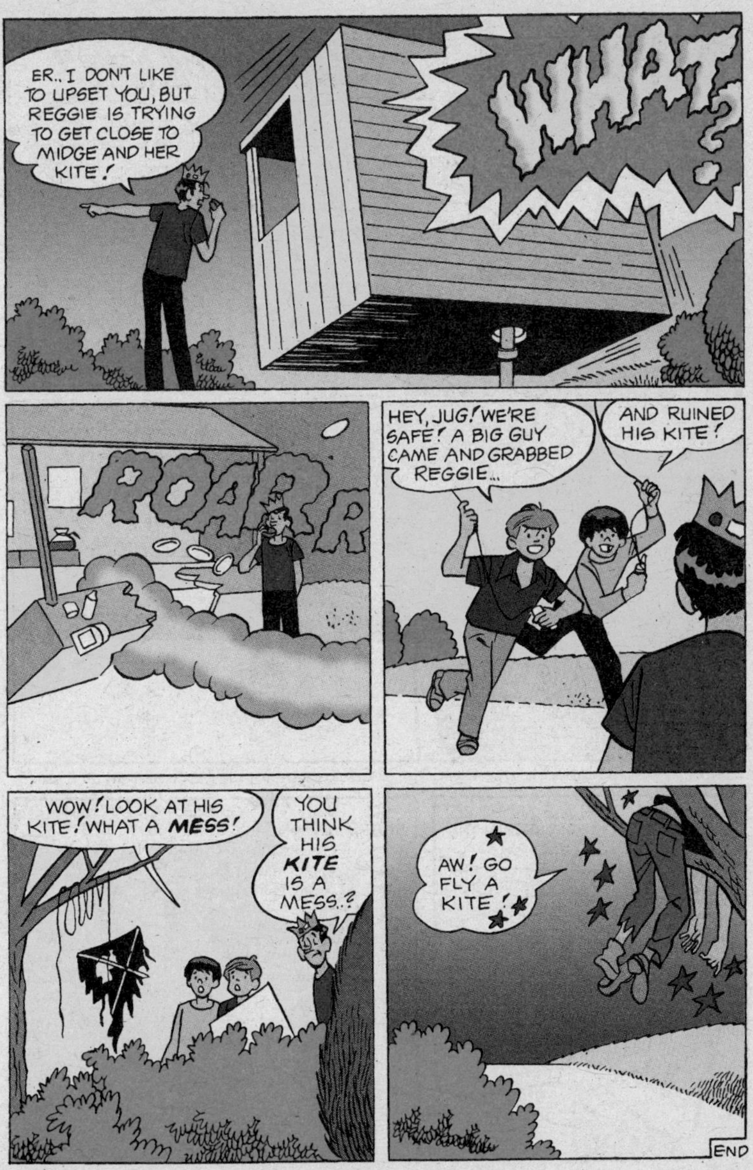
ER.. I DON'T LIKE TO UPSET YOU, BUT REGGIE IS TRYING TO GET CLOSE TO MIDGE AND HER KITE!
WHAT?
ROARR
HEY, JUG! WE'RE SAFE! A BIG GUY CAME AND GRABBED REGGIE...
AND RUINED HIS KITE!
WOW! LOOK AT HIS KITE! WHAT A MESS!
YOU THINK HIS KITE IS A MESS..?
AW! GO FLY A KITE!
END

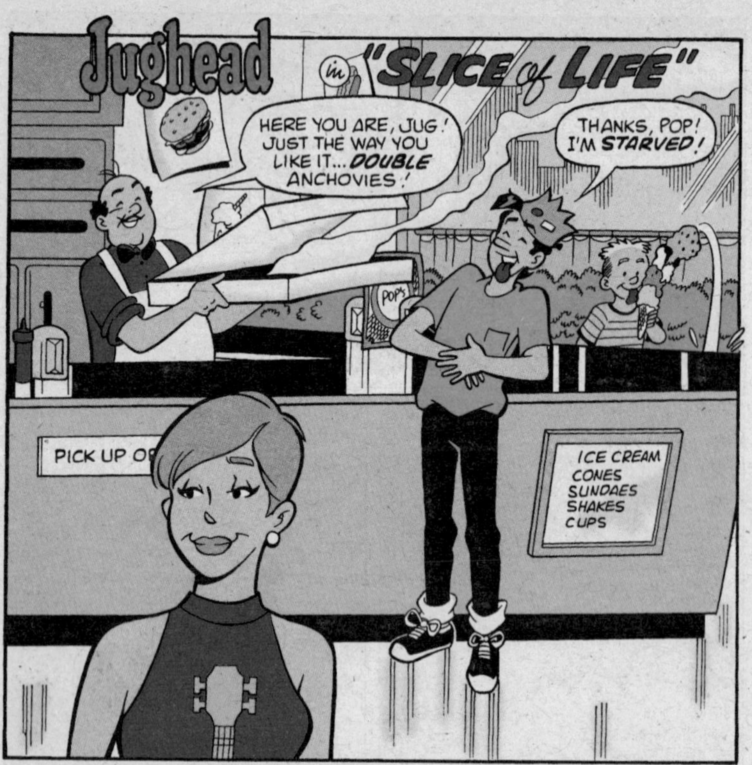
Jughead
in "SLICE of LIFE"
HERE YOU ARE, JUG! JUST THE WAY YOU LIKE IT... DOUBLE ANCHOVIES!
THANKS, POP! I'M STARVED!
POP'S
PICK UP OR
ICE CREAM
CONES
SUNDAES
SHAKES
CUPS

Script: Bill Golliher / Pencils: Fernando Ruiz / Inks: Al Nickerson / Letters: Bill Yoshida / Colors: Barry Grossman

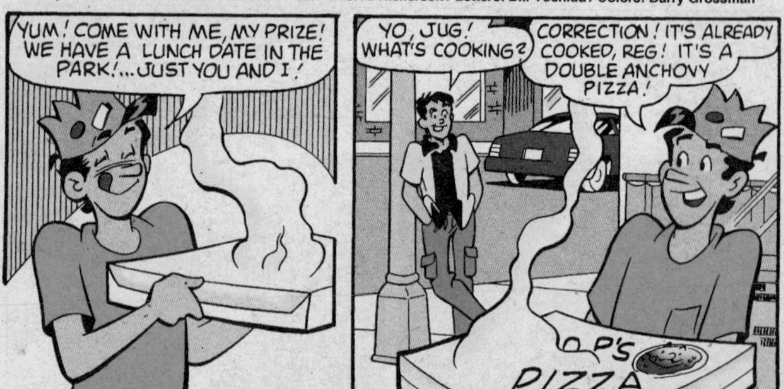
YUM! COME WITH ME, MY PRIZE! WE HAVE A LUNCH DATE IN THE PARK!... JUST YOU AND I!
YO, JUG! WHAT'S COOKING?
CORRECTION! IT'S ALREADY COOKED, REG! IT'S A DOUBLE ANCHOVY PIZZA!
OP'S
PIZZA

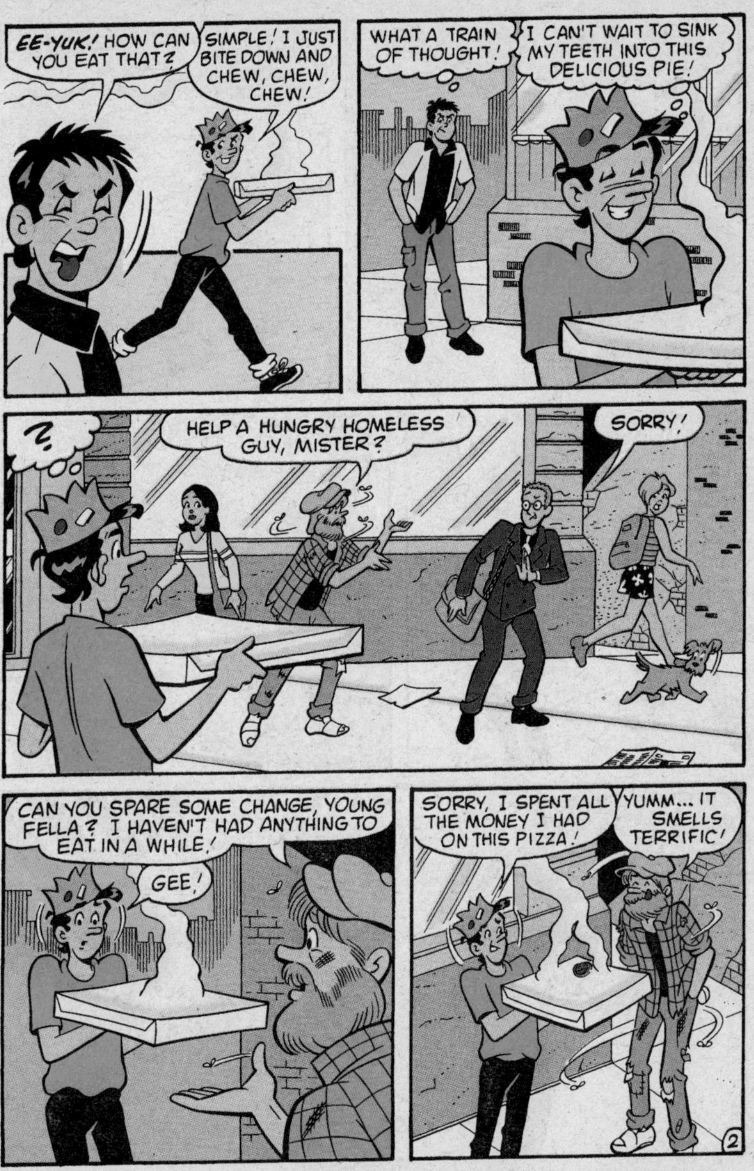

EE-YUK! HOW CAN YOU EAT THAT?
SIMPLE! I JUST BITE DOWN AND CHEW, CHEW, CHEW!
WHAT A TRAIN OF THOUGHT!
I CAN'T WAIT TO SINK MY TEETH INTO THIS DELICIOUS PIE!
?
HELP A HUNGRY HOMELESS GUY, MISTER?
SORRY!
CAN YOU SPARE SOME CHANGE, YOUNG FELLA? I HAVEN'T HAD ANYTHING TO EAT IN A WHILE!
GEE!
SORRY, I SPENT ALL THE MONEY I HAD ON THIS PIZZA!
YUMM... IT SMELLS TERRIFIC!

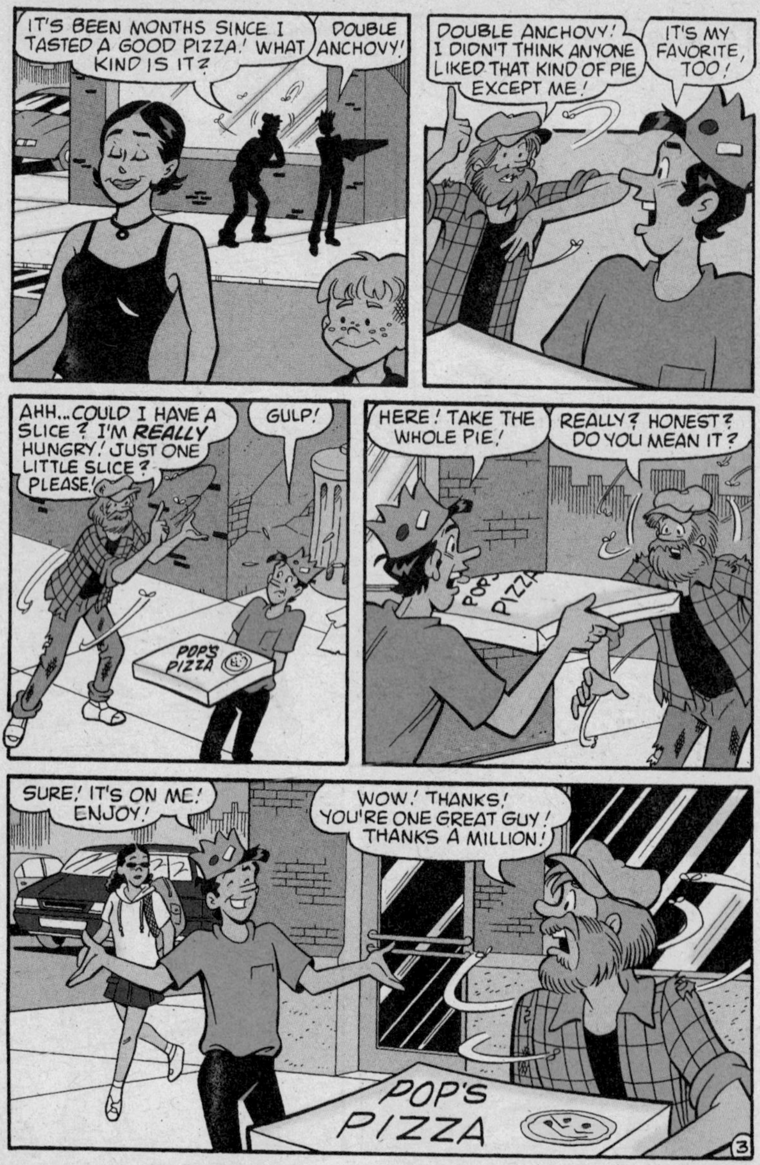
IT'S BEEN MONTHS SINCE I TASTED A GOOD PIZZA! WHAT KIND IS IT?
DOUBLE ANCHOVY!
DOUBLE ANCHOVY! I DIDN'T THINK ANYONE LIKED THAT KIND OF PIE EXCEPT ME!
IT'S MY FAVORITE, TOO!
AHH...COULD I HAVE A SLICE? I'M REALLY HUNGRY! JUST ONE LITTLE SLICE? PLEASE!
GULP!
POP'S PIZZA
HERE! TAKE THE WHOLE PIE!
REALLY? HONEST? DO YOU MEAN IT?
POP'S PIZZA
SURE! IT'S ON ME! ENJOY!
WOW! THANKS! YOU'RE ONE GREAT GUY! THANKS A MILLION!
POP'S PIZZA

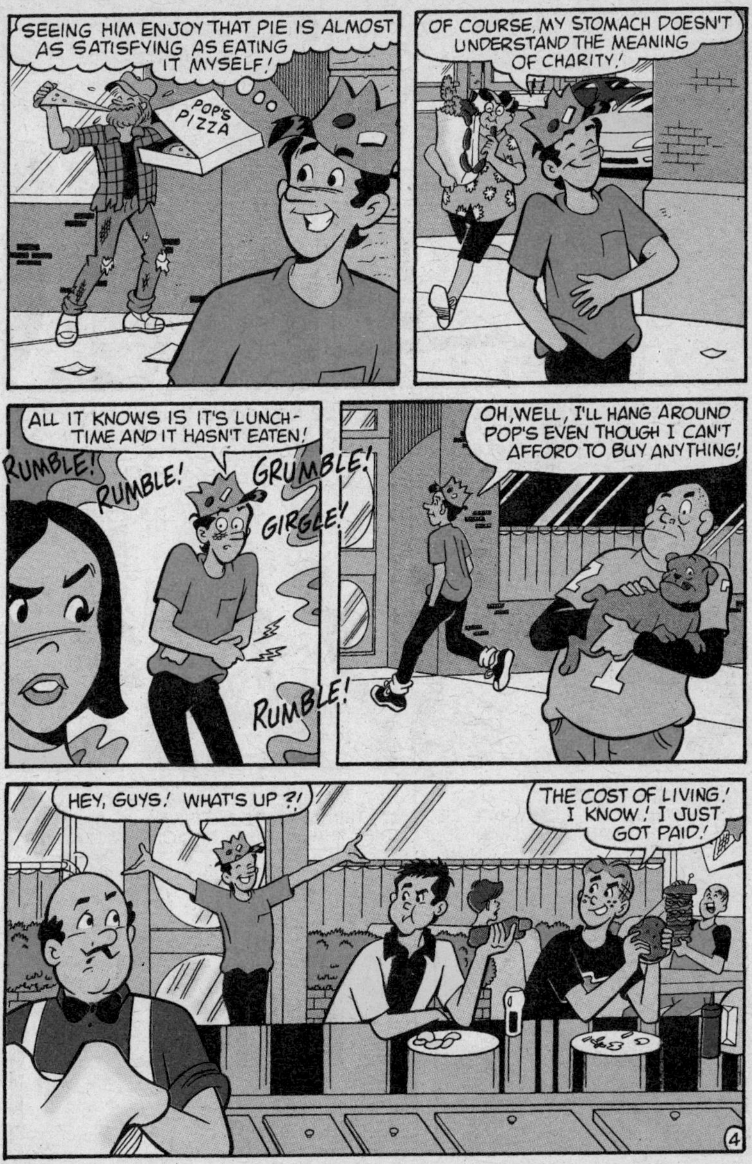

SEEING HIM ENJOY THAT PIE IS ALMOST AS SATISFYING AS EATING IT MYSELF!
POP'S PIZZA
OF COURSE, MY STOMACH DOESN'T UNDERSTAND THE MEANING OF CHARITY!
ALL IT KNOWS IS IT'S LUNCH-TIME AND IT HASN'T EATEN!
RUMBLE!
RUMBLE!
GRUMBLE!
GIRGLE!
RUMBLE!
OH, WELL, I'LL HANG AROUND POP'S EVEN THOUGH I CAN'T AFFORD TO BUY ANYTHING!
HEY, GUYS! WHAT'S UP ?!
THE COST OF LIVING! I KNOW! I JUST GOT PAID!

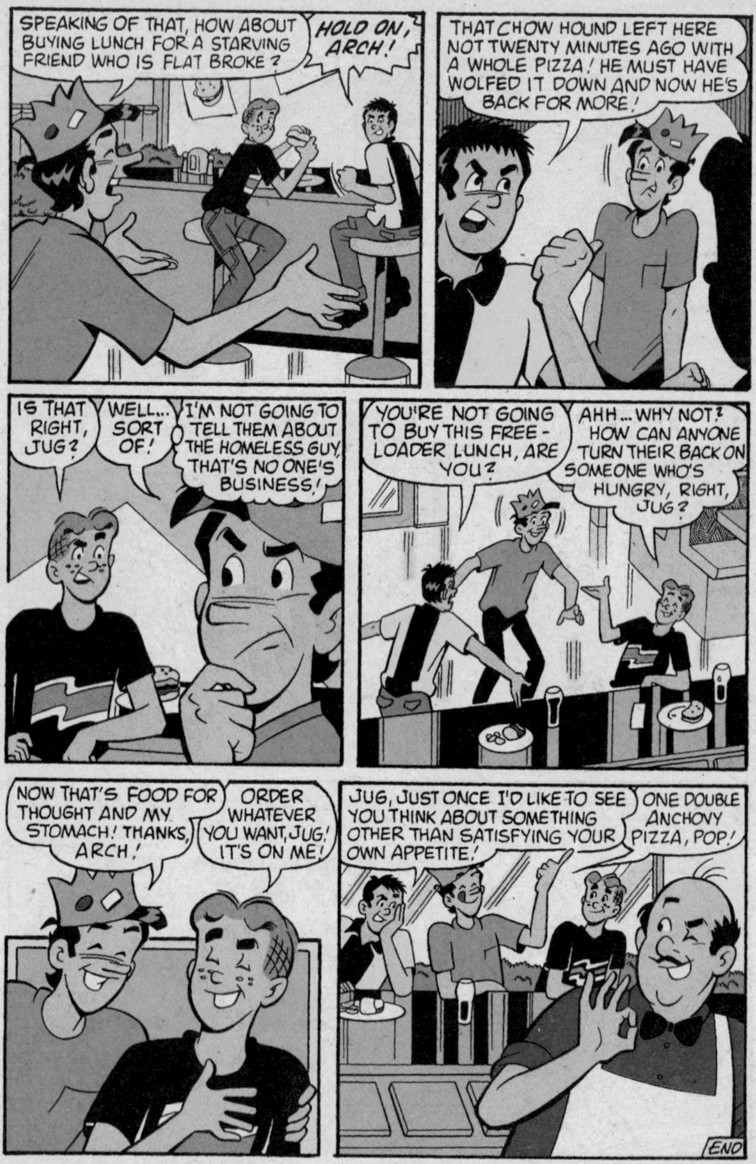
SPEAKING OF THAT, HOW ABOUT BUYING LUNCH FOR A STARVING FRIEND WHO IS FLAT BROKE?
HOLD ON, ARCH!
THAT CHOW HOUND LEFT HERE NOT TWENTY MINUTES AGO WITH A WHOLE PIZZA! HE MUST HAVE WOLFED IT DOWN AND NOW HE'S BACK FOR MORE!
IS THAT RIGHT, JUG?
WELL... SORT OF!
I'M NOT GOING TO TELL THEM ABOUT THE HOMELESS GUY, THAT'S NO ONE'S BUSINESS!
YOU'RE NOT GOING TO BUY THIS FREE-LOADER LUNCH, ARE YOU?
AHH... WHY NOT? HOW CAN ANYONE TURN THEIR BACK ON SOMEONE WHO'S HUNGRY, RIGHT, JUG?
NOW THAT'S FOOD FOR THOUGHT AND MY STOMACH! THANKS, ARCH!
ORDER WHATEVER YOU WANT, JUG! IT'S ON ME!
JUG, JUST ONCE I'D LIKE TO SEE YOU THINK ABOUT SOMETHING OTHER THAN SATISFYING YOUR OWN APPETITE!
ONE DOUBLE ANCHOVY PIZZA, POP!
END

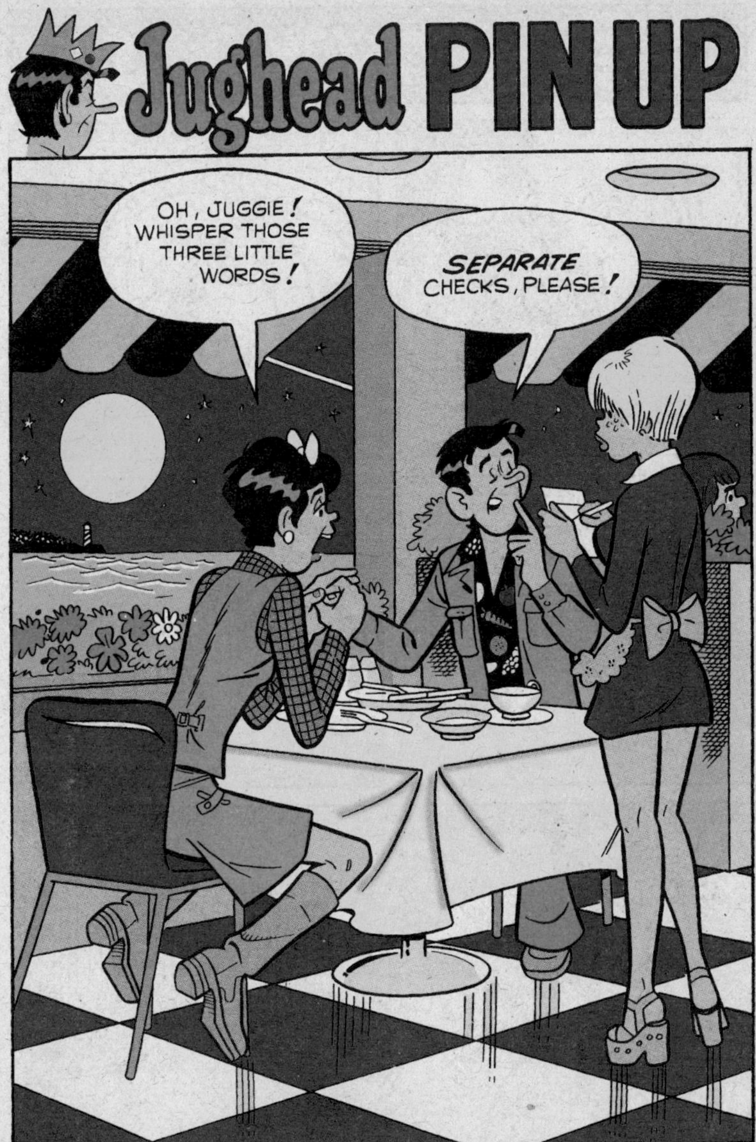
Jughead PIN UP
OH, JUGGIE! WHISPER THOSE THREE LITTLE WORDS!
SEPARATE CHECKS, PLEASE!

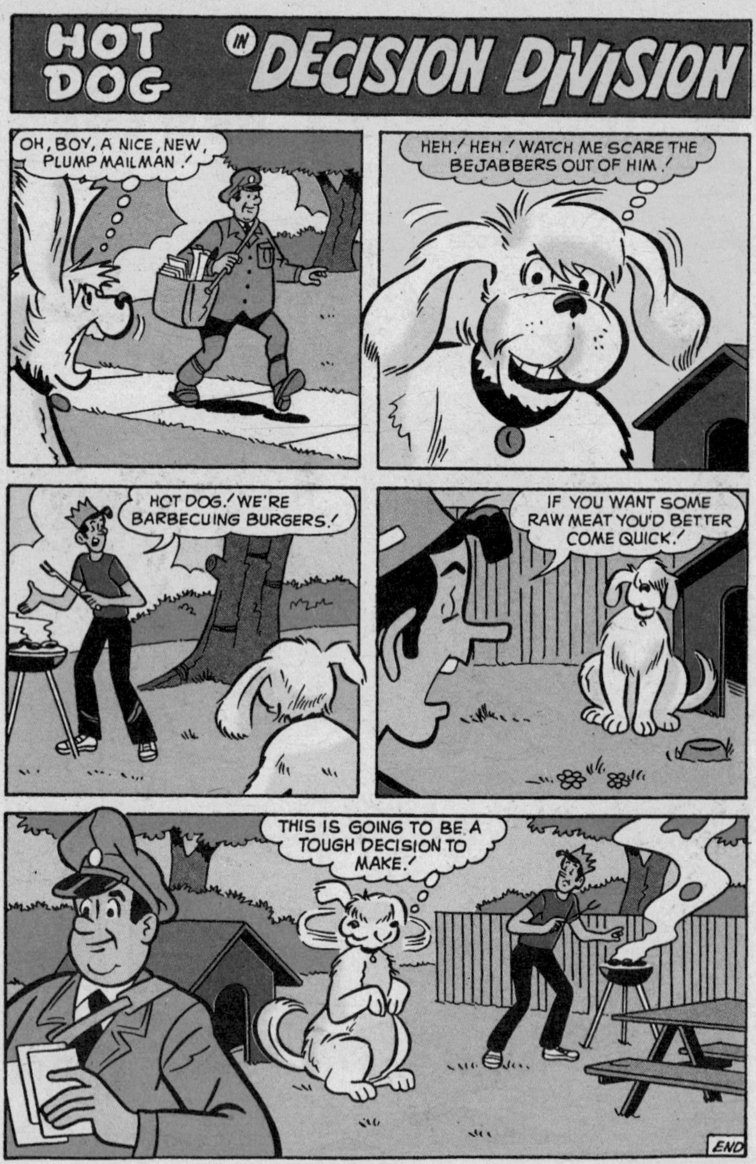

HOT DOG
IN
DECISION DIVISION
OH, BOY, A NICE, NEW, PLUMP MAILMAN!
HEH! HEH! WATCH ME SCARE THE BEJABBERS OUT OF HIM!
HOT DOG! WE'RE BARBECUING BURGERS!
IF YOU WANT SOME RAW MEAT YOU'D BETTER COME QUICK!
THIS IS GOING TO BE A TOUGH DECISION TO MAKE!
END

Jughead

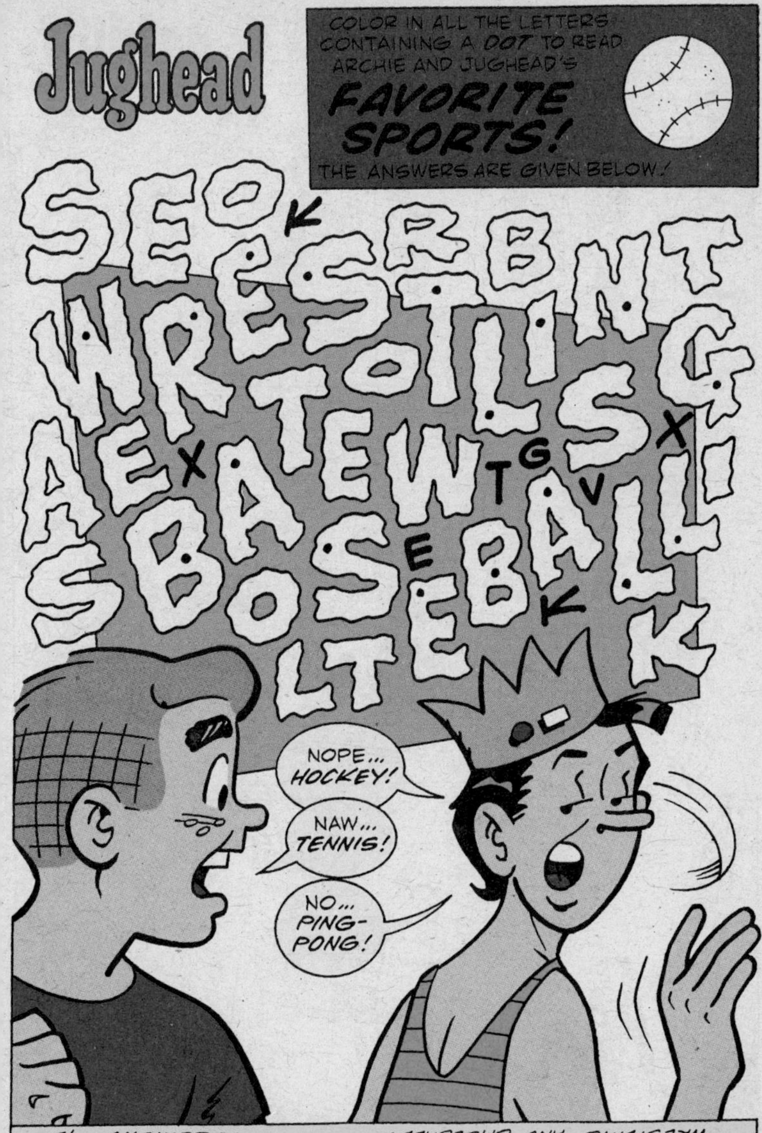

The ANSWERS: WRESTLING AND BASEBALL!

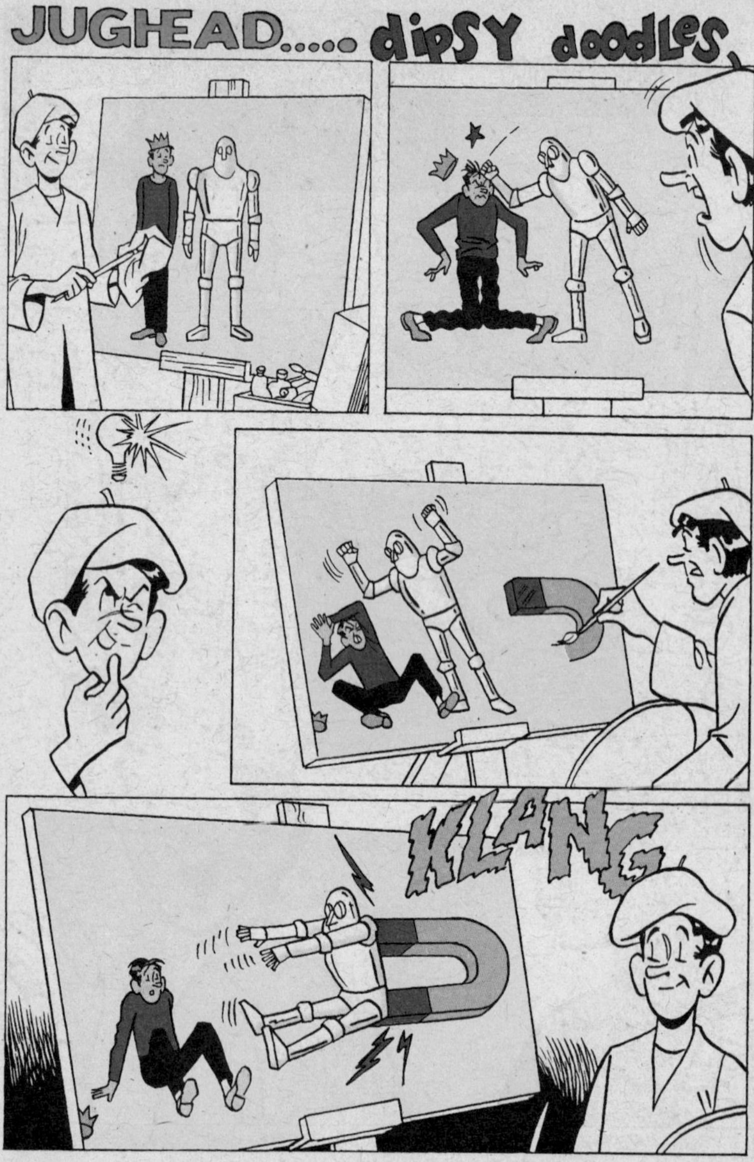
JUGHEAD..... dipsy doodles
KLANG

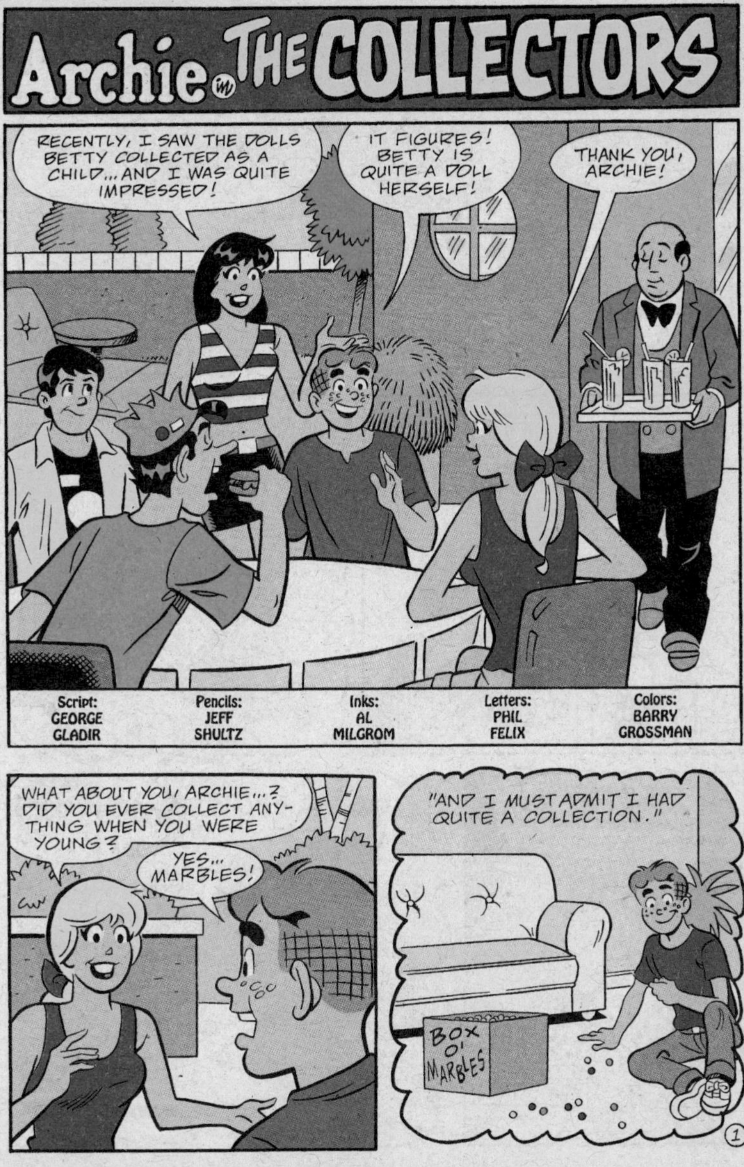
Archie in THE COLLECTORS
RECENTLY, I SAW THE DOLLS BETTY COLLECTED AS A CHILD... AND I WAS QUITE IMPRESSED!
IT FIGURES! BETTY IS QUITE A DOLL HERSELF!
THANK YOU, ARCHIE!
Script: GEORGE GLADIR
Pencils: JEFF SHULTZ
Inks: AL MILGROM
Letters: PHIL FELIX
Colors: BARRY GROSSMAN
WHAT ABOUT YOU, ARCHIE...? DID YOU EVER COLLECT ANYTHING WHEN YOU WERE YOUNG?
YES... MARBLES!
"AND I MUST ADMIT I HAD QUITE A COLLECTION."
BOX O' MARBLES
1

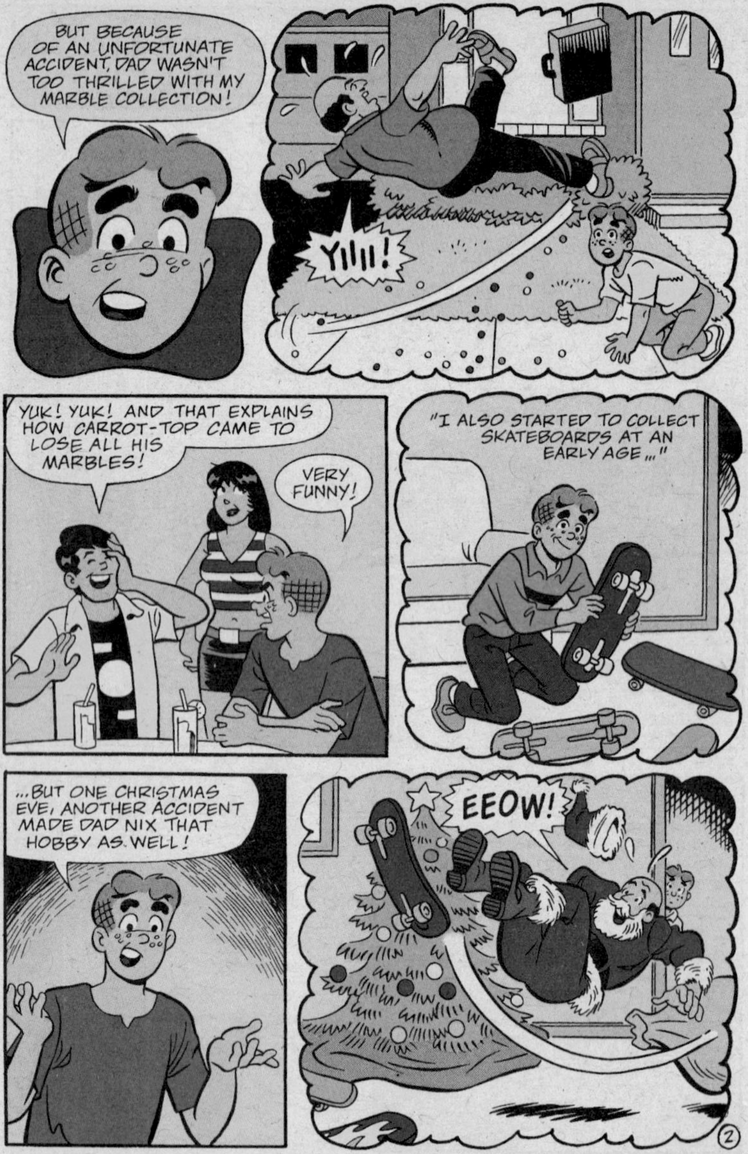
BUT BECAUSE OF AN UNFORTUNATE ACCIDENT, DAD WASN'T TOO THRILLED WITH MY MARBLE COLLECTION!
YIIII!
YUK! YUK! AND THAT EXPLAINS HOW CARROT-TOP CAME TO LOSE ALL HIS MARBLES!
VERY FUNNY!
"I ALSO STARTED TO COLLECT SKATEBOARDS AT AN EARLY AGE..."
...BUT ONE CHRISTMAS EVE, ANOTHER ACCIDENT MADE DAD NIX THAT HOBBY AS WELL!
EEOW!
2

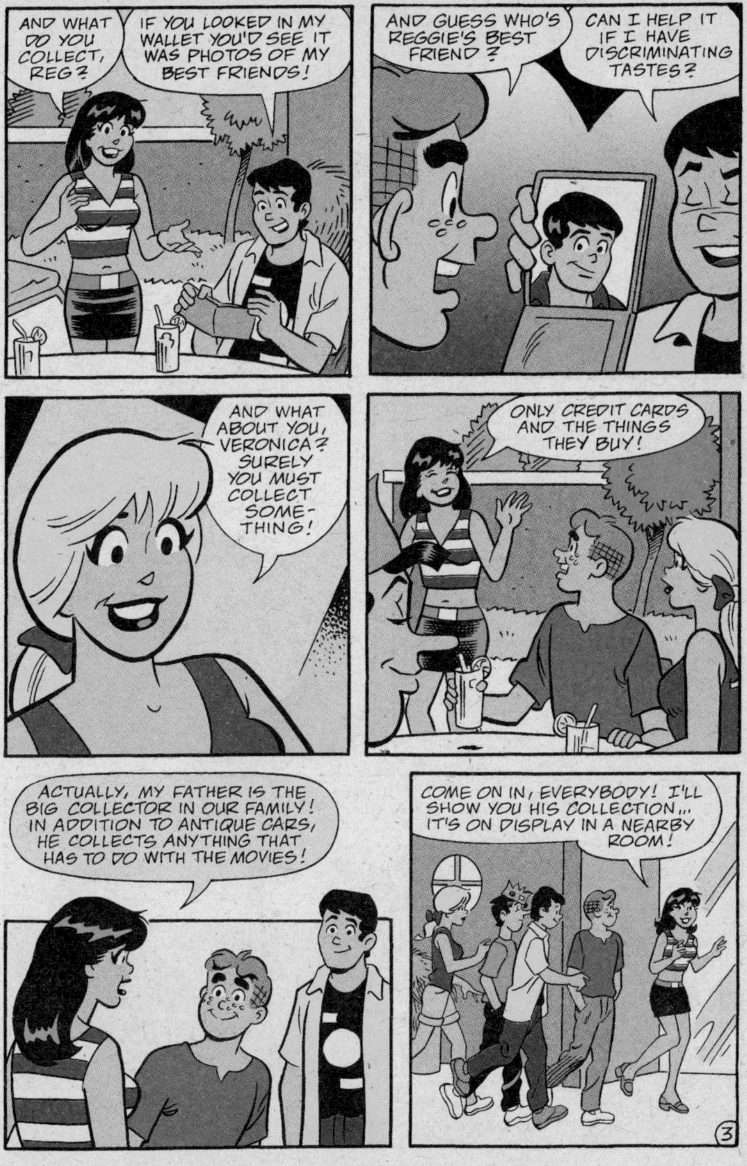
AND WHAT DO YOU COLLECT, REG?
IF YOU LOOKED IN MY WALLET YOU'D SEE IT WAS PHOTOS OF MY BEST FRIENDS!
AND GUESS WHO'S REGGIE'S BEST FRIEND?
CAN I HELP IT IF I HAVE DISCRIMINATING TASTES?
AND WHAT ABOUT YOU, VERONICA? SURELY YOU MUST COLLECT SOME-THING!
ONLY CREDIT CARDS AND THE THINGS THEY BUY!
ACTUALLY, MY FATHER IS THE BIG COLLECTOR IN OUR FAMILY! IN ADDITION TO ANTIQUE CARS, HE COLLECTS ANYTHING THAT HAS TO DO WITH THE MOVIES!
COME ON IN, EVERYBODY! I'LL SHOW YOU HIS COLLECTION... IT'S ON DISPLAY IN A NEARBY ROOM!
3

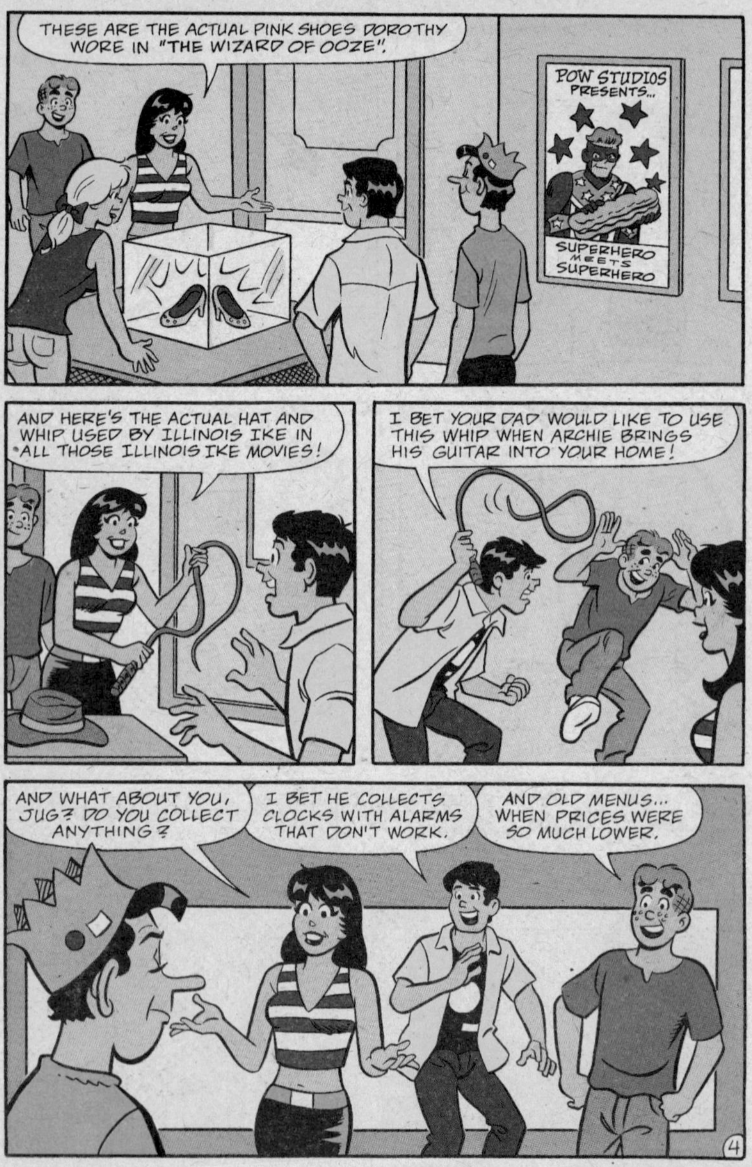
THESE ARE THE ACTUAL PINK SHOES DOROTHY WORE IN "THE WIZARD OF OOZE".
POW STUDIOS PRESENTS...
SUPERHERO MEETS SUPERHERO
AND HERE'S THE ACTUAL HAT AND WHIP USED BY ILLINOIS IKE IN ALL THOSE ILLINOIS IKE MOVIES!
I BET YOUR DAD WOULD LIKE TO USE THIS WHIP WHEN ARCHIE BRINGS HIS GUITAR INTO YOUR HOME!
AND WHAT ABOUT YOU, JUG? DO YOU COLLECT ANYTHING?
I BET HE COLLECTS CLOCKS WITH ALARMS THAT DON'T WORK.
AND OLD MENUS... WHEN PRICES WERE SO MUCH LOWER.
4

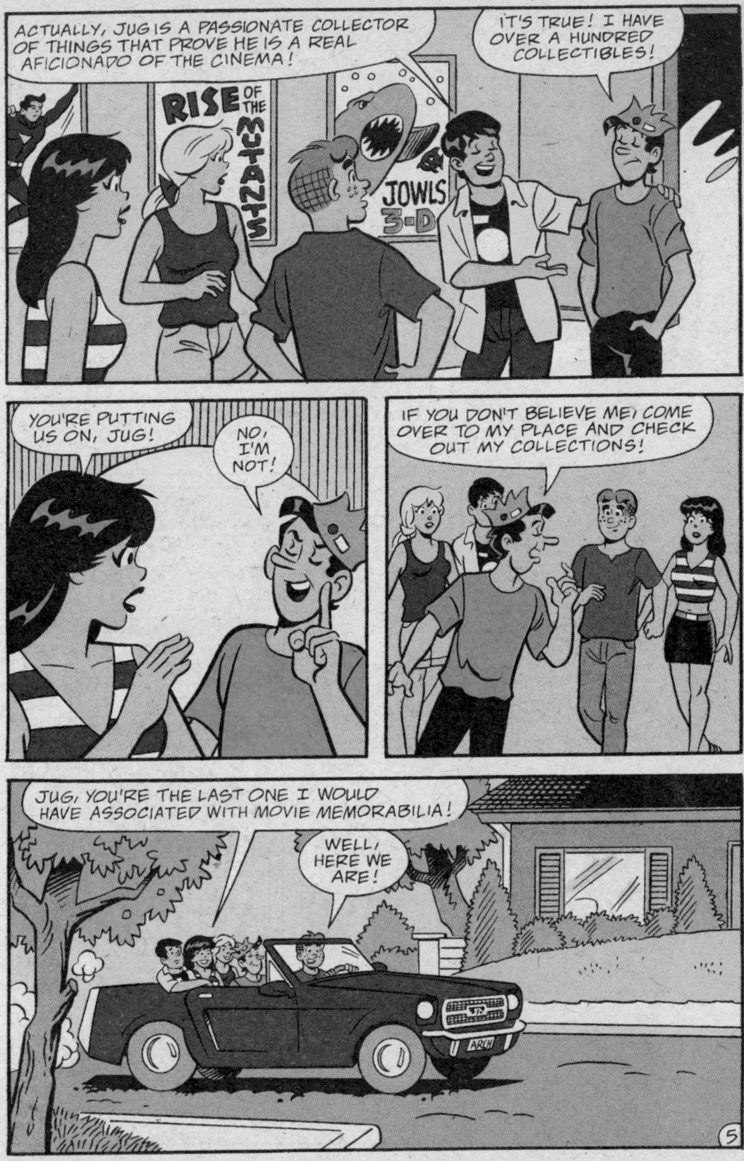
ACTUALLY, JUG IS A PASSIONATE COLLECTOR OF THINGS THAT PROVE HE IS A REAL AFICIONADO OF THE CINEMA!
IT'S TRUE! I HAVE OVER A HUNDRED COLLECTIBLES!
RISE OF THE MUTANTS
JOWLS 3-D
YOU'RE PUTTING US ON, JUG!
NO, I'M NOT!
IF YOU DON'T BELIEVE ME, COME OVER TO MY PLACE AND CHECK OUT MY COLLECTIONS!
JUG, YOU'RE THE LAST ONE I WOULD HAVE ASSOCIATED WITH MOVIE MEMORABILIA!
WELL, HERE WE ARE!
ARCH
5

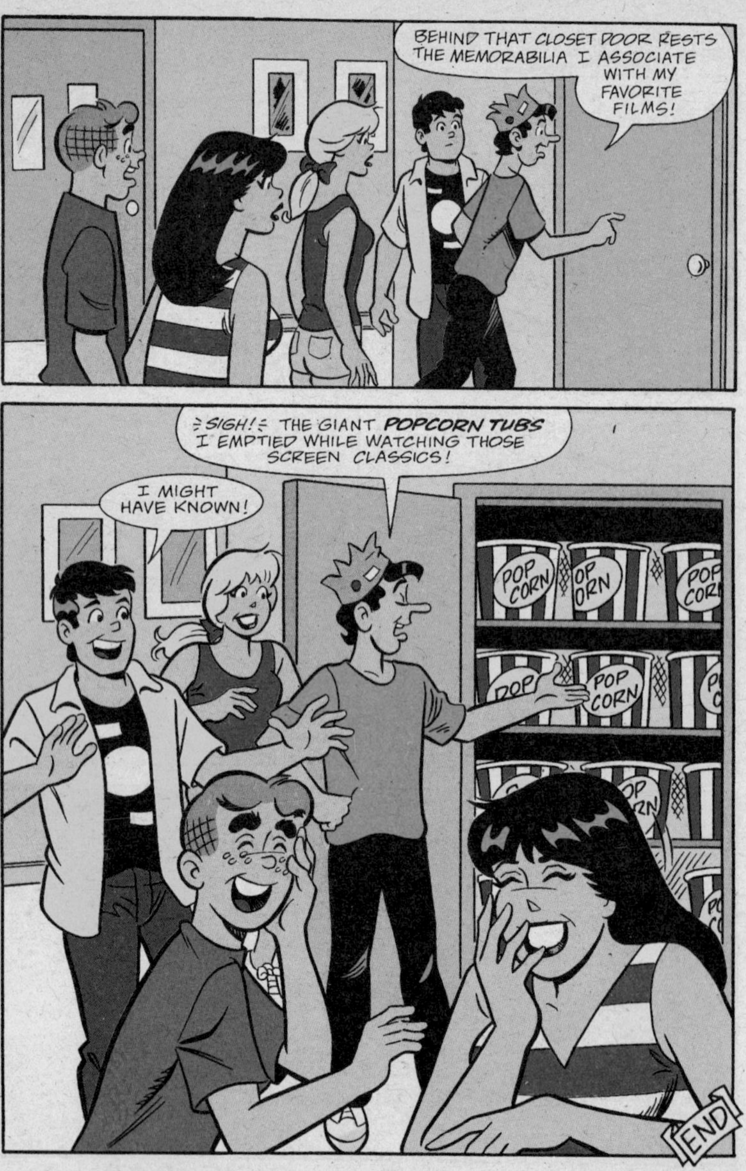
BEHIND THAT CLOSET DOOR RESTS THE MEMORABILIA I ASSOCIATE WITH MY FAVORITE FILMS!
SIGH! THE GIANT POPCORN TUBS I EMPTIED WHILE WATCHING THOSE SCREEN CLASSICS!
I MIGHT HAVE KNOWN!
END

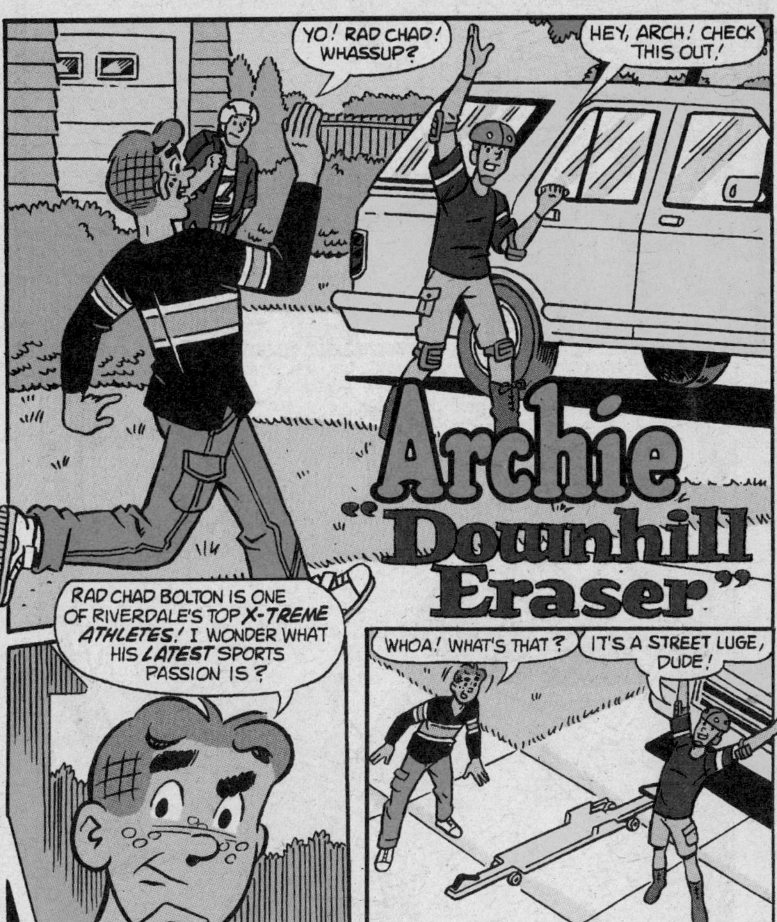
YO! RAD CHAD! WHASSUP?
HEY, ARCH! CHECK THIS OUT!
Archie
"Downhill Eraser"
RAD CHAD BOLTON IS ONE OF RIVERDALE'S TOP X-TREME ATHLETES! I WONDER WHAT HIS LATEST SPORTS PASSION IS?
WHOA! WHAT'S THAT?
IT'S A STREET LUGE, DUDE!

SCRIPT: MIKE PELLOWSKI PENCILS: FERNANDO RUIZ INKS: RUDY LAPICK
LETTERS: BILL YOSHIDA COLORS: BARRY GROSSMAN

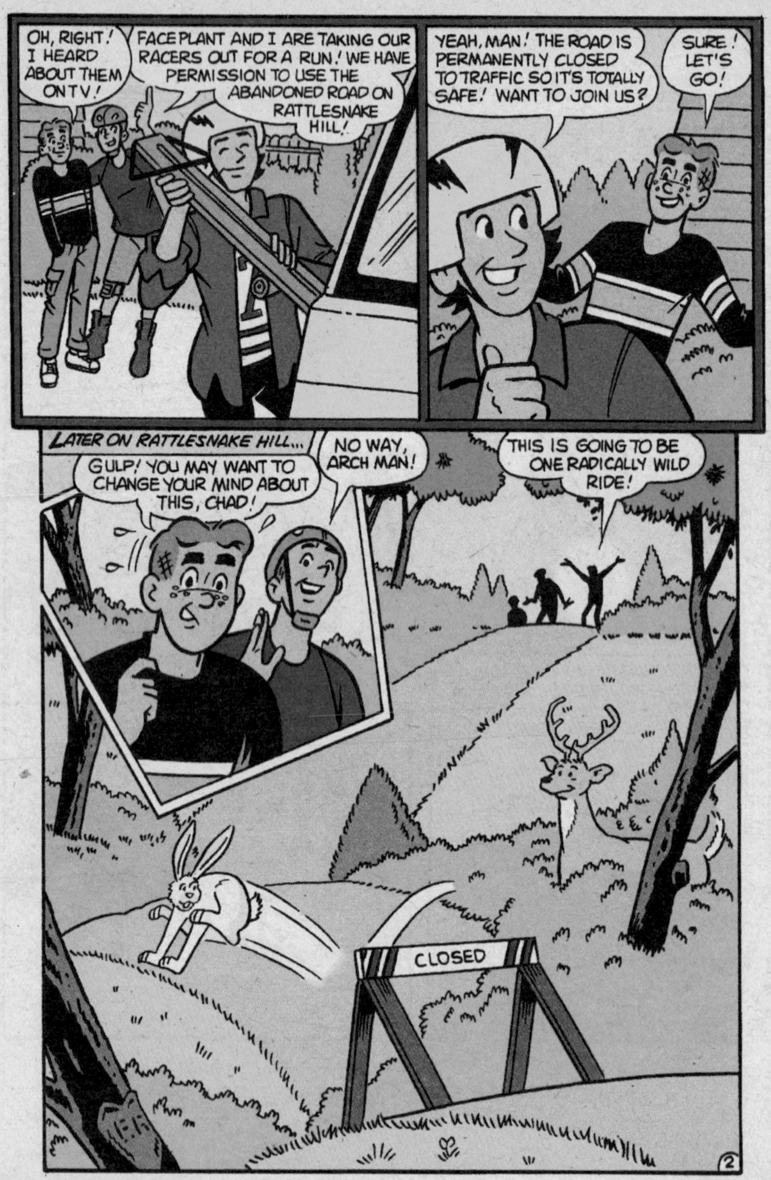

OH, RIGHT! I HEARD ABOUT THEM ON TV!
FACE PLANT AND I ARE TAKING OUR RACERS OUT FOR A RUN! WE HAVE PERMISSION TO USE THE ABANDONED ROAD ON RATTLESNAKE HILL!
YEAH, MAN! THE ROAD IS PERMANENTLY CLOSED TO TRAFFIC SO IT'S TOTALLY SAFE! WANT TO JOIN US?
SURE! LET'S GO!
LATER ON RATTLESNAKE HILL...
GULP! YOU MAY WANT TO CHANGE YOUR MIND ABOUT THIS, CHAD!
NO WAY, ARCH MAN!
THIS IS GOING TO BE ONE RADICALLY WILD RIDE!
CLOSED

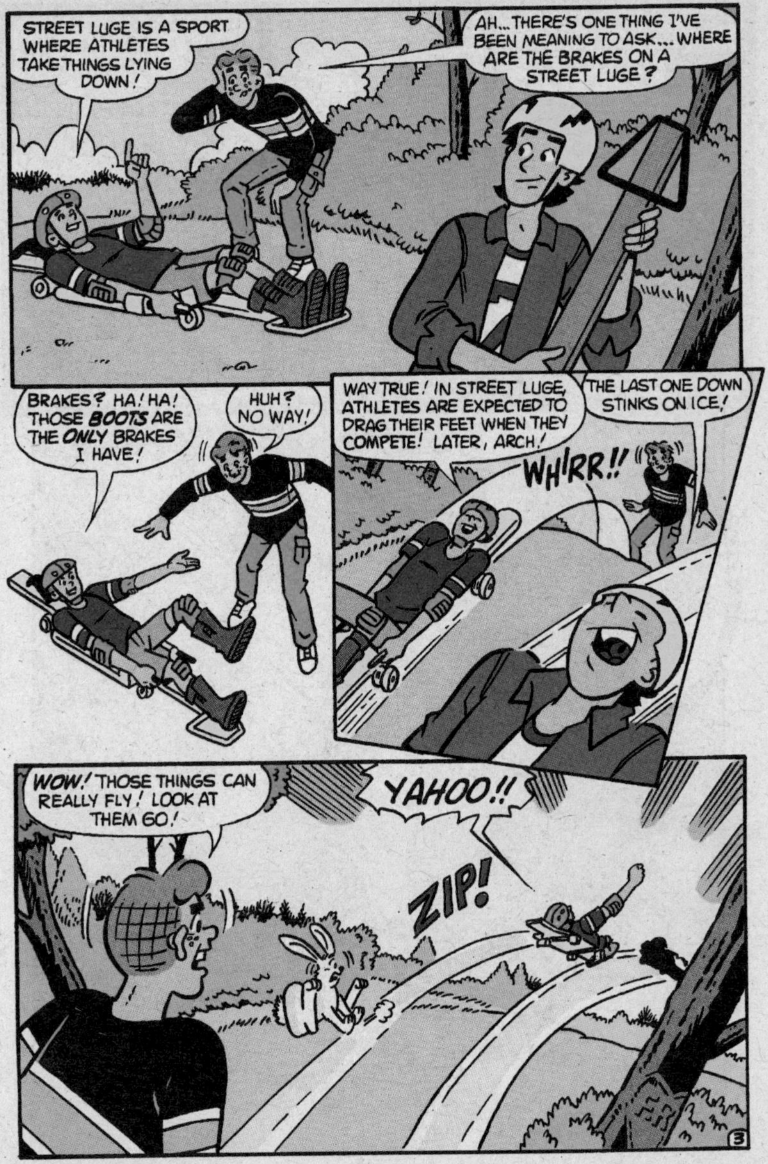
STREET LUGE IS A SPORT WHERE ATHLETES TAKE THINGS LYING DOWN!
AH... THERE'S ONE THING I'VE BEEN MEANING TO ASK... WHERE ARE THE BRAKES ON A STREET LUGE?
BRAKES? HA! HA! THOSE BOOTS ARE THE ONLY BRAKES I HAVE!
HUH? NO WAY!
WAY TRUE! IN STREET LUGE, ATHLETES ARE EXPECTED TO DRAG THEIR FEET WHEN THEY COMPETE! LATER, ARCH!
THE LAST ONE DOWN STINKS ON ICE!
WHIRR!!
WOW! THOSE THINGS CAN REALLY FLY! LOOK AT THEM GO!
YAHOO!!
ZIP!
3

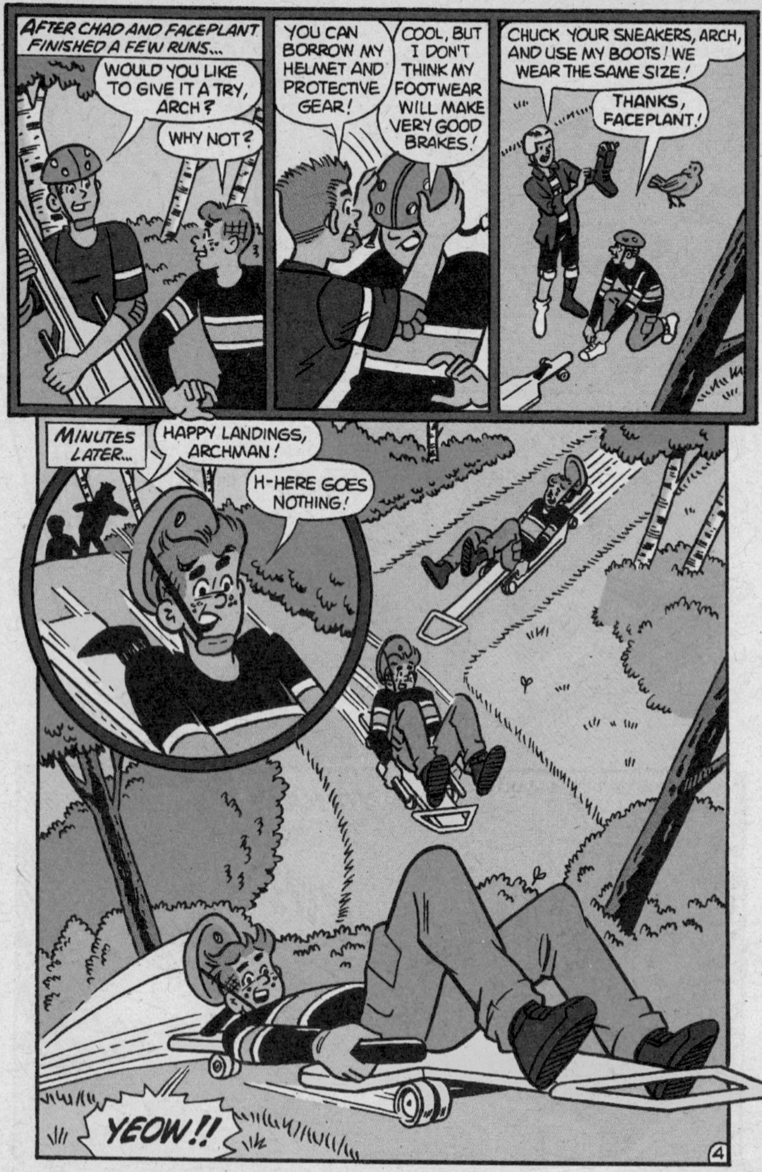
AFTER CHAD AND FACEPLANT FINISHED A FEW RUNS...
WOULD YOU LIKE TO GIVE IT A TRY, ARCH?
WHY NOT?
YOU CAN BORROW MY HELMET AND PROTECTIVE GEAR!
COOL, BUT I DON'T THINK MY FOOTWEAR WILL MAKE VERY GOOD BRAKES!
CHUCK YOUR SNEAKERS, ARCH, AND USE MY BOOTS! WE WEAR THE SAME SIZE!
THANKS, FACEPLANT!
MINUTES LATER...
HAPPY LANDINGS, ARCHMAN!
H-HERE GOES NOTHING!
YEOW!!
4

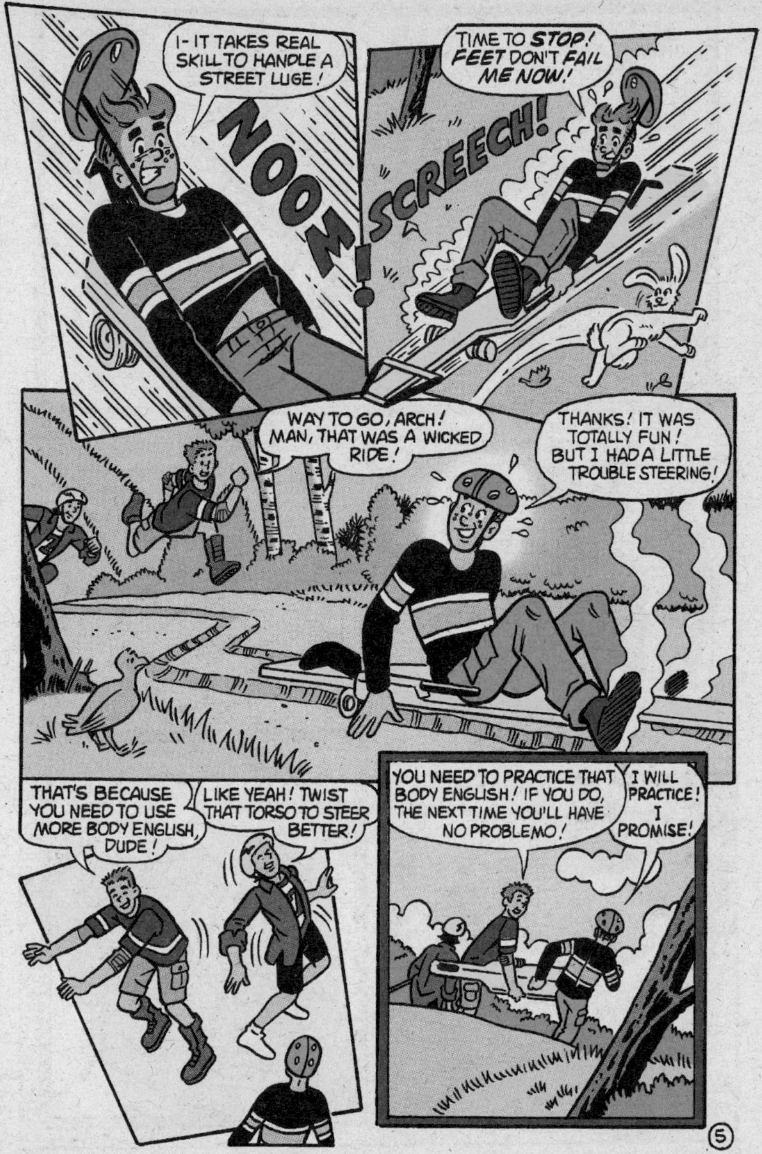

I- IT TAKES REAL SKILL TO HANDLE A STREET LUGE!
NOOM!
TIME TO STOP! FEET DON'T FAIL ME NOW!
SCREECH!
WAY TO GO, ARCH! MAN, THAT WAS A WICKED RIDE!
THANKS! IT WAS TOTALLY FUN! BUT I HAD A LITTLE TROUBLE STEERING!
THAT'S BECAUSE YOU NEED TO USE MORE BODY ENGLISH, DUDE!
LIKE YEAH! TWIST THAT TORSO TO STEER BETTER!
YOU NEED TO PRACTICE THAT BODY ENGLISH! IF YOU DO, THE NEXT TIME YOU'LL HAVE NO PROBLEMO!
I WILL PRACTICE! I PROMISE!

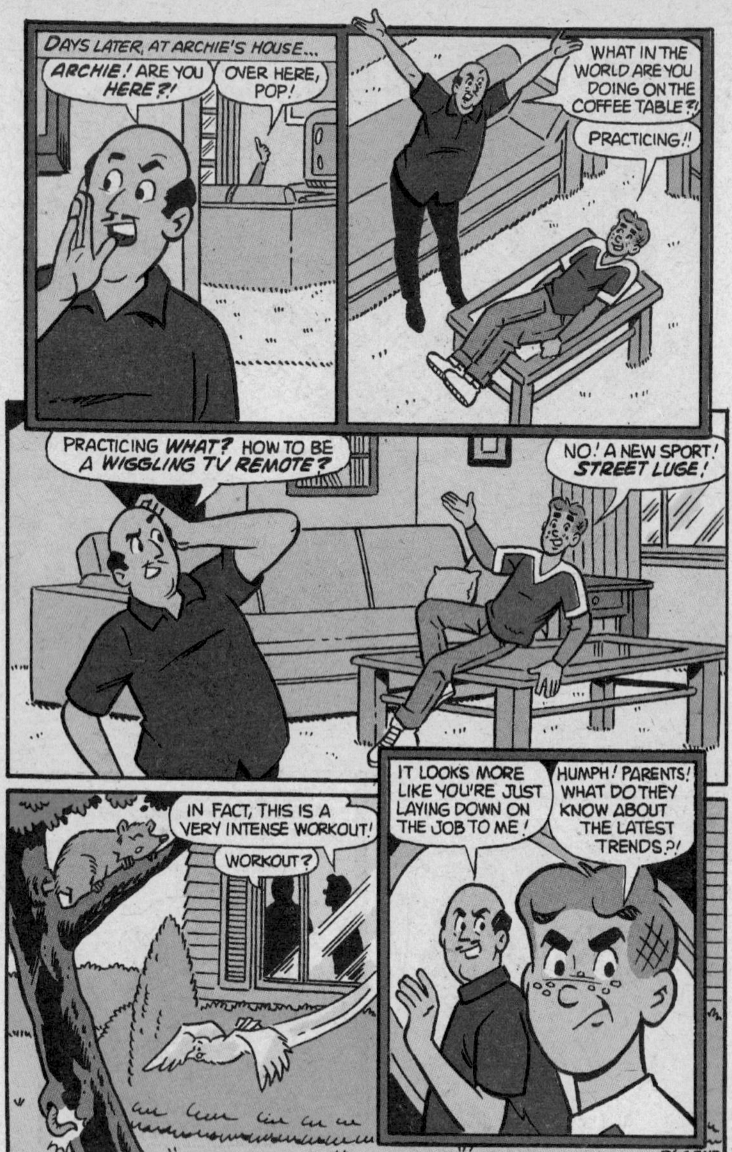
DAYS LATER, AT ARCHIE'S HOUSE...
ARCHIE! ARE YOU HERE?!
OVER HERE, POP!
WHAT IN THE WORLD ARE YOU DOING ON THE COFFEE TABLE?!
PRACTICING!!
PRACTICING WHAT? HOW TO BE A WIGGLING TV REMOTE?
NO! A NEW SPORT! STREET LUGE!
IN FACT, THIS IS A VERY INTENSE WORKOUT!
WORKOUT?
IT LOOKS MORE LIKE YOU'RE JUST LAYING DOWN ON THE JOB TO ME!
HUMPH! PARENTS! WHAT DO THEY KNOW ABOUT THE LATEST TRENDS?!
7KR END

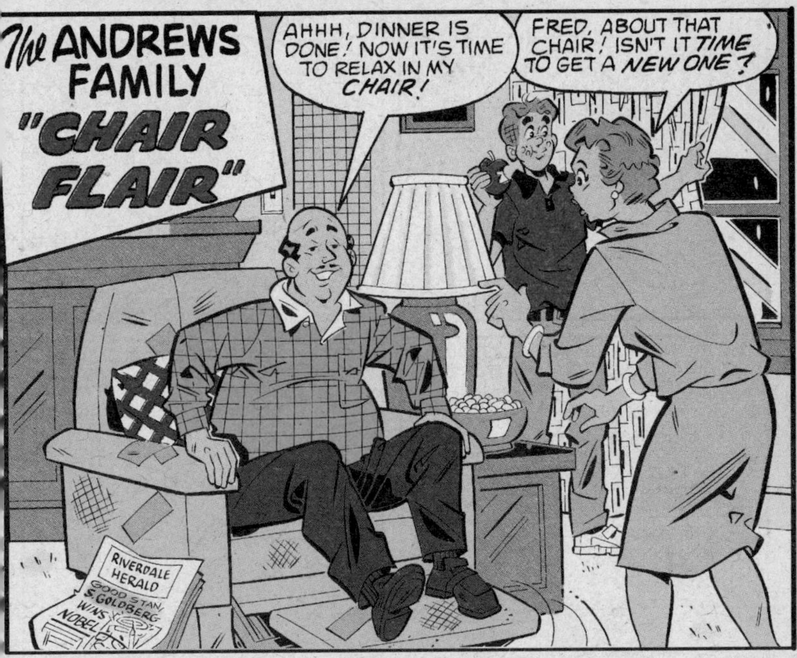

The ANDREWS FAMILY
"CHAIR FLAIR"
AHHH, DINNER IS DONE! NOW IT'S TIME TO RELAX IN MY CHAIR!
FRED, ABOUT THAT CHAIR! ISN'T IT TIME TO GET A NEW ONE?
RIVERDALE HERALD
GOOD STAN, S. GOLDBERG WINS NOBEL

SCRIPT: BILL GOLLIHER PENCILS: PAT KENNEDY INKS: KEN SELIG
LETTERS: BILL YOSHIDA COLORS: FRANK GAGLIARDO

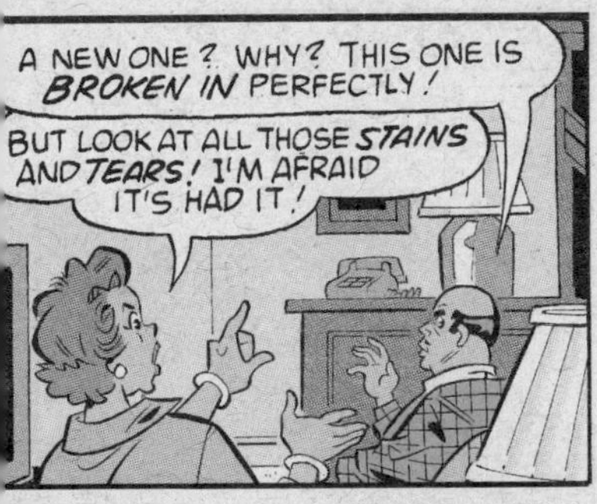

A NEW ONE? WHY? THIS ONE IS BROKEN IN PERFECTLY!
BUT LOOK AT ALL THOSE STAINS AND TEARS! I'M AFRAID IT'S HAD IT!

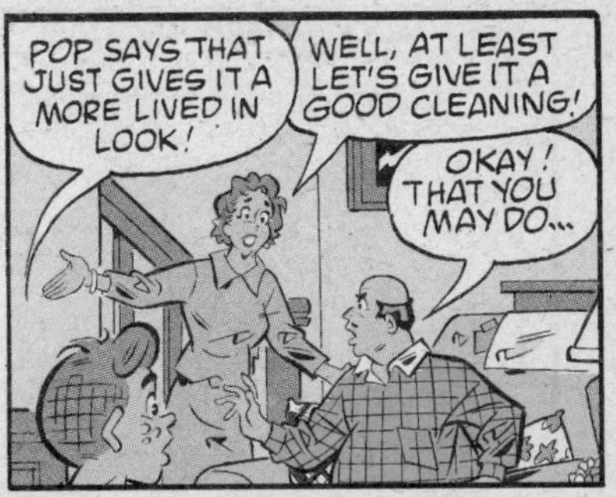

POP SAYS THAT JUST GIVES IT A MORE LIVED IN LOOK!
WELL, AT LEAST LET'S GIVE IT A GOOD CLEANING!
OKAY! THAT YOU MAY DO...

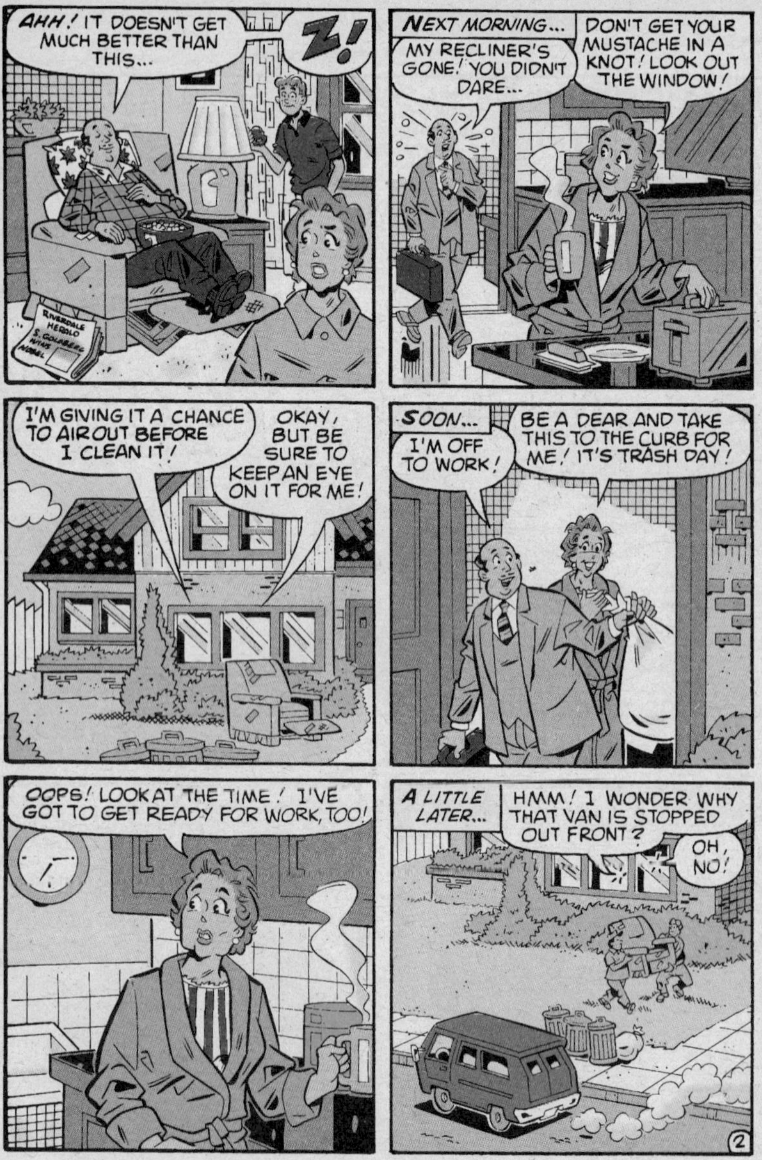
AHH! IT DOESN'T GET MUCH BETTER THAN THIS...
Z!
RIVERDALE HERALD
S. GOLDBERG WINS NOBEL
NEXT MORNING...
MY RECLINER'S GONE! YOU DIDN'T DARE...
DON'T GET YOUR MUSTACHE IN A KNOT! LOOK OUT THE WINDOW!
I'M GIVING IT A CHANCE TO AIR OUT BEFORE I CLEAN IT!
OKAY, BUT BE SURE TO KEEP AN EYE ON IT FOR ME!
SOON...
I'M OFF TO WORK!
BE A DEAR AND TAKE THIS TO THE CURB FOR ME! IT'S TRASH DAY!
OOPS! LOOK AT THE TIME! I'VE GOT TO GET READY FOR WORK, TOO!
A LITTLE LATER...
HMM! I WONDER WHY THAT VAN IS STOPPED OUT FRONT?
OH, NO!
2

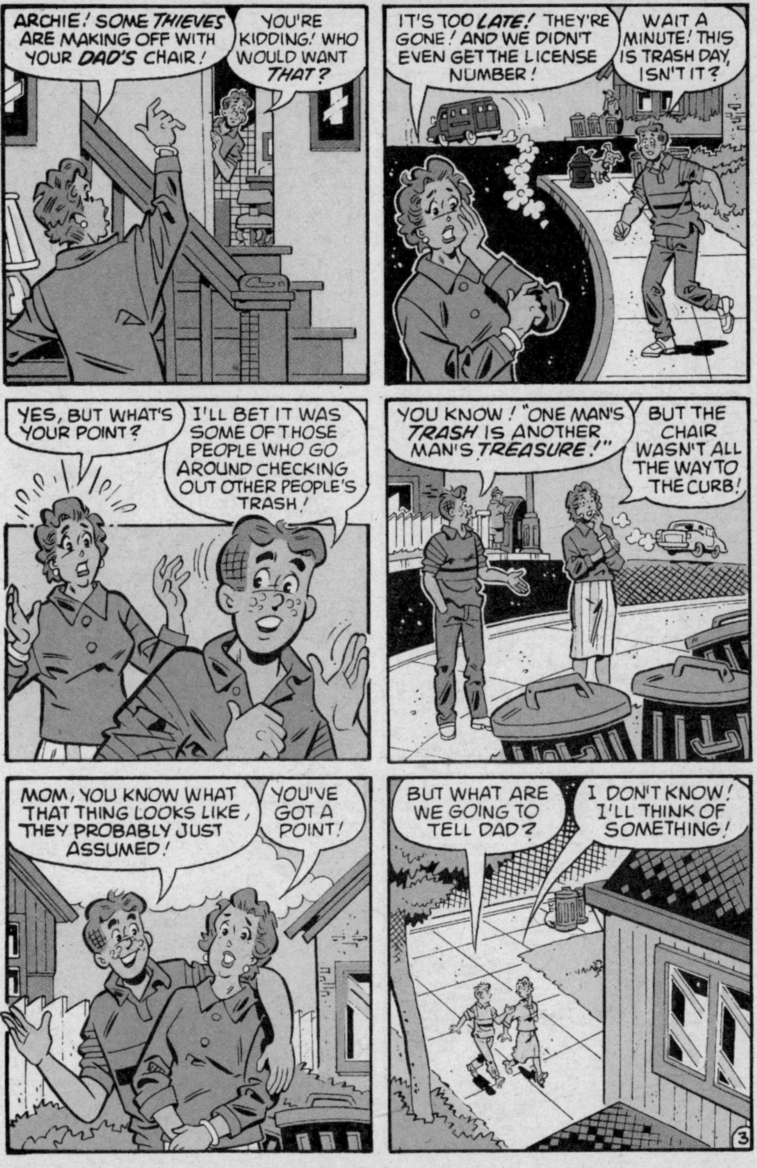
ARCHIE! SOME THIEVES ARE MAKING OFF WITH YOUR DAD'S CHAIR!
YOU'RE KIDDING! WHO WOULD WANT THAT?
IT'S TOO LATE! THEY'RE GONE! AND WE DIDN'T EVEN GET THE LICENSE NUMBER!
WAIT A MINUTE! THIS IS TRASH DAY, ISN'T IT?
YES, BUT WHAT'S YOUR POINT?
I'LL BET IT WAS SOME OF THOSE PEOPLE WHO GO AROUND CHECKING OUT OTHER PEOPLE'S TRASH!
YOU KNOW! "ONE MAN'S TRASH IS ANOTHER MAN'S TREASURE!"
BUT THE CHAIR WASN'T ALL THE WAY TO THE CURB!
MOM, YOU KNOW WHAT THAT THING LOOKS LIKE, THEY PROBABLY JUST ASSUMED!
YOU'VE GOT A POINT!
BUT WHAT ARE WE GOING TO TELL DAD?
I DON'T KNOW! I'LL THINK OF SOMETHING!
3

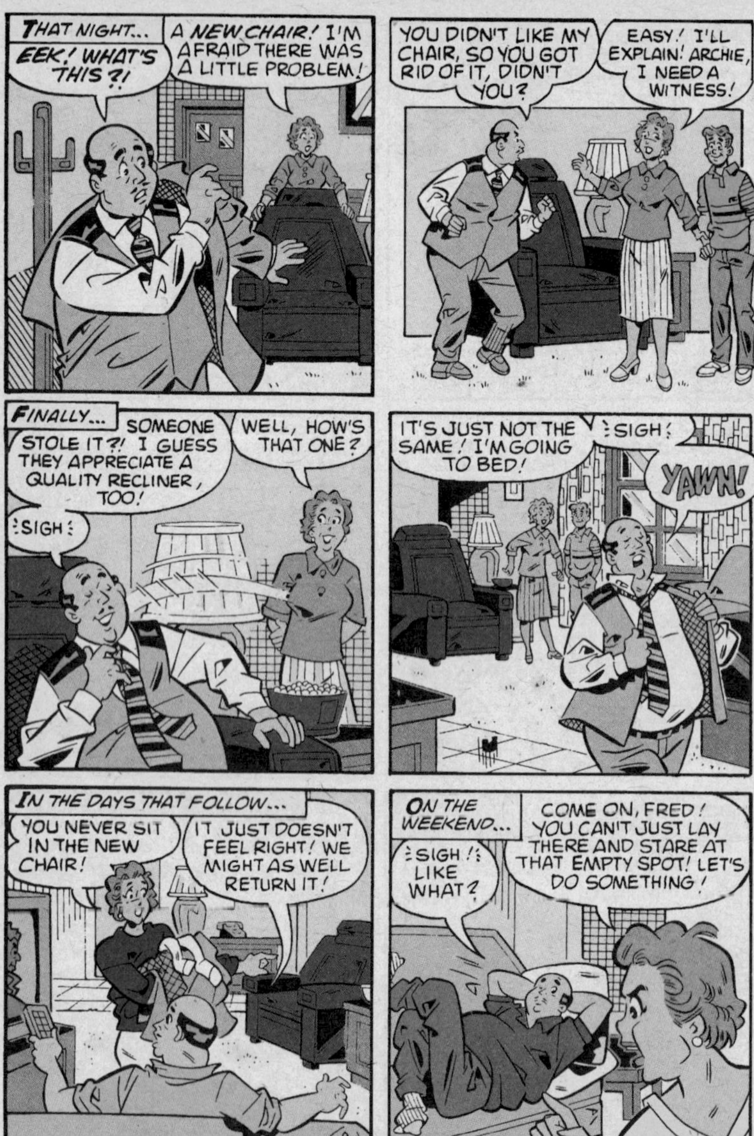
THAT NIGHT...
EEK! WHAT'S THIS?!
A NEW CHAIR! I'M AFRAID THERE WAS A LITTLE PROBLEM!
YOU DIDN'T LIKE MY CHAIR, SO YOU GOT RID OF IT, DIDN'T YOU?
EASY! I'LL EXPLAIN! ARCHIE, I NEED A WITNESS!
FINALLY...
SOMEONE STOLE IT?! I GUESS THEY APPRECIATE A QUALITY RECLINER, TOO!
WELL, HOW'S THAT ONE?
SIGH
IT'S JUST NOT THE SAME! I'M GOING TO BED!
SIGH!
YAWN!
IN THE DAYS THAT FOLLOW...
YOU NEVER SIT IN THE NEW CHAIR!
IT JUST DOESN'T FEEL RIGHT! WE MIGHT AS WELL RETURN IT!
ON THE WEEKEND...
SIGH! LIKE WHAT?
COME ON, FRED! YOU CAN'T JUST LAY THERE AND STARE AT THAT EMPTY SPOT! LET'S DO SOMETHING!
4

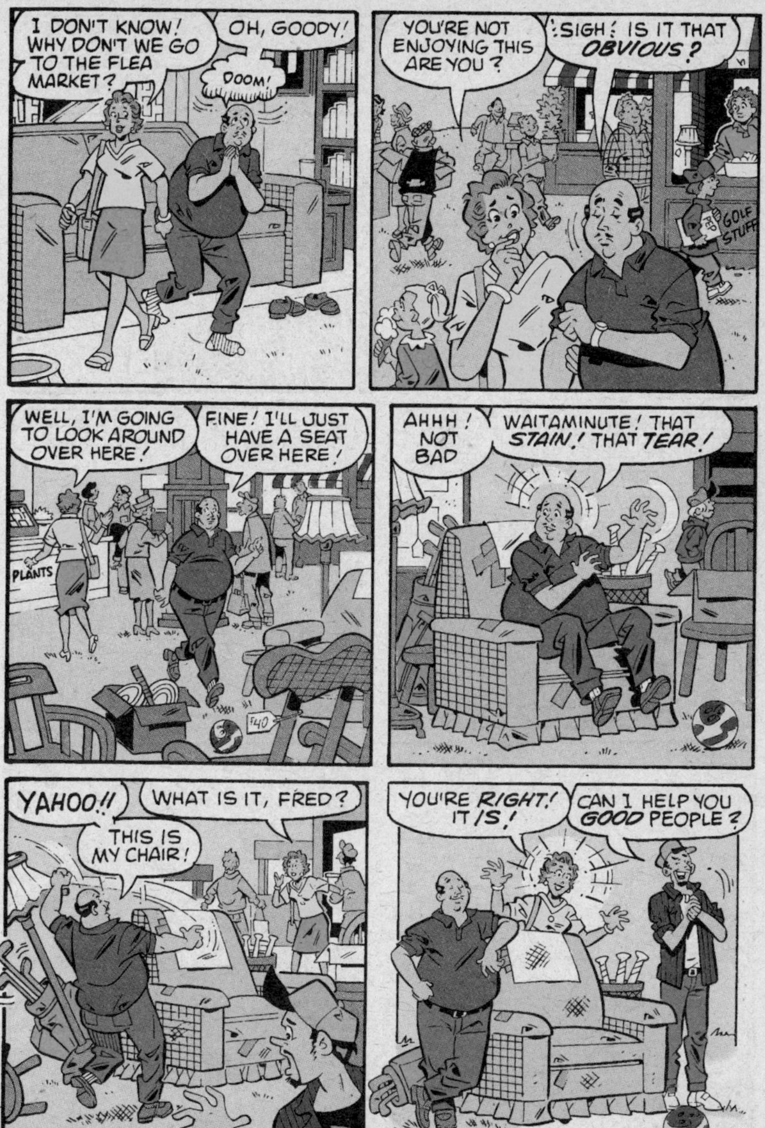
I DON'T KNOW! WHY DON'T WE GO TO THE FLEA MARKET?
OH, GOODY!
DOOM!
YOU'RE NOT ENJOYING THIS ARE YOU?
SIGH! IS IT THAT OBVIOUS?
PEP
GOLF STUFF
WELL, I'M GOING TO LOOK AROUND OVER HERE!
FINE! I'LL JUST HAVE A SEAT OVER HERE!
PLANTS
$40
AHHH! NOT BAD
WAITAMINUTE! THAT STAIN! THAT TEAR!
YAHOO!!
WHAT IS IT, FRED?
THIS IS MY CHAIR!
YOU'RE RIGHT! IT IS!
CAN I HELP YOU GOOD PEOPLE?

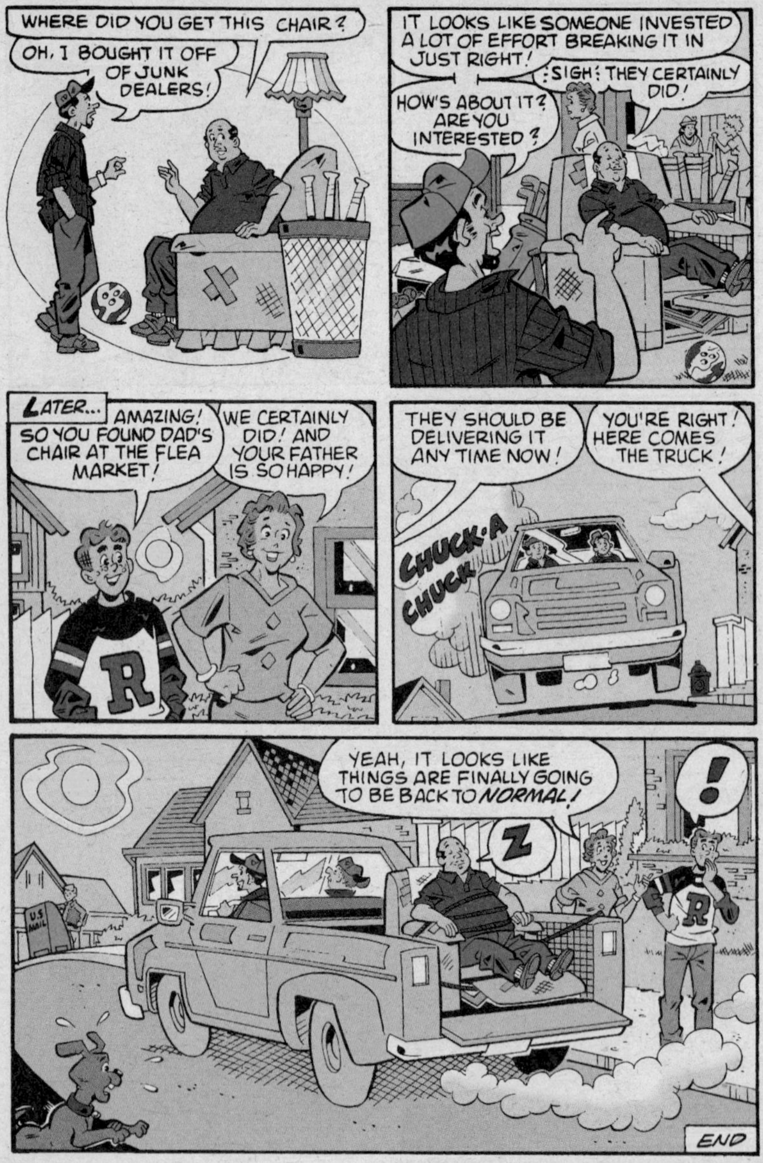
WHERE DID YOU GET THIS CHAIR?
OH, I BOUGHT IT OFF OF JUNK DEALERS!
IT LOOKS LIKE SOMEONE INVESTED A LOT OF EFFORT BREAKING IT IN JUST RIGHT!
HOW'S ABOUT IT? ARE YOU INTERESTED?
SIGH THEY CERTAINLY DID!
LATER...
AMAZING! SO YOU FOUND DAD'S CHAIR AT THE FLEA MARKET!
WE CERTAINLY DID! AND YOUR FATHER IS SO HAPPY!
THEY SHOULD BE DELIVERING IT ANY TIME NOW!
YOU'RE RIGHT! HERE COMES THE TRUCK!
CHUCK-A CHUCK
YEAH, IT LOOKS LIKE THINGS ARE FINALLY GOING TO BE BACK TO NORMAL!
Z
!
U.S. MAIL
END

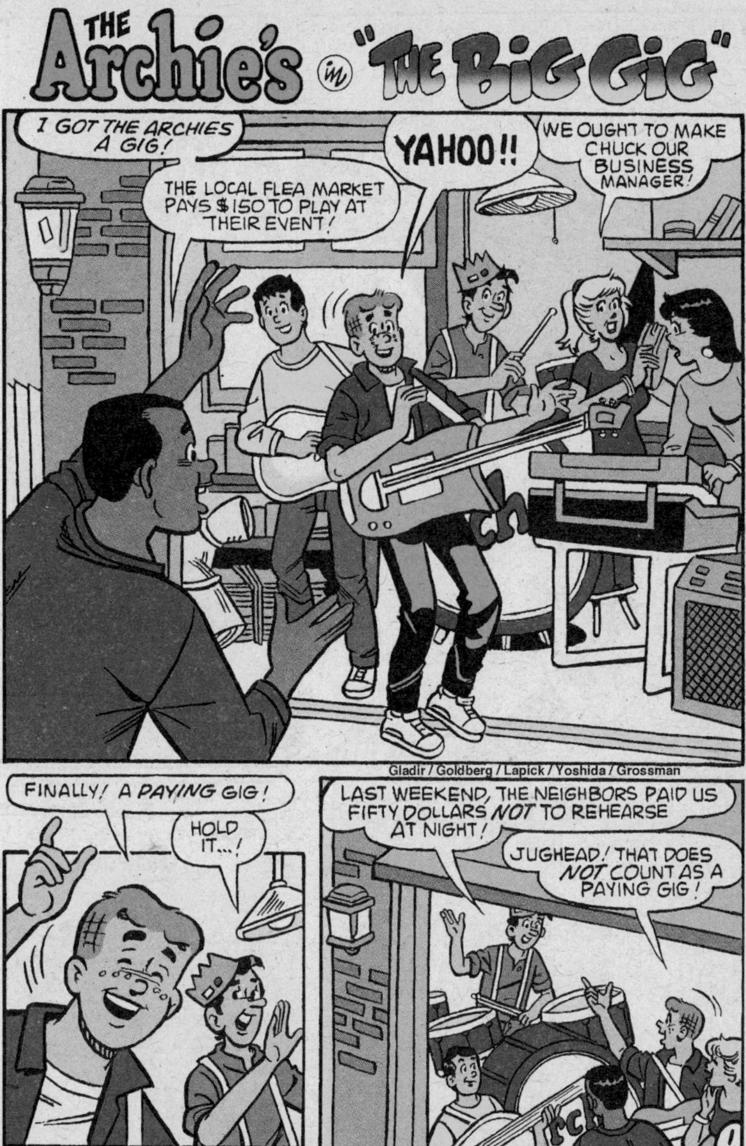
THE Archie's in "THE BIG GIG"
I GOT THE ARCHIES A GIG!
THE LOCAL FLEA MARKET PAYS $150 TO PLAY AT THEIR EVENT!
YAHOO!!
WE OUGHT TO MAKE CHUCK OUR BUSINESS MANAGER!
Gladir / Goldberg / Lapick / Yoshida / Grossman
FINALLY! A PAYING GIG!
HOLD IT...!
LAST WEEKEND, THE NEIGHBORS PAID US FIFTY DOLLARS NOT TO REHEARSE AT NIGHT!
JUGHEAD! THAT DOES NOT COUNT AS A PAYING GIG!
1

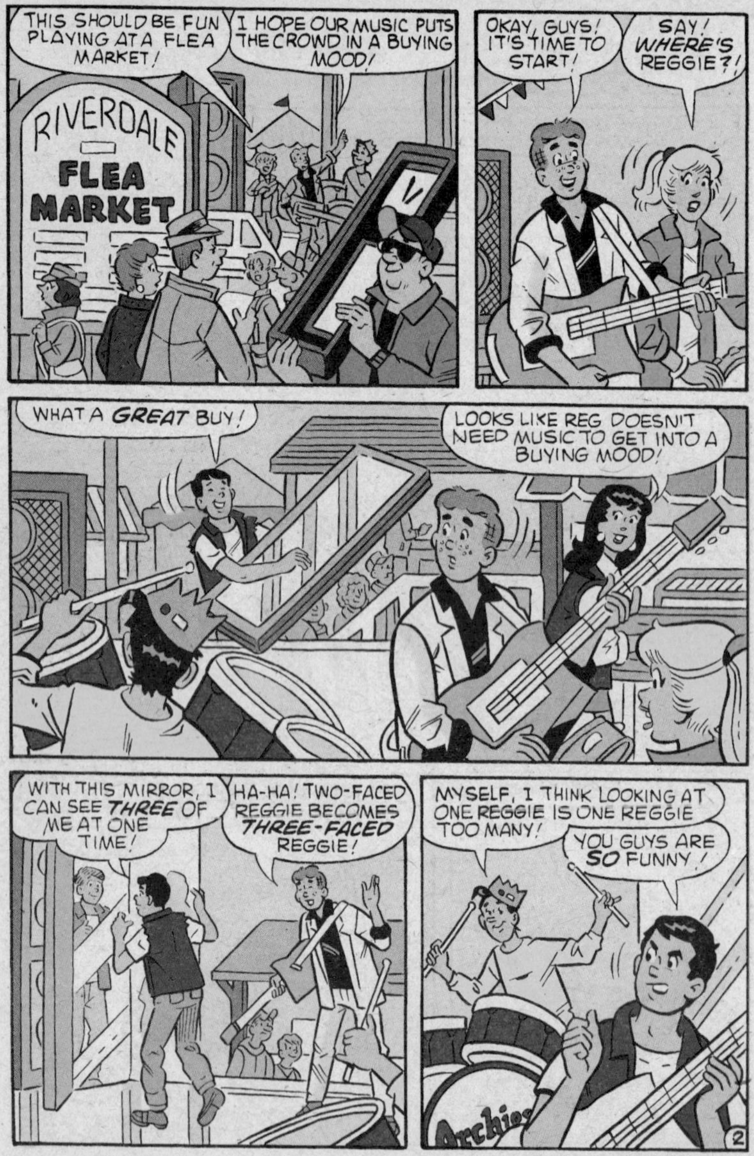
THIS SHOULD BE FUN PLAYING AT A FLEA MARKET!
I HOPE OUR MUSIC PUTS THE CROWD IN A BUYING MOOD!
RIVERDALE FLEA MARKET
OKAY, GUYS! IT'S TIME TO START!
SAY! WHERE'S REGGIE?!
WHAT A GREAT BUY!
LOOKS LIKE REG DOESN'T NEED MUSIC TO GET INTO A BUYING MOOD!
WITH THIS MIRROR, I CAN SEE THREE OF ME AT ONE TIME!
HA-HA! TWO-FACED REGGIE BECOMES THREE-FACED REGGIE!
MYSELF, I THINK LOOKING AT ONE REGGIE IS ONE REGGIE TOO MANY!
YOU GUYS ARE SO FUNNY!
Archies
2

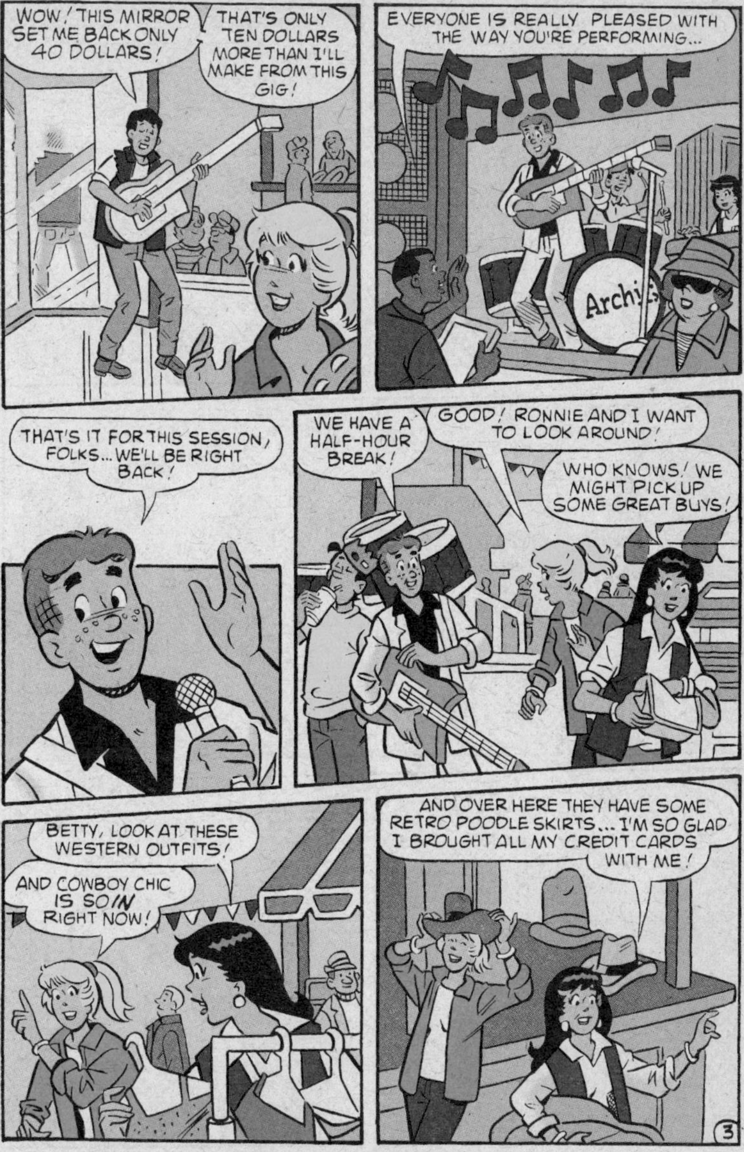

WOW! THIS MIRROR SET ME BACK ONLY 40 DOLLARS!
THAT'S ONLY TEN DOLLARS MORE THAN I'LL MAKE FROM THIS GIG!
EVERYONE IS REALLY PLEASED WITH THE WAY YOU'RE PERFORMING...
Archie's
THAT'S IT FOR THIS SESSION, FOLKS... WE'LL BE RIGHT BACK!
WE HAVE A HALF-HOUR BREAK!
GOOD! RONNIE AND I WANT TO LOOK AROUND!
WHO KNOWS! WE MIGHT PICK UP SOME GREAT BUYS!
BETTY, LOOK AT THESE WESTERN OUTFITS!
AND COWBOY CHIC IS SO *IN* RIGHT NOW!
AND OVER HERE THEY HAVE SOME RETRO POODLE SKIRTS... I'M SO GLAD I BROUGHT ALL MY CREDIT CARDS WITH ME!
3

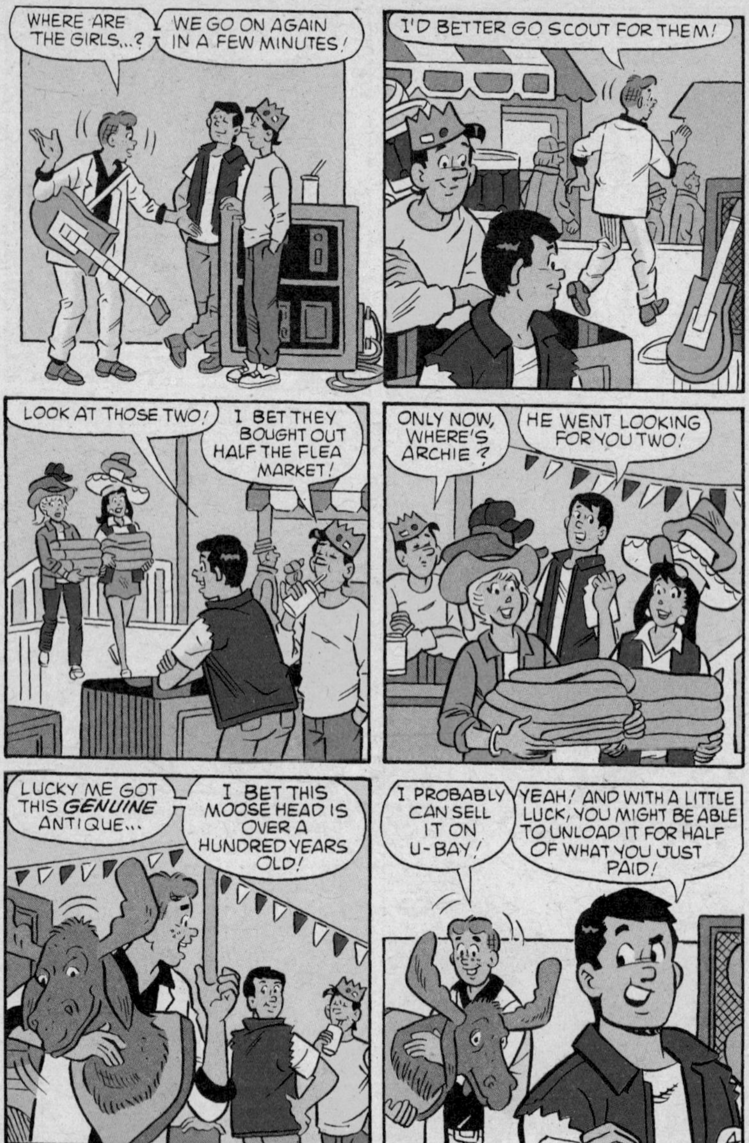
WHERE ARE THE GIRLS...?
WE GO ON AGAIN IN A FEW MINUTES!
I'D BETTER GO SCOUT FOR THEM!
LOOK AT THOSE TWO!
I BET THEY BOUGHT OUT HALF THE FLEA MARKET!
ONLY NOW, WHERE'S ARCHIE?
HE WENT LOOKING FOR YOU TWO!
LUCKY ME GOT THIS *GENUINE* ANTIQUE...
I BET THIS MOOSE HEAD IS OVER A HUNDRED YEARS OLD!
I PROBABLY CAN SELL IT ON U-BAY!
YEAH! AND WITH A LITTLE LUCK, YOU MIGHT BE ABLE TO UNLOAD IT FOR HALF OF WHAT YOU JUST PAID!
4

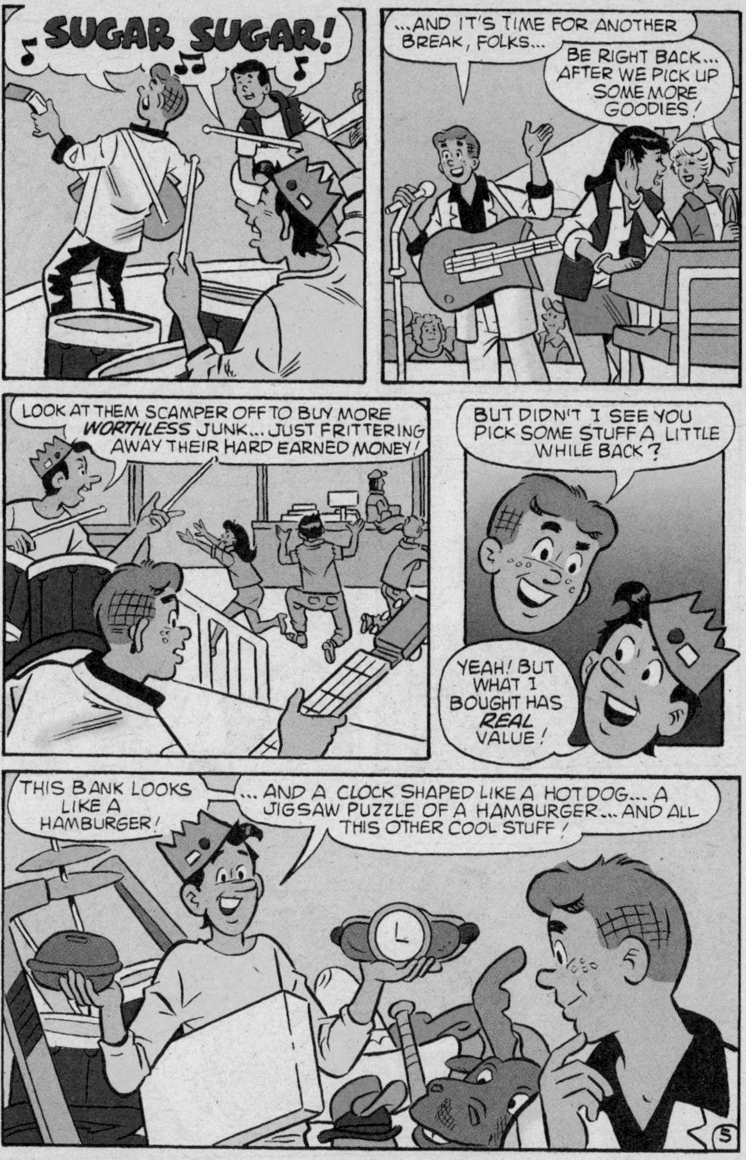

SUGAR SUGAR!
...AND IT'S TIME FOR ANOTHER BREAK, FOLKS...
BE RIGHT BACK... AFTER WE PICK UP SOME MORE GOODIES!
LOOK AT THEM SCAMPER OFF TO BUY MORE WORTHLESS JUNK... JUST FRITTERING AWAY THEIR HARD EARNED MONEY!
BUT DIDN'T I SEE YOU PICK SOME STUFF A LITTLE WHILE BACK?
YEAH! BUT WHAT I BOUGHT HAS REAL VALUE!
THIS BANK LOOKS LIKE A HAMBURGER!
... AND A CLOCK SHAPED LIKE A HOT DOG... A JIGSAW PUZZLE OF A HAMBURGER... AND ALL THIS OTHER COOL STUFF!
5

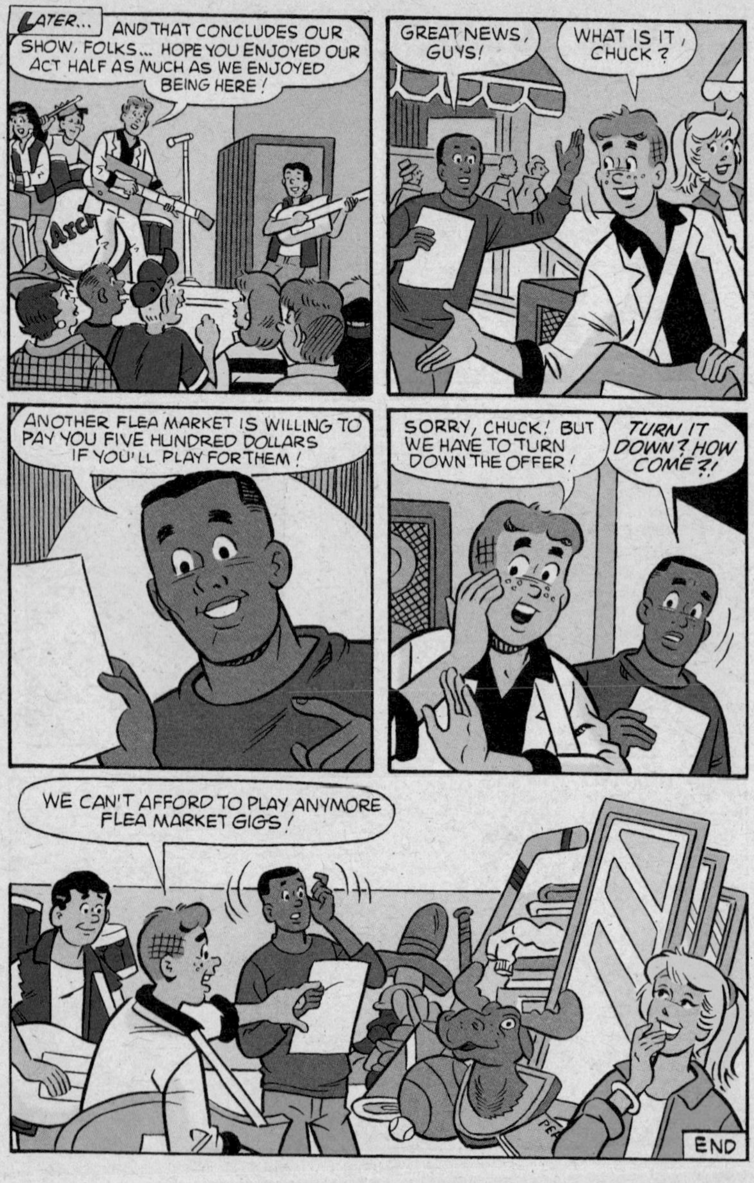
LATER...
AND THAT CONCLUDES OUR SHOW, FOLKS... HOPE YOU ENJOYED OUR ACT HALF AS MUCH AS WE ENJOYED BEING HERE!
GREAT NEWS, GUYS!
WHAT IS IT, CHUCK?
ANOTHER FLEA MARKET IS WILLING TO PAY YOU FIVE HUNDRED DOLLARS IF YOU'LL PLAY FOR THEM!
SORRY, CHUCK! BUT WE HAVE TO TURN DOWN THE OFFER!
TURN IT DOWN? HOW COME?!
WE CAN'T AFFORD TO PLAY ANYMORE FLEA MARKET GIGS!
END

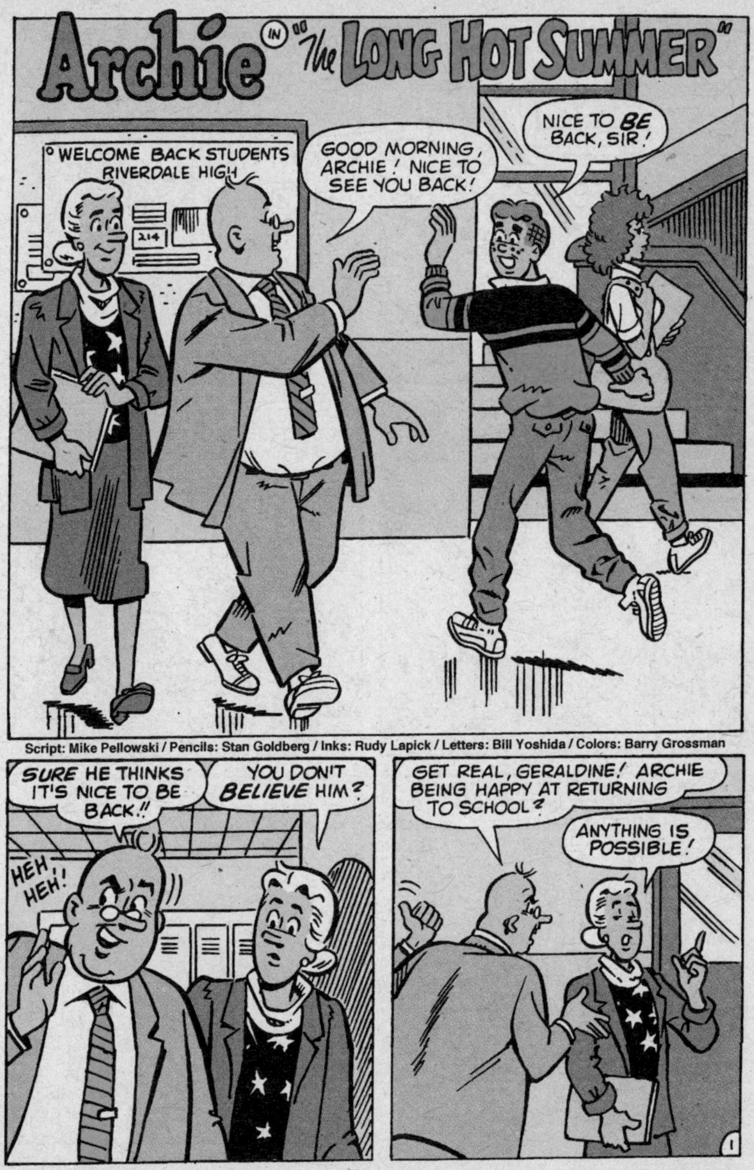
Archie in "The LONG HOT SUMMER"
WELCOME BACK STUDENTS RIVERDALE HIGH
214
GOOD MORNING, ARCHIE! NICE TO SEE YOU BACK!
NICE TO BE BACK, SIR!
Script: Mike Pellowski / Pencils: Stan Goldberg / Inks: Rudy Lapick / Letters: Bill Yoshida / Colors: Barry Grossman
SURE HE THINKS IT'S NICE TO BE BACK!!
YOU DON'T BELIEVE HIM?
HEH HEH!
GET REAL, GERALDINE! ARCHIE BEING HAPPY AT RETURNING TO SCHOOL?
ANYTHING IS POSSIBLE!
1

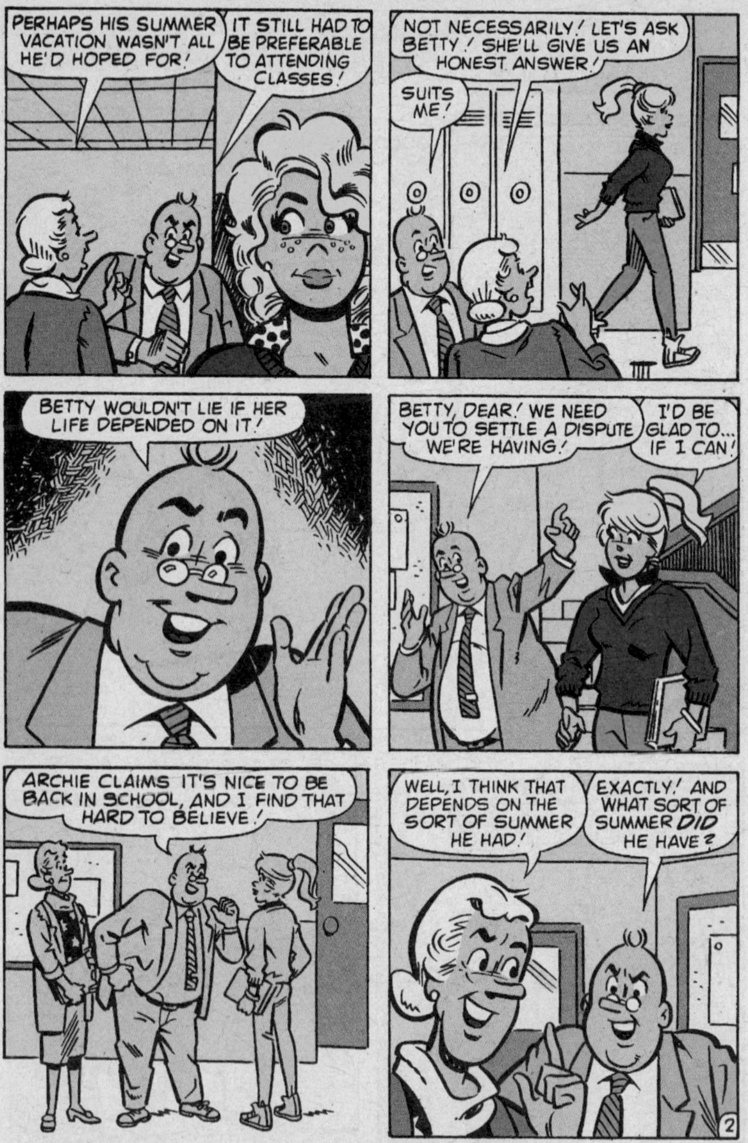
PERHAPS HIS SUMMER VACATION WASN'T ALL HE'D HOPED FOR!
IT STILL HAD TO BE PREFERABLE TO ATTENDING CLASSES!
NOT NECESSARILY! LET'S ASK BETTY! SHE'LL GIVE US AN HONEST ANSWER!
SUITS ME!
BETTY WOULDN'T LIE IF HER LIFE DEPENDED ON IT!
BETTY, DEAR! WE NEED YOU TO SETTLE A DISPUTE WE'RE HAVING!
I'D BE GLAD TO... IF I CAN!
ARCHIE CLAIMS IT'S NICE TO BE BACK IN SCHOOL, AND I FIND THAT HARD TO BELIEVE!
WELL, I THINK THAT DEPENDS ON THE SORT OF SUMMER HE HAD!
EXACTLY! AND WHAT SORT OF SUMMER DID HE HAVE?
2

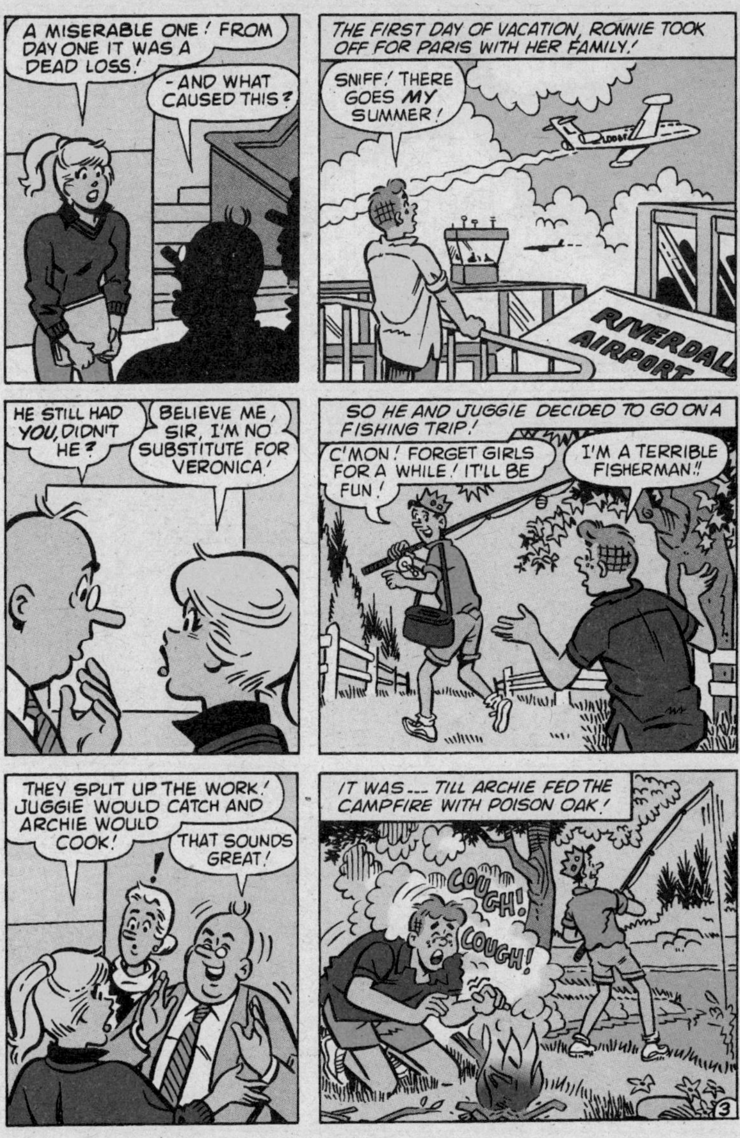
A MISERABLE ONE! FROM DAY ONE IT WAS A DEAD LOSS!
-AND WHAT CAUSED THIS?
THE FIRST DAY OF VACATION, RONNIE TOOK OFF FOR PARIS WITH HER FAMILY!
SNIFF! THERE GOES MY SUMMER!
RIVERDALE AIRPORT
HE STILL HAD YOU, DIDN'T HE?
BELIEVE ME, SIR, I'M NO SUBSTITUTE FOR VERONICA!
SO HE AND JUGGIE DECIDED TO GO ON A FISHING TRIP!
C'MON! FORGET GIRLS FOR A WHILE! IT'LL BE FUN!
I'M A TERRIBLE FISHERMAN!!
THEY SPLIT UP THE WORK! JUGGIE WOULD CATCH AND ARCHIE WOULD COOK!
THAT SOUNDS GREAT!
IT WAS --- TILL ARCHIE FED THE CAMPFIRE WITH POISON OAK!
COUGH!
COUGH!
3

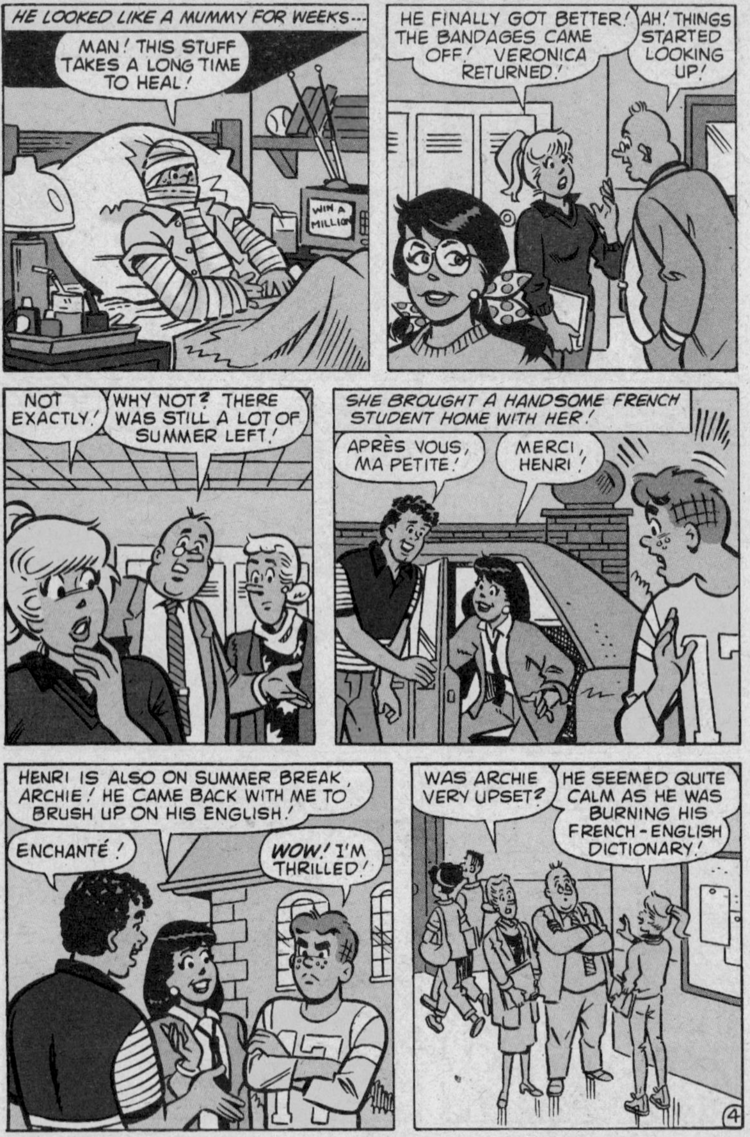
HE LOOKED LIKE A MUMMY FOR WEEKS---
MAN! THIS STUFF TAKES A LONG TIME TO HEAL!
WIN A MILLION
HE FINALLY GOT BETTER! THE BANDAGES CAME OFF! VERONICA RETURNED!
AH! THINGS STARTED LOOKING UP!
NOT EXACTLY!
WHY NOT? THERE WAS STILL A LOT OF SUMMER LEFT!
SHE BROUGHT A HANDSOME FRENCH STUDENT HOME WITH HER!
APRÈS VOUS, MA PETITE!
MERCI, HENRI!
HENRI IS ALSO ON SUMMER BREAK, ARCHIE! HE CAME BACK WITH ME TO BRUSH UP ON HIS ENGLISH!
ENCHANTÉ!
WOW! I'M THRILLED!
WAS ARCHIE VERY UPSET?
HE SEEMED QUITE CALM AS HE WAS BURNING HIS FRENCH-ENGLISH DICTIONARY!
4

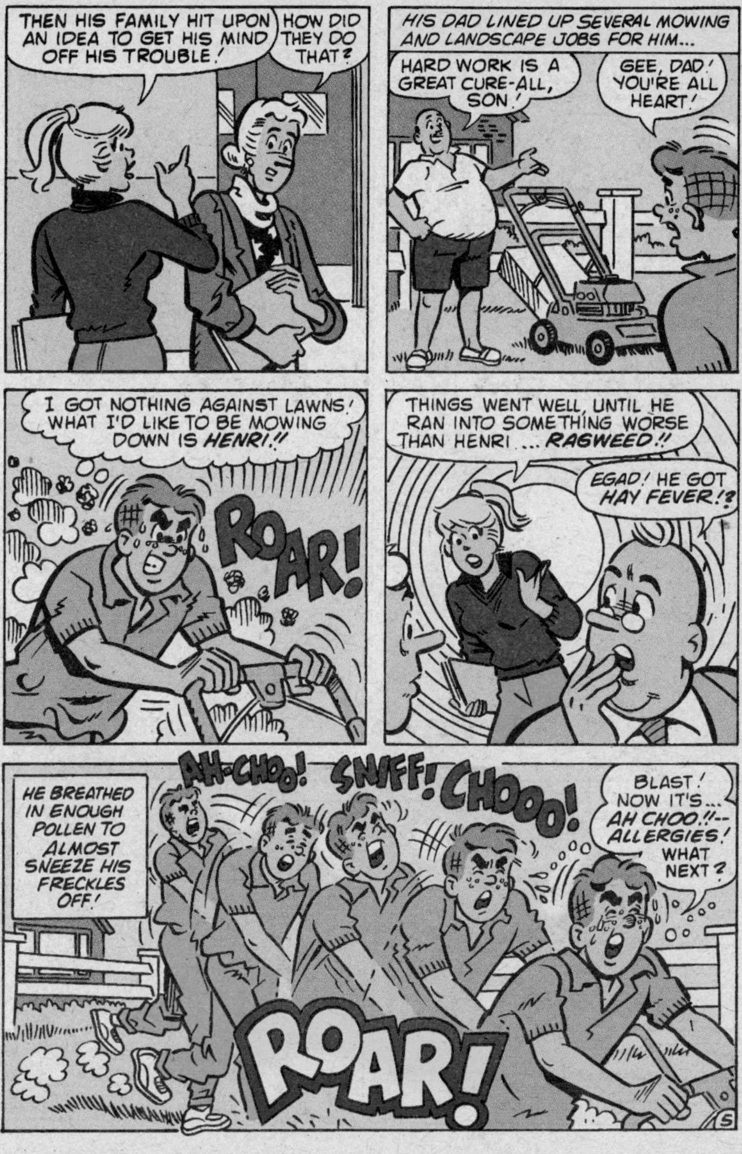
THEN HIS FAMILY HIT UPON AN IDEA TO GET HIS MIND OFF HIS TROUBLE!
HOW DID THEY DO THAT?
HIS DAD LINED UP SEVERAL MOWING AND LANDSCAPE JOBS FOR HIM...
HARD WORK IS A GREAT CURE-ALL, SON!
GEE, DAD! YOU'RE ALL HEART!
I GOT NOTHING AGAINST LAWNS! WHAT I'D LIKE TO BE MOWING DOWN IS HENRI!!
ROAR!
THINGS WENT WELL, UNTIL HE RAN INTO SOMETHING WORSE THAN HENRI ... RAGWEED!!
EGAD! HE GOT HAY FEVER!?
HE BREATHED IN ENOUGH POLLEN TO ALMOST SNEEZE HIS FRECKLES OFF!
AH-CHOO! SNIFF! CHOOOO!
BLAST! NOW IT'S... AH CHOO!!-- ALLERGIES! WHAT NEXT?
ROAR!
5

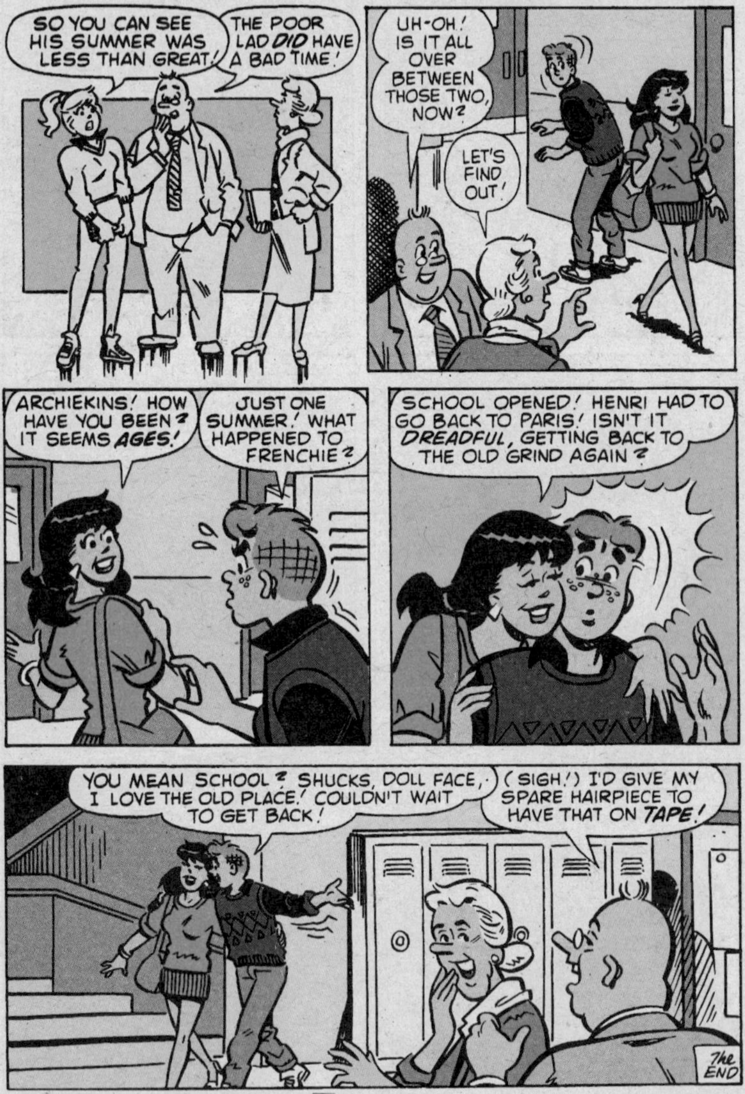
SO YOU CAN SEE HIS SUMMER WAS LESS THAN GREAT!
THE POOR LAD DID HAVE A BAD TIME!
UH-OH! IS IT ALL OVER BETWEEN THOSE TWO, NOW?
LET'S FIND OUT!
ARCHIEKINS! HOW HAVE YOU BEEN? IT SEEMS AGES!
JUST ONE SUMMER! WHAT HAPPENED TO FRENCHIE?
SCHOOL OPENED! HENRI HAD TO GO BACK TO PARIS! ISN'T IT DREADFUL, GETTING BACK TO THE OLD GRIND AGAIN?
YOU MEAN SCHOOL? SHUCKS, DOLL FACE, I LOVE THE OLD PLACE! COULDN'T WAIT TO GET BACK!
(SIGH!) I'D GIVE MY SPARE HAIRPIECE TO HAVE THAT ON TAPE!
The END

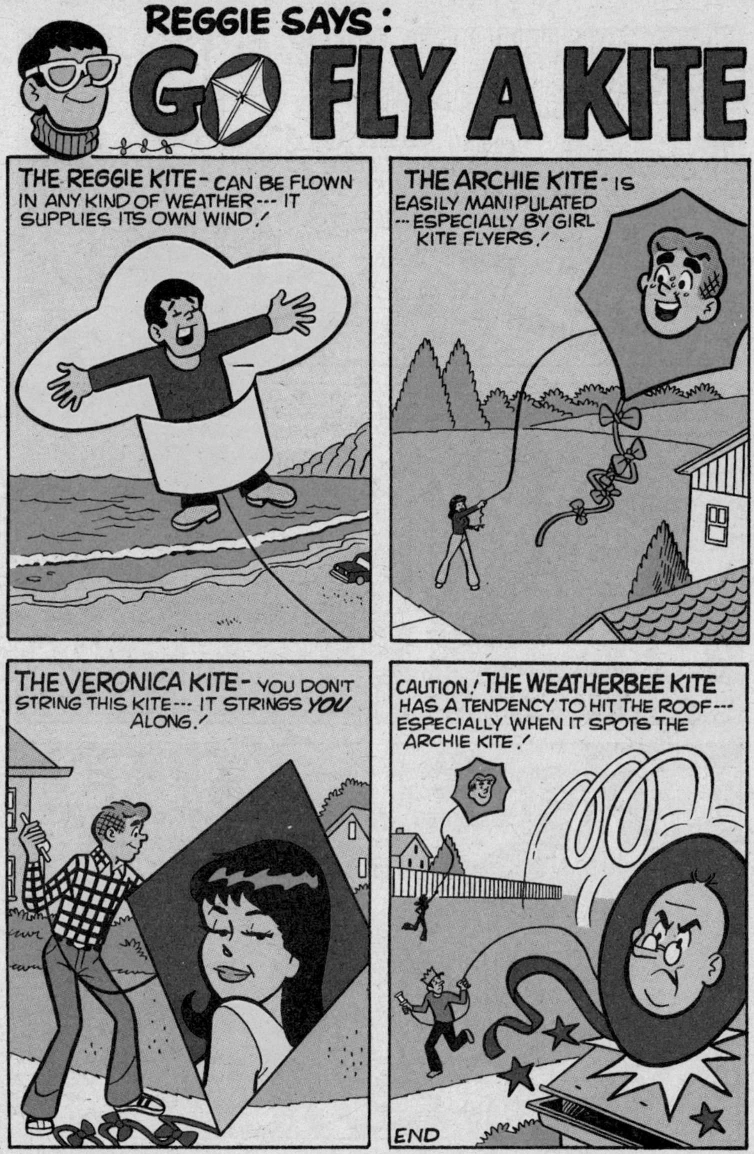
REGGIE SAYS:
GO FLY A KITE
THE REGGIE KITE - CAN BE FLOWN IN ANY KIND OF WEATHER --- IT SUPPLIES ITS OWN WIND!
THE ARCHIE KITE - IS EASILY MANIPULATED --- ESPECIALLY BY GIRL KITE FLYERS!
THE VERONICA KITE - YOU DON'T STRING THIS KITE --- IT STRINGS YOU ALONG!
CAUTION! THE WEATHERBEE KITE HAS A TENDENCY TO HIT THE ROOF --- ESPECIALLY WHEN IT SPOTS THE ARCHIE KITE!
END

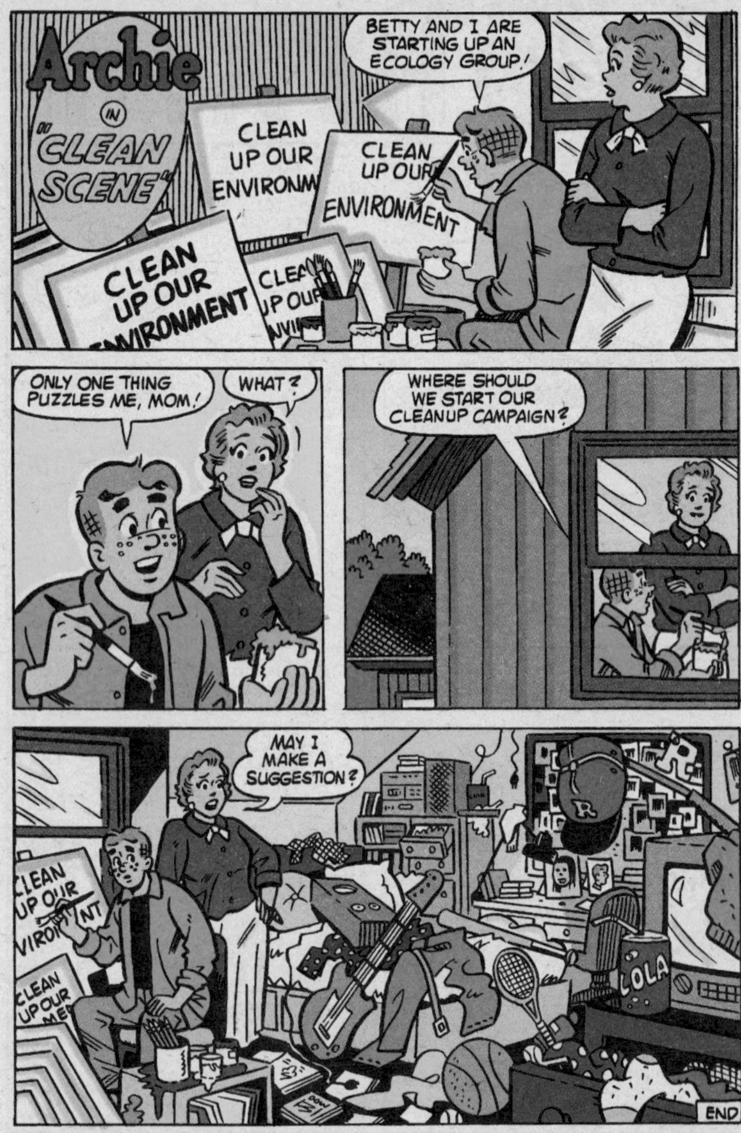
Archie
IN
"CLEAN SCENE"
BETTY AND I ARE STARTING UP AN ECOLOGY GROUP!
CLEAN UP OUR ENVIRONMENT
ONLY ONE THING PUZZLES ME, MOM!
WHAT?
WHERE SHOULD WE START OUR CLEANUP CAMPAIGN?
MAY I MAKE A SUGGESTION?
LOLA
END

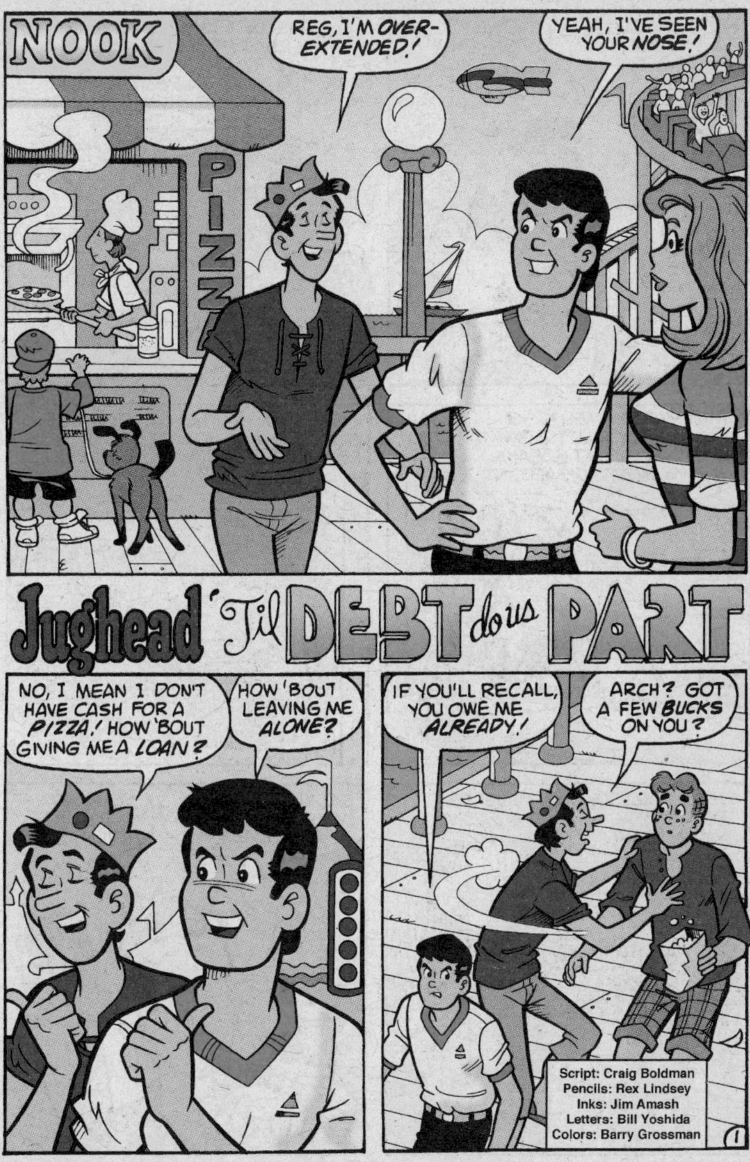
NOOK
PIZZ
REG, I'M OVER-EXTENDED!
YEAH, I'VE SEEN YOUR NOSE!
Jughead 'Til DEBT dous PART
NO, I MEAN I DON'T HAVE CASH FOR A PIZZA! HOW 'BOUT GIVING ME A LOAN?
HOW 'BOUT LEAVING ME ALONE?
IF YOU'LL RECALL, YOU OWE ME ALREADY!
ARCH? GOT A FEW BUCKS ON YOU?
Script: Craig Boldman
Pencils: Rex Lindsey
Inks: Jim Amash
Letters: Bill Yoshida
Colors: Barry Grossman
1

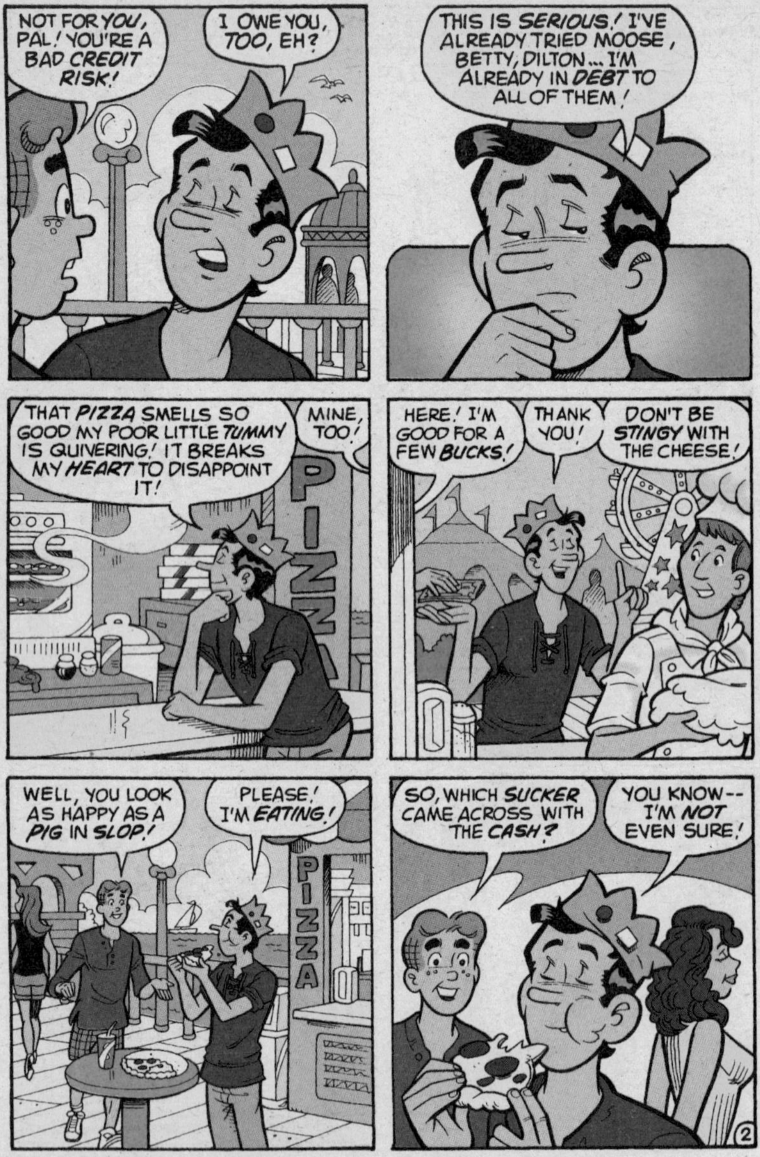

NOT FOR YOU, PAL! YOU'RE A BAD CREDIT RISK!
I OWE YOU, TOO, EH?
THIS IS SERIOUS! I'VE ALREADY TRIED MOOSE, BETTY, DILTON... I'M ALREADY IN DEBT TO ALL OF THEM!
THAT PIZZA SMELLS SO GOOD MY POOR LITTLE TUMMY IS QUIVERING! IT BREAKS MY HEART TO DISAPPOINT IT!
MINE, TOO!
PIZZA
HERE! I'M GOOD FOR A FEW BUCKS!
THANK YOU!
DON'T BE STINGY WITH THE CHEESE!
WELL, YOU LOOK AS HAPPY AS A PIG IN SLOP!
PLEASE! I'M EATING!
PIZZA
SO, WHICH SUCKER CAME ACROSS WITH THE CASH?
YOU KNOW-- I'M NOT EVEN SURE!
2

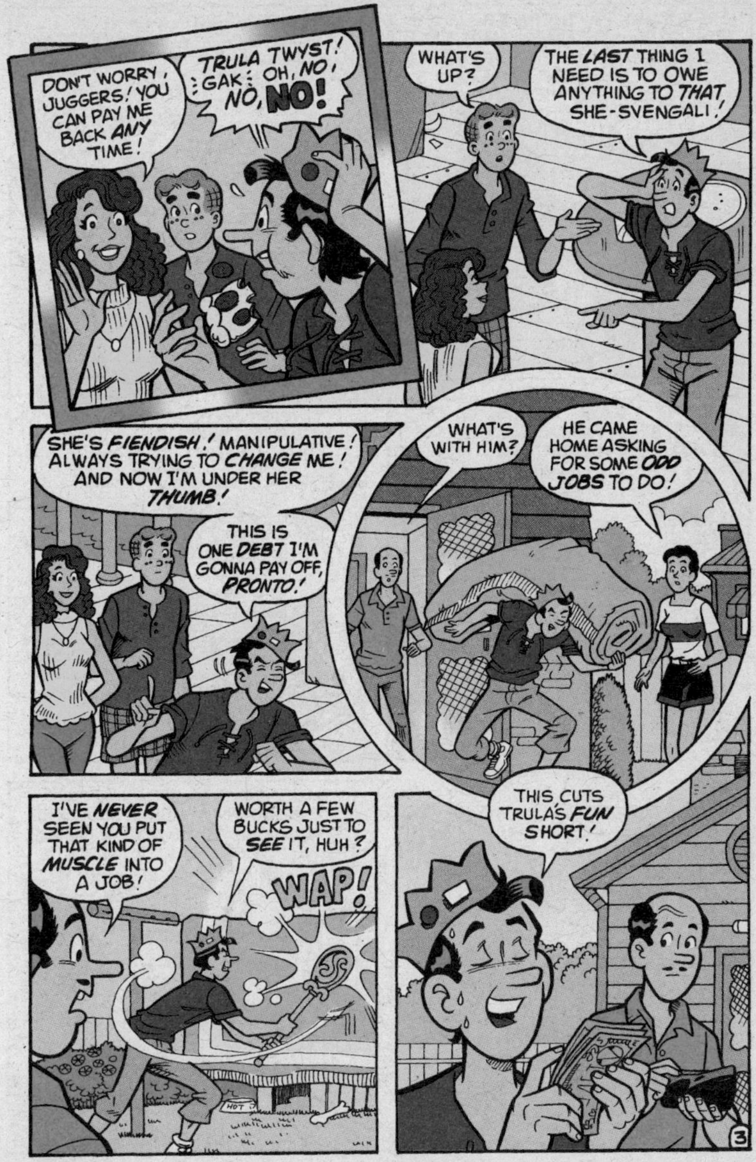
DON'T WORRY, JUGGERS! YOU CAN PAY ME BACK ANY TIME!
TRULA TWYST! GAK OH, NO, NO, NO!
WHAT'S UP?
THE LAST THING I NEED IS TO OWE ANYTHING TO THAT SHE-SVENGALI!
SHE'S FIENDISH! MANIPULATIVE! ALWAYS TRYING TO CHANGE ME! AND NOW I'M UNDER HER THUMB!
THIS IS ONE DEBT I'M GONNA PAY OFF, PRONTO!
WHAT'S WITH HIM?
HE CAME HOME ASKING FOR SOME ODD JOBS TO DO!
I'VE NEVER SEEN YOU PUT THAT KIND OF MUSCLE INTO A JOB!
WORTH A FEW BUCKS JUST TO SEE IT, HUH?
WAP!
HOT
THIS CUTS TRULA'S FUN SHORT!
3

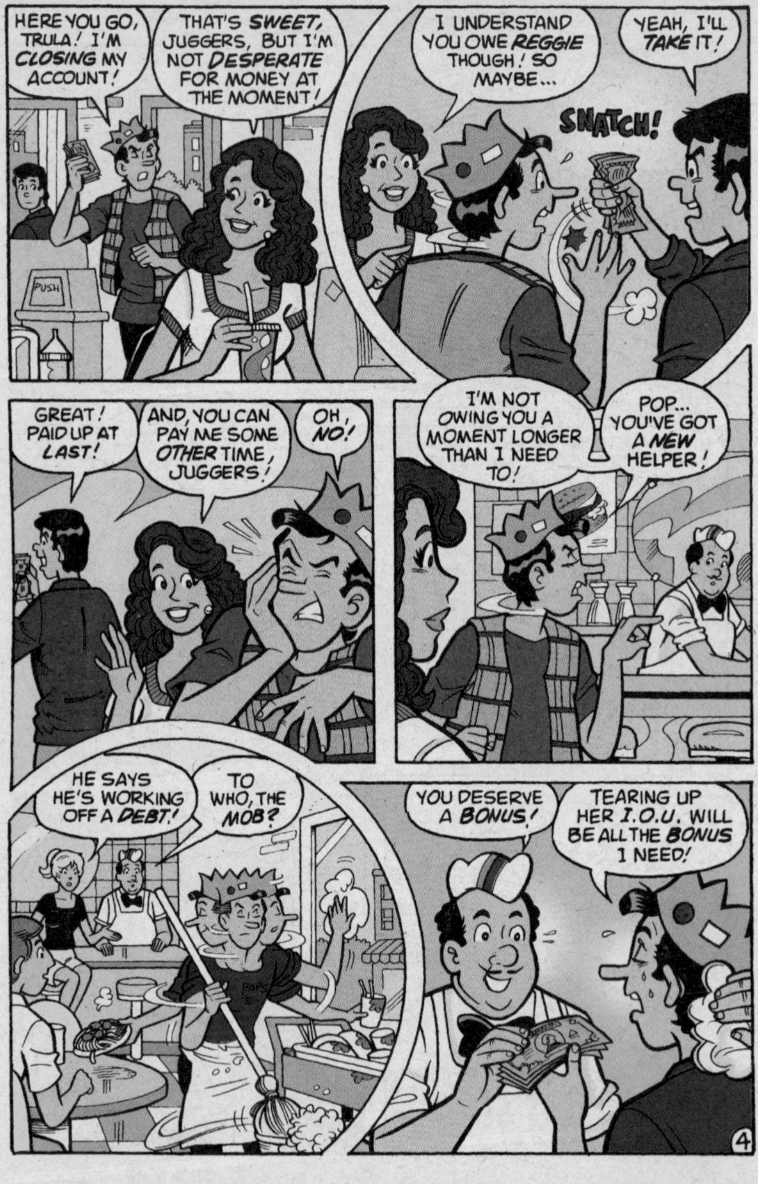
HERE YOU GO, TRULA! I'M CLOSING MY ACCOUNT!
THAT'S SWEET, JUGGERS, BUT I'M NOT DESPERATE FOR MONEY AT THE MOMENT!
I UNDERSTAND YOU OWE REGGIE THOUGH! SO MAYBE...
YEAH, I'LL TAKE IT!
SNATCH!
PUSH
GREAT! PAID UP AT LAST!
AND, YOU CAN PAY ME SOME OTHER TIME, JUGGERS!
OH, NO!
I'M NOT OWING YOU A MOMENT LONGER THAN I NEED TO!
POP... YOU'VE GOT A NEW HELPER!
HE SAYS HE'S WORKING OFF A DEBT!
TO WHO, THE MOB?
YOU DESERVE A BONUS!
TEARING UP HER I.O.U. WILL BE ALL THE BONUS I NEED!
4

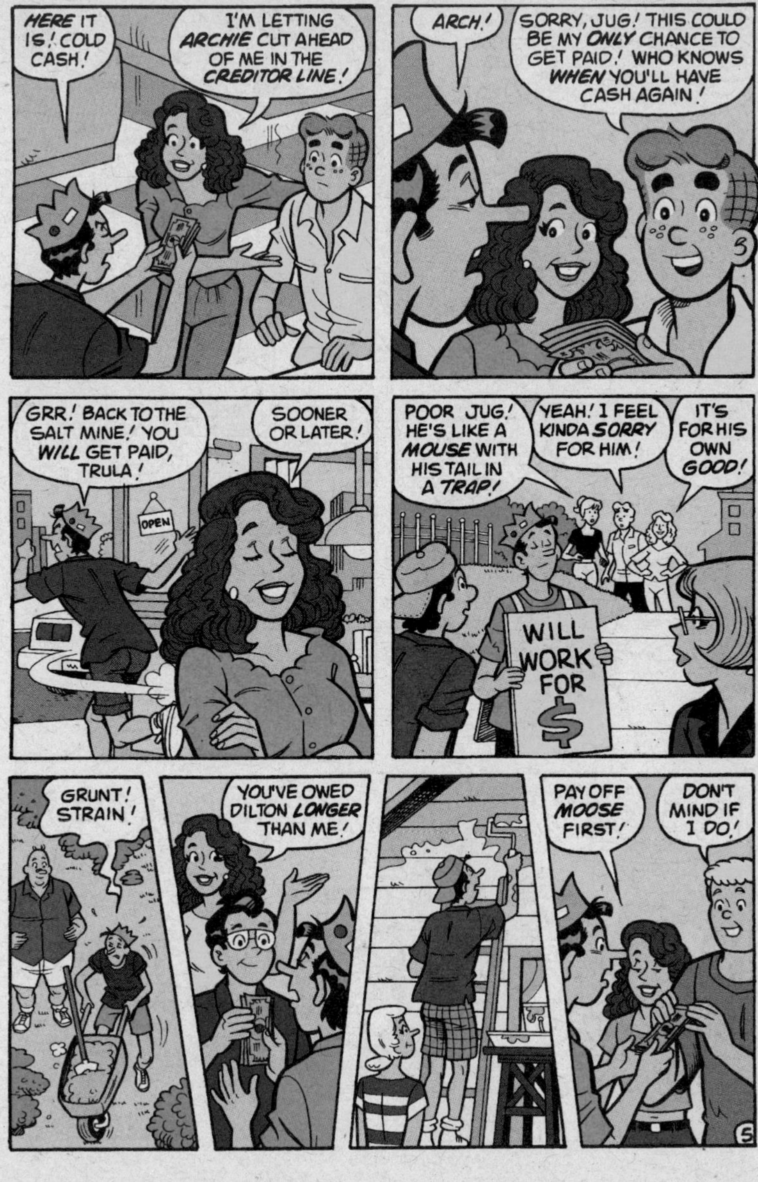
HERE IT IS! COLD CASH!
I'M LETTING ARCHIE CUT AHEAD OF ME IN THE CREDITOR LINE!
ARCH!
SORRY, JUG! THIS COULD BE MY ONLY CHANCE TO GET PAID! WHO KNOWS WHEN YOU'LL HAVE CASH AGAIN!
GRR! BACK TO THE SALT MINE! YOU WILL GET PAID, TRULA!
SOONER OR LATER!
OPEN
POOR JUG! HE'S LIKE A MOUSE WITH HIS TAIL IN A TRAP!
YEAH! I FEEL KINDA SORRY FOR HIM!
IT'S FOR HIS OWN GOOD!
WILL WORK FOR $
GRUNT! STRAIN!
YOU'VE OWED DILTON LONGER THAN ME!
PAY OFF MOOSE FIRST!
DON'T MIND IF I DO!
5

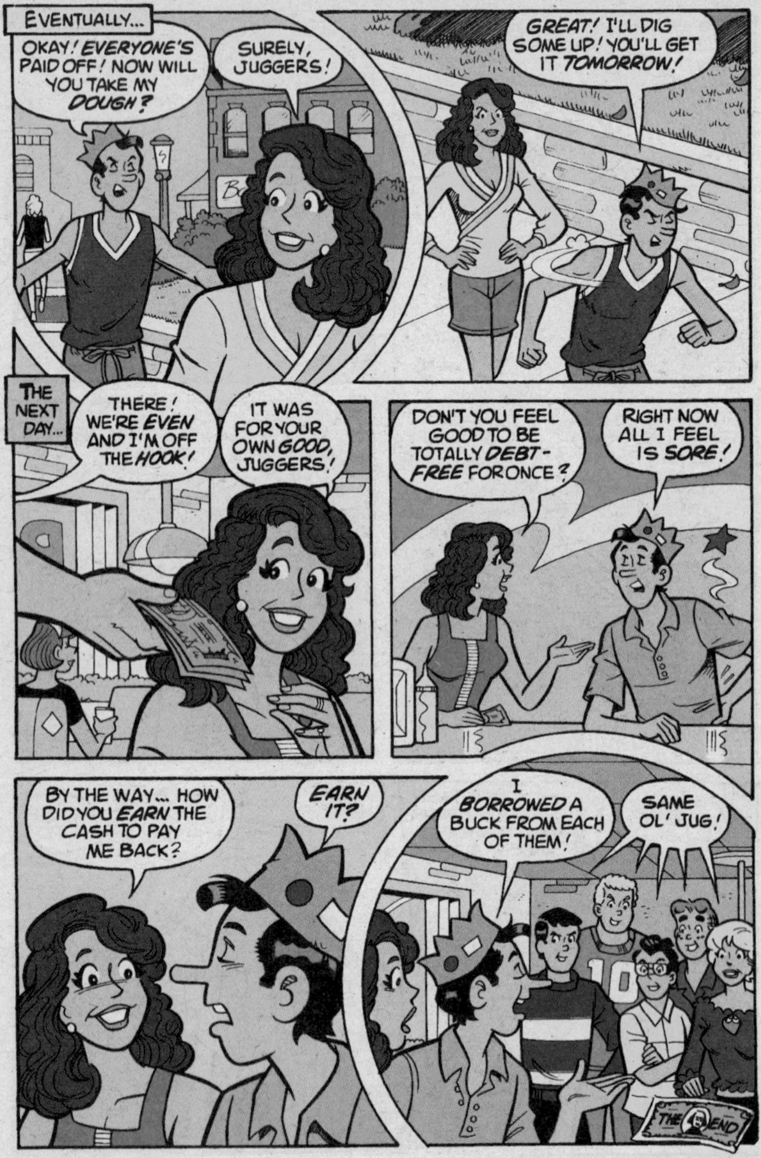
EVENTUALLY...
OKAY! EVERYONE'S PAID OFF! NOW WILL YOU TAKE MY DOUGH?
SURELY, JUGGERS!
GREAT! I'LL DIG SOME UP! YOU'LL GET IT TOMORROW!
THE NEXT DAY...
THERE! WE'RE EVEN AND I'M OFF THE HOOK!
IT WAS FOR YOUR OWN GOOD, JUGGERS!
DON'T YOU FEEL GOOD TO BE TOTALLY DEBT-FREE FOR ONCE?
RIGHT NOW ALL I FEEL IS SORE!
BY THE WAY... HOW DID YOU EARN THE CASH TO PAY ME BACK?
EARN IT?
I BORROWED A BUCK FROM EACH OF THEM!
SAME OL' JUG!
THE END

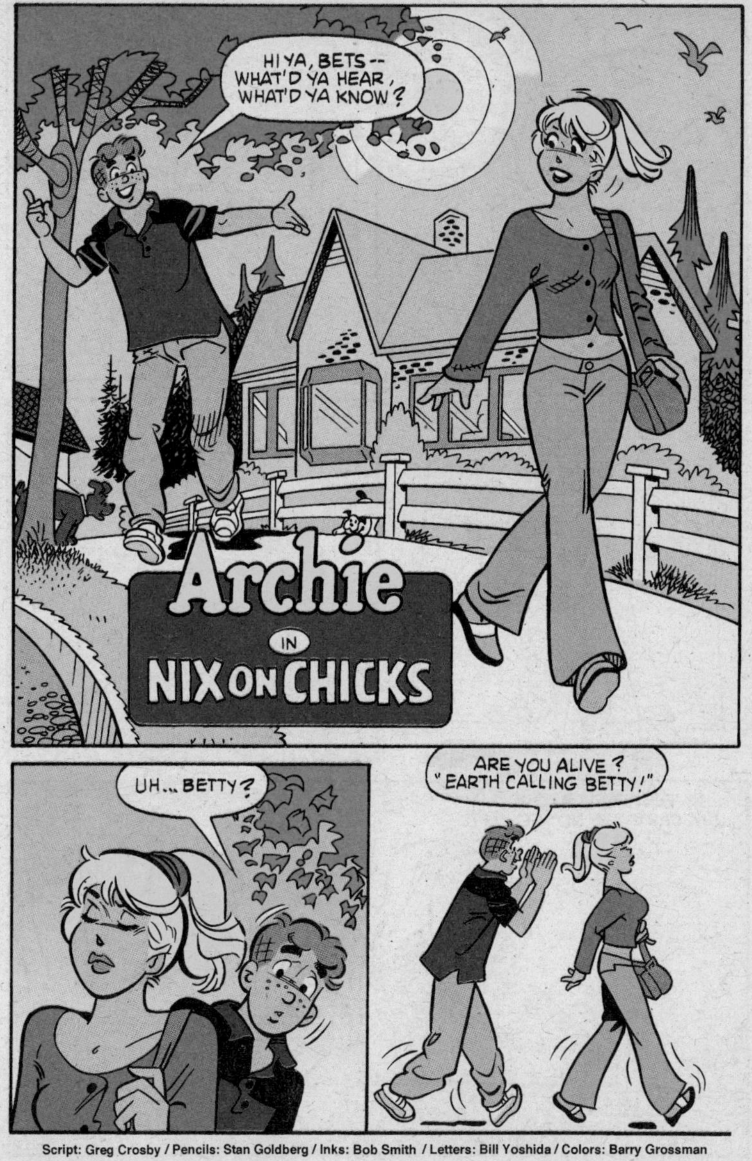
HI YA, BETS -- WHAT'D YA HEAR, WHAT'D YA KNOW?
Archie
IN
NIX ON CHICKS
UH... BETTY?
ARE YOU ALIVE? "EARTH CALLING BETTY!"

Script: Greg Crosby / Pencils: Stan Goldberg / Inks: Bob Smith / Letters: Bill Yoshida / Colors: Barry Grossman

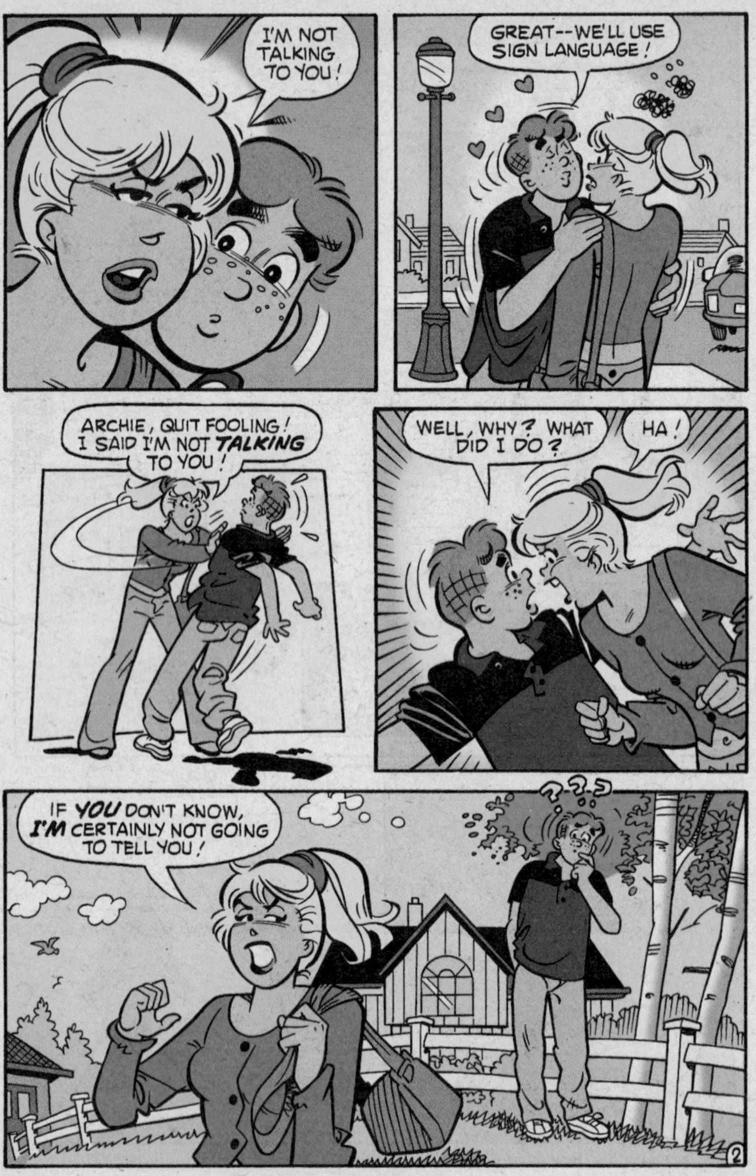
I'M NOT TALKING TO YOU!
GREAT--WE'LL USE SIGN LANGUAGE!
ARCHIE, QUIT FOOLING! I SAID I'M NOT TALKING TO YOU!
WELL, WHY? WHAT DID I DO?
HA!
IF YOU DON'T KNOW, I'M CERTAINLY NOT GOING TO TELL YOU!
2

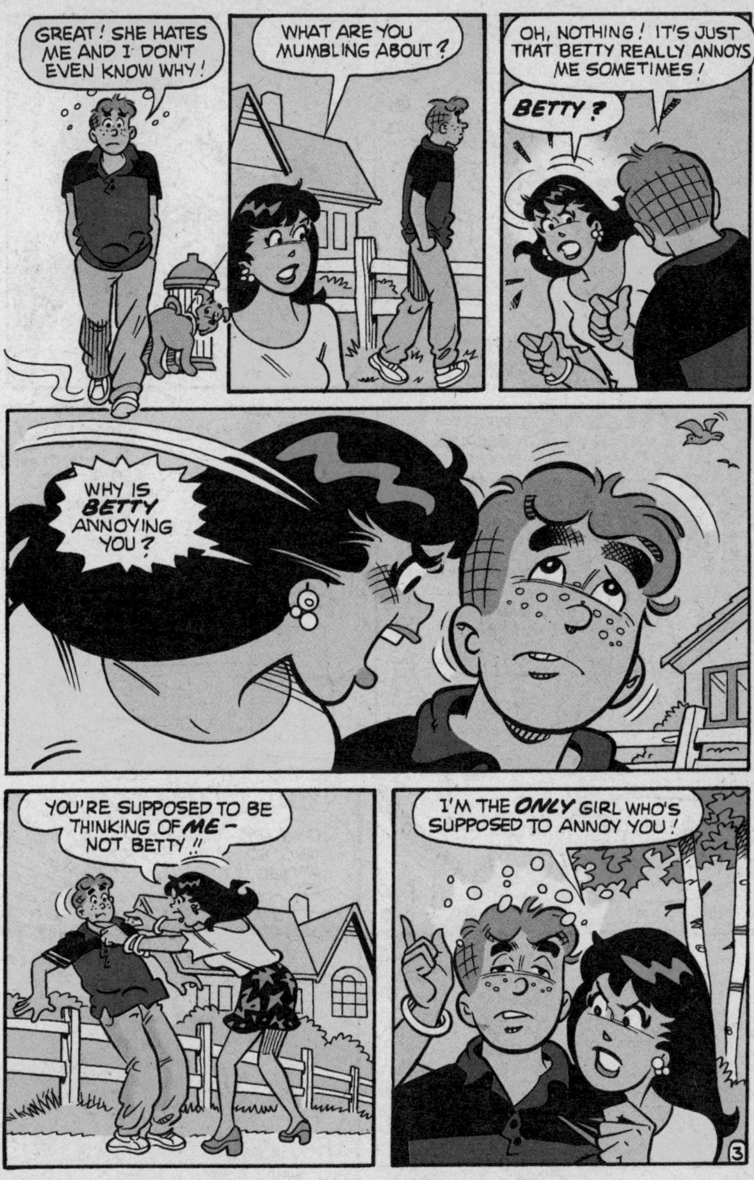

GREAT! SHE HATES ME AND I DON'T EVEN KNOW WHY!
WHAT ARE YOU MUMBLING ABOUT?
OH, NOTHING! IT'S JUST THAT BETTY REALLY ANNOYS ME SOMETIMES!
BETTY?
WHY IS BETTY ANNOYING YOU?
YOU'RE SUPPOSED TO BE THINKING OF ME - NOT BETTY!!
I'M THE ONLY GIRL WHO'S SUPPOSED TO ANNOY YOU!
3

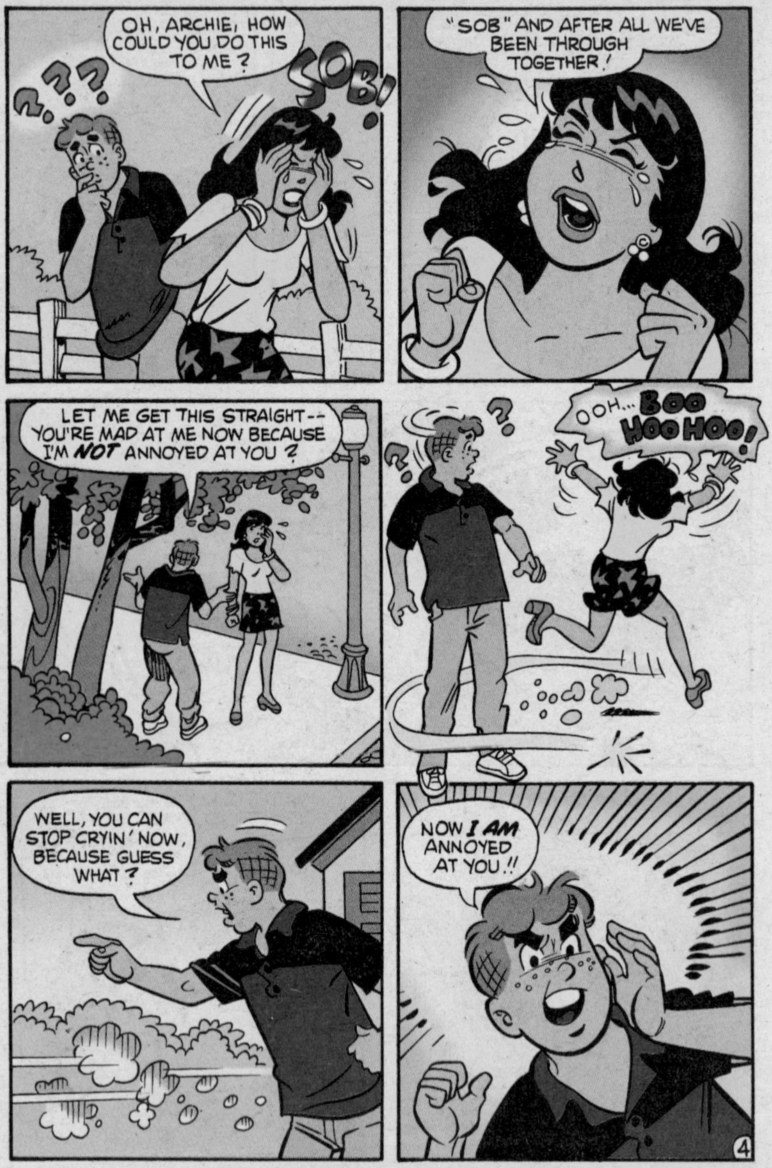

OH, ARCHIE, HOW COULD YOU DO THIS TO ME?
SOB!
"SOB" AND AFTER ALL WE'VE BEEN THROUGH TOGETHER!
LET ME GET THIS STRAIGHT-- YOU'RE MAD AT ME NOW BECAUSE I'M NOT ANNOYED AT YOU?
OOH... BOO HOO HOO!
WELL, YOU CAN STOP CRYIN' NOW, BECAUSE GUESS WHAT?
NOW I AM ANNOYED AT YOU!!
4

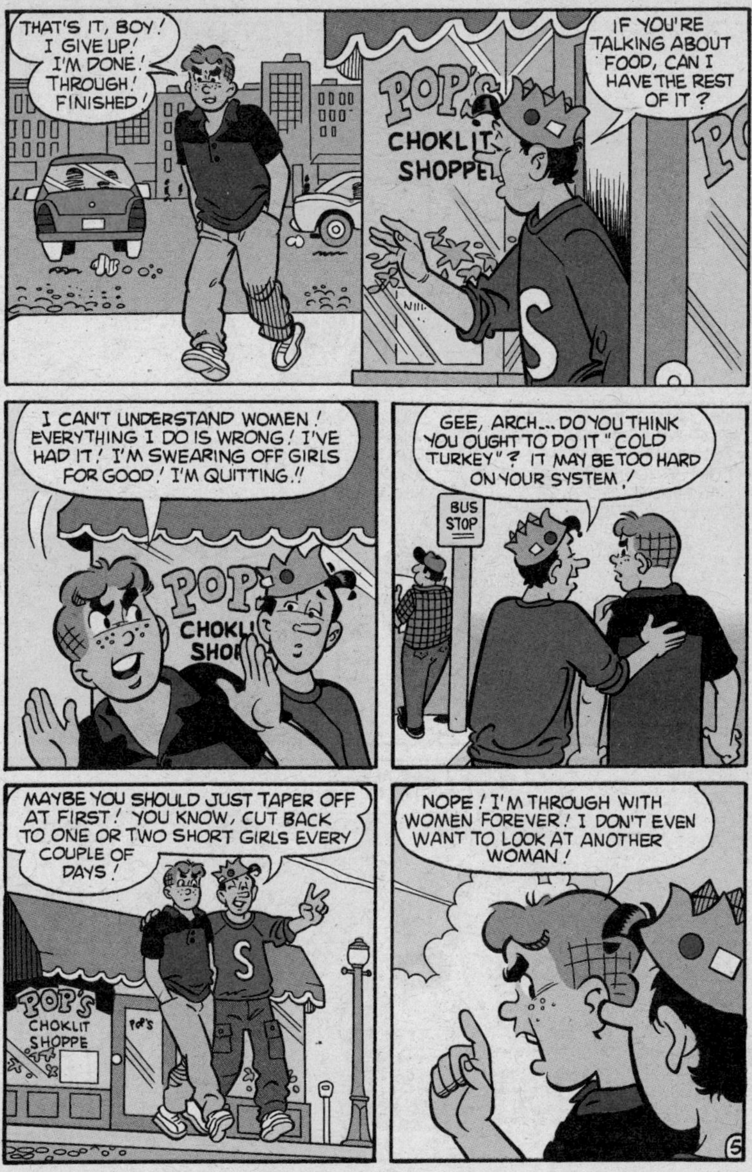
THAT'S IT, BOY! I GIVE UP! I'M DONE! THROUGH! FINISHED!
POP'S CHOKLIT SHOPPE
IF YOU'RE TALKING ABOUT FOOD, CAN I HAVE THE REST OF IT?
I CAN'T UNDERSTAND WOMEN! EVERYTHING I DO IS WRONG! I'VE HAD IT! I'M SWEARING OFF GIRLS FOR GOOD! I'M QUITTING!!
GEE, ARCH... DO YOU THINK YOU OUGHT TO DO IT "COLD TURKEY"? IT MAY BE TOO HARD ON YOUR SYSTEM!
BUS STOP
MAYBE YOU SHOULD JUST TAPER OFF AT FIRST! YOU KNOW, CUT BACK TO ONE OR TWO SHORT GIRLS EVERY COUPLE OF DAYS!
POP'S CHOKLIT SHOPPE
NOPE! I'M THROUGH WITH WOMEN FOREVER! I DON'T EVEN WANT TO LOOK AT ANOTHER WOMAN!
5

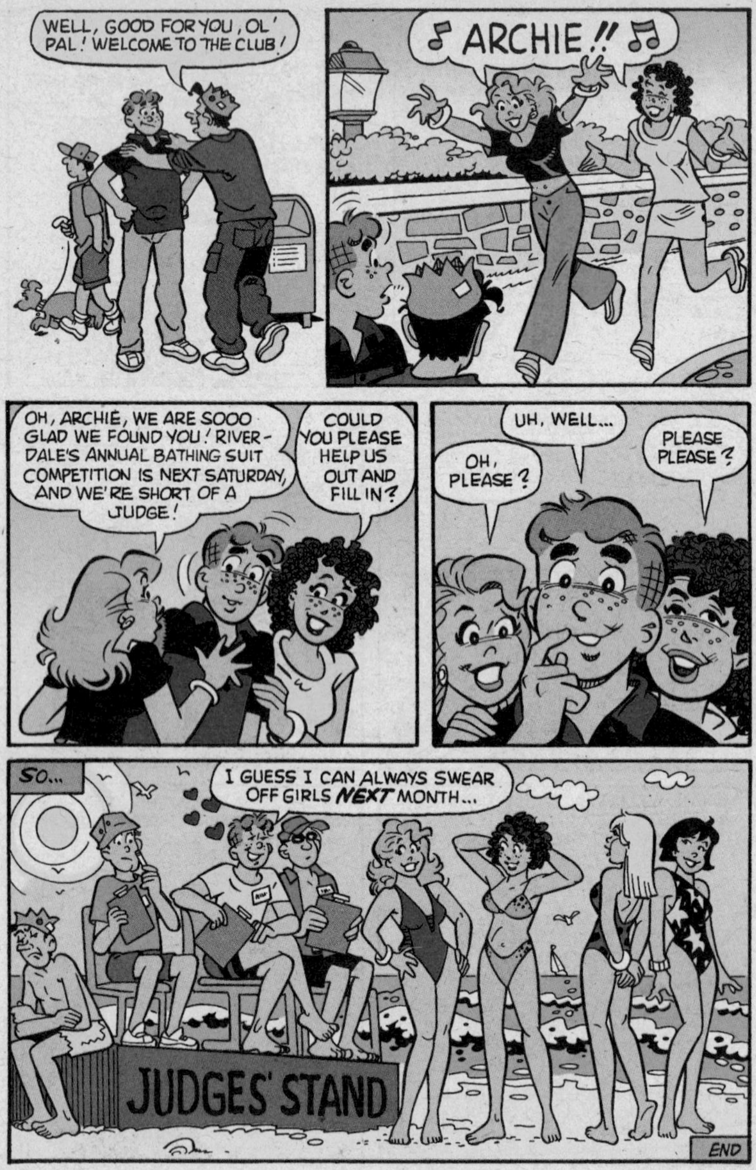
WELL, GOOD FOR YOU, OL' PAL! WELCOME TO THE CLUB!
ARCHIE!!
OH, ARCHIE, WE ARE SOOO GLAD WE FOUND YOU! RIVER-DALE'S ANNUAL BATHING SUIT COMPETITION IS NEXT SATURDAY, AND WE'RE SHORT OF A JUDGE!
COULD YOU PLEASE HELP US OUT AND FILL IN?
OH, PLEASE?
UH, WELL...
PLEASE PLEASE?
SO...
I GUESS I CAN ALWAYS SWEAR OFF GIRLS NEXT MONTH...
JUDGES' STAND
END

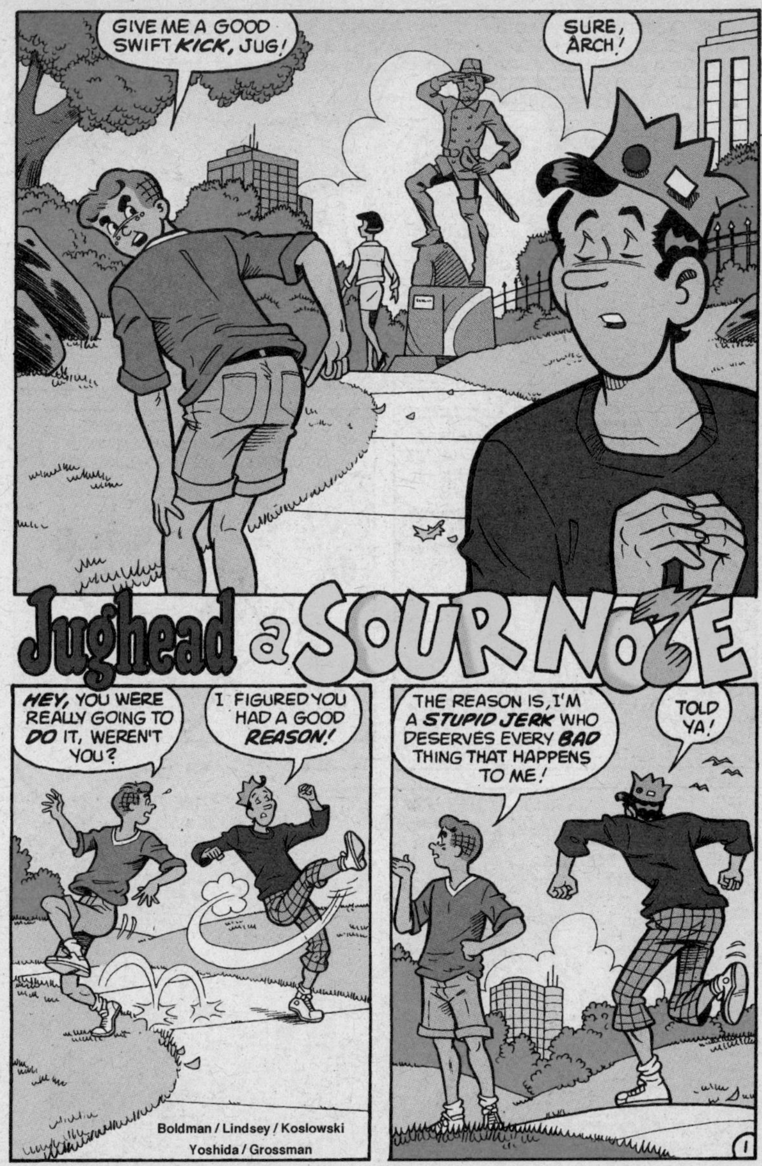
GIVE ME A GOOD SWIFT KICK, JUG!
SURE, ARCH!
Jughead a SOUR NOTE
HEY, YOU WERE REALLY GOING TO DO IT, WEREN'T YOU?
I FIGURED YOU HAD A GOOD REASON!
Boldman / Lindsey / Koslowski
Yoshida / Grossman
THE REASON IS, I'M A STUPID JERK WHO DESERVES EVERY BAD THING THAT HAPPENS TO ME!
TOLD YA!
1

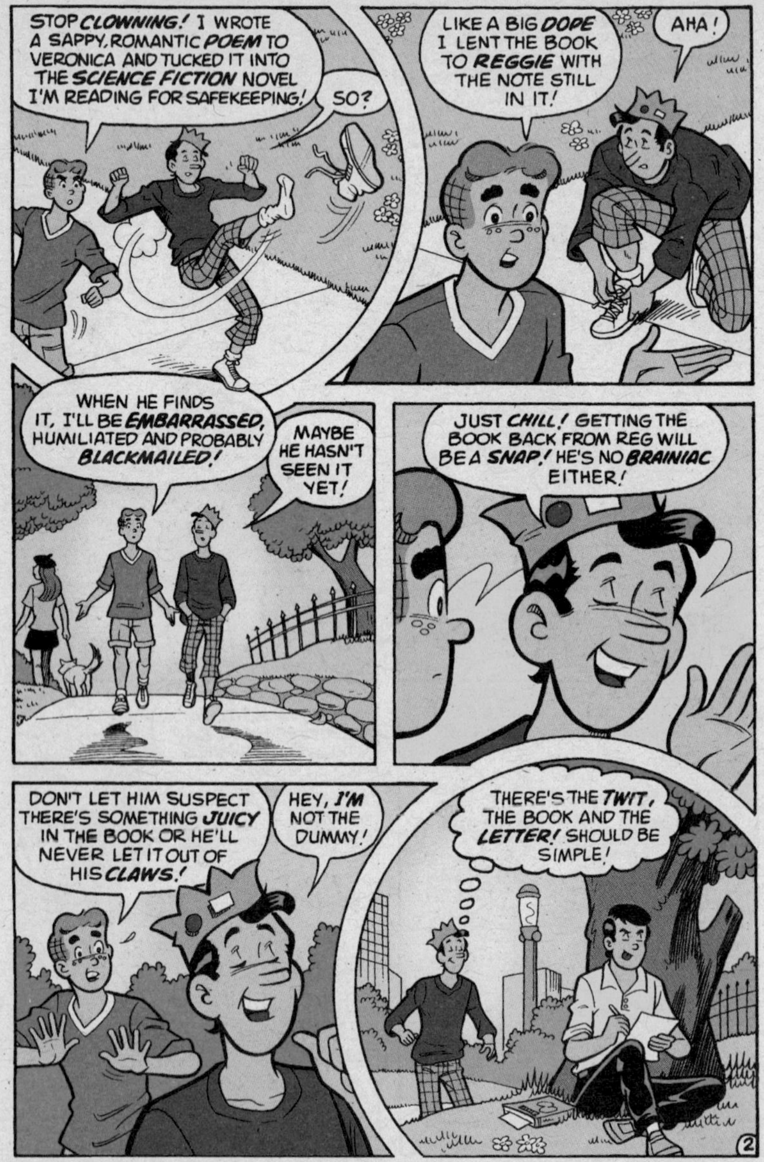
STOP CLOWNING! I WROTE A SAPPY, ROMANTIC POEM TO VERONICA AND TUCKED IT INTO THE SCIENCE FICTION NOVEL I'M READING FOR SAFEKEEPING!
SO?
LIKE A BIG DOPE I LENT THE BOOK TO REGGIE WITH THE NOTE STILL IN IT!
AHA!
WHEN HE FINDS IT, I'LL BE EMBARRASSED, HUMILIATED AND PROBABLY BLACKMAILED!
MAYBE HE HASN'T SEEN IT YET!
JUST CHILL! GETTING THE BOOK BACK FROM REG WILL BE A SNAP! HE'S NO BRAINIAC EITHER!
DON'T LET HIM SUSPECT THERE'S SOMETHING JUICY IN THE BOOK OR HE'LL NEVER LET IT OUT OF HIS CLAWS!
HEY, I'M NOT THE DUMMY!
THERE'S THE TWIT, THE BOOK AND THE LETTER! SHOULD BE SIMPLE!
2

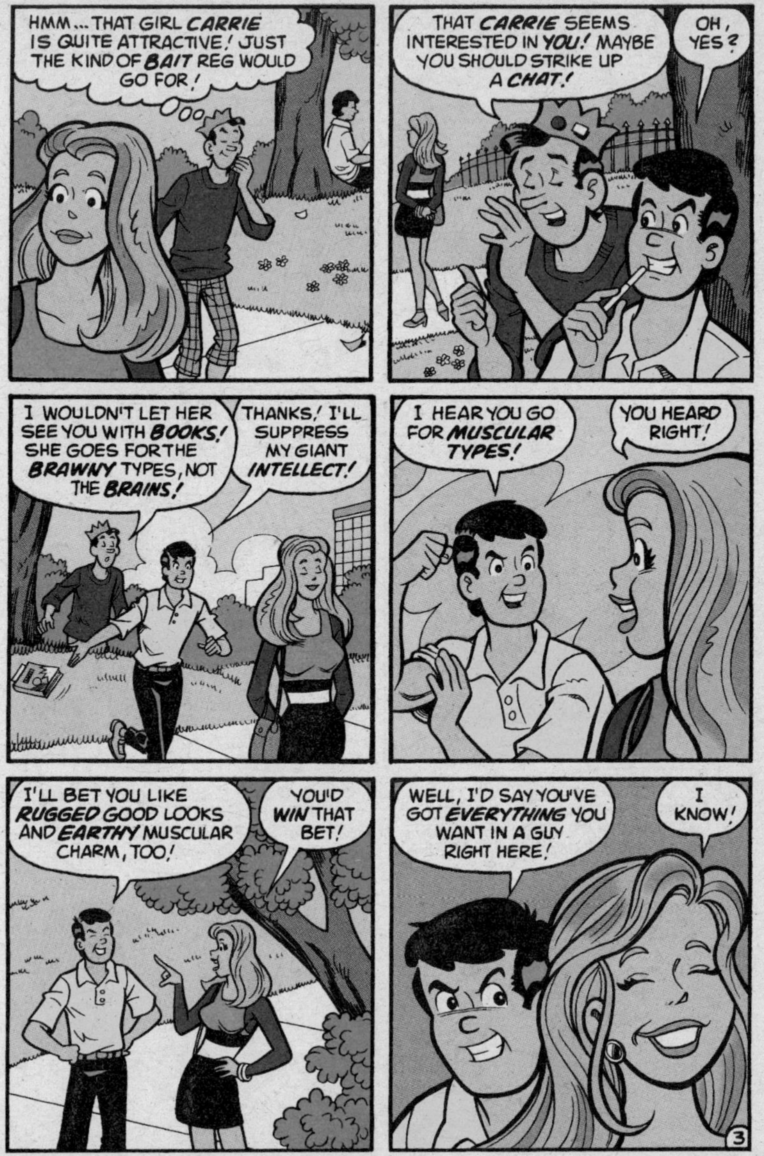
HMM... THAT GIRL CARRIE IS QUITE ATTRACTIVE! JUST THE KIND OF BAIT REG WOULD GO FOR!
THAT CARRIE SEEMS INTERESTED IN YOU! MAYBE YOU SHOULD STRIKE UP A CHAT!
OH, YES?
I WOULDN'T LET HER SEE YOU WITH BOOKS! SHE GOES FOR THE BRAWNY TYPES, NOT THE BRAINS!
THANKS! I'LL SUPPRESS MY GIANT INTELLECT!
I HEAR YOU GO FOR MUSCULAR TYPES!
YOU HEARD RIGHT!
I'LL BET YOU LIKE RUGGED GOOD LOOKS AND EARTHY MUSCULAR CHARM, TOO!
YOU'D WIN THAT BET!
WELL, I'D SAY YOU'VE GOT EVERYTHING YOU WANT IN A GUY RIGHT HERE!
I KNOW!
3

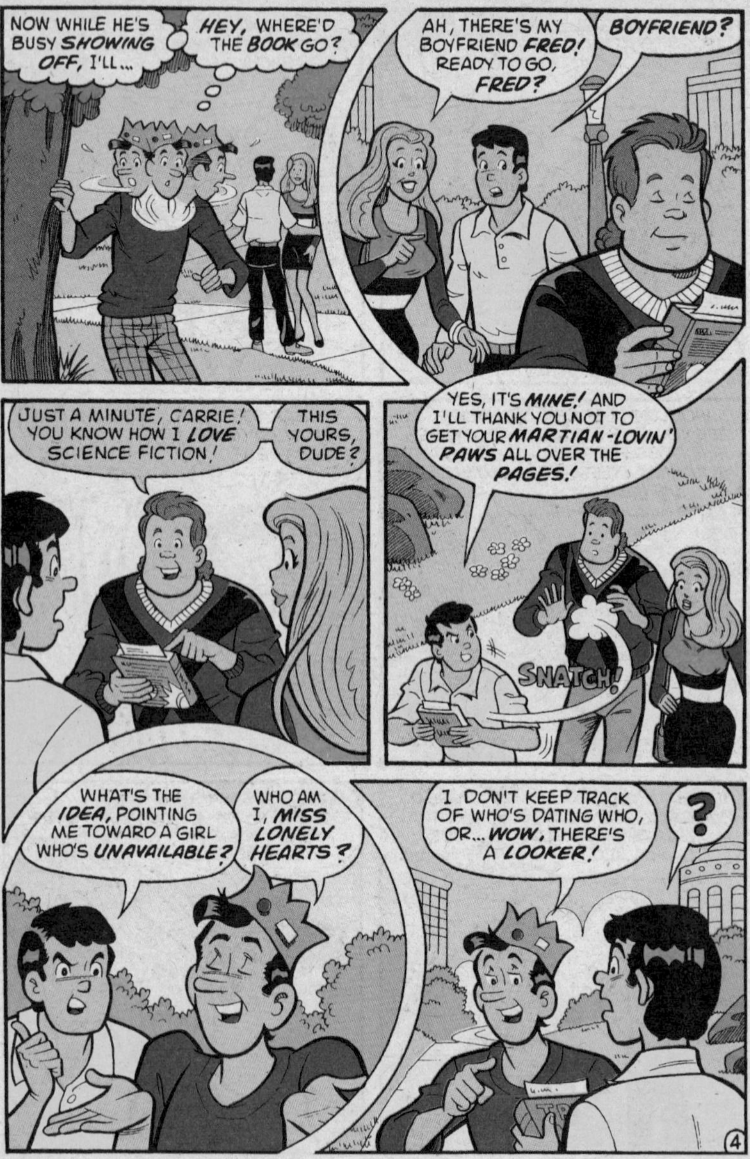
NOW WHILE HE'S BUSY SHOWING OFF, I'LL...
HEY, WHERE'D THE BOOK GO?
AH, THERE'S MY BOYFRIEND FRED! READY TO GO, FRED?
BOYFRIEND?
JUST A MINUTE, CARRIE! YOU KNOW HOW I LOVE SCIENCE FICTION!
THIS YOURS, DUDE?
YES, IT'S MINE! AND I'LL THANK YOU NOT TO GET YOUR MARTIAN-LOVIN' PAWS ALL OVER THE PAGES!
SNATCH!
WHAT'S THE IDEA, POINTING ME TOWARD A GIRL WHO'S UNAVAILABLE?
WHO AM I, MISS LONELY HEARTS?
I DON'T KEEP TRACK OF WHO'S DATING WHO, OR... WOW, THERE'S A LOOKER!
?
4

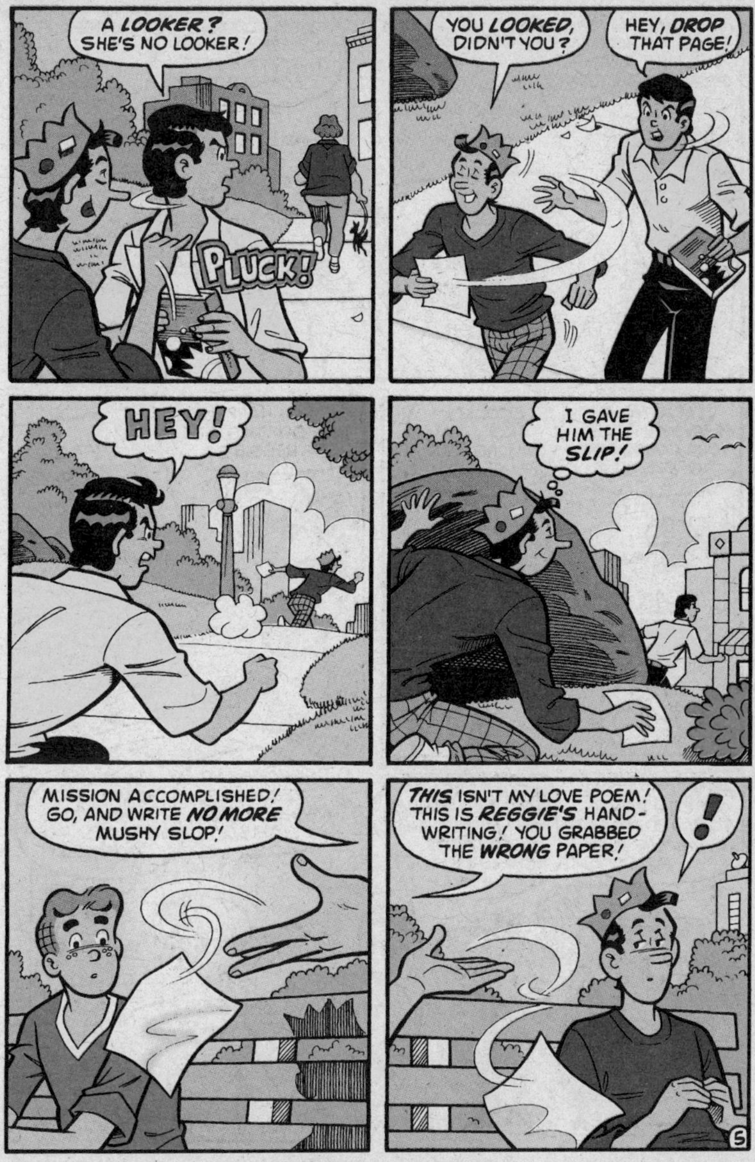

A LOOKER? SHE'S NO LOOKER!
PLUCK!
YOU LOOKED, DIDN'T YOU?
HEY, DROP THAT PAGE!
HEY!
I GAVE HIM THE SLIP!
MISSION ACCOMPLISHED! GO, AND WRITE NO MORE MUSHY SLOP!
THIS ISN'T MY LOVE POEM! THIS IS REGGIE'S HAND-WRITING! YOU GRABBED THE WRONG PAPER!
!
5

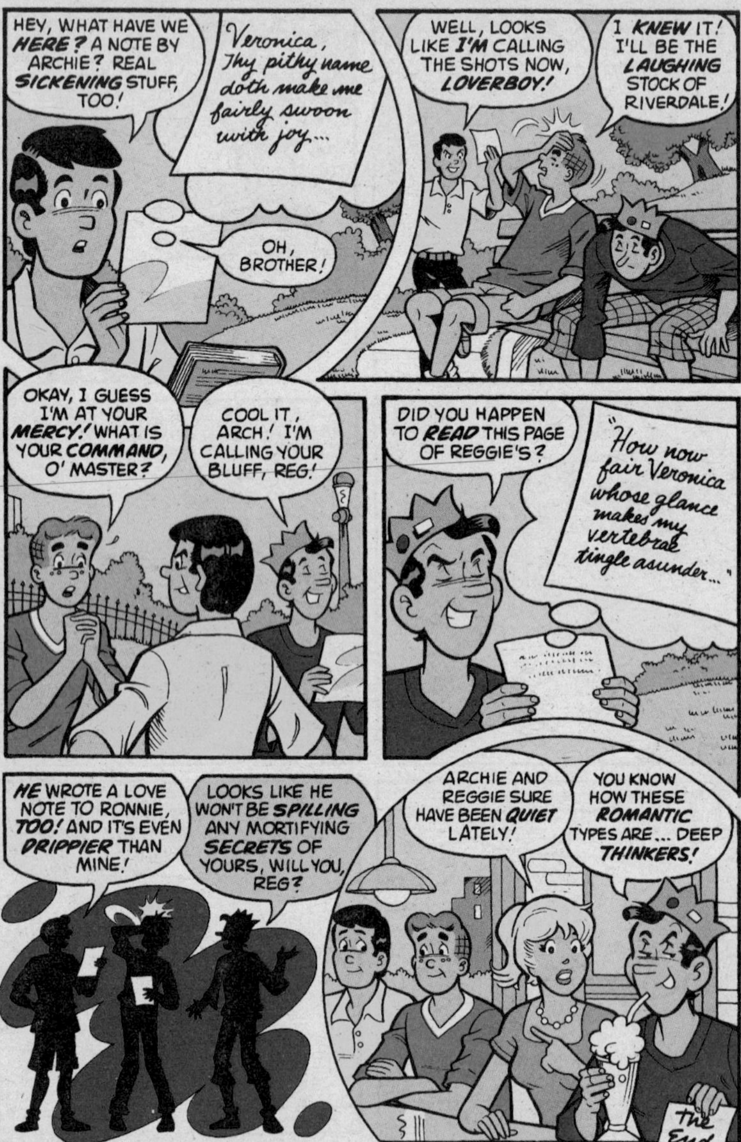
HEY, WHAT HAVE WE HERE? A NOTE BY ARCHIE? REAL SICKENING STUFF, TOO!
Veronica, Thy pithy name doth make me fairly swoon with joy...
OH, BROTHER!
WELL, LOOKS LIKE I'M CALLING THE SHOTS NOW, LOVERBOY!
I KNEW IT! I'LL BE THE LAUGHING STOCK OF RIVERDALE!
OKAY, I GUESS I'M AT YOUR MERCY! WHAT IS YOUR COMMAND, O' MASTER?
COOL IT, ARCH! I'M CALLING YOUR BLUFF, REG!
DID YOU HAPPEN TO READ THIS PAGE OF REGGIE'S?
"How now fair Veronica whose glance makes my vertebrae tingle asunder..."
HE WROTE A LOVE NOTE TO RONNIE, TOO! AND IT'S EVEN DRIPPIER THAN MINE!
LOOKS LIKE HE WON'T BE SPILLING ANY MORTIFYING SECRETS OF YOURS, WILL YOU, REG?
ARCHIE AND REGGIE SURE HAVE BEEN QUIET LATELY!
YOU KNOW HOW THESE ROMANTIC TYPES ARE... DEEP THINKERS!
The End

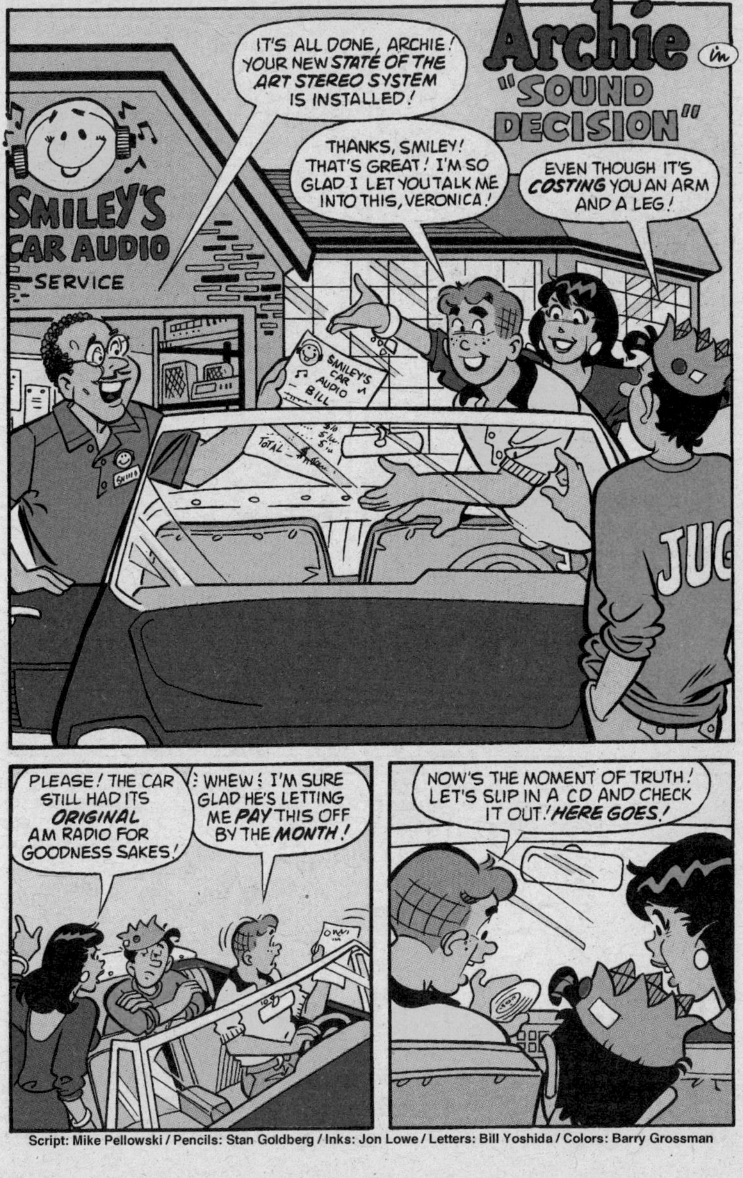
Archie in "SOUND DECISION"
IT'S ALL DONE, ARCHIE! YOUR NEW STATE OF THE ART STEREO SYSTEM IS INSTALLED!
SMILEY'S CAR AUDIO
SERVICE
THANKS, SMILEY! THAT'S GREAT! I'M SO GLAD I LET YOU TALK ME INTO THIS, VERONICA!
EVEN THOUGH IT'S COSTING YOU AN ARM AND A LEG!
SMILEY'S CAR AUDIO BILL
TOTAL
JUG
PLEASE! THE CAR STILL HAD ITS ORIGINAL AM RADIO FOR GOODNESS SAKES!
WHEW! I'M SURE GLAD HE'S LETTING ME PAY THIS OFF BY THE MONTH!
NOW'S THE MOMENT OF TRUTH! LET'S SLIP IN A CD AND CHECK IT OUT! HERE GOES!

Script: Mike Pellowski / Pencils: Stan Goldberg / Inks: Jon Lowe / Letters: Bill Yoshida / Colors: Barry Grossman

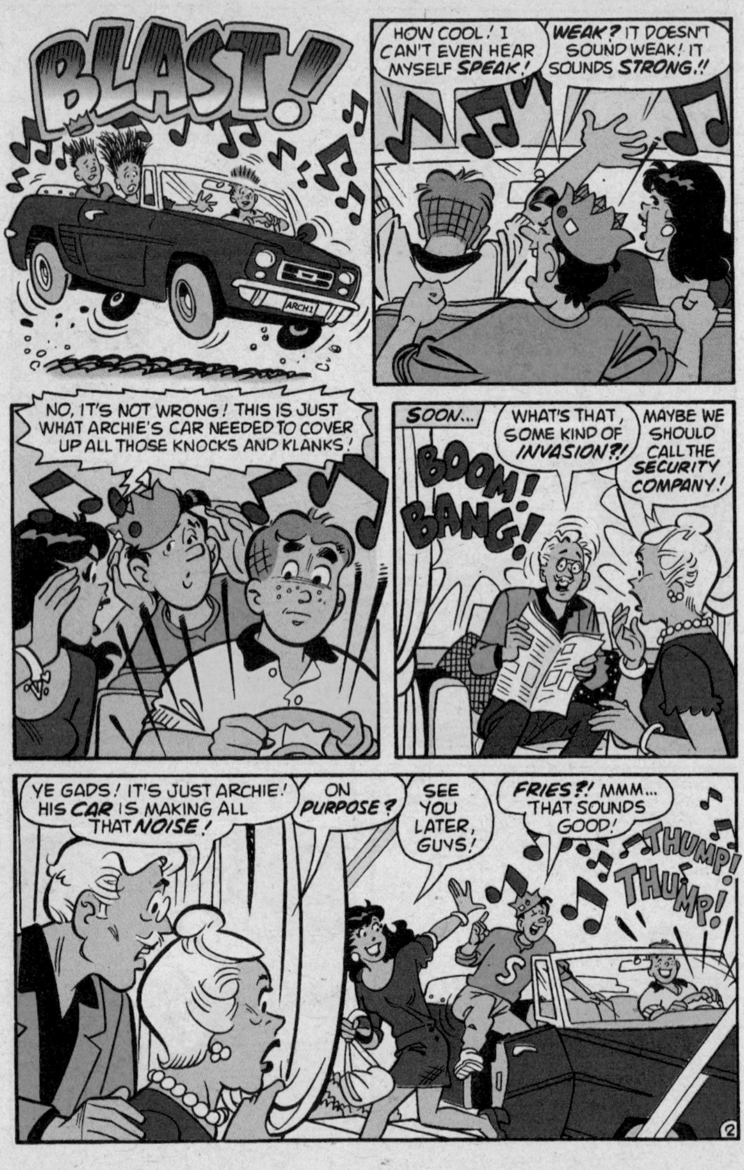
BLAST!
HOW COOL! I CAN'T EVEN HEAR MYSELF SPEAK!
WEAK? IT DOESN'T SOUND WEAK! IT SOUNDS STRONG!!
NO, IT'S NOT WRONG! THIS IS JUST WHAT ARCHIE'S CAR NEEDED TO COVER UP ALL THOSE KNOCKS AND KLANKS!
SOON...
BOOM! BANG!
WHAT'S THAT, SOME KIND OF INVASION?!
MAYBE WE SHOULD CALL THE SECURITY COMPANY!
YE GADS! IT'S JUST ARCHIE! HIS CAR IS MAKING ALL THAT NOISE!
ON PURPOSE?
SEE YOU LATER, GUYS!
FRIES?! MMM... THAT SOUNDS GOOD!
THUMP! THUMP!
2

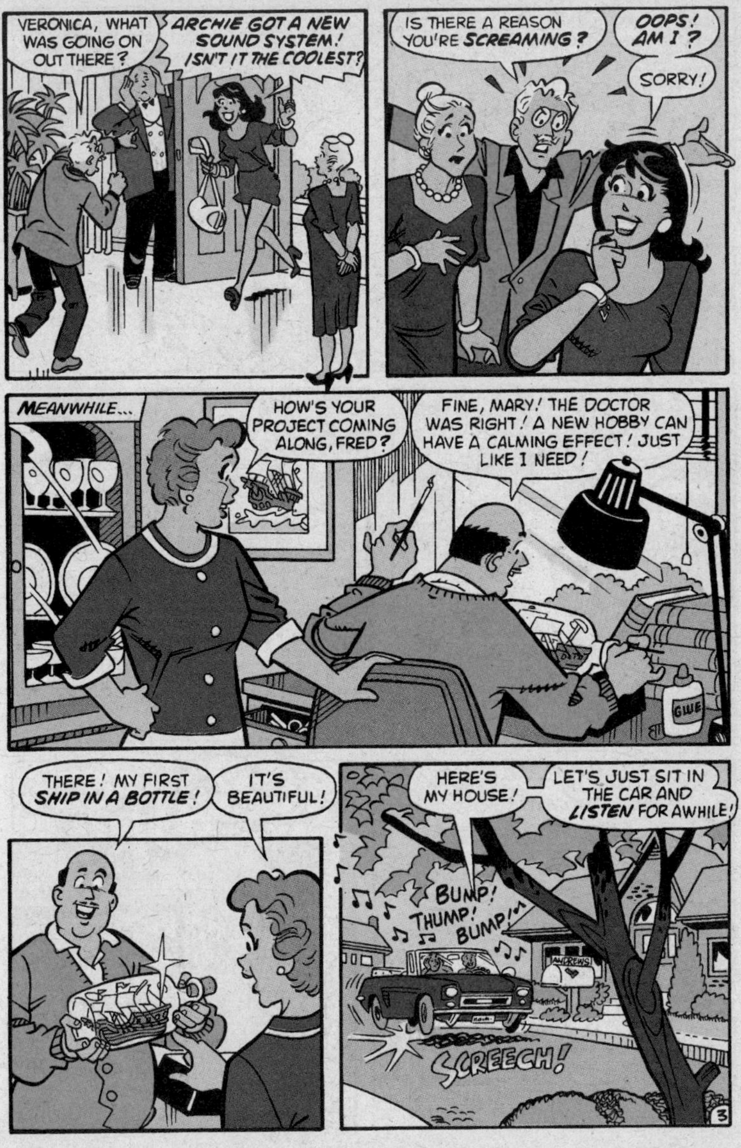

VERONICA, WHAT WAS GOING ON OUT THERE?
ARCHIE GOT A NEW SOUND SYSTEM! ISN'T IT THE COOLEST?
IS THERE A REASON YOU'RE SCREAMING?
OOPS! AM I?
SORRY!
MEANWHILE...
HOW'S YOUR PROJECT COMING ALONG, FRED?
FINE, MARY! THE DOCTOR WAS RIGHT! A NEW HOBBY CAN HAVE A CALMING EFFECT! JUST LIKE I NEED!
GLUE
THERE! MY FIRST SHIP IN A BOTTLE!
IT'S BEAUTIFUL!
HERE'S MY HOUSE!
LET'S JUST SIT IN THE CAR AND LISTEN FOR AWHILE!
BUMP!
THUMP!
BUMP!
ANDREWS
SCREECH!

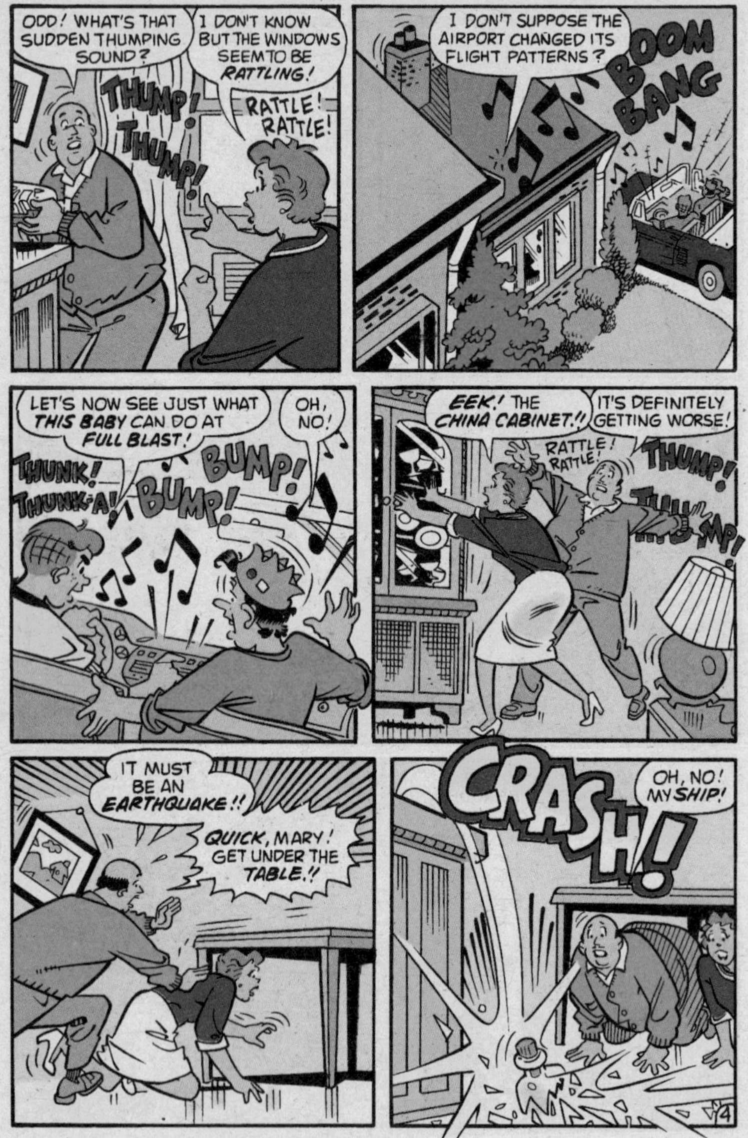
ODD! WHAT'S THAT SUDDEN THUMPING SOUND?
I DON'T KNOW BUT THE WINDOWS SEEM TO BE RATTLING!
THUMP! THUMP!
RATTLE! RATTLE!
I DON'T SUPPOSE THE AIRPORT CHANGED ITS FLIGHT PATTERNS?
BOOM BANG
LET'S NOW SEE JUST WHAT THIS BABY CAN DO AT FULL BLAST!
OH, NO!
THUNK! THUNK-A!
BUMP! BUMP!
EEK! THE CHINA CABINET!!
IT'S DEFINITELY GETTING WORSE!
RATTLE! RATTLE!
THUMP!
IT MUST BE AN EARTHQUAKE!!
QUICK, MARY! GET UNDER THE TABLE!!
CRASH!
OH, NO! MY SHIP!
4

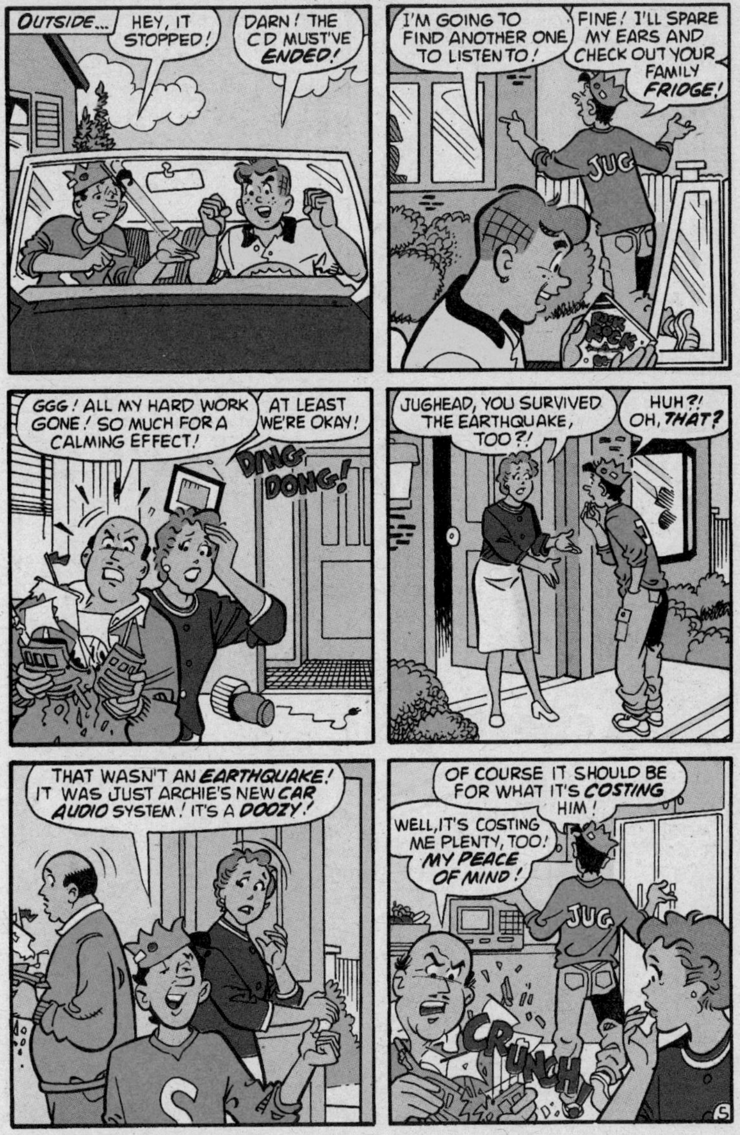
OUTSIDE...
HEY, IT STOPPED!
DARN! THE CD MUST'VE ENDED!
I'M GOING TO FIND ANOTHER ONE TO LISTEN TO!
FINE! I'LL SPARE MY EARS AND CHECK OUT YOUR FAMILY FRIDGE!
JUG
GGG! ALL MY HARD WORK GONE! SO MUCH FOR A CALMING EFFECT!
AT LEAST WE'RE OKAY!
DING DONG!
JUGHEAD, YOU SURVIVED THE EARTHQUAKE, TOO?!
HUH?! OH, THAT?
THAT WASN'T AN EARTHQUAKE! IT WAS JUST ARCHIE'S NEW CAR AUDIO SYSTEM! IT'S A DOOZY!
OF COURSE IT SHOULD BE FOR WHAT IT'S COSTING HIM!
WELL, IT'S COSTING ME PLENTY, TOO! MY PEACE OF MIND!
JUG
CRUNCH!
5

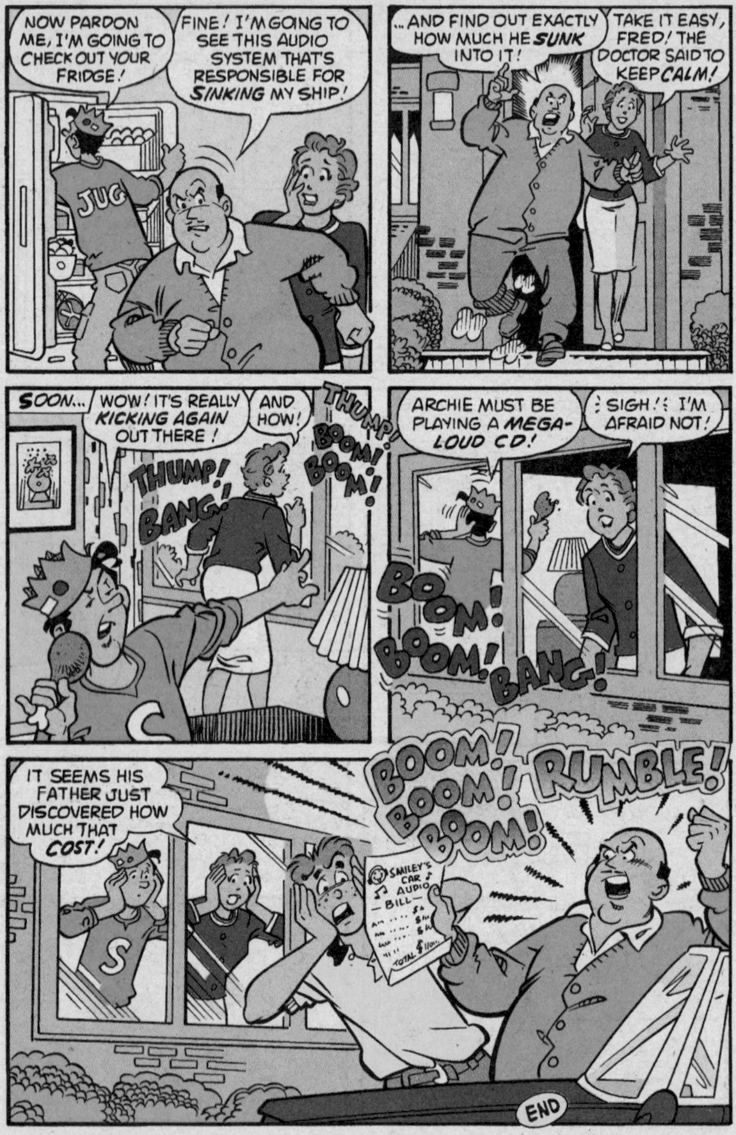
NOW PARDON ME, I'M GOING TO CHECK OUT YOUR FRIDGE!
FINE! I'M GOING TO SEE THIS AUDIO SYSTEM THAT'S RESPONSIBLE FOR SINKING MY SHIP!
...AND FIND OUT EXACTLY HOW MUCH HE SUNK INTO IT!
TAKE IT EASY, FRED! THE DOCTOR SAID TO KEEP CALM!
SOON...
WOW! IT'S REALLY KICKING AGAIN OUT THERE!
AND HOW!
THUMP!
BOOM! BOOM!
THUMP!
BANG!
ARCHIE MUST BE PLAYING A MEGA-LOUD CD!
SIGH! I'M AFRAID NOT!
BOOM!
BOOM!
BANG!
IT SEEMS HIS FATHER JUST DISCOVERED HOW MUCH THAT COST!
BOOM! BOOM! BOOM!
RUMBLE!
SMILEY'S CAR AUDIO
BILL
TOTAL
END

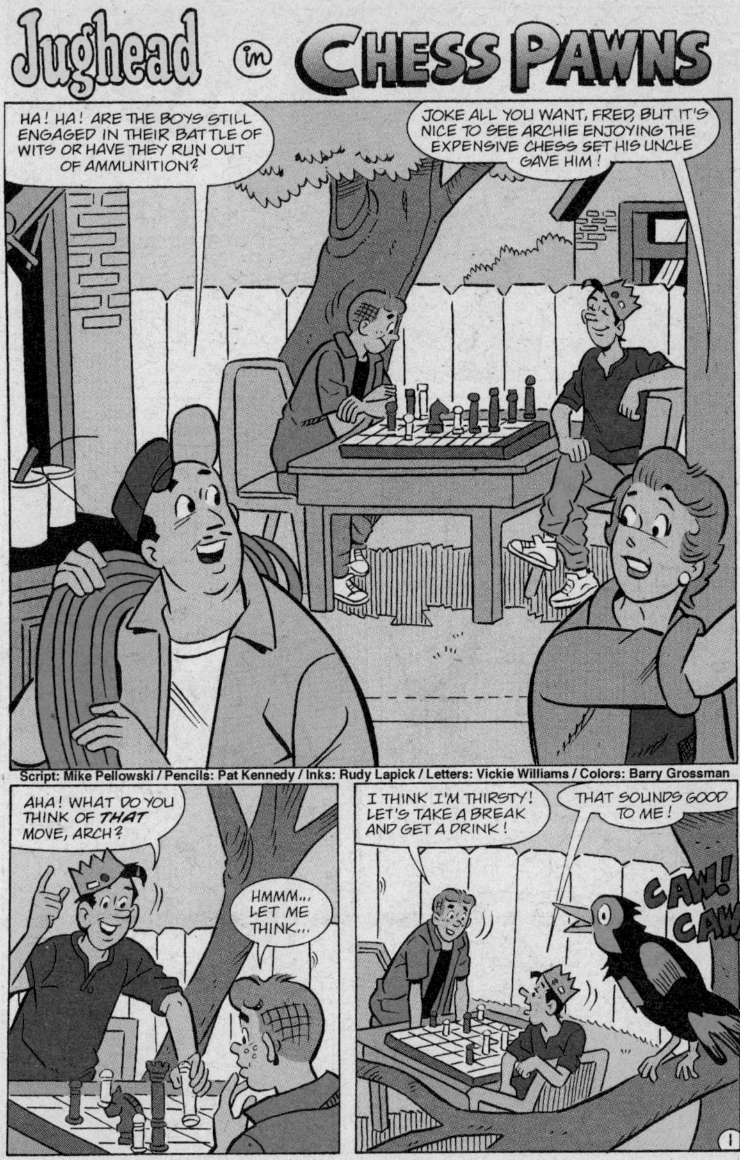
Jughead in CHESS PAWNS
HA! HA! ARE THE BOYS STILL ENGAGED IN THEIR BATTLE OF WITS OR HAVE THEY RUN OUT OF AMMUNITION?
JOKE ALL YOU WANT, FRED, BUT IT'S NICE TO SEE ARCHIE ENJOYING THE EXPENSIVE CHESS SET HIS UNCLE GAVE HIM!
Script: Mike Pellowski / Pencils: Pat Kennedy / Inks: Rudy Lapick / Letters: Vickie Williams / Colors: Barry Grossman
AHA! WHAT DO YOU THINK OF THAT MOVE, ARCH?
HMMM... LET ME THINK...
I THINK I'M THIRSTY! LET'S TAKE A BREAK AND GET A DRINK!
THAT SOUNDS GOOD TO ME!
CAW! CAW!
1

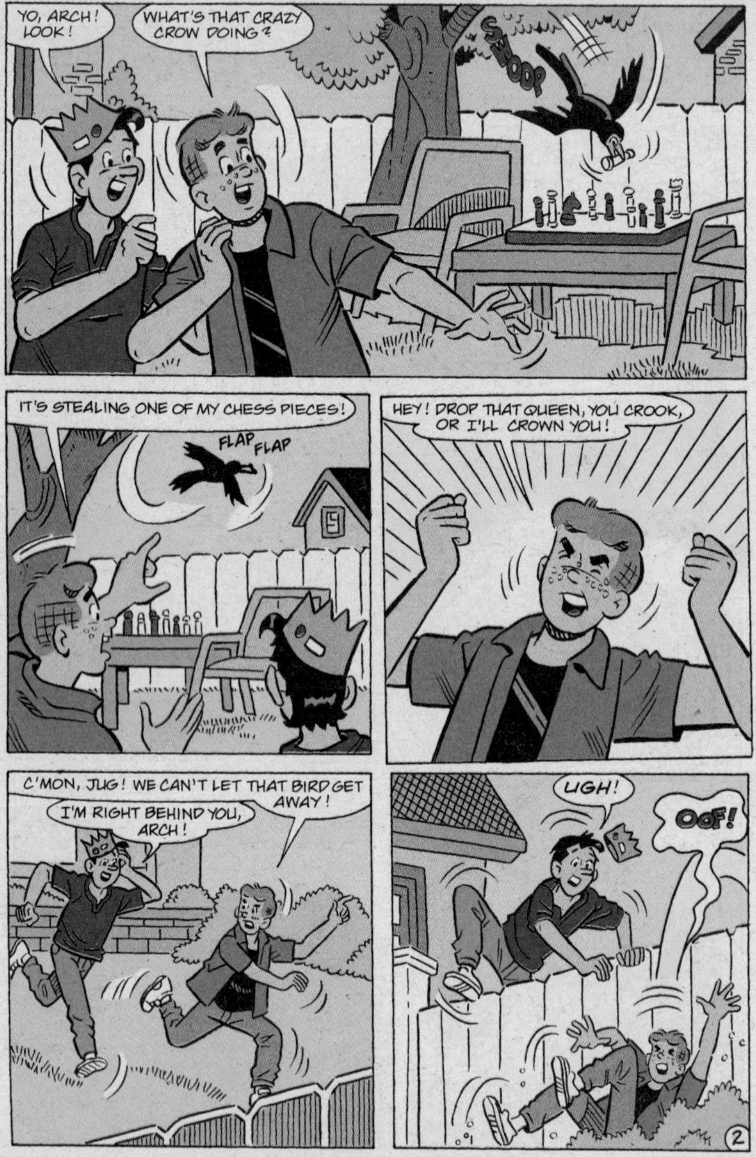
YO, ARCH! LOOK!
WHAT'S THAT CRAZY CROW DOING?
SWOOP
IT'S STEALING ONE OF MY CHESS PIECES!
FLAP FLAP
HEY! DROP THAT QUEEN, YOU CROOK, OR I'LL CROWN YOU!
C'MON, JUG! WE CAN'T LET THAT BIRD GET AWAY!
I'M RIGHT BEHIND YOU, ARCH!
UGH!
OOF!
2

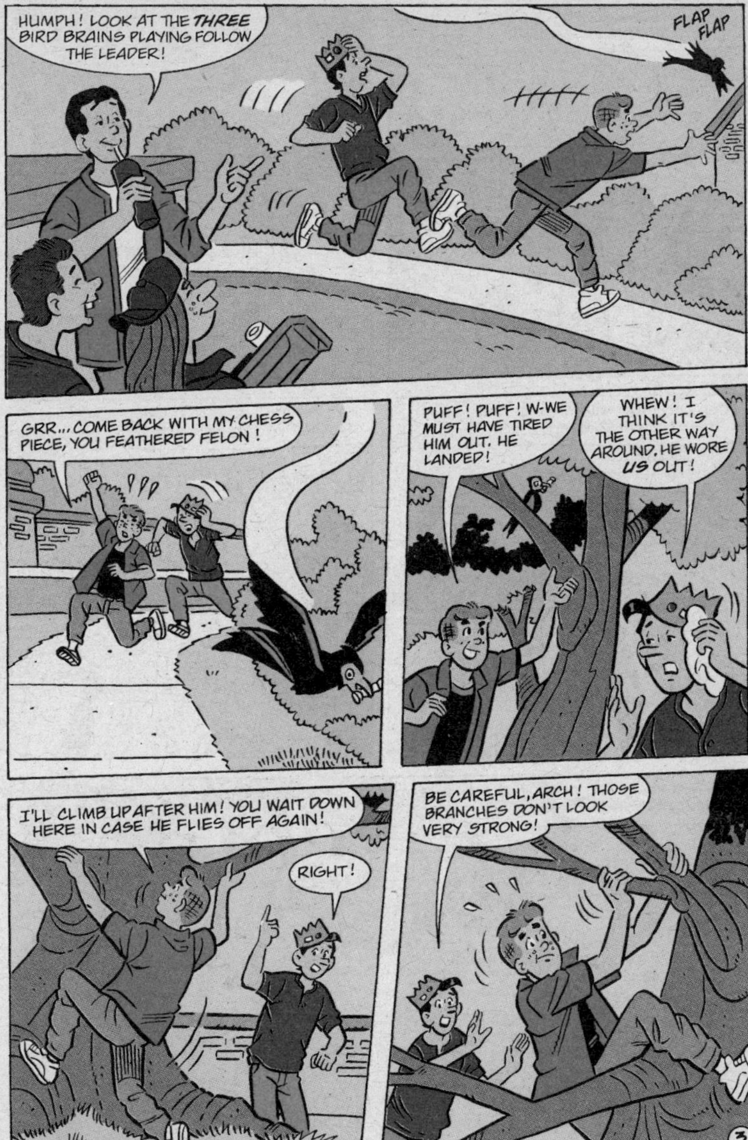
HUMPH! LOOK AT THE *THREE* BIRD BRAINS PLAYING FOLLOW THE LEADER!
FLAP FLAP
GRR... COME BACK WITH MY CHESS PIECE, YOU FEATHERED FELON!
PUFF! PUFF! W-WE MUST HAVE TIRED HIM OUT. HE LANDED!
WHEW! I THINK IT'S THE OTHER WAY AROUND. HE WORE *US* OUT!
I'LL CLIMB UP AFTER HIM! YOU WAIT DOWN HERE IN CASE HE FLIES OFF AGAIN!
RIGHT!
BE CAREFUL, ARCH! THOSE BRANCHES DON'T LOOK VERY STRONG!

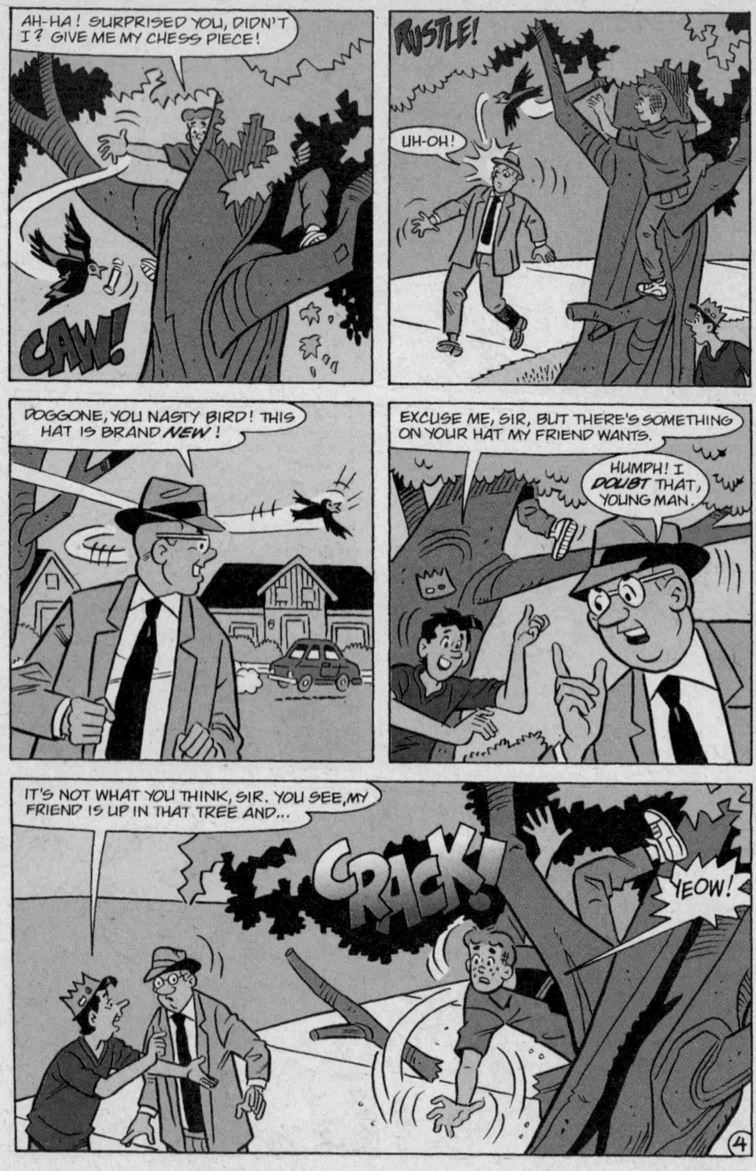
AH-HA! SURPRISED YOU, DIDN'T I? GIVE ME MY CHESS PIECE!
CAW!
RUSTLE!
UH-OH!
DOGGONE, YOU NASTY BIRD! THIS HAT IS BRAND NEW!
EXCUSE ME, SIR, BUT THERE'S SOMETHING ON YOUR HAT MY FRIEND WANTS.
HUMPH! I DOUBT THAT, YOUNG MAN.
IT'S NOT WHAT YOU THINK, SIR. YOU SEE, MY FRIEND IS UP IN THAT TREE AND...
CRACK!
YEOW!
4

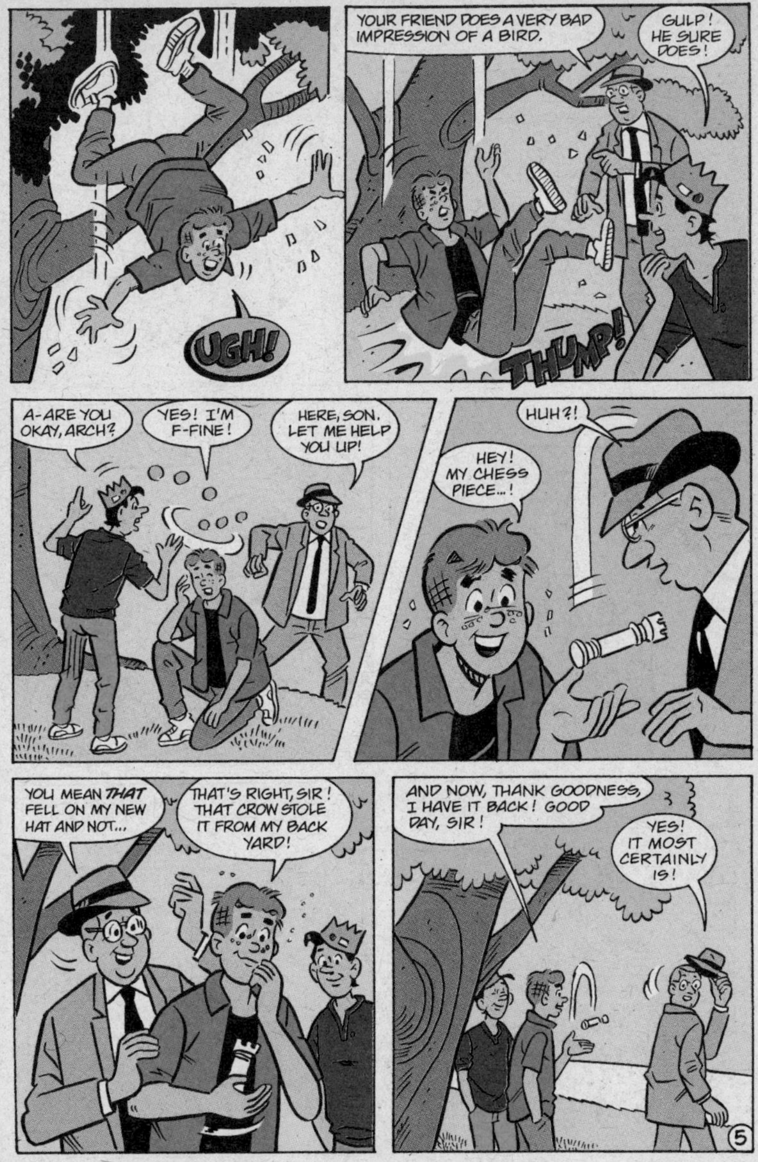
UGH!
YOUR FRIEND DOES A VERY BAD IMPRESSION OF A BIRD.
GULP! HE SURE DOES!
THUMP!
A-ARE YOU OKAY, ARCH?
YES! I'M F-FINE!
HERE, SON. LET ME HELP YOU UP!
HUH?!
HEY! MY CHESS PIECE...!
YOU MEAN THAT FELL ON MY NEW HAT AND NOT...
THAT'S RIGHT, SIR! THAT CROW STOLE IT FROM MY BACK YARD!
AND NOW, THANK GOODNESS, I HAVE IT BACK! GOOD DAY, SIR!
YES! IT MOST CERTAINLY IS!
5

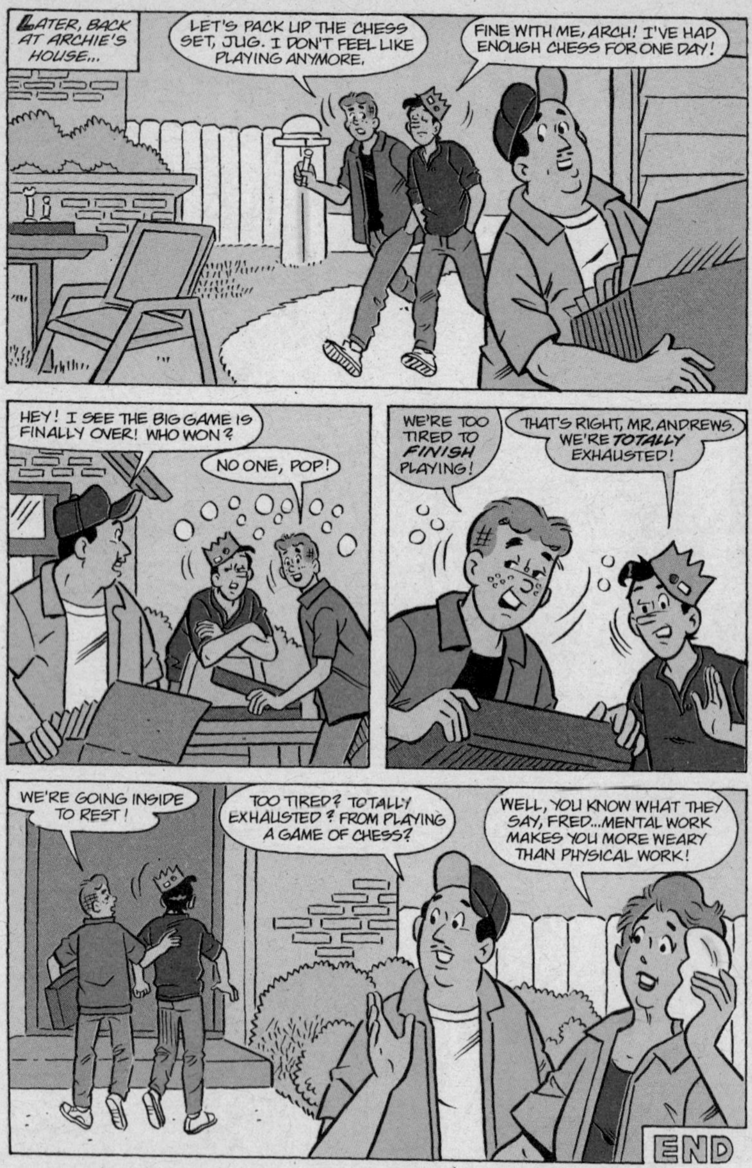
LATER, BACK AT ARCHIE'S HOUSE...
LET'S PACK UP THE CHESS SET, JUG. I DON'T FEEL LIKE PLAYING ANYMORE.
FINE WITH ME, ARCH! I'VE HAD ENOUGH CHESS FOR ONE DAY!
HEY! I SEE THE BIG GAME IS FINALLY OVER! WHO WON?
NO ONE, POP!
WE'RE TOO TIRED TO FINISH PLAYING!
THAT'S RIGHT, MR. ANDREWS. WE'RE TOTALLY EXHAUSTED!
WE'RE GOING INSIDE TO REST!
TOO TIRED? TOTALLY EXHAUSTED? FROM PLAYING A GAME OF CHESS?
WELL, YOU KNOW WHAT THEY SAY, FRED...MENTAL WORK MAKES YOU MORE WEARY THAN PHYSICAL WORK!
END

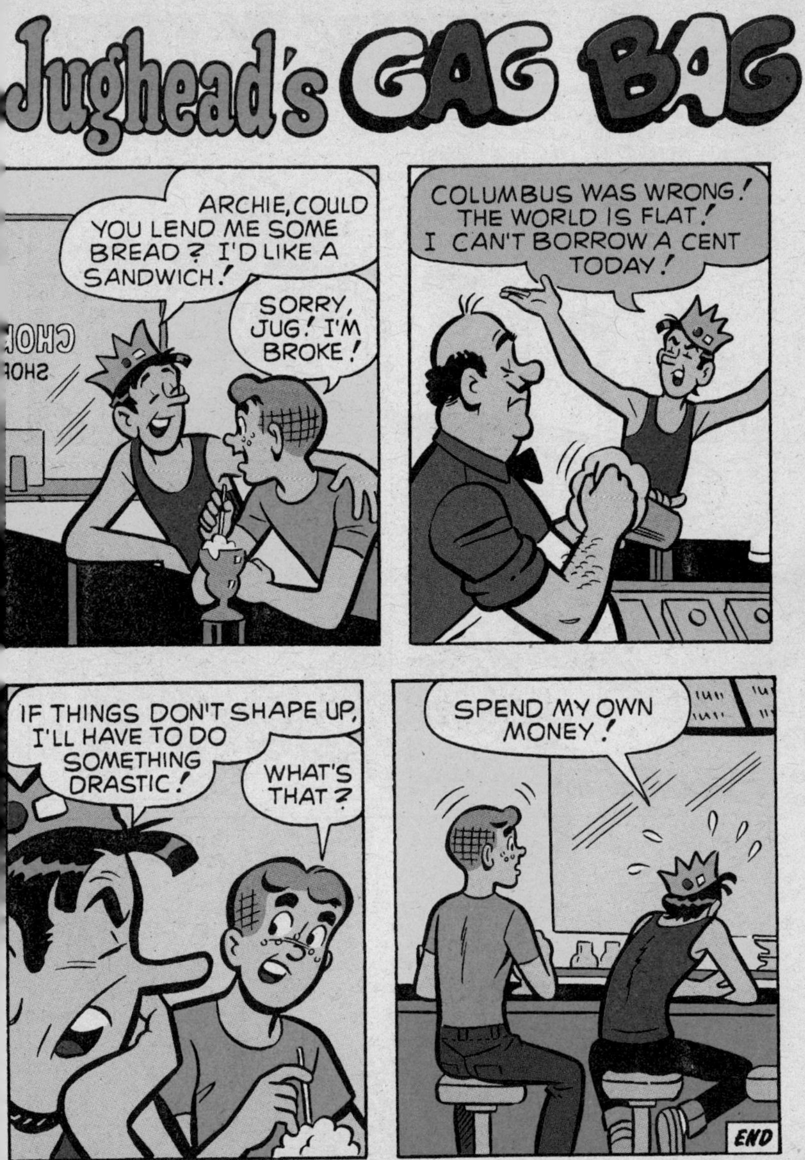
Jughead's GAG BAG
ARCHIE, COULD YOU LEND ME SOME BREAD? I'D LIKE A SANDWICH!
SORRY, JUG! I'M BROKE!
CHO
SHO
COLUMBUS WAS WRONG! THE WORLD IS FLAT! I CAN'T BORROW A CENT TODAY!
IF THINGS DON'T SHAPE UP, I'LL HAVE TO DO SOMETHING DRASTIC!
WHAT'S THAT?
SPEND MY OWN MONEY!
END

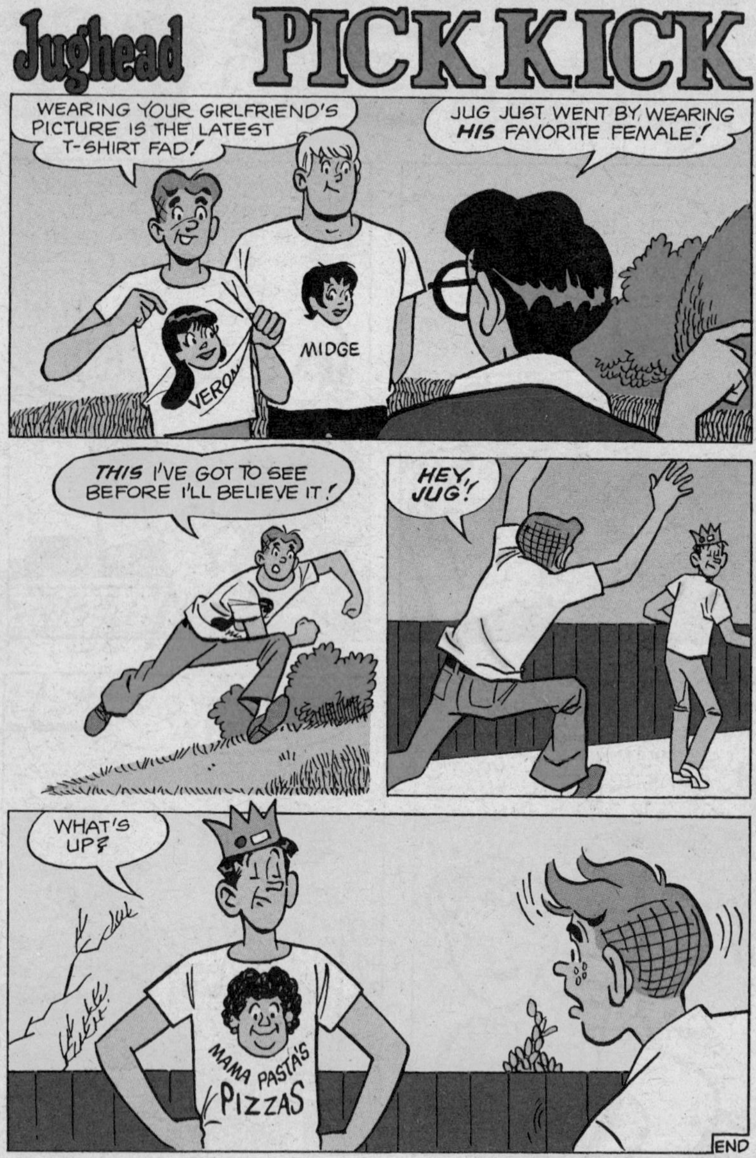
Jughead
PICK KICK
WEARING YOUR GIRLFRIEND'S PICTURE IS THE LATEST T-SHIRT FAD!
MIDGE
JUG JUST WENT BY, WEARING HIS FAVORITE FEMALE!
THIS I'VE GOT TO SEE BEFORE I'LL BELIEVE IT!
HEY, JUG!
WHAT'S UP?
MAMA PASTA'S PIZZAS
END

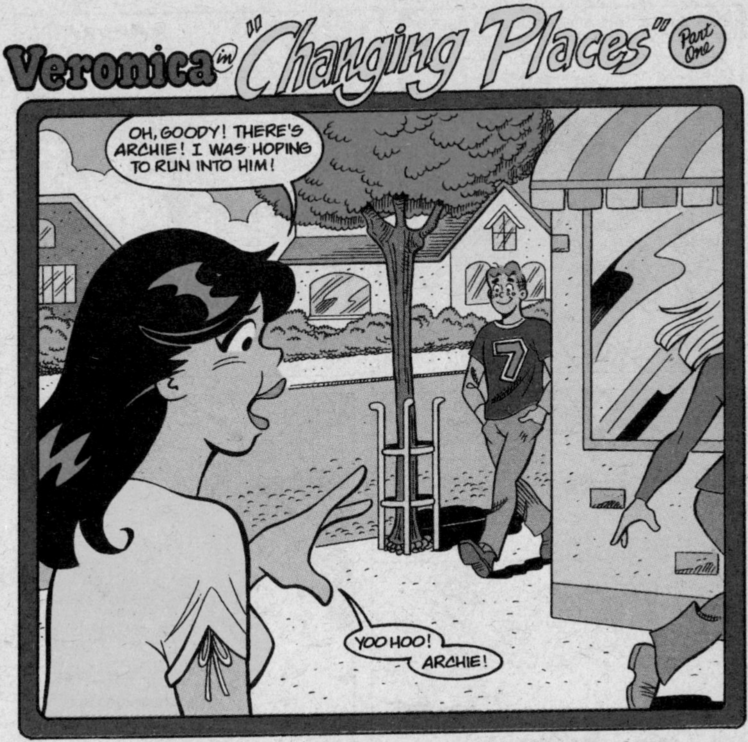
Veronica in "Changing Places" Part One
OH, GOODY! THERE'S ARCHIE! I WAS HOPING TO RUN INTO HIM!
YOO HOO! ARCHIE!

Script & Pencils: Dan Parent / Inks: Jim Amash / Letters: Vickie Williams / Colors: Barry Grossman

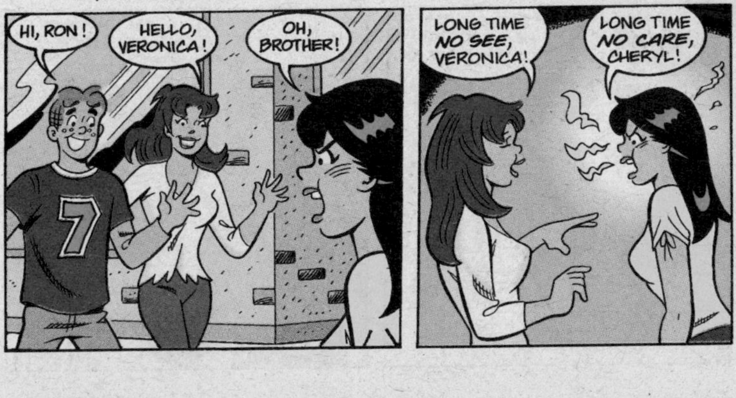
HI, RON!
HELLO, VERONICA!
OH, BROTHER!
LONG TIME NO SEE, VERONICA!
LONG TIME NO CARE, CHERYL!

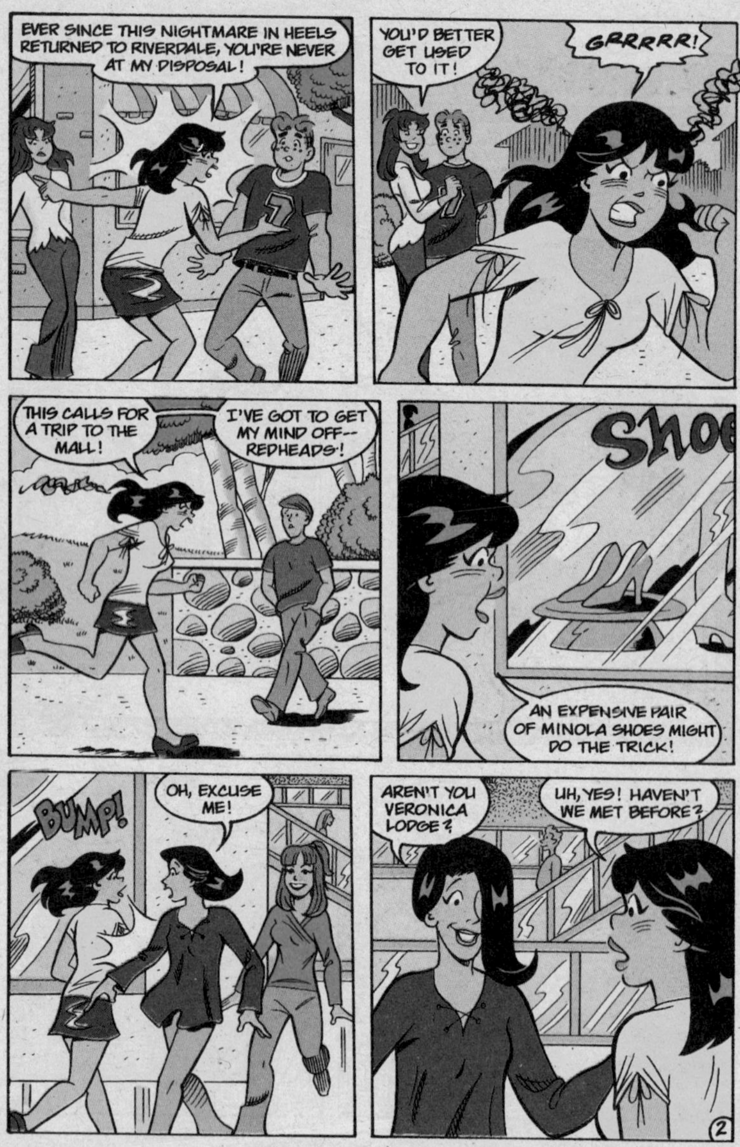
EVER SINCE THIS NIGHTMARE IN HEELS RETURNED TO RIVERDALE, YOU'RE NEVER AT MY DISPOSAL!
YOU'D BETTER GET USED TO IT!
GRRRRR!
THIS CALLS FOR A TRIP TO THE MALL!
I'VE GOT TO GET MY MIND OFF-- REDHEADS!
SHOE
AN EXPENSIVE PAIR OF MINOLA SHOES MIGHT DO THE TRICK!
BUMP!
OH, EXCUSE ME!
AREN'T YOU VERONICA LODGE?
UH, YES! HAVEN'T WE MET BEFORE?

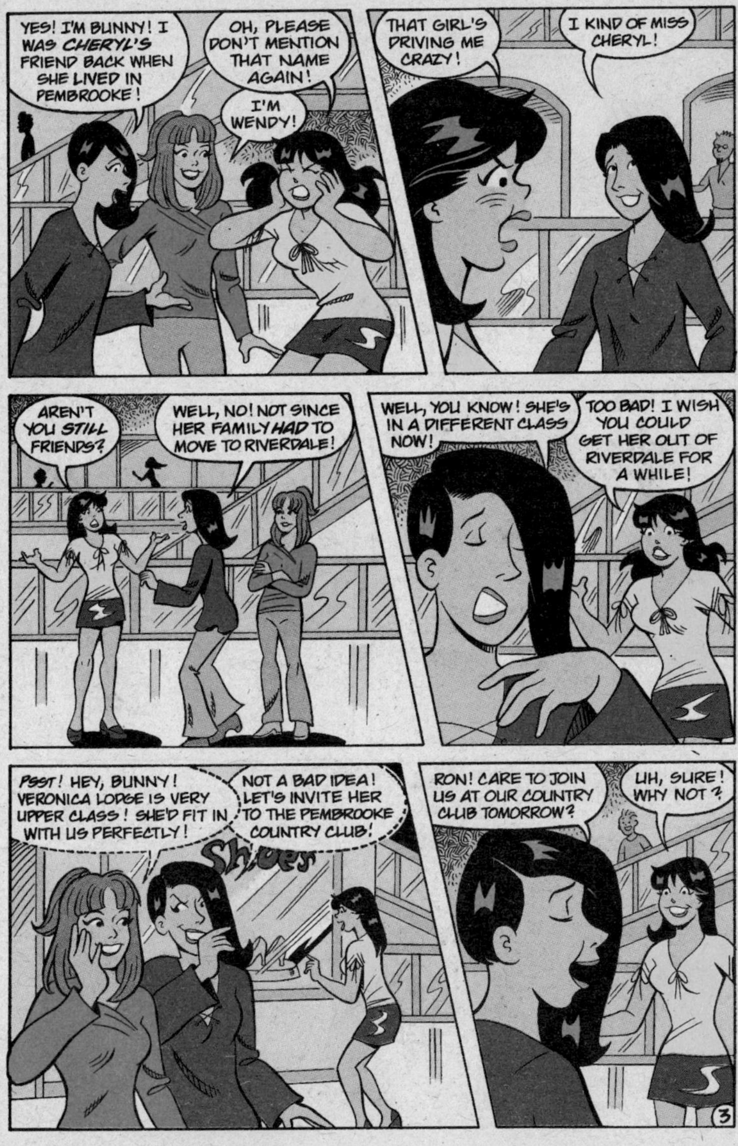
YES! I'M BUNNY! I WAS CHERYL'S FRIEND BACK WHEN SHE LIVED IN PEMBROOKE!
OH, PLEASE DON'T MENTION THAT NAME AGAIN!
I'M WENDY!
THAT GIRL'S DRIVING ME CRAZY!
I KIND OF MISS CHERYL!
AREN'T YOU STILL FRIENDS?
WELL, NO! NOT SINCE HER FAMILY HAD TO MOVE TO RIVERDALE!
WELL, YOU KNOW! SHE'S IN A DIFFERENT CLASS NOW!
TOO BAD! I WISH YOU COULD GET HER OUT OF RIVERDALE FOR A WHILE!
PSST! HEY, BUNNY! VERONICA LODGE IS VERY UPPER CLASS! SHE'D FIT IN WITH US PERFECTLY!
NOT A BAD IDEA! LET'S INVITE HER TO THE PEMBROOKE COUNTRY CLUB!
SHOES
RON! CARE TO JOIN US AT OUR COUNTRY CLUB TOMORROW?
UH, SURE! WHY NOT?
3

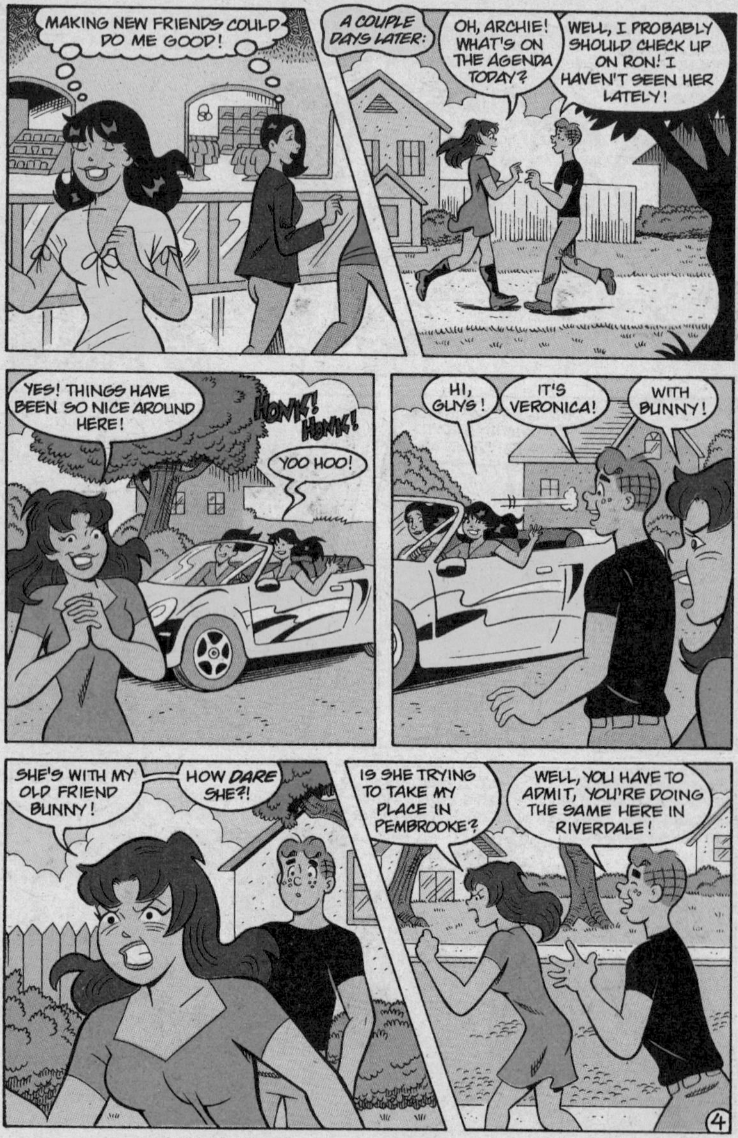
MAKING NEW FRIENDS COULD DO ME GOOD!
A COUPLE DAYS LATER:
OH, ARCHIE! WHAT'S ON THE AGENDA TODAY?
WELL, I PROBABLY SHOULD CHECK UP ON RON! I HAVEN'T SEEN HER LATELY!
YES! THINGS HAVE BEEN SO NICE AROUND HERE!
HONK! HONK!
YOO HOO!
HI, GUYS!
IT'S VERONICA!
WITH BUNNY!
SHE'S WITH MY OLD FRIEND BUNNY!
HOW DARE SHE?!
IS SHE TRYING TO TAKE MY PLACE IN PEMBROOKE?
WELL, YOU HAVE TO ADMIT, YOU'RE DOING THE SAME HERE IN RIVERDALE!
4

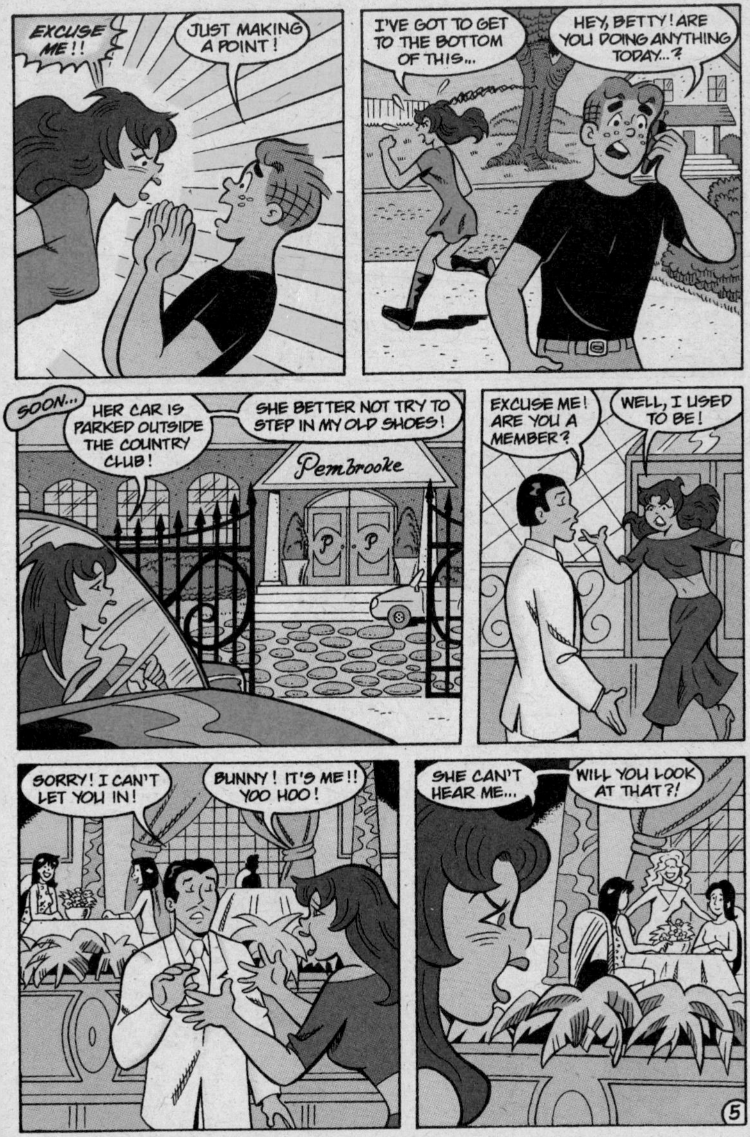
EXCUSE ME!!
JUST MAKING A POINT!
I'VE GOT TO GET TO THE BOTTOM OF THIS...
HEY, BETTY! ARE YOU DOING ANYTHING TODAY...?
SOON...
HER CAR IS PARKED OUTSIDE THE COUNTRY CLUB!
SHE BETTER NOT TRY TO STEP IN MY OLD SHOES!
Pembrooke
EXCUSE ME! ARE YOU A MEMBER?
WELL, I USED TO BE!
SORRY! I CAN'T LET YOU IN!
BUNNY! IT'S ME!! YOO HOO!
SHE CAN'T HEAR ME...
WILL YOU LOOK AT THAT?!
5

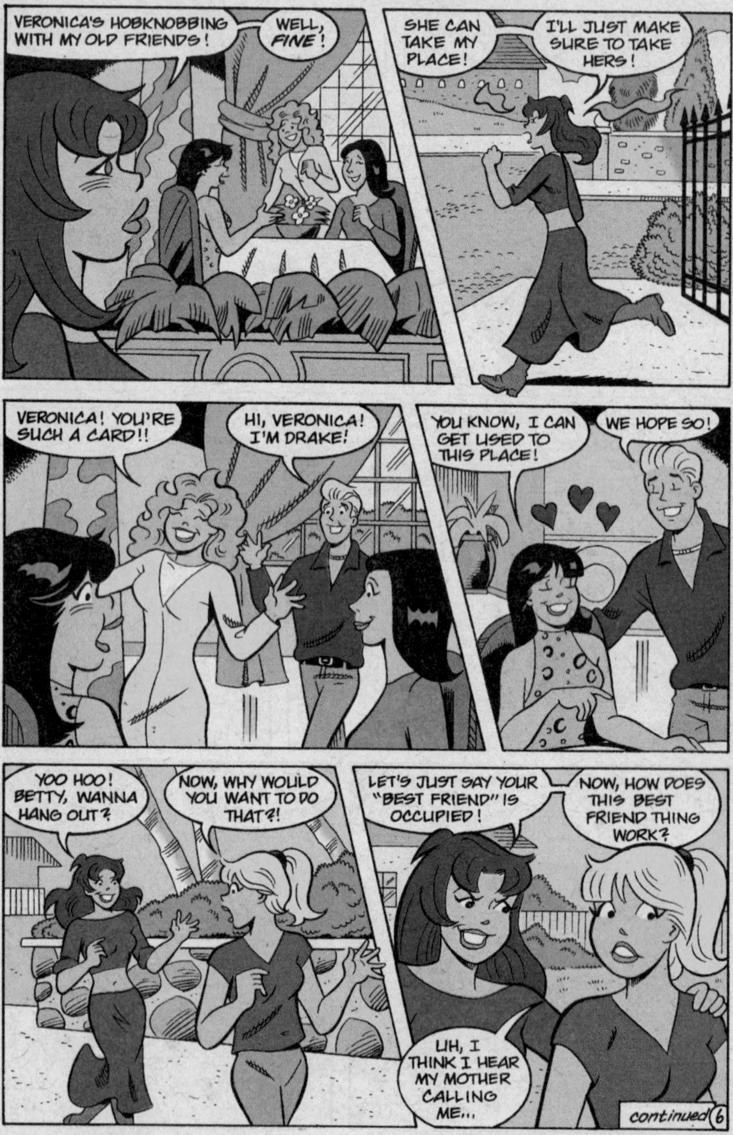
VERONICA'S HOBKNOBBING WITH MY OLD FRIENDS!
WELL, FINE!
SHE CAN TAKE MY PLACE!
I'LL JUST MAKE SURE TO TAKE HERS!
VERONICA! YOU'RE SUCH A CARD!!
HI, VERONICA! I'M DRAKE!
YOU KNOW, I CAN GET USED TO THIS PLACE!
WE HOPE SO!
YOO HOO! BETTY, WANNA HANG OUT?
NOW, WHY WOULD YOU WANT TO DO THAT?!
LET'S JUST SAY YOUR "BEST FRIEND" IS OCCUPIED!
NOW, HOW DOES THIS BEST FRIEND THING WORK?
UH, I THINK I HEAR MY MOTHER CALLING ME...
continued 6

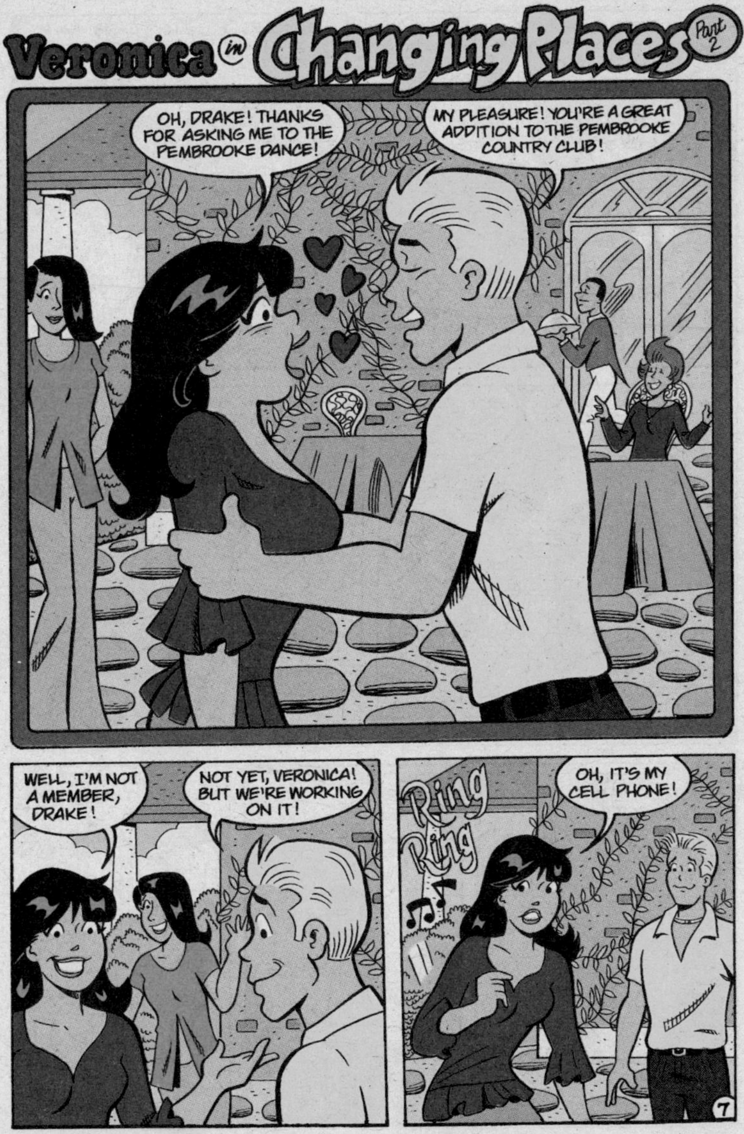
Veronica in Changing Places Part 2
OH, DRAKE! THANKS FOR ASKING ME TO THE PEMBROOKE DANCE!
MY PLEASURE! YOU'RE A GREAT ADDITION TO THE PEMBROOKE COUNTRY CLUB!
WELL, I'M NOT A MEMBER, DRAKE!
NOT YET, VERONICA! BUT WE'RE WORKING ON IT!
Ring Ring
OH, IT'S MY CELL PHONE!
7

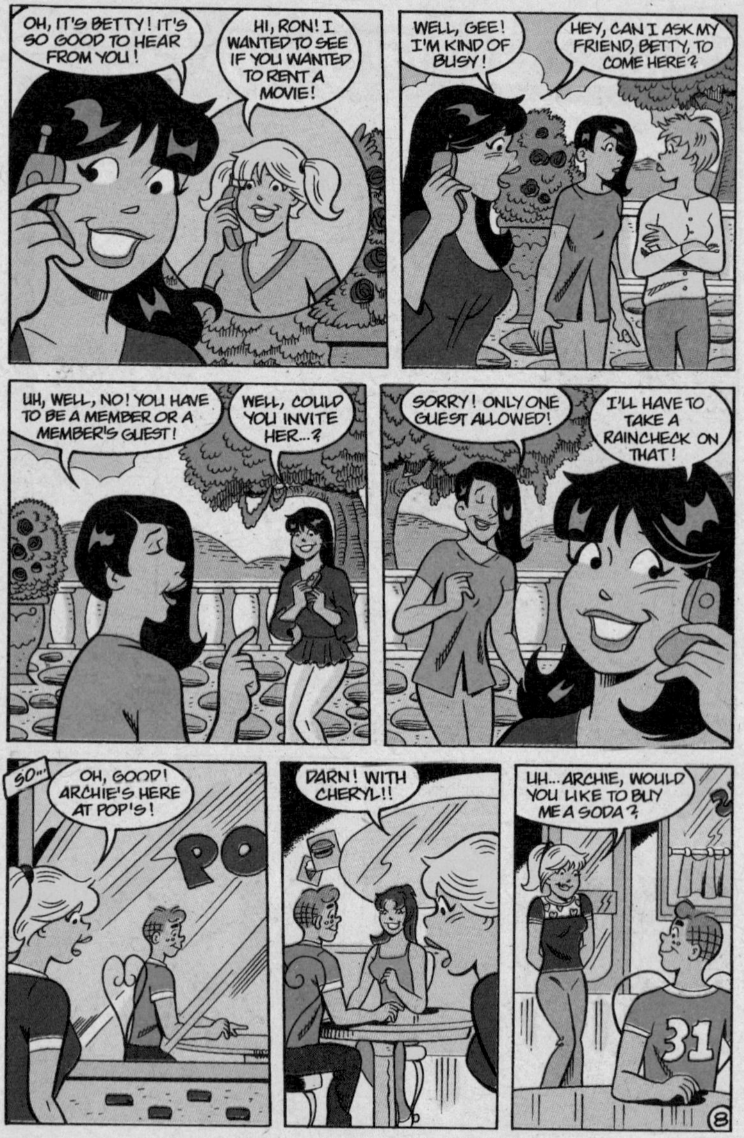
OH, IT'S BETTY! IT'S SO GOOD TO HEAR FROM YOU!
HI, RON! I WANTED TO SEE IF YOU WANTED TO RENT A MOVIE!
WELL, GEE! I'M KIND OF BUSY!
HEY, CAN I ASK MY FRIEND, BETTY, TO COME HERE?
UH, WELL, NO! YOU HAVE TO BE A MEMBER OR A MEMBER'S GUEST!
WELL, COULD YOU INVITE HER...?
SORRY! ONLY ONE GUEST ALLOWED!
I'LL HAVE TO TAKE A RAINCHECK ON THAT!
SO...
OH, GOOD! ARCHIE'S HERE AT POP'S!
PO
DARN! WITH CHERYL!!
UH... ARCHIE, WOULD YOU LIKE TO BUY ME A SODA?
31
8

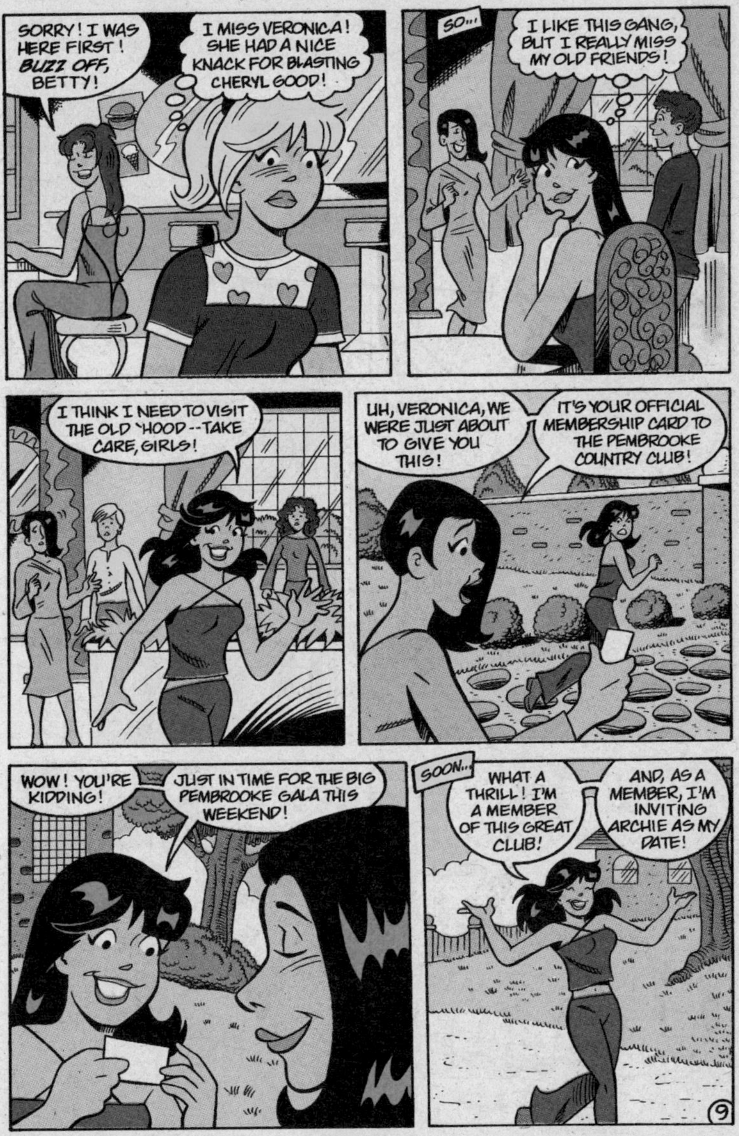
SORRY! I WAS HERE FIRST! BUZZ OFF, BETTY!
I MISS VERONICA! SHE HAD A NICE KNACK FOR BLASTING CHERYL GOOD!
SO...
I LIKE THIS GANG, BUT I REALLY MISS MY OLD FRIENDS!
I THINK I NEED TO VISIT THE OLD 'HOOD--TAKE CARE, GIRLS!
UH, VERONICA, WE WERE JUST ABOUT TO GIVE YOU THIS!
IT'S YOUR OFFICIAL MEMBERSHIP CARD TO THE PEMBROOKE COUNTRY CLUB!
WOW! YOU'RE KIDDING!
JUST IN TIME FOR THE BIG PEMBROOKE GALA THIS WEEKEND!
SOON...
WHAT A THRILL! I'M A MEMBER OF THIS GREAT CLUB!
AND, AS A MEMBER, I'M INVITING ARCHIE AS MY DATE!
9

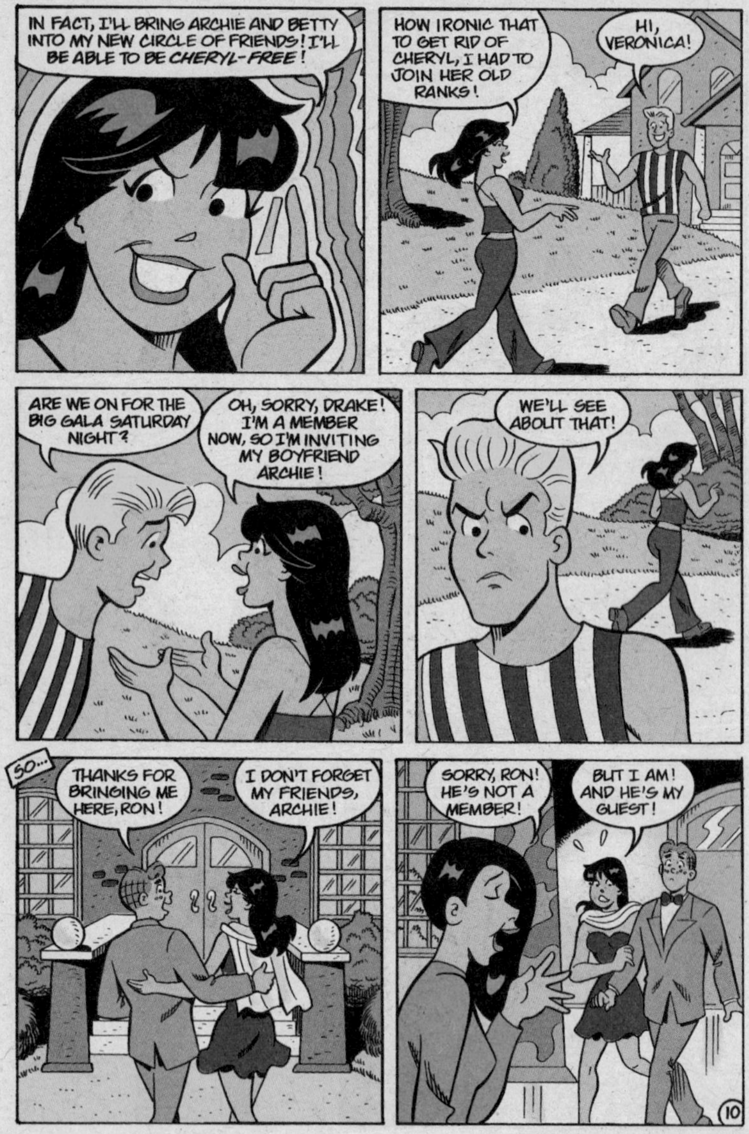
IN FACT, I'LL BRING ARCHIE AND BETTY INTO MY NEW CIRCLE OF FRIENDS! I'LL BE ABLE TO BE CHERYL-FREE!
HOW IRONIC THAT TO GET RID OF CHERYL, I HAD TO JOIN HER OLD RANKS!
HI, VERONICA!
ARE WE ON FOR THE BIG GALA SATURDAY NIGHT?
OH, SORRY, DRAKE! I'M A MEMBER NOW, SO I'M INVITING MY BOYFRIEND ARCHIE!
WE'LL SEE ABOUT THAT!
SO...
THANKS FOR BRINGING ME HERE, RON!
I DON'T FORGET MY FRIENDS, ARCHIE!
SORRY, RON! HE'S NOT A MEMBER!
BUT I AM! AND HE'S MY GUEST!
10

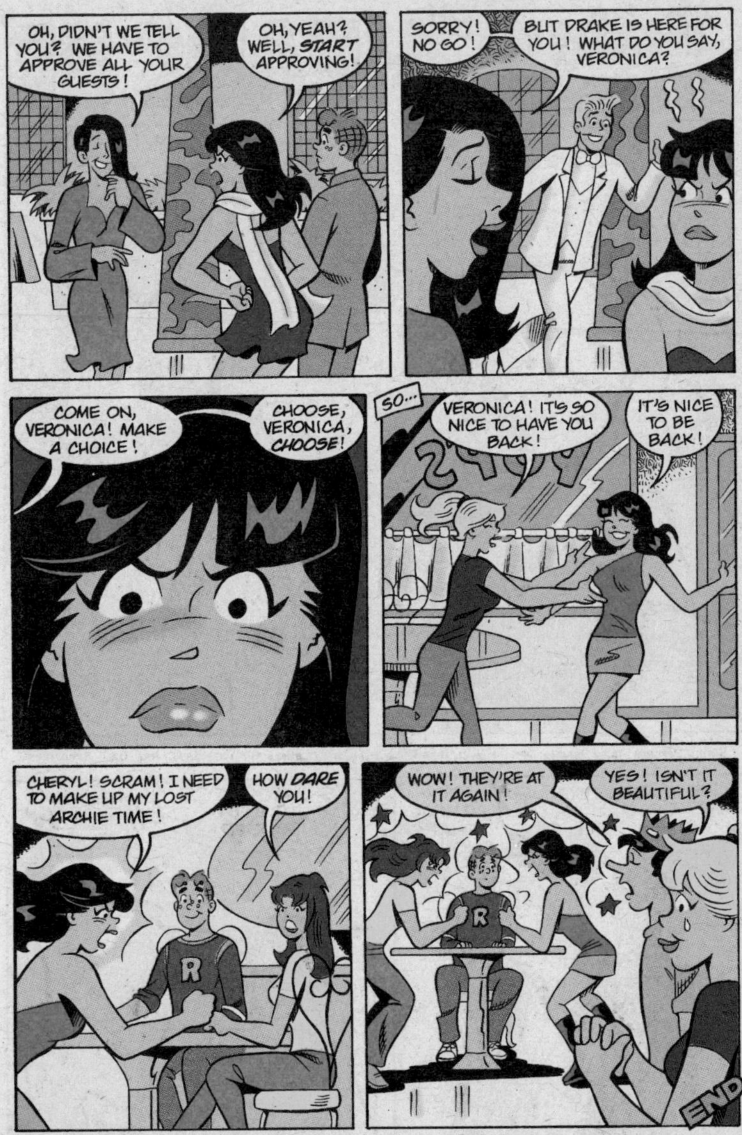
OH, DIDN'T WE TELL YOU? WE HAVE TO APPROVE ALL YOUR GUESTS!
OH, YEAH? WELL, START APPROVING!
SORRY! NO GO!
BUT DRAKE IS HERE FOR YOU! WHAT DO YOU SAY, VERONICA?
COME ON, VERONICA! MAKE A CHOICE!
CHOOSE, VERONICA, CHOOSE!
SO...
VERONICA! IT'S SO NICE TO HAVE YOU BACK!
IT'S NICE TO BE BACK!
CHERYL! SCRAM! I NEED TO MAKE UP MY LOST ARCHIE TIME!
HOW DARE YOU!
WOW! THEY'RE AT IT AGAIN!
YES! ISN'T IT BEAUTIFUL?
END

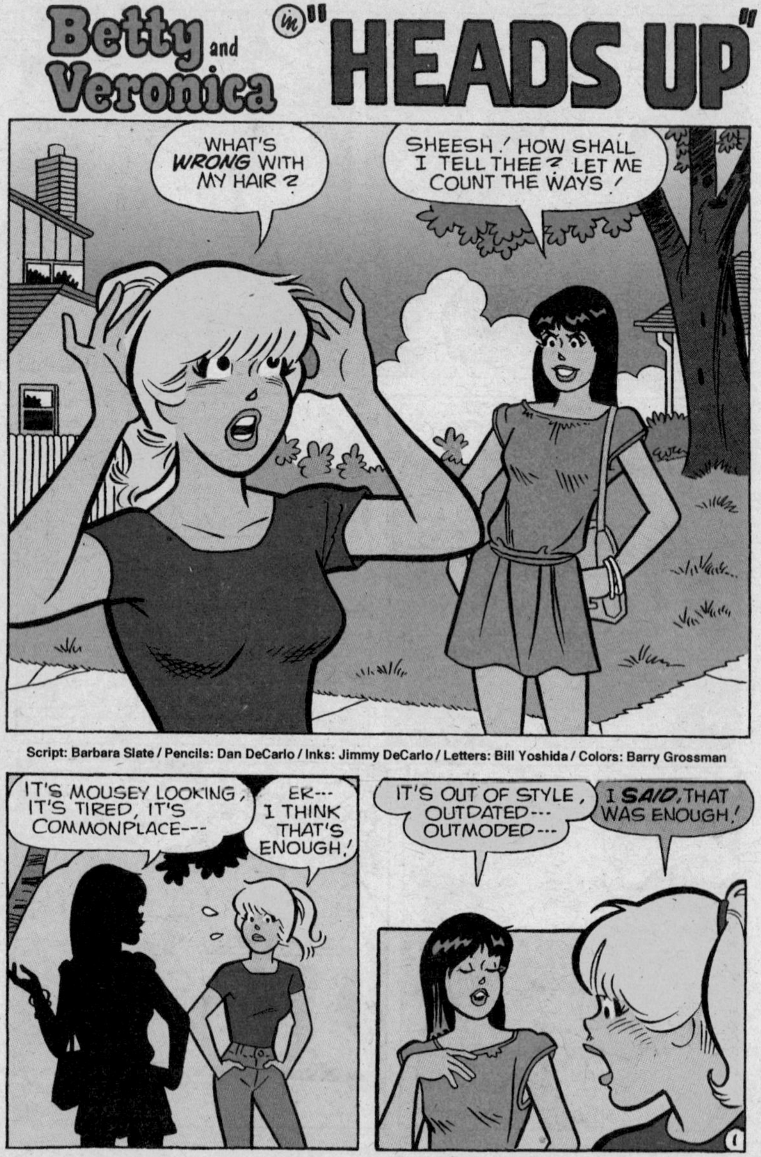
Betty and Veronica in "HEADS UP"
WHAT'S WRONG WITH MY HAIR?
SHEESH! HOW SHALL I TELL THEE? LET ME COUNT THE WAYS!
Script: Barbara Slate / Pencils: Dan DeCarlo / Inks: Jimmy DeCarlo / Letters: Bill Yoshida / Colors: Barry Grossman
IT'S MOUSEY LOOKING, IT'S TIRED, IT'S COMMONPLACE---
ER--- I THINK THAT'S ENOUGH!
IT'S OUT OF STYLE, OUTDATED--- OUTMODED---
I SAID, THAT WAS ENOUGH!
1

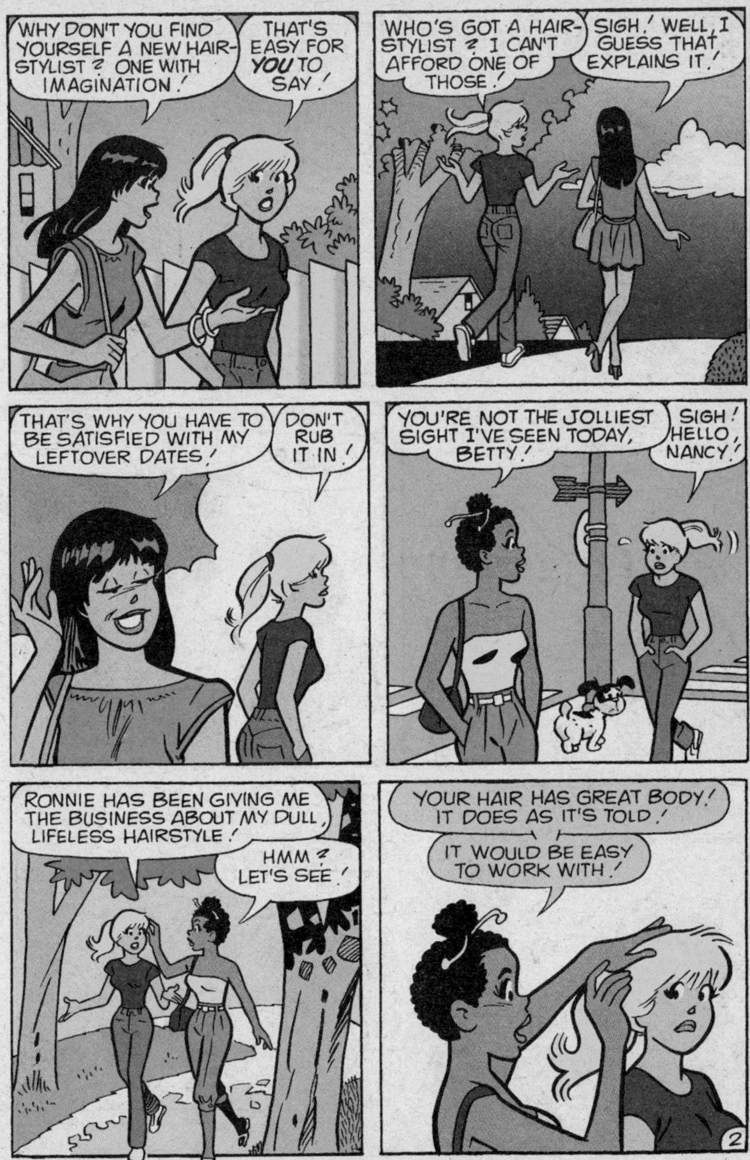
WHY DON'T YOU FIND YOURSELF A NEW HAIR-STYLIST? ONE WITH IMAGINATION!
THAT'S EASY FOR YOU TO SAY!
WHO'S GOT A HAIR-STYLIST? I CAN'T AFFORD ONE OF THOSE!
SIGH! WELL, I GUESS THAT EXPLAINS IT!
THAT'S WHY YOU HAVE TO BE SATISFIED WITH MY LEFTOVER DATES!
DON'T RUB IT IN!
YOU'RE NOT THE JOLLIEST SIGHT I'VE SEEN TODAY, BETTY!
SIGH! HELLO, NANCY!
RONNIE HAS BEEN GIVING ME THE BUSINESS ABOUT MY DULL, LIFELESS HAIRSTYLE!
HMM? LET'S SEE!
YOUR HAIR HAS GREAT BODY! IT DOES AS IT'S TOLD!
IT WOULD BE EASY TO WORK WITH!
2

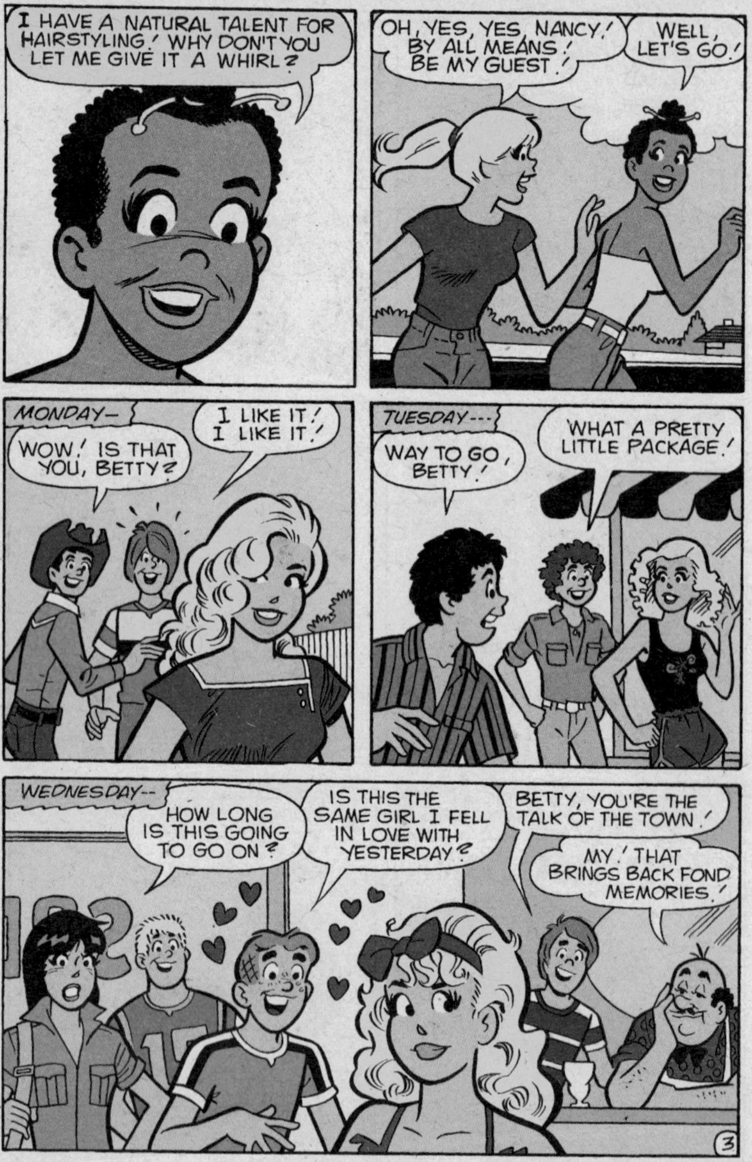
I HAVE A NATURAL TALENT FOR HAIRSTYLING! WHY DON'T YOU LET ME GIVE IT A WHIRL?
OH, YES, YES, NANCY! BY ALL MEANS! BE MY GUEST!
WELL, LET'S GO!
MONDAY—
WOW! IS THAT YOU, BETTY?
I LIKE IT! I LIKE IT!
TUESDAY---
WAY TO GO, BETTY!
WHAT A PRETTY LITTLE PACKAGE!
WEDNESDAY--
HOW LONG IS THIS GOING TO GO ON?
IS THIS THE SAME GIRL I FELL IN LOVE WITH YESTERDAY?
BETTY, YOU'RE THE TALK OF THE TOWN!
MY! THAT BRINGS BACK FOND MEMORIES!
3

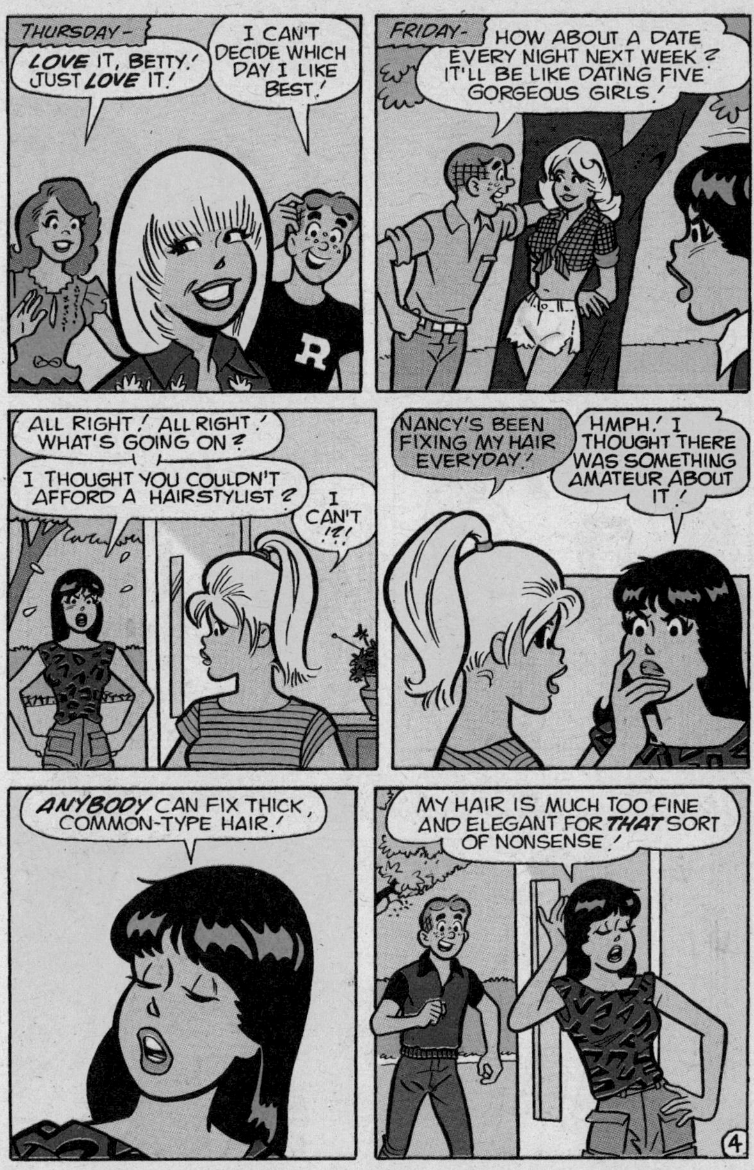
THURSDAY -
LOVE IT, BETTY! JUST LOVE IT!
I CAN'T DECIDE WHICH DAY I LIKE BEST!
FRIDAY -
HOW ABOUT A DATE EVERY NIGHT NEXT WEEK? IT'LL BE LIKE DATING FIVE GORGEOUS GIRLS!
ALL RIGHT! ALL RIGHT! WHAT'S GOING ON?
I THOUGHT YOU COULDN'T AFFORD A HAIRSTYLIST?
I CAN'T !?!
NANCY'S BEEN FIXING MY HAIR EVERYDAY!
HMPH! I THOUGHT THERE WAS SOMETHING AMATEUR ABOUT IT!
ANYBODY CAN FIX THICK, COMMON-TYPE HAIR!
MY HAIR IS MUCH TOO FINE AND ELEGANT FOR THAT SORT OF NONSENSE!
4

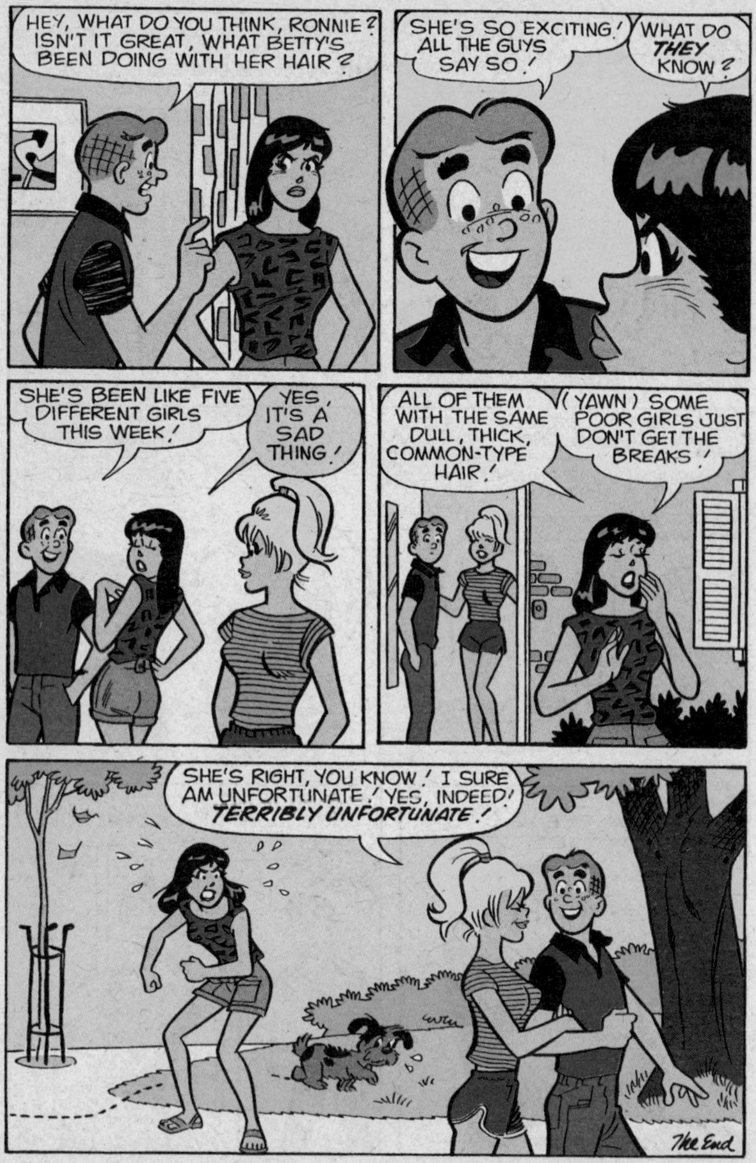
HEY, WHAT DO YOU THINK, RONNIE? ISN'T IT GREAT, WHAT BETTY'S BEEN DOING WITH HER HAIR?
SHE'S SO EXCITING! ALL THE GUYS SAY SO!
WHAT DO THEY KNOW?
SHE'S BEEN LIKE FIVE DIFFERENT GIRLS THIS WEEK!
YES, IT'S A SAD THING!
ALL OF THEM WITH THE SAME DULL, THICK, COMMON-TYPE HAIR!
(YAWN) SOME POOR GIRLS JUST DON'T GET THE BREAKS!
SHE'S RIGHT, YOU KNOW! I SURE AM UNFORTUNATE! YES, INDEED! TERRIBLY UNFORTUNATE!
The End

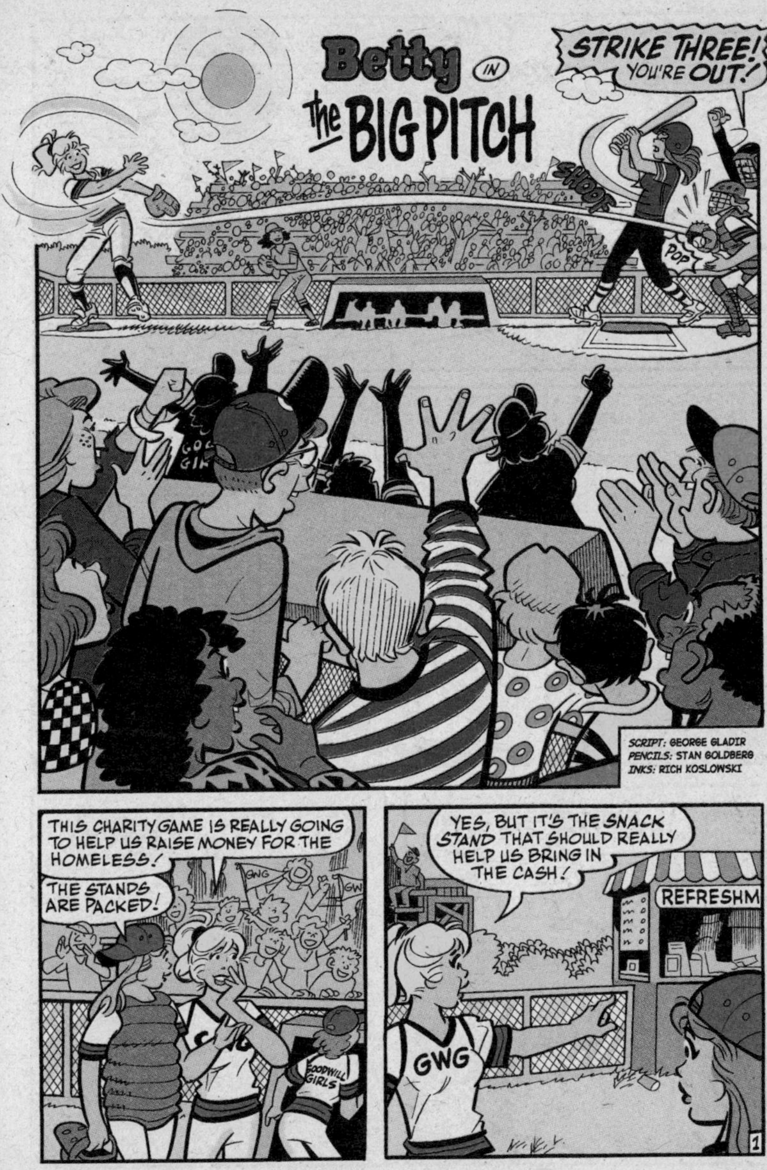

Betty IN the BIG PITCH
STRIKE THREE! YOU'RE OUT!
SHOOP
POP
SCRIPT: GEORGE GLADIR
PENCILS: STAN GOLDBERG
INKS: RICH KOSLOWSKI
THIS CHARITY GAME IS REALLY GOING TO HELP US RAISE MONEY FOR THE HOMELESS!
THE STANDS ARE PACKED!
GWG
GOODWILL GIRLS
YES, BUT IT'S THE SNACK STAND THAT SHOULD REALLY HELP US BRING IN THE CASH!
REFRESHM
GWG

ARCHIE, WE REALLY APPRECIATE YOU VOLUNTEERING TO HELP SELL HOT DOGS!

THE FOLKS ARE COMPLAINING THAT THEY'RE A BIT *BURNED!*

GOODWILL GIRLS BETTY

HOT★ DOGS

LET'S GO CHECK OUT THE *REFRESHMENT* STAND!

WG

VERONICA, YOU HAVE THE GRILL FLAMES UP MUCH TOO HIGH! THE FRANKS ARE GETTING *BURNED!*

Oh, DEAR!

THERE! I TURNED THE FLAMES DOWN A BIT. THAT SHOULD TAKE CARE OF THE PROBLEM!

GOODWILL GIRLS

C'MON, BETTY! WE HAVE TO TAKE THE FIELD!

ARCHIE, WHY DON'T YOU RUN UP TO THE PRESS BOX AND MAKE A PITCH FOR OUR SNACK BAR?

GWG

GOODWILL GIRLS BETTY

GWG

PRESS BOX

2

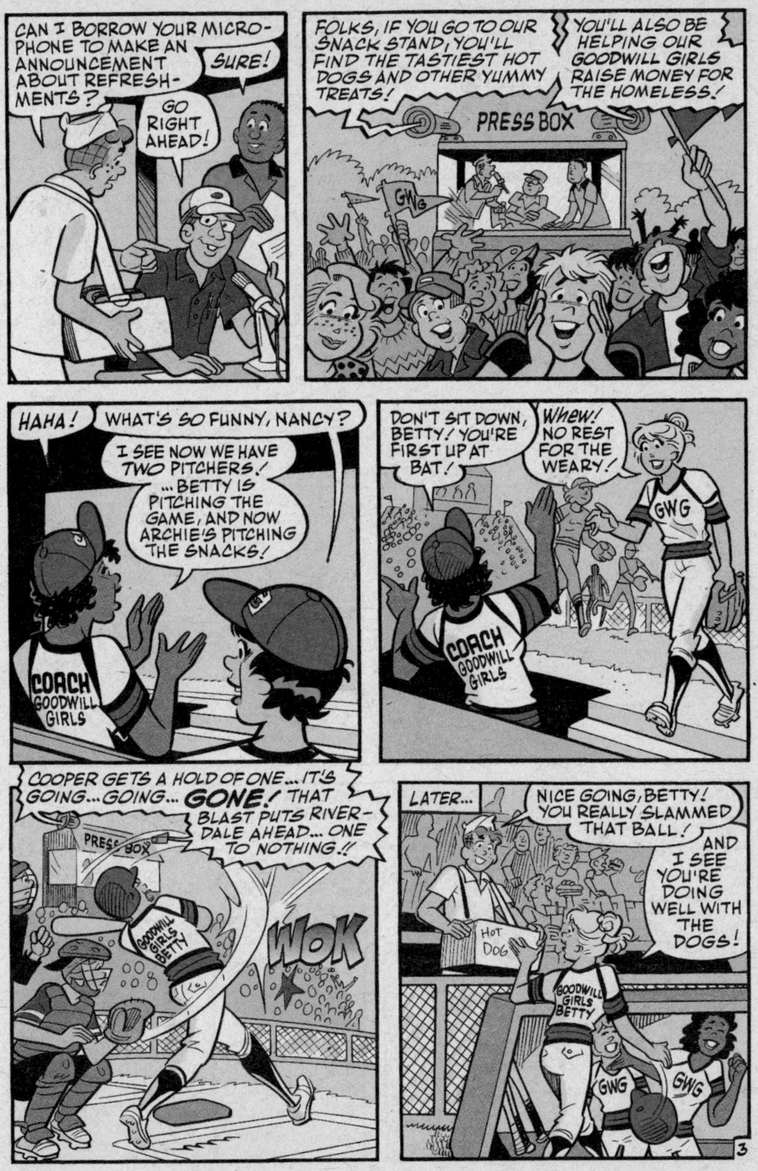
CAN I BORROW YOUR MICRO-PHONE TO MAKE AN ANNOUNCEMENT ABOUT REFRESH-MENTS?
SURE!
GO RIGHT AHEAD!
FOLKS, IF YOU GO TO OUR SNACK STAND, YOU'LL FIND THE TASTIEST HOT DOGS AND OTHER YUMMY TREATS!
YOU'LL ALSO BE HELPING OUR GOODWILL GIRLS RAISE MONEY FOR THE HOMELESS!
PRESS BOX
GWG
HAHA!
WHAT'S SO FUNNY, NANCY?
I SEE NOW WE HAVE TWO PITCHERS! ...BETTY IS PITCHING THE GAME, AND NOW ARCHIE'S PITCHING THE SNACKS!
COACH GOODWILL GIRLS
DON'T SIT DOWN, BETTY! YOU'RE FIRST UP AT BAT!
WHEW! NO REST FOR THE WEARY!
GWG
COACH GOODWILL GIRLS
COOPER GETS A HOLD OF ONE... IT'S GOING... GOING... GONE! THAT BLAST PUTS RIVER-DALE AHEAD... ONE TO NOTHING!!
PRESS BOX
GOODWILL GIRLS BETTY
WOK
LATER...
NICE GOING, BETTY! YOU REALLY SLAMMED THAT BALL!
AND I SEE YOU'RE DOING WELL WITH THE DOGS!
HOT DOG
GOODWILL GIRLS BETTY
GWG
GWG

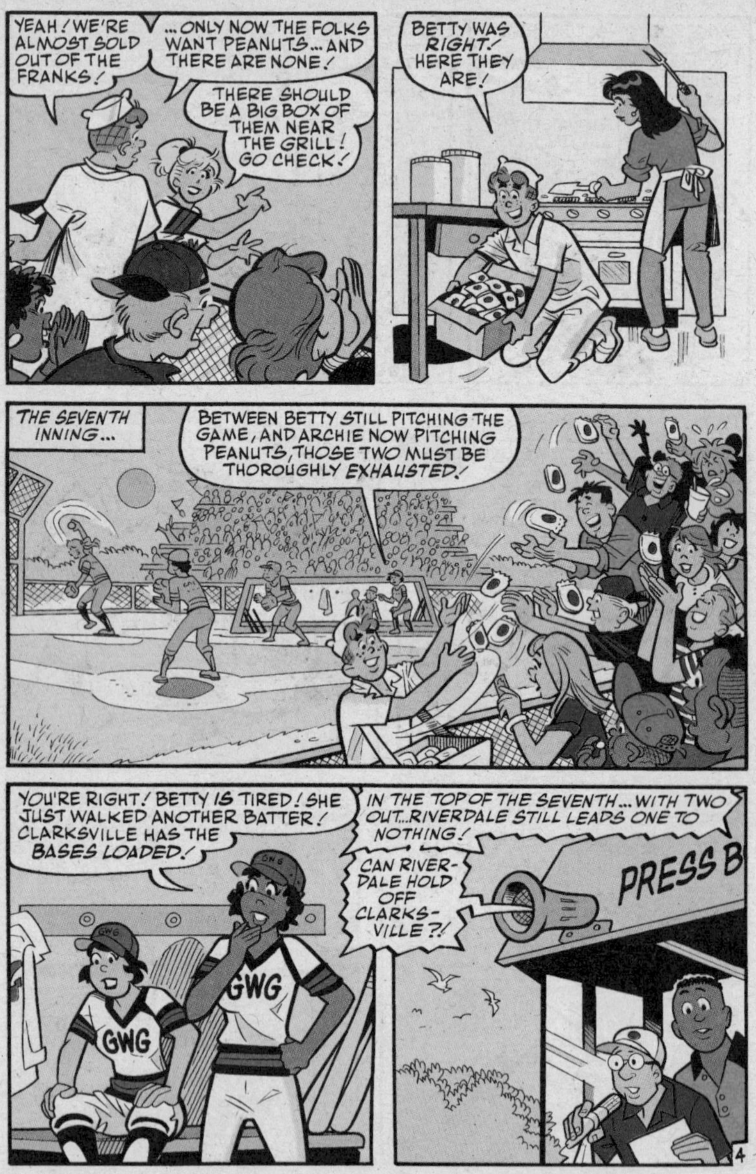
YEAH! WE'RE ALMOST SOLD OUT OF THE FRANKS!
...ONLY NOW THE FOLKS WANT PEANUTS... AND THERE ARE NONE!
THERE SHOULD BE A BIG BOX OF THEM NEAR THE GRILL! GO CHECK!
BETTY WAS RIGHT! HERE THEY ARE!
THE SEVENTH INNING...
BETWEEN BETTY STILL PITCHING THE GAME, AND ARCHIE NOW PITCHING PEANUTS, THOSE TWO MUST BE THOROUGHLY EXHAUSTED!
YOU'RE RIGHT! BETTY IS TIRED! SHE JUST WALKED ANOTHER BATTER! CLARKSVILLE HAS THE BASES LOADED!
GWG
GWG
IN THE TOP OF THE SEVENTH... WITH TWO OUT...RIVERDALE STILL LEADS ONE TO NOTHING!
CAN RIVERDALE HOLD OFF CLARKSVILLE?!
PRESS B
4

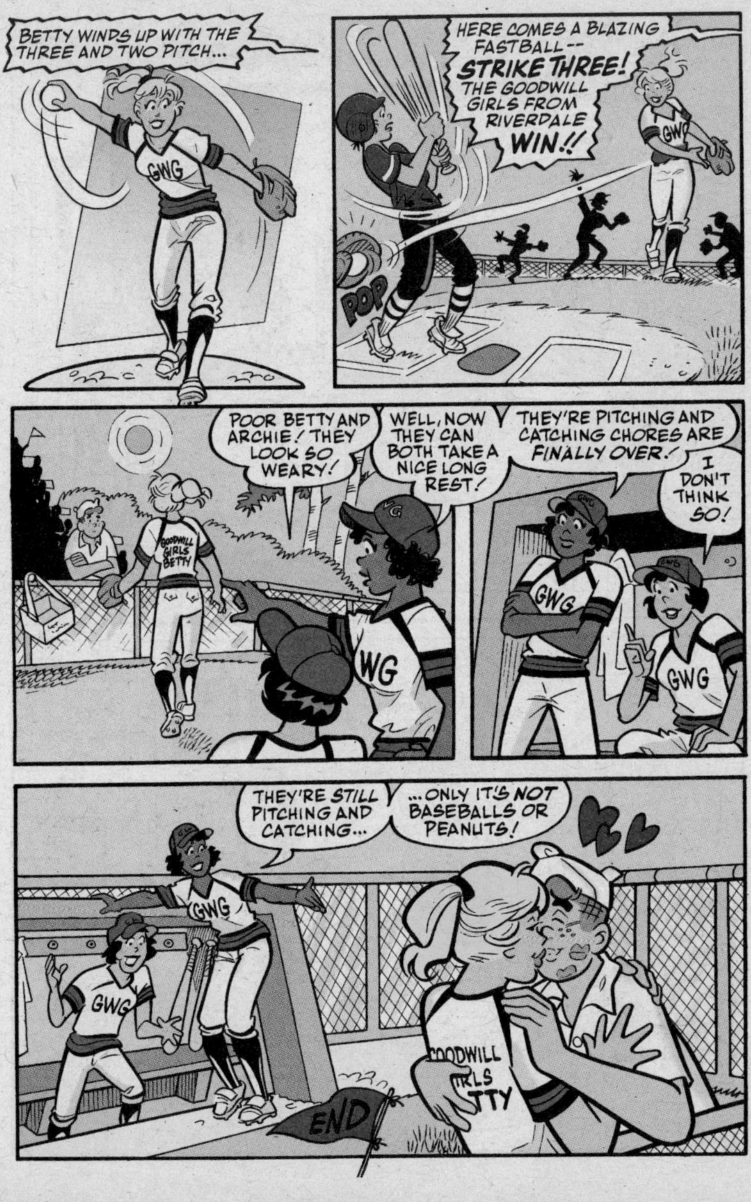
BETTY WINDS UP WITH THE THREE AND TWO PITCH...
HERE COMES A BLAZING FASTBALL-- STRIKE THREE! THE GOODWILL GIRLS FROM RIVERDALE WIN!!
POP
GWG
POOR BETTY AND ARCHIE! THEY LOOK SO WEARY!
WELL, NOW THEY CAN BOTH TAKE A NICE LONG REST!
GOODWILL GIRLS BETTY
THEY'RE PITCHING AND CATCHING CHORES ARE FINALLY OVER!
I DON'T THINK SO!
THEY'RE STILL PITCHING AND CATCHING...
...ONLY IT'S NOT BASEBALLS OR PEANUTS!
END

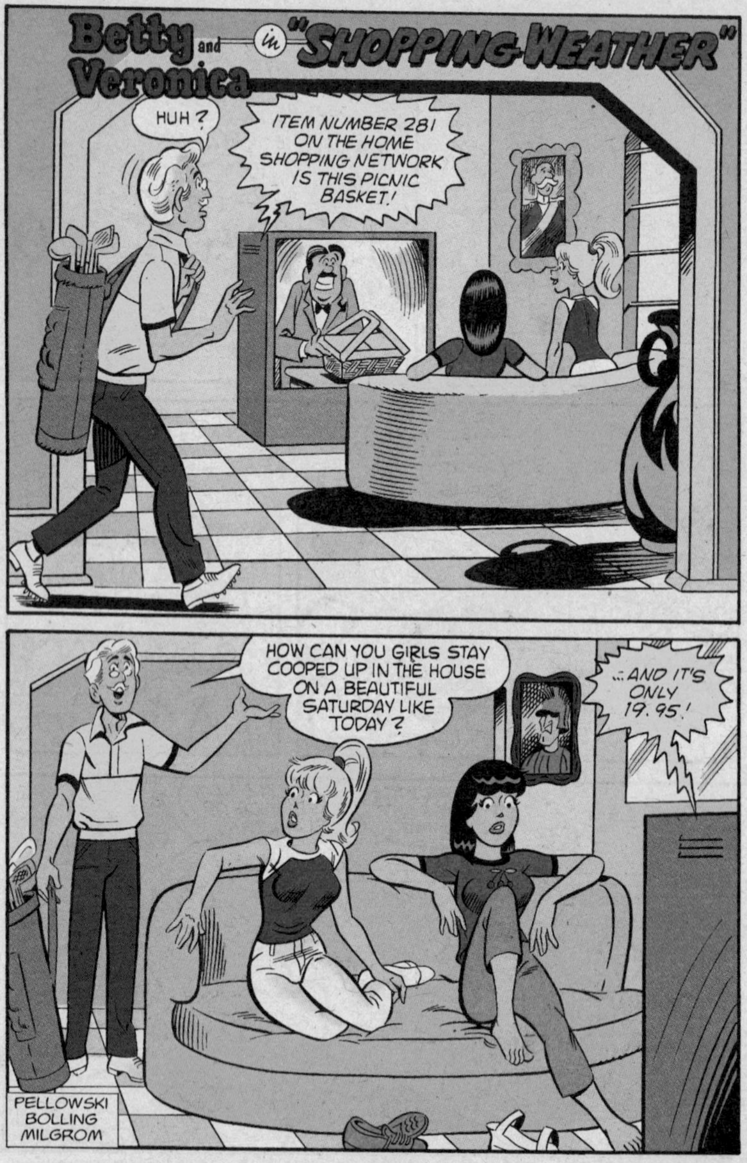

Betty and Veronica in "SHOPPING WEATHER"
HUH ?
ITEM NUMBER 281 ON THE HOME SHOPPING NETWORK IS THIS PICNIC BASKET!
HOW CAN YOU GIRLS STAY COOPED UP IN THE HOUSE ON A BEAUTIFUL SATURDAY LIKE TODAY ?
...AND IT'S ONLY 19.95!
PELLOWSKI BOLLING MILGROM

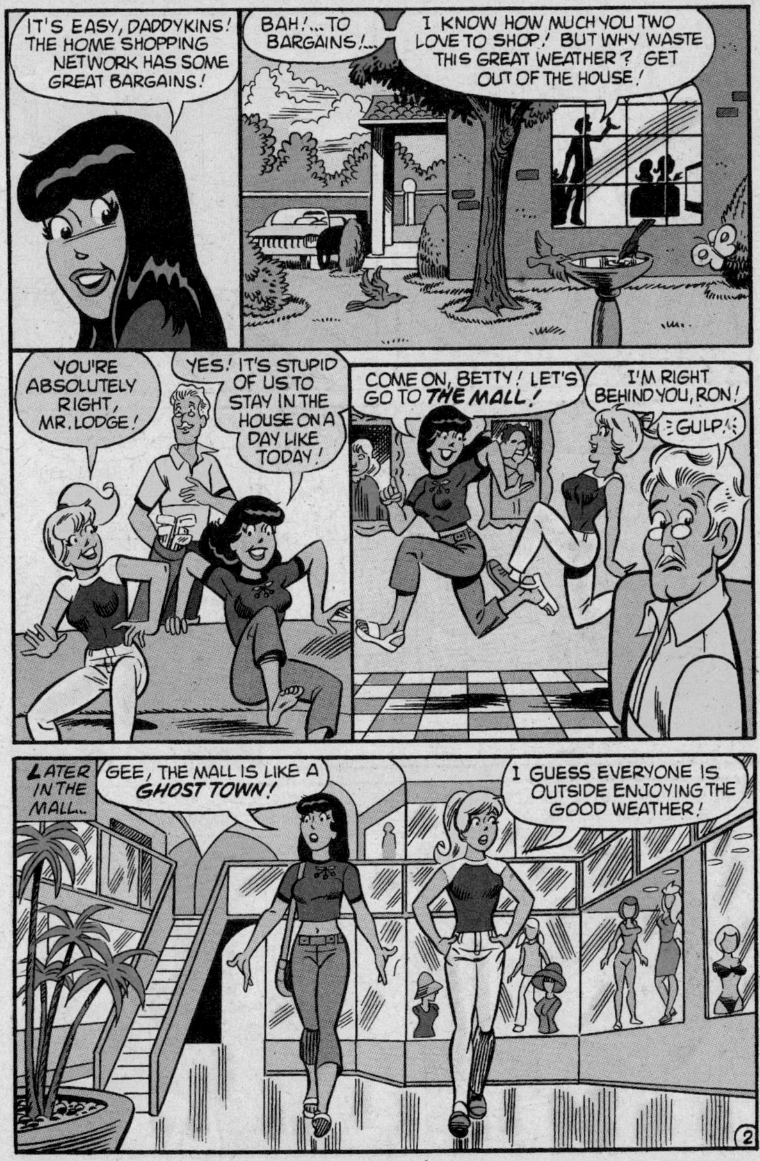
IT'S EASY, DADDYKINS! THE HOME SHOPPING NETWORK HAS SOME GREAT BARGAINS!
BAH!...TO BARGAINS!...
I KNOW HOW MUCH YOU TWO LOVE TO SHOP! BUT WHY WASTE THIS GREAT WEATHER? GET OUT OF THE HOUSE!
YOU'RE ABSOLUTELY RIGHT, MR. LODGE!
YES! IT'S STUPID OF US TO STAY IN THE HOUSE ON A DAY LIKE TODAY!
COME ON, BETTY! LET'S GO TO THE MALL!
I'M RIGHT BEHIND YOU, RON!
GULP!
LATER IN THE MALL...
GEE, THE MALL IS LIKE A GHOST TOWN!
I GUESS EVERYONE IS OUTSIDE ENJOYING THE GOOD WEATHER!
2

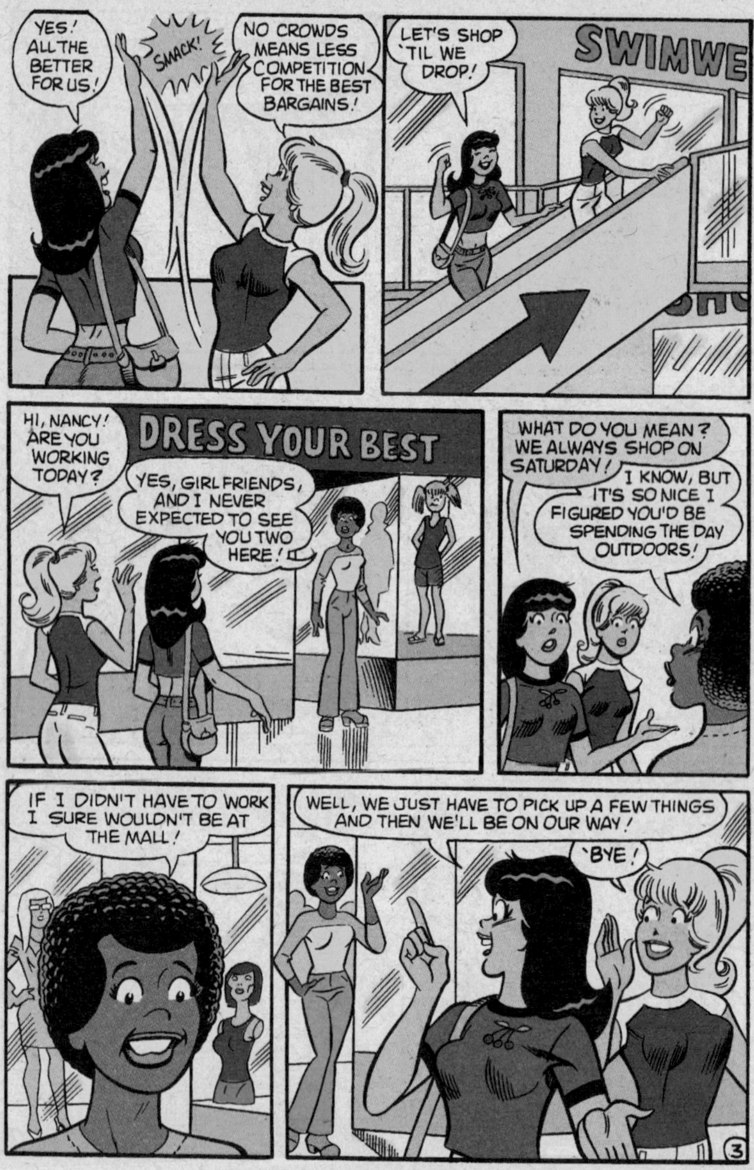
YES! ALL THE BETTER FOR US!
SMACK!
NO CROWDS MEANS LESS COMPETITION FOR THE BEST BARGAINS!
LET'S SHOP 'TIL WE DROP!
SWIMWE
HI, NANCY! ARE YOU WORKING TODAY?
DRESS YOUR BEST
YES, GIRLFRIENDS, AND I NEVER EXPECTED TO SEE YOU TWO HERE!
WHAT DO YOU MEAN? WE ALWAYS SHOP ON SATURDAY!
I KNOW, BUT IT'S SO NICE I FIGURED YOU'D BE SPENDING THE DAY OUTDOORS!
IF I DIDN'T HAVE TO WORK I SURE WOULDN'T BE AT THE MALL!
WELL, WE JUST HAVE TO PICK UP A FEW THINGS AND THEN WE'LL BE ON OUR WAY!
'BYE!

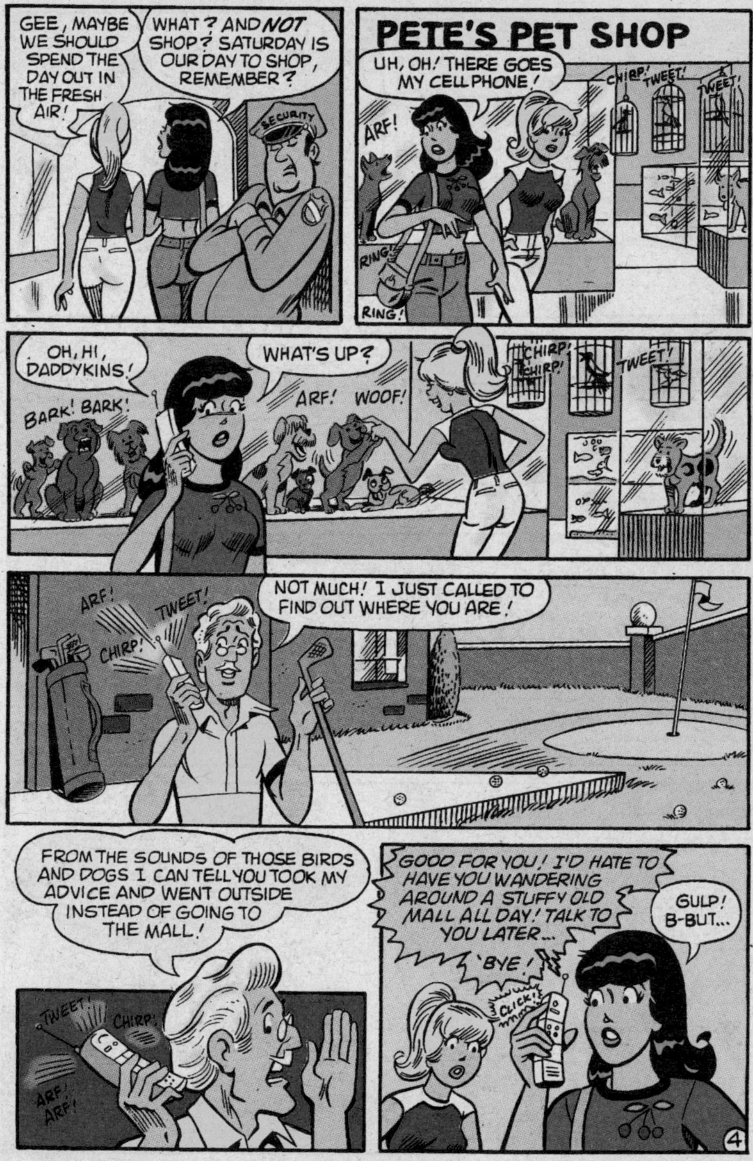
GEE, MAYBE WE SHOULD SPEND THE DAY OUT IN THE FRESH AIR!
WHAT? AND NOT SHOP? SATURDAY IS OUR DAY TO SHOP, REMEMBER?
SECURITY
PETE'S PET SHOP
UH, OH! THERE GOES MY CELLPHONE!
ARF!
CHIRP! TWEET! TWEET!
RING!
RING!
OH, HI, DADDYKINS!
WHAT'S UP?
BARK! BARK!
ARF! WOOF!
CHIRP! CHIRP!
TWEET!
ARF!
TWEET!
CHIRP!
NOT MUCH! I JUST CALLED TO FIND OUT WHERE YOU ARE!
FROM THE SOUNDS OF THOSE BIRDS AND DOGS I CAN TELL YOU TOOK MY ADVICE AND WENT OUTSIDE INSTEAD OF GOING TO THE MALL!
TWEET!
CHIRP!
ARF! ARF!
GOOD FOR YOU! I'D HATE TO HAVE YOU WANDERING AROUND A STUFFY OLD MALL ALL DAY! TALK TO YOU LATER... 'BYE!
GULP! B-BUT...
CLICK!
4

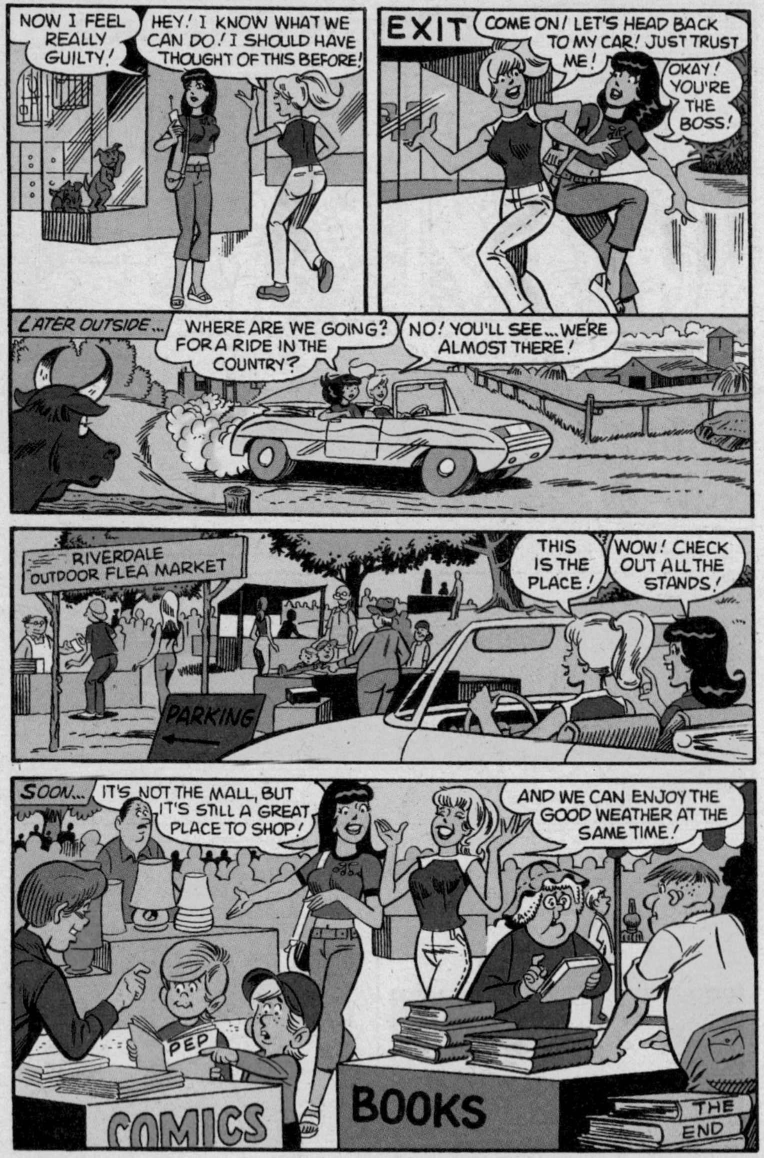
NOW I FEEL REALLY GUILTY!
HEY! I KNOW WHAT WE CAN DO! I SHOULD HAVE THOUGHT OF THIS BEFORE!
EXIT
COME ON! LET'S HEAD BACK TO MY CAR! JUST TRUST ME!
OKAY! YOU'RE THE BOSS!
LATER OUTSIDE...
WHERE ARE WE GOING? FOR A RIDE IN THE COUNTRY?
NO! YOU'LL SEE... WE'RE ALMOST THERE!
RIVERDALE OUTDOOR FLEA MARKET
PARKING
THIS IS THE PLACE!
WOW! CHECK OUT ALL THE STANDS!
SOON...
IT'S NOT THE MALL, BUT IT'S STILL A GREAT PLACE TO SHOP!
AND WE CAN ENJOY THE GOOD WEATHER AT THE SAME TIME!
PEP
COMICS
BOOKS
THE END

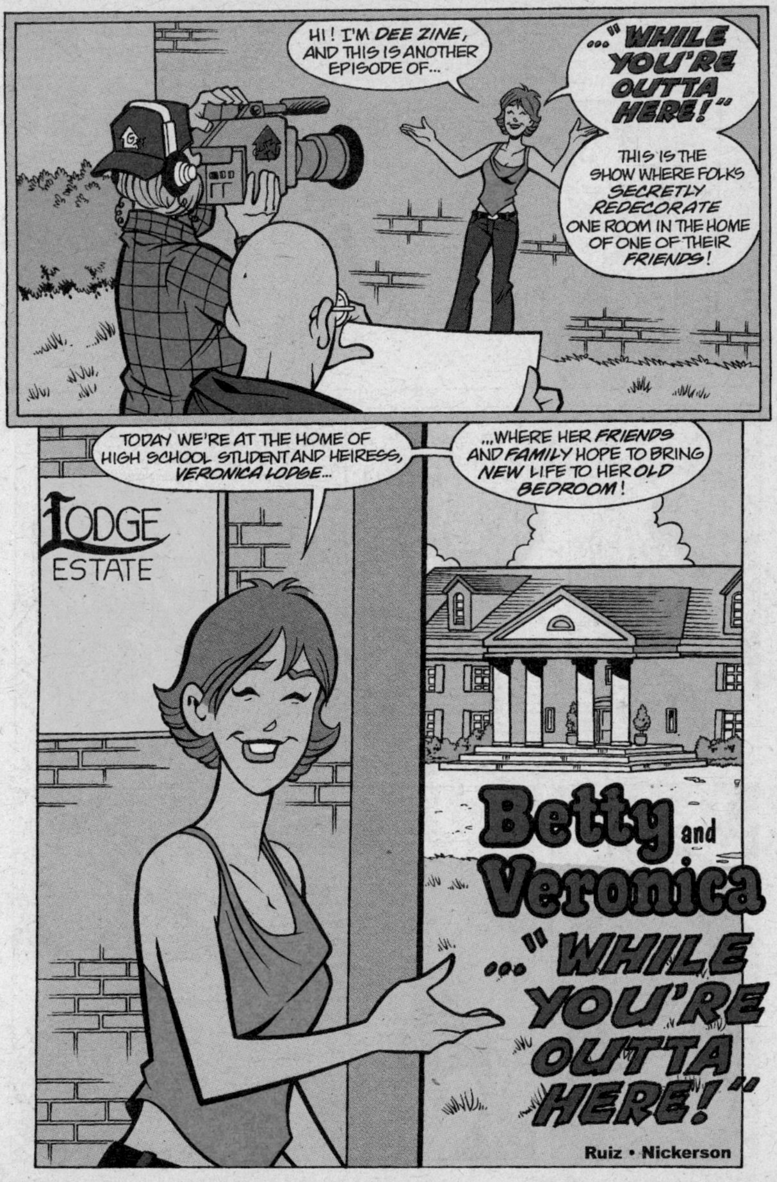
HI! I'M DEE ZINE, AND THIS IS ANOTHER EPISODE OF...
..."WHILE YOU'RE OUTTA HERE!"
THIS IS THE SHOW WHERE FOLKS SECRETLY REDECORATE ONE ROOM IN THE HOME OF ONE OF THEIR FRIENDS!
TODAY WE'RE AT THE HOME OF HIGH SCHOOL STUDENT AND HEIRESS, VERONICA LODGE...
...WHERE HER FRIENDS AND FAMILY HOPE TO BRING NEW LIFE TO HER OLD BEDROOM!
LODGE ESTATE
Betty and Veronica
..."WHILE YOU'RE OUTTA HERE!"
Ruiz • Nickerson

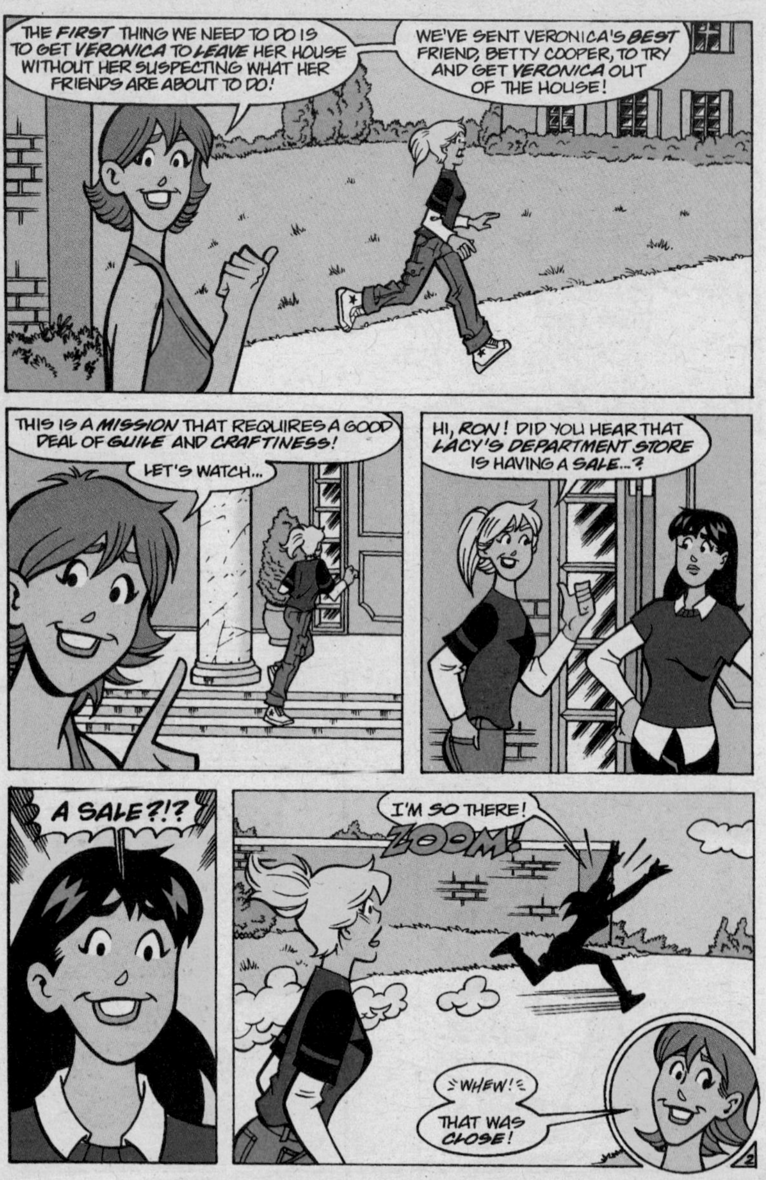
THE FIRST THING WE NEED TO DO IS TO GET VERONICA TO LEAVE HER HOUSE WITHOUT HER SUSPECTING WHAT HER FRIENDS ARE ABOUT TO DO!
WE'VE SENT VERONICA'S BEST FRIEND, BETTY COOPER, TO TRY AND GET VERONICA OUT OF THE HOUSE!
THIS IS A MISSION THAT REQUIRES A GOOD DEAL OF GUILE AND CRAFTINESS!
LET'S WATCH...
HI, RON! DID YOU HEAR THAT LACY'S DEPARTMENT STORE IS HAVING A SALE...?
A SALE?!?
I'M SO THERE!
ZOOM!
WHEW!
THAT WAS CLOSE!
2

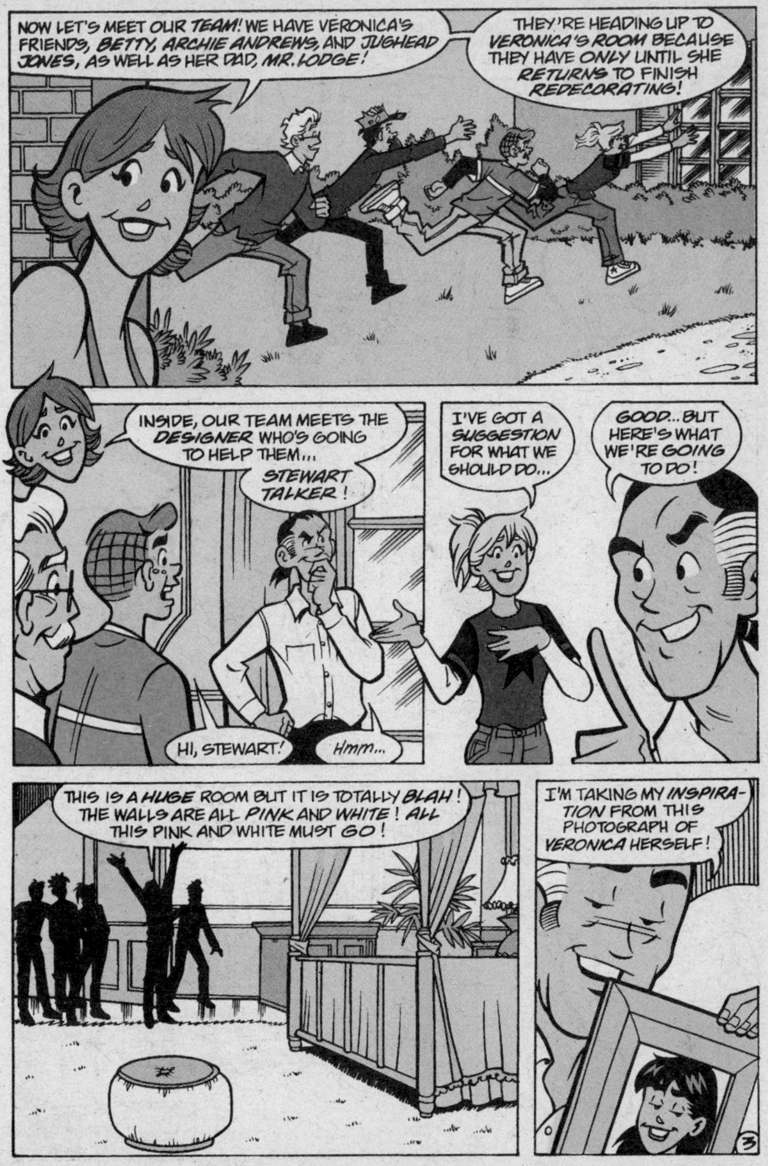
NOW LET'S MEET OUR TEAM! WE HAVE VERONICA'S FRIENDS, BETTY, ARCHIE ANDREWS, AND JUGHEAD JONES, AS WELL AS HER DAD, MR. LODGE!
THEY'RE HEADING UP TO VERONICA'S ROOM BECAUSE THEY HAVE ONLY UNTIL SHE RETURNS TO FINISH REDECORATING!
INSIDE, OUR TEAM MEETS THE DESIGNER WHO'S GOING TO HELP THEM...
STEWART TALKER!
HI, STEWART!
Hmm...
I'VE GOT A SUGGESTION FOR WHAT WE SHOULD DO...
GOOD... BUT HERE'S WHAT WE'RE GOING TO DO!
THIS IS A HUGE ROOM BUT IT IS TOTALLY BLAH! THE WALLS ARE ALL PINK AND WHITE! ALL THIS PINK AND WHITE MUST GO!
I'M TAKING MY INSPIRATION FROM THIS PHOTOGRAPH OF VERONICA HERSELF!
3

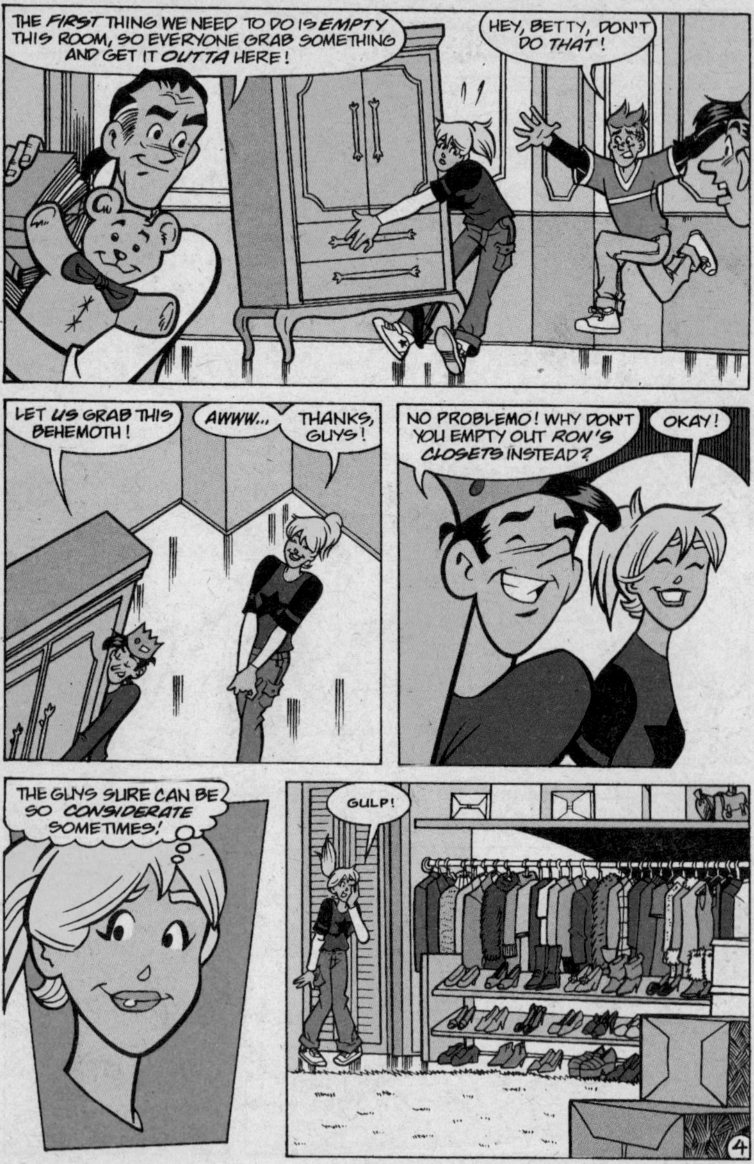
THE *FIRST* THING WE NEED TO DO IS *EMPTY* THIS ROOM, SO EVERYONE GRAB SOMETHING AND GET IT *OUTTA* HERE!
HEY, BETTY, DON'T DO *THAT*!
LET *US* GRAB THIS BEHEMOTH!
AWWW...
THANKS, GUYS!
NO PROBLEMO! WHY DON'T YOU EMPTY OUT *RON'S CLOSETS* INSTEAD?
OKAY!
THE GUYS SURE CAN BE SO *CONSIDERATE* SOMETIMES!
GULP!

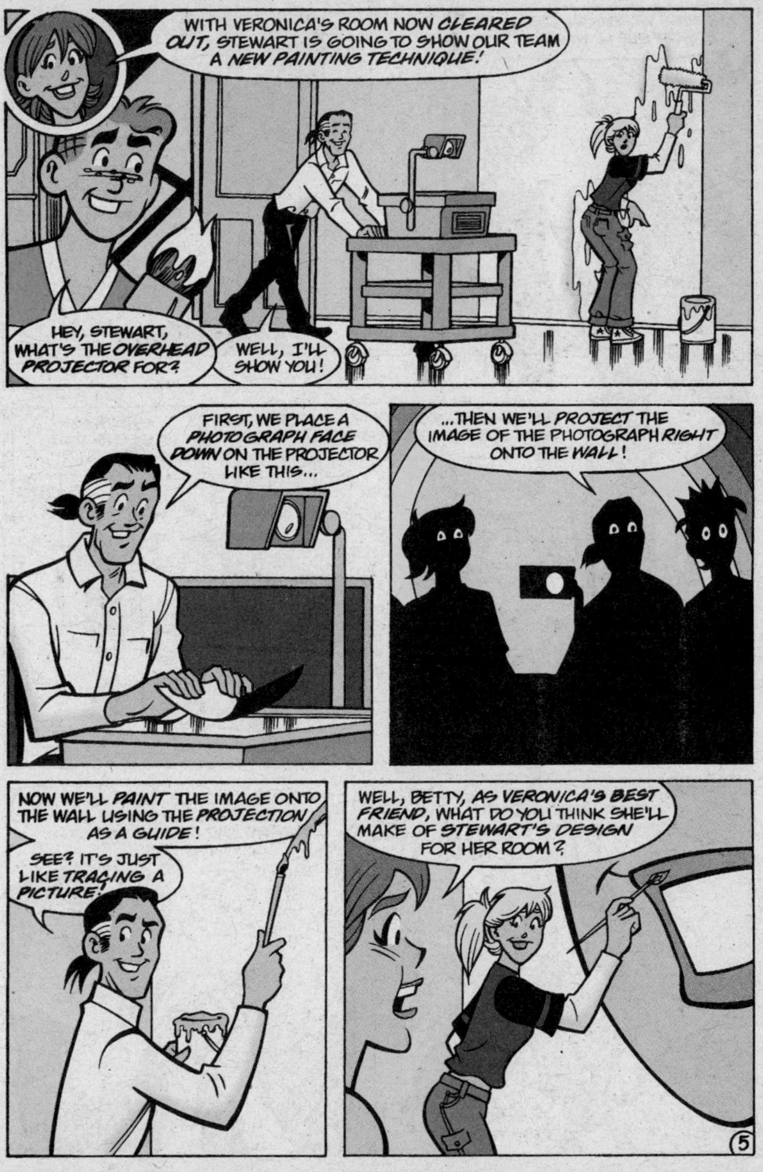
WITH VERONICA'S ROOM NOW CLEARED OUT, STEWART IS GOING TO SHOW OUR TEAM A NEW PAINTING TECHNIQUE!
HEY, STEWART, WHAT'S THE OVERHEAD PROJECTOR FOR?
WELL, I'LL SHOW YOU!
FIRST, WE PLACE A PHOTOGRAPH FACE DOWN ON THE PROJECTOR LIKE THIS...
...THEN WE'LL PROJECT THE IMAGE OF THE PHOTOGRAPH RIGHT ONTO THE WALL!
NOW WE'LL PAINT THE IMAGE ONTO THE WALL USING THE PROJECTION AS A GUIDE!
SEE? IT'S JUST LIKE TRACING A PICTURE!
WELL, BETTY, AS VERONICA'S BEST FRIEND, WHAT DO YOU THINK SHE'LL MAKE OF STEWART'S DESIGN FOR HER ROOM?
5

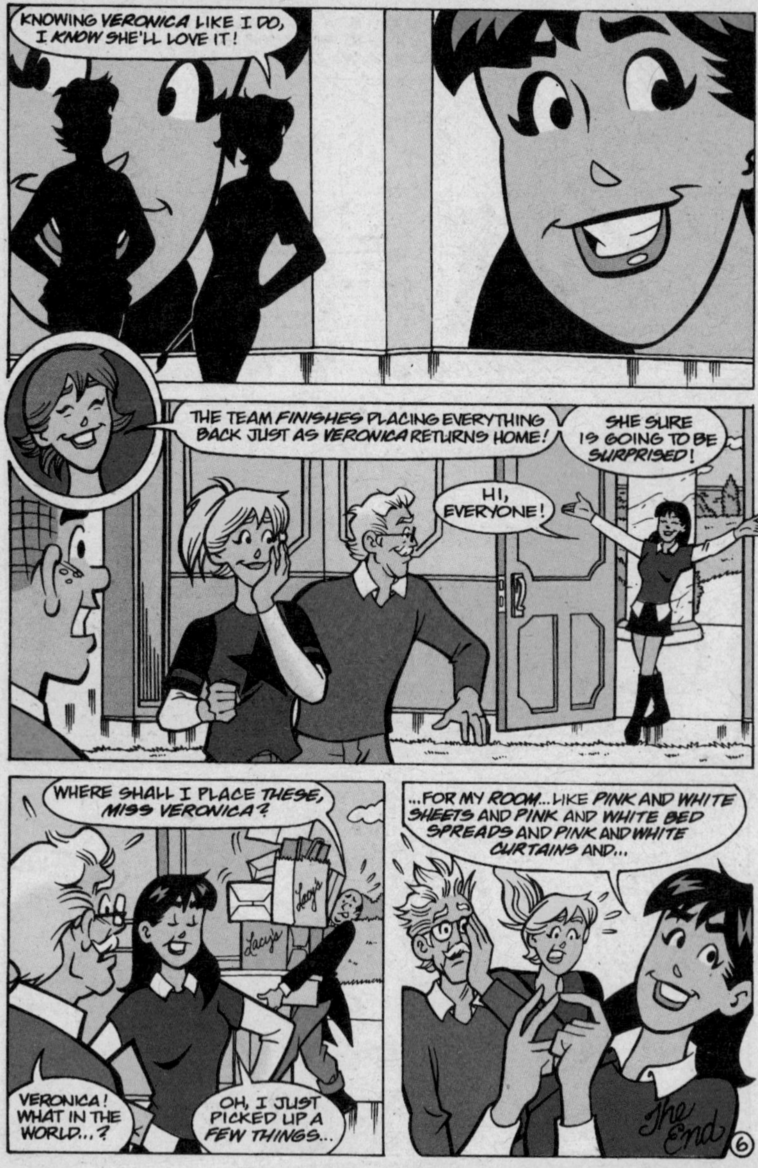
KNOWING VERONICA LIKE I DO, I KNOW SHE'LL LOVE IT!
THE TEAM FINISHES PLACING EVERYTHING BACK JUST AS VERONICA RETURNS HOME!
SHE SURE IS GOING TO BE SURPRISED!
HI, EVERYONE!
WHERE SHALL I PLACE THESE, MISS VERONICA?
VERONICA! WHAT IN THE WORLD...?
OH, I JUST PICKED UP A FEW THINGS...
...FOR MY ROOM... LIKE PINK AND WHITE SHEETS AND PINK AND WHITE BED SPREADS AND PINK AND WHITE CURTAINS AND...
The End
6

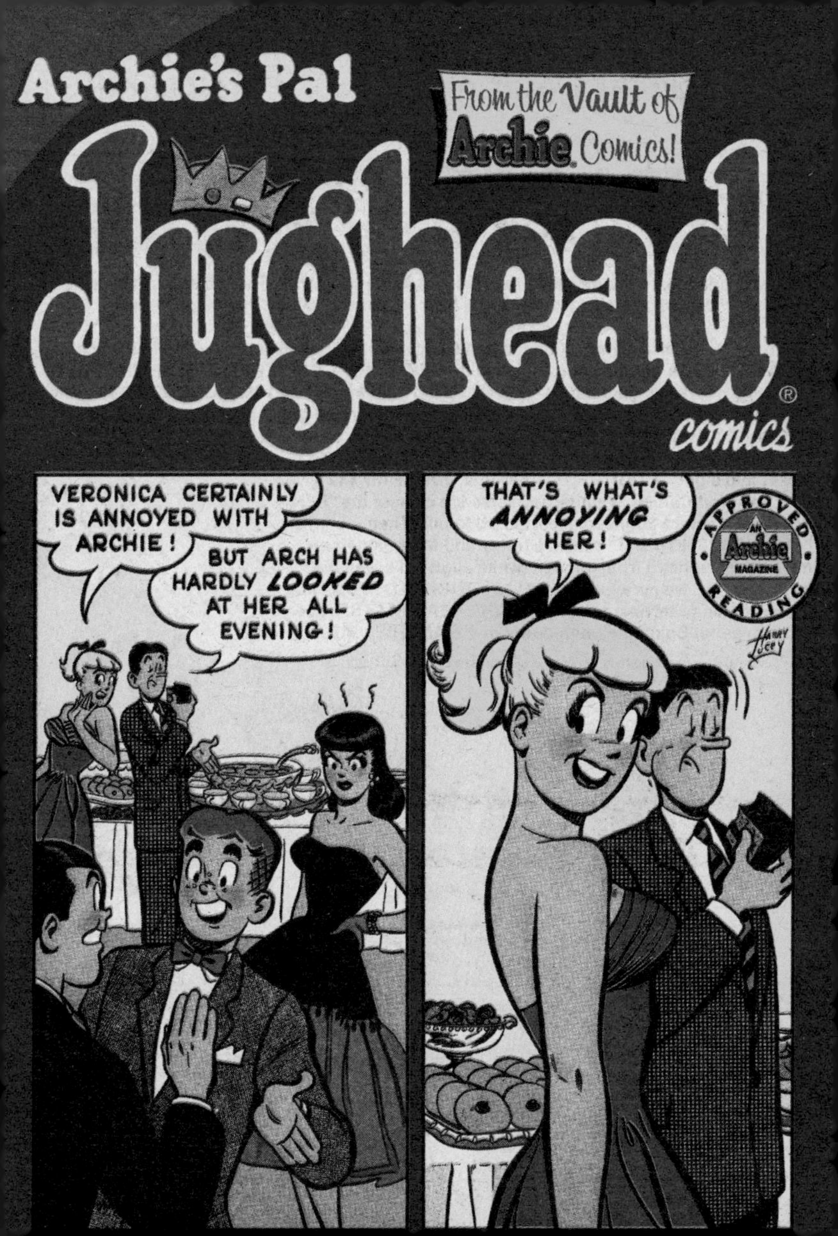
Archie's Pal
From the Vault of Archie Comics!
Jughead®
comics
VERONICA CERTAINLY IS ANNOYED WITH ARCHIE!
BUT ARCH HAS HARDLY LOOKED AT HER ALL EVENING!
THAT'S WHAT'S ANNOYING HER!
APPROVED AN Archie MAGAZINE READING

From the Vault of Archie Comics!

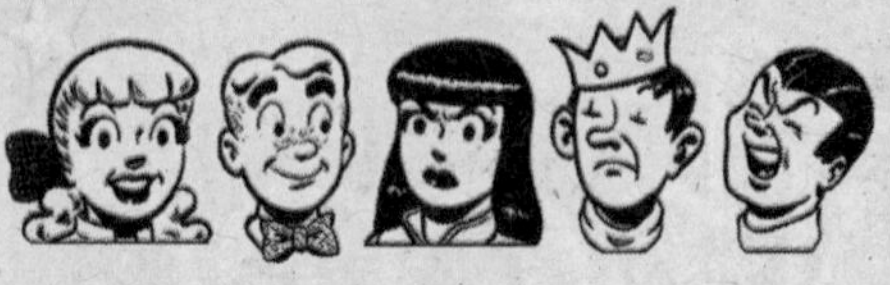

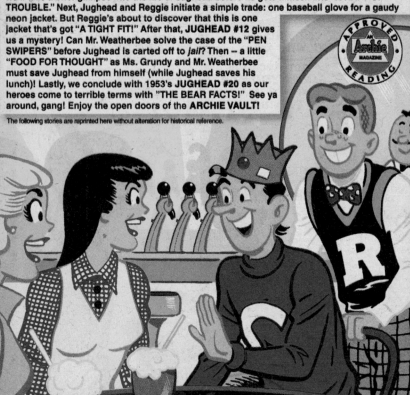

THE FABULOUS FIFTIES

Welcome, friends, to the rollicking return of the **ARCHIE VAULT!** The fabulous fifties are back with only ***the best*** of Archie Andrews and his burger-eatin' buddy, Jughead Jones!

From 1951's **JUGHEAD #7**, Jughead and Reggie are ready to clobber each other -- again. But Mr. Weatherbee's got the soggy solution in "BEWITCHED, BATTERED AND BEWILDERED!" Switching gears, it's gonna be a "FIGHT! FIGHT!" as we shift to 1952's **JUGHEAD #11** where **we'll take a brief glimpse into the life of Jughead before he gets himself into "A RAFT OF TROUBLE." Next, Jughead and Reggie initiate a simple trade: one baseball glove for a gaudy neon jacket. But Reggie's about to discover that this is one jacket that's got "A TIGHT FIT!" After that, JUGHEAD #12 gives us a mystery! Can Mr. Weatherbee solve the case of the "PEN SWIPERS" before Jughead is carted off to *jail*? Then -- a little "FOOD FOR THOUGHT" as Ms. Grundy and Mr. Weatherbee must save Jughead from himself (while Jughead saves his lunch)! Lastly, we conclude with 1953's JUGHEAD #20 as our heroes come to terrible terms with "THE BEAR FACTS!" See ya around, gang! Enjoy the open doors of the ARCHIE VAULT!**

The following stories are reprinted here without alteration for historical reference.

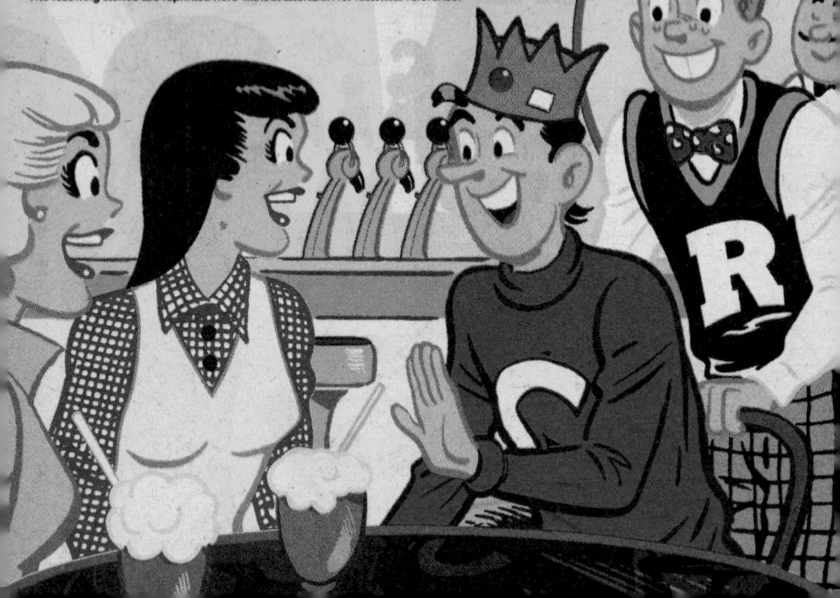

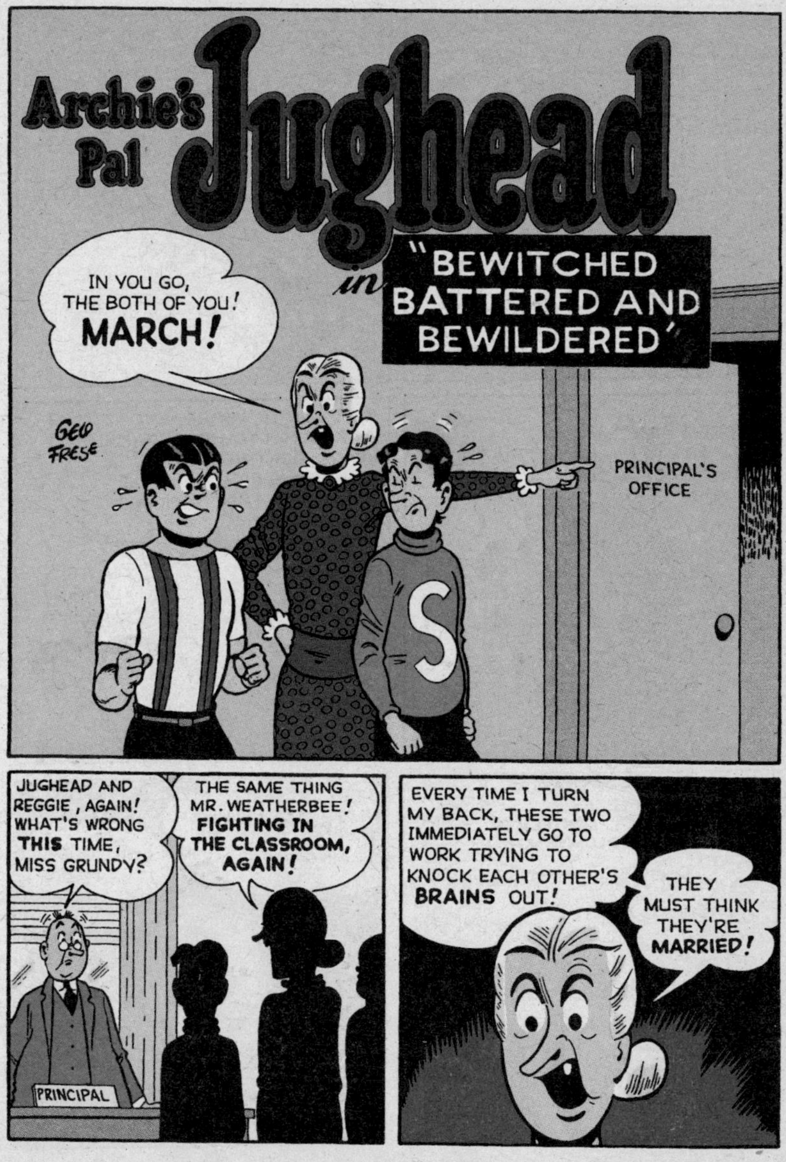
Archie's Pal Jughead
in "BEWITCHED BATTERED AND BEWILDERED"
IN YOU GO, THE BOTH OF YOU! MARCH!
GEO FRESE
PRINCIPAL'S OFFICE
JUGHEAD AND REGGIE, AGAIN! WHAT'S WRONG THIS TIME, MISS GRUNDY?
THE SAME THING MR. WEATHERBEE! FIGHTING IN THE CLASSROOM, AGAIN!
PRINCIPAL
EVERY TIME I TURN MY BACK, THESE TWO IMMEDIATELY GO TO WORK TRYING TO KNOCK EACH OTHER'S BRAINS OUT!
THEY MUST THINK THEY'RE MARRIED!

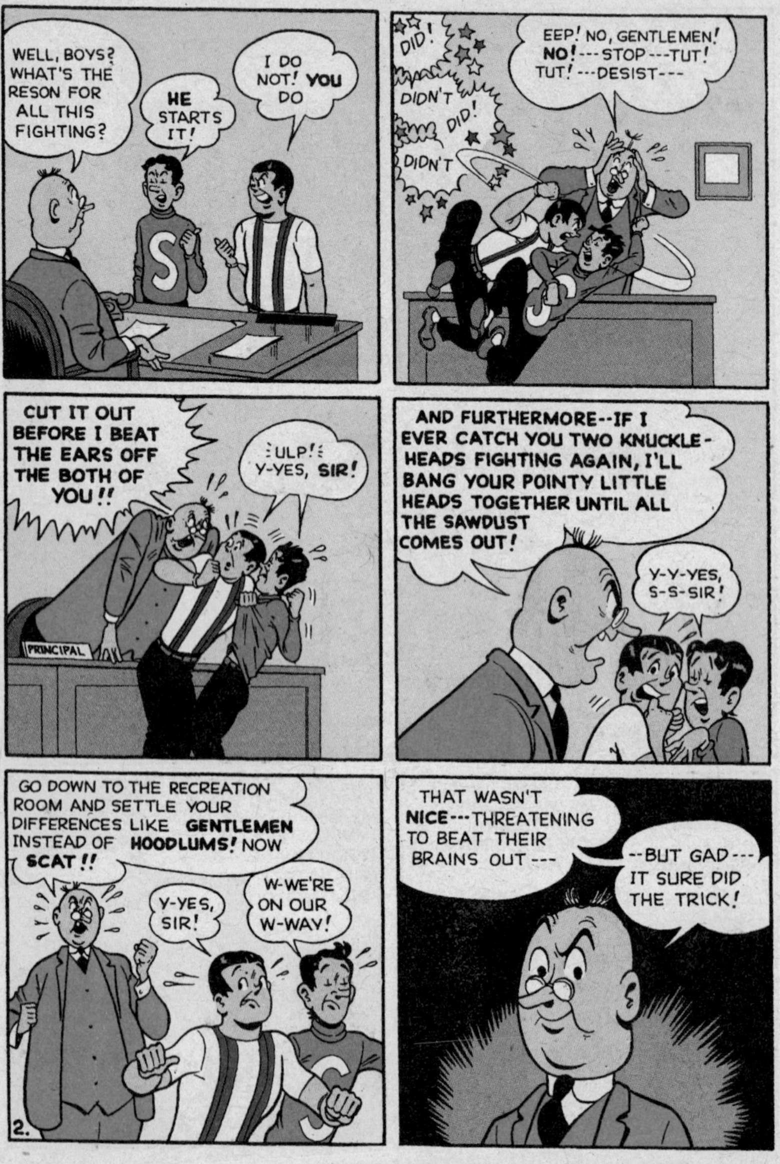
WELL, BOYS? WHAT'S THE RESON FOR ALL THIS FIGHTING?
HE STARTS IT!
I DO NOT! YOU DO
DID!
DIDN'T
DID!
DIDN'T
EEP! NO, GENTLEMEN! NO! --- STOP --- TUT! TUT! --- DESIST ---
CUT IT OUT BEFORE I BEAT THE EARS OFF THE BOTH OF YOU!!
ULP! Y-YES, SIR!
PRINCIPAL
AND FURTHERMORE--IF I EVER CATCH YOU TWO KNUCKLE-HEADS FIGHTING AGAIN, I'LL BANG YOUR POINTY LITTLE HEADS TOGETHER UNTIL ALL THE SAWDUST COMES OUT!
Y-Y-YES, S-S-SIR!
GO DOWN TO THE RECREATION ROOM AND SETTLE YOUR DIFFERENCES LIKE GENTLEMEN INSTEAD OF HOODLUMS! NOW SCAT!!
Y-YES, SIR!
W-WE'RE ON OUR W-WAY!
2.
THAT WASN'T NICE --- THREATENING TO BEAT THEIR BRAINS OUT ---
-- BUT GAD --- IT SURE DID THE TRICK!

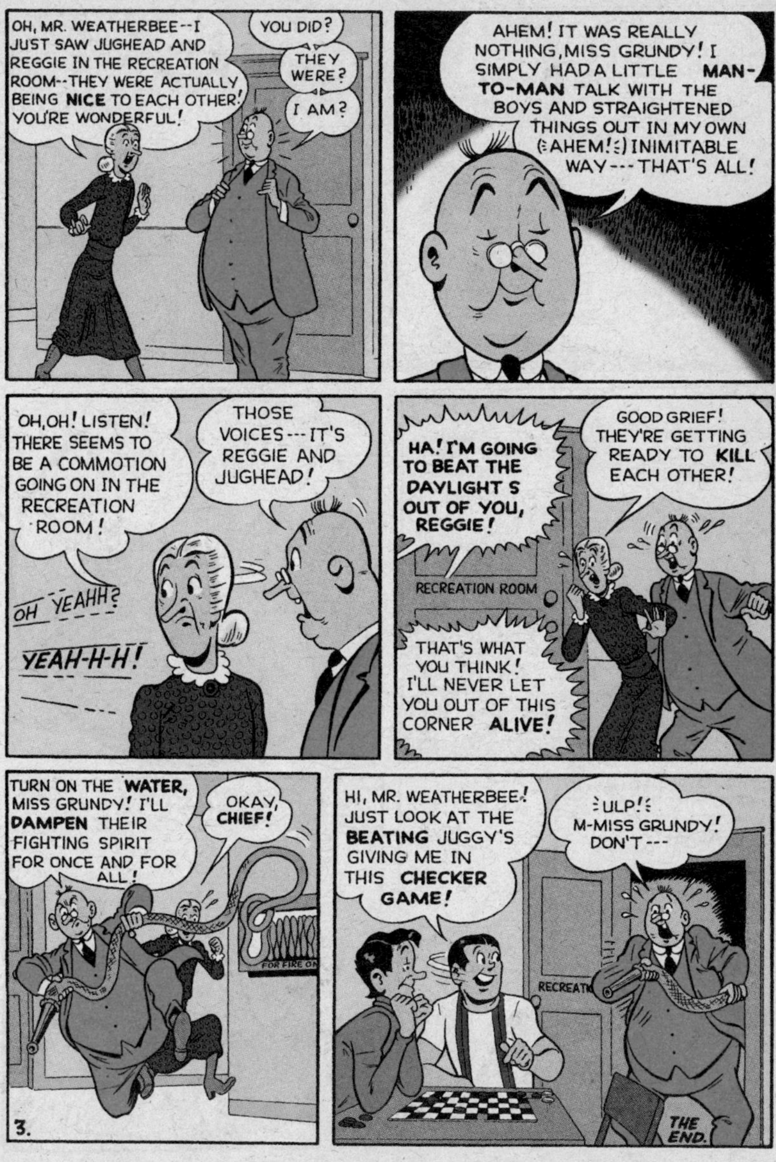
OH, MR. WEATHERBEE--I JUST SAW JUGHEAD AND REGGIE IN THE RECREATION ROOM--THEY WERE ACTUALLY BEING NICE TO EACH OTHER! YOU'RE WONDERFUL!
YOU DID?
THEY WERE?
I AM?
AHEM! IT WAS REALLY NOTHING, MISS GRUNDY! I SIMPLY HAD A LITTLE MAN-TO-MAN TALK WITH THE BOYS AND STRAIGHTENED THINGS OUT IN MY OWN (AHEM!) INIMITABLE WAY--- THAT'S ALL!
OH, OH! LISTEN! THERE SEEMS TO BE A COMMOTION GOING ON IN THE RECREATION ROOM!
THOSE VOICES--- IT'S REGGIE AND JUGHEAD!
OH YEAHH?
YEAH-H-H!
HA! I'M GOING TO BEAT THE DAYLIGHT S OUT OF YOU, REGGIE!
RECREATION ROOM
THAT'S WHAT YOU THINK! I'LL NEVER LET YOU OUT OF THIS CORNER ALIVE!
GOOD GRIEF! THEY'RE GETTING READY TO KILL EACH OTHER!
TURN ON THE WATER, MISS GRUNDY! I'LL DAMPEN THEIR FIGHTING SPIRIT FOR ONCE AND FOR ALL!
OKAY, CHIEF!
FOR FIRE ON
3.
HI, MR. WEATHERBEE! JUST LOOK AT THE BEATING JUGGY'S GIVING ME IN THIS CHECKER GAME!
ULP! M-MISS GRUNDY! DON'T ---
RECREAT
THE END.

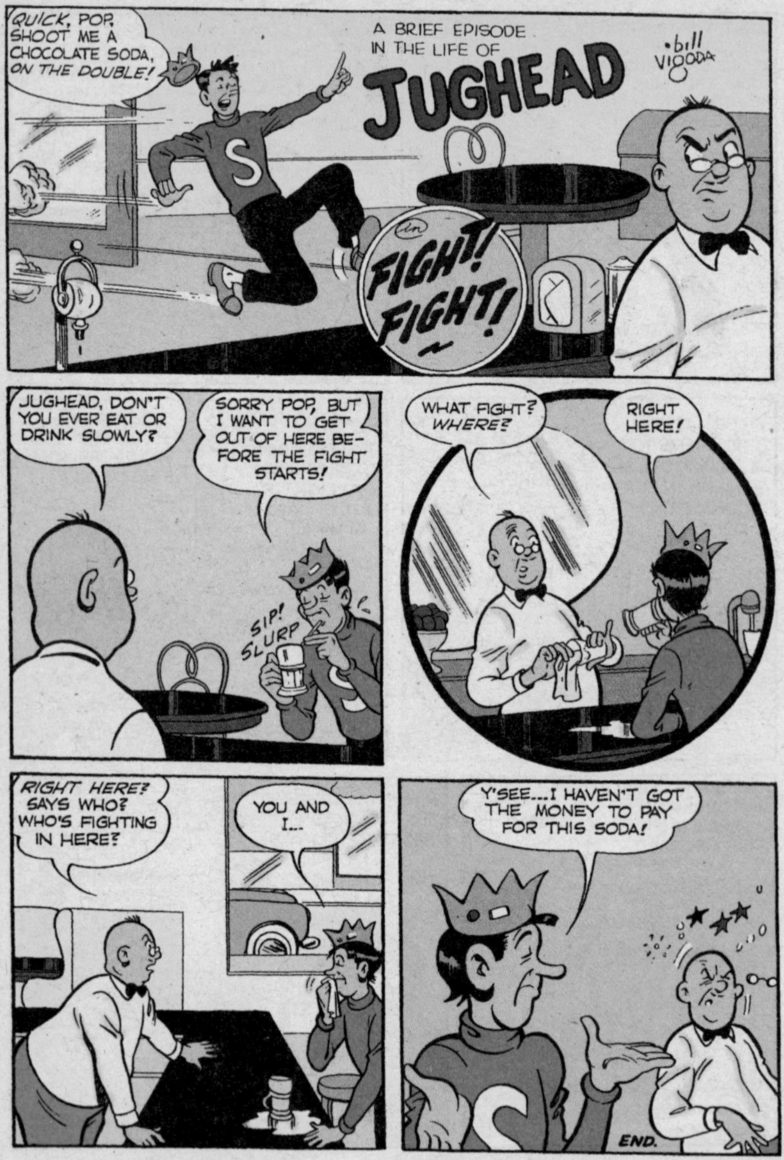
QUICK, POP, SHOOT ME A CHOCOLATE SODA, ON THE DOUBLE!
A BRIEF EPISODE IN THE LIFE OF
JUGHEAD
in
FIGHT! FIGHT!
bill VIGODA
JUGHEAD, DON'T YOU EVER EAT OR DRINK SLOWLY?
SORRY POP, BUT I WANT TO GET OUT OF HERE BEFORE THE FIGHT STARTS!
SIP! SLURP
WHAT FIGHT? WHERE?
RIGHT HERE!
RIGHT HERE? SAYS WHO? WHO'S FIGHTING IN HERE?
YOU AND I...
Y'SEE...I HAVEN'T GOT THE MONEY TO PAY FOR THIS SODA!
END.

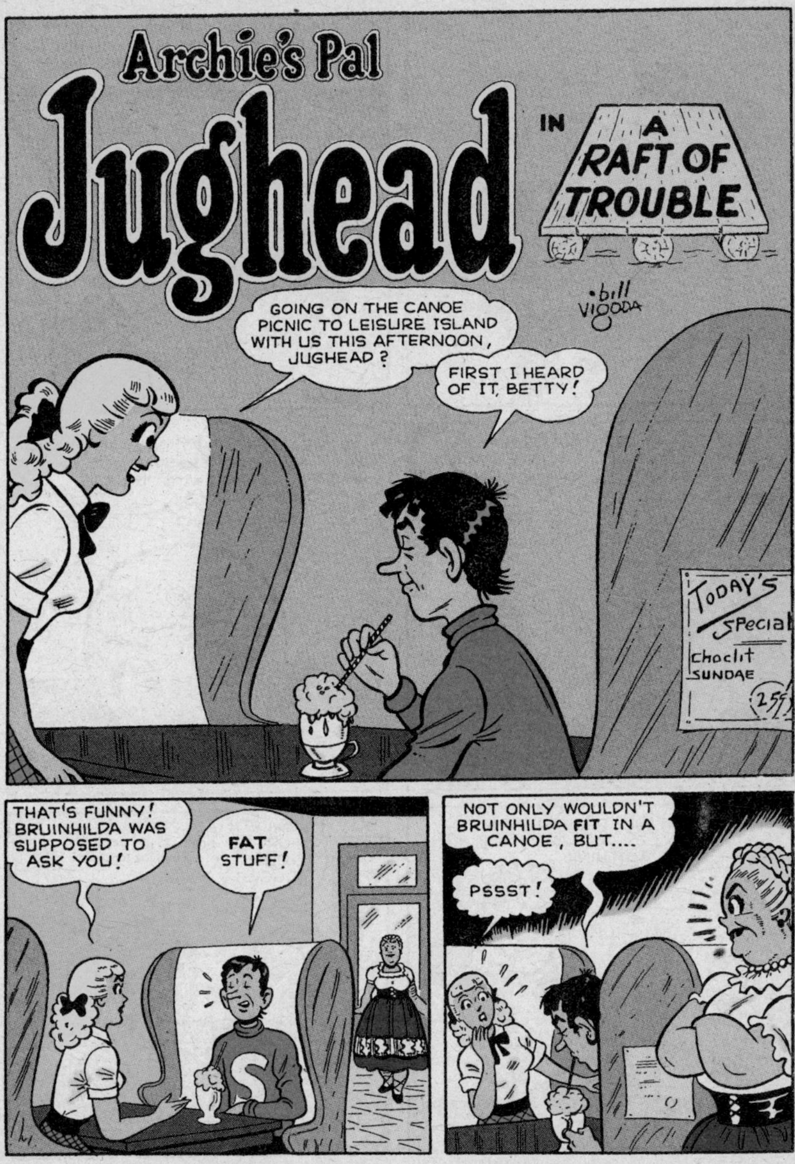

Archie's Pal
Jughead
IN
A RAFT OF TROUBLE
bill VIGODA
GOING ON THE CANOE PICNIC TO LEISURE ISLAND WITH US THIS AFTERNOON, JUGHEAD?
FIRST I HEARD OF IT, BETTY!
TODAY'S Special
choclit SUNDAE
25¢
THAT'S FUNNY! BRUINHILDA WAS SUPPOSED TO ASK YOU!
FAT STUFF!
NOT ONLY WOULDN'T BRUINHILDA FIT IN A CANOE, BUT....
PSSST!

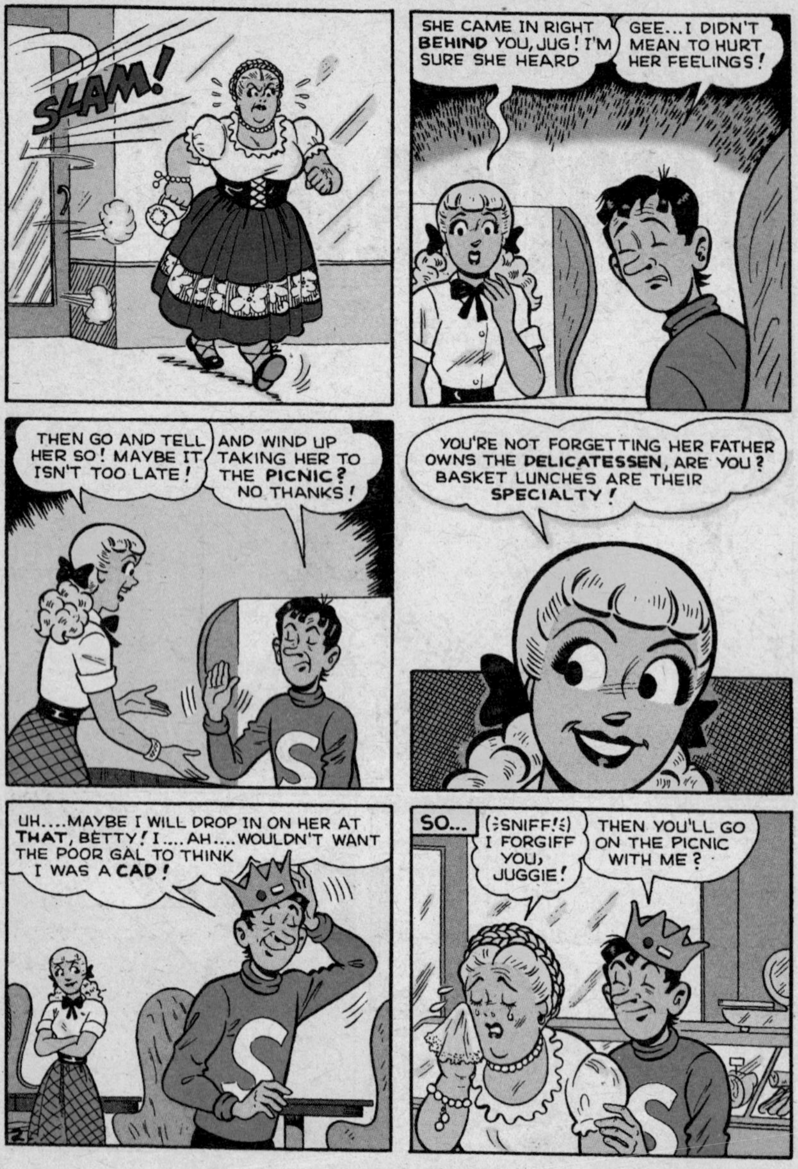
SLAM!
SHE CAME IN RIGHT BEHIND YOU, JUG! I'M SURE SHE HEARD
GEE...I DIDN'T MEAN TO HURT HER FEELINGS!
THEN GO AND TELL HER SO! MAYBE IT ISN'T TOO LATE!
AND WIND UP TAKING HER TO THE PICNIC? NO THANKS!
YOU'RE NOT FORGETTING HER FATHER OWNS THE DELICATESSEN, ARE YOU? BASKET LUNCHES ARE THEIR SPECIALTY!
UH....MAYBE I WILL DROP IN ON HER AT THAT, BETTY! I....AH....WOULDN'T WANT THE POOR GAL TO THINK I WAS A CAD!
SO...
(SNIFF!) I FORGIFF YOU, JUGGIE!
THEN YOU'LL GO ON THE PICNIC WITH ME?

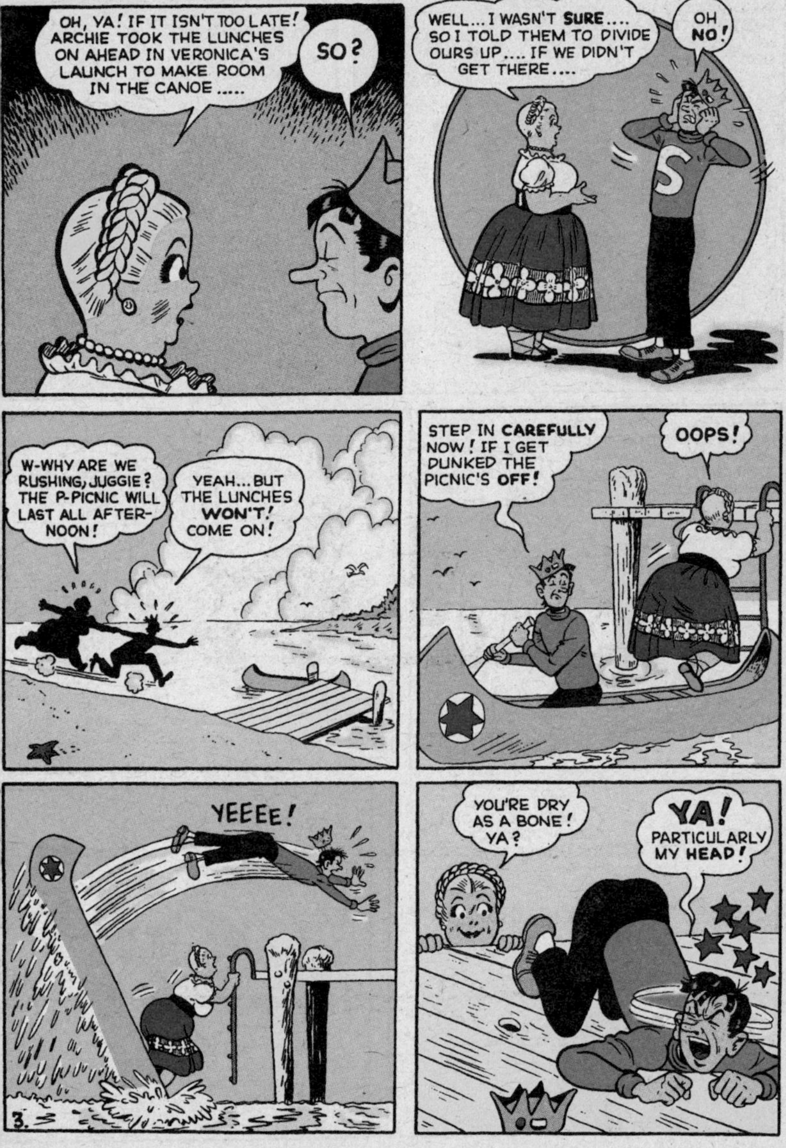

OH, YA! IF IT ISN'T TOO LATE! ARCHIE TOOK THE LUNCHES ON AHEAD IN VERONICA'S LAUNCH TO MAKE ROOM IN THE CANOE .....
SO?
WELL... I WASN'T SURE.... SO I TOLD THEM TO DIVIDE OURS UP.... IF WE DIDN'T GET THERE....
OH NO!
W-WHY ARE WE RUSHING, JUGGIE? THE P-PICNIC WILL LAST ALL AFTER-NOON!
YEAH... BUT THE LUNCHES WON'T! COME ON!
STEP IN CAREFULLY NOW! IF I GET DUNKED THE PICNIC'S OFF!
OOPS!
YEEEE!
YOU'RE DRY AS A BONE! YA?
YA! PARTICULARLY MY HEAD!

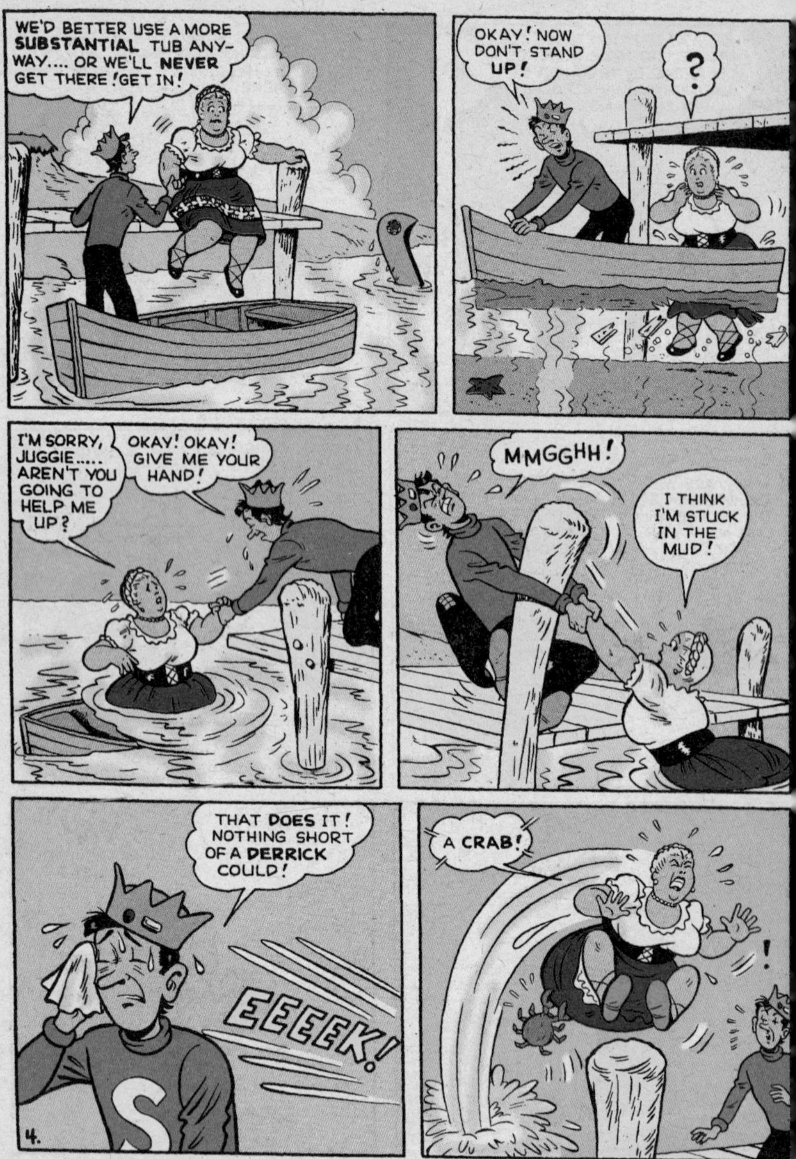
WE'D BETTER USE A MORE SUBSTANTIAL TUB ANY-WAY.... OR WE'LL NEVER GET THERE! GET IN!
OKAY! NOW DON'T STAND UP!
?
I'M SORRY, JUGGIE..... AREN'T YOU GOING TO HELP ME UP?
OKAY! OKAY! GIVE ME YOUR HAND!
MMGGHH!
I THINK I'M STUCK IN THE MUD!
THAT DOES IT! NOTHING SHORT OF A DERRICK COULD!
EEEEK!
A CRAB!
!
4.

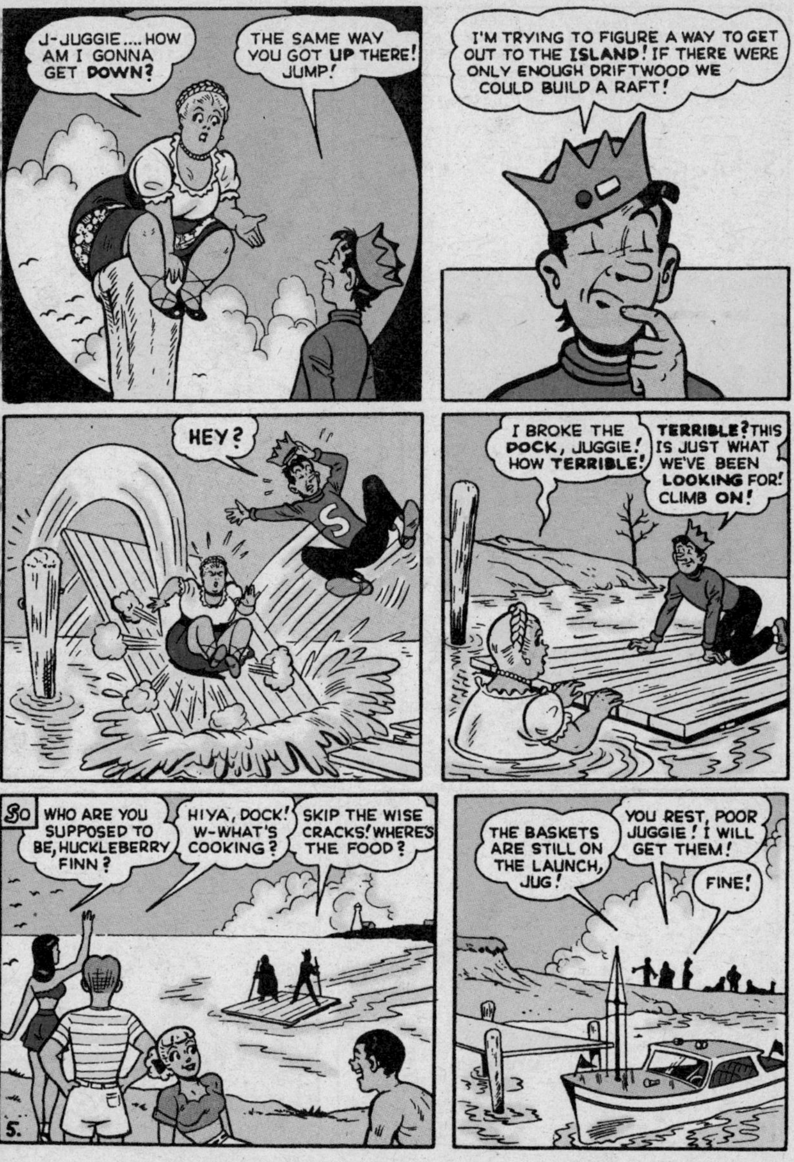
J-JUGGIE.... HOW AM I GONNA GET DOWN?
THE SAME WAY YOU GOT UP THERE! JUMP!
I'M TRYING TO FIGURE A WAY TO GET OUT TO THE ISLAND! IF THERE WERE ONLY ENOUGH DRIFTWOOD WE COULD BUILD A RAFT!
HEY?
I BROKE THE DOCK, JUGGIE! HOW TERRIBLE!
TERRIBLE? THIS IS JUST WHAT WE'VE BEEN LOOKING FOR! CLIMB ON!
SO
WHO ARE YOU SUPPOSED TO BE, HUCKLEBERRY FINN?
HIYA, DOCK! W-WHAT'S COOKING?
SKIP THE WISE CRACKS! WHERE'S THE FOOD?
THE BASKETS ARE STILL ON THE LAUNCH, JUG!
YOU REST, POOR JUGGIE! I WILL GET THEM!
FINE!

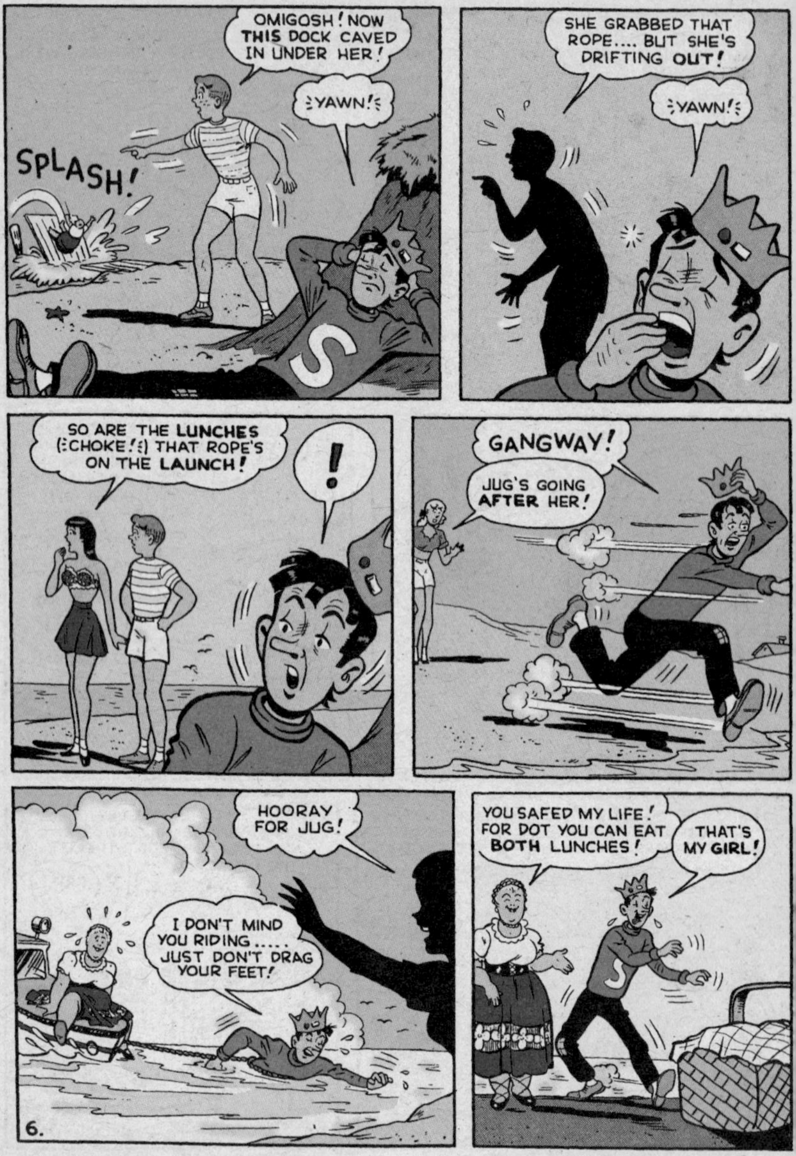
OMIGOSH! NOW THIS DOCK CAVED IN UNDER HER!
SPLASH!
YAWN!
SHE GRABBED THAT ROPE.... BUT SHE'S DRIFTING OUT!
YAWN!
SO ARE THE LUNCHES (CHOKE!) THAT ROPE'S ON THE LAUNCH!
!
GANGWAY!
JUG'S GOING AFTER HER!
HOORAY FOR JUG!
I DON'T MIND YOU RIDING..... JUST DON'T DRAG YOUR FEET!
6.
YOU SAFED MY LIFE! FOR DOT YOU CAN EAT BOTH LUNCHES!
THAT'S MY GIRL!

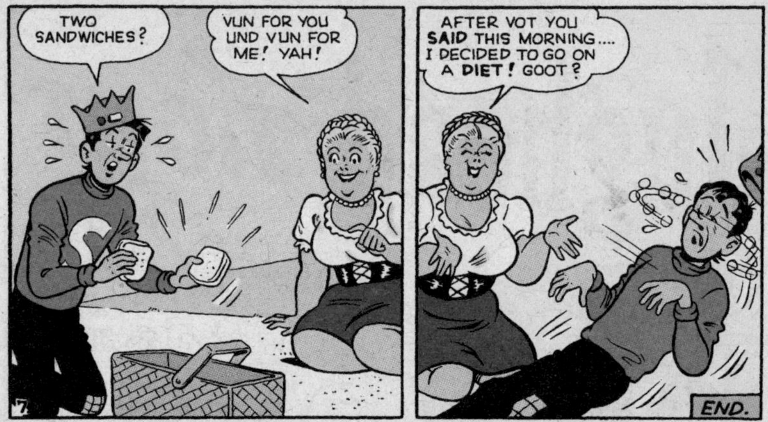

TWO SANDWICHES?
VUN FOR YOU UND VUN FOR ME! YAH!
AFTER VOT YOU SAID THIS MORNING.... I DECIDED TO GO ON A DIET! GOOT?
END.

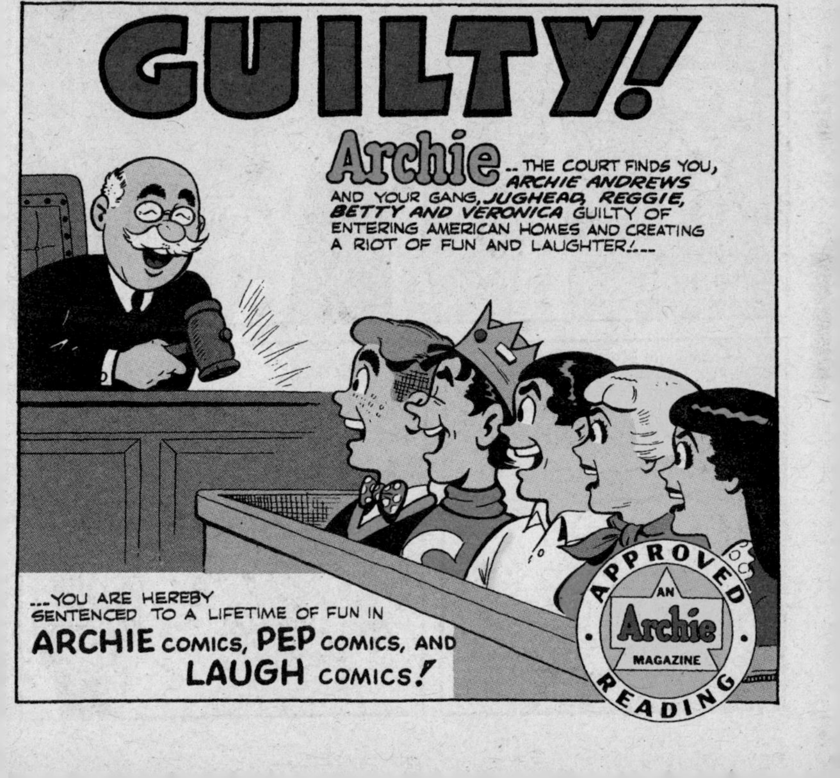

GUILTY!
Archie.. THE COURT FINDS YOU, ARCHIE ANDREWS AND YOUR GANG, JUGHEAD, REGGIE, BETTY AND VERONICA GUILTY OF ENTERING AMERICAN HOMES AND CREATING A RIOT OF FUN AND LAUGHTER!...
...YOU ARE HEREBY SENTENCED TO A LIFETIME OF FUN IN ARCHIE COMICS, PEP COMICS, AND LAUGH COMICS!
APPROVED
AN Archie MAGAZINE
READING

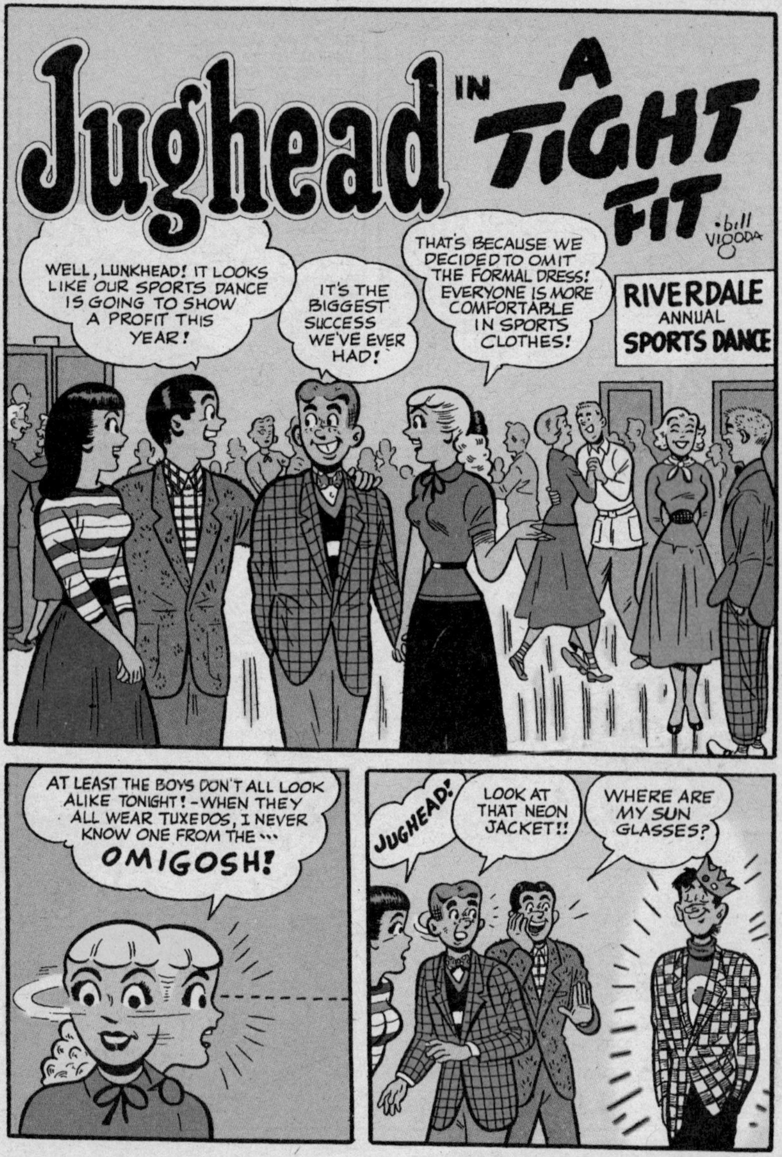
Jughead IN A TIGHT FIT
bill VIGODA
WELL, LUNKHEAD! IT LOOKS LIKE OUR SPORTS DANCE IS GOING TO SHOW A PROFIT THIS YEAR!
IT'S THE BIGGEST SUCCESS WE'VE EVER HAD!
THAT'S BECAUSE WE DECIDED TO OMIT THE FORMAL DRESS! EVERYONE IS MORE COMFORTABLE IN SPORTS CLOTHES!
RIVERDALE ANNUAL SPORTS DANCE
AT LEAST THE BOYS DON'T ALL LOOK ALIKE TONIGHT! -WHEN THEY ALL WEAR TUXEDOS, I NEVER KNOW ONE FROM THE ...
OMIGOSH!
JUGHEAD!
LOOK AT THAT NEON JACKET!!
WHERE ARE MY SUN GLASSES?

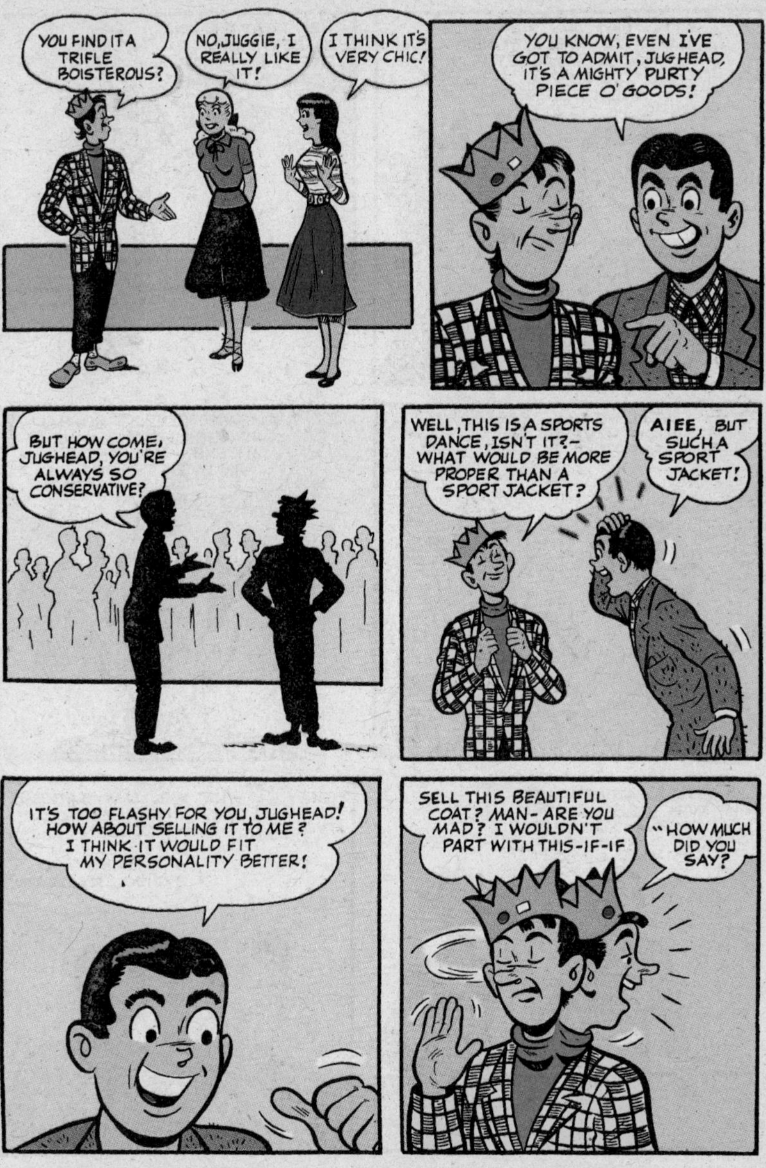

YOU FIND IT A TRIFLE BOISTEROUS?
NO, JUGGIE, I REALLY LIKE IT!
I THINK IT'S VERY CHIC!
YOU KNOW, EVEN I'VE GOT TO ADMIT, JUGHEAD, IT'S A MIGHTY PURTY PIECE O' GOODS!
BUT HOW COME, JUGHEAD, YOU'RE ALWAYS SO CONSERVATIVE?
WELL, THIS IS A SPORTS DANCE, ISN'T IT? – WHAT WOULD BE MORE PROPER THAN A SPORT JACKET?
AIEE, BUT SUCH A SPORT JACKET!
IT'S TOO FLASHY FOR YOU, JUGHEAD! HOW ABOUT SELLING IT TO ME? I THINK IT WOULD FIT MY PERSONALITY BETTER!
SELL THIS BEAUTIFUL COAT? MAN - ARE YOU MAD? I WOULDN'T PART WITH THIS-IF-IF
"HOW MUCH DID YOU SAY?

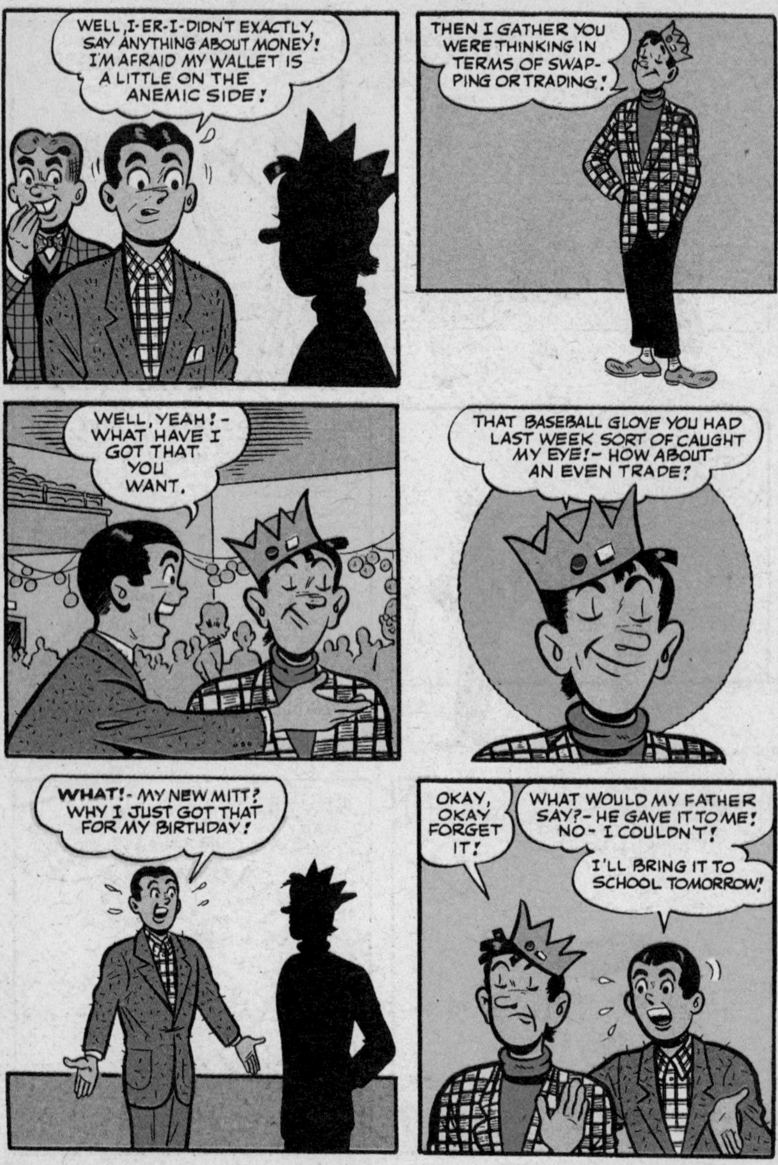
WELL, I-ER-I-DIDN'T EXACTLY SAY ANYTHING ABOUT MONEY! I'M AFRAID MY WALLET IS A LITTLE ON THE ANEMIC SIDE!
THEN I GATHER YOU WERE THINKING IN TERMS OF SWAP-PING OR TRADING!
WELL, YEAH! - WHAT HAVE I GOT THAT YOU WANT.
THAT BASEBALL GLOVE YOU HAD LAST WEEK SORT OF CAUGHT MY EYE! - HOW ABOUT AN EVEN TRADE?
WHAT! - MY NEW MITT? WHY I JUST GOT THAT FOR MY BIRTHDAY!
WHAT WOULD MY FATHER SAY? - HE GAVE IT TO ME! NO - I COULDN'T!
OKAY, OKAY FORGET IT!
I'LL BRING IT TO SCHOOL TOMORROW!

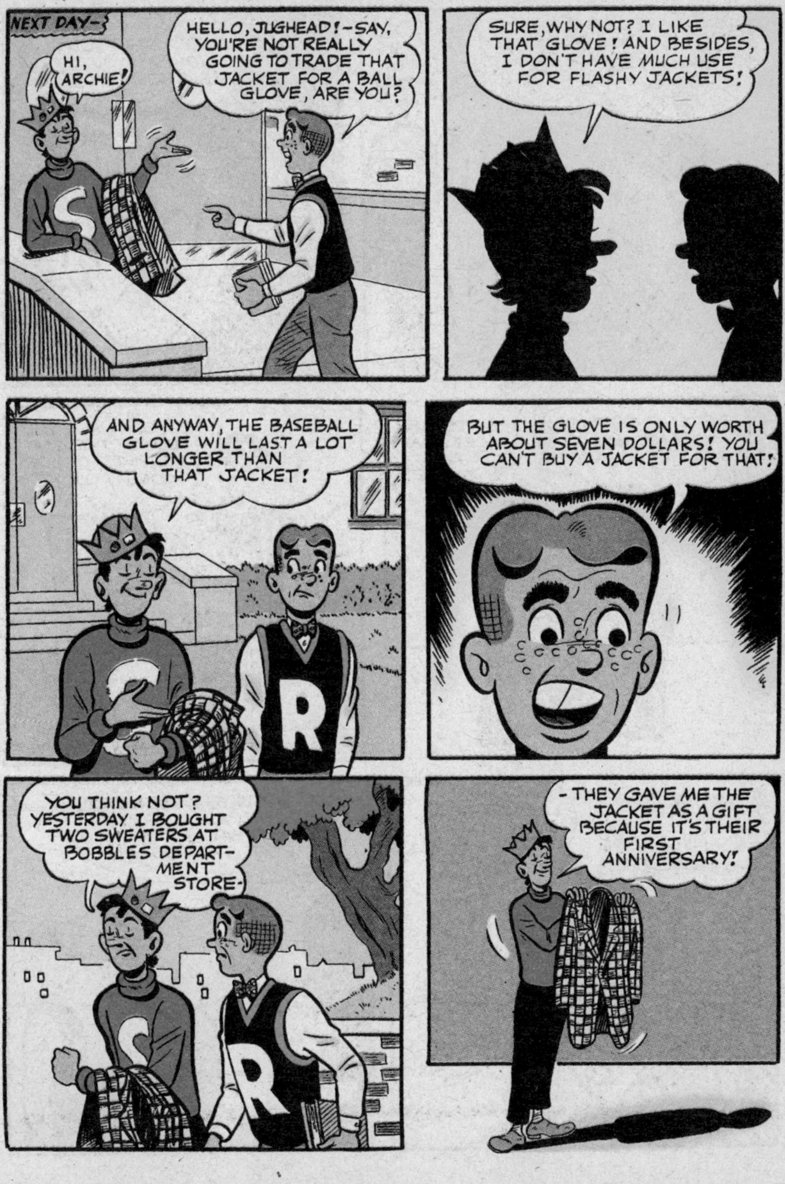
NEXT DAY-
HI, ARCHIE!
HELLO, JUGHEAD! -SAY, YOU'RE NOT REALLY GOING TO TRADE THAT JACKET FOR A BALL GLOVE, ARE YOU?
SURE, WHY NOT? I LIKE THAT GLOVE! AND BESIDES, I DON'T HAVE MUCH USE FOR FLASHY JACKETS!
AND ANYWAY, THE BASEBALL GLOVE WILL LAST A LOT LONGER THAN THAT JACKET!
BUT THE GLOVE IS ONLY WORTH ABOUT SEVEN DOLLARS! YOU CAN'T BUY A JACKET FOR THAT!
YOU THINK NOT? YESTERDAY I BOUGHT TWO SWEATERS AT BOBBLES DEPARTMENT STORE-
- THEY GAVE ME THE JACKET AS A GIFT BECAUSE IT'S THEIR FIRST ANNIVERSARY!

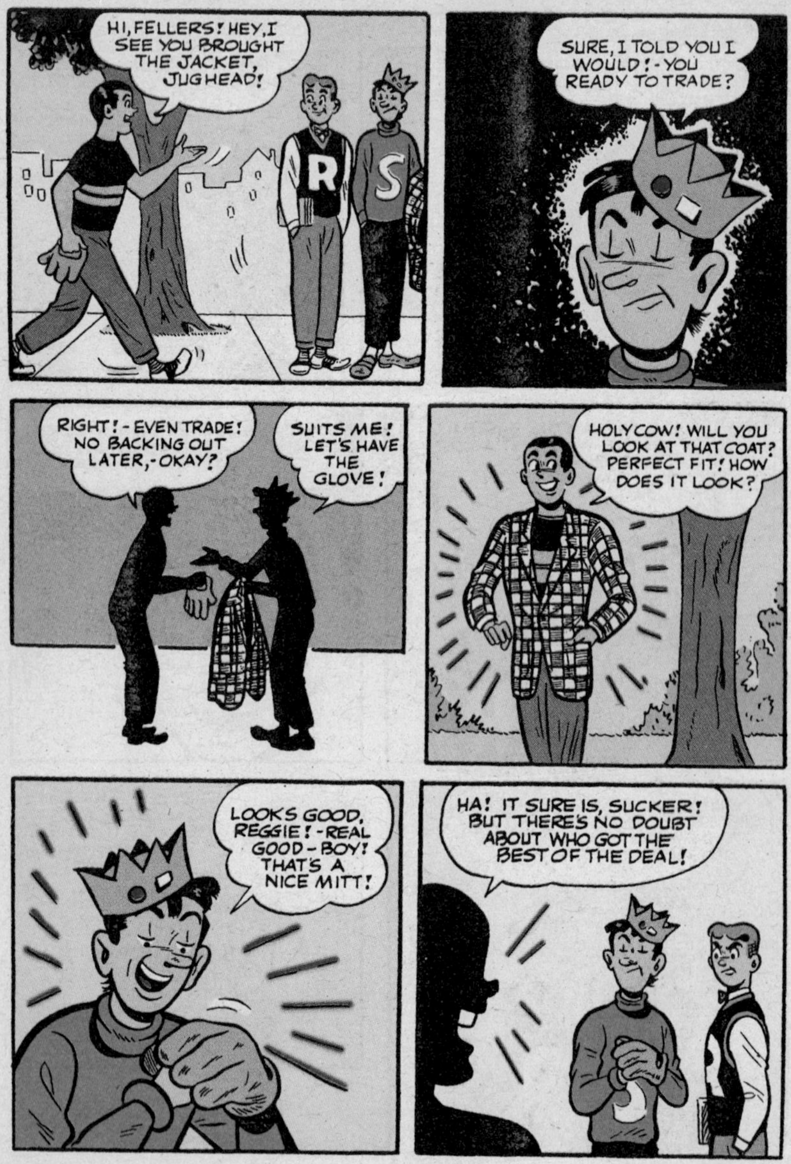
HI, FELLERS! HEY, I SEE YOU BROUGHT THE JACKET, JUGHEAD!
SURE, I TOLD YOU I WOULD! - YOU READY TO TRADE?
RIGHT! - EVEN TRADE! NO BACKING OUT LATER, - OKAY?
SUITS ME! LET'S HAVE THE GLOVE!
HOLY COW! WILL YOU LOOK AT THAT COAT? PERFECT FIT! HOW DOES IT LOOK?
LOOKS GOOD, REGGIE! - REAL GOOD - BOY! THAT'S A NICE MITT!
HA! IT SURE IS, SUCKER! BUT THERE'S NO DOUBT ABOUT WHO GOT THE BEST OF THE DEAL!

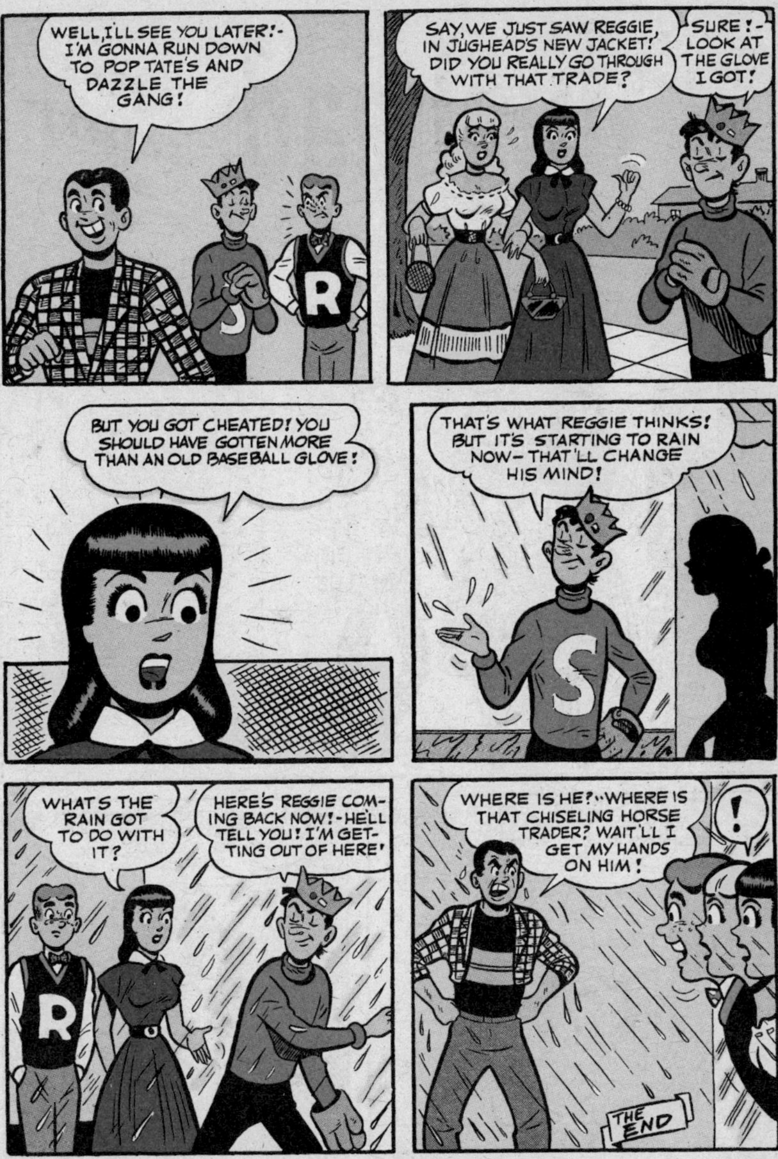
WELL, I'LL SEE YOU LATER! - I'M GONNA RUN DOWN TO POP TATE'S AND DAZZLE THE GANG!
SAY, WE JUST SAW REGGIE, IN JUGHEAD'S NEW JACKET! DID YOU REALLY GO THROUGH WITH THAT TRADE?
SURE! - LOOK AT THE GLOVE I GOT!
BUT YOU GOT CHEATED! YOU SHOULD HAVE GOTTEN MORE THAN AN OLD BASEBALL GLOVE!
THAT'S WHAT REGGIE THINKS! BUT IT'S STARTING TO RAIN NOW - THAT'LL CHANGE HIS MIND!
WHAT'S THE RAIN GOT TO DO WITH IT?
HERE'S REGGIE COMING BACK NOW! - HE'LL TELL YOU! I'M GETTING OUT OF HERE!
WHERE IS HE? - WHERE IS THAT CHISELING HORSE TRADER? WAIT'LL I GET MY HANDS ON HIM!
!
THE END

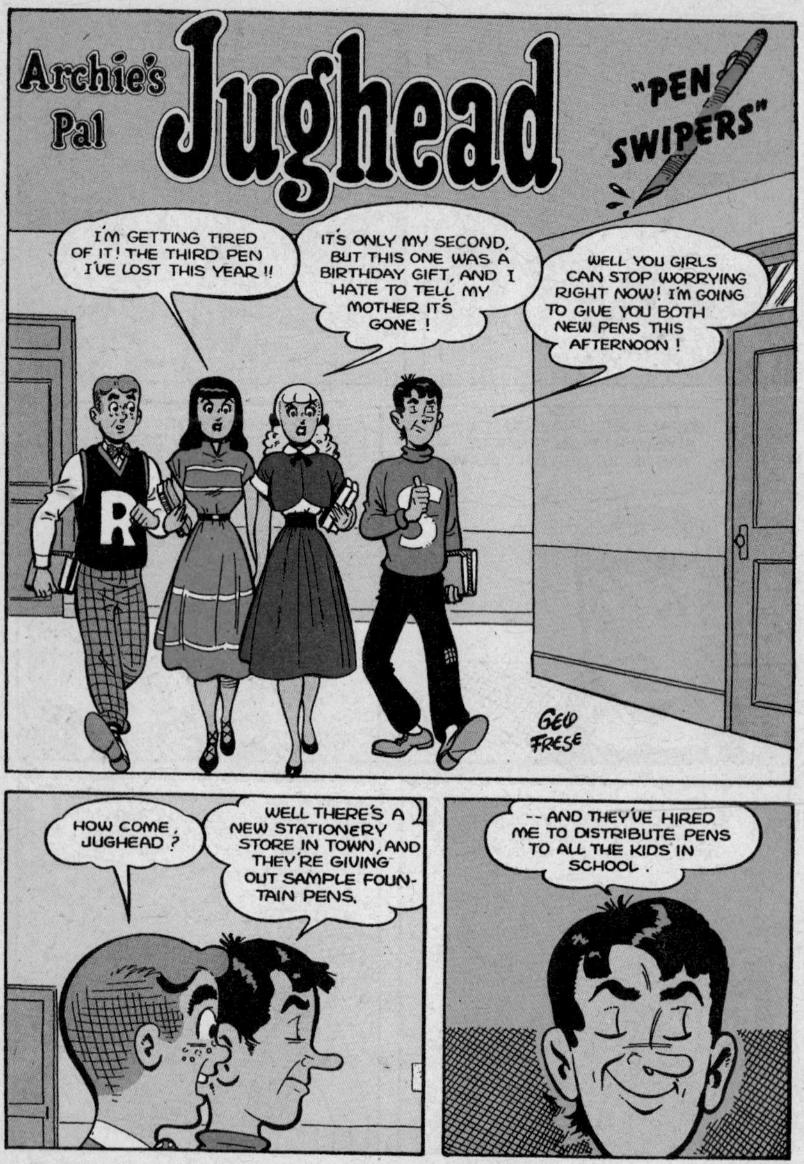
Archie's Pal
Jughead
"PEN SWIPERS"
I'M GETTING TIRED OF IT! THE THIRD PEN I'VE LOST THIS YEAR !!
IT'S ONLY MY SECOND, BUT THIS ONE WAS A BIRTHDAY GIFT, AND I HATE TO TELL MY MOTHER IT'S GONE !
WELL YOU GIRLS CAN STOP WORRYING RIGHT NOW! I'M GOING TO GIVE YOU BOTH NEW PENS THIS AFTERNOON !
GEO FRESE
HOW COME, JUGHEAD ?
WELL THERE'S A NEW STATIONERY STORE IN TOWN, AND THEY'RE GIVING OUT SAMPLE FOUNTAIN PENS.
-- AND THEY'VE HIRED ME TO DISTRIBUTE PENS TO ALL THE KIDS IN SCHOOL .

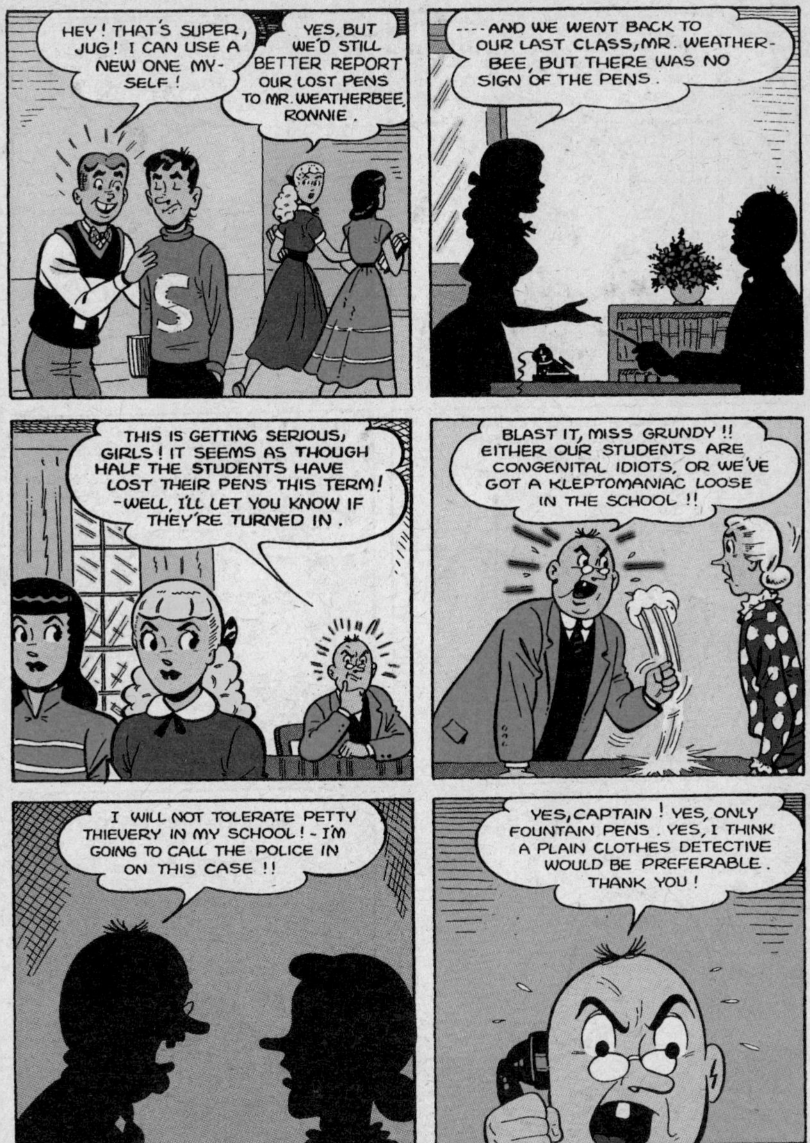
HEY! THAT'S SUPER, JUG! I CAN USE A NEW ONE MY-SELF!
YES, BUT WE'D STILL BETTER REPORT OUR LOST PENS TO MR. WEATHERBEE, RONNIE.
----AND WE WENT BACK TO OUR LAST CLASS, MR. WEATHER-BEE, BUT THERE WAS NO SIGN OF THE PENS.
THIS IS GETTING SERIOUS, GIRLS! IT SEEMS AS THOUGH HALF THE STUDENTS HAVE LOST THEIR PENS THIS TERM! -WELL, I'LL LET YOU KNOW IF THEY'RE TURNED IN.
BLAST IT, MISS GRUNDY!! EITHER OUR STUDENTS ARE CONGENITAL IDIOTS, OR WE'VE GOT A KLEPTOMANIAC LOOSE IN THE SCHOOL!!
I WILL NOT TOLERATE PETTY THIEVERY IN MY SCHOOL! - I'M GOING TO CALL THE POLICE IN ON THIS CASE!!
YES, CAPTAIN! YES, ONLY FOUNTAIN PENS. YES, I THINK A PLAIN CLOTHES DETECTIVE WOULD BE PREFERABLE. THANK YOU!

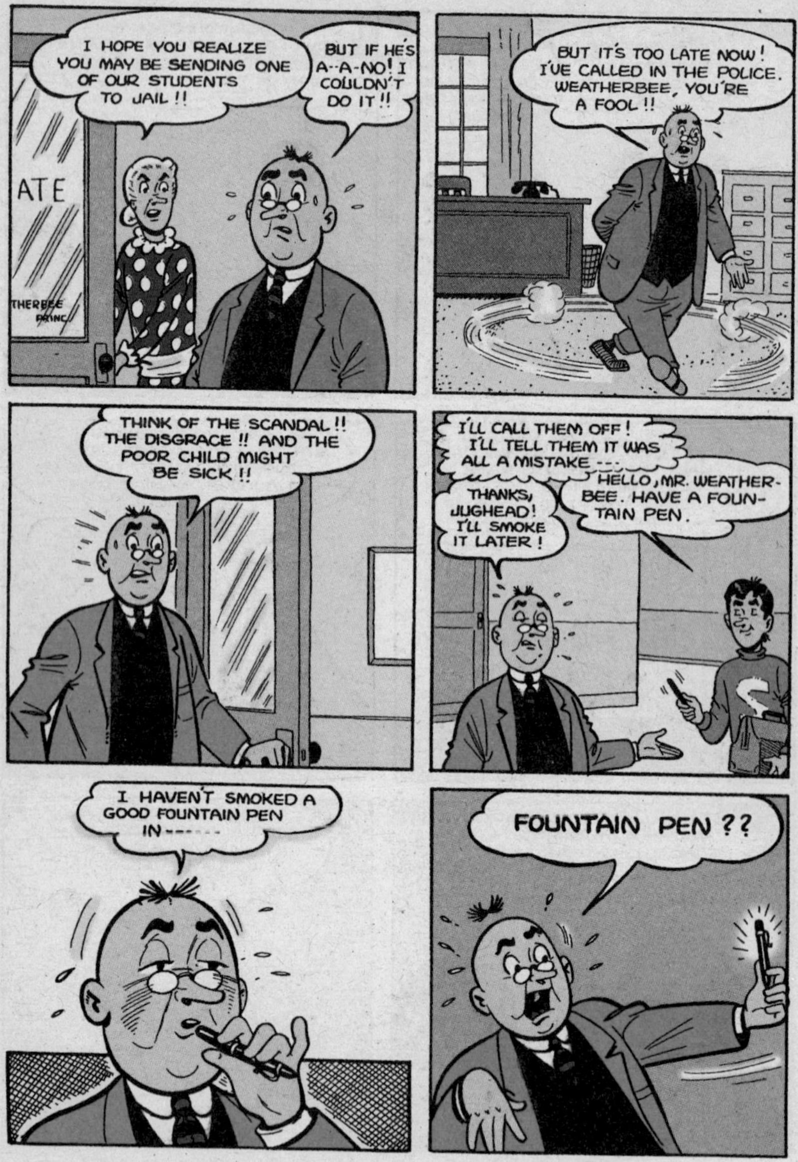
I HOPE YOU REALIZE YOU MAY BE SENDING ONE OF OUR STUDENTS TO JAIL !!
BUT IF HE'S A--A-NO! I COULDN'T DO IT !!
ATE
BUT IT'S TOO LATE NOW! I'VE CALLED IN THE POLICE. WEATHERBEE, YOU'RE A FOOL !!
THINK OF THE SCANDAL !! THE DISGRACE !! AND THE POOR CHILD MIGHT BE SICK !!
I'LL CALL THEM OFF! I'LL TELL THEM IT WAS ALL A MISTAKE ---
HELLO, MR. WEATHER-BEE. HAVE A FOUN-TAIN PEN.
THANKS, JUGHEAD! I'LL SMOKE IT LATER!
I HAVEN'T SMOKED A GOOD FOUNTAIN PEN IN ------
FOUNTAIN PEN ??

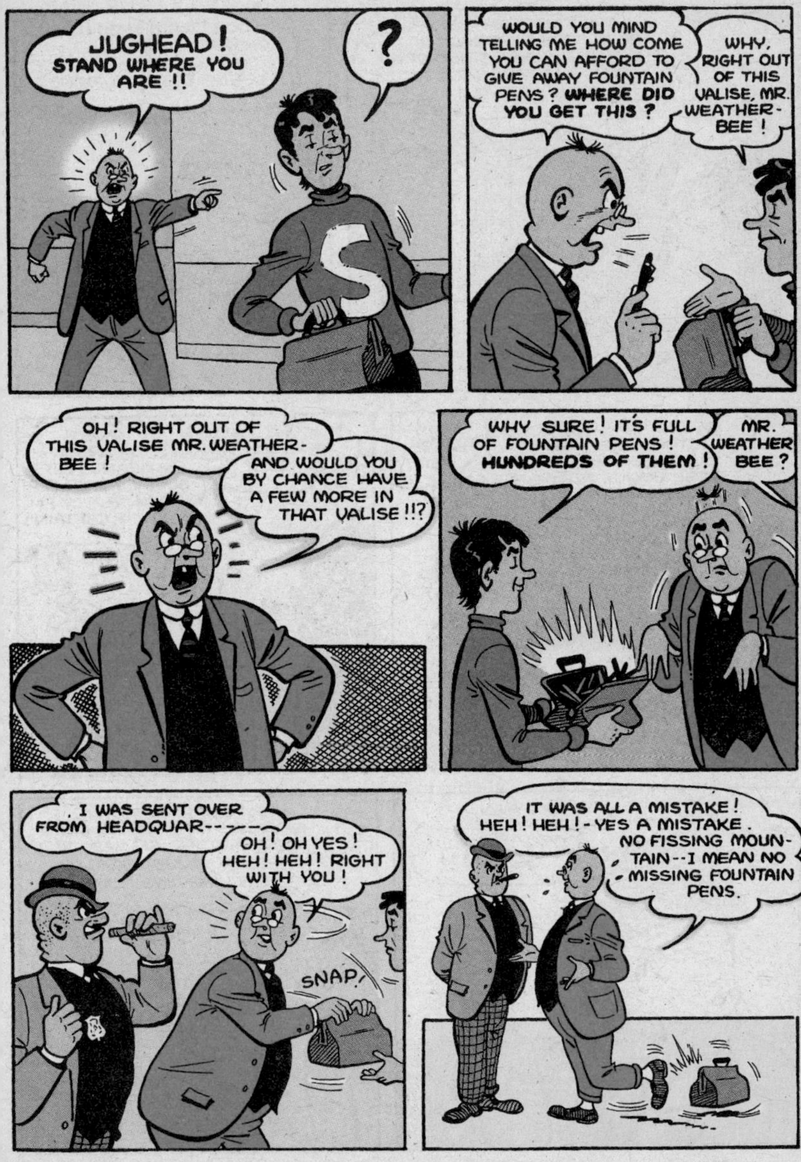
JUGHEAD! STAND WHERE YOU ARE !!
?
WOULD YOU MIND TELLING ME HOW COME YOU CAN AFFORD TO GIVE AWAY FOUNTAIN PENS? WHERE DID YOU GET THIS?
WHY, RIGHT OUT OF THIS VALISE, MR. WEATHER-BEE!
OH! RIGHT OUT OF THIS VALISE MR. WEATHER-BEE!
AND WOULD YOU BY CHANCE HAVE A FEW MORE IN THAT VALISE !!?
WHY SURE! IT'S FULL OF FOUNTAIN PENS! HUNDREDS OF THEM!
MR. WEATHER BEE?
I WAS SENT OVER FROM HEADQUAR-----
OH! OH YES! HEH! HEH! RIGHT WITH YOU!
SNAP!
IT WAS ALL A MISTAKE! HEH! HEH! - YES A MISTAKE. NO FISSING MOUN-TAIN--I MEAN NO MISSING FOUNTAIN PENS.

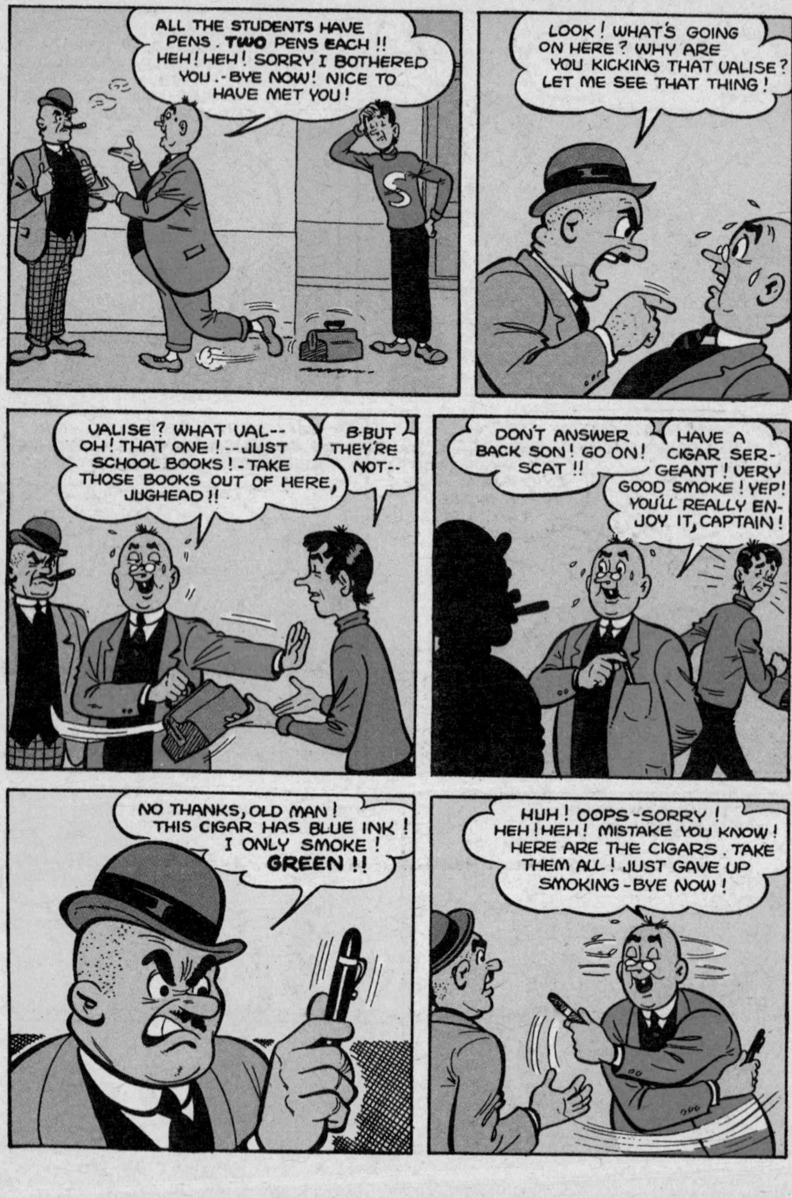
ALL THE STUDENTS HAVE PENS. TWO PENS EACH !! HEH! HEH! SORRY I BOTHERED YOU.- BYE NOW! NICE TO HAVE MET YOU!
LOOK! WHAT'S GOING ON HERE? WHY ARE YOU KICKING THAT VALISE? LET ME SEE THAT THING!
VALISE? WHAT VAL-- OH! THAT ONE! --JUST SCHOOL BOOKS! - TAKE THOSE BOOKS OUT OF HERE, JUGHEAD !!
B-BUT THEY'RE NOT--
DON'T ANSWER BACK SON! GO ON! SCAT !!
HAVE A CIGAR SERGEANT! VERY GOOD SMOKE! YEP! YOU'LL REALLY ENJOY IT, CAPTAIN!
NO THANKS, OLD MAN! THIS CIGAR HAS BLUE INK! I ONLY SMOKE! GREEN !!
HUH! OOPS-SORRY! HEH! HEH! MISTAKE YOU KNOW! HERE ARE THE CIGARS. TAKE THEM ALL! JUST GAVE UP SMOKING-BYE NOW!

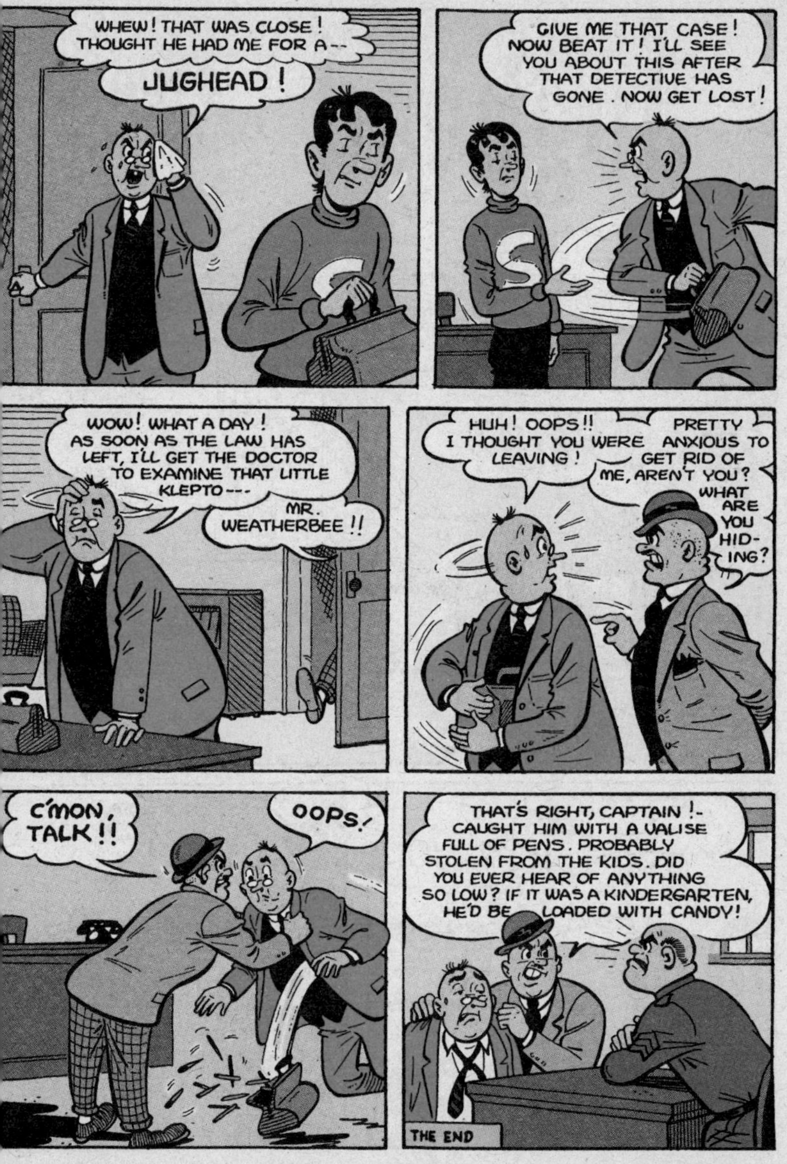

WHEW! THAT WAS CLOSE! THOUGHT HE HAD ME FOR A--
JUGHEAD!
GIVE ME THAT CASE! NOW BEAT IT! I'LL SEE YOU ABOUT THIS AFTER THAT DETECTIVE HAS GONE. NOW GET LOST!
WOW! WHAT A DAY! AS SOON AS THE LAW HAS LEFT, I'LL GET THE DOCTOR TO EXAMINE THAT LITTLE KLEPTO---
MR. WEATHERBEE!!
HUH! OOPS!! I THOUGHT YOU WERE LEAVING!
PRETTY ANXIOUS TO GET RID OF ME, AREN'T YOU? WHAT ARE YOU HIDING?
C'MON, TALK!!
OOPS!
THAT'S RIGHT, CAPTAIN!- CAUGHT HIM WITH A VALISE FULL OF PENS. PROBABLY STOLEN FROM THE KIDS. DID YOU EVER HEAR OF ANYTHING SO LOW? IF IT WAS A KINDERGARTEN, HE'D BE LOADED WITH CANDY!
THE END

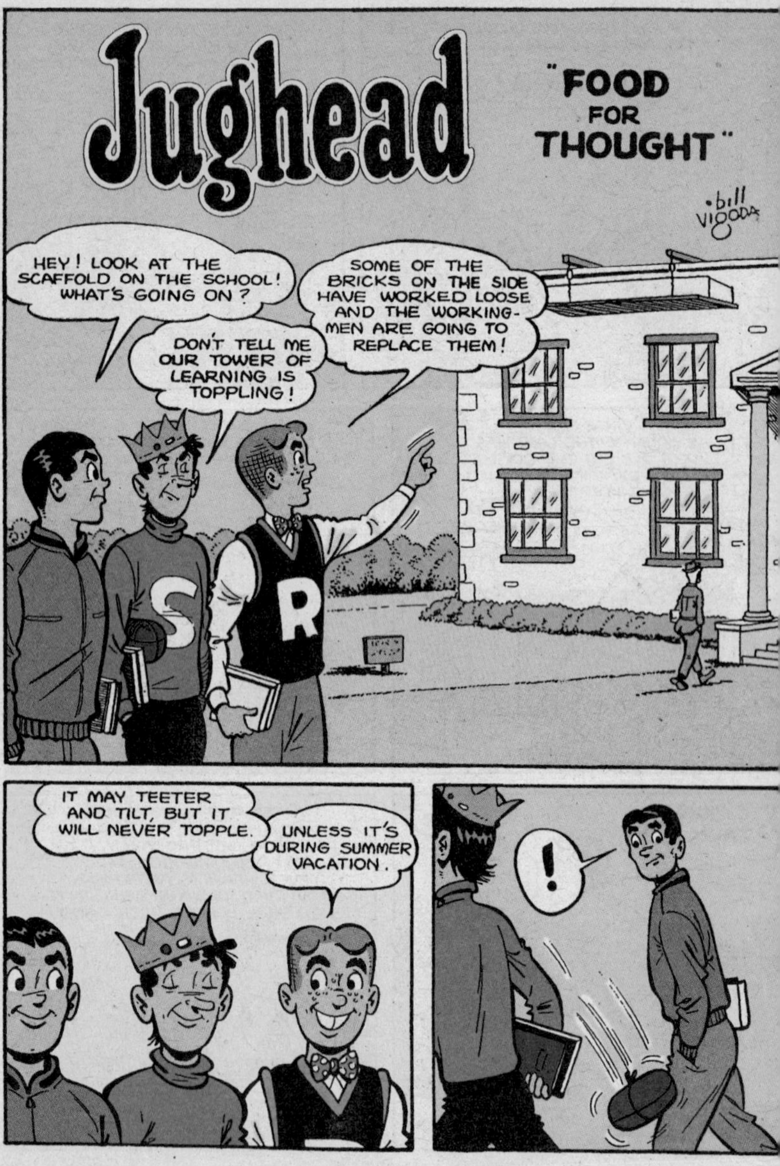
Jughead
"FOOD FOR THOUGHT"
bill VIGODA
HEY! LOOK AT THE SCAFFOLD ON THE SCHOOL! WHAT'S GOING ON?
SOME OF THE BRICKS ON THE SIDE HAVE WORKED LOOSE AND THE WORKINGMEN ARE GOING TO REPLACE THEM!
DON'T TELL ME OUR TOWER OF LEARNING IS TOPPLING!
S
R
IT MAY TEETER AND TILT, BUT IT WILL NEVER TOPPLE.
UNLESS IT'S DURING SUMMER VACATION.
!

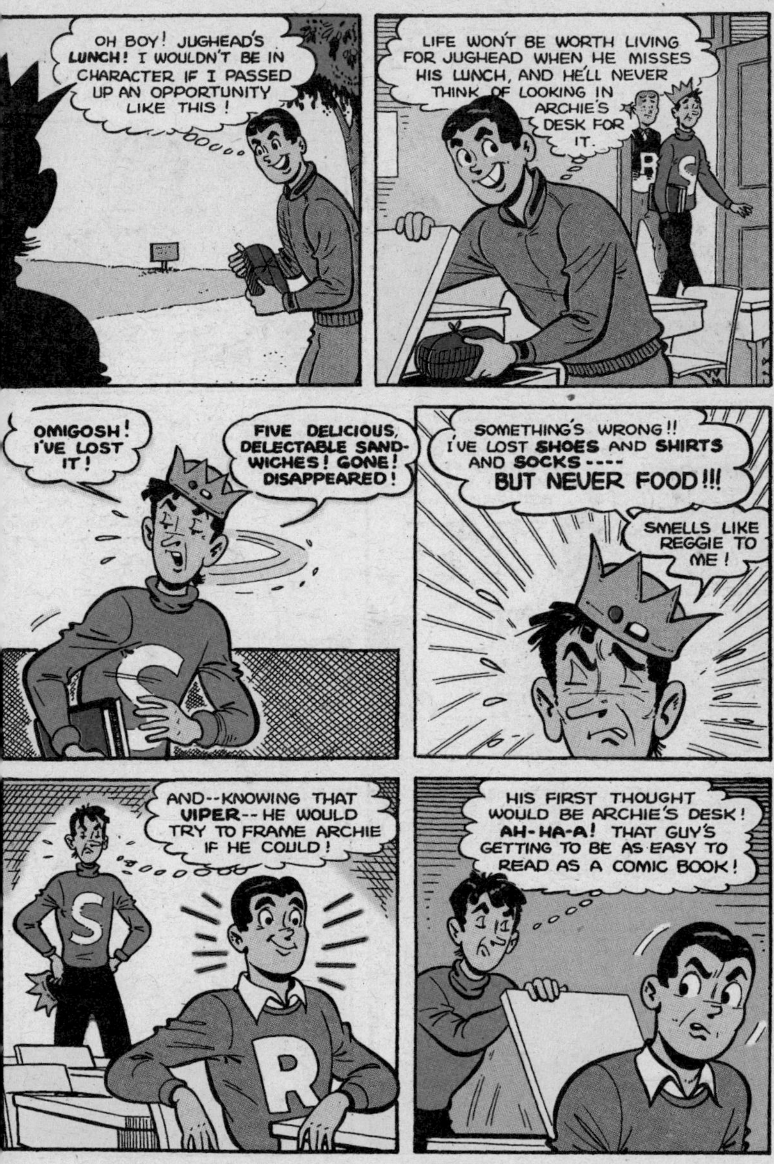
OH BOY! JUGHEAD'S LUNCH! I WOULDN'T BE IN CHARACTER IF I PASSED UP AN OPPORTUNITY LIKE THIS!
LIFE WON'T BE WORTH LIVING FOR JUGHEAD WHEN HE MISSES HIS LUNCH, AND HE'LL NEVER THINK OF LOOKING IN ARCHIE'S DESK FOR IT.
OMIGOSH! I'VE LOST IT!
FIVE DELICIOUS, DELECTABLE SANDWICHES! GONE! DISAPPEARED!
SOMETHING'S WRONG!! I'VE LOST SHOES AND SHIRTS AND SOCKS ---- BUT NEVER FOOD!!!
SMELLS LIKE REGGIE TO ME!
AND--KNOWING THAT VIPER-- HE WOULD TRY TO FRAME ARCHIE IF HE COULD!
HIS FIRST THOUGHT WOULD BE ARCHIE'S DESK! AH-HA-A! THAT GUY'S GETTING TO BE AS EASY TO READ AS A COMIC BOOK!

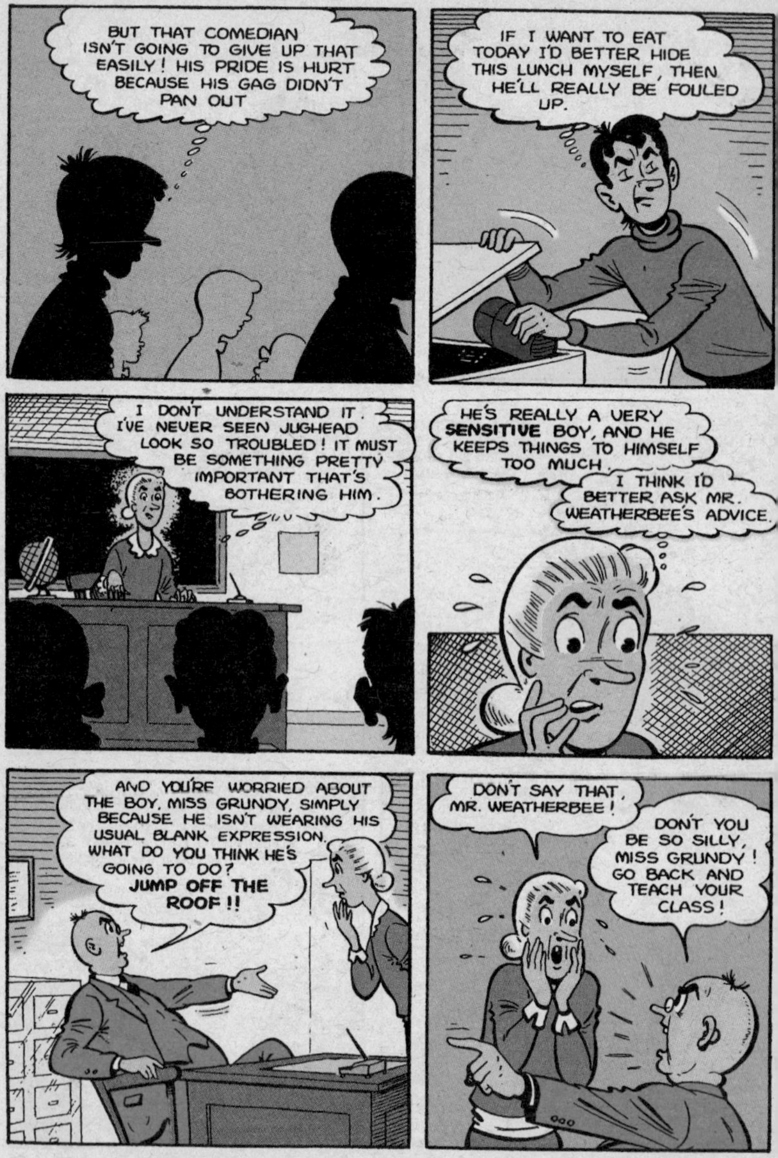
BUT THAT COMEDIAN ISN'T GOING TO GIVE UP THAT EASILY! HIS PRIDE IS HURT BECAUSE HIS GAG DIDN'T PAN OUT
IF I WANT TO EAT TODAY I'D BETTER HIDE THIS LUNCH MYSELF, THEN HE'LL REALLY BE FOULED UP.
I DON'T UNDERSTAND IT. I'VE NEVER SEEN JUGHEAD LOOK SO TROUBLED! IT MUST BE SOMETHING PRETTY IMPORTANT THAT'S BOTHERING HIM.
HE'S REALLY A VERY SENSITIVE BOY, AND HE KEEPS THINGS TO HIMSELF TOO MUCH.
I THINK I'D BETTER ASK MR. WEATHERBEE'S ADVICE.
AND YOU'RE WORRIED ABOUT THE BOY, MISS GRUNDY, SIMPLY BECAUSE HE ISN'T WEARING HIS USUAL BLANK EXPRESSION. WHAT DO YOU THINK HE'S GOING TO DO? JUMP OFF THE ROOF!!
DON'T SAY THAT, MR. WEATHERBEE!
DON'T YOU BE SO SILLY, MISS GRUNDY! GO BACK AND TEACH YOUR CLASS!

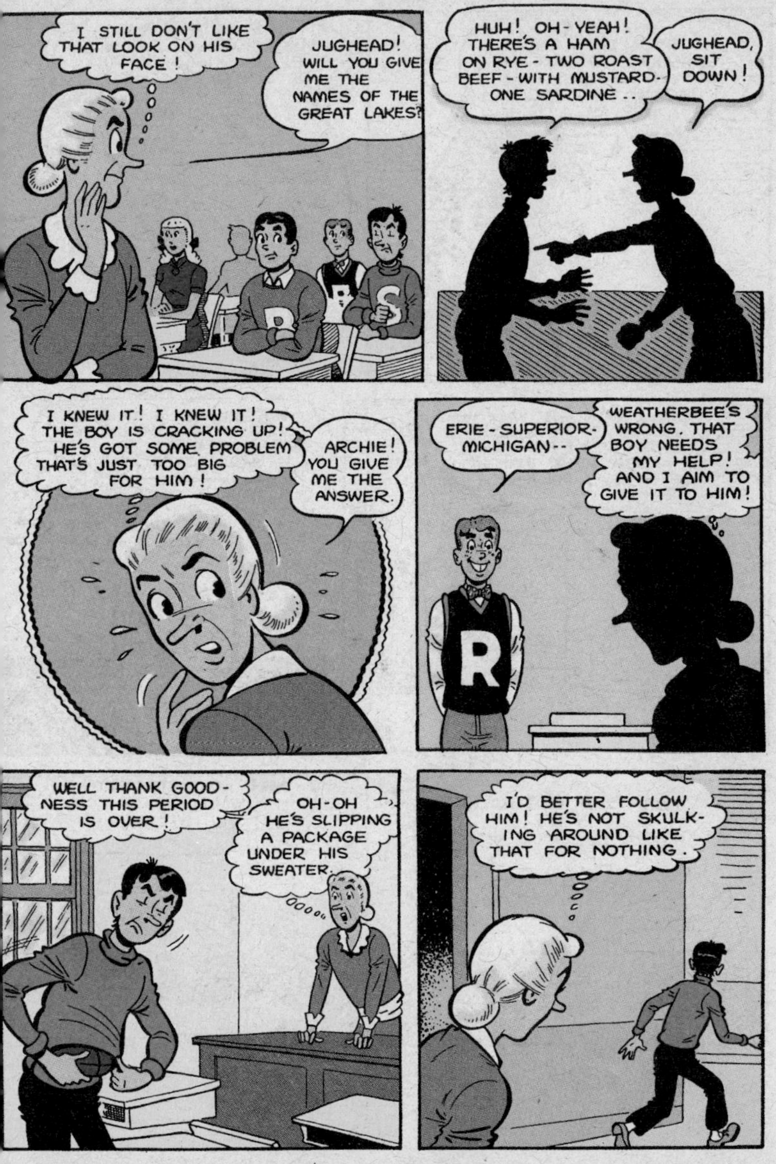
I STILL DON'T LIKE THAT LOOK ON HIS FACE!
JUGHEAD! WILL YOU GIVE ME THE NAMES OF THE GREAT LAKES?
HUH! OH-YEAH! THERE'S A HAM ON RYE - TWO ROAST BEEF - WITH MUSTARD - ONE SARDINE..
JUGHEAD, SIT DOWN!
I KNEW IT! I KNEW IT! THE BOY IS CRACKING UP! HE'S GOT SOME PROBLEM THAT'S JUST TOO BIG FOR HIM!
ARCHIE! YOU GIVE ME THE ANSWER.
ERIE - SUPERIOR - MICHIGAN--
WEATHERBEE'S WRONG. THAT BOY NEEDS MY HELP! AND I AIM TO GIVE IT TO HIM!
WELL THANK GOODNESS THIS PERIOD IS OVER!
OH-OH HE'S SLIPPING A PACKAGE UNDER HIS SWEATER.
I'D BETTER FOLLOW HIM! HE'S NOT SKULKING AROUND LIKE THAT FOR NOTHING.

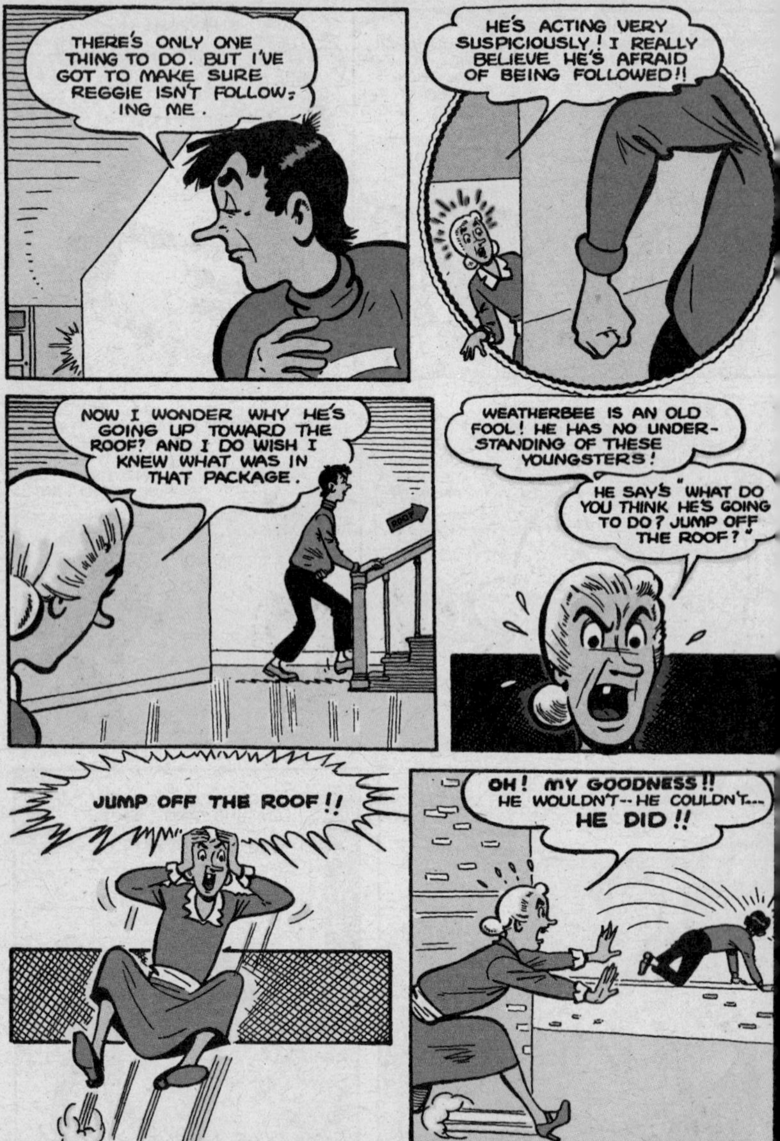
THERE'S ONLY ONE THING TO DO. BUT I'VE GOT TO MAKE SURE REGGIE ISN'T FOLLOW-ING ME.
HE'S ACTING VERY SUSPICIOUSLY! I REALLY BELIEVE HE'S AFRAID OF BEING FOLLOWED!!
NOW I WONDER WHY HE'S GOING UP TOWARD THE ROOF? AND I DO WISH I KNEW WHAT WAS IN THAT PACKAGE.
ROOF
WEATHERBEE IS AN OLD FOOL! HE HAS NO UNDER-STANDING OF THESE YOUNGSTERS!
HE SAY'S "WHAT DO YOU THINK HE'S GOING TO DO? JUMP OFF THE ROOF?"
JUMP OFF THE ROOF!!
OH! MY GOODNESS!! HE WOULDN'T-- HE COULDN'T--- HE DID!!

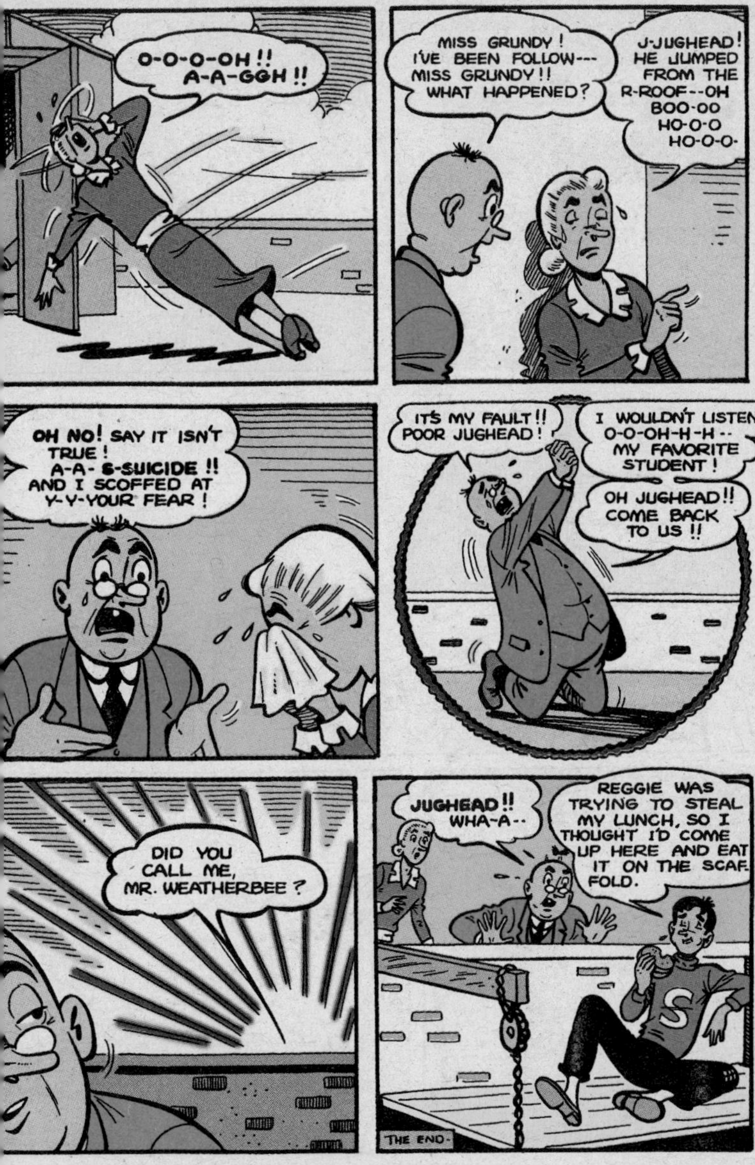
O-O-O-OH!!
A-A-GGH!!
MISS GRUNDY! I'VE BEEN FOLLOW--- MISS GRUNDY!! WHAT HAPPENED?
J-JUGHEAD! HE JUMPED FROM THE R-ROOF--OH BOO-OO HO-O-O HO-O-O-
OH NO! SAY IT ISN'T TRUE! A-A- S-SUICIDE!! AND I SCOFFED AT Y-Y-YOUR FEAR!
IT'S MY FAULT!! POOR JUGHEAD!
I WOULDN'T LISTEN O-O-OH-H-H -- MY FAVORITE STUDENT!
OH JUGHEAD!! COME BACK TO US!!
DID YOU CALL ME, MR. WEATHERBEE?
JUGHEAD!! WHA-A--
REGGIE WAS TRYING TO STEAL MY LUNCH, SO I THOUGHT I'D COME UP HERE AND EAT IT ON THE SCAF-FOLD.
THE END-

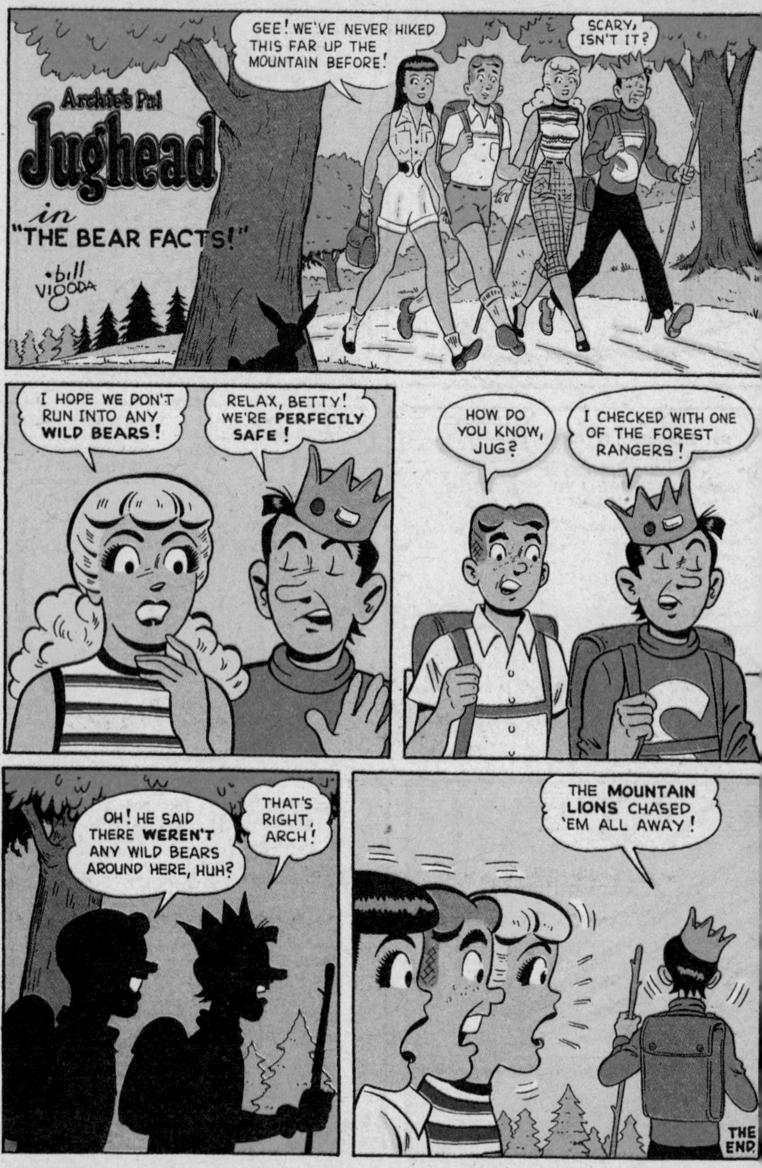
Archie's Pal
Jughead
in
"THE BEAR FACTS!"
bill VIGODA
GEE! WE'VE NEVER HIKED THIS FAR UP THE MOUNTAIN BEFORE!
SCARY, ISN'T IT?
I HOPE WE DON'T RUN INTO ANY WILD BEARS!
RELAX, BETTY! WE'RE PERFECTLY SAFE!
HOW DO YOU KNOW, JUG?
I CHECKED WITH ONE OF THE FOREST RANGERS!
OH! HE SAID THERE WEREN'T ANY WILD BEARS AROUND HERE, HUH?
THAT'S RIGHT, ARCH!
THE MOUNTAIN LIONS CHASED 'EM ALL AWAY!
THE END.

Veronica in ARCHIE -or- Archie?!

Chapter One

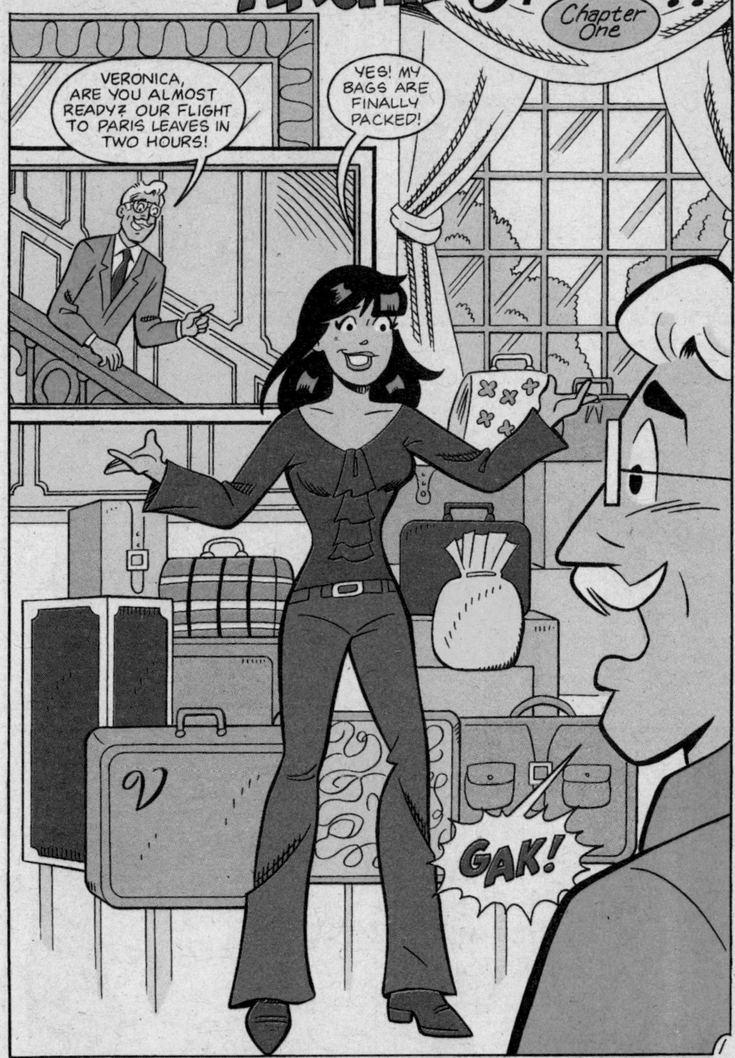
VERONICA, ARE YOU ALMOST READY? OUR FLIGHT TO PARIS LEAVES IN TWO HOURS!
YES! MY BAGS ARE FINALLY PACKED!
GAK!

Script & Pencils: **Dan Parent** Inks: **Jim Amash** Letters: **Teresa Davidson** Colors: **Barry Grossman**
Editor-In-Chief: **Victor Gorelick** President: **Mike Pellerito** Publisher: **Jon Goldwater**

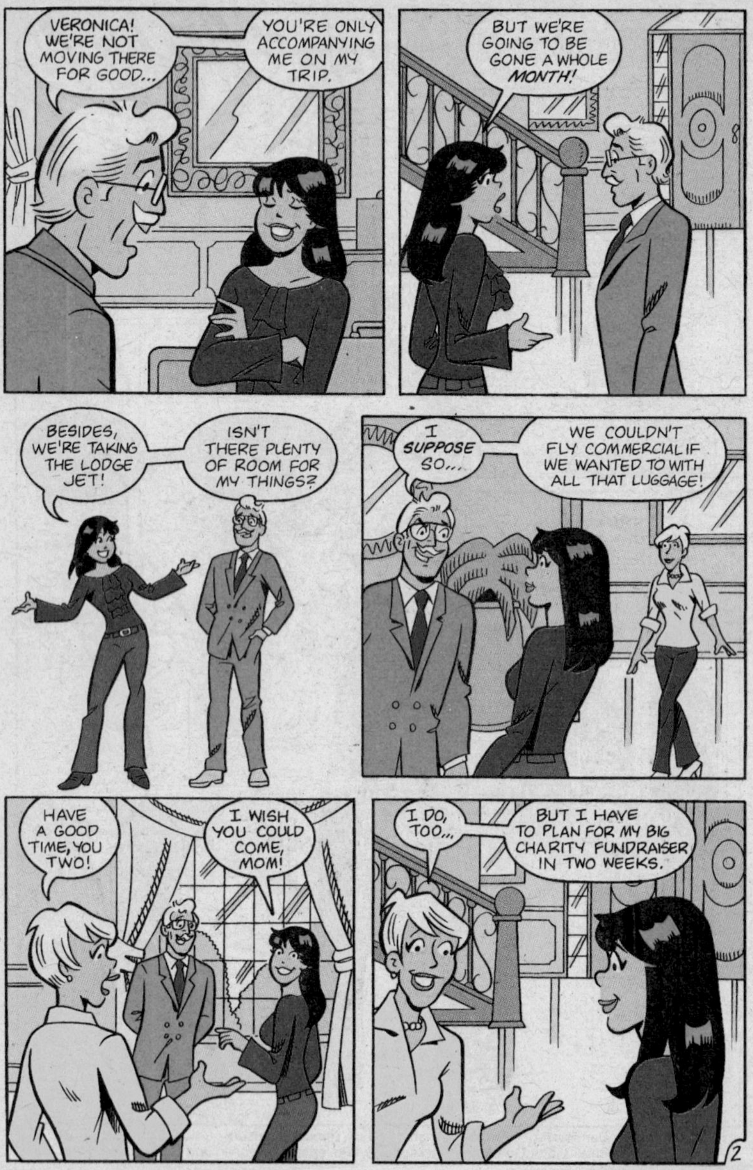
VERONICA! WE'RE NOT MOVING THERE FOR GOOD...
YOU'RE ONLY ACCOMPANYING ME ON MY TRIP.
BUT WE'RE GOING TO BE GONE A WHOLE MONTH!
BESIDES, WE'RE TAKING THE LODGE JET!
ISN'T THERE PLENTY OF ROOM FOR MY THINGS?
I SUPPOSE SO...
WE COULDN'T FLY COMMERCIAL IF WE WANTED TO WITH ALL THAT LUGGAGE!
HAVE A GOOD TIME, YOU TWO!
I WISH YOU COULD COME, MOM!
I DO, TOO...
BUT I HAVE TO PLAN FOR MY BIG CHARITY FUNDRAISER IN TWO WEEKS.

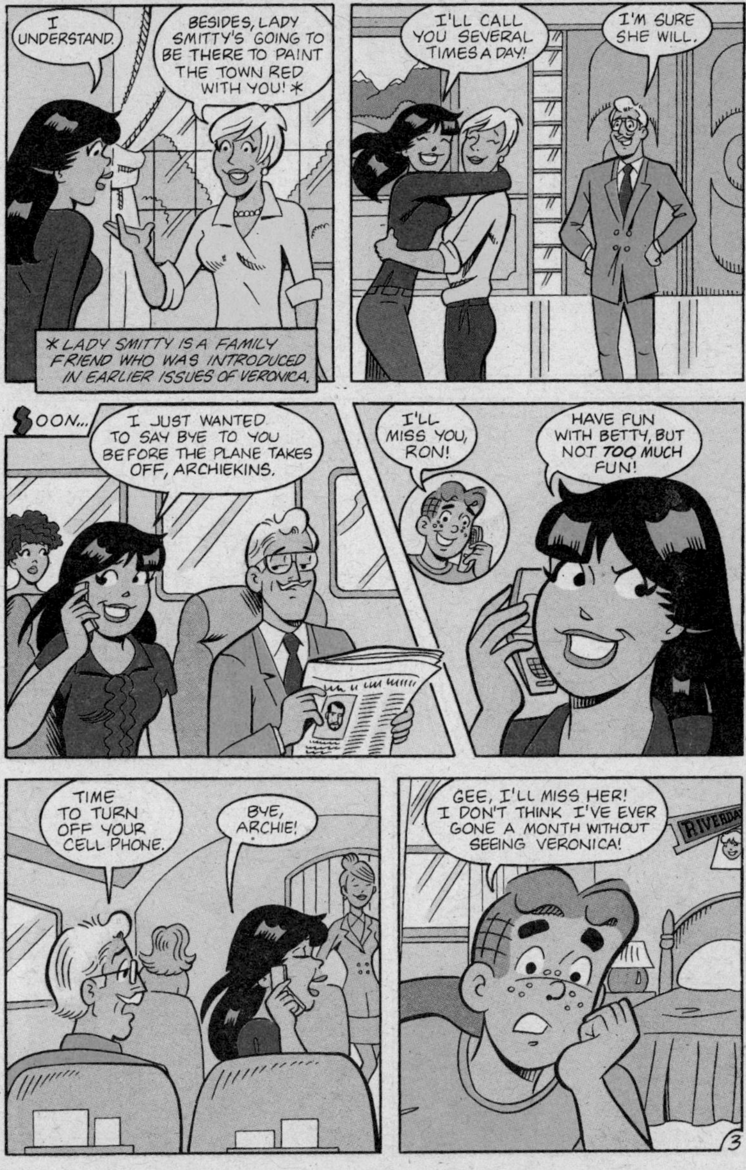
I UNDERSTAND.
BESIDES, LADY SMITTY'S GOING TO BE THERE TO PAINT THE TOWN RED WITH YOU! *
* LADY SMITTY IS A FAMILY FRIEND WHO WAS INTRODUCED IN EARLIER ISSUES OF VERONICA.
I'LL CALL YOU SEVERAL TIMES A DAY!
I'M SURE SHE WILL.
SOON...
I JUST WANTED TO SAY BYE TO YOU BEFORE THE PLANE TAKES OFF, ARCHIEKINS.
I'LL MISS YOU, RON!
HAVE FUN WITH BETTY, BUT NOT TOO MUCH FUN!
TIME TO TURN OFF YOUR CELL PHONE.
BYE, ARCHIE!
GEE, I'LL MISS HER! I DON'T THINK I'VE EVER GONE A MONTH WITHOUT SEEING VERONICA!
RIVERDA

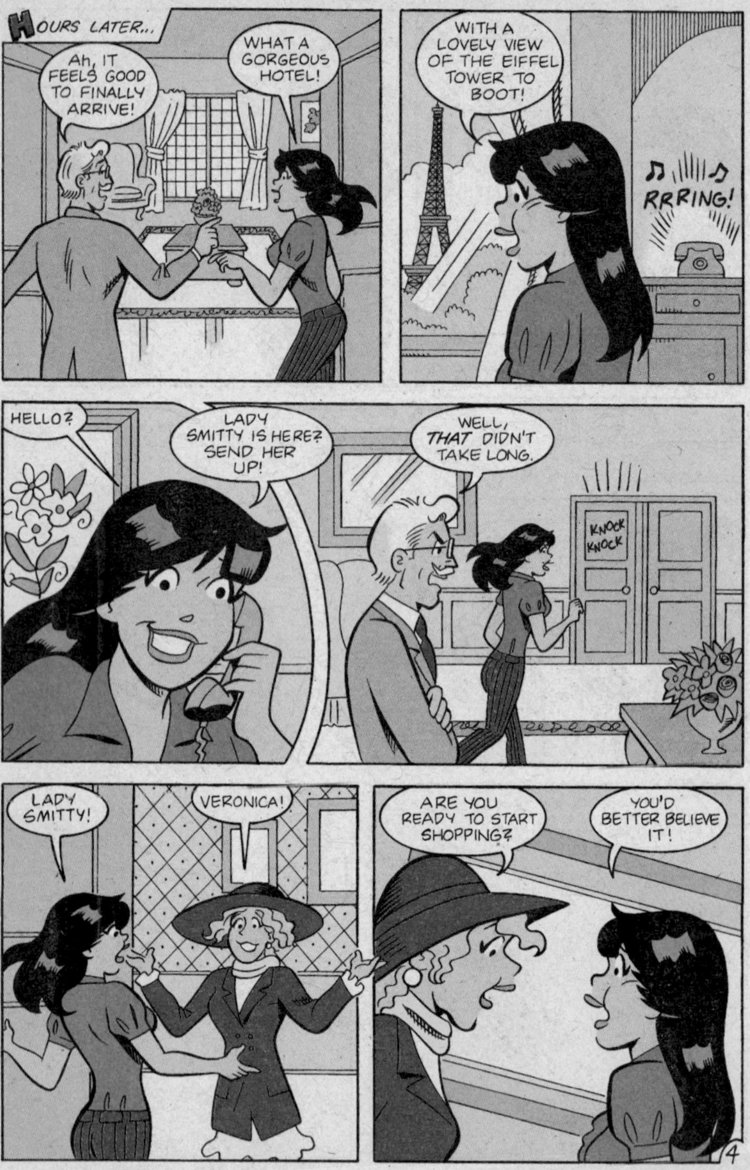
HOURS LATER...
Ah, IT FEELS GOOD TO FINALLY ARRIVE!
WHAT A GORGEOUS HOTEL!
WITH A LOVELY VIEW OF THE EIFFEL TOWER TO BOOT!
RRRING!
HELLO?
LADY SMITTY IS HERE? SEND HER UP!
WELL, THAT DIDN'T TAKE LONG.
KNOCK KNOCK
LADY SMITTY!
VERONICA!
ARE YOU READY TO START SHOPPING?
YOU'D BETTER BELIEVE IT!
4

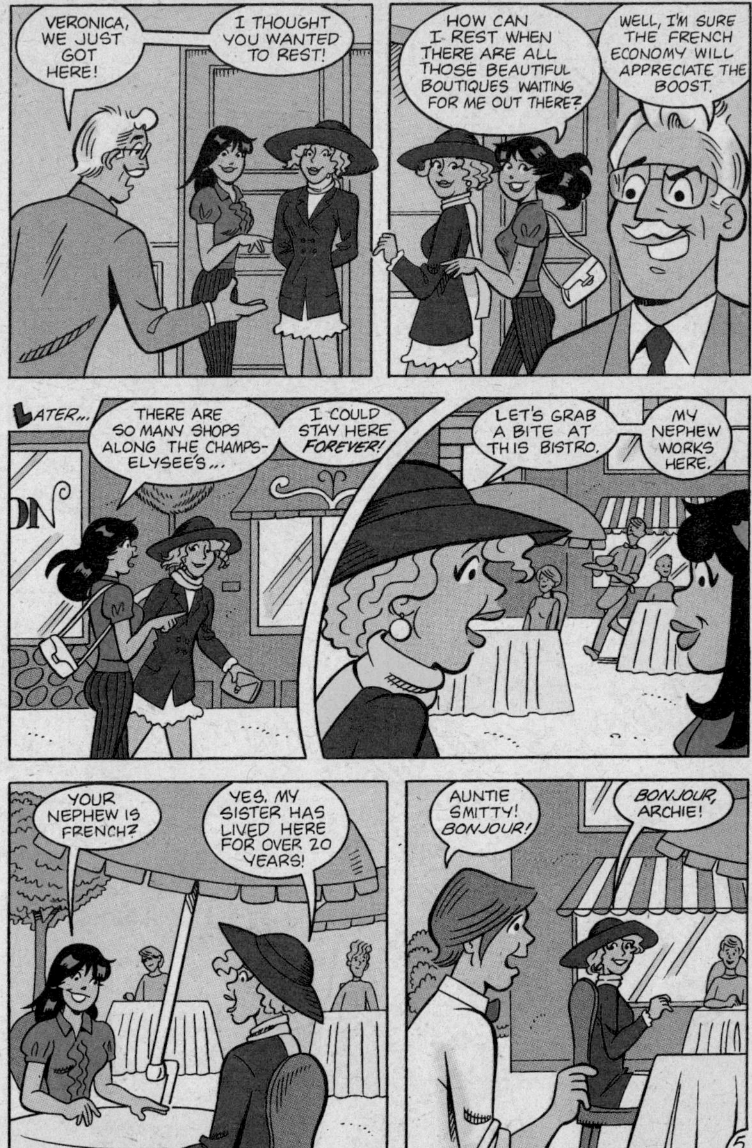

VERONICA, WE JUST GOT HERE!
I THOUGHT YOU WANTED TO REST!
HOW CAN I REST WHEN THERE ARE ALL THOSE BEAUTIFUL BOUTIQUES WAITING FOR ME OUT THERE?
WELL, I'M SURE THE FRENCH ECONOMY WILL APPRECIATE THE BOOST.
LATER...
THERE ARE SO MANY SHOPS ALONG THE CHAMPS-ELYSEE'S...
I COULD STAY HERE *FOREVER!*
LET'S GRAB A BITE AT THIS BISTRO.
MY NEPHEW WORKS HERE.
YOUR NEPHEW IS FRENCH?
YES. MY SISTER HAS LIVED HERE FOR OVER 20 YEARS!
AUNTIE SMITTY! *BONJOUR!*
BONJOUR, ARCHIE!

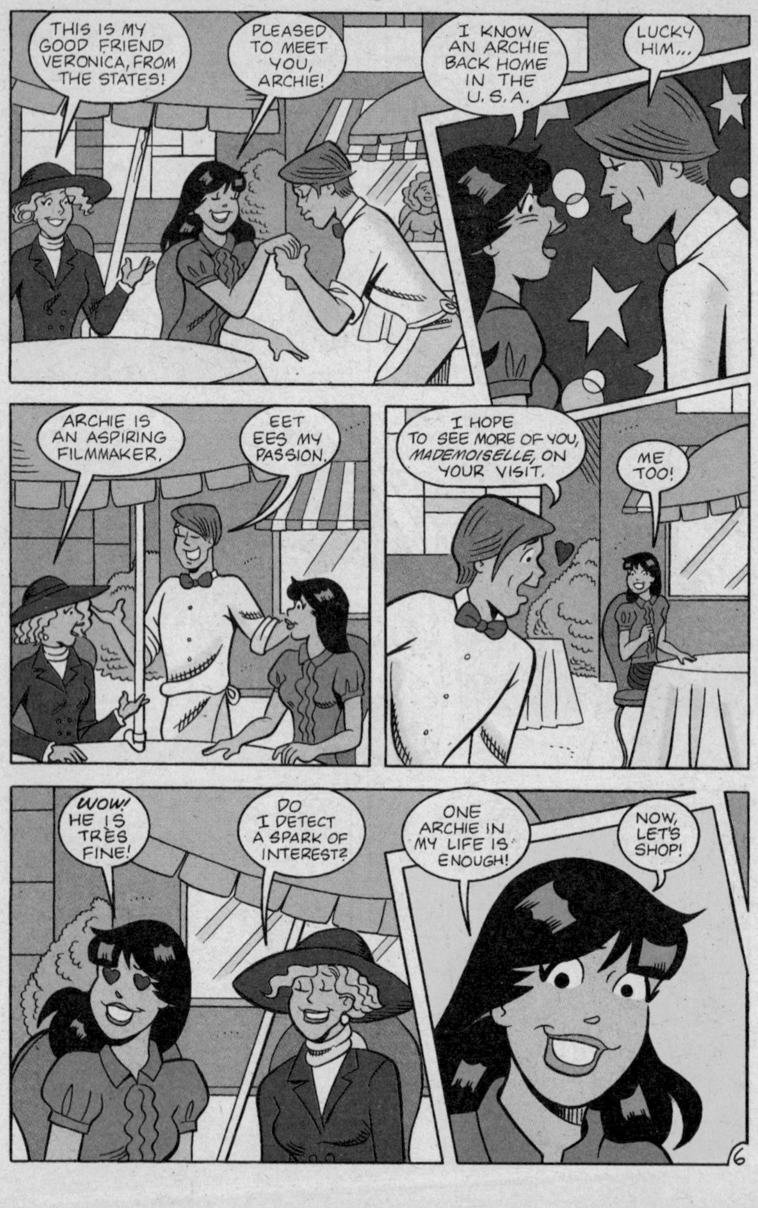
THIS IS MY GOOD FRIEND VERONICA, FROM THE STATES!
PLEASED TO MEET YOU, ARCHIE!
I KNOW AN ARCHIE BACK HOME IN THE U.S.A.
LUCKY HIM...
ARCHIE IS AN ASPIRING FILMMAKER.
EET EES MY PASSION.
I HOPE TO SEE MORE OF YOU, *MADEMOISELLE*, ON YOUR VISIT.
ME TOO!
WOW! HE IS TRÈS FINE!
DO I DETECT A SPARK OF INTEREST?
ONE ARCHIE IN MY LIFE IS ENOUGH!
NOW, LET'S SHOP!

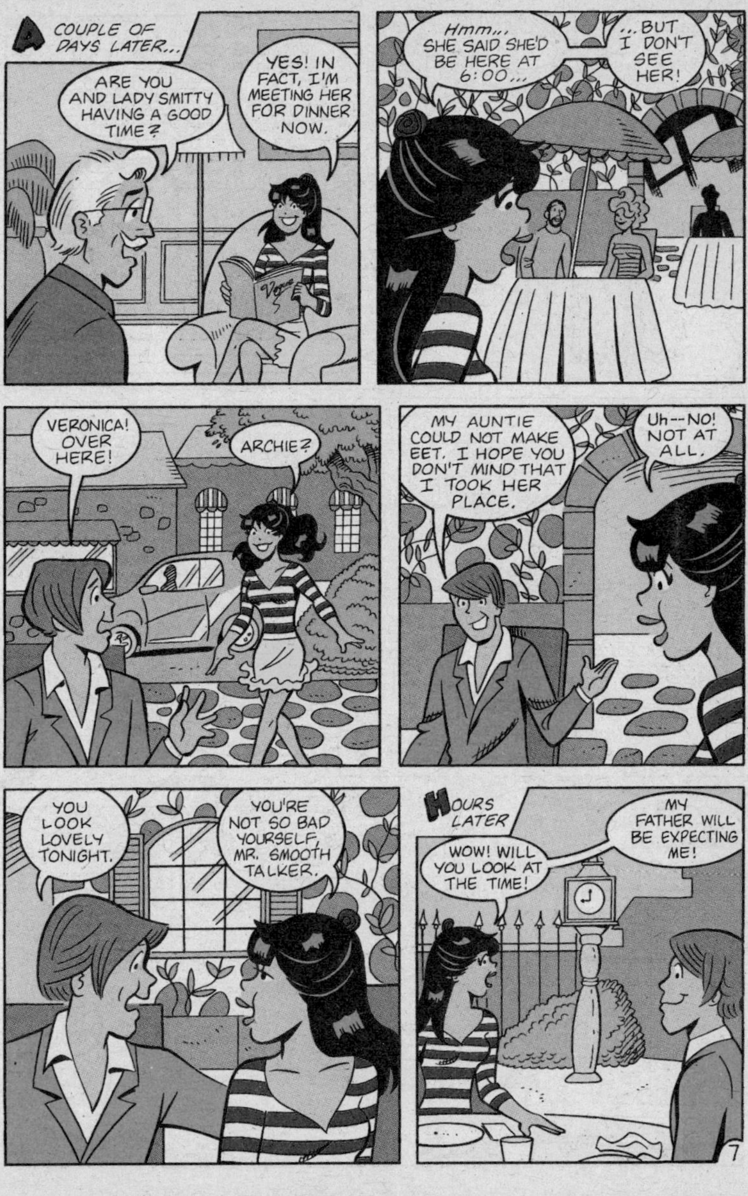
A COUPLE OF DAYS LATER...
ARE YOU AND LADY SMITTY HAVING A GOOD TIME?
YES! IN FACT, I'M MEETING HER FOR DINNER NOW.
Vogue
Hmm... SHE SAID SHE'D BE HERE AT 6:00...
...BUT I DON'T SEE HER!
VERONICA! OVER HERE!
ARCHIE?
MY AUNTIE COULD NOT MAKE EET. I HOPE YOU DON'T MIND THAT I TOOK HER PLACE.
Uh--NO! NOT AT ALL.
YOU LOOK LOVELY TONIGHT.
YOU'RE NOT SO BAD YOURSELF, MR. SMOOTH TALKER.
HOURS LATER
WOW! WILL YOU LOOK AT THE TIME!
MY FATHER WILL BE EXPECTING ME!

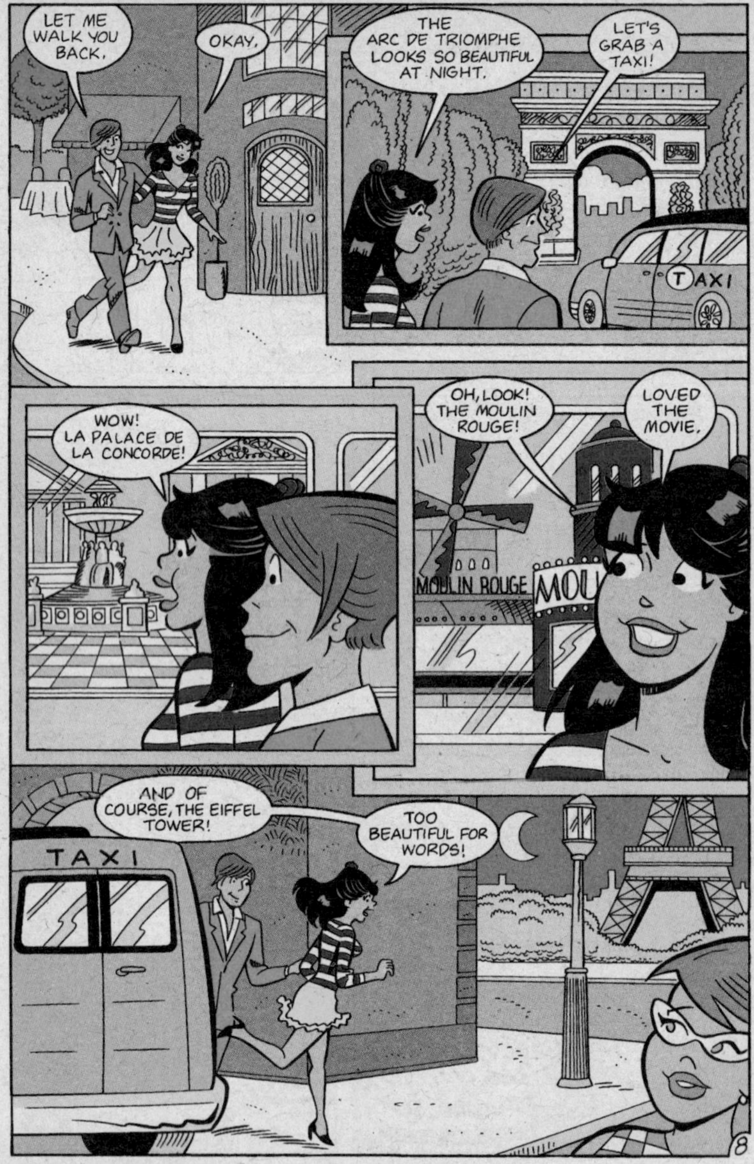
LET ME WALK YOU BACK.
OKAY.
THE ARC DE TRIOMPHE LOOKS SO BEAUTIFUL AT NIGHT.
LET'S GRAB A TAXI!
TAXI
WOW! LA PALACE DE LA CONCORDE!
OH, LOOK! THE MOULIN ROUGE!
LOVED THE MOVIE.
MOULIN ROUGE
MOU
AND OF COURSE, THE EIFFEL TOWER!
TOO BEAUTIFUL FOR WORDS!
TAXI

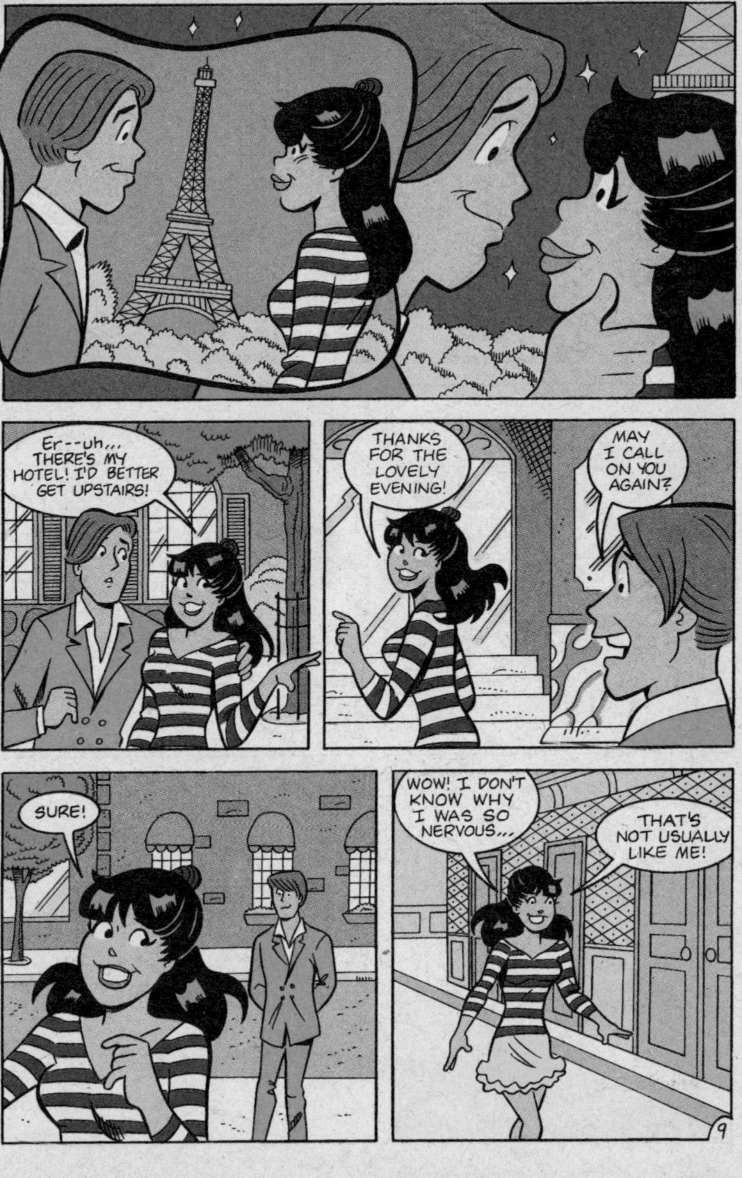

Er--uh... THERE'S MY HOTEL! I'D BETTER GET UPSTAIRS!
THANKS FOR THE LOVELY EVENING!
MAY I CALL ON YOU AGAIN?
SURE!
WOW! I DON'T KNOW WHY I WAS SO NERVOUS...
THAT'S NOT USUALLY LIKE ME!

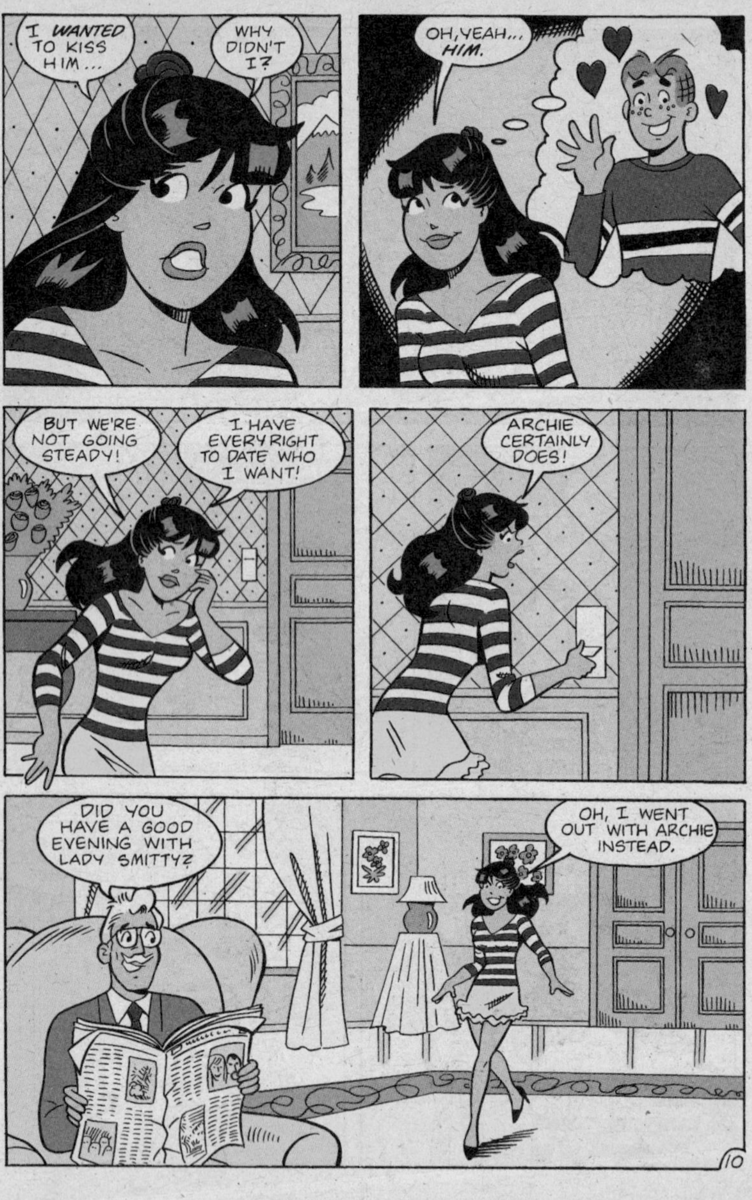
I *WANTED* TO KISS HIM...
WHY DIDN'T I?
OH, YEAH... *HIM.*
BUT WE'RE NOT GOING STEADY!
I HAVE EVERY RIGHT TO DATE WHO I WANT!
ARCHIE CERTAINLY DOES!
DID YOU HAVE A GOOD EVENING WITH LADY SMITTY?
OH, I WENT OUT WITH ARCHIE INSTEAD.

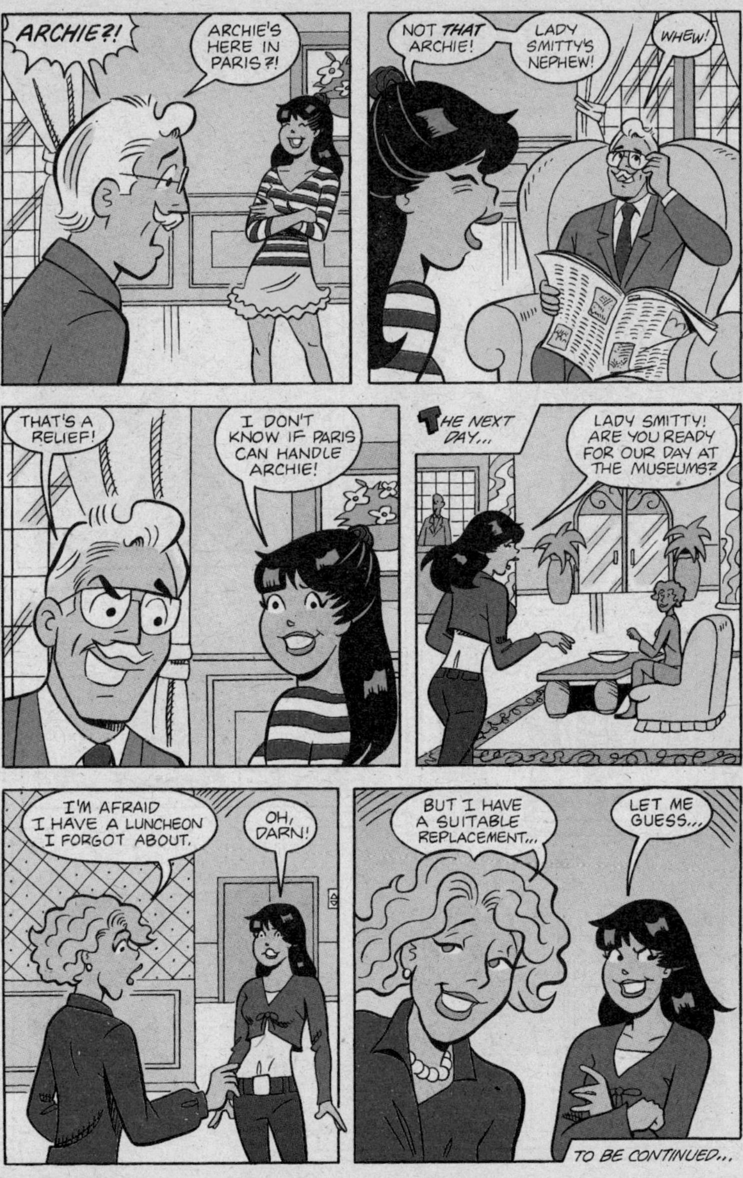
ARCHIE?!
ARCHIE'S HERE IN PARIS?!
NOT THAT ARCHIE!
LADY SMITTY'S NEPHEW!
WHEW!
THAT'S A RELIEF!
I DON'T KNOW IF PARIS CAN HANDLE ARCHIE!
THE NEXT DAY...
LADY SMITTY! ARE YOU READY FOR OUR DAY AT THE MUSEUMS?
I'M AFRAID I HAVE A LUNCHEON I FORGOT ABOUT.
OH, DARN!
BUT I HAVE A SUITABLE REPLACEMENT...
LET ME GUESS...
TO BE CONTINUED...

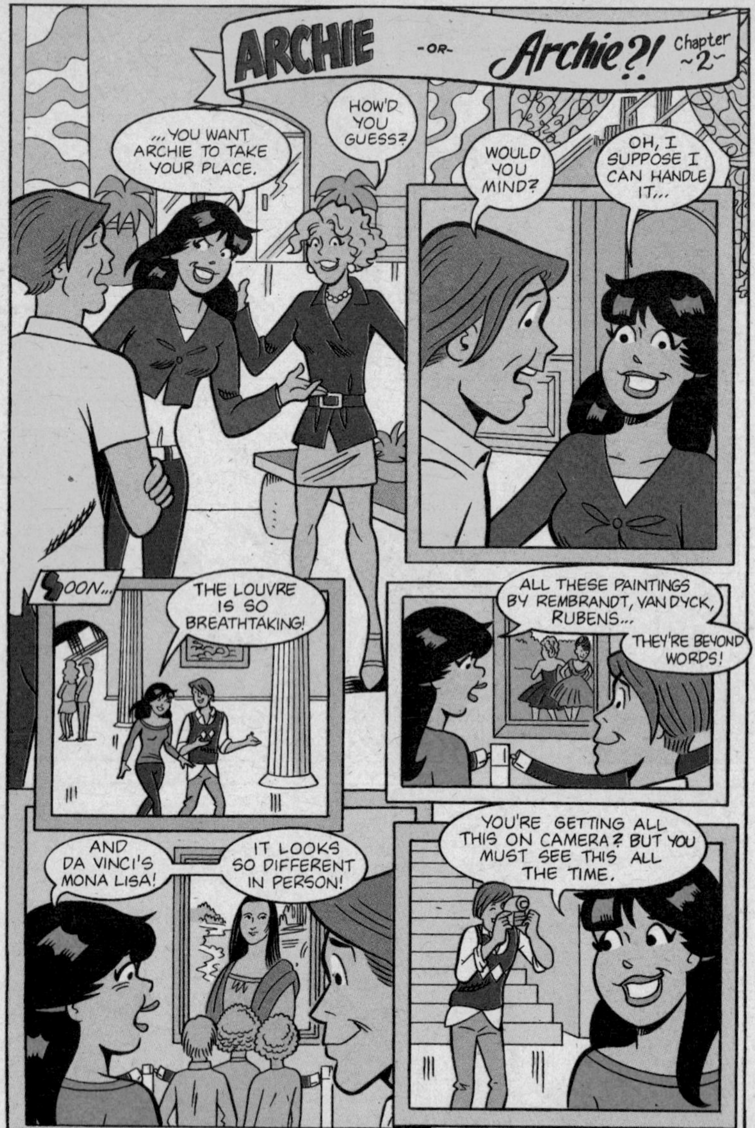

ARCHIE -OR- Archie?! Chapter ~2~
...YOU WANT ARCHIE TO TAKE YOUR PLACE.
HOW'D YOU GUESS?
WOULD YOU MIND?
OH, I SUPPOSE I CAN HANDLE IT...
SOON...
THE LOUVRE IS SO BREATHTAKING!
ALL THESE PAINTINGS BY REMBRANDT, VAN DYCK, RUBENS...
THEY'RE BEYOND WORDS!
AND DA VINCI'S MONA LISA!
IT LOOKS SO DIFFERENT IN PERSON!
YOU'RE GETTING ALL THIS ON CAMERA? BUT YOU MUST SEE THIS ALL THE TIME.

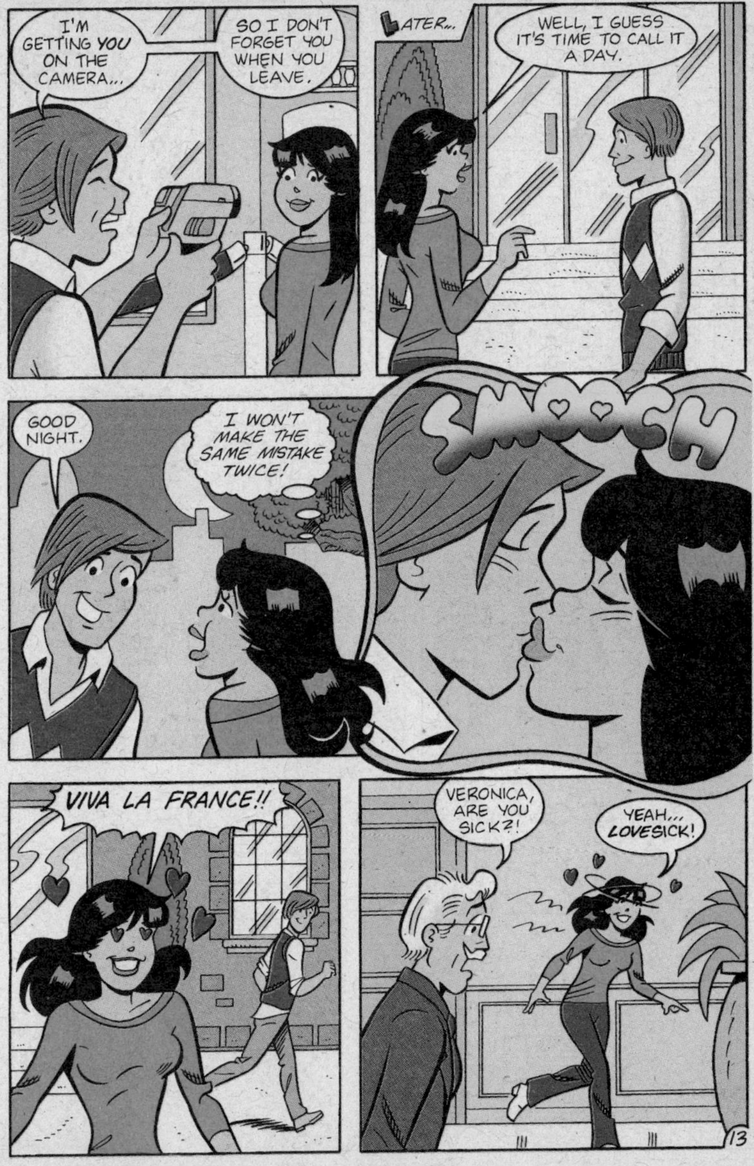

I'M GETTING YOU ON THE CAMERA...
SO I DON'T FORGET YOU WHEN YOU LEAVE.
LATER...
WELL, I GUESS IT'S TIME TO CALL IT A DAY.
GOOD NIGHT.
I WON'T MAKE THE SAME MISTAKE TWICE!
SMOOCH
VIVA LA FRANCE!!
VERONICA, ARE YOU SICK?!
YEAH... LOVESICK!
13

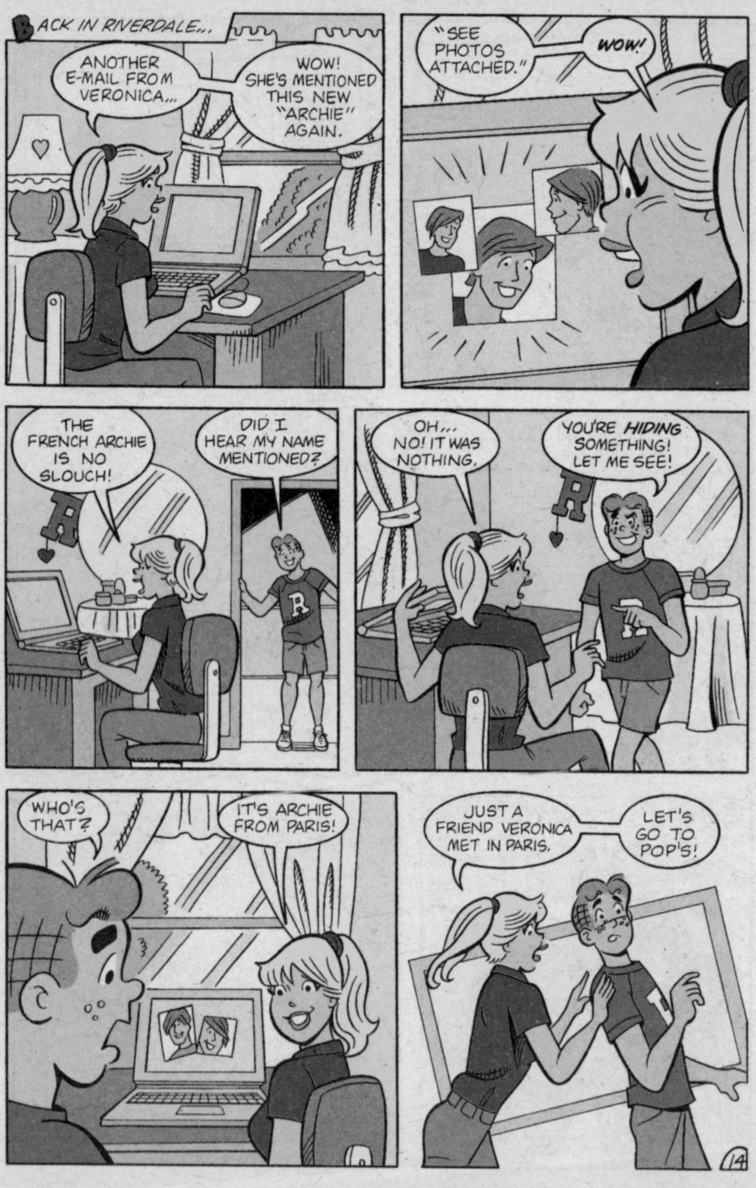
BACK IN RIVERDALE...
ANOTHER E-MAIL FROM VERONICA...
WOW! SHE'S MENTIONED THIS NEW "ARCHIE" AGAIN.
"SEE PHOTOS ATTACHED."
WOW!
THE FRENCH ARCHIE IS NO SLOUCH!
DID I HEAR MY NAME MENTIONED?
OH... NO! IT WAS NOTHING.
YOU'RE HIDING SOMETHING! LET ME SEE!
WHO'S THAT?
IT'S ARCHIE FROM PARIS!
JUST A FRIEND VERONICA MET IN PARIS.
LET'S GO TO POP'S!
14

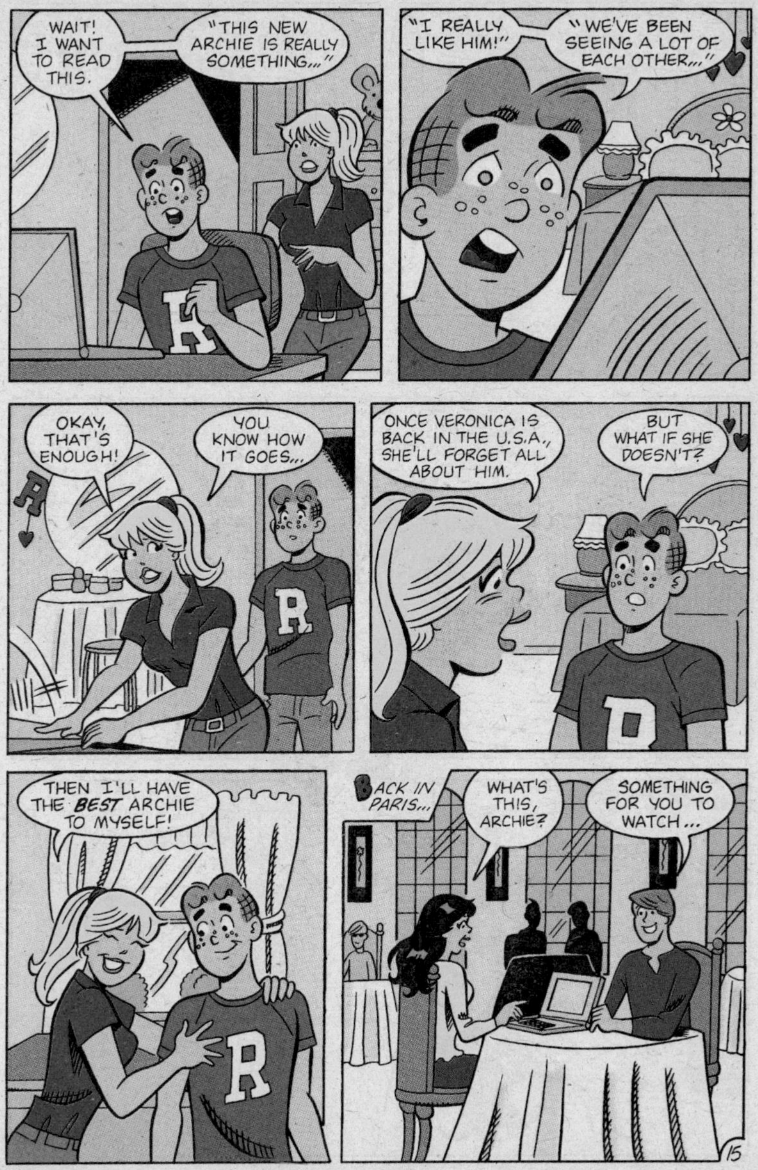
WAIT! I WANT TO READ THIS.
"THIS NEW ARCHIE IS REALLY SOMETHING..."
"I REALLY LIKE HIM!"
"WE'VE BEEN SEEING A LOT OF EACH OTHER..."
OKAY, THAT'S ENOUGH!
YOU KNOW HOW IT GOES...
ONCE VERONICA IS BACK IN THE U.S.A., SHE'LL FORGET ALL ABOUT HIM.
BUT WHAT IF SHE DOESN'T?
THEN I'LL HAVE THE BEST ARCHIE TO MYSELF!
BACK IN PARIS...
WHAT'S THIS, ARCHIE?
SOMETHING FOR YOU TO WATCH...

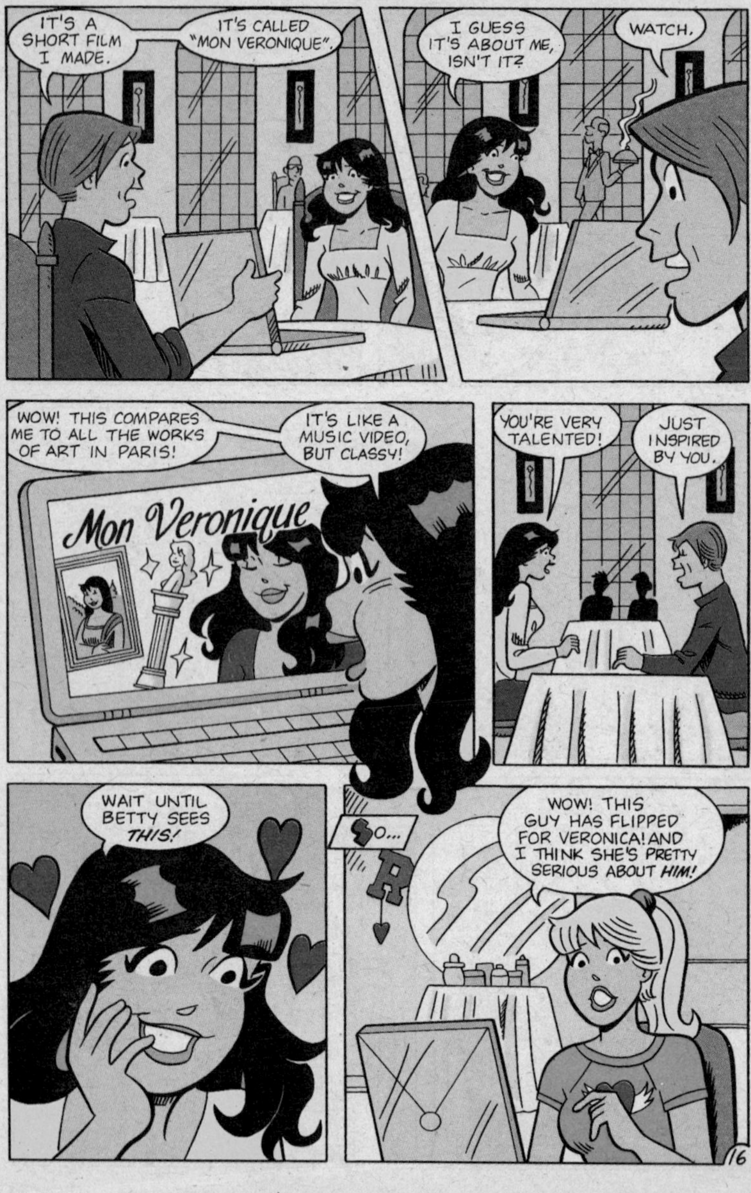
IT'S A SHORT FILM I MADE.
IT'S CALLED "MON VERONIQUE".
I GUESS IT'S ABOUT ME, ISN'T IT?
WATCH.
WOW! THIS COMPARES ME TO ALL THE WORKS OF ART IN PARIS!
IT'S LIKE A MUSIC VIDEO, BUT CLASSY!
Mon Veronique
YOU'RE VERY TALENTED!
JUST INSPIRED BY YOU.
WAIT UNTIL BETTY SEES *THIS!*
SO...
WOW! THIS GUY HAS FLIPPED FOR VERONICA! AND I THINK SHE'S PRETTY SERIOUS ABOUT *HIM!*

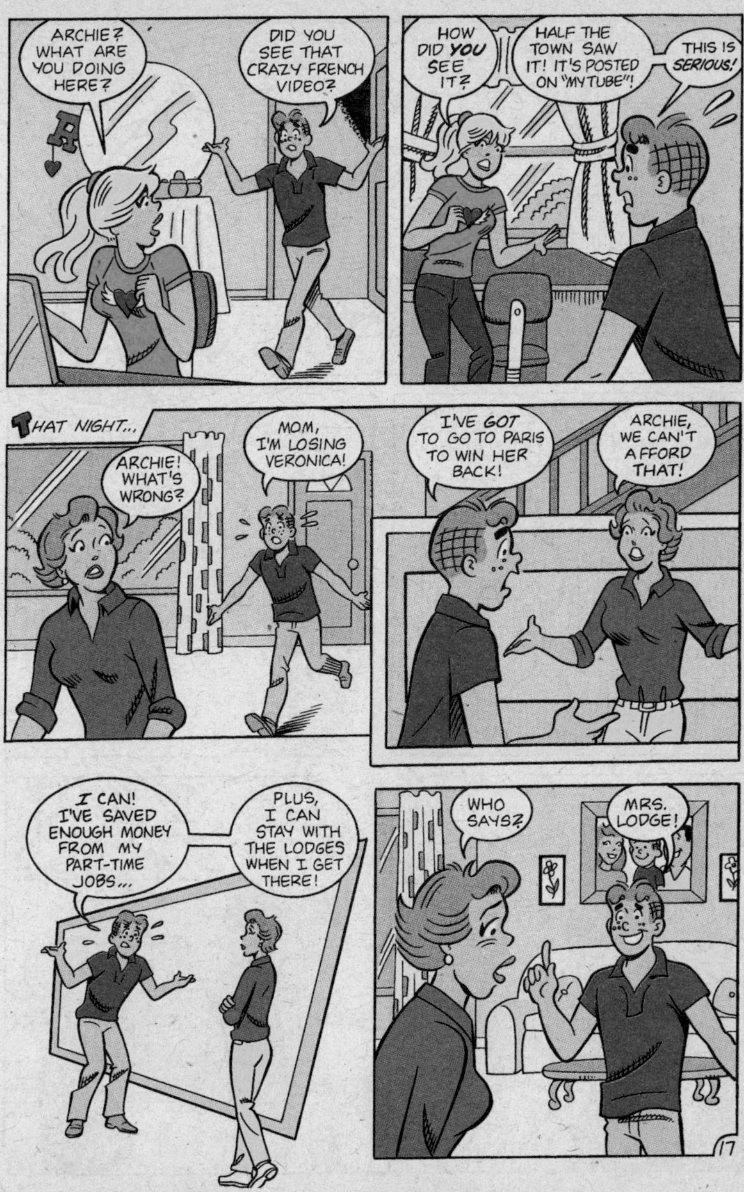

ARCHIE? WHAT ARE YOU DOING HERE?
DID YOU SEE THAT CRAZY FRENCH VIDEO?
HOW DID YOU SEE IT?
HALF THE TOWN SAW IT! IT'S POSTED ON "MYTUBE"!
THIS IS SERIOUS!
THAT NIGHT...
ARCHIE! WHAT'S WRONG?
MOM, I'M LOSING VERONICA!
I'VE GOT TO GO TO PARIS TO WIN HER BACK!
ARCHIE, WE CAN'T AFFORD THAT!
I CAN! I'VE SAVED ENOUGH MONEY FROM MY PART-TIME JOBS...
PLUS, I CAN STAY WITH THE LODGES WHEN I GET THERE!
WHO SAYS?
MRS. LODGE!

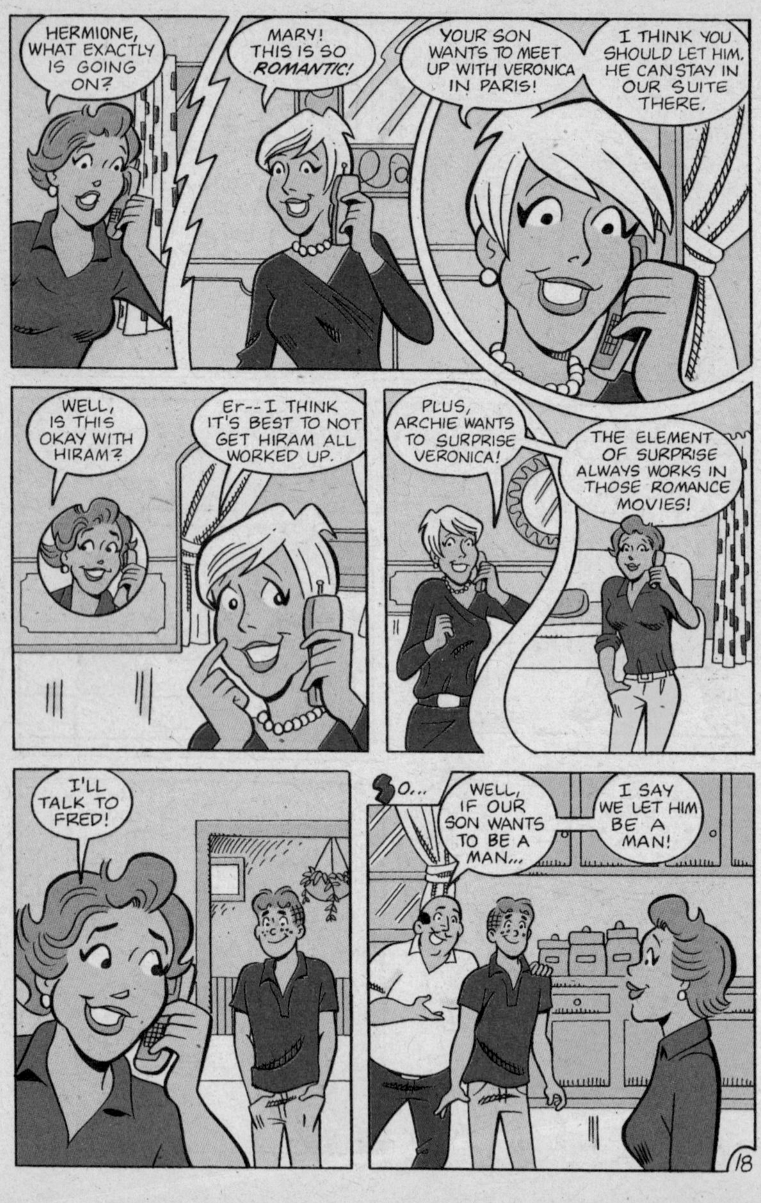
HERMIONE, WHAT EXACTLY IS GOING ON?
MARY! THIS IS SO ROMANTIC!
YOUR SON WANTS TO MEET UP WITH VERONICA IN PARIS!
I THINK YOU SHOULD LET HIM. HE CAN STAY IN OUR SUITE THERE.
WELL, IS THIS OKAY WITH HIRAM?
Er-- I THINK IT'S BEST TO NOT GET HIRAM ALL WORKED UP.
PLUS, ARCHIE WANTS TO SURPRISE VERONICA!
THE ELEMENT OF SURPRISE ALWAYS WORKS IN THOSE ROMANCE MOVIES!
I'LL TALK TO FRED!
SO...
WELL, IF OUR SON WANTS TO BE A MAN...
I SAY WE LET HIM BE A MAN!

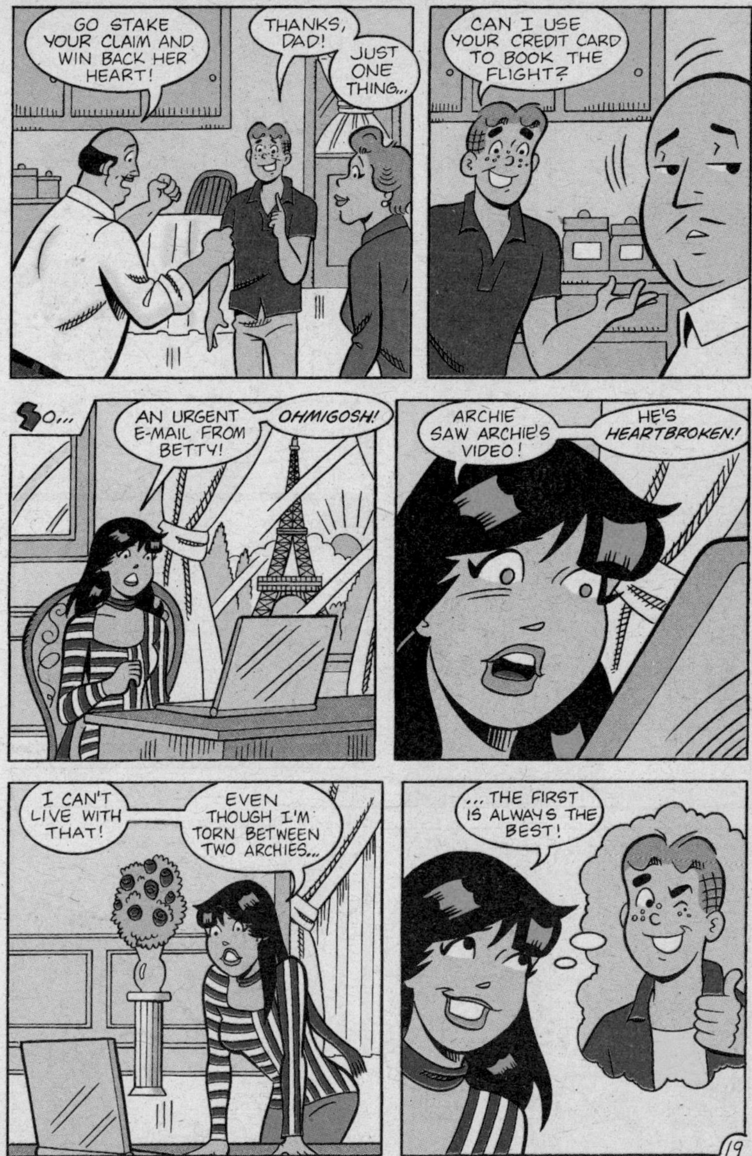
GO STAKE YOUR CLAIM AND WIN BACK HER HEART!
THANKS, DAD!
JUST ONE THING...
CAN I USE YOUR CREDIT CARD TO BOOK THE FLIGHT?
SO...
AN URGENT E-MAIL FROM BETTY!
OHMIGOSH!
ARCHIE SAW ARCHIE'S VIDEO!
HE'S HEARTBROKEN!
I CAN'T LIVE WITH THAT!
EVEN THOUGH I'M TORN BETWEEN TWO ARCHIES...
...THE FIRST IS ALWAYS THE BEST!

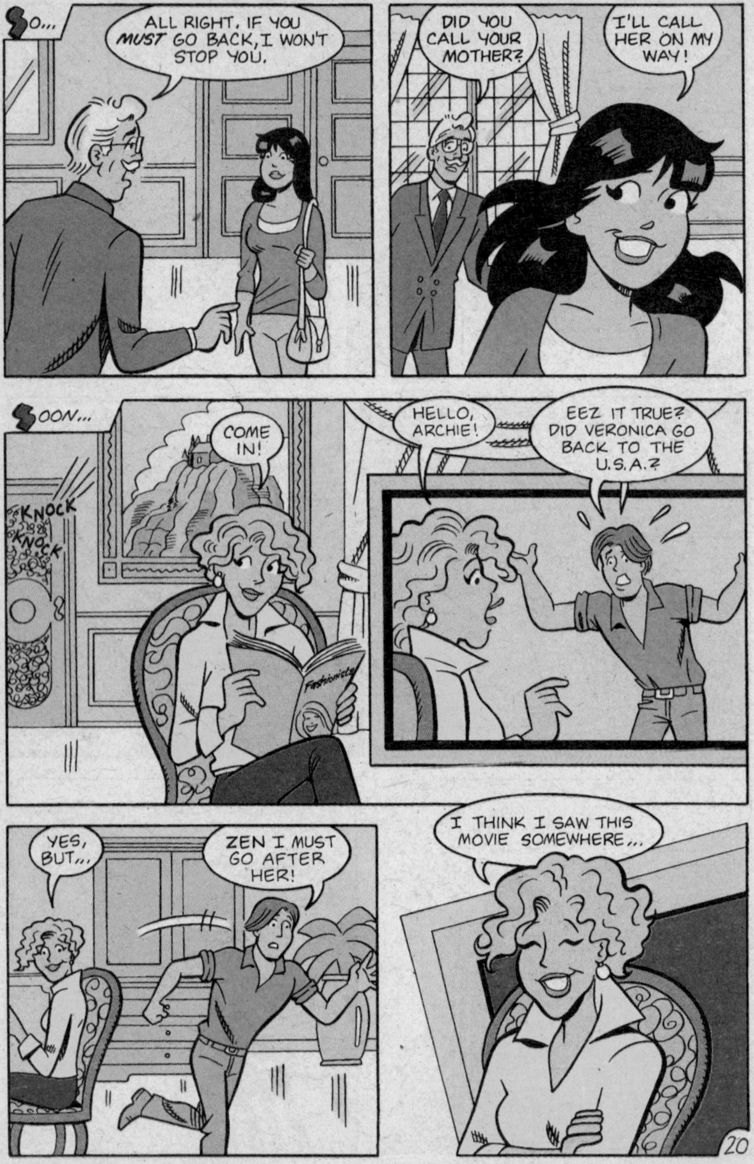
SO...
ALL RIGHT. IF YOU MUST GO BACK, I WON'T STOP YOU.
DID YOU CALL YOUR MOTHER?
I'LL CALL HER ON MY WAY!
SOON...
KNOCK KNOCK
COME IN!
HELLO, ARCHIE!
EEZ IT TRUE? DID VERONICA GO BACK TO THE U.S.A.?
Fashionista
YES, BUT...
ZEN I MUST GO AFTER HER!
I THINK I SAW THIS MOVIE SOMEWHERE...

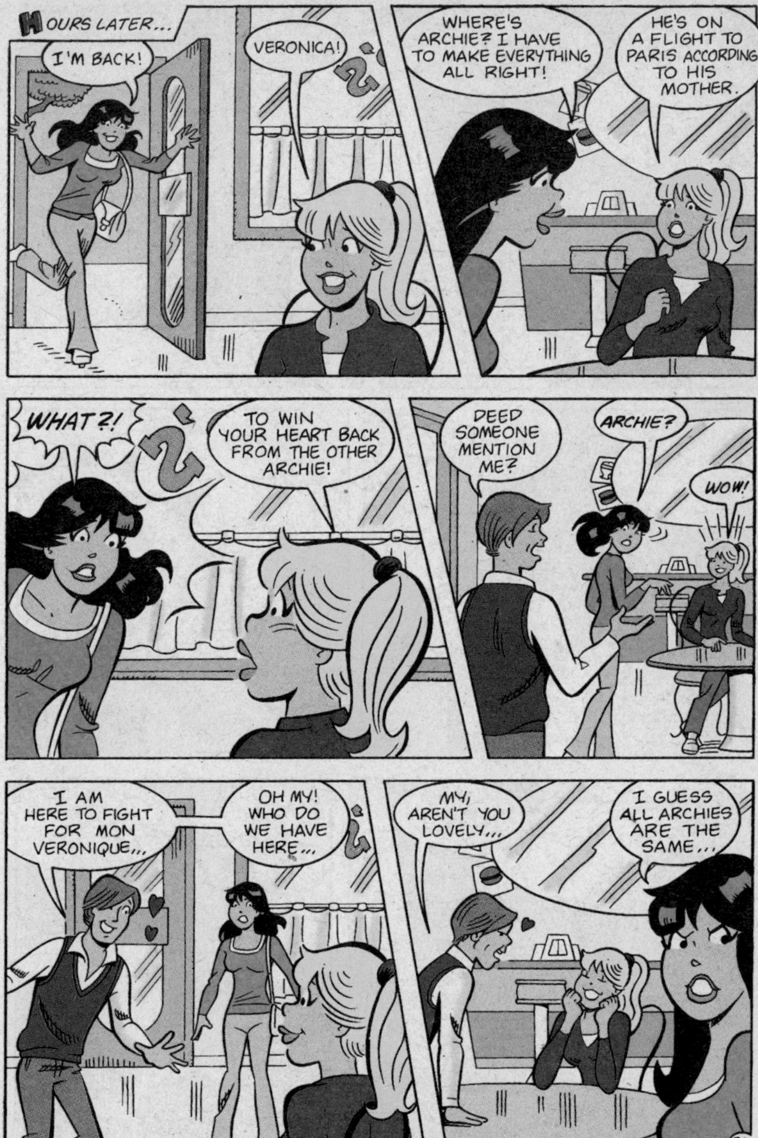
HOURS LATER...
I'M BACK!
VERONICA!
WHERE'S ARCHIE? I HAVE TO MAKE EVERYTHING ALL RIGHT!
HE'S ON A FLIGHT TO PARIS ACCORDING TO HIS MOTHER.
WHAT?!
TO WIN YOUR HEART BACK FROM THE OTHER ARCHIE!
DEED SOMEONE MENTION ME?
ARCHIE?
WOW!
I AM HERE TO FIGHT FOR MON VERONIQUE...
OH MY! WHO DO WE HAVE HERE...
MY, AREN'T YOU LOVELY...
I GUESS ALL ARCHIES ARE THE SAME...

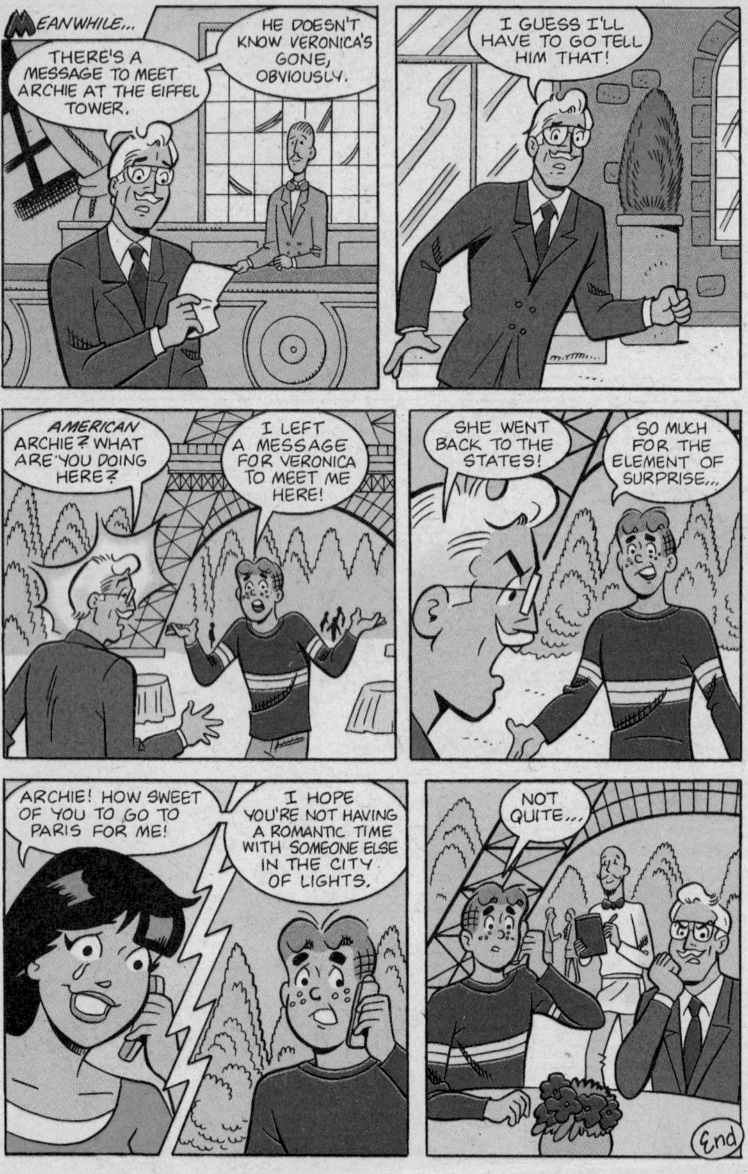
MEANWHILE...
THERE'S A MESSAGE TO MEET ARCHIE AT THE EIFFEL TOWER.
HE DOESN'T KNOW VERONICA'S GONE, OBVIOUSLY.
I GUESS I'LL HAVE TO GO TELL HIM THAT!
AMERICAN ARCHIE? WHAT ARE YOU DOING HERE?
I LEFT A MESSAGE FOR VERONICA TO MEET ME HERE!
SHE WENT BACK TO THE STATES!
SO MUCH FOR THE ELEMENT OF SURPRISE...
ARCHIE! HOW SWEET OF YOU TO GO TO PARIS FOR ME!
I HOPE YOU'RE NOT HAVING A ROMANTIC TIME WITH SOMEONE ELSE IN THE CITY OF LIGHTS.
NOT QUITE...
End

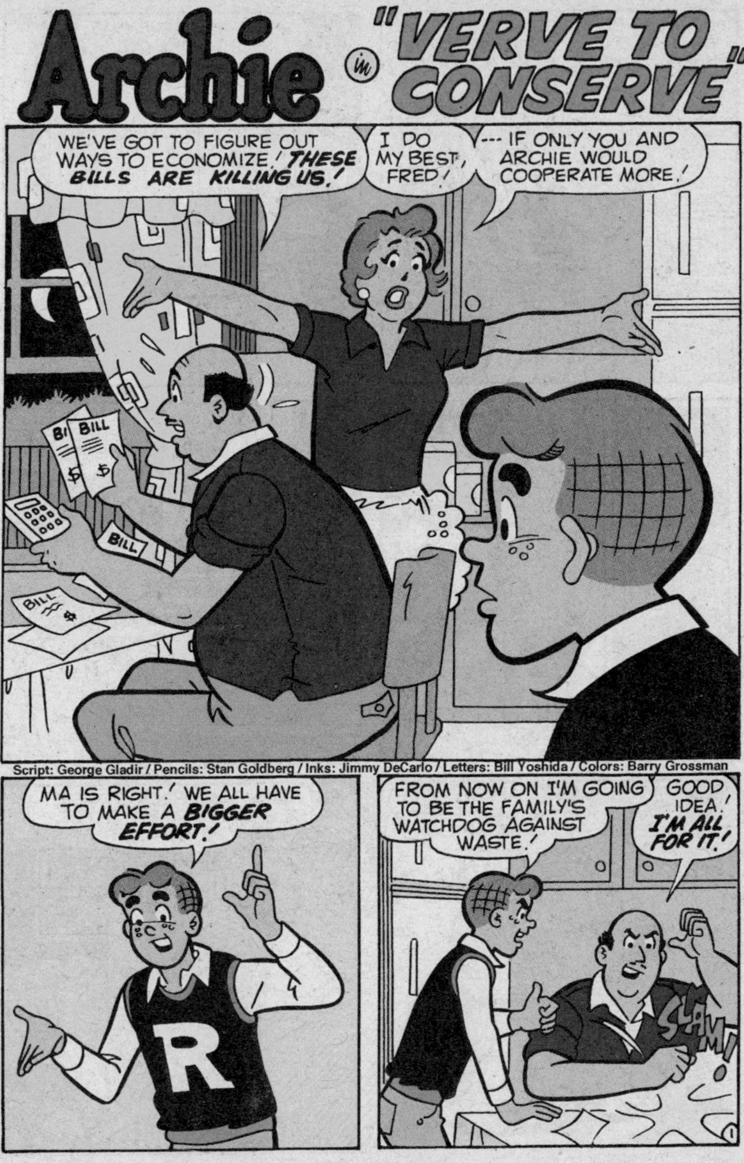
Archie in "VERVE TO CONSERVE"
WE'VE GOT TO FIGURE OUT WAYS TO ECONOMIZE! THESE BILLS ARE KILLING US!
I DO MY BEST, FRED!
--- IF ONLY YOU AND ARCHIE WOULD COOPERATE MORE!
BILL
BILL
BILL
BILL
Script: George Gladir / Pencils: Stan Goldberg / Inks: Jimmy DeCarlo / Letters: Bill Yoshida / Colors: Barry Grossman
MA IS RIGHT! WE ALL HAVE TO MAKE A BIGGER EFFORT!
FROM NOW ON I'M GOING TO BE THE FAMILY'S WATCHDOG AGAINST WASTE!
GOOD IDEA! I'M ALL FOR IT!
SLAM!
1

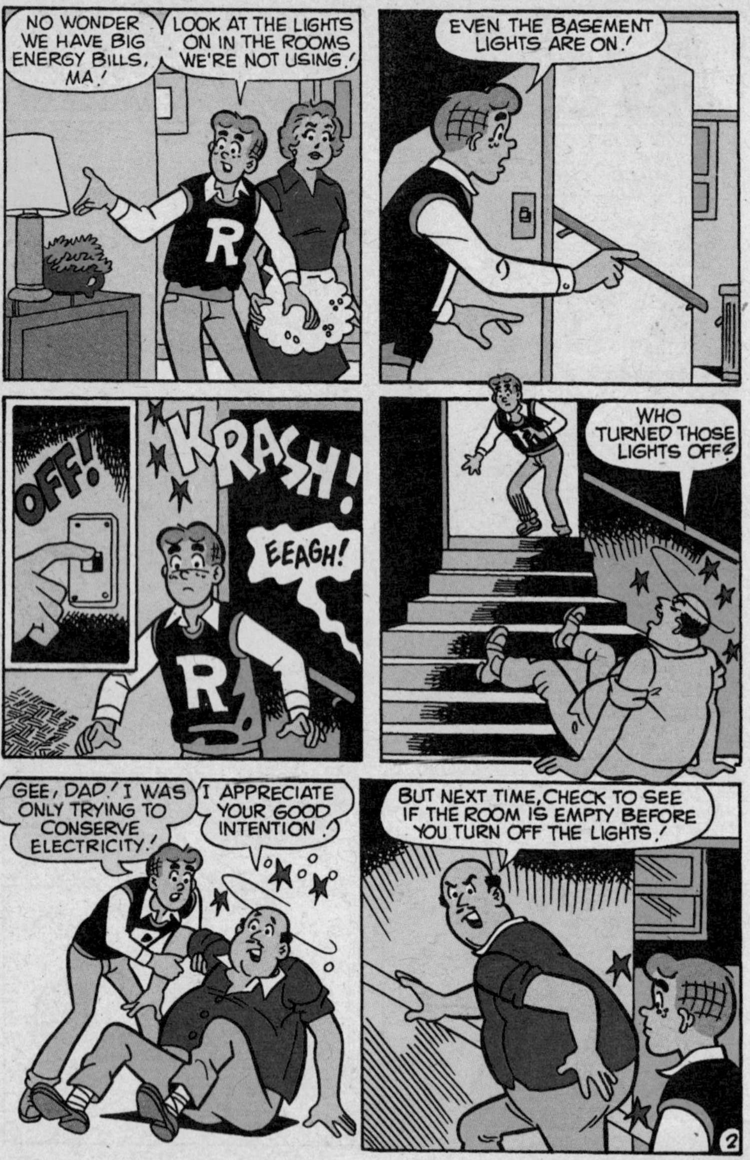
NO WONDER WE HAVE BIG ENERGY BILLS, MA!
LOOK AT THE LIGHTS ON IN THE ROOMS WE'RE NOT USING!
EVEN THE BASEMENT LIGHTS ARE ON!
OFF!
KRASH!
EEAGH!
WHO TURNED THOSE LIGHTS OFF?
GEE, DAD! I WAS ONLY TRYING TO CONSERVE ELECTRICITY!
I APPRECIATE YOUR GOOD INTENTION!
BUT NEXT TIME, CHECK TO SEE IF THE ROOM IS EMPTY BEFORE YOU TURN OFF THE LIGHTS!
2

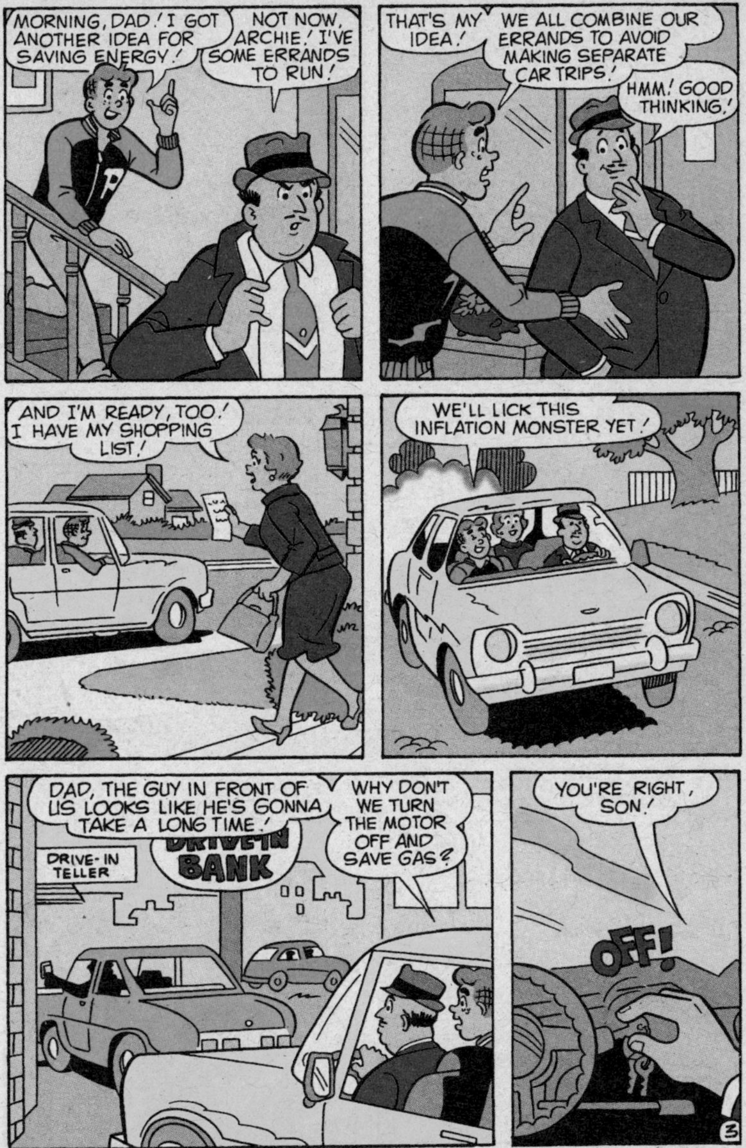
MORNING, DAD! I GOT ANOTHER IDEA FOR SAVING ENERGY!
NOT NOW, ARCHIE! I'VE SOME ERRANDS TO RUN!
THAT'S MY IDEA!
WE ALL COMBINE OUR ERRANDS TO AVOID MAKING SEPARATE CAR TRIPS!
HMM! GOOD THINKING!
AND I'M READY, TOO! I HAVE MY SHOPPING LIST!
WE'LL LICK THIS INFLATION MONSTER YET!
DAD, THE GUY IN FRONT OF US LOOKS LIKE HE'S GONNA TAKE A LONG TIME!
WHY DON'T WE TURN THE MOTOR OFF AND SAVE GAS?
DRIVE-IN TELLER
DRIVE-IN BANK
YOU'RE RIGHT, SON!
OFF!
3

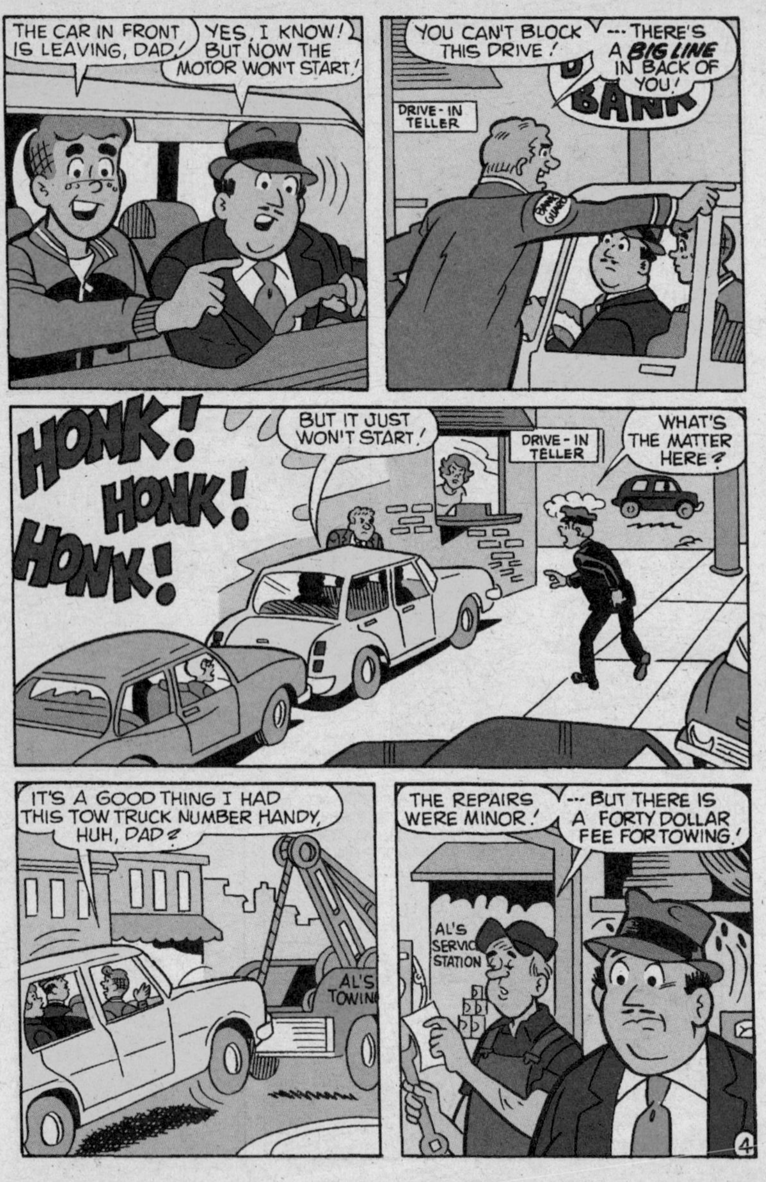
THE CAR IN FRONT IS LEAVING, DAD!
YES, I KNOW! BUT NOW THE MOTOR WON'T START!
YOU CAN'T BLOCK THIS DRIVE!
--- THERE'S A BIG LINE IN BACK OF YOU!
DRIVE-IN TELLER
HONK! HONK! HONK!
BUT IT JUST WON'T START!
DRIVE-IN TELLER
WHAT'S THE MATTER HERE?
IT'S A GOOD THING I HAD THIS TOW TRUCK NUMBER HANDY, HUH, DAD?
THE REPAIRS WERE MINOR!
--- BUT THERE IS A FORTY DOLLAR FEE FOR TOWING!
AL'S SERVIC STATION
4

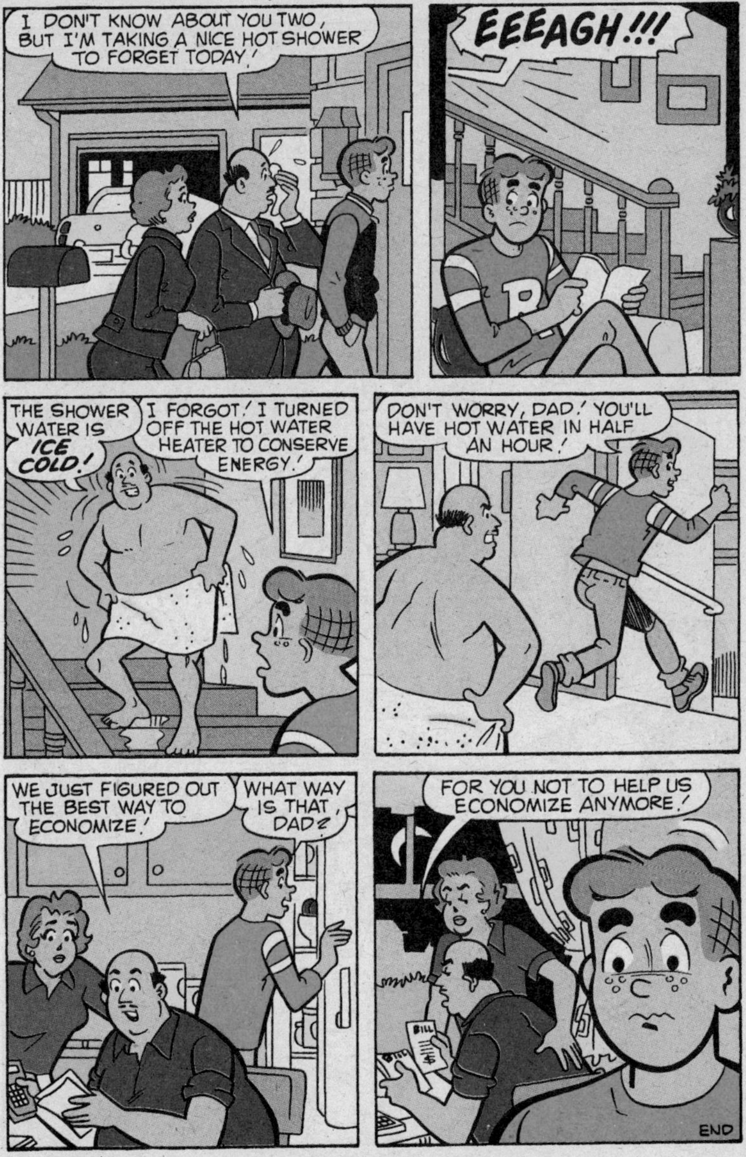
I DON'T KNOW ABOUT YOU TWO, BUT I'M TAKING A NICE HOT SHOWER TO FORGET TODAY!
EEEAGH!!!
THE SHOWER WATER IS ICE COLD!
I FORGOT! I TURNED OFF THE HOT WATER HEATER TO CONSERVE ENERGY!
DON'T WORRY, DAD! YOU'LL HAVE HOT WATER IN HALF AN HOUR!
WE JUST FIGURED OUT THE BEST WAY TO ECONOMIZE!
WHAT WAY IS THAT, DAD?
FOR YOU NOT TO HELP US ECONOMIZE ANYMORE!
BILL
END

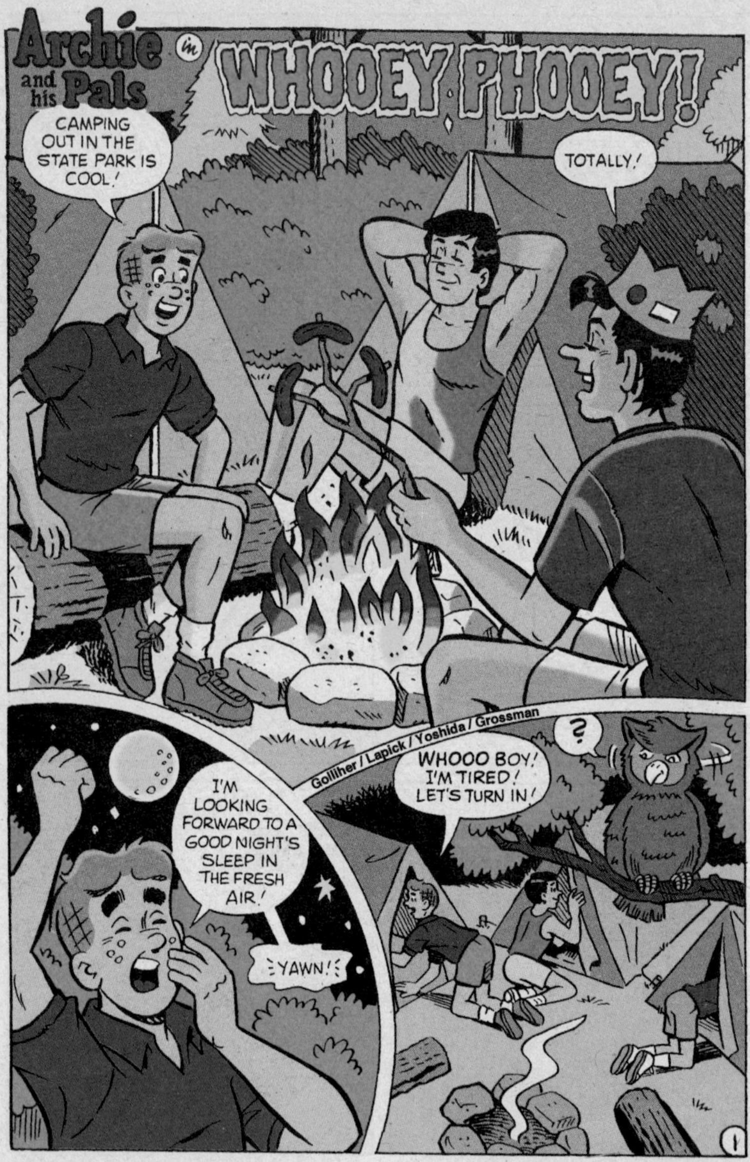
Archie and his Pals in
WHOOEY PHOOEY!
CAMPING OUT IN THE STATE PARK IS COOL!
TOTALLY!
Golliher / Lapick / Yoshida / Grossman
I'M LOOKING FORWARD TO A GOOD NIGHT'S SLEEP IN THE FRESH AIR!
YAWN!
WHOOO BOY! I'M TIRED! LET'S TURN IN!
?
1

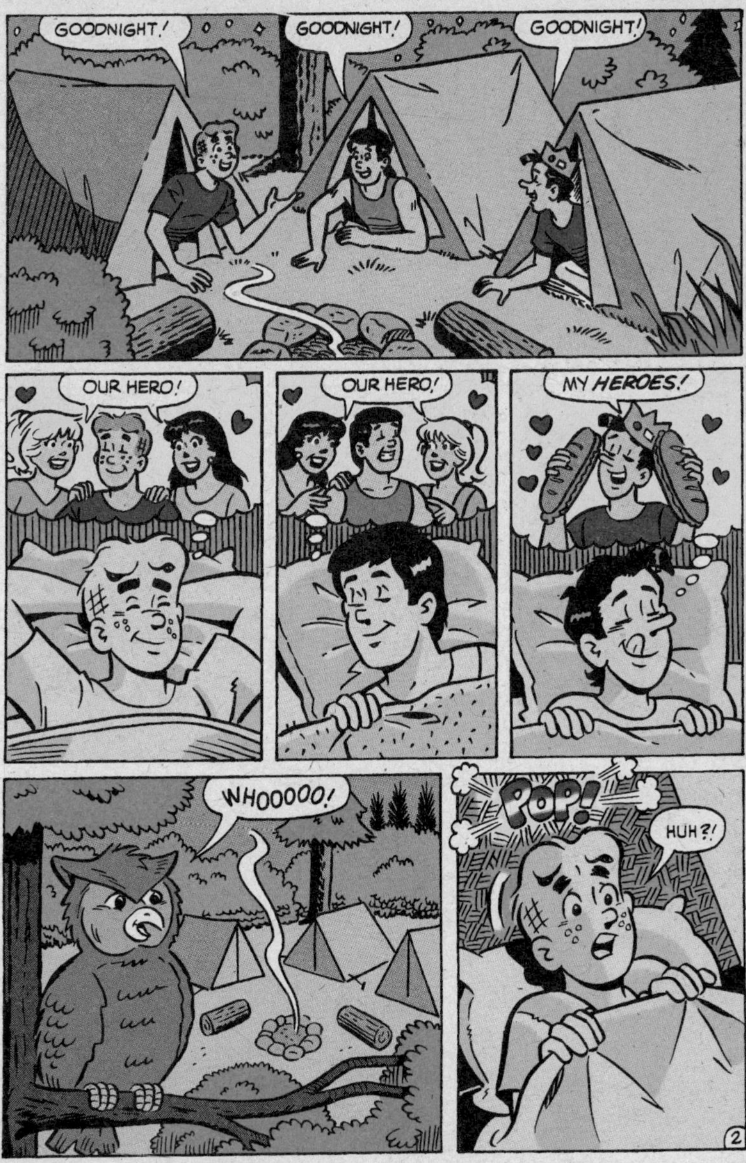
GOODNIGHT!
GOODNIGHT!
GOODNIGHT!
OUR HERO!
OUR HERO!
MY HEROES!
WHOOOOO!
POP!
HUH?!
2

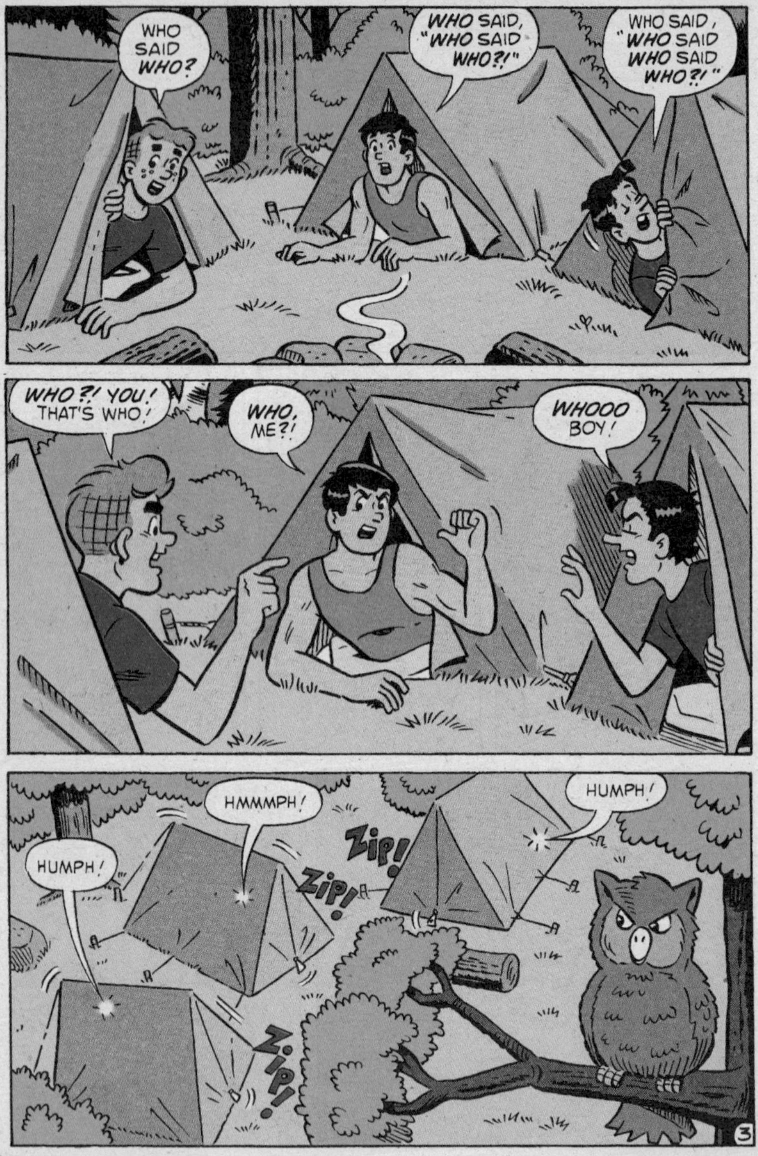
WHO SAID WHO?
WHO SAID, "WHO SAID WHO?!"
WHO SAID, "WHO SAID WHO SAID WHO?!"
WHO?! YOU! THAT'S WHO!
WHO, ME?!
WHOOO BOY!
HUMPH!
HMMMPH!
ZIP!
ZIP!
HUMPH!
ZIP!
3

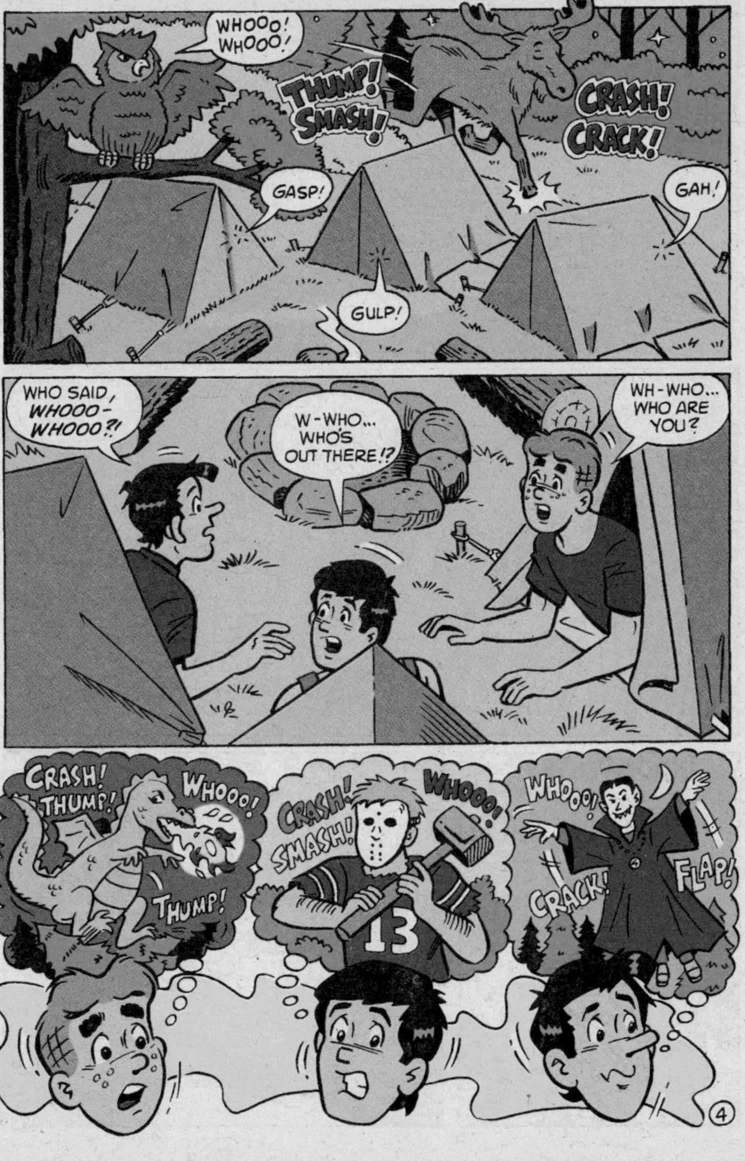
WHOOO! WHOOO!
THUMP! SMASH!
CRASH! CRACK!
GASP!
GAH!
GULP!
WHO SAID, WHOOO-WHOOO?!
W-WHO... WHO'S OUT THERE!?
WH-WHO... WHO ARE YOU?
CRASH! THUMP!
WHOOO!
THUMP!
CRASH! SMASH!
WHOOO!
13
WHOOO!
CRACK!
FLAP!

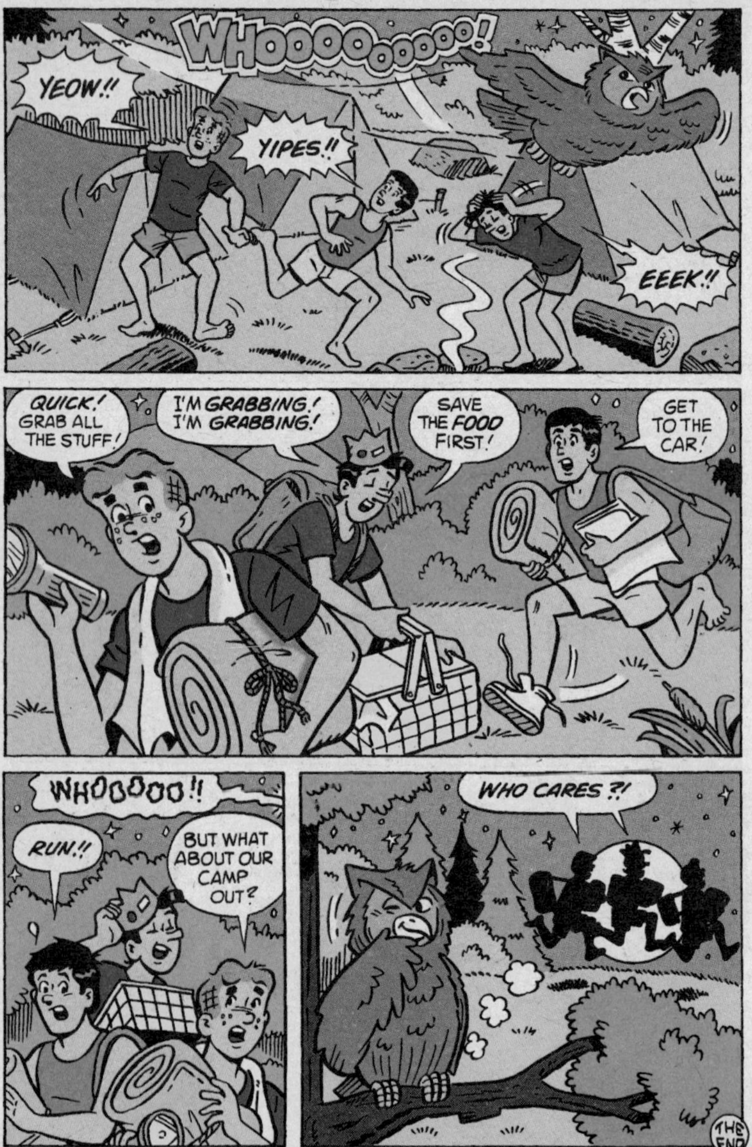
WHOOOOOOOOOO!
YEOW!!
YIPES!!
EEEK!!
QUICK! GRAB ALL THE STUFF!
I'M GRABBING! I'M GRABBING!
SAVE THE FOOD FIRST!
GET TO THE CAR!
WHOOOOO!!
RUN!!
BUT WHAT ABOUT OUR CAMP OUT?
WHO CARES?!
THE END

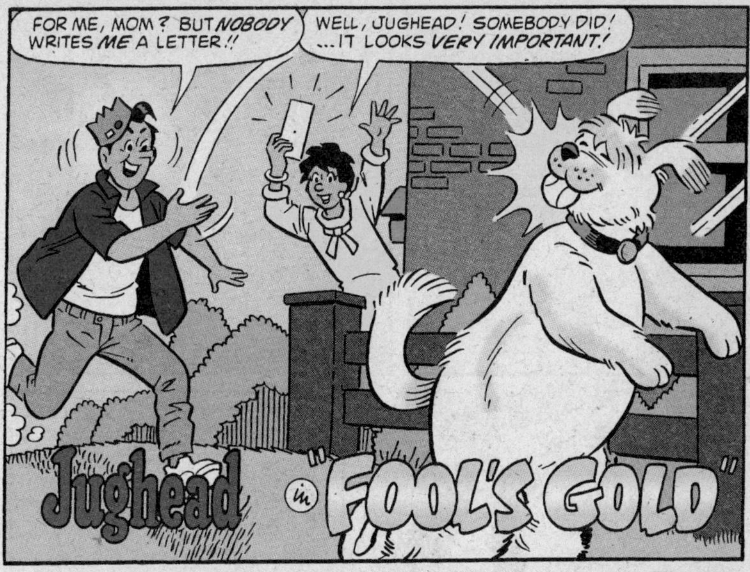

FOR ME, MOM? BUT NOBODY WRITES ME A LETTER!!
WELL, JUGHEAD! SOMEBODY DID! ...IT LOOKS VERY IMPORTANT!
Jughead in "FOOL'S GOLD"

Script: George Gladir / Pencils: Stan Goldberg / Inks: Rudy Lapick / Letters: Bill Yoshida / Colors: Barry Grossman

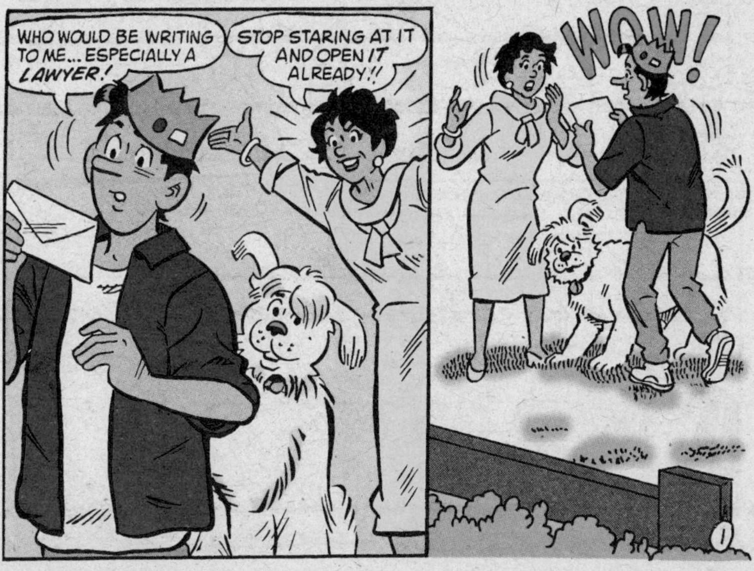

WHO WOULD BE WRITING TO ME... ESPECIALLY A LAWYER!
STOP STARING AT IT AND OPEN IT ALREADY!!
WOW!

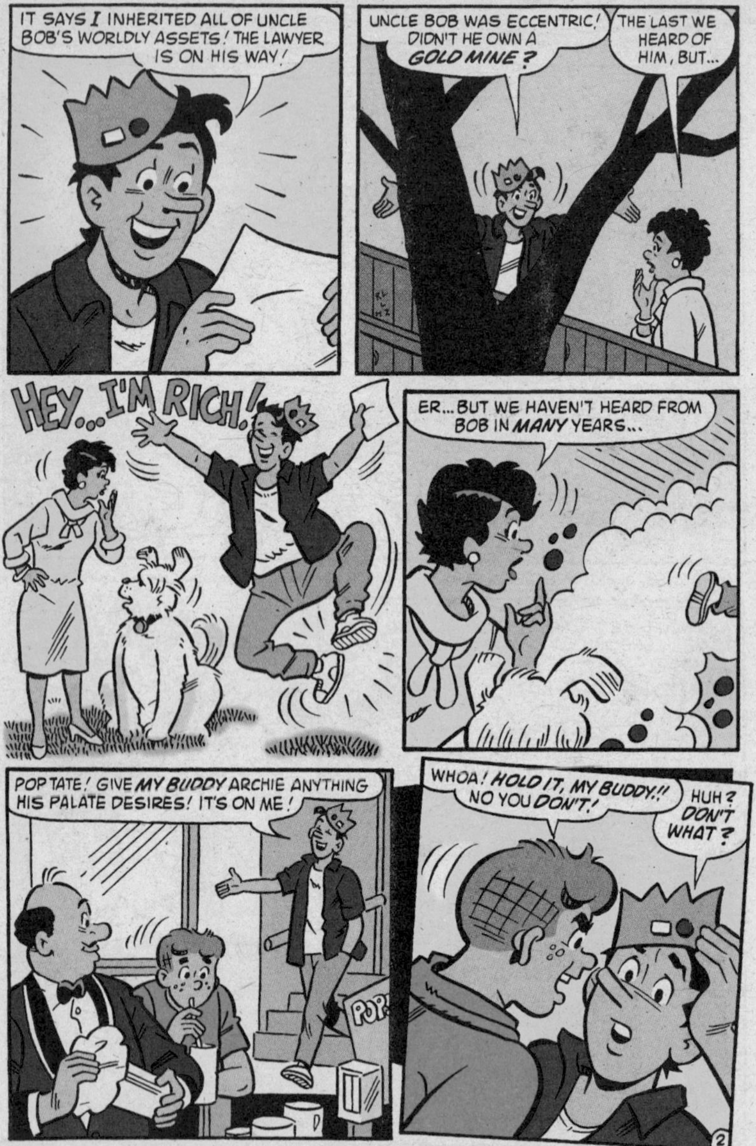
IT SAYS I INHERITED ALL OF UNCLE BOB'S WORLDLY ASSETS! THE LAWYER IS ON HIS WAY!
UNCLE BOB WAS ECCENTRIC! DIDN'T HE OWN A GOLD MINE?
THE LAST WE HEARD OF HIM, BUT...
HEY... I'M RICH!
ER... BUT WE HAVEN'T HEARD FROM BOB IN MANY YEARS...
POP TATE! GIVE MY BUDDY ARCHIE ANYTHING HIS PALATE DESIRES! IT'S ON ME!
POP'S
WHOA! HOLD IT, MY BUDDY!! NO YOU DON'T!
HUH? DON'T WHAT?
2

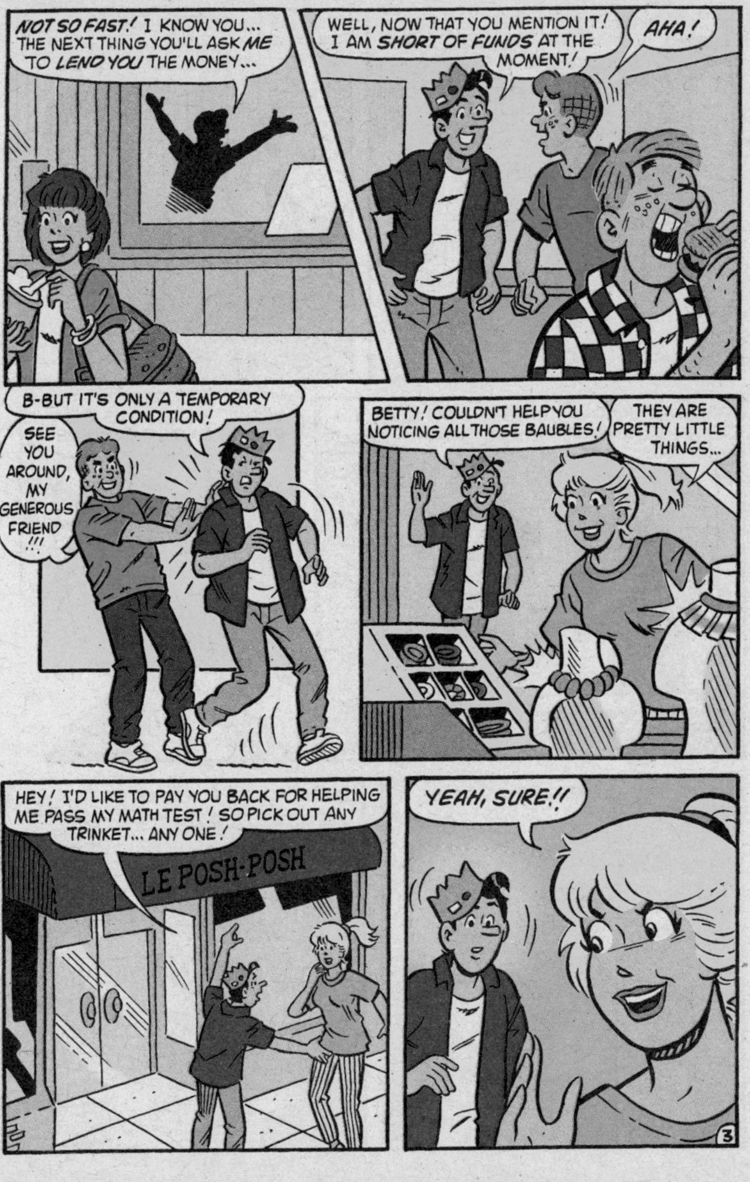
NOT SO FAST! I KNOW YOU... THE NEXT THING YOU'LL ASK ME TO LEND YOU THE MONEY...
WELL, NOW THAT YOU MENTION IT! I AM SHORT OF FUNDS AT THE MOMENT!
AHA!
B-BUT IT'S ONLY A TEMPORARY CONDITION!
SEE YOU AROUND, MY GENEROUS FRIEND!!!
BETTY! COULDN'T HELP YOU NOTICING ALL THOSE BAUBLES!
THEY ARE PRETTY LITTLE THINGS...
HEY! I'D LIKE TO PAY YOU BACK FOR HELPING ME PASS MY MATH TEST! SO PICK OUT ANY TRINKET... ANY ONE!
LE POSH-POSH
YEAH, SURE!!
3

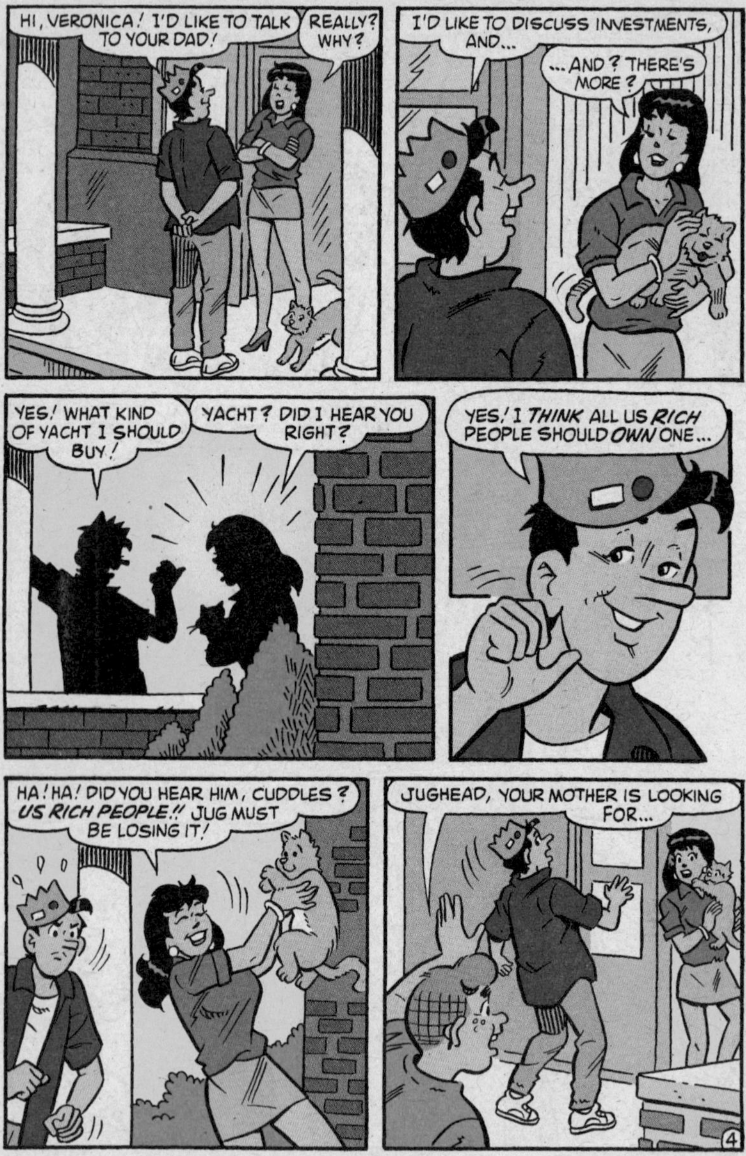
HI, VERONICA! I'D LIKE TO TALK TO YOUR DAD!
REALLY? WHY?
I'D LIKE TO DISCUSS INVESTMENTS, AND...
...AND? THERE'S MORE?
YES! WHAT KIND OF YACHT I SHOULD BUY!
YACHT? DID I HEAR YOU RIGHT?
YES! I THINK ALL US RICH PEOPLE SHOULD OWN ONE...
HA! HA! DID YOU HEAR HIM, CUDDLES? US RICH PEOPLE!! JUG MUST BE LOSING IT!
JUGHEAD, YOUR MOTHER IS LOOKING FOR...
4

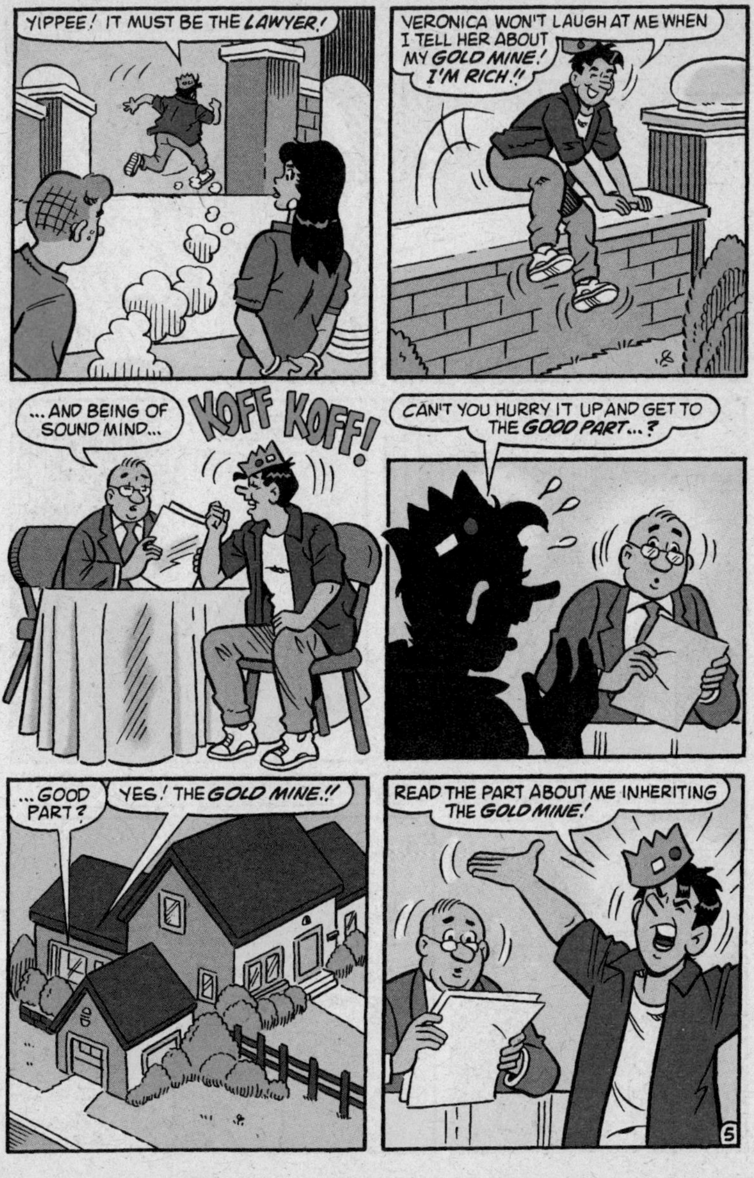
YIPPEE! IT MUST BE THE LAWYER!
VERONICA WON'T LAUGH AT ME WHEN I TELL HER ABOUT MY GOLD MINE! I'M RICH!!
... AND BEING OF SOUND MIND...
KOFF KOFF!
CAN'T YOU HURRY IT UP AND GET TO THE GOOD PART...?
... GOOD PART?
YES! THE GOLD MINE!!
READ THE PART ABOUT ME INHERITING THE GOLD MINE!
5

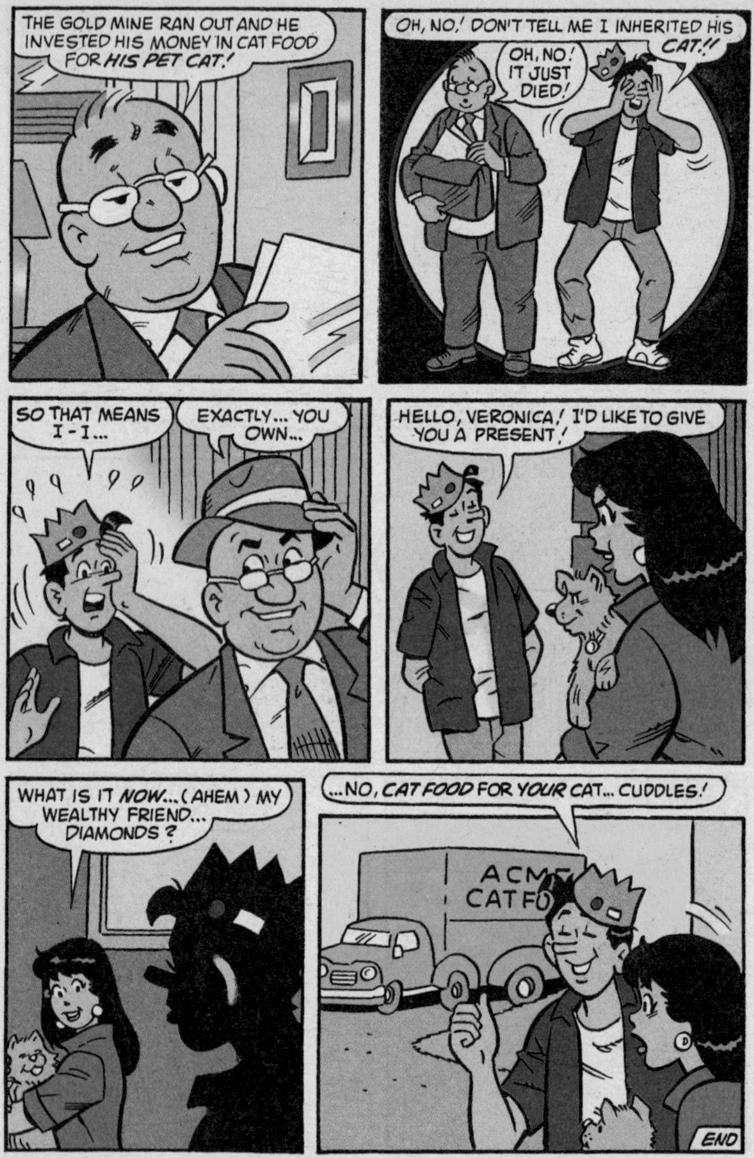
THE GOLD MINE RAN OUT AND HE INVESTED HIS MONEY IN CAT FOOD FOR HIS PET CAT!
OH, NO! DON'T TELL ME I INHERITED HIS CAT!!
OH, NO! IT JUST DIED!
SO THAT MEANS I - I...
EXACTLY... YOU OWN...
HELLO, VERONICA! I'D LIKE TO GIVE YOU A PRESENT!
WHAT IS IT NOW...(AHEM) MY WEALTHY FRIEND... DIAMONDS?
...NO, CAT FOOD FOR YOUR CAT... CUDDLES!
ACME CAT FO
END

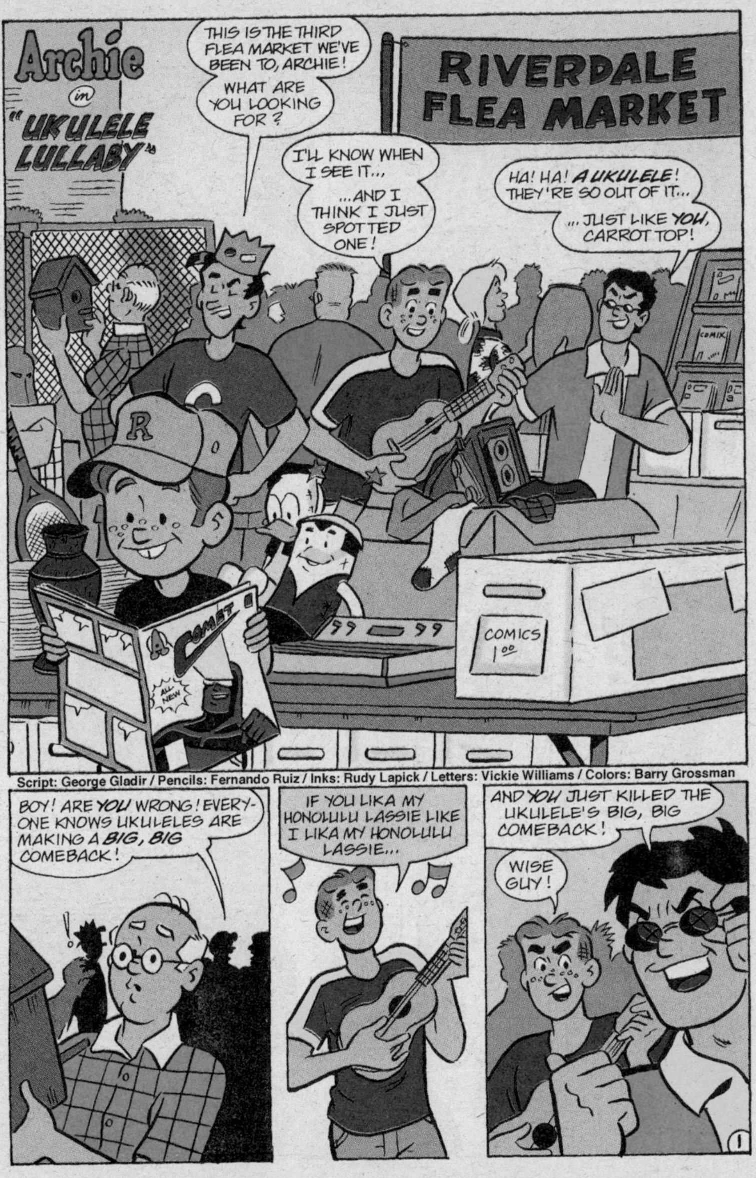

Archie in "UKULELE LULLABY"
THIS IS THE THIRD FLEA MARKET WE'VE BEEN TO, ARCHIE! WHAT ARE YOU LOOKING FOR?
RIVERDALE FLEA MARKET
I'LL KNOW WHEN I SEE IT... ...AND I THINK I JUST SPOTTED ONE!
HA! HA! A UKULELE! THEY'RE SO OUT OF IT... ...JUST LIKE YOU, CARROT TOP!
COMIX
COMET
ALL NEW
COMICS 1.00
Script: George Gladir / Pencils: Fernando Ruiz / Inks: Rudy Lapick / Letters: Vickie Williams / Colors: Barry Grossman
BOY! ARE YOU WRONG! EVERYONE KNOWS UKULELES ARE MAKING A BIG, BIG COMEBACK!
IF YOU LIKA MY HONOLULU LASSIE LIKE I LIKA MY HONOLULU LASSIE...
AND YOU JUST KILLED THE UKULELE'S BIG, BIG COMEBACK!
WISE GUY!
1

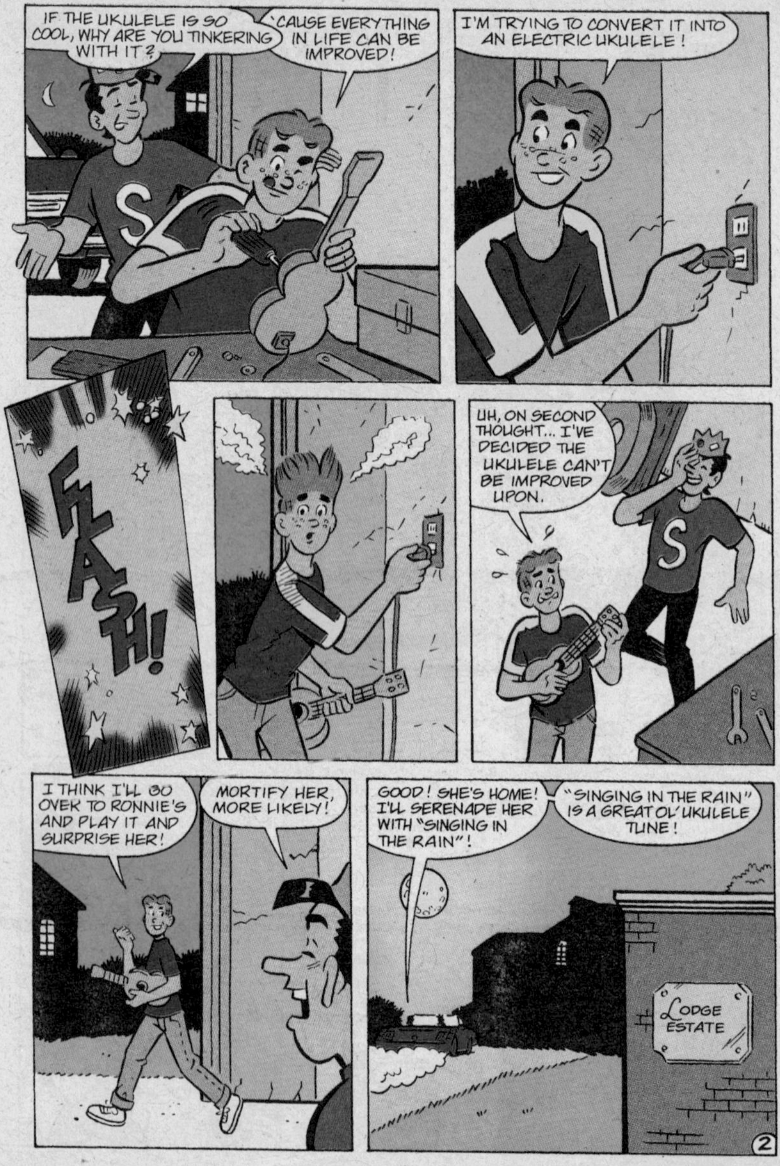
IF THE UKULELE IS SO COOL, WHY ARE YOU TINKERING WITH IT?
'CAUSE EVERYTHING IN LIFE CAN BE IMPROVED!
I'M TRYING TO CONVERT IT INTO AN ELECTRIC UKULELE!
FLASH!
UH, ON SECOND THOUGHT... I'VE DECIDED THE UKULELE CAN'T BE IMPROVED UPON.
I THINK I'LL GO OVER TO RONNIE'S AND PLAY IT AND SURPRISE HER!
MORTIFY HER, MORE LIKELY!
GOOD! SHE'S HOME! I'LL SERENADE HER WITH "SINGING IN THE RAIN"!
"SINGING IN THE RAIN" IS A GREAT OL' UKULELE TUNE!
LODGE ESTATE
2

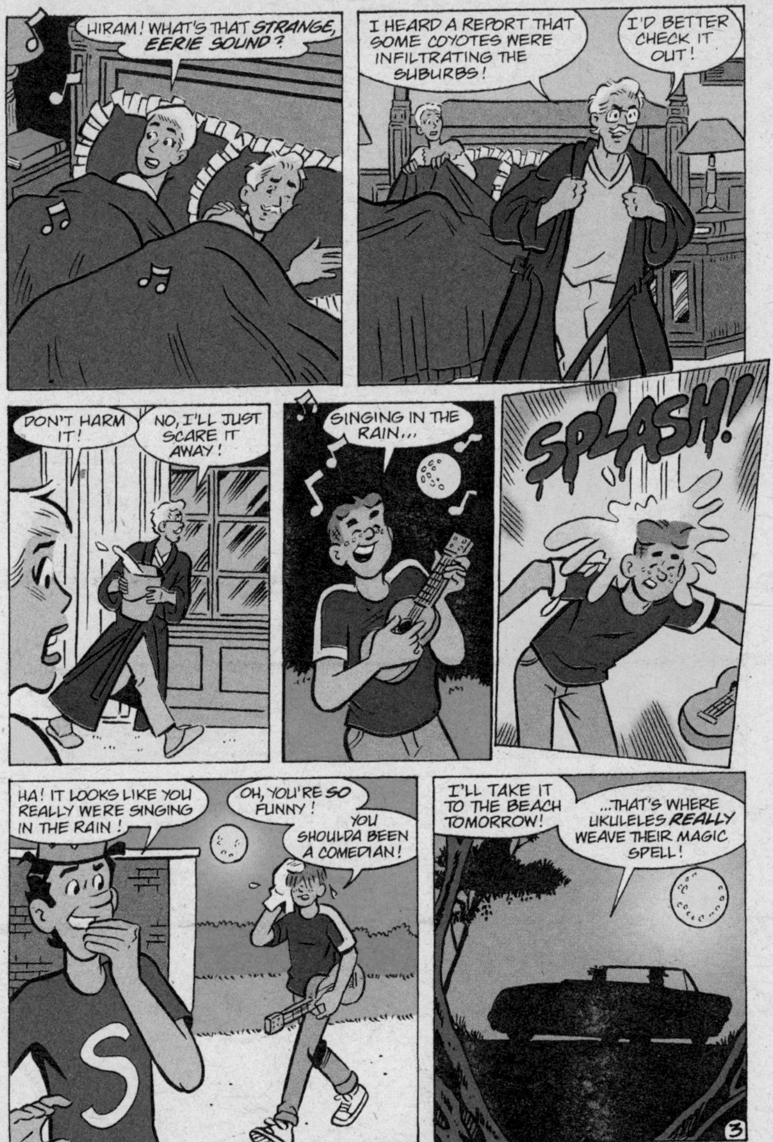
HIRAM! WHAT'S THAT STRANGE, EERIE SOUND?
I HEARD A REPORT THAT SOME COYOTES WERE INFILTRATING THE SUBURBS!
I'D BETTER CHECK IT OUT!
DON'T HARM IT!
NO, I'LL JUST SCARE IT AWAY!
SINGING IN THE RAIN...
SPLASH!
HA! IT LOOKS LIKE YOU REALLY WERE SINGING IN THE RAIN!
OH, YOU'RE SO FUNNY!
YOU SHOULDA BEEN A COMEDIAN!
I'LL TAKE IT TO THE BEACH TOMORROW!
...THAT'S WHERE UKULELES REALLY WEAVE THEIR MAGIC SPELL!
3

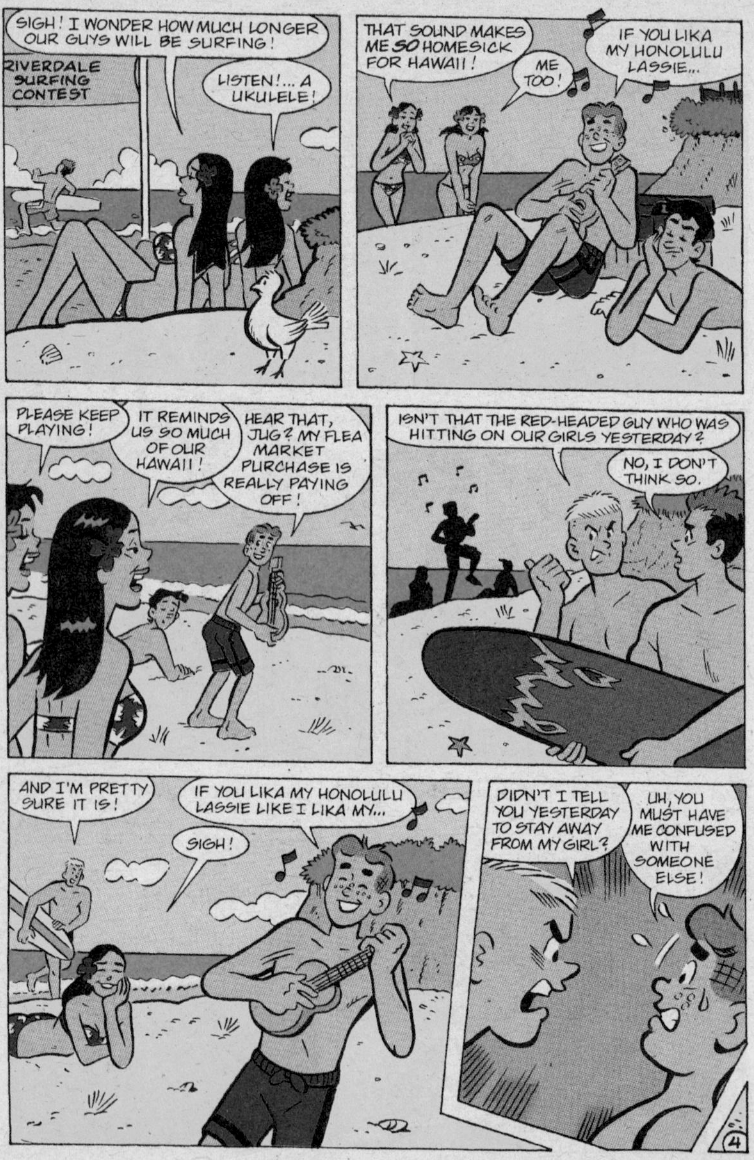
SIGH! I WONDER HOW MUCH LONGER OUR GUYS WILL BE SURFING!
RIVERDALE SURFING CONTEST
LISTEN!... A UKULELE!
THAT SOUND MAKES ME SO HOMESICK FOR HAWAII!
ME TOO!
IF YOU LIKA MY HONOLULU LASSIE...
PLEASE KEEP PLAYING!
IT REMINDS US SO MUCH OF OUR HAWAII!
HEAR THAT, JUG? MY FLEA MARKET PURCHASE IS REALLY PAYING OFF!
ISN'T THAT THE RED-HEADED GUY WHO WAS HITTING ON OUR GIRLS YESTERDAY?
NO, I DON'T THINK SO.
AND I'M PRETTY SURE IT IS!
IF YOU LIKA MY HONOLULU LASSIE LIKE I LIKA MY...
SIGH!
DIDN'T I TELL YOU YESTERDAY TO STAY AWAY FROM MY GIRL?
UH, YOU MUST HAVE ME CONFUSED WITH SOMEONE ELSE!
4

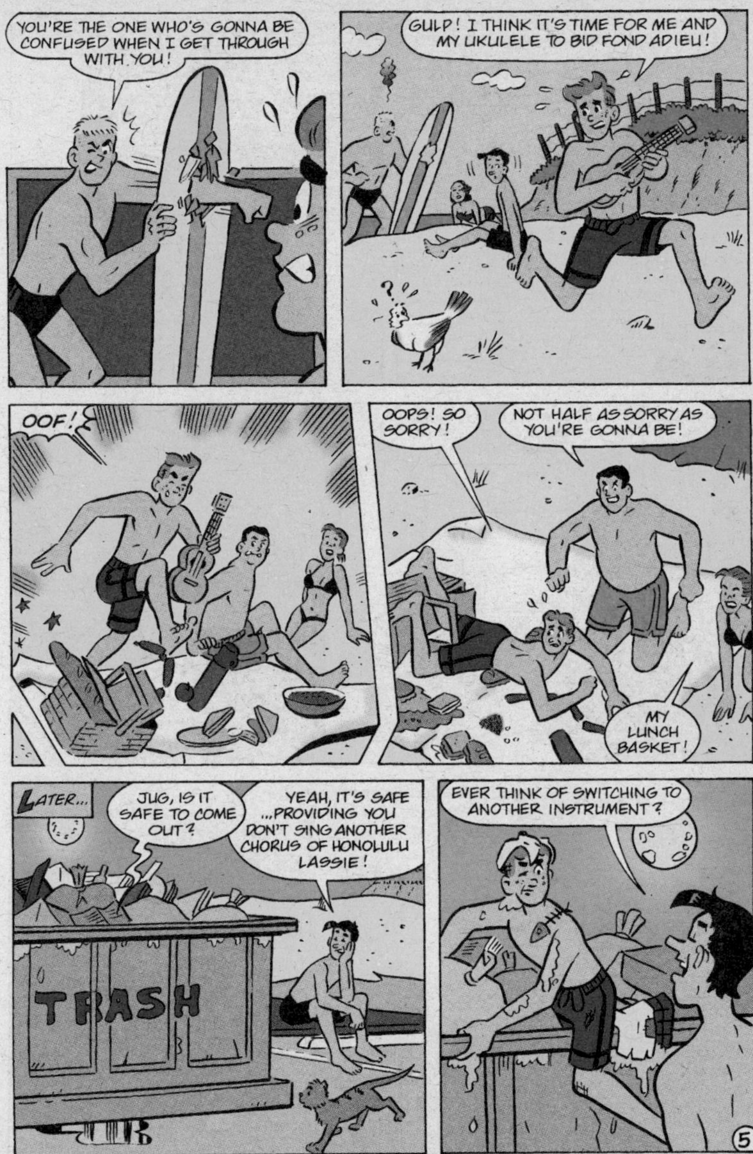
YOU'RE THE ONE WHO'S GONNA BE CONFUSED WHEN I GET THROUGH WITH YOU!
GULP! I THINK IT'S TIME FOR ME AND MY UKULELE TO BID FOND ADIEU!
OOF!
OOPS! SO SORRY!
NOT HALF AS SORRY AS YOU'RE GONNA BE!
MY LUNCH BASKET!
LATER...
JUG, IS IT SAFE TO COME OUT?
YEAH, IT'S SAFE ...PROVIDING YOU DON'T SING ANOTHER CHORUS OF HONOLULU LASSIE!
TRASH
EVER THINK OF SWITCHING TO ANOTHER INSTRUMENT?
5

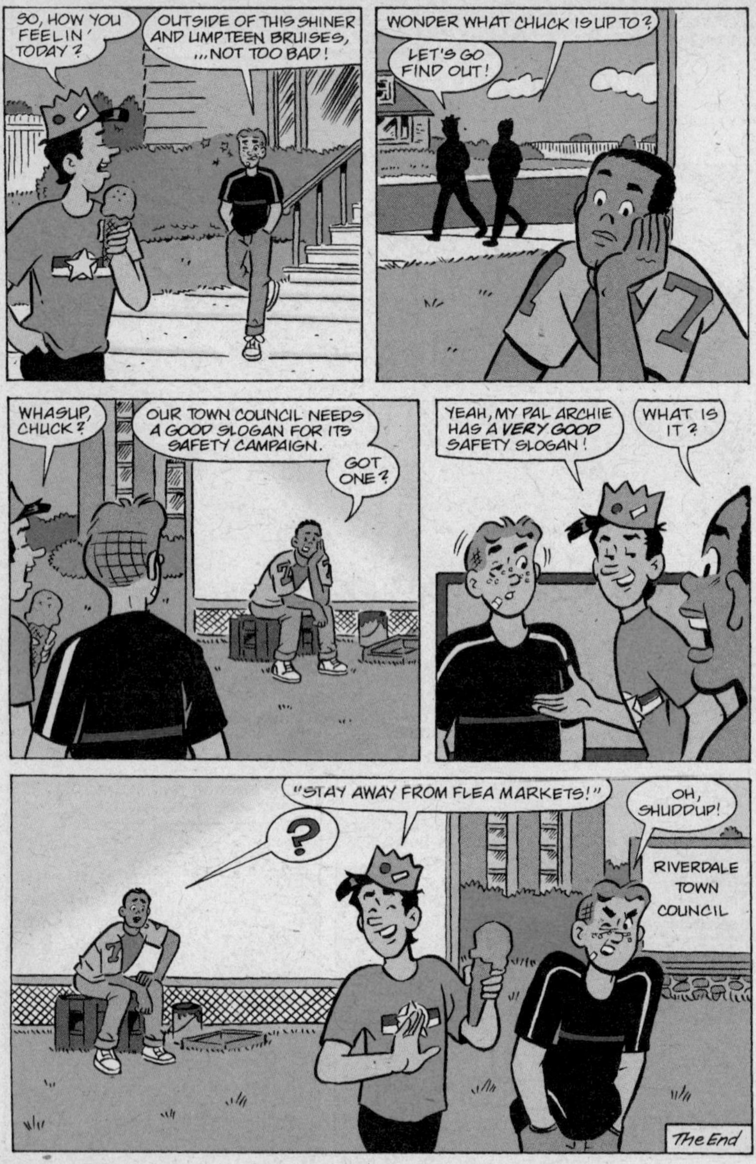
SO, HOW YOU FEELIN' TODAY?
OUTSIDE OF THIS SHINER AND UMPTEEN BRUISES, ...NOT TOO BAD!
WONDER WHAT CHUCK IS UP TO?
LET'S GO FIND OUT!
WHASUP, CHUCK?
OUR TOWN COUNCIL NEEDS A GOOD SLOGAN FOR ITS SAFETY CAMPAIGN.
GOT ONE?
YEAH, MY PAL ARCHIE HAS A VERY GOOD SAFETY SLOGAN!
WHAT IS IT?
"STAY AWAY FROM FLEA MARKETS!"
?
OH, SHUDDUP!
RIVERDALE TOWN COUNCIL
The End

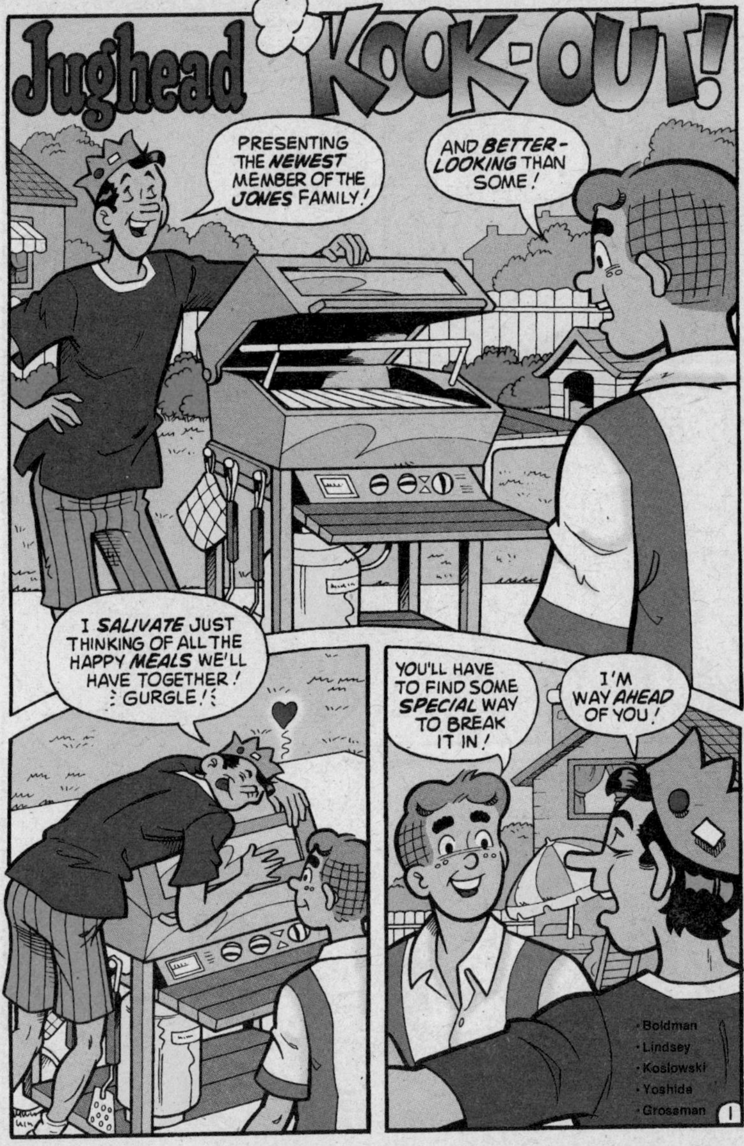
Jughead
KOOK-OUT!
PRESENTING THE NEWEST MEMBER OF THE JONES FAMILY!
AND BETTER-LOOKING THAN SOME!
I SALIVATE JUST THINKING OF ALL THE HAPPY MEALS WE'LL HAVE TOGETHER! GURGLE!
YOU'LL HAVE TO FIND SOME SPECIAL WAY TO BREAK IT IN!
I'M WAY AHEAD OF YOU!
•Boldman
•Lindsey
•Koslowski
•Yoshida
•Grossman

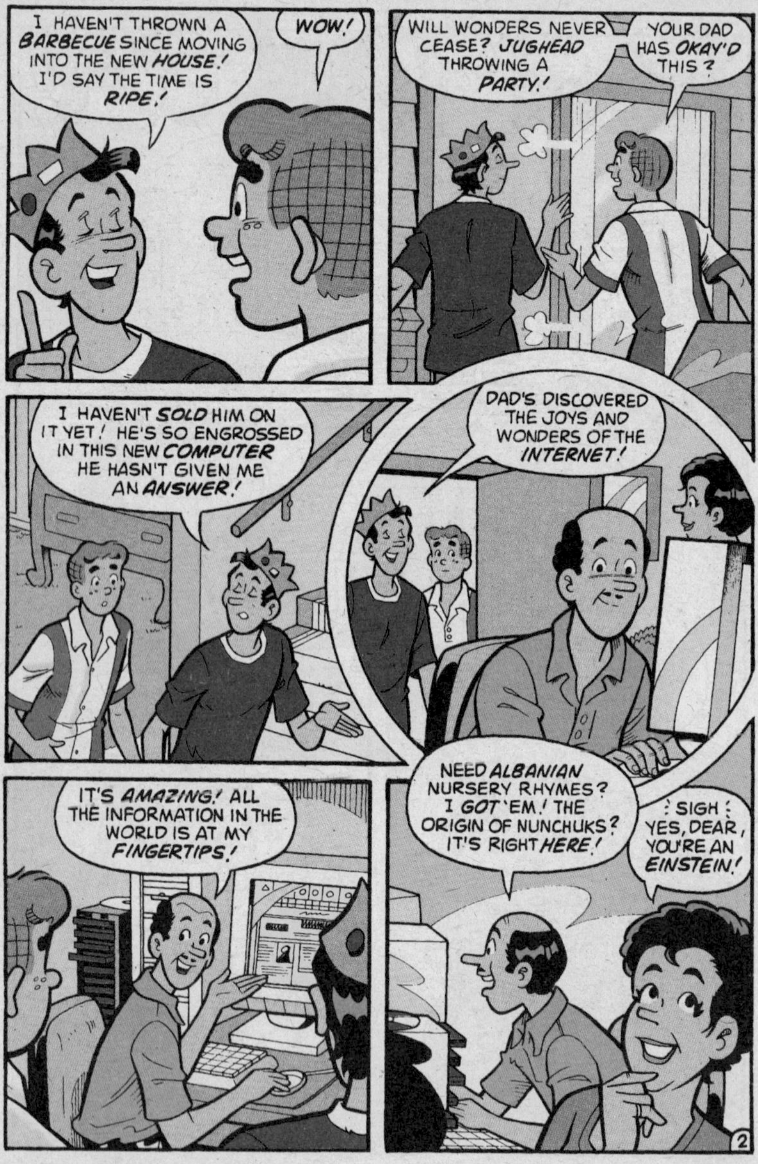

I HAVEN'T THROWN A BARBECUE SINCE MOVING INTO THE NEW HOUSE! I'D SAY THE TIME IS RIPE!
WOW!
WILL WONDERS NEVER CEASE? JUGHEAD THROWING A PARTY!
YOUR DAD HAS OKAY'D THIS?
I HAVEN'T SOLD HIM ON IT YET! HE'S SO ENGROSSED IN THIS NEW COMPUTER HE HASN'T GIVEN ME AN ANSWER!
DAD'S DISCOVERED THE JOYS AND WONDERS OF THE INTERNET!
IT'S AMAZING! ALL THE INFORMATION IN THE WORLD IS AT MY FINGERTIPS!
NEED ALBANIAN NURSERY RHYMES? I GOT 'EM! THE ORIGIN OF NUNCHUKS? IT'S RIGHT HERE!
:SIGH: YES, DEAR, YOU'RE AN EINSTEIN!
2

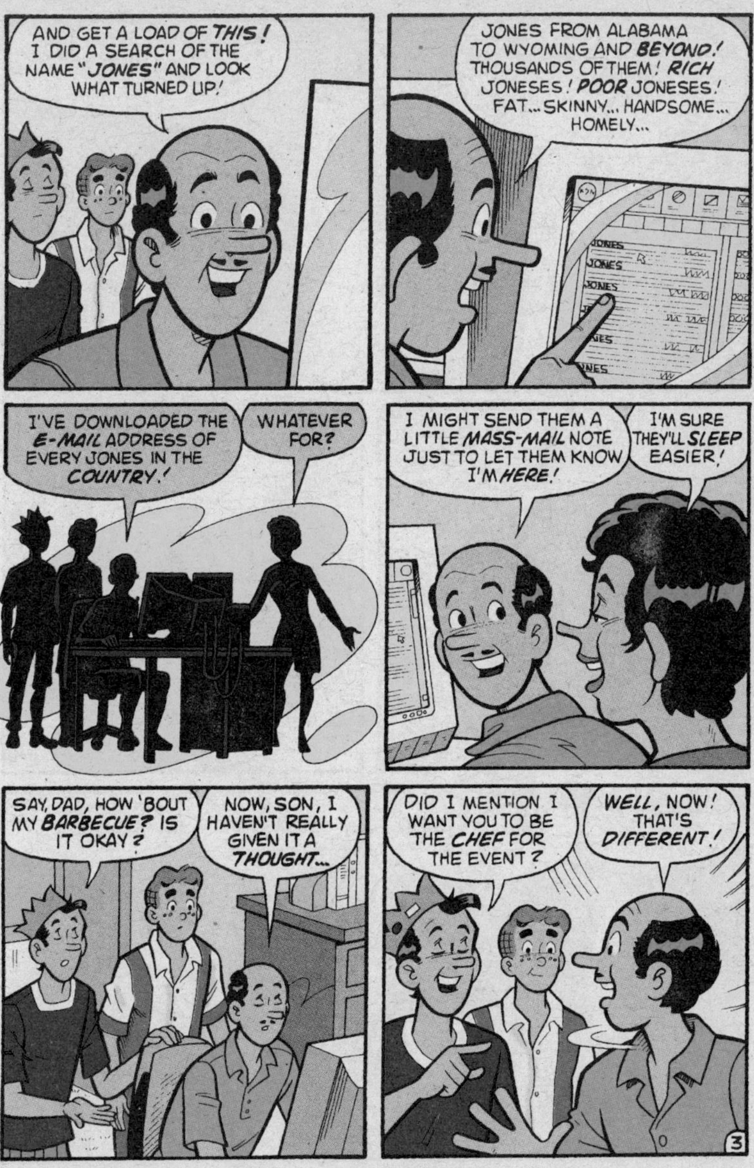
AND GET A LOAD OF THIS! I DID A SEARCH OF THE NAME "JONES" AND LOOK WHAT TURNED UP!
JONES FROM ALABAMA TO WYOMING AND BEYOND! THOUSANDS OF THEM! RICH JONESES! POOR JONESES! FAT... SKINNY... HANDSOME... HOMELY...
JONES
JONES
JONES
I'VE DOWNLOADED THE E-MAIL ADDRESS OF EVERY JONES IN THE COUNTRY!
WHATEVER FOR?
I MIGHT SEND THEM A LITTLE MASS-MAIL NOTE JUST TO LET THEM KNOW I'M HERE!
I'M SURE THEY'LL SLEEP EASIER!
SAY, DAD, HOW 'BOUT MY BARBECUE? IS IT OKAY?
NOW, SON, I HAVEN'T REALLY GIVEN IT A THOUGHT...
DID I MENTION I WANT YOU TO BE THE CHEF FOR THE EVENT?
WELL, NOW! THAT'S DIFFERENT!
3

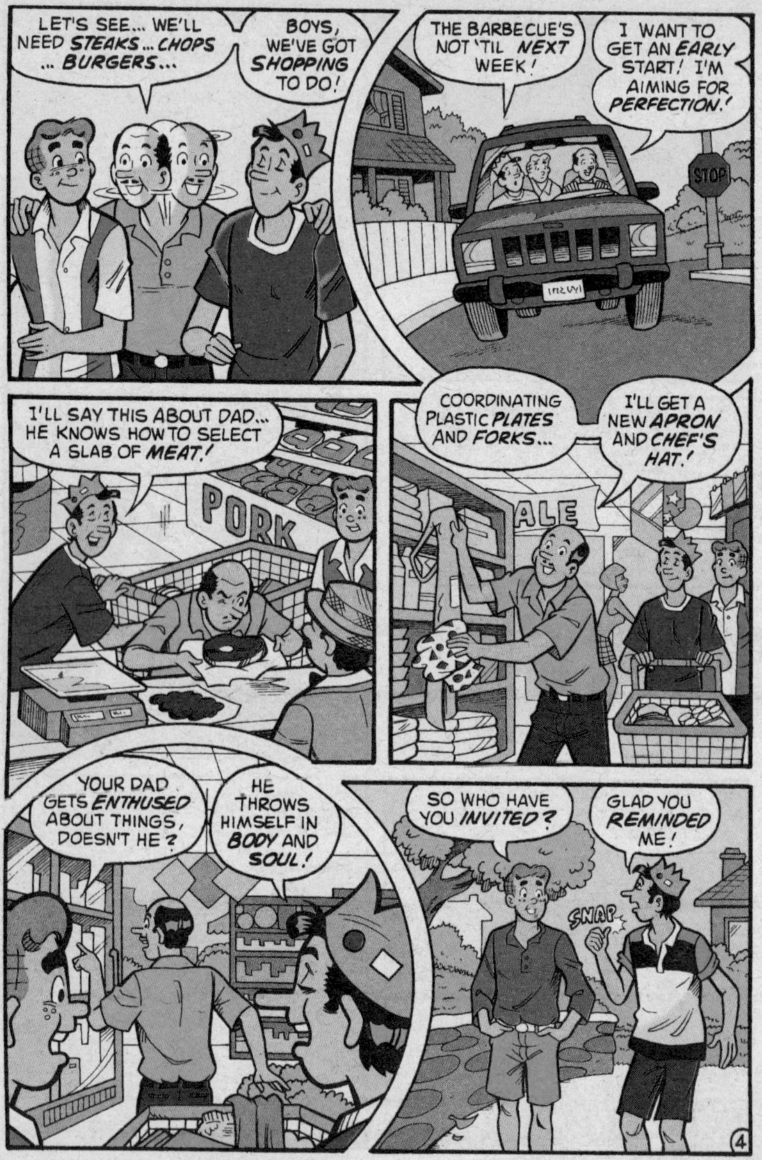
LET'S SEE... WE'LL NEED STEAKS ... CHOPS ... BURGERS...
BOYS, WE'VE GOT SHOPPING TO DO!
THE BARBECUE'S NOT 'TIL NEXT WEEK!
I WANT TO GET AN EARLY START! I'M AIMING FOR PERFECTION!
STOP
I'LL SAY THIS ABOUT DAD... HE KNOWS HOW TO SELECT A SLAB OF MEAT!
PORK
COORDINATING PLASTIC PLATES AND FORKS...
I'LL GET A NEW APRON AND CHEF'S HAT!
ALE
YOUR DAD GETS ENTHUSED ABOUT THINGS, DOESN'T HE?
HE THROWS HIMSELF IN BODY AND SOUL!
SO WHO HAVE YOU INVITED?
GLAD YOU REMINDED ME!
SNAP
4

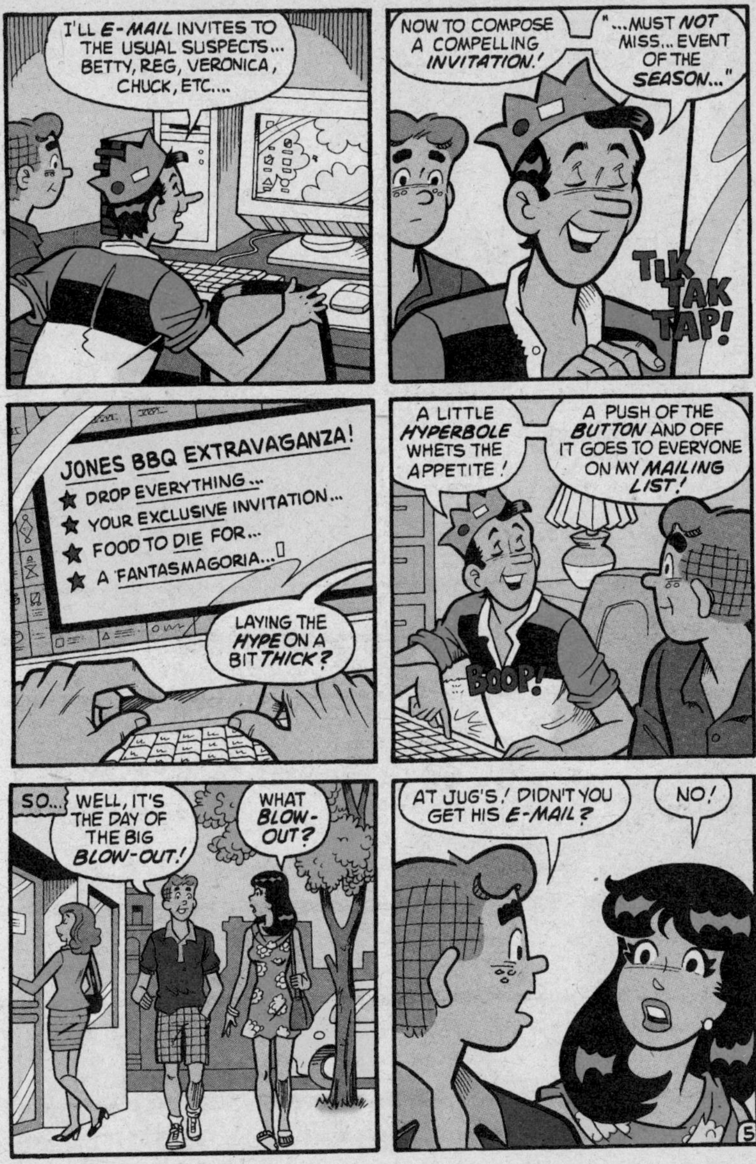

I'LL E-MAIL INVITES TO THE USUAL SUSPECTS... BETTY, REG, VERONICA, CHUCK, ETC....
NOW TO COMPOSE A COMPELLING INVITATION!
"...MUST NOT MISS... EVENT OF THE SEASON..."
TIK TAK TAP!
JONES BBQ EXTRAVAGANZA!
DROP EVERYTHING...
YOUR EXCLUSIVE INVITATION...
FOOD TO DIE FOR...
A 'FANTASMAGORIA...
LAYING THE HYPE ON A BIT THICK?
A LITTLE HYPERBOLE WHETS THE APPETITE!
A PUSH OF THE BUTTON AND OFF IT GOES TO EVERYONE ON MY MAILING LIST!
BOOP!
SO...
WELL, IT'S THE DAY OF THE BIG BLOW-OUT!
WHAT BLOW-OUT?
AT JUG'S! DIDN'T YOU GET HIS E-MAIL?
NO!
5

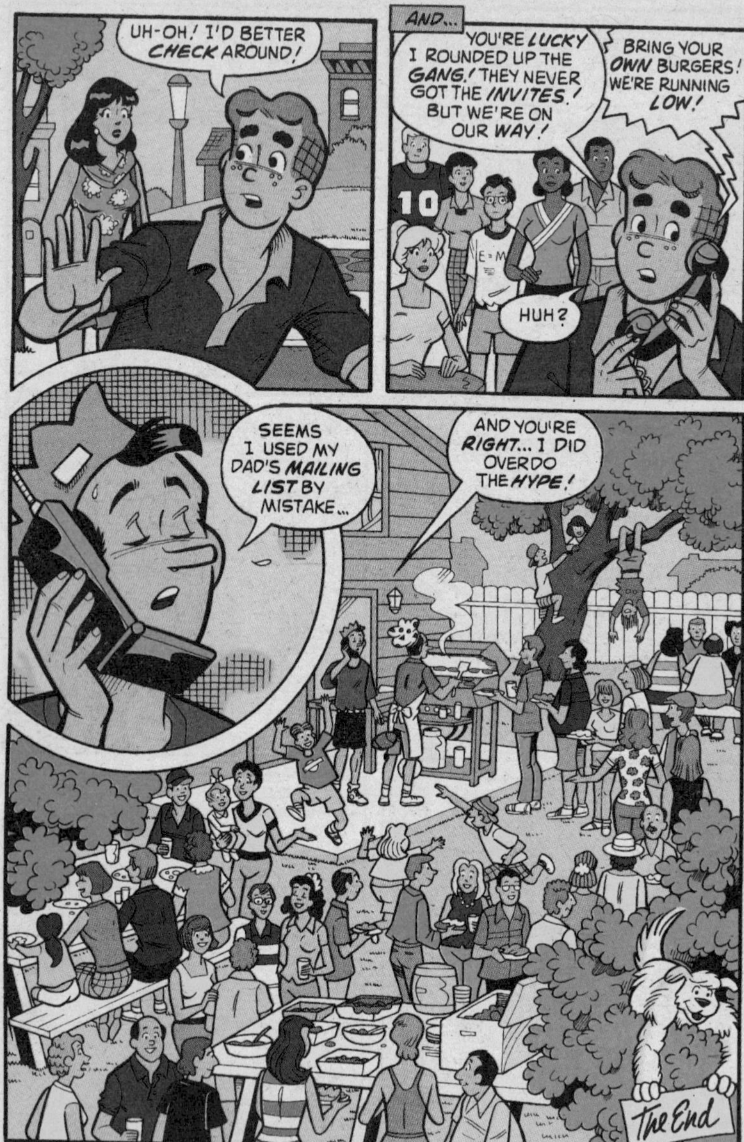
UH-OH! I'D BETTER CHECK AROUND!
AND...
YOU'RE LUCKY I ROUNDED UP THE GANG! THEY NEVER GOT THE INVITES! BUT WE'RE ON OUR WAY!
BRING YOUR OWN BURGERS! WE'RE RUNNING LOW!
HUH?
SEEMS I USED MY DAD'S MAILING LIST BY MISTAKE...
AND YOU'RE RIGHT... I DID OVERDO THE HYPE!
The End

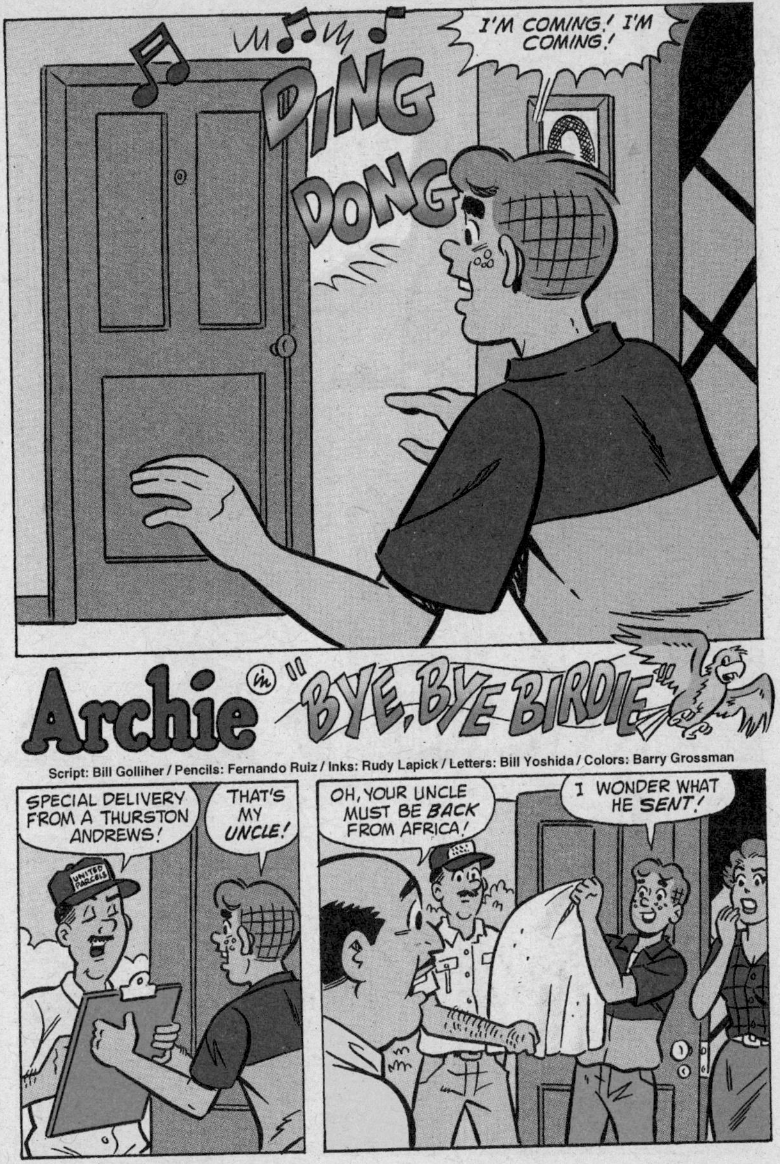
DING DONG
I'M COMING! I'M COMING!
Archie in "BYE, BYE BIRDIE"
Script: Bill Golliher / Pencils: Fernando Ruiz / Inks: Rudy Lapick / Letters: Bill Yoshida / Colors: Barry Grossman
SPECIAL DELIVERY FROM A THURSTON ANDREWS!
UNITED PARCELS
THAT'S MY *UNCLE*!
OH, YOUR UNCLE MUST BE *BACK* FROM AFRICA!
I WONDER WHAT HE *SENT*!

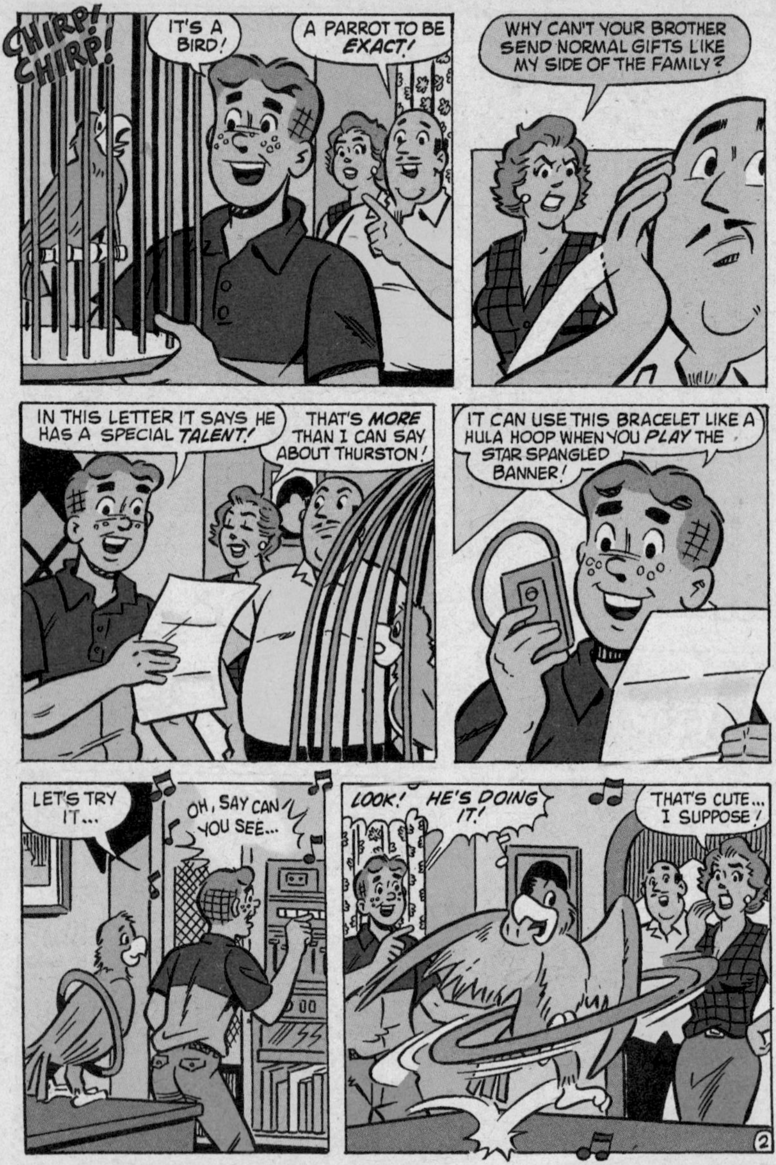

CHIRP! CHIRP!
IT'S A BIRD!
A PARROT TO BE EXACT!
WHY CAN'T YOUR BROTHER SEND NORMAL GIFTS LIKE MY SIDE OF THE FAMILY?
IN THIS LETTER IT SAYS HE HAS A SPECIAL TALENT!
THAT'S MORE THAN I CAN SAY ABOUT THURSTON!
IT CAN USE THIS BRACELET LIKE A HULA HOOP WHEN YOU PLAY THE STAR SPANGLED BANNER!
LET'S TRY IT...
OH, SAY CAN YOU SEE...
LOOK! HE'S DOING IT!
THAT'S CUTE... I SUPPOSE!

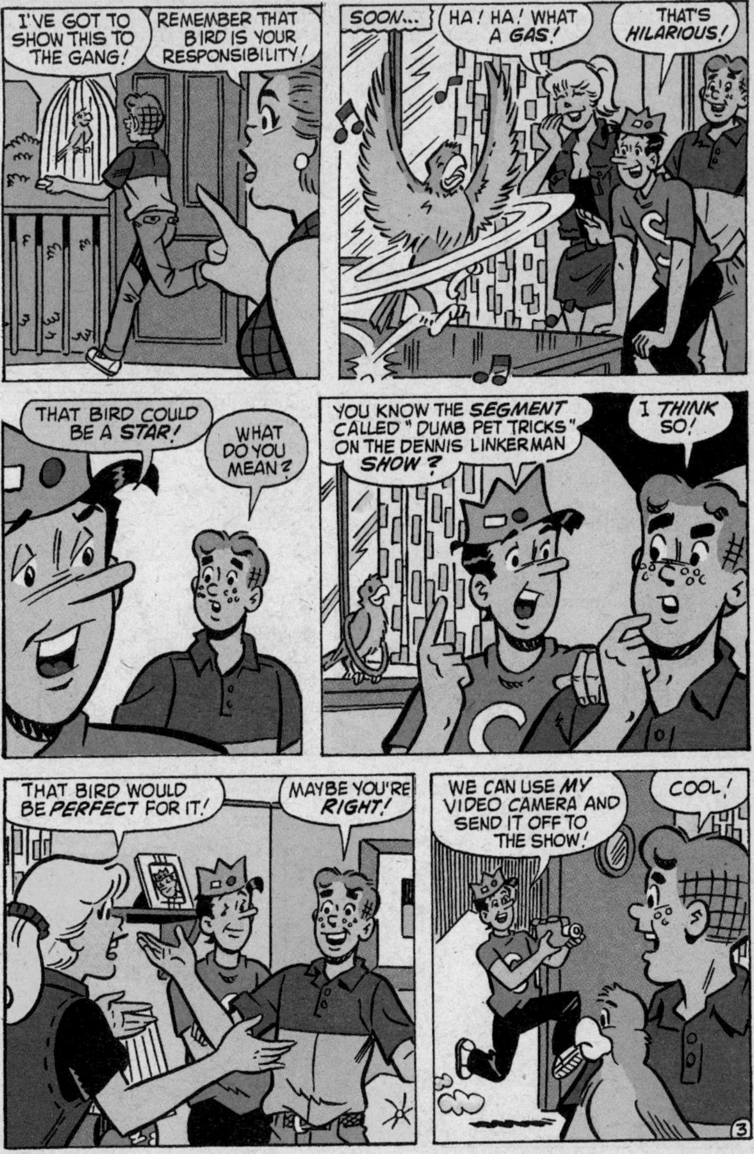
I'VE GOT TO SHOW THIS TO THE GANG!
REMEMBER THAT BIRD IS YOUR RESPONSIBILITY!
SOON...
HA! HA! WHAT A GAS!
THAT'S HILARIOUS!
THAT BIRD COULD BE A STAR!
WHAT DO YOU MEAN?
YOU KNOW THE SEGMENT CALLED "DUMB PET TRICKS" ON THE DENNIS LINKERMAN SHOW?
I THINK SO!
THAT BIRD WOULD BE PERFECT FOR IT!
MAYBE YOU'RE RIGHT!
WE CAN USE MY VIDEO CAMERA AND SEND IT OFF TO THE SHOW!
COOL!
3

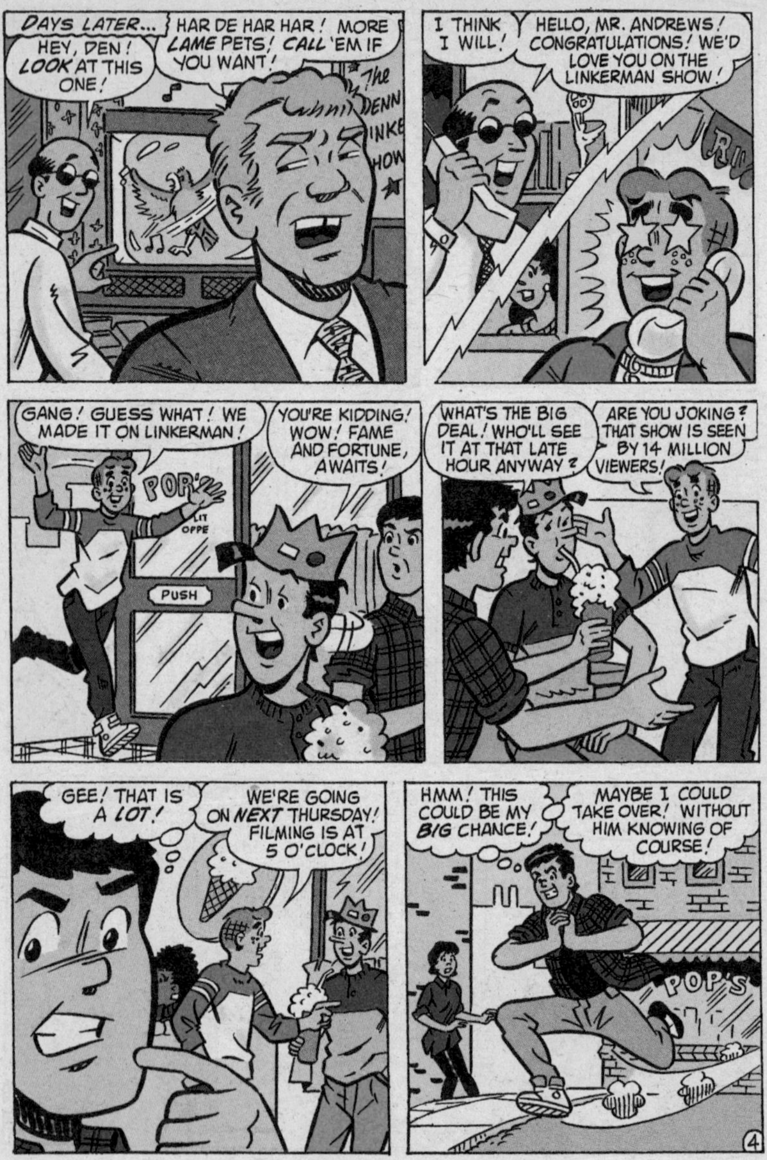
DAYS LATER...
HEY, DEN! LOOK AT THIS ONE!
HAR DE HAR HAR! MORE LAME PETS! CALL 'EM IF YOU WANT!
The DENN INKE HOW
I THINK I WILL!
HELLO, MR. ANDREWS! CONGRATULATIONS! WE'D LOVE YOU ON THE LINKERMAN SHOW!
GANG! GUESS WHAT! WE MADE IT ON LINKERMAN!
YOU'RE KIDDING! WOW! FAME AND FORTUNE, AWAITS!
POP'S
PUSH
WHAT'S THE BIG DEAL! WHO'LL SEE IT AT THAT LATE HOUR ANYWAY?
ARE YOU JOKING? THAT SHOW IS SEEN BY 14 MILLION VIEWERS!
GEE! THAT IS A LOT!
WE'RE GOING ON NEXT THURSDAY! FILMING IS AT 5 O'CLOCK!
HMM! THIS COULD BE MY BIG CHANCE!
MAYBE I COULD TAKE OVER! WITHOUT HIM KNOWING OF COURSE!
POP'S
4

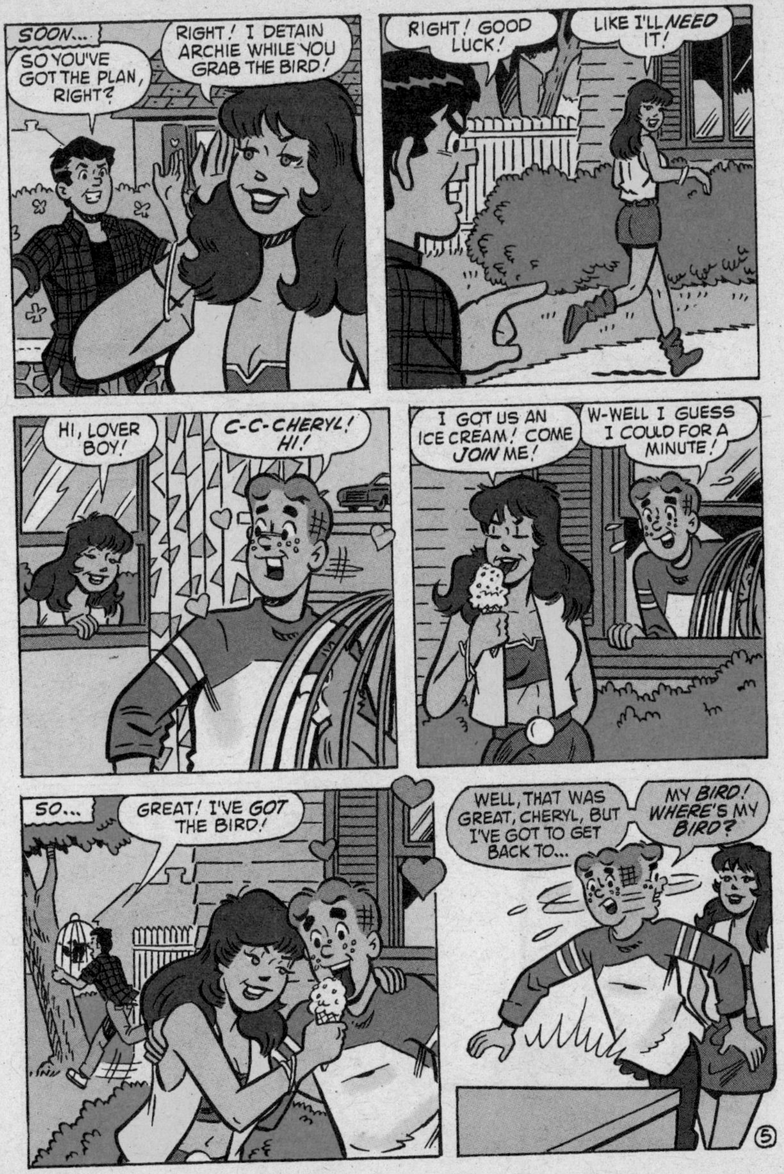
SOON...
SO YOU'VE GOT THE PLAN, RIGHT?
RIGHT! I DETAIN ARCHIE WHILE YOU GRAB THE BIRD!
RIGHT! GOOD LUCK!
LIKE I'LL NEED IT!
HI, LOVER BOY!
C-C-CHERYL! HI!
I GOT US AN ICE CREAM! COME JOIN ME!
W-WELL I GUESS I COULD FOR A MINUTE!
SO...
GREAT! I'VE GOT THE BIRD!
WELL, THAT WAS GREAT, CHERYL, BUT I'VE GOT TO GET BACK TO...
MY BIRD! WHERE'S MY BIRD?
5

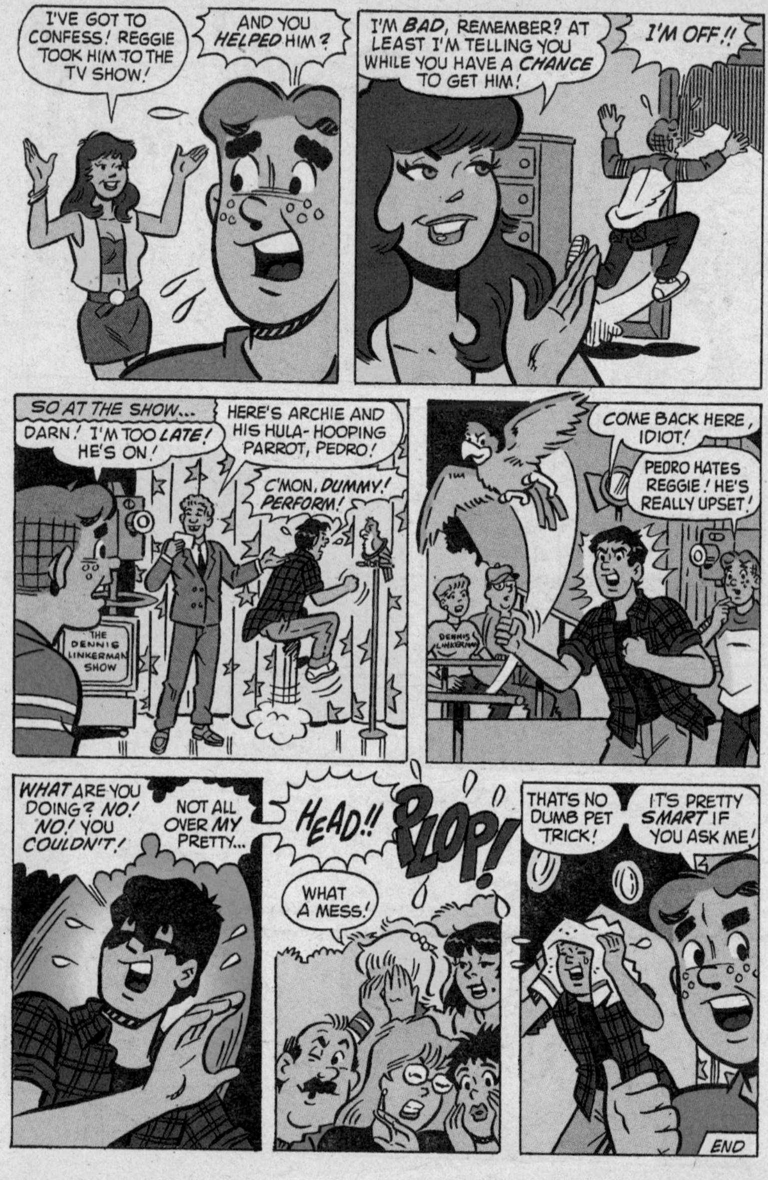

I'VE GOT TO CONFESS! REGGIE TOOK HIM TO THE TV SHOW!
AND YOU HELPED HIM?
I'M BAD, REMEMBER? AT LEAST I'M TELLING YOU WHILE YOU HAVE A CHANCE TO GET HIM!
I'M OFF!!
SO AT THE SHOW...
DARN! I'M TOO LATE! HE'S ON!
HERE'S ARCHIE AND HIS HULA-HOOPING PARROT, PEDRO!
C'MON, DUMMY! PERFORM!
THE DENNIS LINKERMAN SHOW
COME BACK HERE, IDIOT!
PEDRO HATES REGGIE! HE'S REALLY UPSET!
DENNIS LINKERMAN
WHAT ARE YOU DOING? NO! NO! YOU COULDN'T!
NOT ALL OVER MY PRETTY...
HEAD!!
PLOP!
WHAT A MESS!
THAT'S NO DUMB PET TRICK!
IT'S PRETTY SMART IF YOU ASK ME!
END

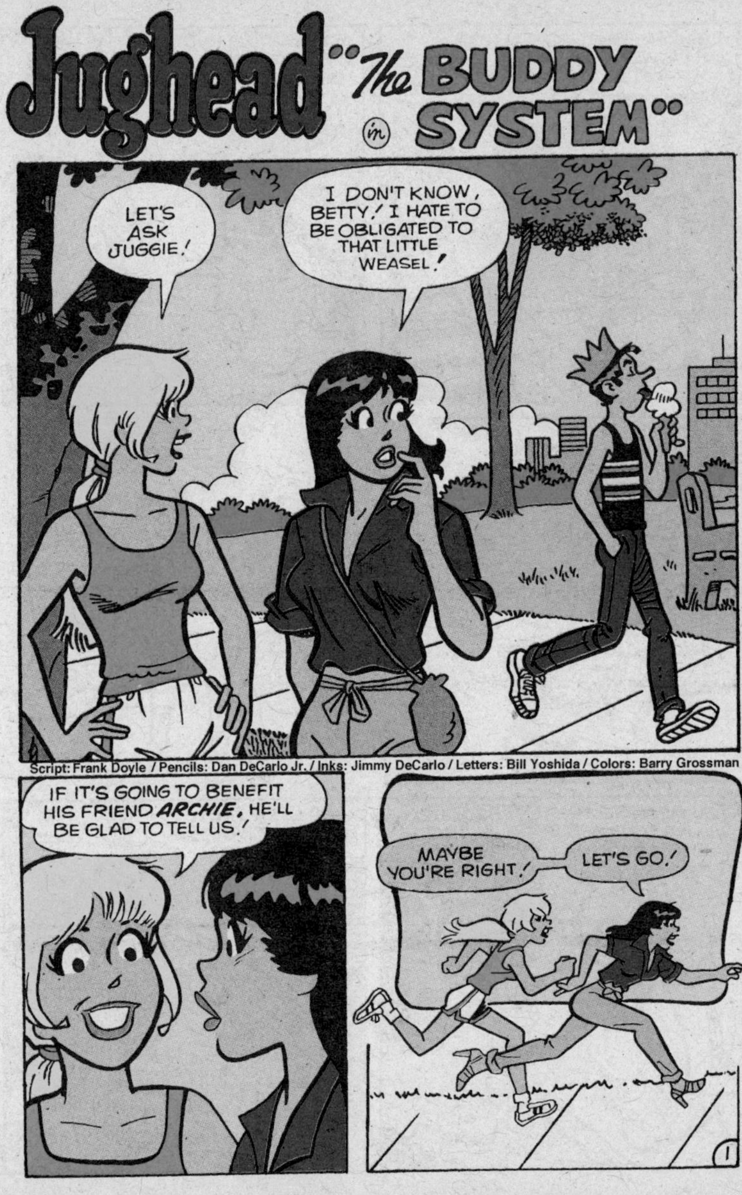
Jughead in "The BUDDY SYSTEM"
LET'S ASK JUGGIE!
I DON'T KNOW, BETTY! I HATE TO BE OBLIGATED TO THAT LITTLE WEASEL!
Script: Frank Doyle / Pencils: Dan DeCarlo Jr. / Inks: Jimmy DeCarlo / Letters: Bill Yoshida / Colors: Barry Grossman
IF IT'S GOING TO BENEFIT HIS FRIEND ARCHIE, HE'LL BE GLAD TO TELL US!
MAYBE YOU'RE RIGHT!
LET'S GO!
1

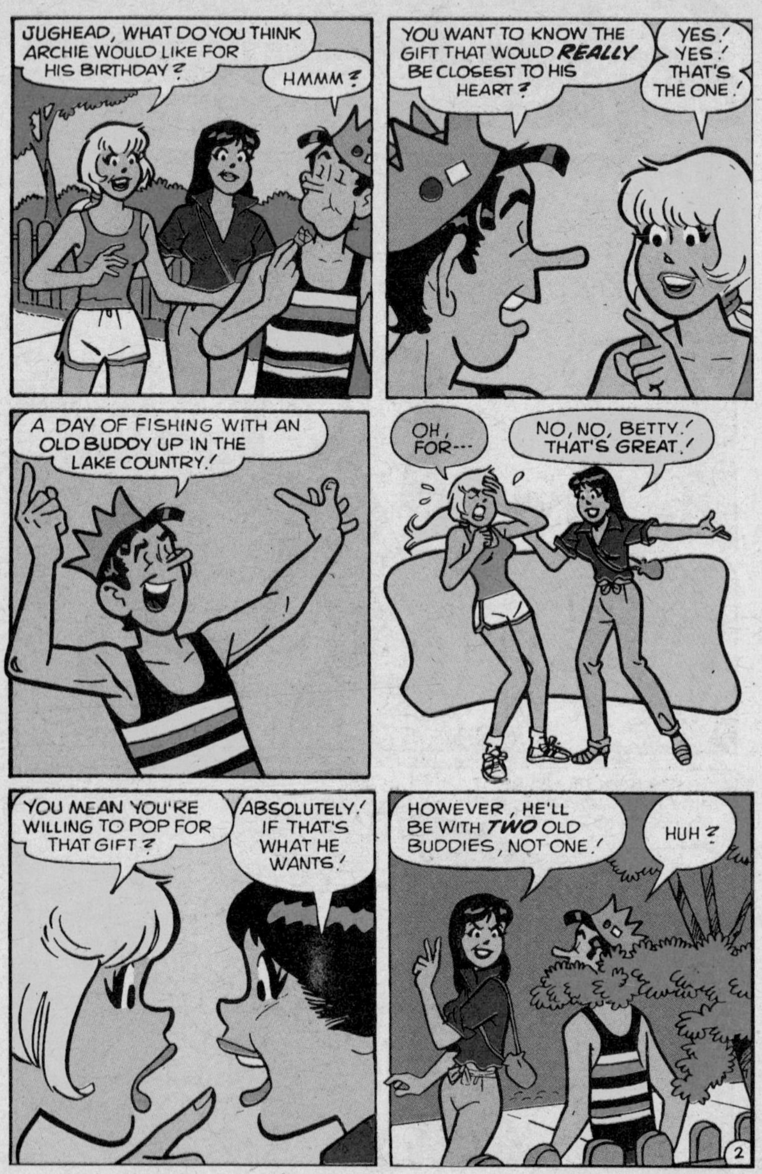
JUGHEAD, WHAT DO YOU THINK ARCHIE WOULD LIKE FOR HIS BIRTHDAY?
HMMM?
YOU WANT TO KNOW THE GIFT THAT WOULD REALLY BE CLOSEST TO HIS HEART?
YES! YES! THAT'S THE ONE!
A DAY OF FISHING WITH AN OLD BUDDY UP IN THE LAKE COUNTRY!
OH, FOR---
NO, NO, BETTY! THAT'S GREAT!
YOU MEAN YOU'RE WILLING TO POP FOR THAT GIFT?
ABSOLUTELY! IF THAT'S WHAT HE WANTS!
HOWEVER, HE'LL BE WITH TWO OLD BUDDIES, NOT ONE!
HUH?
2

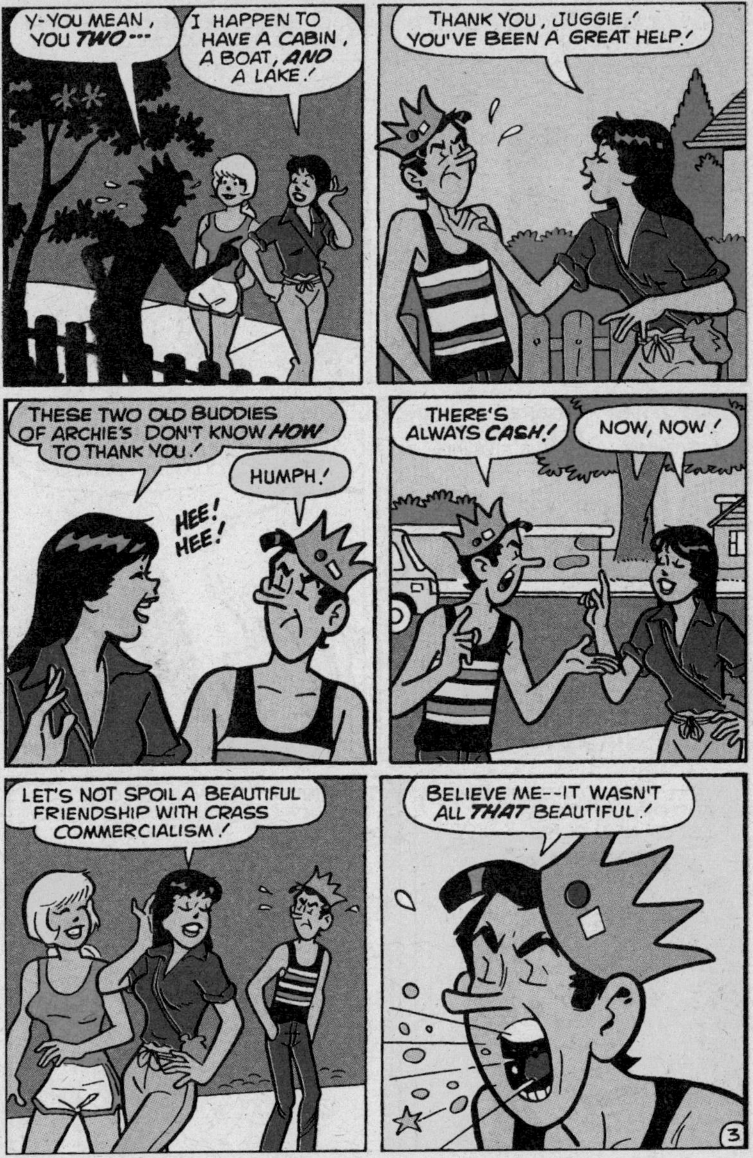

Y-YOU MEAN, YOU TWO...
I HAPPEN TO HAVE A CABIN, A BOAT, AND A LAKE!
THANK YOU, JUGGIE! YOU'VE BEEN A GREAT HELP!
THESE TWO OLD BUDDIES OF ARCHIE'S DON'T KNOW HOW TO THANK YOU!
HEE! HEE!
HUMPH!
THERE'S ALWAYS CASH!
NOW, NOW!
LET'S NOT SPOIL A BEAUTIFUL FRIENDSHIP WITH CRASS COMMERCIALISM!
BELIEVE ME--IT WASN'T ALL THAT BEAUTIFUL!
3

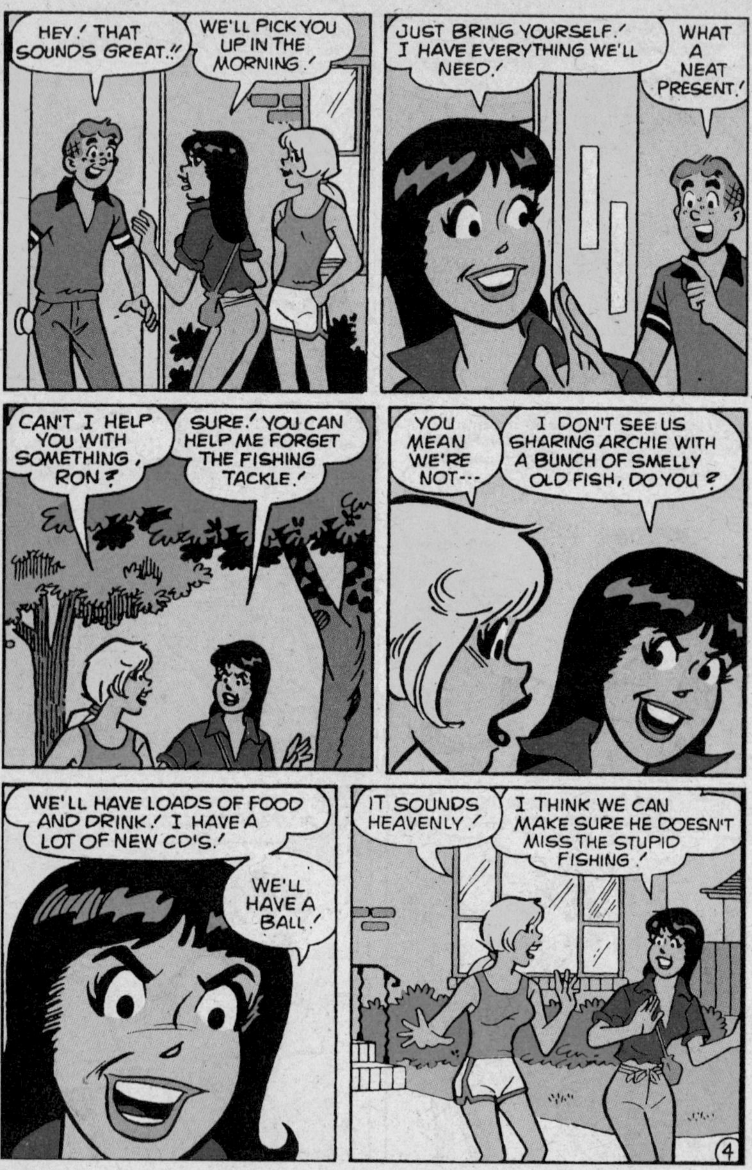
HEY! THAT SOUNDS GREAT.!!
WE'LL PICK YOU UP IN THE MORNING.!
JUST BRING YOURSELF.! I HAVE EVERYTHING WE'LL NEED.!
WHAT A NEAT PRESENT.!
CAN'T I HELP YOU WITH SOMETHING, RON?
SURE.! YOU CAN HELP ME FORGET THE FISHING TACKLE.!
YOU MEAN WE'RE NOT---
I DON'T SEE US SHARING ARCHIE WITH A BUNCH OF SMELLY OLD FISH, DO YOU?
WE'LL HAVE LOADS OF FOOD AND DRINK.! I HAVE A LOT OF NEW CD'S.!
WE'LL HAVE A BALL.!
IT SOUNDS HEAVENLY.!
I THINK WE CAN MAKE SURE HE DOESN'T MISS THE STUPID FISHING.!
4

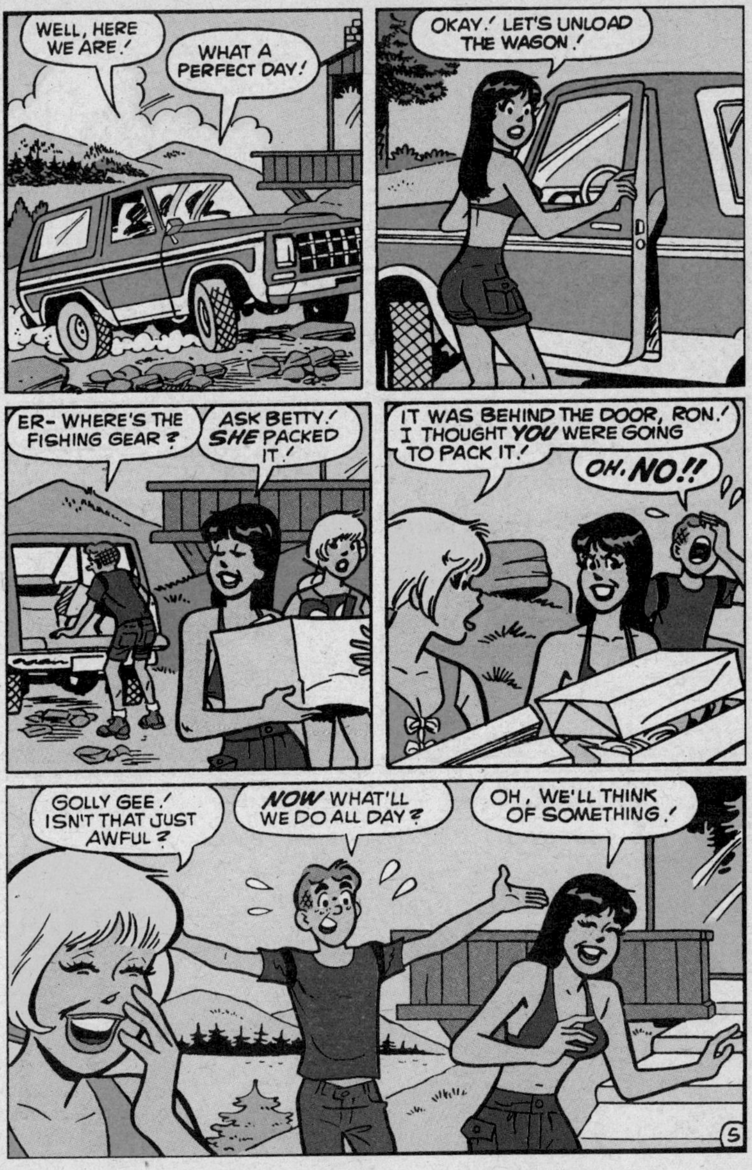
WELL, HERE WE ARE!
WHAT A PERFECT DAY!
OKAY! LET'S UNLOAD THE WAGON!
ER- WHERE'S THE FISHING GEAR?
ASK BETTY! SHE PACKED IT!
IT WAS BEHIND THE DOOR, RON! I THOUGHT YOU WERE GOING TO PACK IT!
OH, NO!!
GOLLY GEE! ISN'T THAT JUST AWFUL?
NOW WHAT'LL WE DO ALL DAY?
OH, WE'LL THINK OF SOMETHING!
5

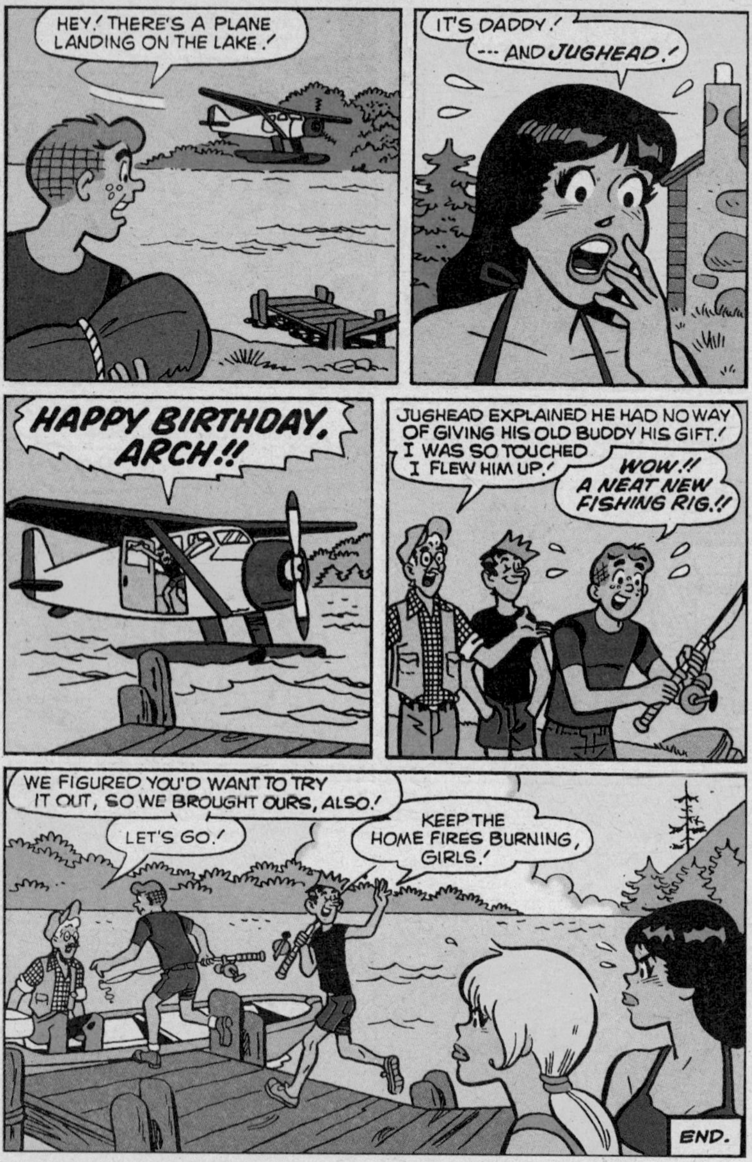
HEY! THERE'S A PLANE LANDING ON THE LAKE!
IT'S DADDY!
--- AND JUGHEAD!
HAPPY BIRTHDAY, ARCH!!
JUGHEAD EXPLAINED HE HAD NO WAY OF GIVING HIS OLD BUDDY HIS GIFT! I WAS SO TOUCHED I FLEW HIM UP!
WOW!! A NEAT NEW FISHING RIG!!
WE FIGURED YOU'D WANT TO TRY IT OUT, SO WE BROUGHT OURS, ALSO!
LET'S GO!
KEEP THE HOME FIRES BURNING, GIRLS!
END.

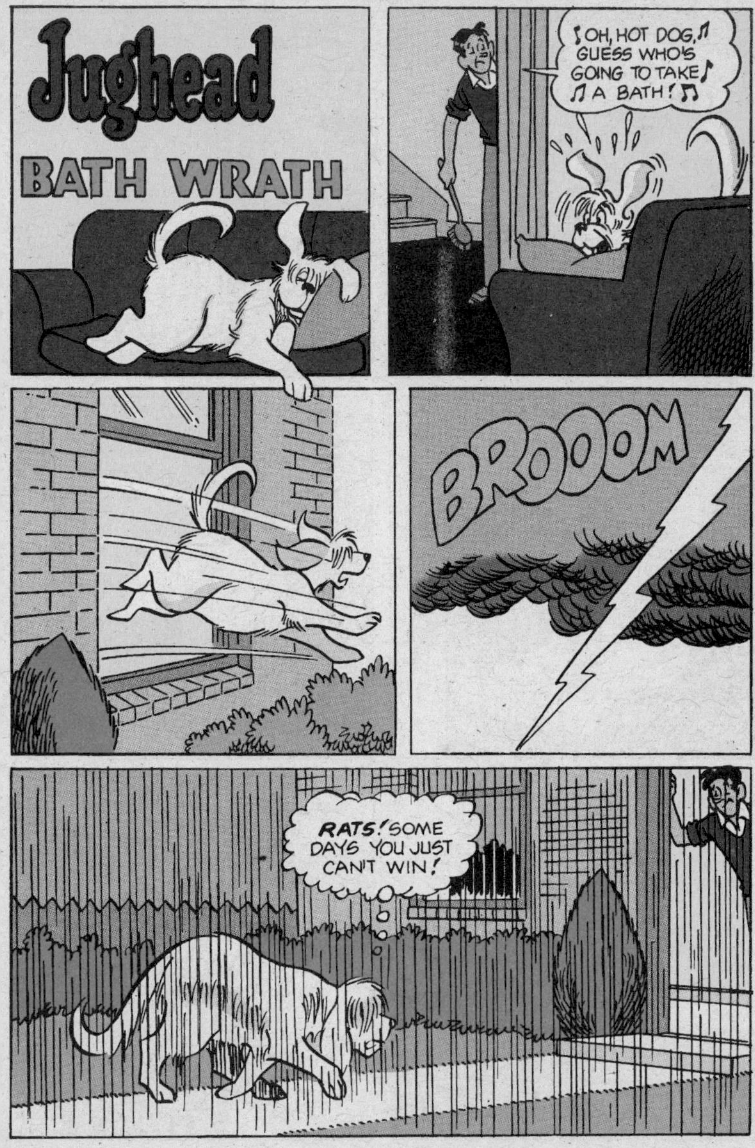
Jughead
BATH WRATH
♪OH, HOT DOG,♪ GUESS WHO'S GOING TO TAKE♪ ♫A BATH!♫
BROOOM
RATS! SOME DAYS YOU JUST CAN'T WIN!

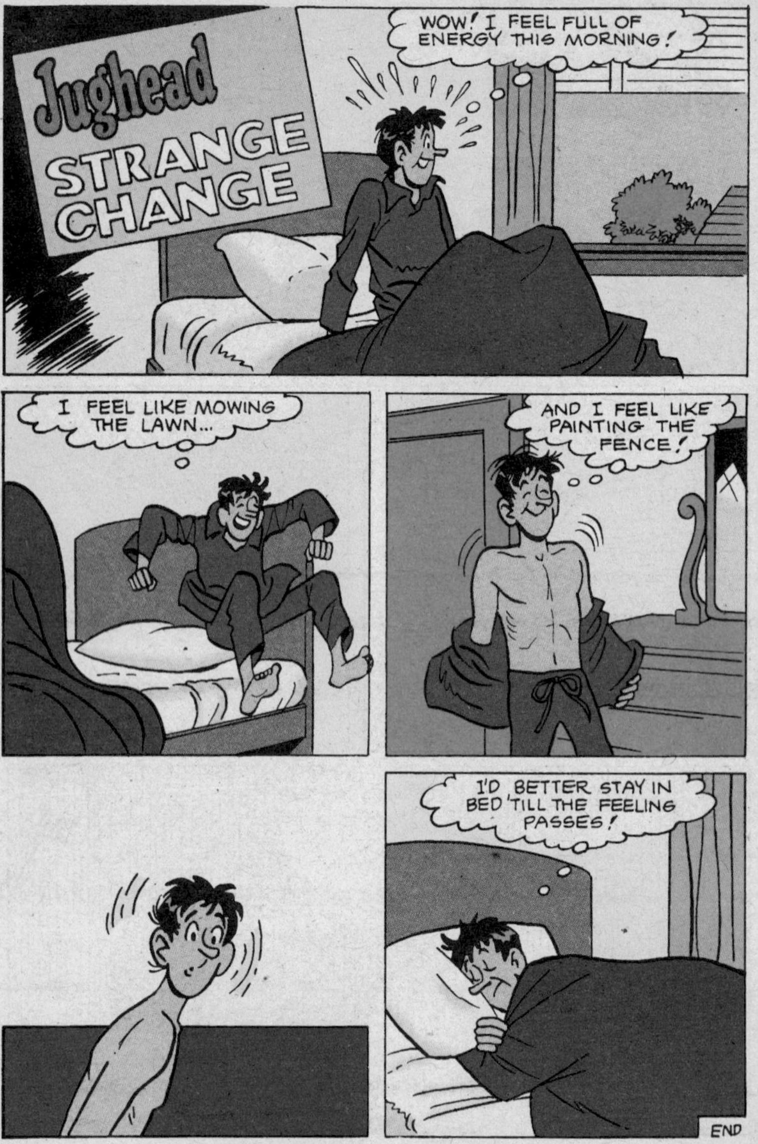
Jughead
STRANGE CHANGE
WOW! I FEEL FULL OF ENERGY THIS MORNING!
I FEEL LIKE MOWING THE LAWN...
AND I FEEL LIKE PAINTING THE FENCE!
I'D BETTER STAY IN BED 'TILL THE FEELING PASSES!
END

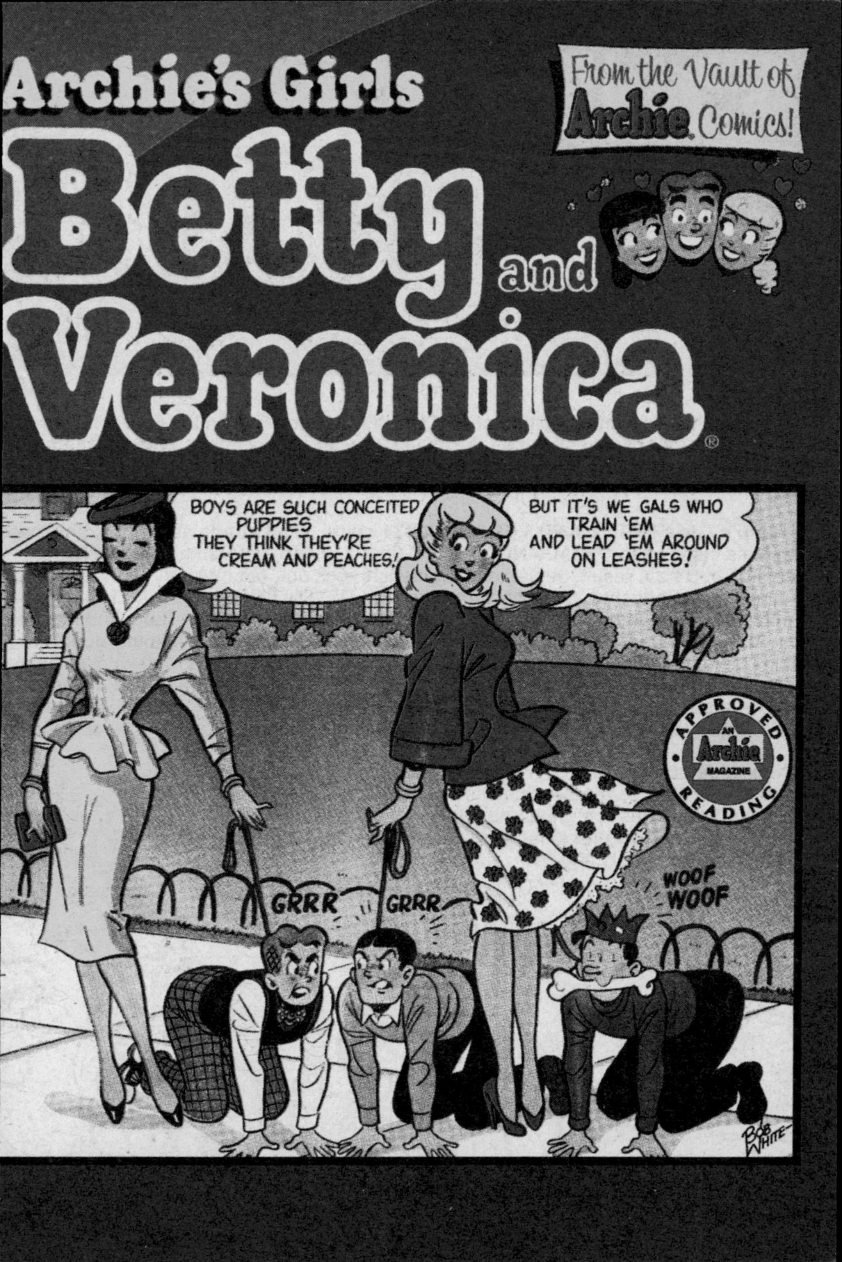

Archie's Girls
Betty and Veronica®
From the Vault of Archie Comics!
BOYS ARE SUCH CONCEITED PUPPIES THEY THINK THEY'RE CREAM AND PEACHES!
BUT IT'S WE GALS WHO TRAIN 'EM AND LEAD 'EM AROUND ON LEASHES!
APPROVED AN Archie MAGAZINE READING
GRRR
GRRR
WOOF WOOF
BOB WHITE

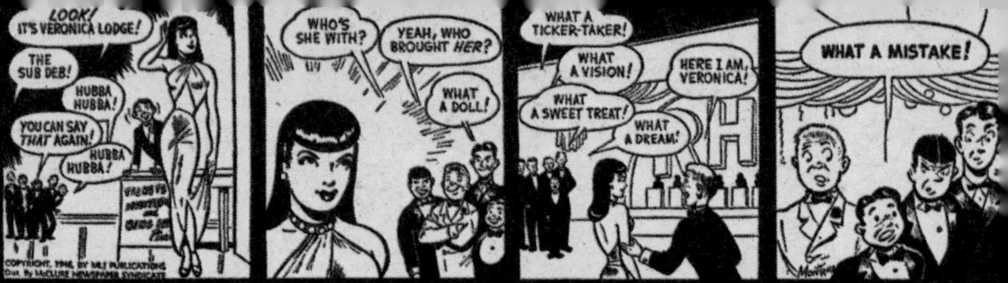
LOOK! IT'S VERONICA LODGE!
THE SUB DEB!
HUBBA, HUBBA!
YOU CAN SAY THAT AGAIN!
HUBBA HUBBA!
COPYRIGHT, 1946, BY MLJ PUBLICATIONS
Dist. By McCLURE NEWSPAPER SYNDICATE
WHO'S SHE WITH?
YEAH, WHO BROUGHT HER?
WHAT A DOLL!
WHAT A TICKER-TAKER!
WHAT A VISION!
HERE I AM, VERONICA!
WHAT A SWEET TREAT!
WHAT A DREAM!
WHAT A MISTAKE!

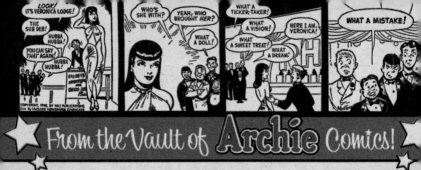

From the Vault of Archie Comics!

Howdy, gang! This latest edition of **ARCHIE VAULT** zeros in on the year 1957 as we take yet another casual peek into the lovingly lavish and luxurious lives of America's favorite comedy glamour girls (and bestest gal pals), Betty and Veronica! Five tales o merriment await you -- along with a certain freckled redhead for good measure!

Archie's Girls BETTY AND VERONICA #31 starts us off strong as Betty experience Archie's insensitive "TRIAL AND ERROR" firsthand and, unfortunately, gets her feelings hurt as a result. Jughead straightens things out, but instantly regrets it once he becomes Betty and Veronica's unwitting "GLUTTON FOR PUNISHMENT!" Next, Archie and Reggie encounter a logic bomb to end all reason when Betty and Veronic put forth the paradox of the "DRESS DILEMMA!" Once that snafu has unwound, we shift gears to **#32** as we look in on our "CAST OF CHARACTERS" and wonder how they don't break each others' limbs (You'll get the pun once you read it)! Finally, we h **#33** where all the gang's at play for a little "MUSIC DEPRECIATION," but Betty's "on note" crusade to get Archie for herself causes some big "trouble-clef" for everybody!

Thousands of men, women, teens and kids all over the country and in the armed forces read Archie Comics during this period and it's no wonder: the stories are great and the artists were in their prime! We hope you enjoy this presentation of classic tales from Archie Comics' past! Take care, pals n' gals!

APPROVED AN Archie MAGAZINE READING

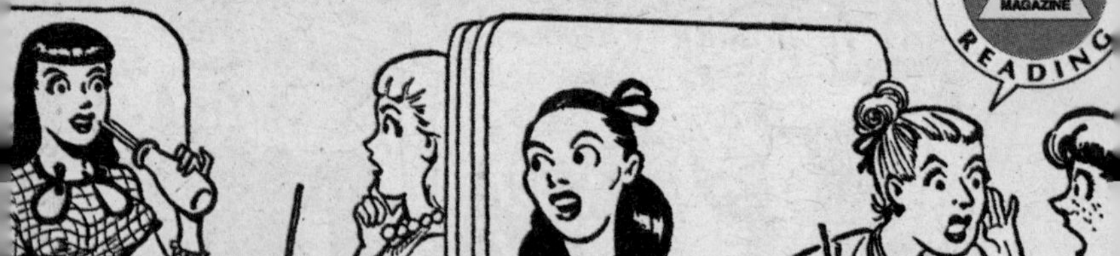

The following stories are reprinted here without alteration for historical reference.

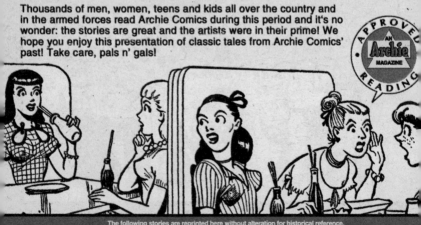

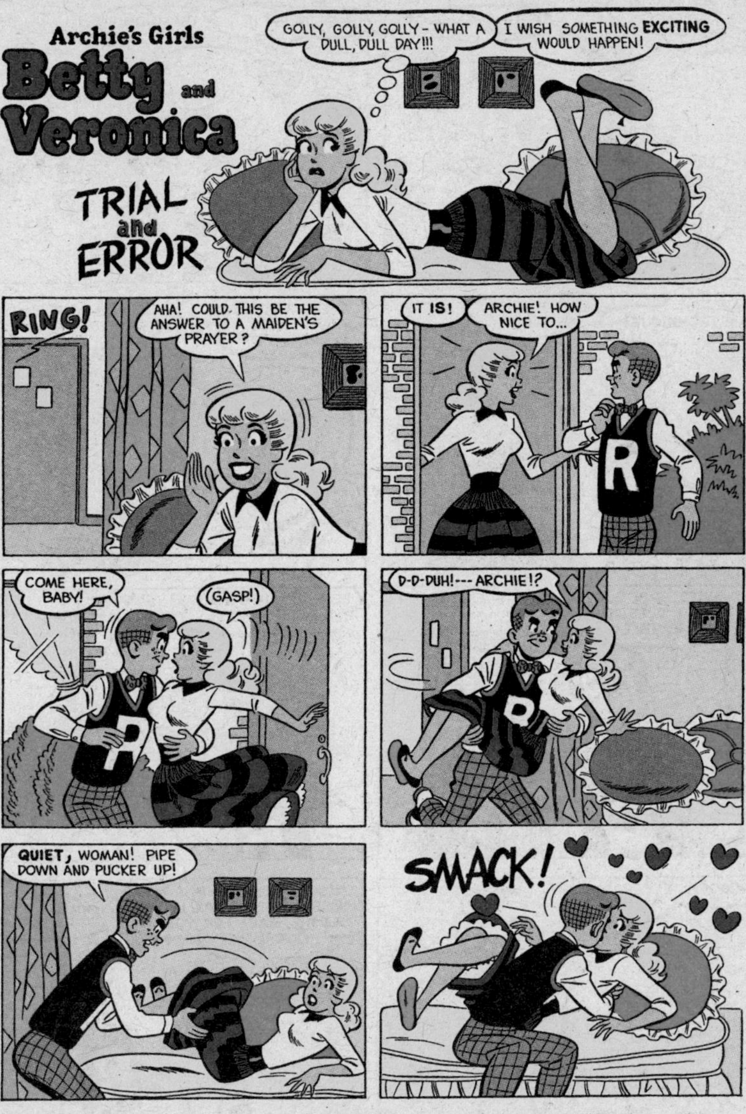
Archie's Girls Betty and Veronica
TRIAL and ERROR
GOLLY, GOLLY, GOLLY - WHAT A DULL, DULL DAY!!!
I WISH SOMETHING EXCITING WOULD HAPPEN!
RING!
AHA! COULD THIS BE THE ANSWER TO A MAIDEN'S PRAYER?
IT IS!
ARCHIE! HOW NICE TO...
COME HERE, BABY!
(GASP!)
D-D-DUH!--- ARCHIE!?
QUIET, WOMAN! PIPE DOWN AND PUCKER UP!
SMACK!

SCRIPT:
SY REIT

PENCILS:
DAN DECARLO

INKS:
RUDY LAPICK

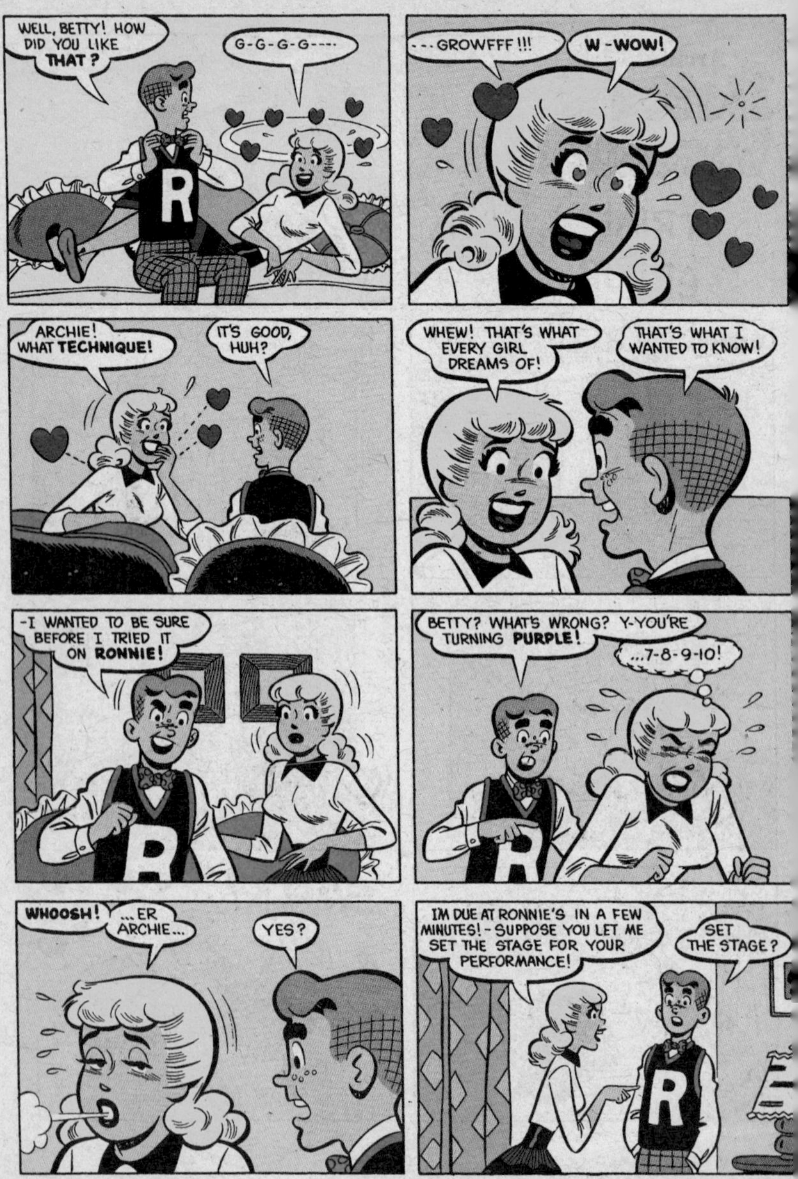
WELL, BETTY! HOW DID YOU LIKE THAT?
G-G-G-G----
---GROWFFF!!!
W-WOW!
ARCHIE! WHAT TECHNIQUE!
IT'S GOOD, HUH?
WHEW! THAT'S WHAT EVERY GIRL DREAMS OF!
THAT'S WHAT I WANTED TO KNOW!
-I WANTED TO BE SURE BEFORE I TRIED IT ON RONNIE!
BETTY? WHAT'S WRONG? Y-YOU'RE TURNING PURPLE!
...7-8-9-10!
WHOOSH!
...ER ARCHIE...
YES?
I'M DUE AT RONNIE'S IN A FEW MINUTES! - SUPPOSE YOU LET ME SET THE STAGE FOR YOUR PERFORMANCE!
SET THE STAGE?

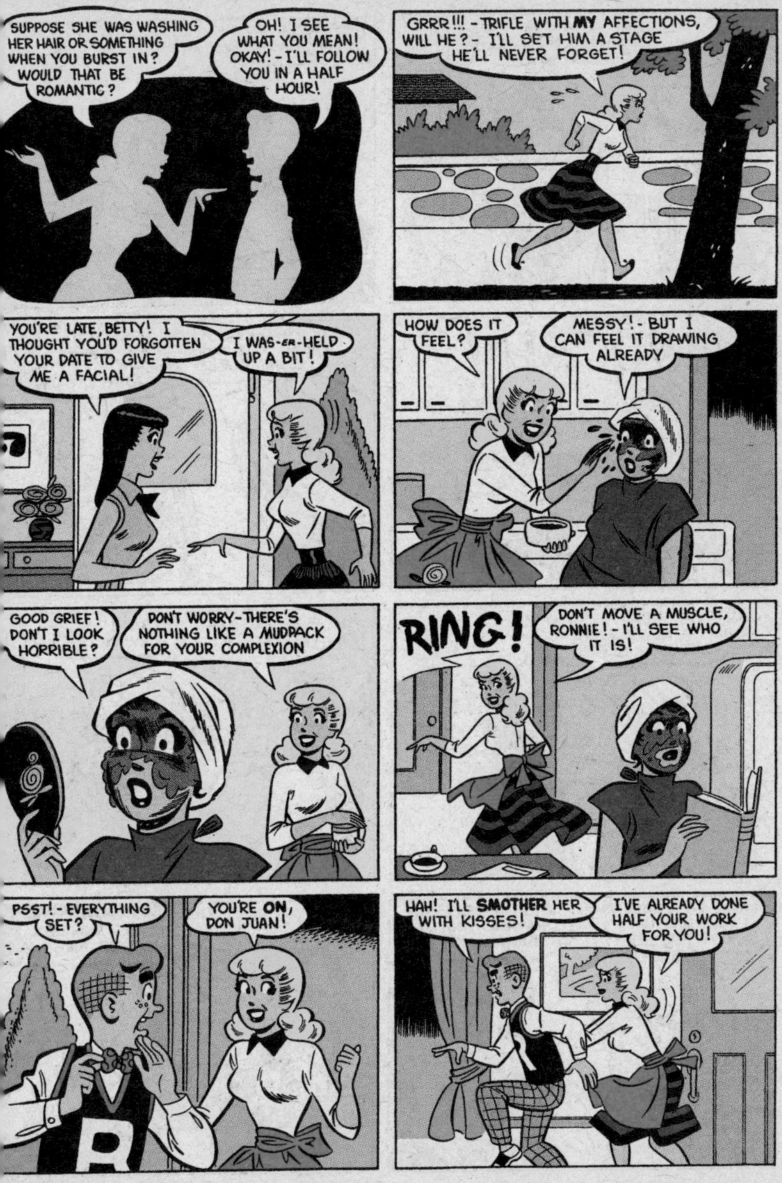
SUPPOSE SHE WAS WASHING HER HAIR OR SOMETHING WHEN YOU BURST IN? WOULD THAT BE ROMANTIC?
OH! I SEE WHAT YOU MEAN! OKAY! - I'LL FOLLOW YOU IN A HALF HOUR!
GRRR!!! - TRIFLE WITH MY AFFECTIONS, WILL HE? - I'LL SET HIM A STAGE HE'LL NEVER FORGET!
YOU'RE LATE, BETTY! I THOUGHT YOU'D FORGOTTEN YOUR DATE TO GIVE ME A FACIAL!
I WAS-ER-HELD UP A BIT!
HOW DOES IT FEEL?
MESSY! - BUT I CAN FEEL IT DRAWING ALREADY
GOOD GRIEF! DON'T I LOOK HORRIBLE?
DON'T WORRY-THERE'S NOTHING LIKE A MUDPACK FOR YOUR COMPLEXION
RING!
DON'T MOVE A MUSCLE, RONNIE! - I'LL SEE WHO IT IS!
PSST! - EVERYTHING SET?
YOU'RE ON, DON JUAN!
HAH! I'LL SMOTHER HER WITH KISSES!
I'VE ALREADY DONE HALF YOUR WORK FOR YOU!

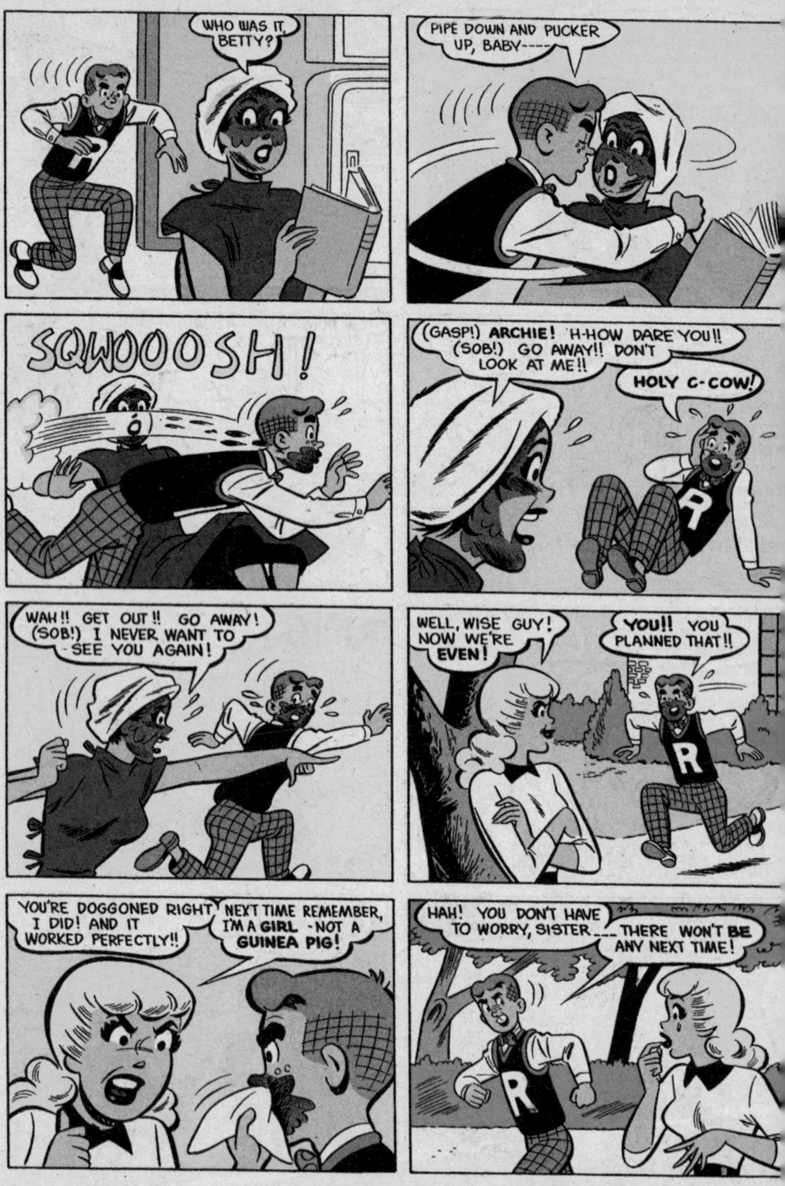
WHO WAS IT, BETTY?
PIPE DOWN AND PUCKER UP, BABY----
SQWOOOSH!
(GASP!) ARCHIE! H-HOW DARE YOU!! (SOB!) GO AWAY!! DON'T LOOK AT ME!!
HOLY C-COW!
WAH!! GET OUT!! GO AWAY! (SOB!) I NEVER WANT TO SEE YOU AGAIN!
WELL, WISE GUY! NOW WE'RE EVEN!
YOU!! YOU PLANNED THAT!!
YOU'RE DOGGONED RIGHT I DID! AND IT WORKED PERFECTLY!!
NEXT TIME REMEMBER, I'M A GIRL -NOT A GUINEA PIG!
HAH! YOU DON'T HAVE TO WORRY, SISTER ___ THERE WON'T BE ANY NEXT TIME!

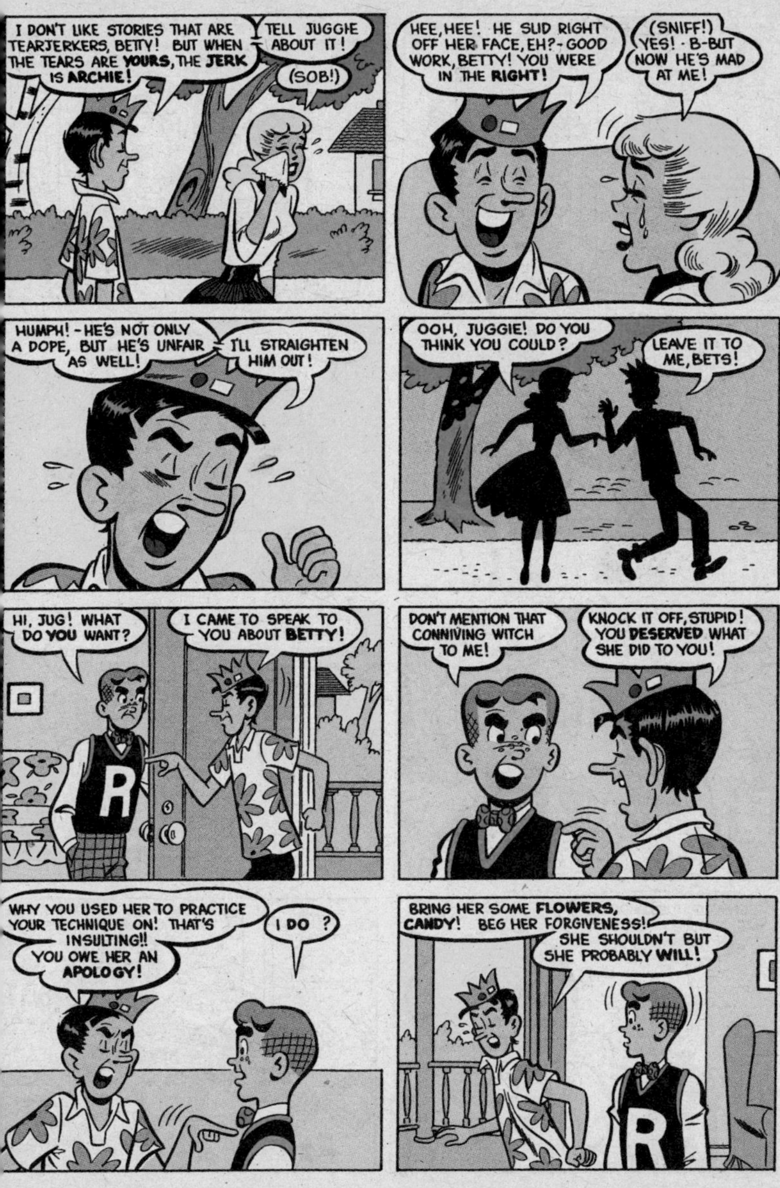
I DON'T LIKE STORIES THAT ARE TEARJERKERS, BETTY! BUT WHEN THE TEARS ARE YOURS, THE JERK IS ARCHIE!
TELL JUGGIE ABOUT IT!
(SOB!)
HEE, HEE! HE SLID RIGHT OFF HER FACE, EH?- GOOD WORK, BETTY! YOU WERE IN THE RIGHT!
(SNIFF!) YES! - B-BUT NOW HE'S MAD AT ME!
HUMPH! - HE'S NOT ONLY A DOPE, BUT HE'S UNFAIR AS WELL!
I'LL STRAIGHTEN HIM OUT!
OOH, JUGGIE! DO YOU THINK YOU COULD?
LEAVE IT TO ME, BETS!
HI, JUG! WHAT DO YOU WANT?
I CAME TO SPEAK TO YOU ABOUT BETTY!
DON'T MENTION THAT CONNIVING WITCH TO ME!
KNOCK IT OFF, STUPID! YOU DESERVED WHAT SHE DID TO YOU!
WHY YOU USED HER TO PRACTICE YOUR TECHNIQUE ON! THAT'S INSULTING!!
YOU OWE HER AN APOLOGY!
I DO?
BRING HER SOME FLOWERS, CANDY! BEG HER FORGIVENESS!
SHE SHOULDN'T BUT SHE PROBABLY WILL!

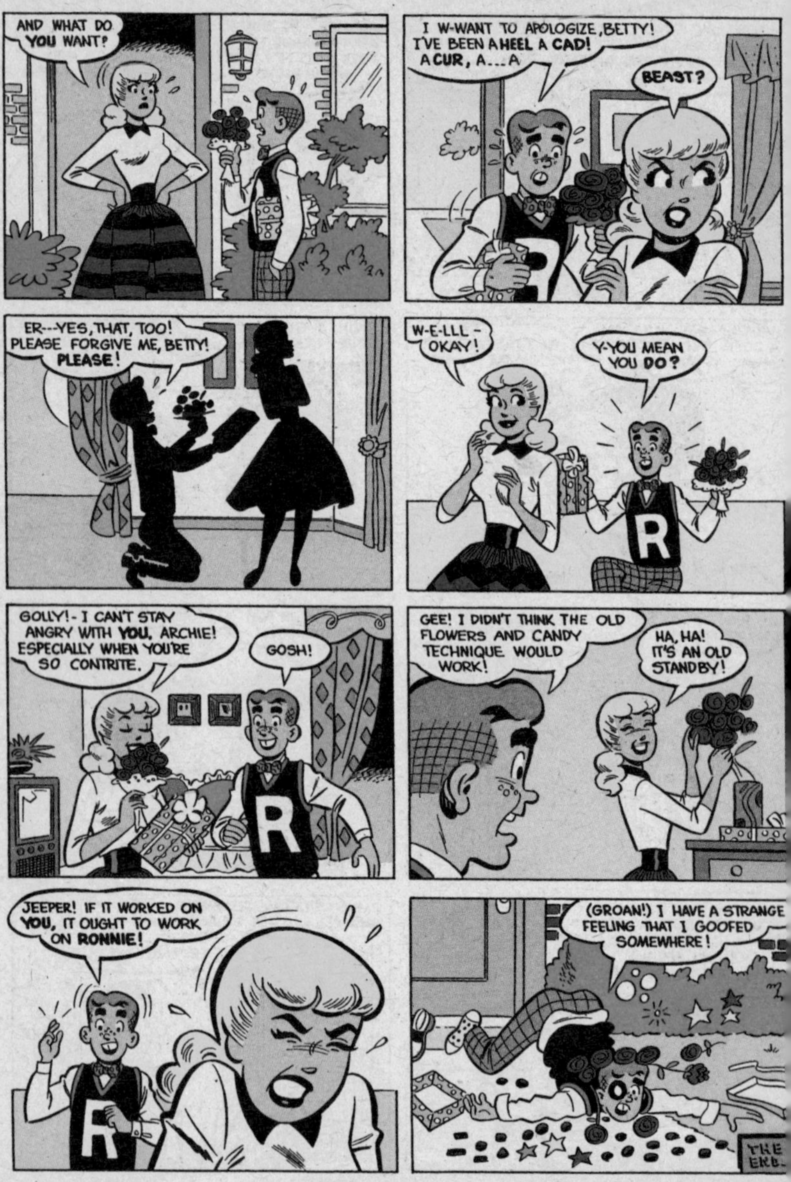
AND WHAT DO YOU WANT?
I W-WANT TO APOLOGIZE, BETTY! I'VE BEEN A HEEL A CAD! A CUR, A... A
BEAST?
ER---YES, THAT, TOO! PLEASE FORGIVE ME, BETTY! PLEASE!
W-E-LLL - OKAY!
Y-YOU MEAN YOU DO?
GOLLY! - I CAN'T STAY ANGRY WITH YOU, ARCHIE! ESPECIALLY WHEN YOU'RE SO CONTRITE.
GOSH!
GEE! I DIDN'T THINK THE OLD FLOWERS AND CANDY TECHNIQUE WOULD WORK!
HA, HA! IT'S AN OLD STANDBY!
JEEPER! IF IT WORKED ON YOU, IT OUGHT TO WORK ON RONNIE!
(GROAN!) I HAVE A STRANGE FEELING THAT I GOOFED SOMEWHERE!
THE END.

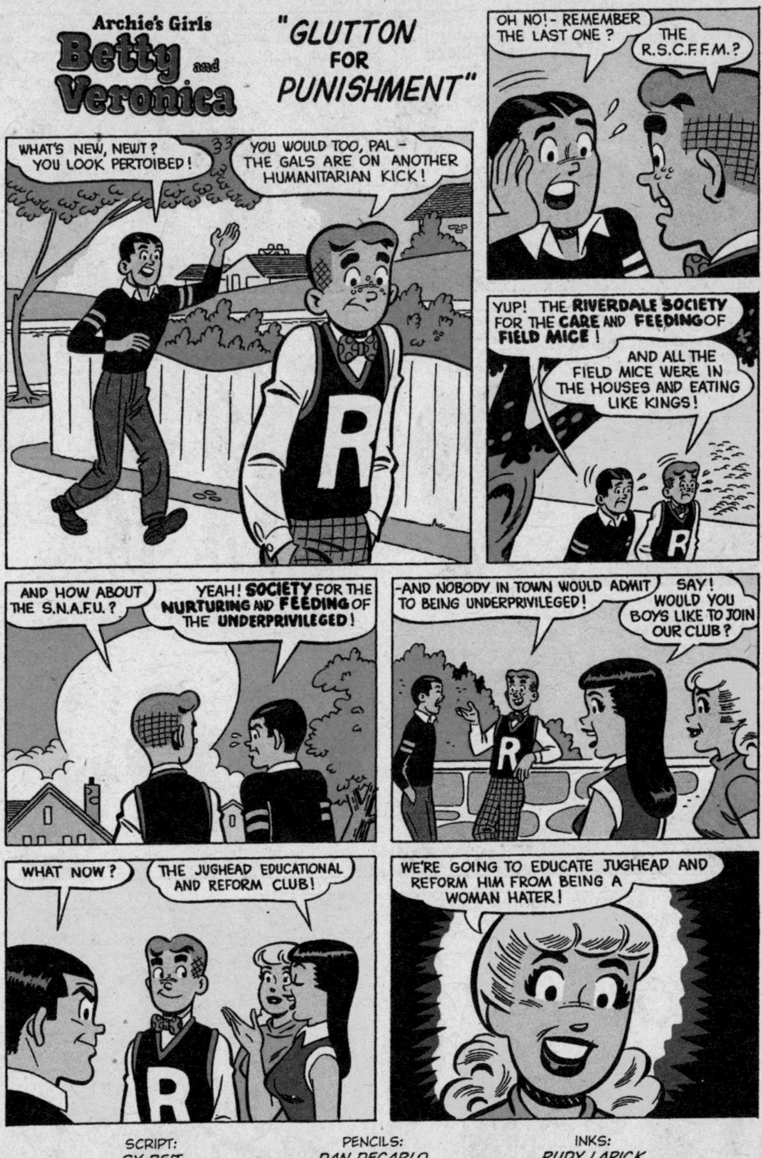
Archie's Girls Betty and Veronica
"GLUTTON FOR PUNISHMENT"
WHAT'S NEW, NEWT? YOU LOOK PERTOIBED!
YOU WOULD TOO, PAL - THE GALS ARE ON ANOTHER HUMANITARIAN KICK!
OH NO! - REMEMBER THE LAST ONE?
THE R.S.C.F.F.M.?
YUP! THE RIVERDALE SOCIETY FOR THE CARE AND FEEDING OF FIELD MICE!
AND ALL THE FIELD MICE WERE IN THE HOUSES AND EATING LIKE KINGS!
AND HOW ABOUT THE S.N.A.F.U.?
YEAH! SOCIETY FOR THE NURTURING AND FEEDING OF THE UNDERPRIVILEGED!
-AND NOBODY IN TOWN WOULD ADMIT TO BEING UNDERPRIVILEGED!
SAY! WOULD YOU BOYS LIKE TO JOIN OUR CLUB?
WHAT NOW?
THE JUGHEAD EDUCATIONAL AND REFORM CLUB!
WE'RE GOING TO EDUCATE JUGHEAD AND REFORM HIM FROM BEING A WOMAN HATER!

SCRIPT: *SY REIT*　PENCILS: *DAN DECARLO*　INKS: *RUDY LAPICK*

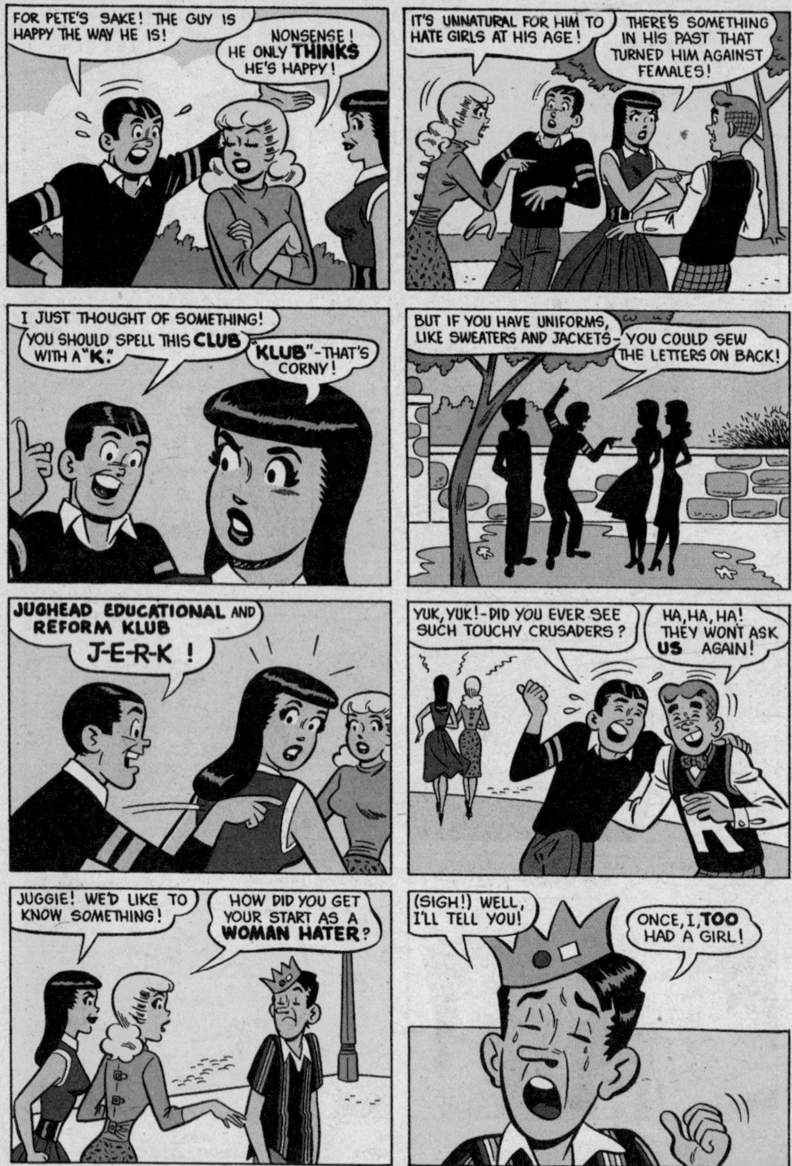
FOR PETE'S SAKE! THE GUY IS HAPPY THE WAY HE IS!
NONSENSE! HE ONLY THINKS HE'S HAPPY!
IT'S UNNATURAL FOR HIM TO HATE GIRLS AT HIS AGE!
THERE'S SOMETHING IN HIS PAST THAT TURNED HIM AGAINST FEMALES!
I JUST THOUGHT OF SOMETHING! YOU SHOULD SPELL THIS CLUB WITH A "K."
"KLUB"-THAT'S CORNY!
BUT IF YOU HAVE UNIFORMS, LIKE SWEATERS AND JACKETS-
YOU COULD SEW THE LETTERS ON BACK!
JUGHEAD EDUCATIONAL AND REFORM KLUB
J-E-R-K !
YUK, YUK!-DID YOU EVER SEE SUCH TOUCHY CRUSADERS?
HA, HA, HA! THEY WON'T ASK US AGAIN!
JUGGIE! WE'D LIKE TO KNOW SOMETHING!
HOW DID YOU GET YOUR START AS A WOMAN HATER?
(SIGH!) WELL, I'LL TELL YOU!
ONCE, I, TOO HAD A GIRL!

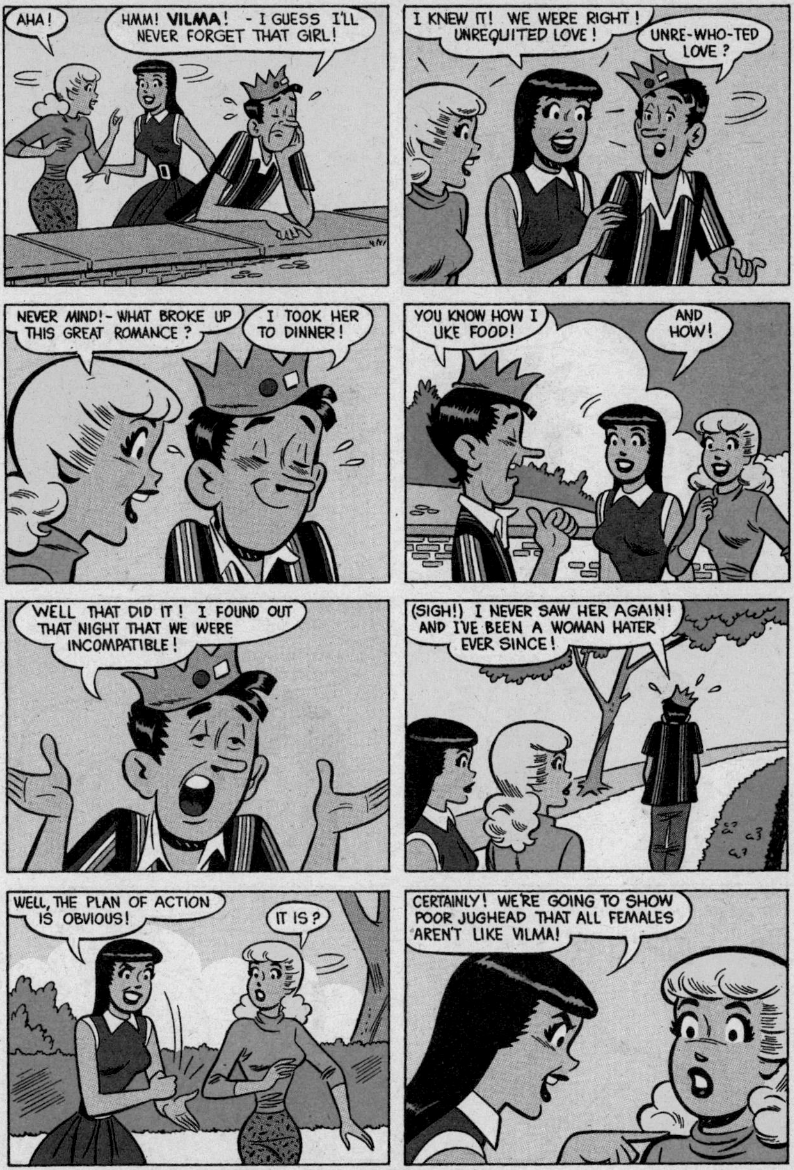
AHA!
HMM! VILMA! - I GUESS I'LL NEVER FORGET THAT GIRL!
I KNEW IT! WE WERE RIGHT! UNREQUITED LOVE!
UNRE-WHO-TED LOVE?
NEVER MIND! - WHAT BROKE UP THIS GREAT ROMANCE?
I TOOK HER TO DINNER!
YOU KNOW HOW I LIKE FOOD!
AND HOW!
WELL THAT DID IT! I FOUND OUT THAT NIGHT THAT WE WERE INCOMPATIBLE!
(SIGH!) I NEVER SAW HER AGAIN! AND I'VE BEEN A WOMAN HATER EVER SINCE!
WELL, THE PLAN OF ACTION IS OBVIOUS!
IT IS?
CERTAINLY! WE'RE GOING TO SHOW POOR JUGHEAD THAT ALL FEMALES AREN'T LIKE VILMA!

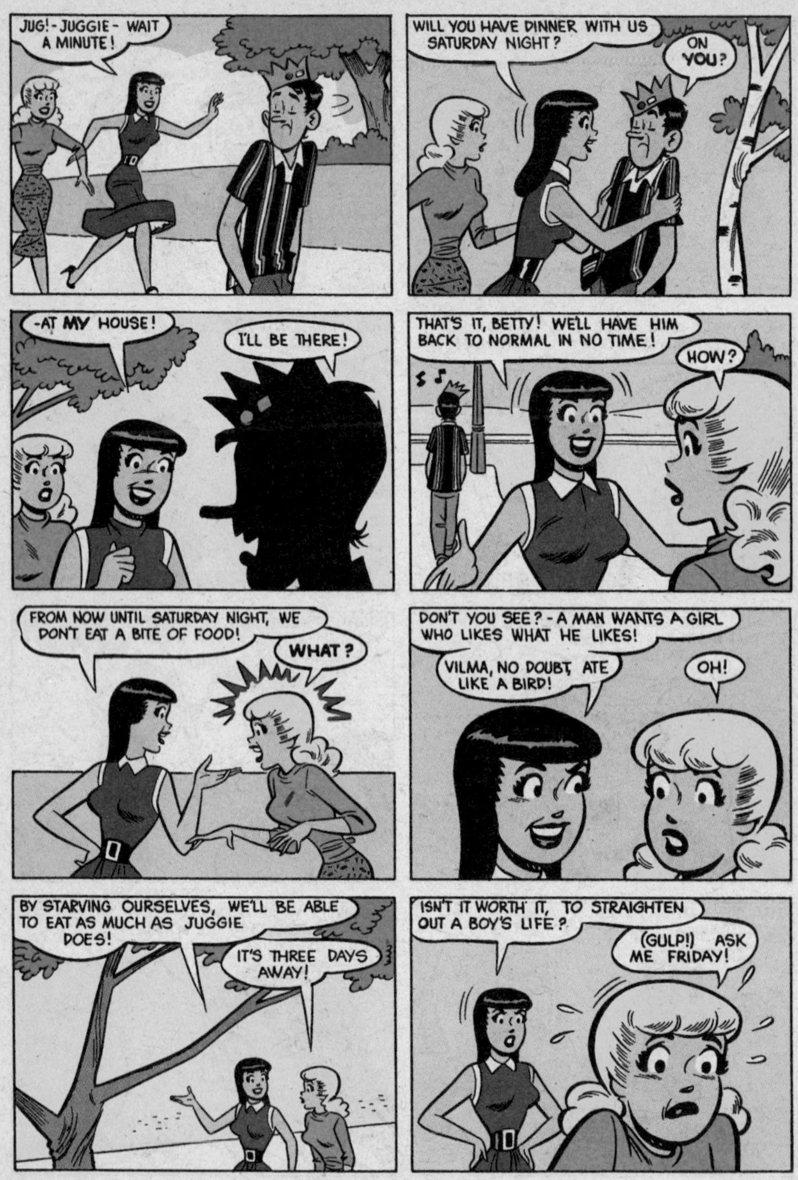
JUG! - JUGGIE - WAIT A MINUTE!
WILL YOU HAVE DINNER WITH US SATURDAY NIGHT?
ON YOU?
-AT MY HOUSE!
I'LL BE THERE!
THAT'S IT, BETTY! WE'LL HAVE HIM BACK TO NORMAL IN NO TIME!
HOW?
FROM NOW UNTIL SATURDAY NIGHT, WE DON'T EAT A BITE OF FOOD!
WHAT?
DON'T YOU SEE? - A MAN WANTS A GIRL WHO LIKES WHAT HE LIKES!
VILMA, NO DOUBT, ATE LIKE A BIRD!
OH!
BY STARVING OURSELVES, WE'LL BE ABLE TO EAT AS MUCH AS JUGGIE DOES!
IT'S THREE DAYS AWAY!
ISN'T IT WORTH IT, TO STRAIGHTEN OUT A BOY'S LIFE?
(GULP!) ASK ME FRIDAY!

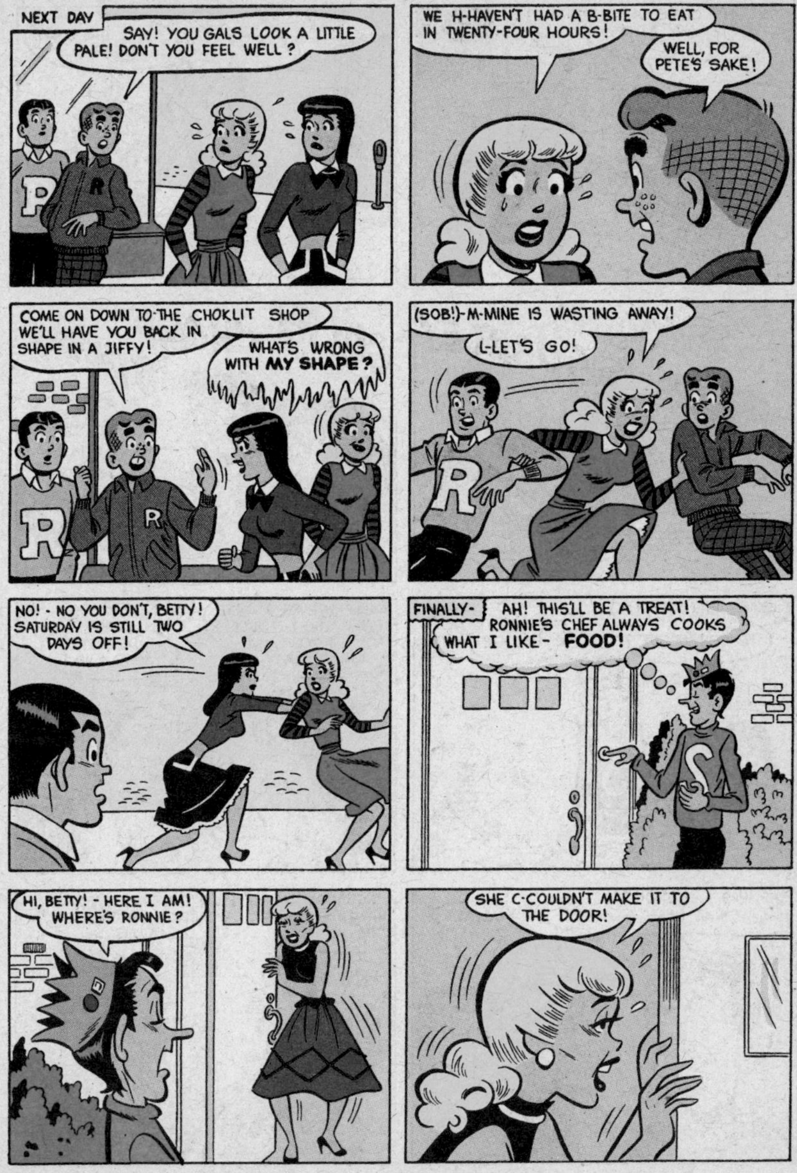
NEXT DAY
SAY! YOU GALS LOOK A LITTLE PALE! DON'T YOU FEEL WELL ?
WE H-HAVEN'T HAD A B-BITE TO EAT IN TWENTY-FOUR HOURS!
WELL, FOR PETE'S SAKE!
COME ON DOWN TO THE CHOKLIT SHOP WE'LL HAVE YOU BACK IN SHAPE IN A JIFFY!
WHAT'S WRONG WITH MY SHAPE ?
(SOB!)-M-MINE IS WASTING AWAY!
L-LET'S GO!
NO! - NO YOU DON'T, BETTY! SATURDAY IS STILL TWO DAYS OFF!
FINALLY-
AH! THIS'LL BE A TREAT! RONNIE'S CHEF ALWAYS COOKS WHAT I LIKE- FOOD!
HI, BETTY! - HERE I AM! WHERE'S RONNIE ?
SHE C-COULDN'T MAKE IT TO THE DOOR!

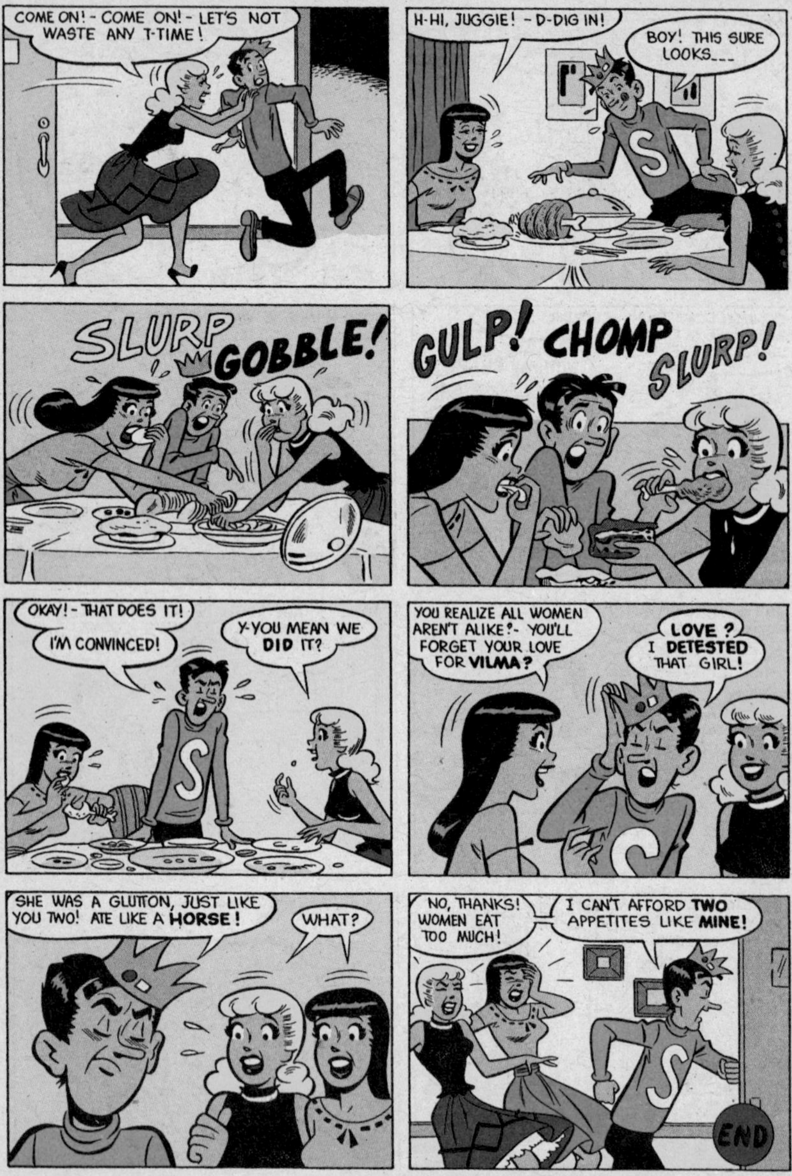

COME ON! - COME ON! - LET'S NOT WASTE ANY T-TIME!
H-HI, JUGGIE! - D-DIG IN!
BOY! THIS SURE LOOKS---
SLURP
GOBBLE!
GULP!
CHOMP
SLURP!
OKAY! - THAT DOES IT!
I'M CONVINCED!
Y-YOU MEAN WE DID IT?
YOU REALIZE ALL WOMEN AREN'T ALIKE?- YOU'LL FORGET YOUR LOVE FOR VILMA?
LOVE? I DETESTED THAT GIRL!
SHE WAS A GLUTTON, JUST LIKE YOU TWO! ATE LIKE A HORSE!
WHAT?
NO, THANKS! WOMEN EAT TOO MUCH!
I CAN'T AFFORD TWO APPETITES LIKE MINE!
END

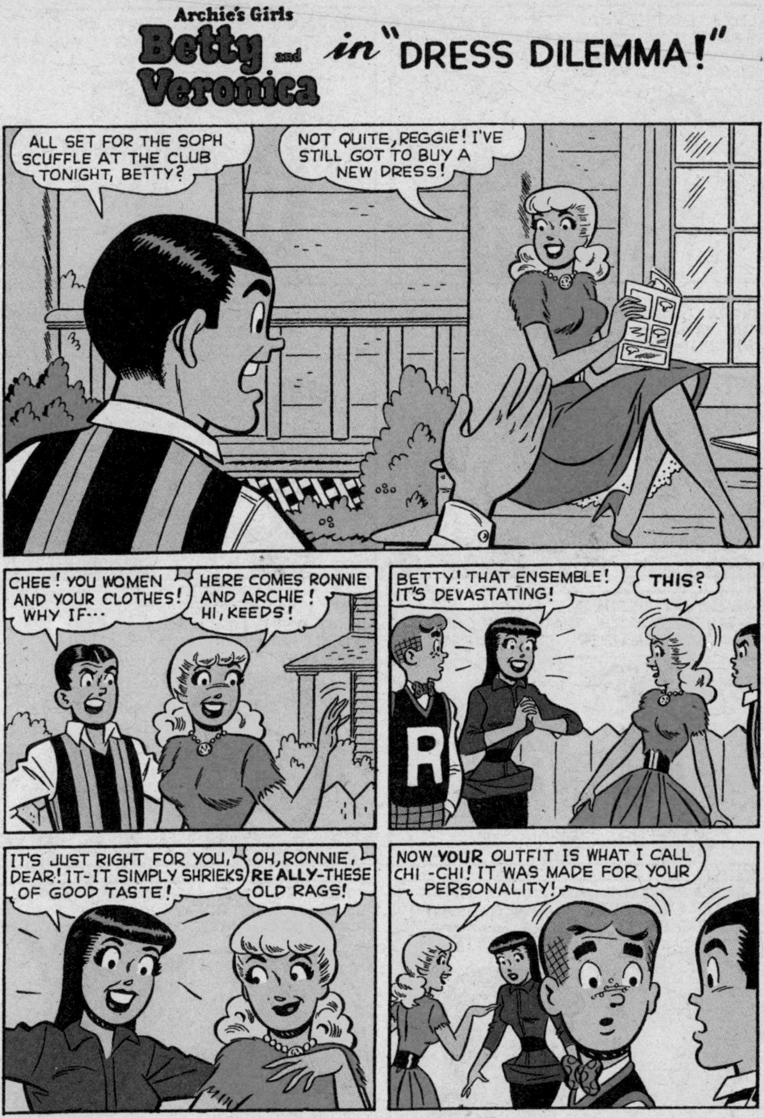
Archie's Girls Betty and Veronica in "DRESS DILEMMA!"
ALL SET FOR THE SOPH SCUFFLE AT THE CLUB TONIGHT, BETTY?
NOT QUITE, REGGIE! I'VE STILL GOT TO BUY A NEW DRESS!
CHEE! YOU WOMEN AND YOUR CLOTHES! WHY IF···
HERE COMES RONNIE AND ARCHIE! HI, KEEDS!
BETTY! THAT ENSEMBLE! IT'S DEVASTATING!
THIS?
IT'S JUST RIGHT FOR YOU, DEAR! IT-IT SIMPLY SHRIEKS OF GOOD TASTE!
OH, RONNIE, REALLY-THESE OLD RAGS!
NOW YOUR OUTFIT IS WHAT I CALL CHI -CHI! IT WAS MADE FOR YOUR PERSONALITY!

SCRIPT: *FRANK DOYLE* PENCILS: *DAN DECARLO* INKS: *RUDY LAPICK* LETTERS: *VINCE DECARLO*

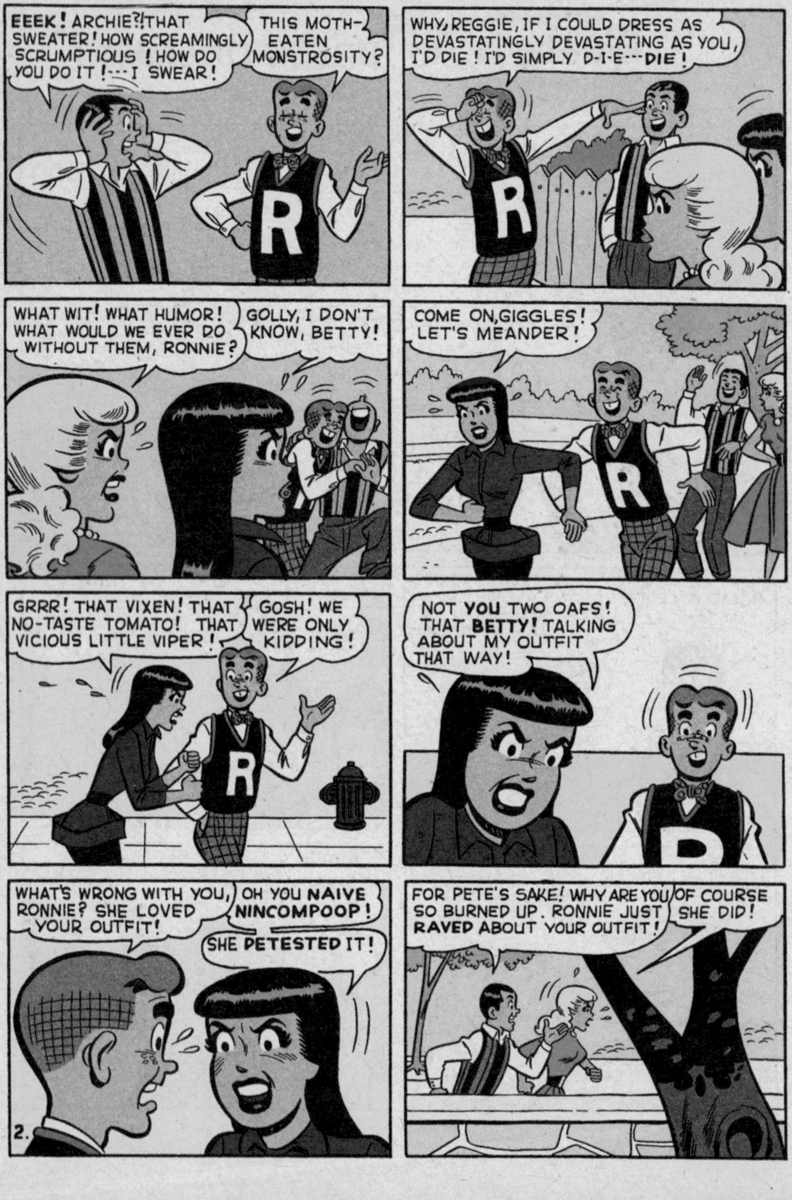
EEEK! ARCHIE?! THAT SWEATER! HOW SCREAMINGLY SCRUMPTIOUS! HOW DO YOU DO IT!--- I SWEAR!
THIS MOTH-EATEN MONSTROSITY?
WHY, REGGIE, IF I COULD DRESS AS DEVASTATINGLY DEVASTATING AS YOU, I'D DIE! I'D SIMPLY D-I-E---DIE!
WHAT WIT! WHAT HUMOR! WHAT WOULD WE EVER DO WITHOUT THEM, RONNIE?
GOLLY, I DON'T KNOW, BETTY!
COME ON, GIGGLES! LET'S MEANDER!
GRRR! THAT VIXEN! THAT NO-TASTE TOMATO! THAT VICIOUS LITTLE VIPER!
GOSH! WE WERE ONLY KIDDING!
NOT YOU TWO OAFS! THAT BETTY! TALKING ABOUT MY OUTFIT THAT WAY!
WHAT'S WRONG WITH YOU, RONNIE? SHE LOVED YOUR OUTFIT!
OH YOU NAIVE NINCOMPOOP!
SHE DETESTED IT!
FOR PETE'S SAKE! WHY ARE YOU SO BURNED UP. RONNIE JUST RAVED ABOUT YOUR OUTFIT!
OF COURSE SHE DID!
2.

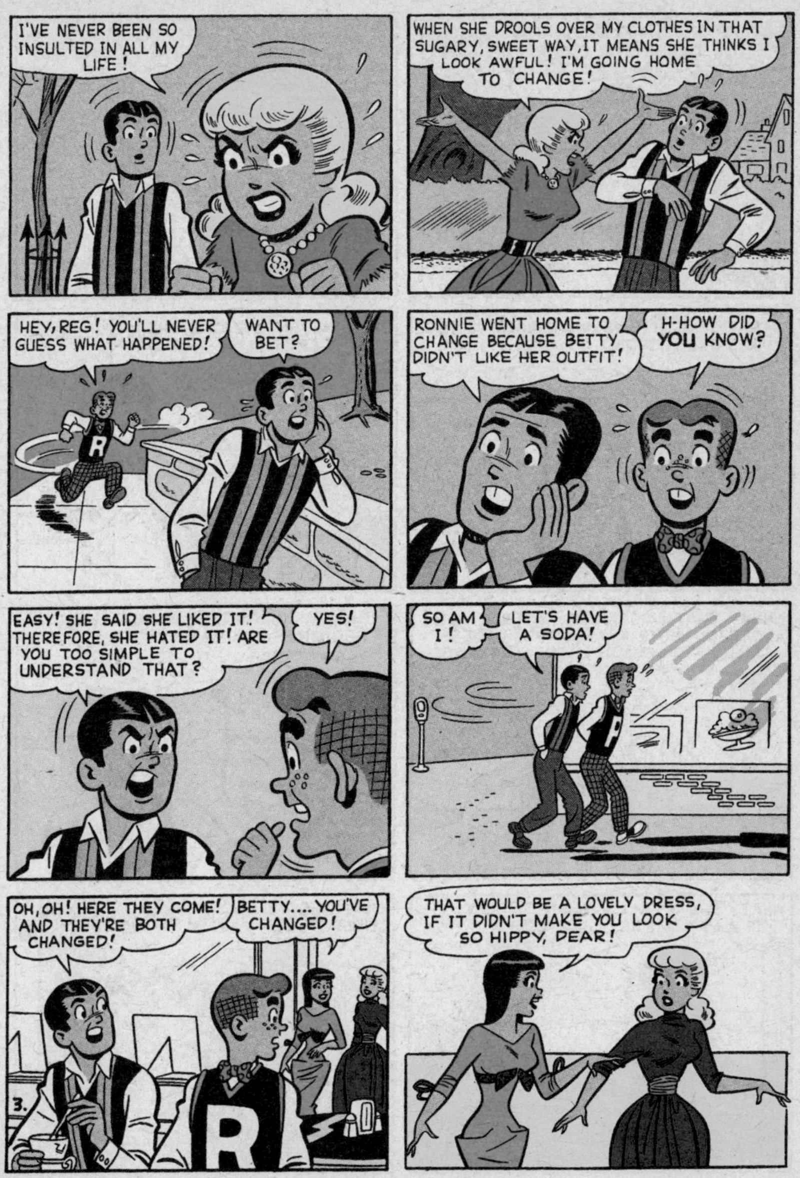
I'VE NEVER BEEN SO INSULTED IN ALL MY LIFE!
WHEN SHE DROOLS OVER MY CLOTHES IN THAT SUGARY, SWEET WAY, IT MEANS SHE THINKS I LOOK AWFUL! I'M GOING HOME TO CHANGE!
HEY, REG! YOU'LL NEVER GUESS WHAT HAPPENED!
WANT TO BET?
RONNIE WENT HOME TO CHANGE BECAUSE BETTY DIDN'T LIKE HER OUTFIT!
H-HOW DID YOU KNOW?
EASY! SHE SAID SHE LIKED IT! THEREFORE, SHE HATED IT! ARE YOU TOO SIMPLE TO UNDERSTAND THAT?
YES!
SO AM I!
LET'S HAVE A SODA!
3.
OH, OH! HERE THEY COME! AND THEY'RE BOTH CHANGED!
BETTY.... YOU'VE CHANGED!
THAT WOULD BE A LOVELY DRESS, IF IT DIDN'T MAKE YOU LOOK SO HIPPY, DEAR!

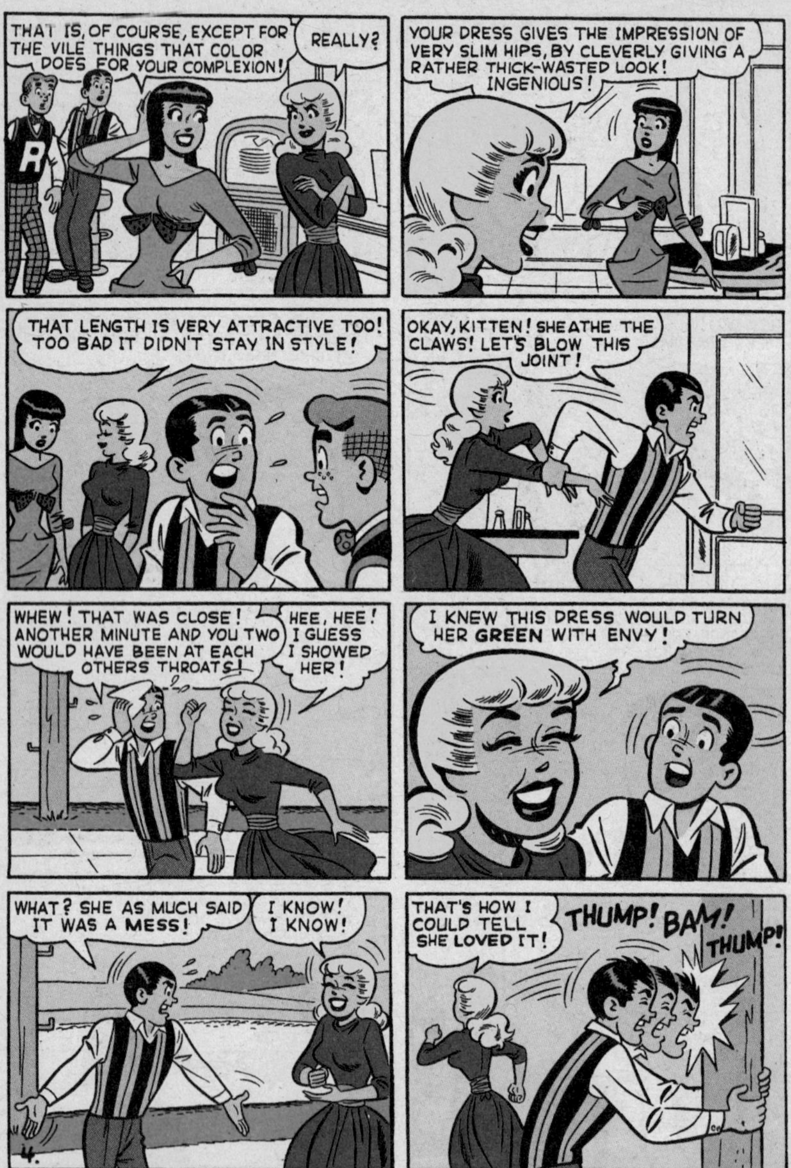
THAT IS, OF COURSE, EXCEPT FOR THE VILE THINGS THAT COLOR DOES FOR YOUR COMPLEXION!
REALLY?
YOUR DRESS GIVES THE IMPRESSION OF VERY SLIM HIPS, BY CLEVERLY GIVING A RATHER THICK-WASTED LOOK! INGENIOUS!
THAT LENGTH IS VERY ATTRACTIVE TOO! TOO BAD IT DIDN'T STAY IN STYLE!
OKAY, KITTEN! SHEATHE THE CLAWS! LET'S BLOW THIS JOINT!
WHEW! THAT WAS CLOSE! ANOTHER MINUTE AND YOU TWO WOULD HAVE BEEN AT EACH OTHERS THROATS!
HEE, HEE! I GUESS I SHOWED HER!
I KNEW THIS DRESS WOULD TURN HER **GREEN** WITH ENVY!
WHAT? SHE AS MUCH SAID IT WAS A **MESS**!
I KNOW! I KNOW!
THAT'S HOW I COULD TELL SHE **LOVED** IT!
THUMP! BAM! THUMP!
4.

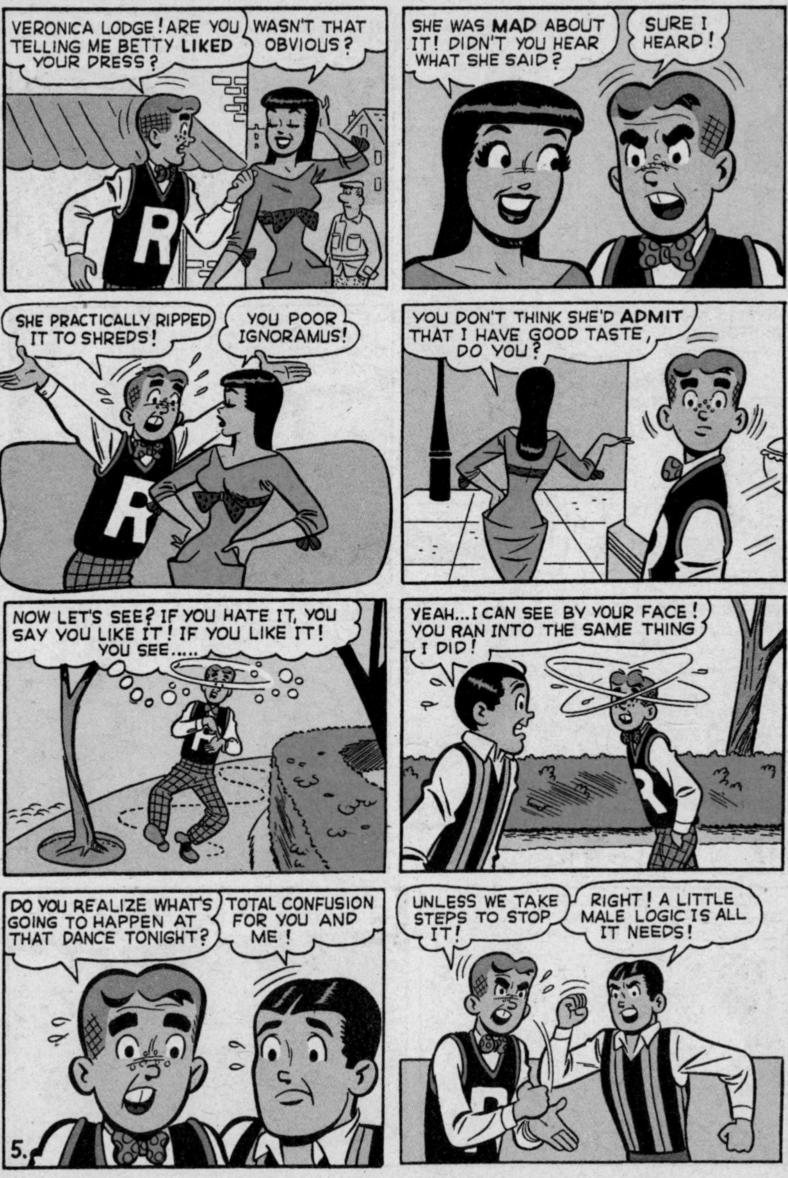

VERONICA LODGE! ARE YOU TELLING ME BETTY LIKED YOUR DRESS?
WASN'T THAT OBVIOUS?
SHE WAS MAD ABOUT IT! DIDN'T YOU HEAR WHAT SHE SAID?
SURE I HEARD!
SHE PRACTICALLY RIPPED IT TO SHREDS!
YOU POOR IGNORAMUS!
YOU DON'T THINK SHE'D ADMIT THAT I HAVE GOOD TASTE, DO YOU?
NOW LET'S SEE? IF YOU HATE IT, YOU SAY YOU LIKE IT! IF YOU LIKE IT! YOU SEE.....
YEAH...I CAN SEE BY YOUR FACE! YOU RAN INTO THE SAME THING I DID!
DO YOU REALIZE WHAT'S GOING TO HAPPEN AT THAT DANCE TONIGHT?
TOTAL CONFUSION FOR YOU AND ME!
UNLESS WE TAKE STEPS TO STOP IT!
RIGHT! A LITTLE MALE LOGIC IS ALL IT NEEDS!

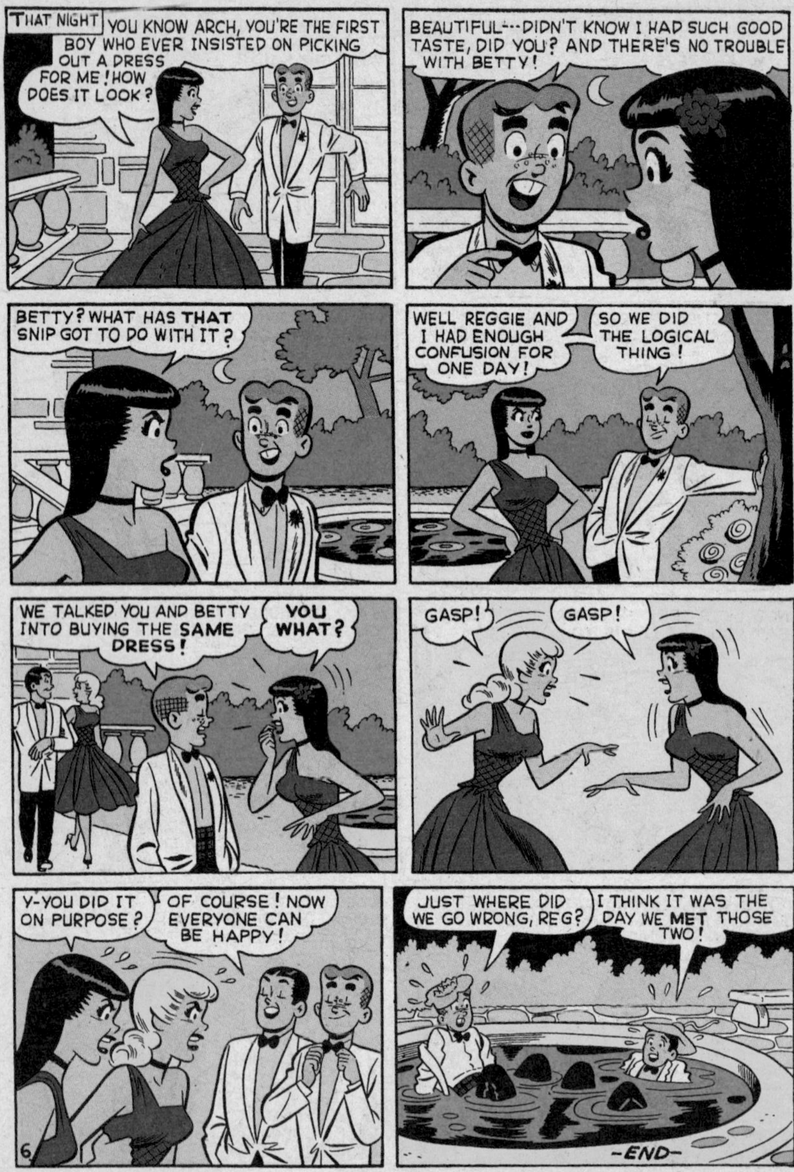
THAT NIGHT
YOU KNOW ARCH, YOU'RE THE FIRST BOY WHO EVER INSISTED ON PICKING OUT A DRESS FOR ME! HOW DOES IT LOOK?
BEAUTIFUL---DIDN'T KNOW I HAD SUCH GOOD TASTE, DID YOU? AND THERE'S NO TROUBLE WITH BETTY!
BETTY? WHAT HAS THAT SNIP GOT TO DO WITH IT?
WELL REGGIE AND I HAD ENOUGH CONFUSION FOR ONE DAY!
SO WE DID THE LOGICAL THING!
WE TALKED YOU AND BETTY INTO BUYING THE SAME DRESS!
YOU WHAT?
GASP!
GASP!
Y-YOU DID IT ON PURPOSE?
OF COURSE! NOW EVERYONE CAN BE HAPPY!
JUST WHERE DID WE GO WRONG, REG?
I THINK IT WAS THE DAY WE MET THOSE TWO!
-END-
6

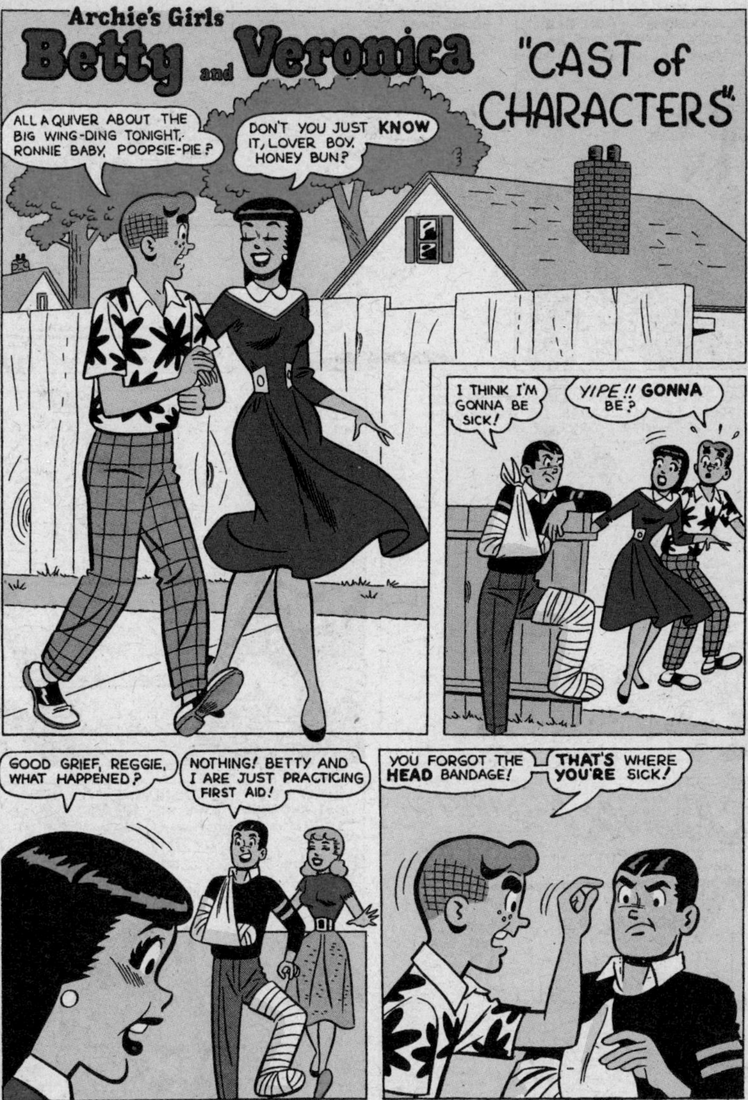
Archie's Girls
Betty and Veronica
"CAST of CHARACTERS"
ALL A QUIVER ABOUT THE BIG WING-DING TONIGHT, RONNIE BABY, POOPSIE-PIE?
DON'T YOU JUST KNOW IT, LOVER BOY, HONEY BUN?
I THINK I'M GONNA BE SICK!
YIPE!! GONNA BE?
GOOD GRIEF, REGGIE, WHAT HAPPENED?
NOTHING! BETTY AND I ARE JUST PRACTICING FIRST AID!
YOU FORGOT THE HEAD BANDAGE!
THAT'S WHERE YOU'RE SICK!

SCRIPT: *FRANK DOYLE* PENCILS: *DAN DECARLO* INKS: *RUDY LAPICK*

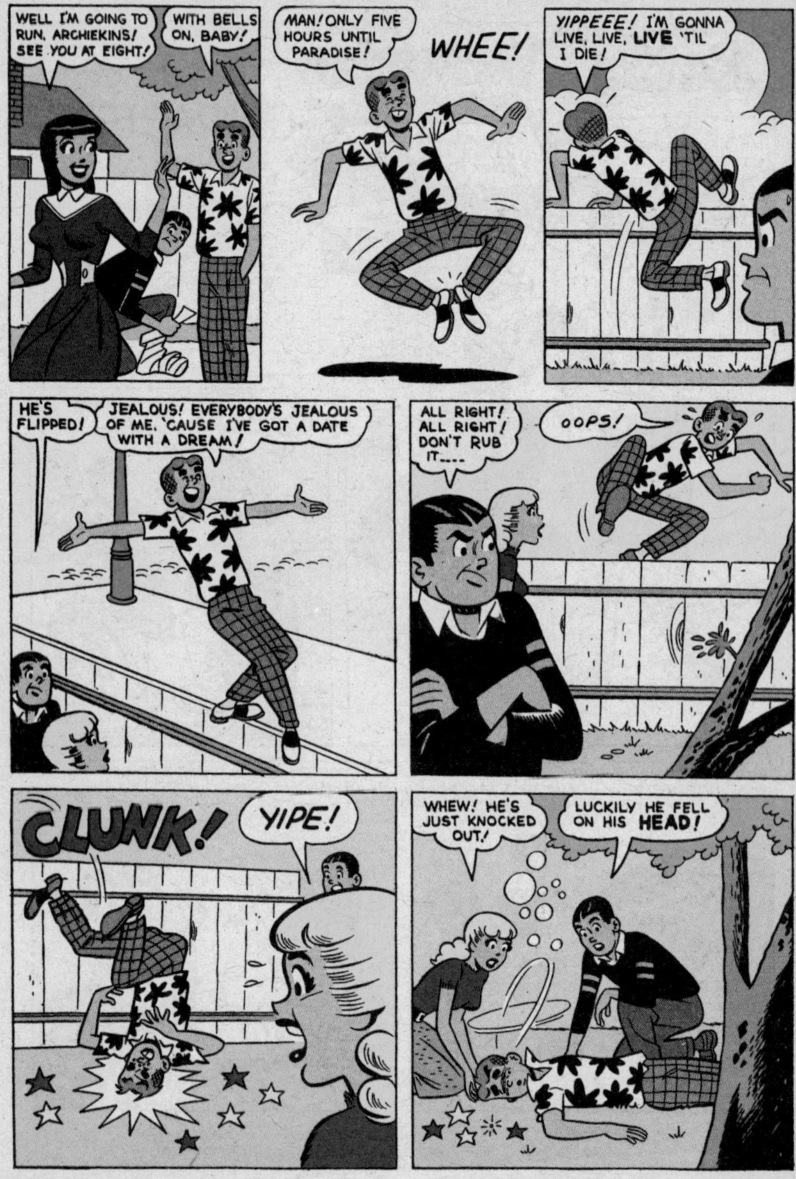
WELL I'M GOING TO RUN, ARCHIEKINS! SEE YOU AT EIGHT!
WITH BELLS ON, BABY!
MAN! ONLY FIVE HOURS UNTIL PARADISE!
WHEE!
YIPPEEE! I'M GONNA LIVE, LIVE, LIVE 'TIL I DIE!
HE'S FLIPPED!
JEALOUS! EVERYBODY'S JEALOUS OF ME. 'CAUSE I'VE GOT A DATE WITH A DREAM!
ALL RIGHT! ALL RIGHT! DON'T RUB IT....
OOPS!
CLUNK!
YIPE!
WHEW! HE'S JUST KNOCKED OUT!
LUCKILY HE FELL ON HIS HEAD!

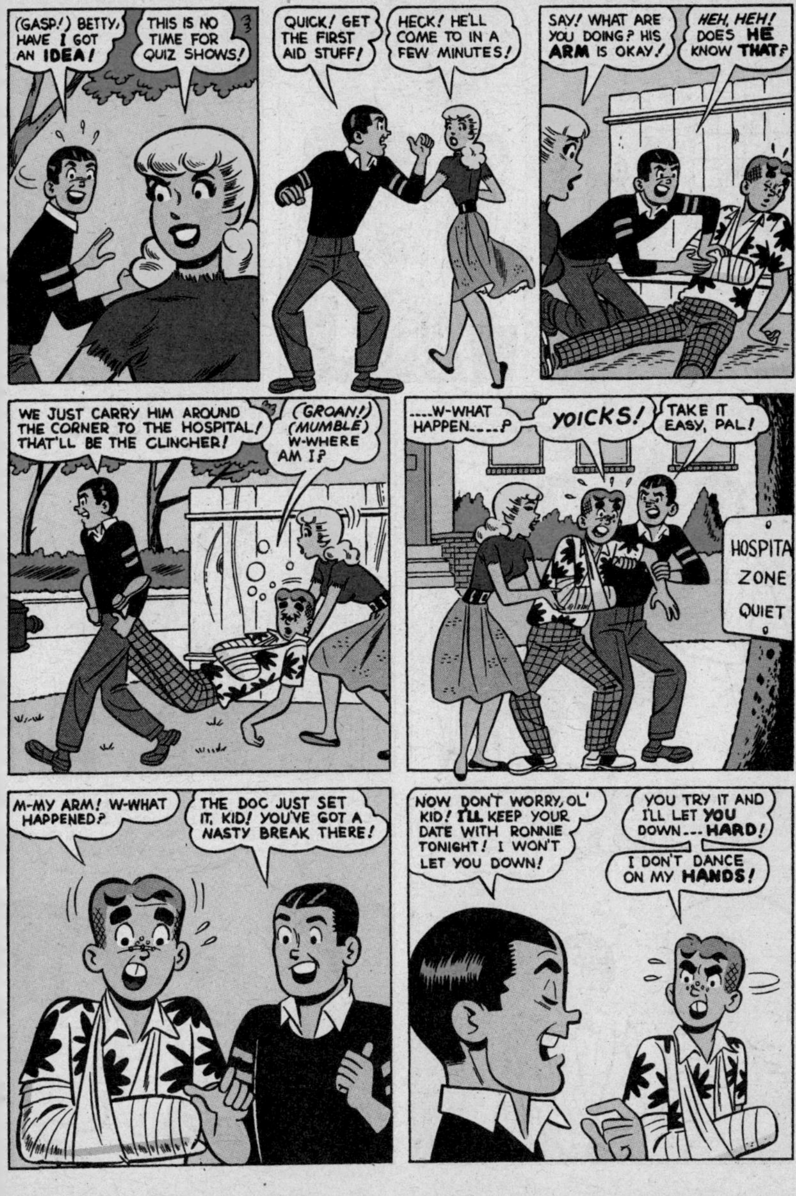
(GASP!) BETTY, HAVE I GOT AN IDEA!
THIS IS NO TIME FOR QUIZ SHOWS!
QUICK! GET THE FIRST AID STUFF!
HECK! HE'LL COME TO IN A FEW MINUTES!
SAY! WHAT ARE YOU DOING? HIS ARM IS OKAY!
HEH, HEH! DOES HE KNOW THAT?
WE JUST CARRY HIM AROUND THE CORNER TO THE HOSPITAL! THAT'LL BE THE CLINCHER!
(GROAN!) (MUMBLE) W-WHERE AM I?
....W-WHAT HAPPEN....?
YOICKS!
TAKE IT EASY, PAL!
HOSPITA ZONE QUIET
M-MY ARM! W-WHAT HAPPENED?
THE DOC JUST SET IT, KID! YOU'VE GOT A NASTY BREAK THERE!
NOW DON'T WORRY, OL' KID! I'LL KEEP YOUR DATE WITH RONNIE TONIGHT! I WON'T LET YOU DOWN!
YOU TRY IT AND I'LL LET YOU DOWN... HARD!
I DON'T DANCE ON MY HANDS!

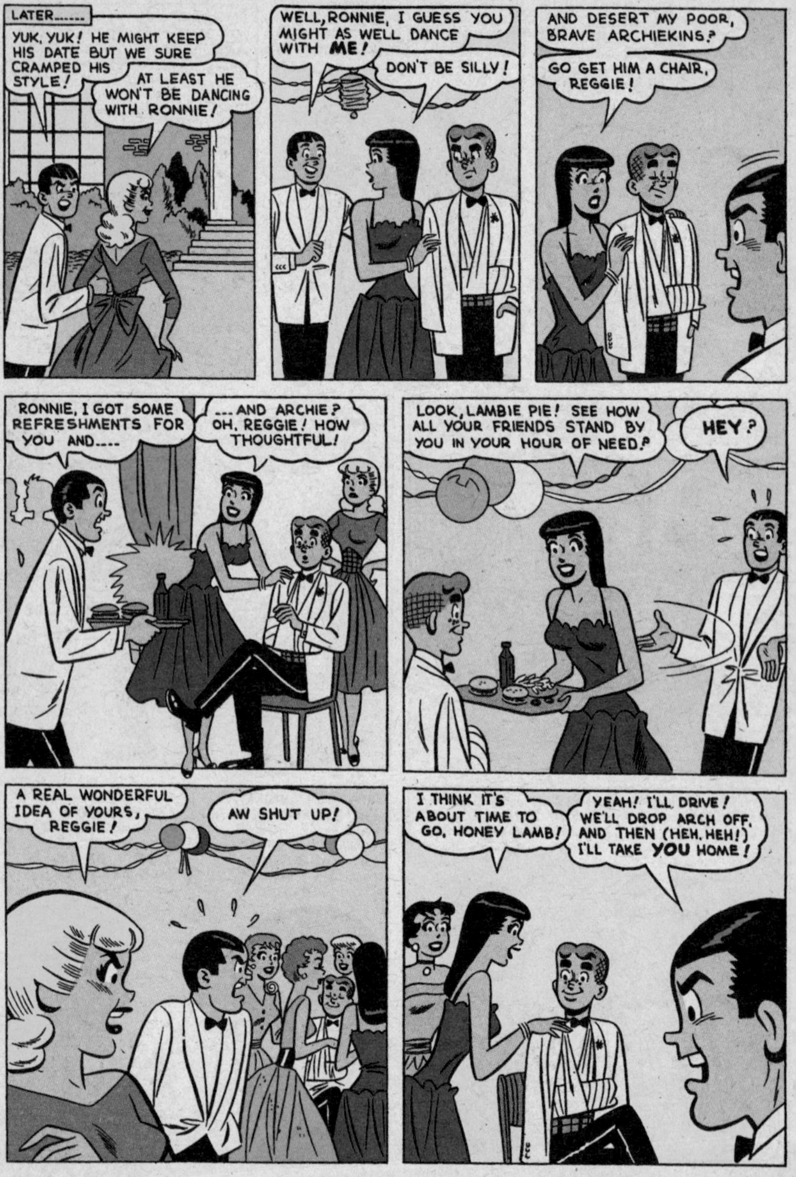
LATER......
YUK, YUK! HE MIGHT KEEP HIS DATE BUT WE SURE CRAMPED HIS STYLE!
AT LEAST HE WON'T BE DANCING WITH RONNIE!
WELL, RONNIE, I GUESS YOU MIGHT AS WELL DANCE WITH ME!
DON'T BE SILLY!
AND DESERT MY POOR, BRAVE ARCHIEKINS?
GO GET HIM A CHAIR, REGGIE!
RONNIE, I GOT SOME REFRESHMENTS FOR YOU AND....
...AND ARCHIE? OH, REGGIE! HOW THOUGHTFUL!
LOOK, LAMBIE PIE! SEE HOW ALL YOUR FRIENDS STAND BY YOU IN YOUR HOUR OF NEED?
HEY?
A REAL WONDERFUL IDEA OF YOURS, REGGIE!
AW SHUT UP!
I THINK IT'S ABOUT TIME TO GO, HONEY LAMB!
YEAH! I'LL DRIVE! WE'LL DROP ARCH OFF, AND THEN (HEH, HEH!) I'LL TAKE YOU HOME!

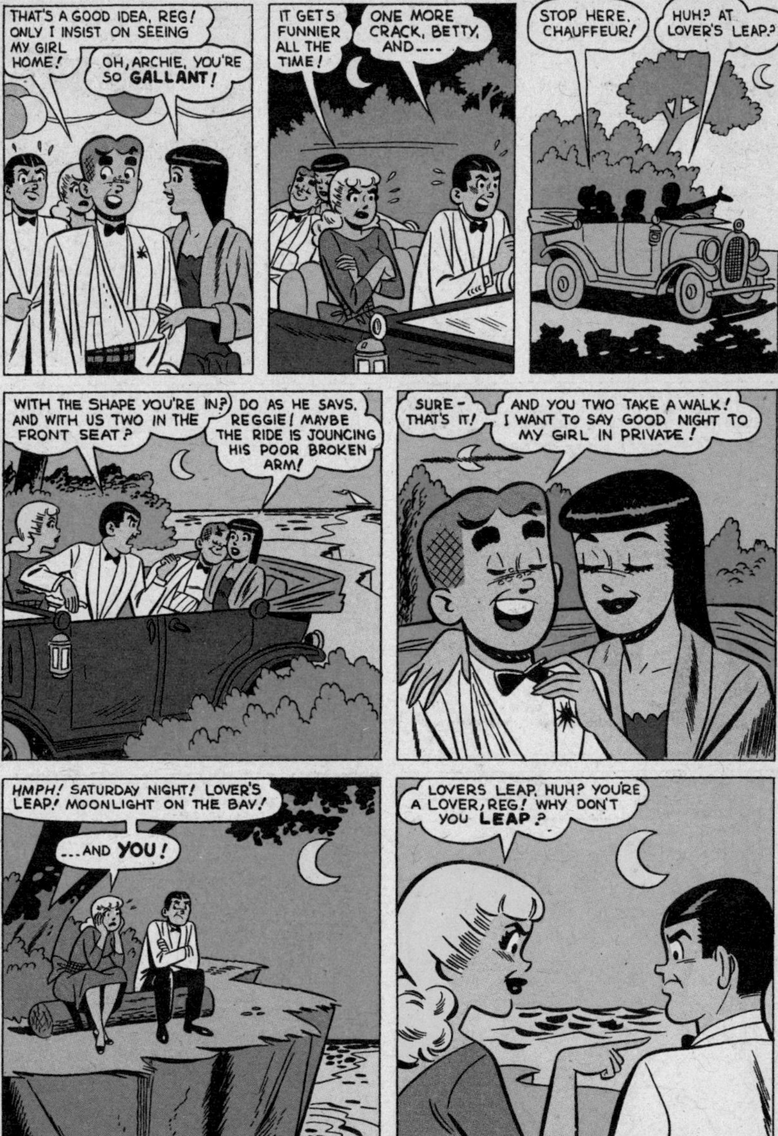
THAT'S A GOOD IDEA, REG! ONLY I INSIST ON SEEING MY GIRL HOME!
OH, ARCHIE, YOU'RE SO GALLANT!
IT GETS FUNNIER ALL THE TIME!
ONE MORE CRACK, BETTY, AND....
STOP HERE, CHAUFFEUR!
HUH? AT LOVER'S LEAP?
WITH THE SHAPE YOU'RE IN? AND WITH US TWO IN THE FRONT SEAT?
DO AS HE SAYS, REGGIE! MAYBE THE RIDE IS JOUNCING HIS POOR BROKEN ARM!
SURE - THAT'S IT!
AND YOU TWO TAKE A WALK! I WANT TO SAY GOOD NIGHT TO MY GIRL IN PRIVATE!
HMPH! SATURDAY NIGHT! LOVER'S LEAP! MOONLIGHT ON THE BAY!
...AND YOU!
LOVERS LEAP, HUH? YOU'RE A LOVER, REG! WHY DON'T YOU LEAP?

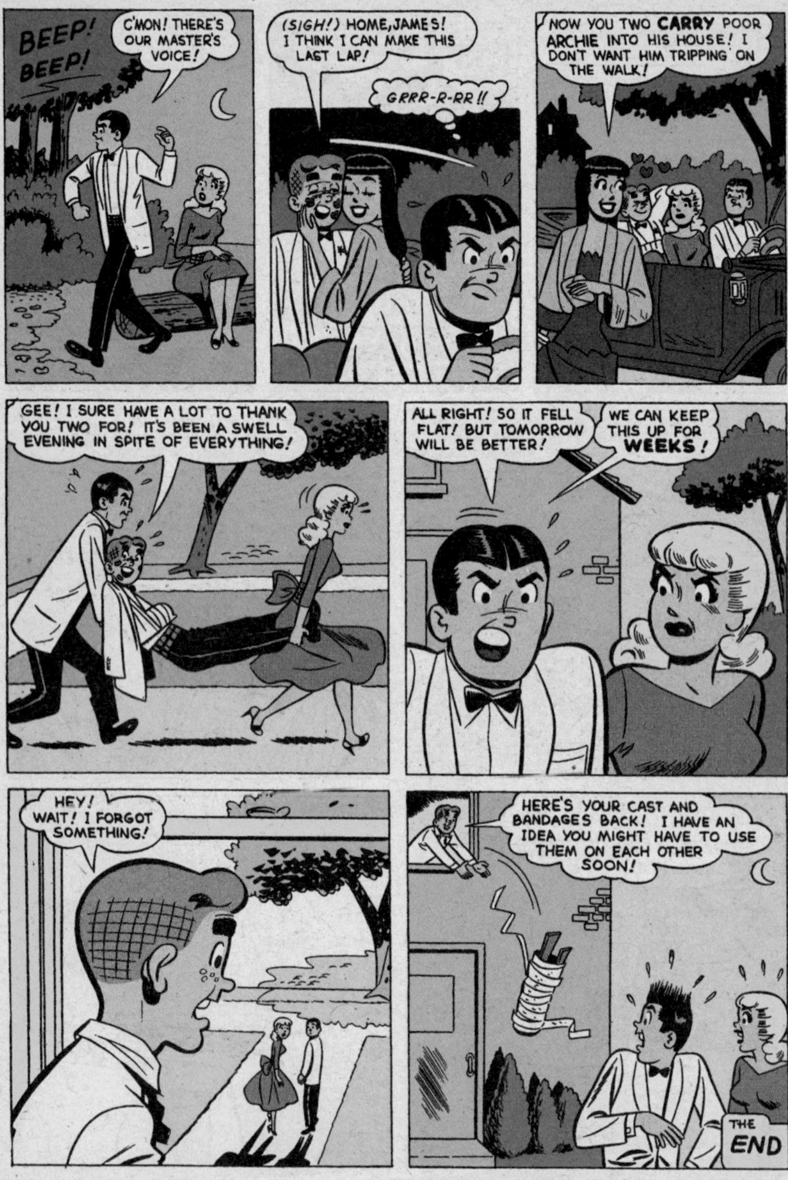
BEEP! BEEP!
C'MON! THERE'S OUR MASTER'S VOICE!
(SIGH!) HOME, JAMES! I THINK I CAN MAKE THIS LAST LAP!
GRRR-R-RR!!
NOW YOU TWO **CARRY** POOR ARCHIE INTO HIS HOUSE! I DON'T WANT HIM TRIPPING ON THE WALK!
GEE! I SURE HAVE A LOT TO THANK YOU TWO FOR! IT'S BEEN A SWELL EVENING IN SPITE OF EVERYTHING!
ALL RIGHT! SO IT FELL FLAT! BUT TOMORROW WILL BE BETTER!
WE CAN KEEP THIS UP FOR **WEEKS**!
HEY! WAIT! I FORGOT SOMETHING!
HERE'S YOUR CAST AND BANDAGES BACK! I HAVE AN IDEA YOU MIGHT HAVE TO USE THEM ON EACH OTHER SOON!
THE END

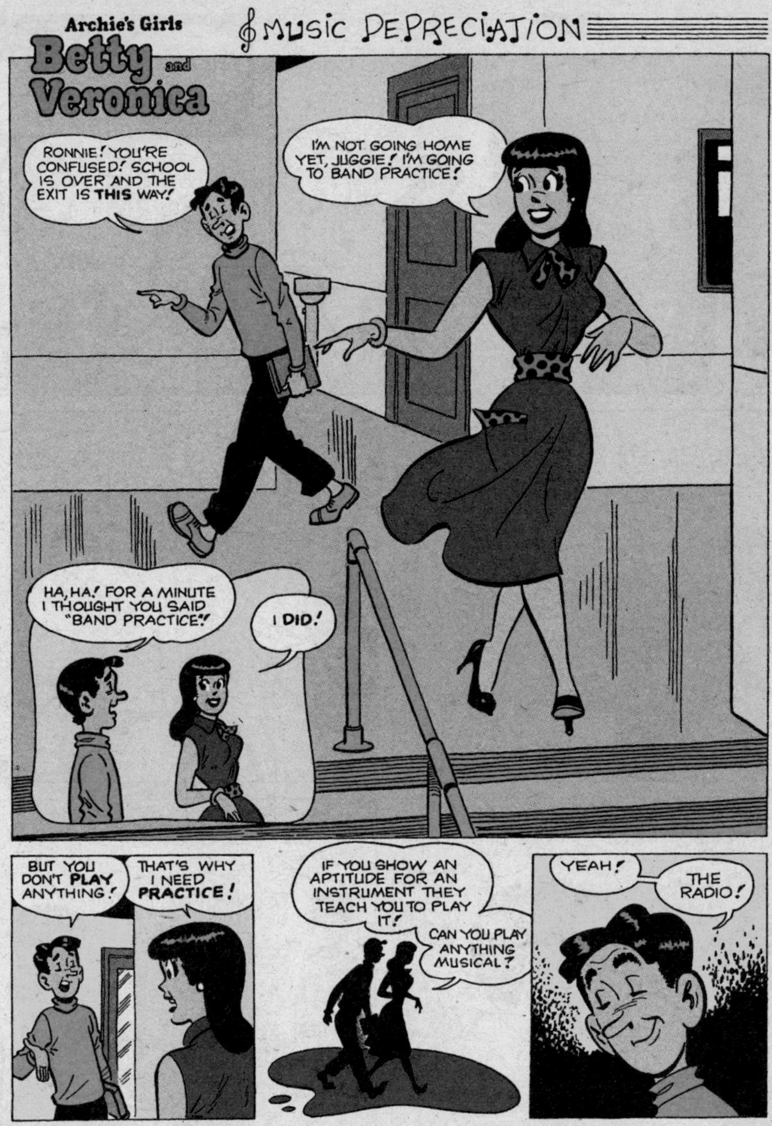
Archie's Girls
Betty and Veronica
MUSIC DEPRECIATION
RONNIE! YOU'RE CONFUSED! SCHOOL IS OVER AND THE EXIT IS **THIS** WAY!
I'M NOT GOING HOME YET, JUGGIE! I'M GOING TO BAND PRACTICE!
HA, HA! FOR A MINUTE I THOUGHT YOU SAID "BAND PRACTICE"!
I **DID**!
BUT YOU DON'T **PLAY** ANYTHING!
THAT'S WHY I NEED **PRACTICE**!
IF YOU SHOW AN APTITUDE FOR AN INSTRUMENT THEY TEACH YOU TO PLAY IT!
CAN YOU PLAY ANYTHING MUSICAL?
YEAH!
THE RADIO!

SCRIPT:
FRANK DOYLE

PENCILS, INKS & LETTERS:
SAMM SCHWARTZ

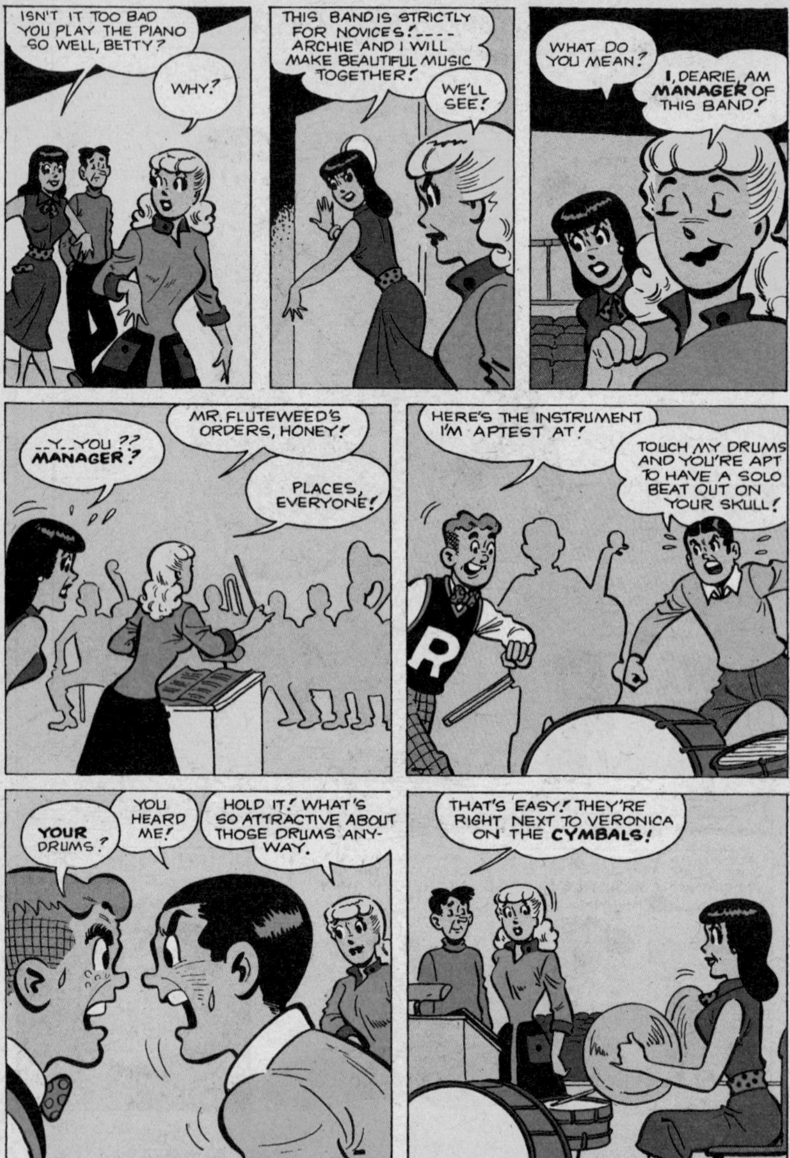
ISN'T IT TOO BAD YOU PLAY THE PIANO SO WELL, BETTY?
WHY?
THIS BAND IS STRICTLY FOR NOVICES!---- ARCHIE AND I WILL MAKE BEAUTIFUL MUSIC TOGETHER!
WE'LL SEE!
WHAT DO YOU MEAN?
I, DEARIE, AM **MANAGER** OF THIS BAND!
--Y--YOU?? **MANAGER**?
MR. FLUTEWEED'S ORDERS, HONEY!
PLACES, EVERYONE!
HERE'S THE INSTRUMENT I'M APTEST AT!
TOUCH MY DRUMS AND YOU'RE APT TO HAVE A SOLO BEAT OUT ON YOUR SKULL!
YOUR DRUMS?
YOU HEARD ME!
HOLD IT! WHAT'S SO ATTRACTIVE ABOUT THOSE DRUMS ANY-WAY.
THAT'S EASY! THEY'RE RIGHT NEXT TO VERONICA ON THE **CYMBALS**!

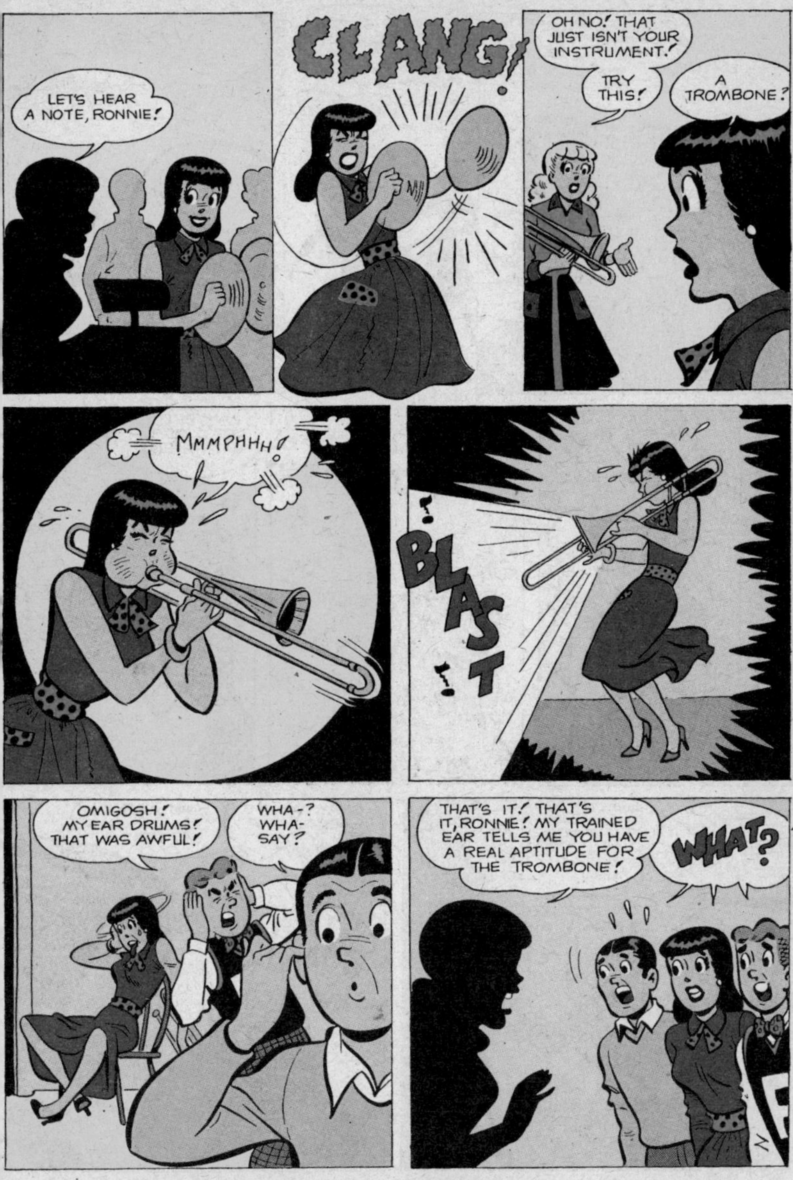
LET'S HEAR A NOTE, RONNIE!
CLANG!
OH NO! THAT JUST ISN'T YOUR INSTRUMENT!
TRY THIS!
A TROMBONE?
MMMPHHH!
BLAST
OMIGOSH! MY EAR DRUMS! THAT WAS AWFUL!
WHA-? WHA-SAY?
THAT'S IT! THAT'S IT, RONNIE! MY TRAINED EAR TELLS ME YOU HAVE A REAL APTITUDE FOR THE TROMBONE!
WHAT?

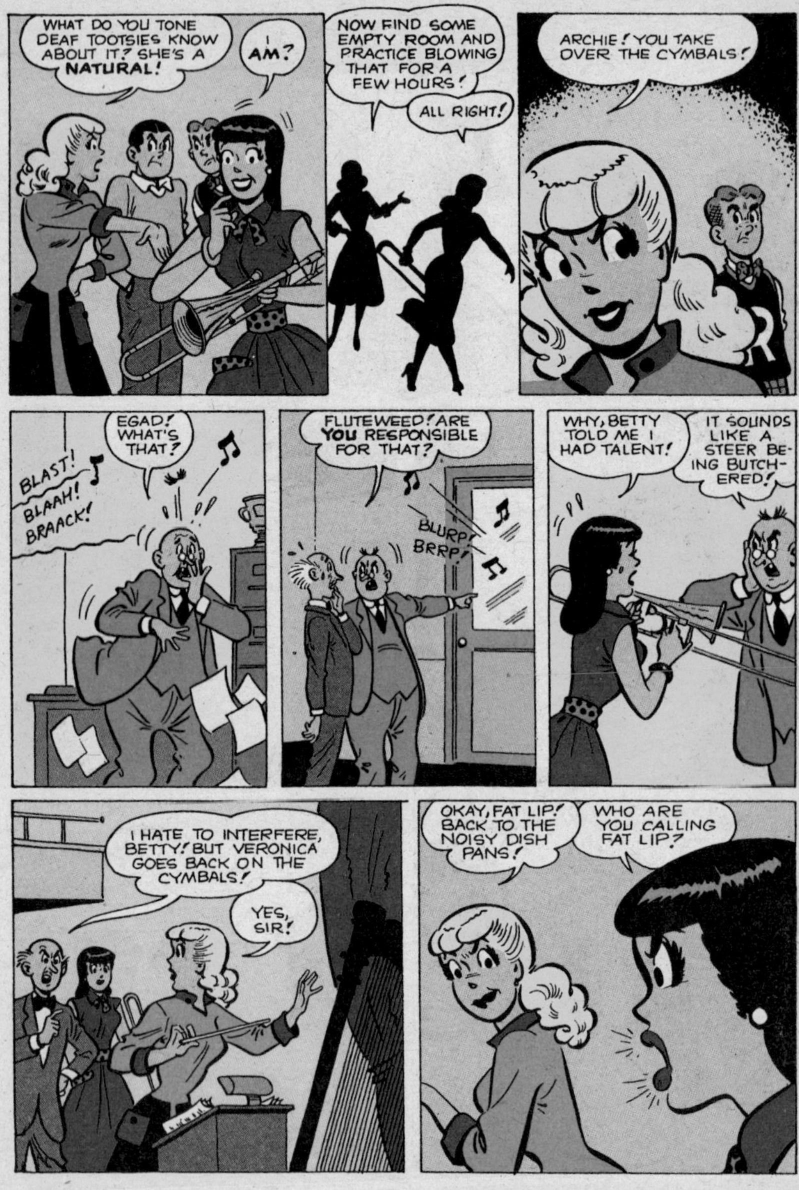
WHAT DO YOU TONE DEAF TOOTSIES KNOW ABOUT IT? SHE'S A NATURAL!
I AM?
NOW FIND SOME EMPTY ROOM AND PRACTICE BLOWING THAT FOR A FEW HOURS!
ALL RIGHT!
ARCHIE! YOU TAKE OVER THE CYMBALS!
BLAST! BLAAH! BRAACK!
EGAD! WHAT'S THAT?
FLUTEWEED! ARE YOU RESPONSIBLE FOR THAT?
BLURP! BRRP!
WHY, BETTY TOLD ME I HAD TALENT!
IT SOUNDS LIKE A STEER BE-ING BUTCH-ERED!
I HATE TO INTERFERE, BETTY! BUT VERONICA GOES BACK ON THE CYMBALS!
YES, SIR!
OKAY, FAT LIP! BACK TO THE NOISY DISH PANS!
WHO ARE YOU CALLING FAT LIP?

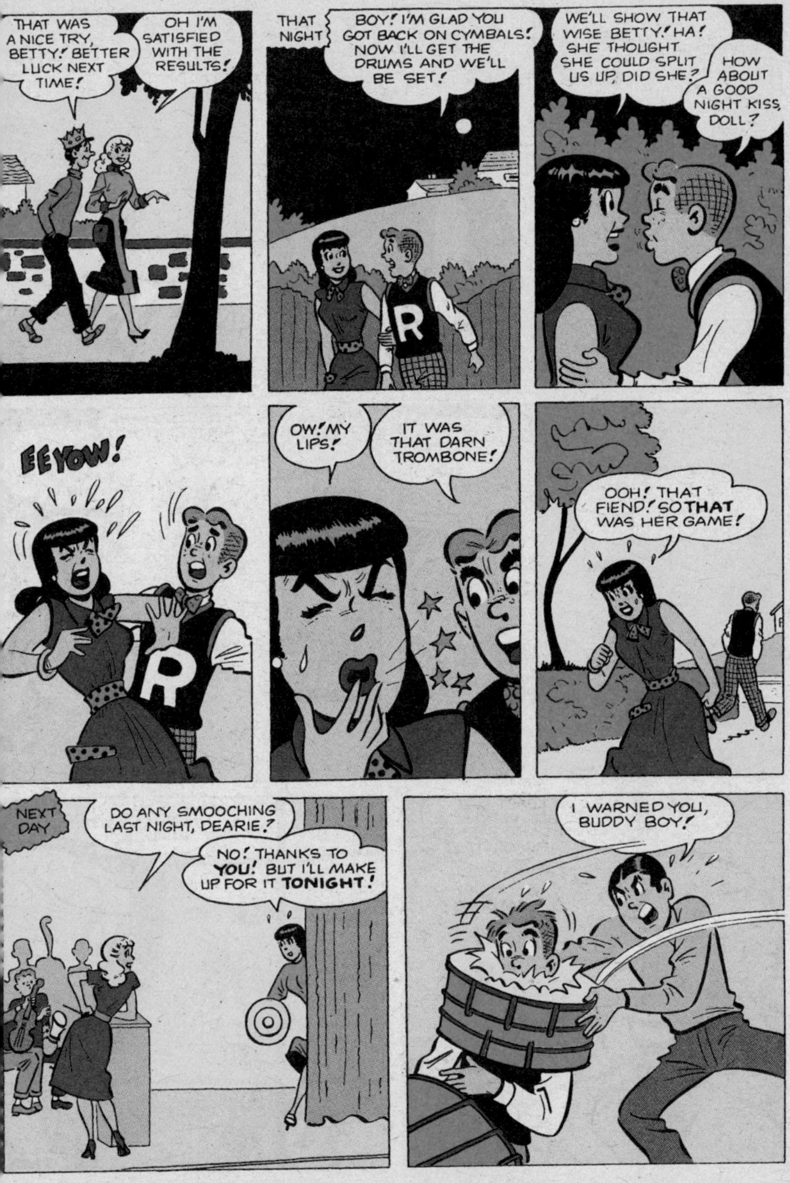
THAT WAS A NICE TRY, BETTY! BETTER LUCK NEXT TIME!
OH I'M SATISFIED WITH THE RESULTS!
THAT NIGHT
BOY! I'M GLAD YOU GOT BACK ON CYMBALS! NOW I'LL GET THE DRUMS AND WE'LL BE SET!
WE'LL SHOW THAT WISE BETTY! HA! SHE THOUGHT SHE COULD SPLIT US UP, DID SHE?
HOW ABOUT A GOOD NIGHT KISS, DOLL?
EEYOW!
OW! MY LIPS!
IT WAS THAT DARN TROMBONE!
OOH! THAT FIEND! SO THAT WAS HER GAME!
NEXT DAY
DO ANY SMOOCHING LAST NIGHT, DEARIE?
NO! THANKS TO YOU! BUT I'LL MAKE UP FOR IT TONIGHT!
I WARNED YOU, BUDDY BOY!

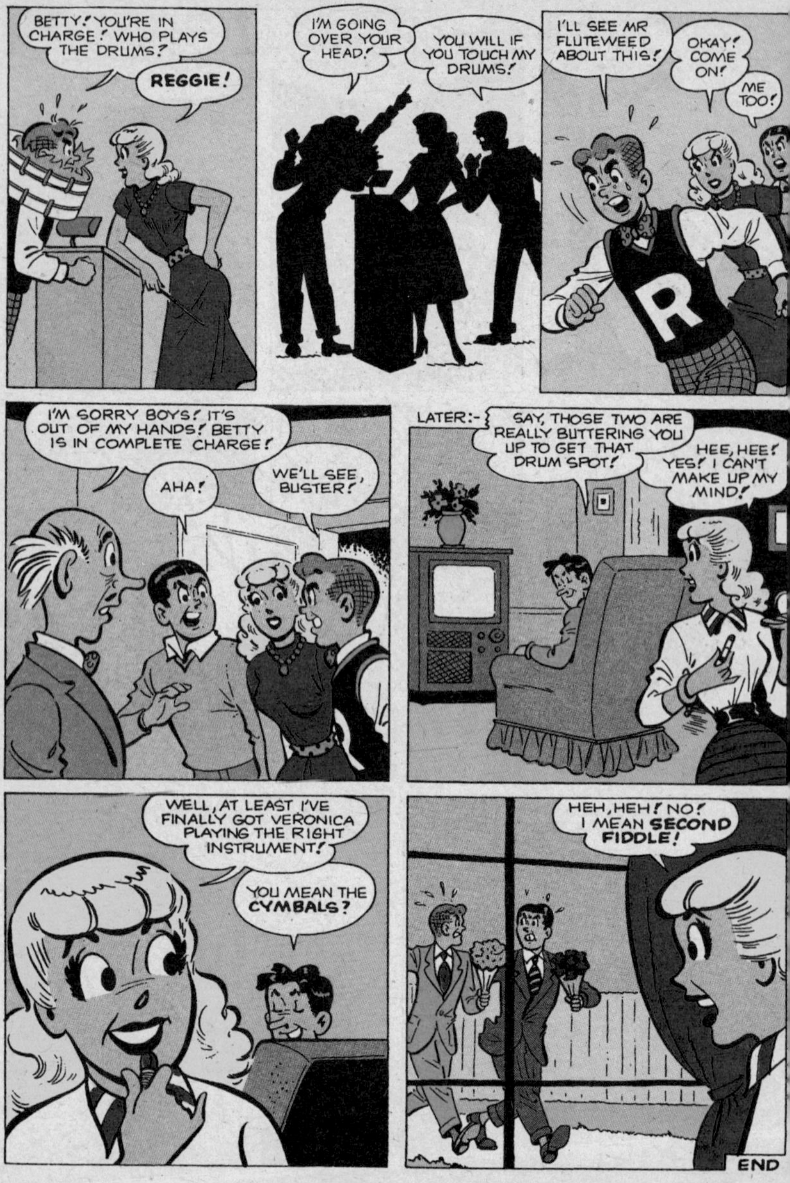
BETTY! YOU'RE IN CHARGE! WHO PLAYS THE DRUMS?
REGGIE!
I'M GOING OVER YOUR HEAD!
YOU WILL IF YOU TOUCH MY DRUMS!
I'LL SEE MR FLUTEWEED ABOUT THIS!
OKAY! COME ON!
ME TOO!
I'M SORRY BOYS! IT'S OUT OF MY HANDS! BETTY IS IN COMPLETE CHARGE!
AHA!
WE'LL SEE, BUSTER!
LATER:-
SAY, THOSE TWO ARE REALLY BUTTERING YOU UP TO GET THAT DRUM SPOT!
HEE, HEE! YES! I CAN'T MAKE UP MY MIND!
WELL, AT LEAST I'VE FINALLY GOT VERONICA PLAYING THE RIGHT INSTRUMENT!
YOU MEAN THE CYMBALS?
HEH, HEH! NO! I MEAN SECOND FIDDLE!
END

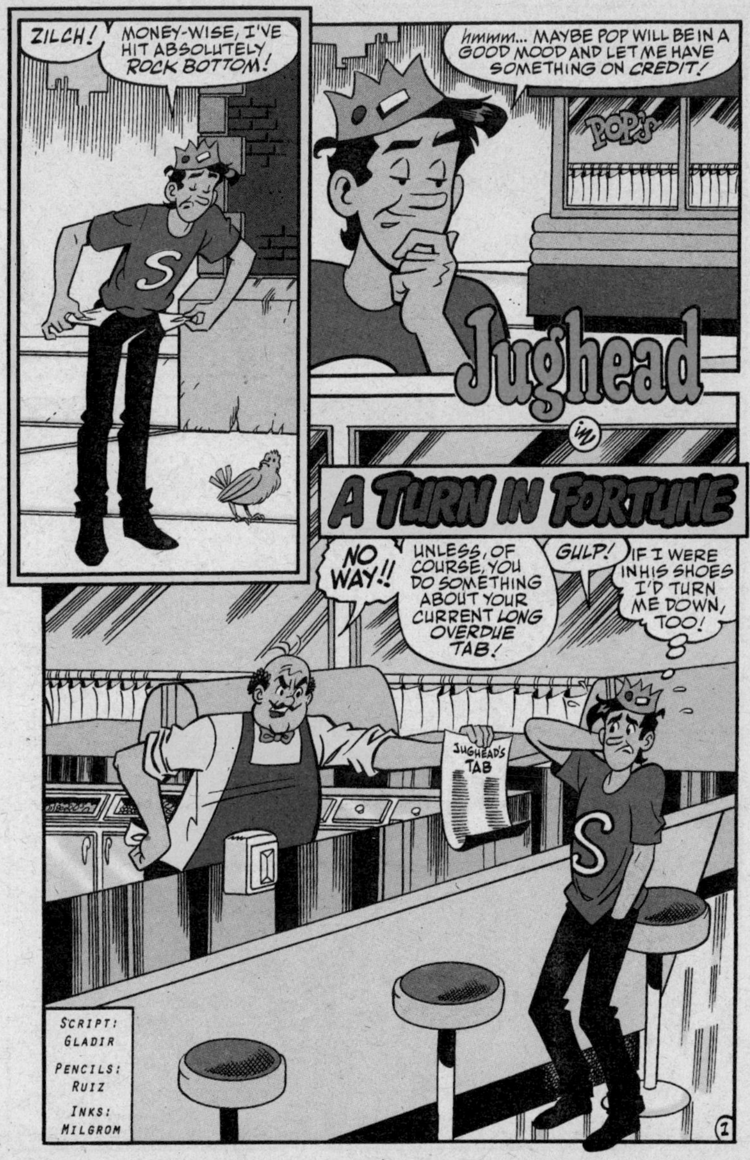

ZILCH!
MONEY-WISE, I'VE HIT ABSOLUTELY ROCK BOTTOM!
hmmm... MAYBE POP WILL BE IN A GOOD MOOD AND LET ME HAVE SOMETHING ON CREDIT!
POP'S
Jughead
in
A TURN IN FORTUNE
NO WAY!!
UNLESS, OF COURSE, YOU DO SOMETHING ABOUT YOUR CURRENT LONG OVERDUE TAB!
GULP!
IF I WERE IN HIS SHOES I'D TURN ME DOWN, TOO!
JUGHEAD'S TAB
SCRIPT: GLADIR
PENCILS: RUIZ
INKS: MILGROM
1

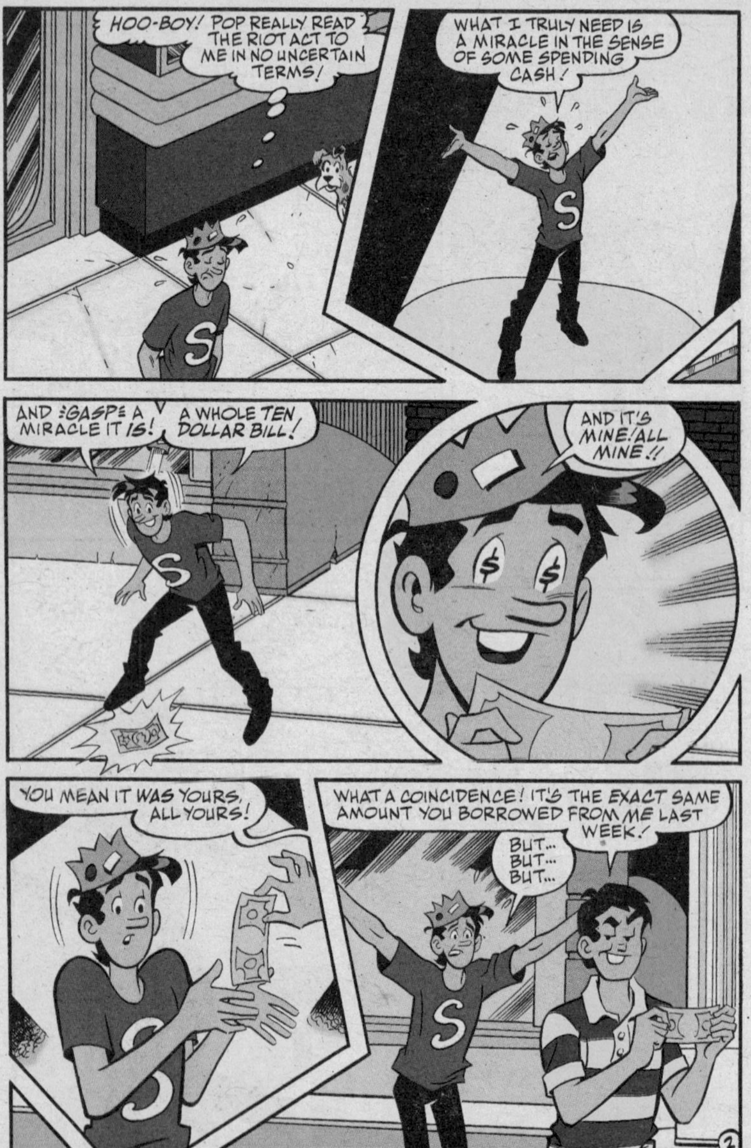
HOO-BOY! POP REALLY READ THE RIOT ACT TO ME IN NO UNCERTAIN TERMS!
WHAT I TRULY NEED IS A MIRACLE IN THE SENSE OF SOME SPENDING CASH!
AND ≡GASP≡ A MIRACLE IT IS!
A WHOLE TEN DOLLAR BILL!
AND IT'S MINE! ALL MINE!!
YOU MEAN IT WAS YOURS, ALL YOURS!
WHAT A COINCIDENCE! IT'S THE EXACT SAME AMOUNT YOU BORROWED FROM ME LAST WEEK!
BUT... BUT... BUT...
2

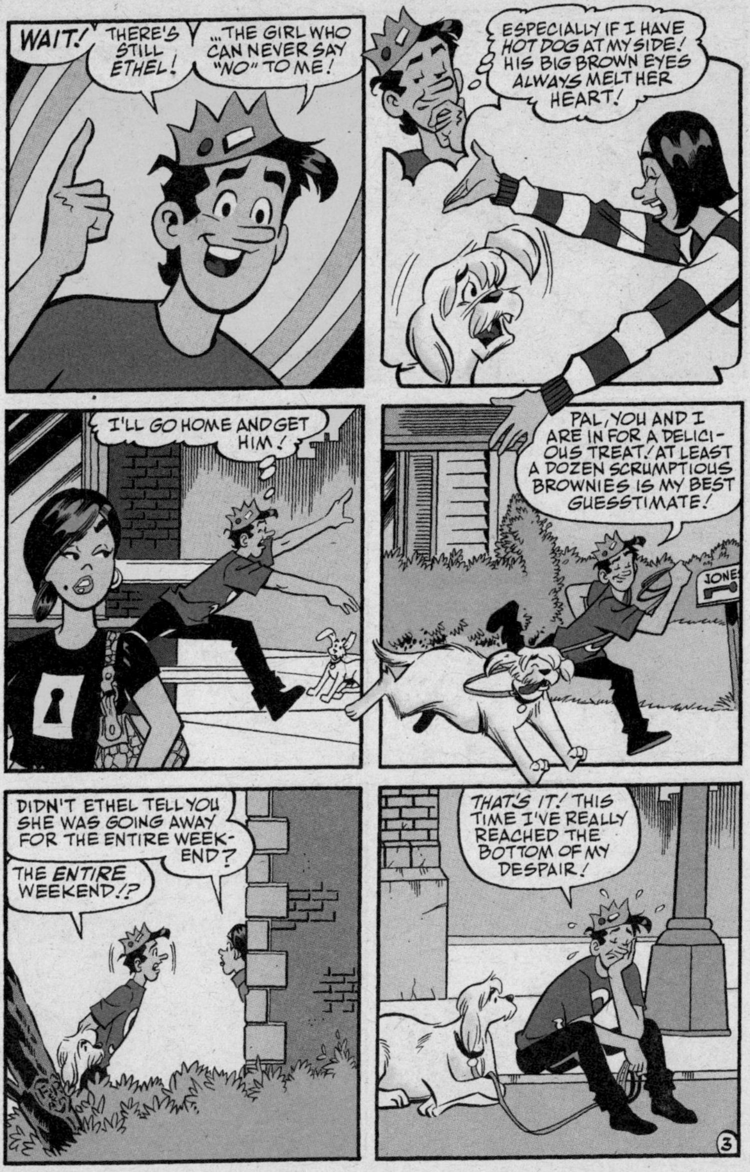
WAIT!
THERE'S STILL ETHEL!
...THE GIRL WHO CAN NEVER SAY "NO" TO ME!
ESPECIALLY IF I HAVE HOT DOG AT MY SIDE! HIS BIG BROWN EYES ALWAYS MELT HER HEART!
I'LL GO HOME AND GET HIM!
PAL, YOU AND I ARE IN FOR A DELICIOUS TREAT! AT LEAST A DOZEN SCRUMPTIOUS BROWNIES IS MY BEST GUESSTIMATE!
JONE
DIDN'T ETHEL TELL YOU SHE WAS GOING AWAY FOR THE ENTIRE WEEKEND?
THE ENTIRE WEEKEND!?
THAT'S IT! THIS TIME I'VE REALLY REACHED THE BOTTOM OF MY DESPAIR!
3

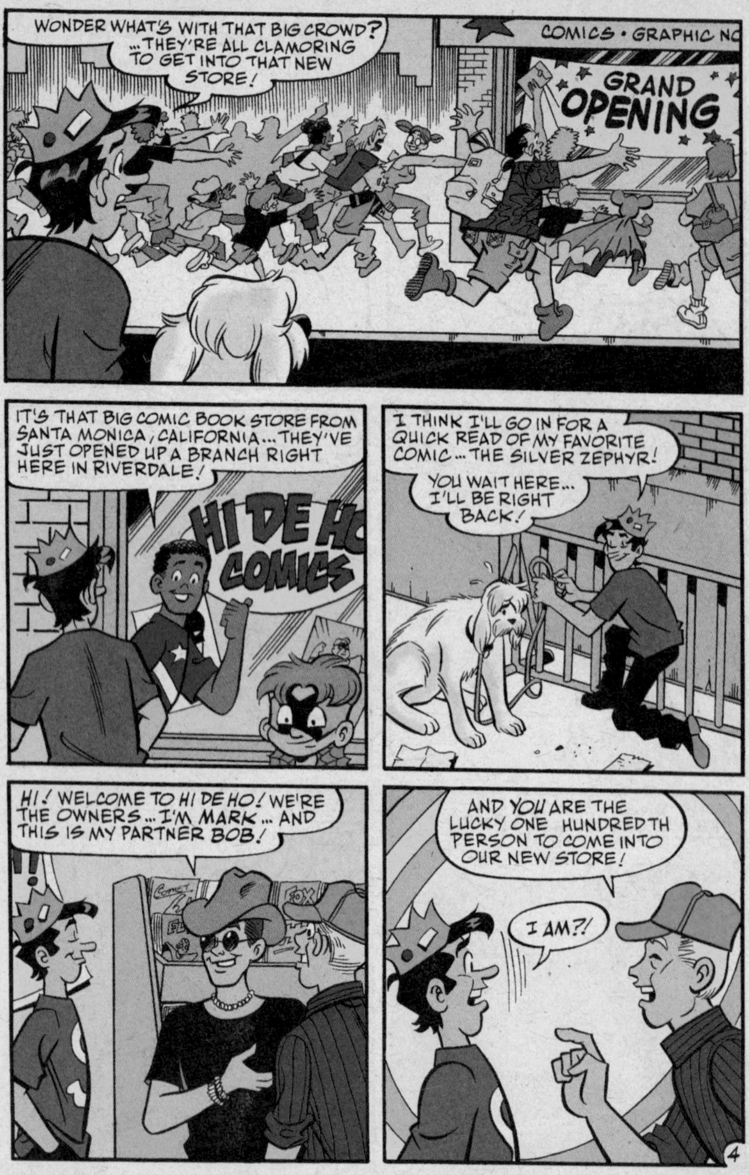
WONDER WHAT'S WITH THAT BIG CROWD?
...THEY'RE ALL CLAMORING TO GET INTO THAT NEW STORE!
COMICS • GRAPHIC N
GRAND OPENING
IT'S THAT BIG COMIC BOOK STORE FROM SANTA MONICA, CALIFORNIA... THEY'VE JUST OPENED UP A BRANCH RIGHT HERE IN RIVERDALE!
HI DE HO COMICS
I THINK I'LL GO IN FOR A QUICK READ OF MY FAVORITE COMIC... THE SILVER ZEPHYR!
YOU WAIT HERE... I'LL BE RIGHT BACK!
HI! WELCOME TO HI DE HO! WE'RE THE OWNERS... I'M MARK... AND THIS IS MY PARTNER BOB!
!!
AND YOU ARE THE LUCKY ONE HUNDREDTH PERSON TO COME INTO OUR NEW STORE!
I AM?!
4

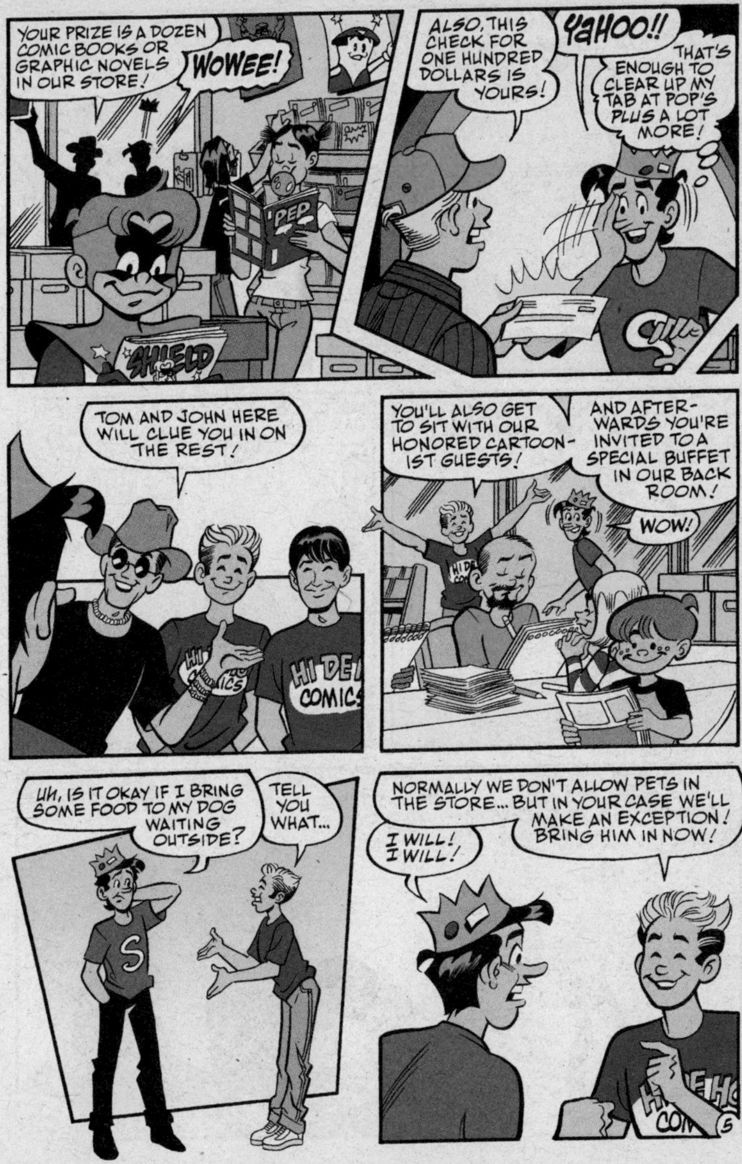
YOUR PRIZE IS A DOZEN COMIC BOOKS OR GRAPHIC NOVELS IN OUR STORE!
WOWEE!
PEP
SHIELD
ALSO, THIS CHECK FOR ONE HUNDRED DOLLARS IS YOURS!
YAHOO!!
THAT'S ENOUGH TO CLEAR UP MY TAB AT POP'S PLUS A LOT MORE!
TOM AND JOHN HERE WILL CLUE YOU IN ON THE REST!
HI DE HO COMICS
HI DE HO COMICS
YOU'LL ALSO GET TO SIT WITH OUR HONORED CARTOON-IST GUESTS!
AND AFTER-WARDS YOU'RE INVITED TO A SPECIAL BUFFET IN OUR BACK ROOM!
WOW!
UH, IS IT OKAY IF I BRING SOME FOOD TO MY DOG WAITING OUTSIDE?
TELL YOU WHAT...
NORMALLY WE DON'T ALLOW PETS IN THE STORE... BUT IN YOUR CASE WE'LL MAKE AN EXCEPTION! BRING HIM IN NOW!
I WILL! I WILL!
5

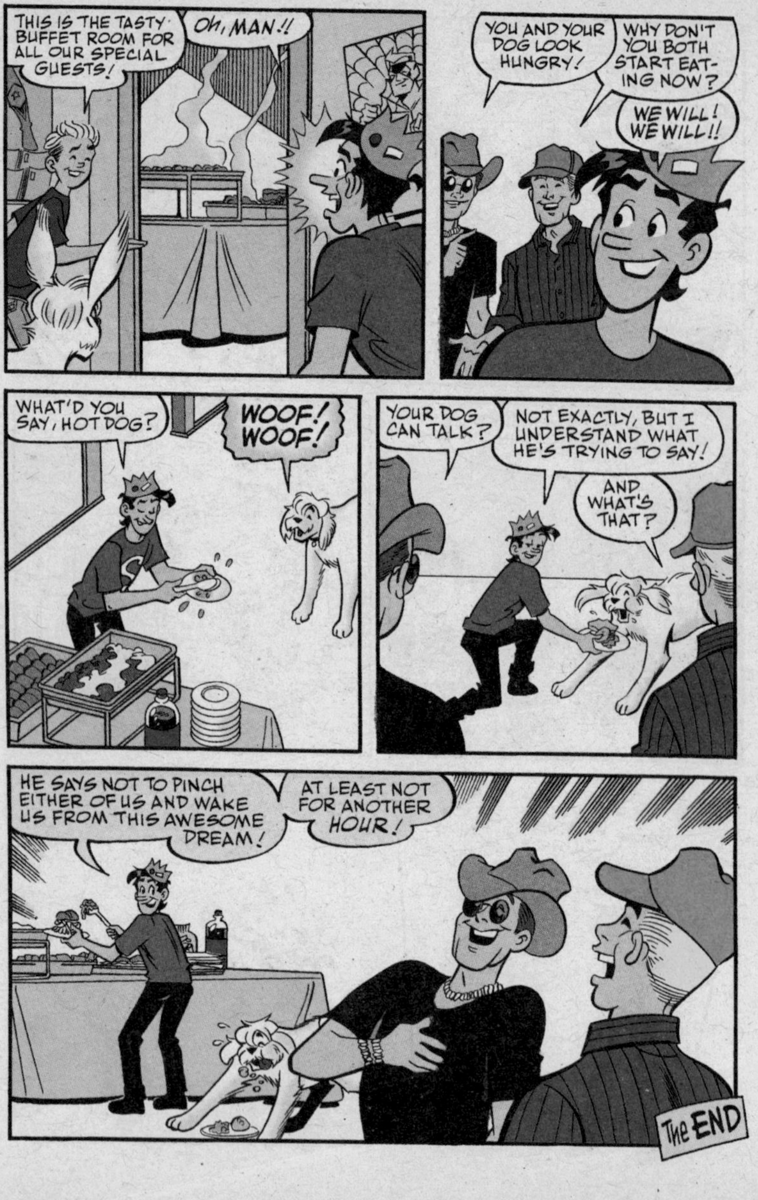
THIS IS THE TASTY BUFFET ROOM FOR ALL OUR SPECIAL GUESTS!
Oh, MAN!!
YOU AND YOUR DOG LOOK HUNGRY!
WHY DON'T YOU BOTH START EATING NOW?
WE WILL! WE WILL!!
WHAT'D YOU SAY, HOT DOG?
WOOF! WOOF!
YOUR DOG CAN TALK?
NOT EXACTLY, BUT I UNDERSTAND WHAT HE'S TRYING TO SAY!
AND WHAT'S THAT?
HE SAYS NOT TO PINCH EITHER OF US AND WAKE US FROM THIS AWESOME DREAM!
AT LEAST NOT FOR ANOTHER HOUR!
The END

Archie in ALL IN THE FAMILY

WHAT'S THE PROB, ARCHIE, GIRL TROUBLE AGAIN?

YOU'VE GOT THAT "WHO DO I LOVE-- VERONICA OR BETTY?" LOOK!

HOW DID YOU KNOW, JUGHEAD?

RIVERDALE PARK

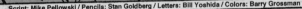

Script: Mike Pellowski / Pencils: Stan Goldberg / Letters: Bill Yoshida / Colors: Barry Grossman

SOMETIMES I WISH I WAS YOU, JUG!

YOUR BIG CONFLICT IS WHETHER TO HAVE A HOT DOG OR HAMBURGER FOR LUNCH!

DON'T KNOCK MY PROBS, ARCHIE!

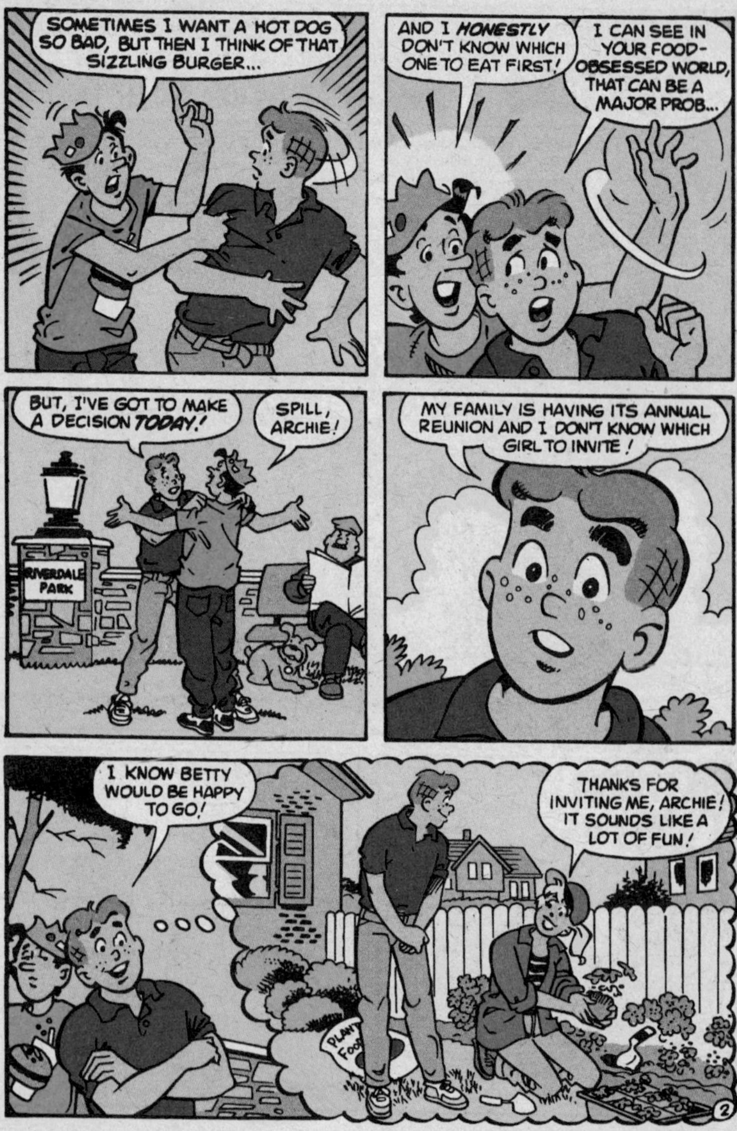
SOMETIMES I WANT A HOT DOG SO BAD, BUT THEN I THINK OF THAT SIZZLING BURGER...
AND I HONESTLY DON'T KNOW WHICH ONE TO EAT FIRST!
I CAN SEE IN YOUR FOOD-OBSESSED WORLD, THAT CAN BE A MAJOR PROB...
BUT, I'VE GOT TO MAKE A DECISION TODAY!
SPILL, ARCHIE!
RIVERDALE PARK
MY FAMILY IS HAVING ITS ANNUAL REUNION AND I DON'T KNOW WHICH GIRL TO INVITE!
I KNOW BETTY WOULD BE HAPPY TO GO!
THANKS FOR INVITING ME, ARCHIE! IT SOUNDS LIKE A LOT OF FUN!
PLANT FOOD
2

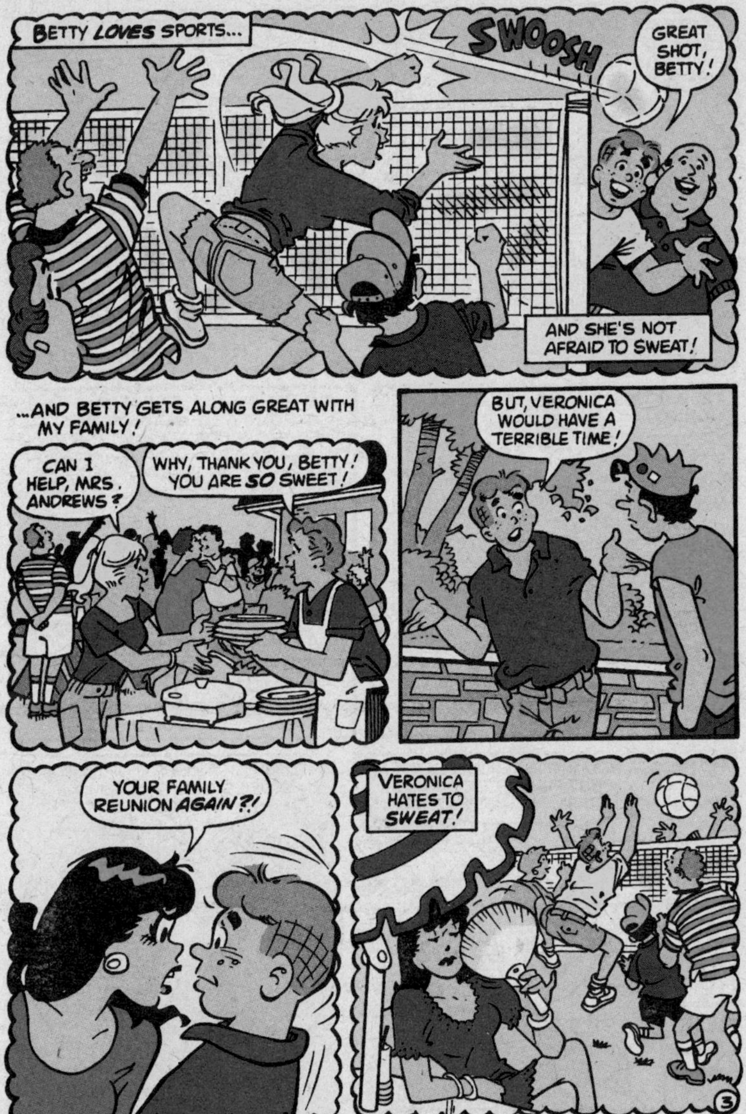
BETTY LOVES SPORTS...
SWOOSH
GREAT SHOT, BETTY!
AND SHE'S NOT AFRAID TO SWEAT!
...AND BETTY GETS ALONG GREAT WITH MY FAMILY!
CAN I HELP, MRS. ANDREWS?
WHY, THANK YOU, BETTY! YOU ARE SO SWEET!
BUT, VERONICA WOULD HAVE A TERRIBLE TIME!
YOUR FAMILY REUNION AGAIN?!
VERONICA HATES TO SWEAT!
3

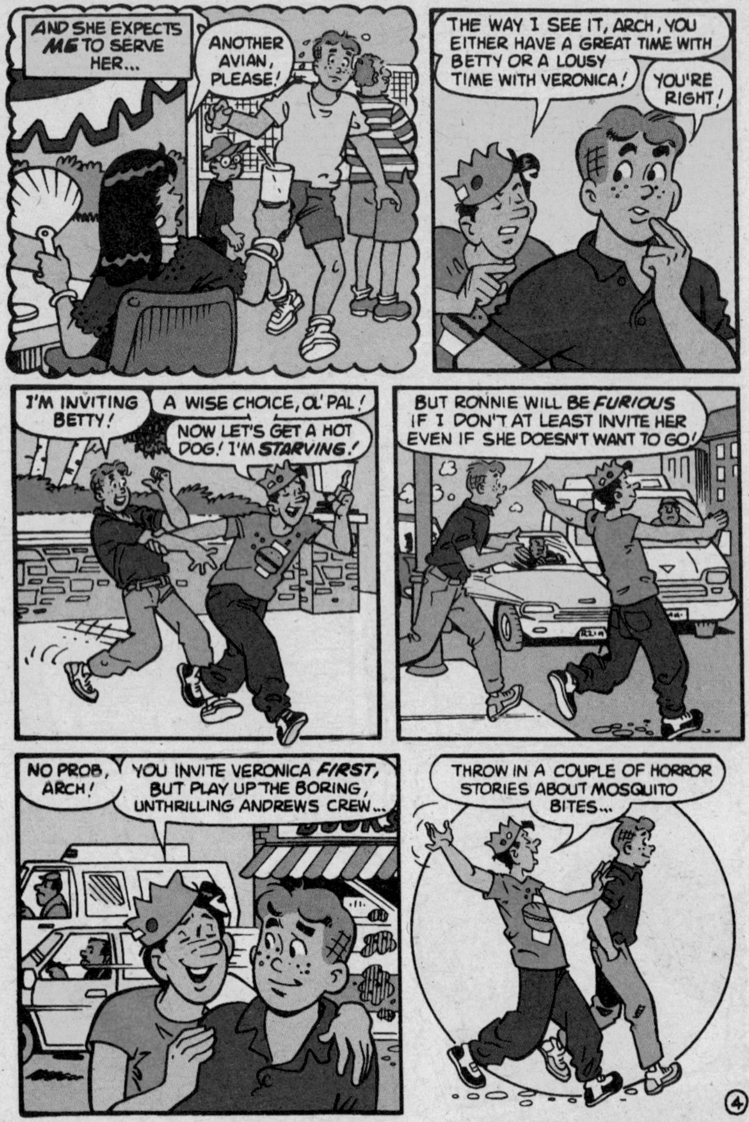

AND SHE EXPECTS ME TO SERVE HER...
ANOTHER AVIAN, PLEASE!
THE WAY I SEE IT, ARCH, YOU EITHER HAVE A GREAT TIME WITH BETTY OR A LOUSY TIME WITH VERONICA!
YOU'RE RIGHT!
I'M INVITING BETTY!
A WISE CHOICE, OL' PAL!
NOW LET'S GET A HOT DOG! I'M STARVING!
BUT RONNIE WILL BE FURIOUS IF I DON'T AT LEAST INVITE HER EVEN IF SHE DOESN'T WANT TO GO!
NO PROB, ARCH!
YOU INVITE VERONICA FIRST, BUT PLAY UP THE BORING, UNTHRILLING ANDREWS CREW...
THROW IN A COUPLE OF HORROR STORIES ABOUT MOSQUITO BITES...
4

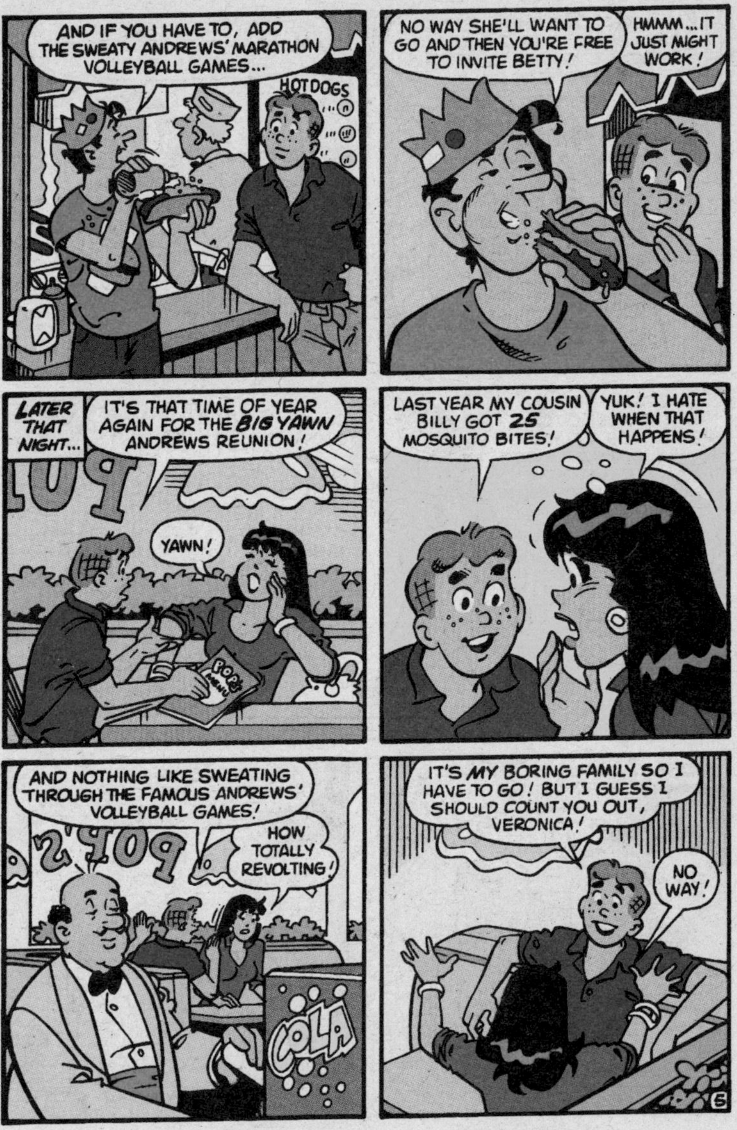

AND IF YOU HAVE TO, ADD THE SWEATY ANDREWS' MARATHON VOLLEYBALL GAMES...
HOT DOGS
NO WAY SHE'LL WANT TO GO AND THEN YOU'RE FREE TO INVITE BETTY!
HMMM...IT JUST MIGHT WORK!
LATER THAT NIGHT...
IT'S THAT TIME OF YEAR AGAIN FOR THE BIG YAWN ANDREWS REUNION!
YAWN!
LAST YEAR MY COUSIN BILLY GOT 25 MOSQUITO BITES!
YUK! I HATE WHEN THAT HAPPENS!
AND NOTHING LIKE SWEATING THROUGH THE FAMOUS ANDREWS' VOLLEYBALL GAMES!
HOW TOTALLY REVOLTING!
COLA
IT'S MY BORING FAMILY SO I HAVE TO GO! BUT I GUESS I SHOULD COUNT YOU OUT, VERONICA!
NO WAY!
6

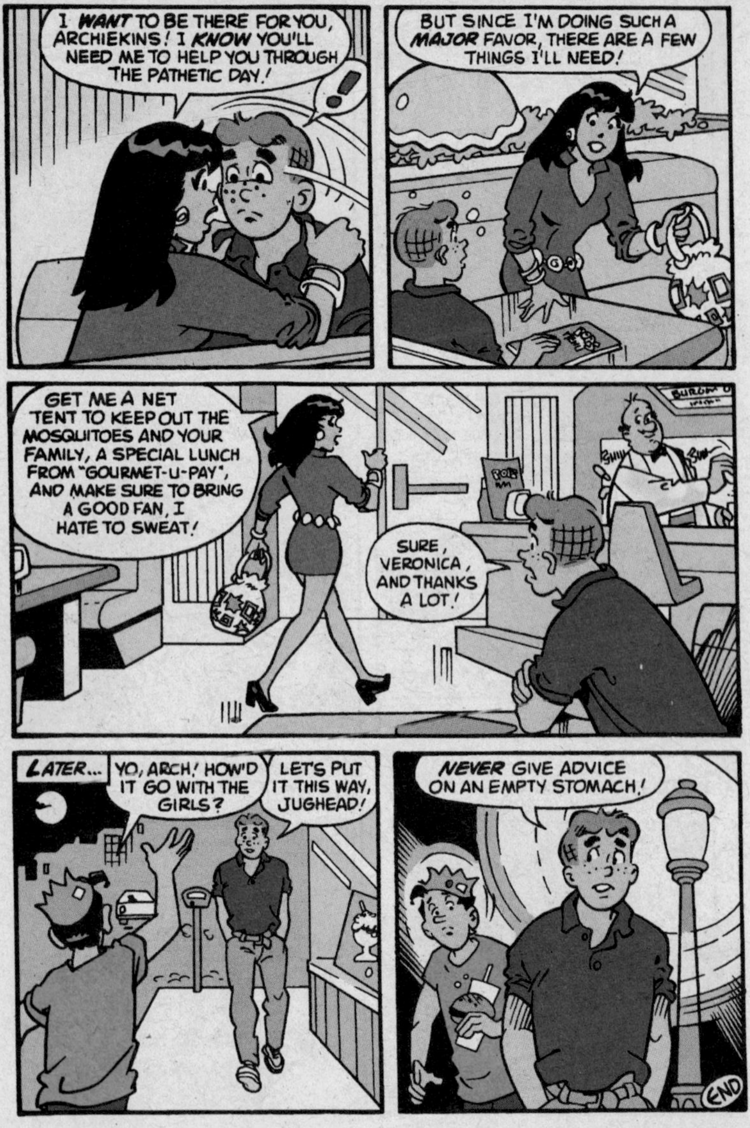

I WANT TO BE THERE FOR YOU, ARCHIEKINS! I KNOW YOU'LL NEED ME TO HELP YOU THROUGH THE PATHETIC DAY!
!
BUT SINCE I'M DOING SUCH A MAJOR FAVOR, THERE ARE A FEW THINGS I'LL NEED!
GET ME A NET TENT TO KEEP OUT THE MOSQUITOES AND YOUR FAMILY, A SPECIAL LUNCH FROM "GOURMET-U-PAY", AND MAKE SURE TO BRING A GOOD FAN, I HATE TO SWEAT!
SURE, VERONICA, AND THANKS A LOT!
LATER...
YO, ARCH! HOW'D IT GO WITH THE GIRLS?
LET'S PUT IT THIS WAY, JUGHEAD!
NEVER GIVE ADVICE ON AN EMPTY STOMACH!
END

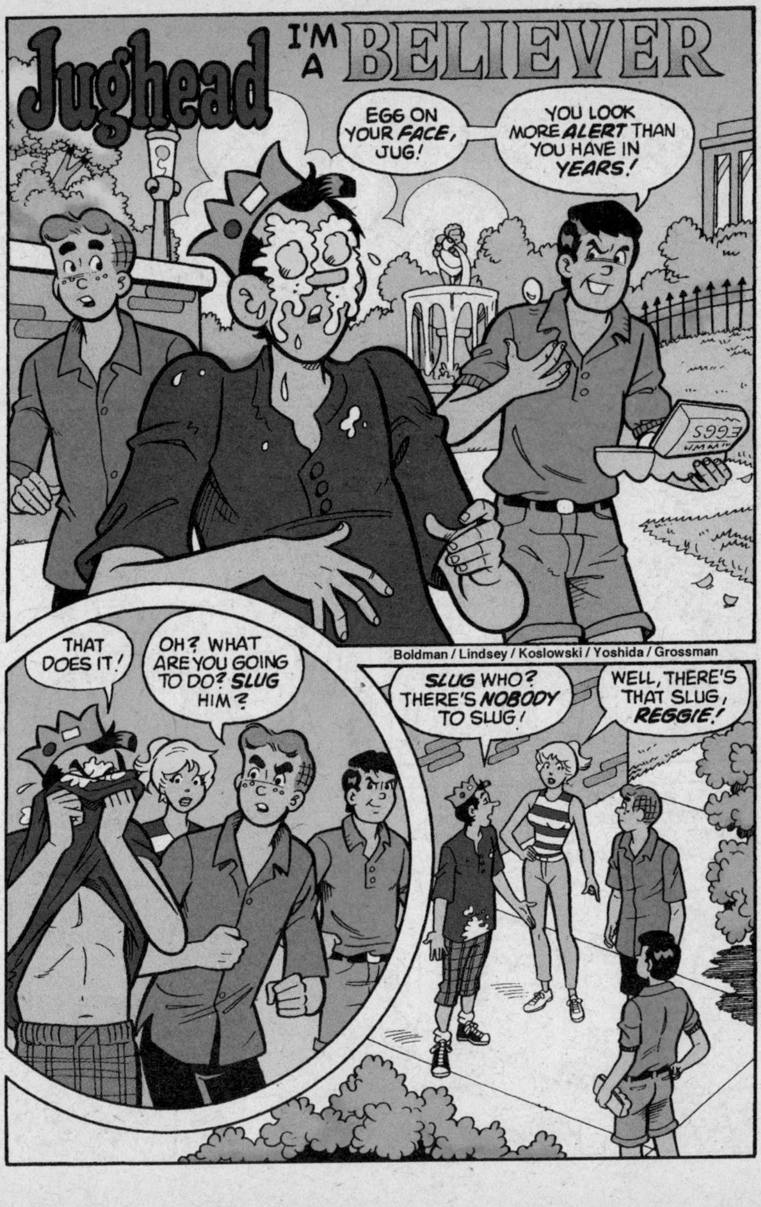

Jughead
I'M A BELIEVER
EGG ON YOUR FACE, JUG!
YOU LOOK MORE ALERT THAN YOU HAVE IN YEARS!
EGGS
Boldman / Lindsey / Koslowski / Yoshida / Grossman
THAT DOES IT!
OH? WHAT ARE YOU GOING TO DO? SLUG HIM?
SLUG WHO? THERE'S NOBODY TO SLUG!
WELL, THERE'S THAT SLUG, REGGIE!

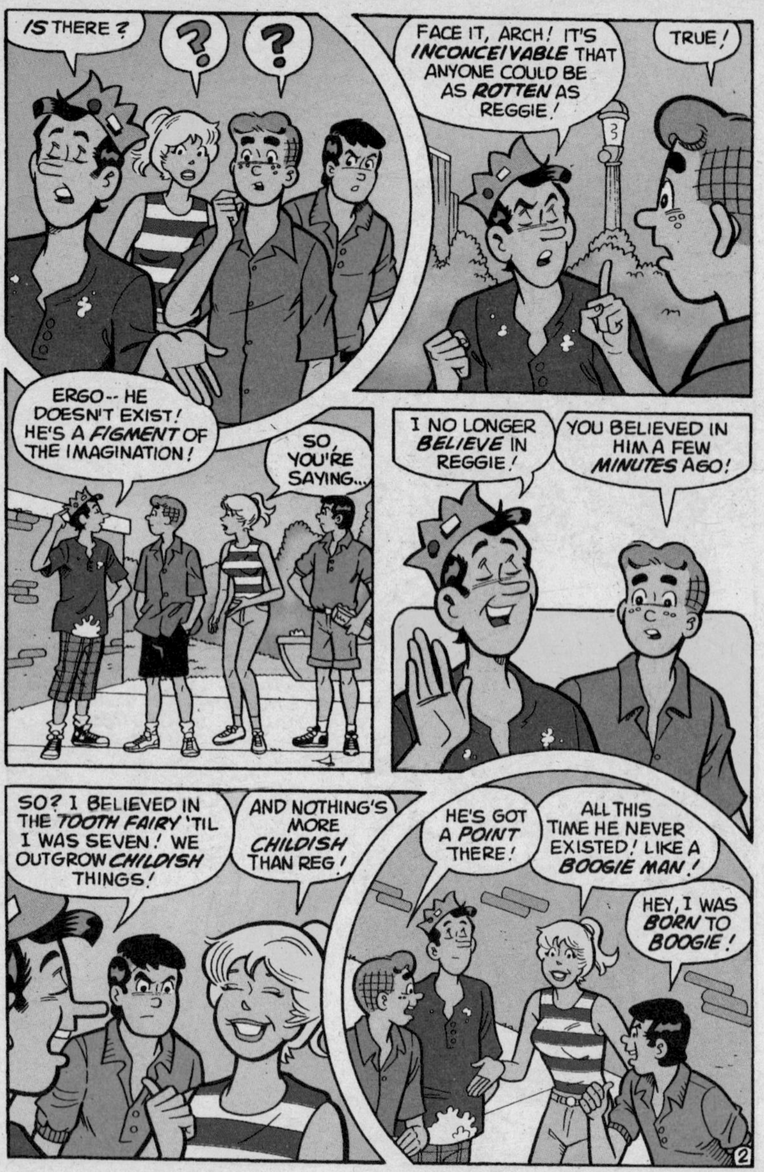
IS THERE?
?
?
FACE IT, ARCH! IT'S INCONCEIVABLE THAT ANYONE COULD BE AS ROTTEN AS REGGIE!
TRUE!
ERGO-- HE DOESN'T EXIST! HE'S A FIGMENT OF THE IMAGINATION!
SO, YOU'RE SAYING...
I NO LONGER BELIEVE IN REGGIE!
YOU BELIEVED IN HIM A FEW MINUTES AGO!
SO? I BELIEVED IN THE TOOTH FAIRY 'TIL I WAS SEVEN! WE OUTGROW CHILDISH THINGS!
AND NOTHING'S MORE CHILDISH THAN REG!
HE'S GOT A POINT THERE!
ALL THIS TIME HE NEVER EXISTED! LIKE A BOOGIE MAN!
HEY, I WAS BORN TO BOOGIE!
2

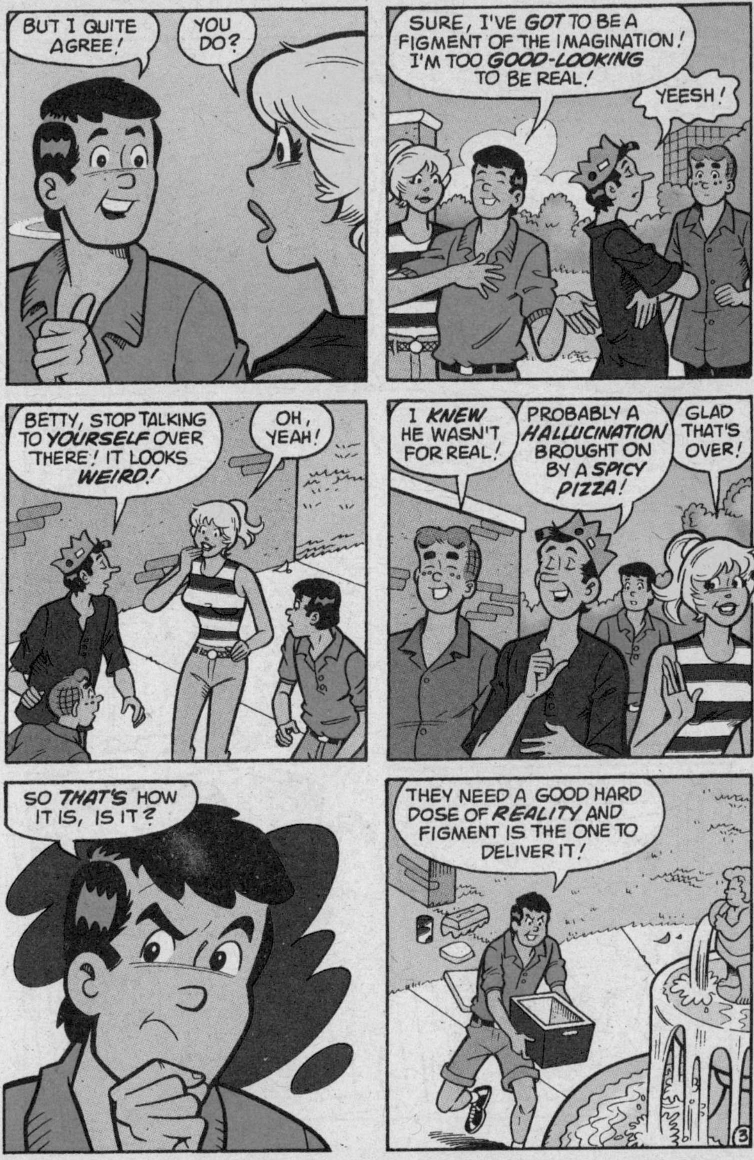

BUT I QUITE AGREE!
YOU DO?
SURE, I'VE GOT TO BE A FIGMENT OF THE IMAGINATION! I'M TOO GOOD-LOOKING TO BE REAL!
YEESH!
BETTY, STOP TALKING TO YOURSELF OVER THERE! IT LOOKS WEIRD!
OH, YEAH!
I KNEW HE WASN'T FOR REAL!
PROBABLY A HALLUCINATION BROUGHT ON BY A SPICY PIZZA!
GLAD THAT'S OVER!
SO THAT'S HOW IT IS, IS IT?
THEY NEED A GOOD HARD DOSE OF REALITY AND FIGMENT IS THE ONE TO DELIVER IT!
3

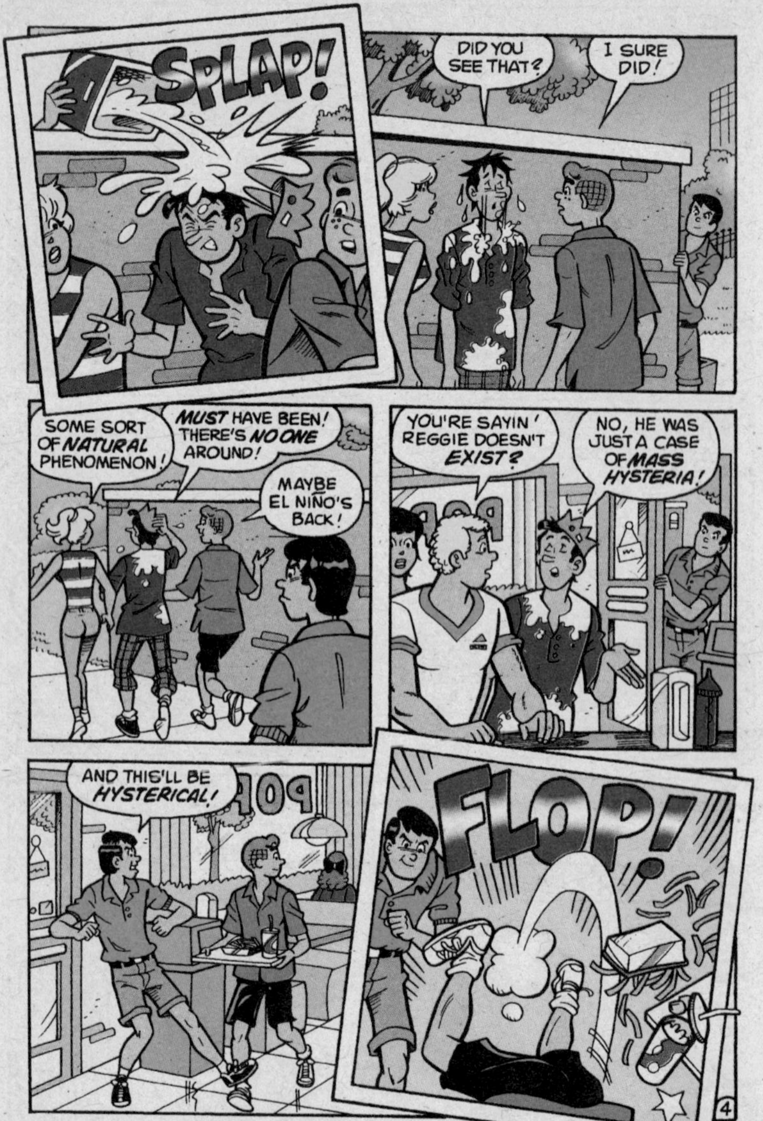
SPLAP!
DID YOU SEE THAT?
I SURE DID!
SOME SORT OF NATURAL PHENOMENON!
MUST HAVE BEEN! THERE'S NO ONE AROUND!
MAYBE EL NIÑO'S BACK!
YOU'RE SAYIN' REGGIE DOESN'T EXIST?
NO, HE WAS JUST A CASE OF MASS HYSTERIA!
POP
AND THIS'LL BE HYSTERICAL!
POP
FLOP!
4

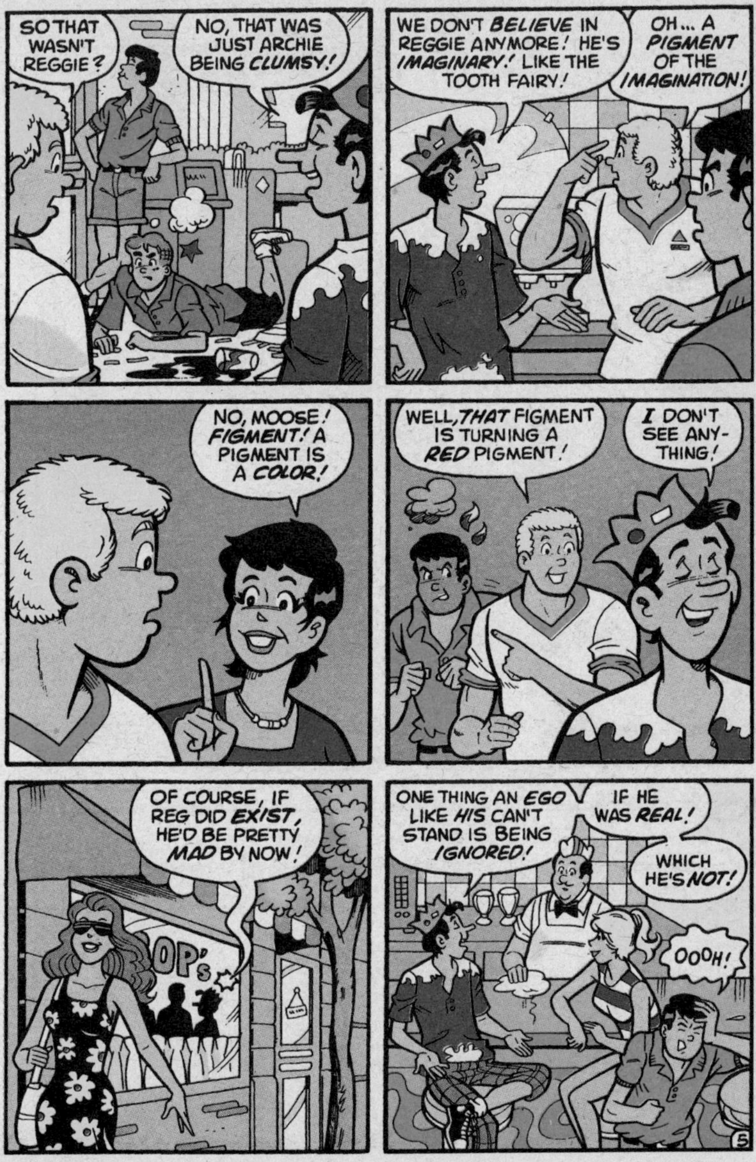
SO THAT WASN'T REGGIE?
NO, THAT WAS JUST ARCHIE BEING *CLUMSY!*
WE DON'T *BELIEVE* IN REGGIE ANYMORE! HE'S *IMAGINARY!* LIKE THE TOOTH FAIRY!
OH... A *PIGMENT* OF THE *IMAGINATION!*
NO, MOOSE! *FIGMENT!* A PIGMENT IS A *COLOR!*
WELL, *THAT* FIGMENT IS TURNING A *RED* PIGMENT!
I DON'T SEE ANY-THING!
OF COURSE, IF REG DID *EXIST*, HE'D BE PRETTY *MAD* BY NOW!
ONE THING AN *EGO* LIKE *HIS* CAN'T STAND IS BEING *IGNORED!*
IF HE WAS *REAL!*
WHICH HE'S *NOT!*
OOOH!
5

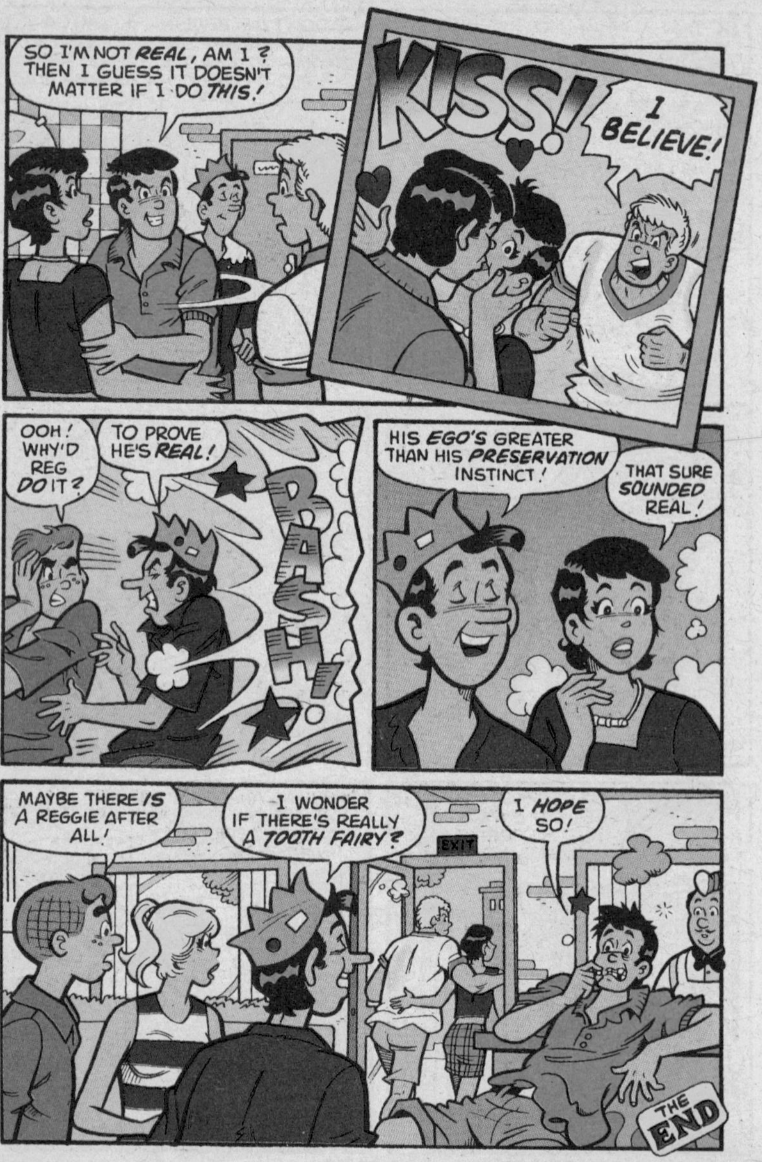
SO I'M NOT REAL, AM I? THEN I GUESS IT DOESN'T MATTER IF I DO THIS!
KISS!
I BELIEVE!
OOH! WHY'D REG DO IT?
TO PROVE HE'S REAL!
BASH!
HIS EGO'S GREATER THAN HIS PRESERVATION INSTINCT!
THAT SURE SOUNDED REAL!
MAYBE THERE IS A REGGIE AFTER ALL!
I WONDER IF THERE'S REALLY A TOOTH FAIRY?
EXIT
I HOPE SO!
THE END

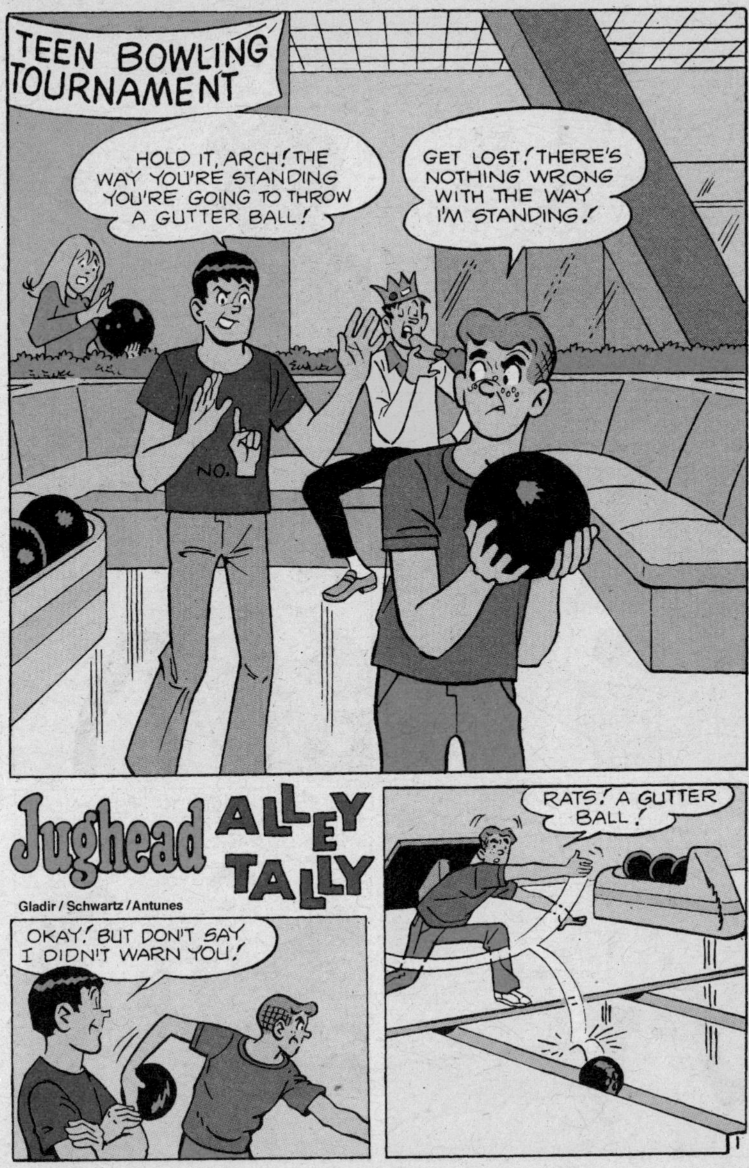

TEEN BOWLING TOURNAMENT
HOLD IT, ARCH! THE WAY YOU'RE STANDING YOU'RE GOING TO THROW A GUTTER BALL!
GET LOST! THERE'S NOTHING WRONG WITH THE WAY I'M STANDING!
NO.
Jughead
ALLEY TALLY
Gladir / Schwartz / Antunes
OKAY! BUT DON'T SAY I DIDN'T WARN YOU!
RATS! A GUTTER BALL!

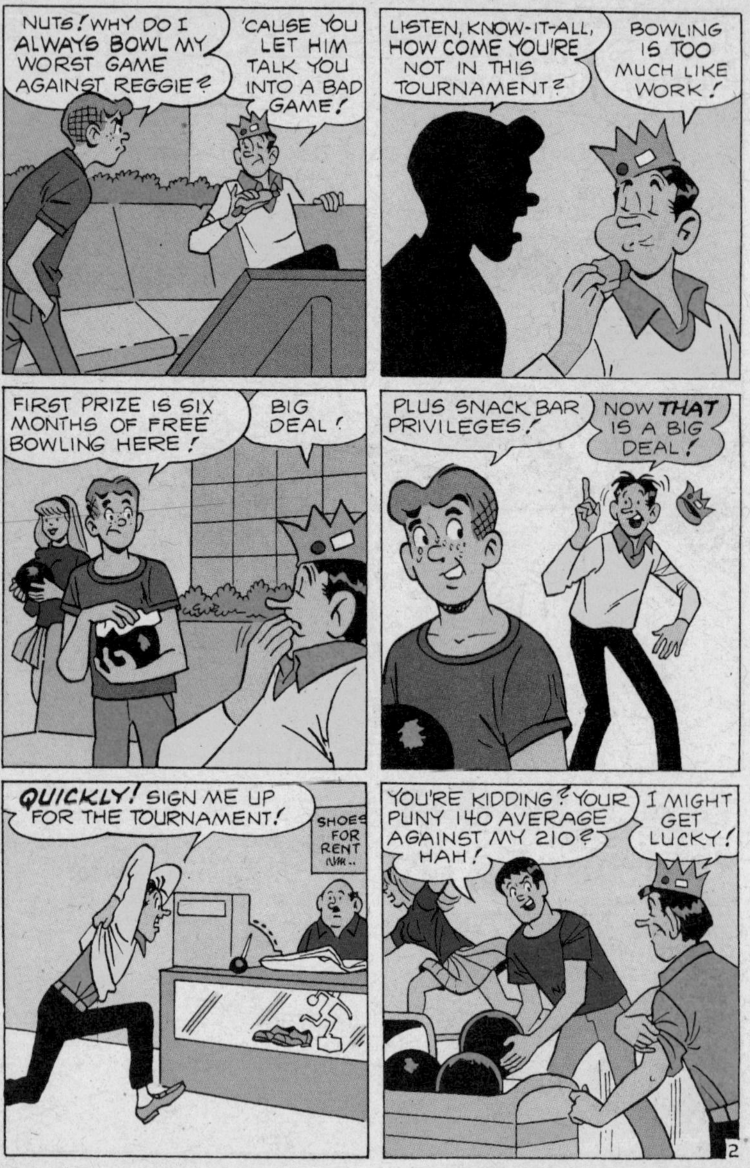
NUTS! WHY DO I ALWAYS BOWL MY WORST GAME AGAINST REGGIE?
'CAUSE YOU LET HIM TALK YOU INTO A BAD GAME!
LISTEN, KNOW-IT-ALL, HOW COME YOU'RE NOT IN THIS TOURNAMENT?
BOWLING IS TOO MUCH LIKE WORK!
FIRST PRIZE IS SIX MONTHS OF FREE BOWLING HERE!
BIG DEAL!
PLUS SNACK BAR PRIVILEGES!
NOW THAT IS A BIG DEAL!
QUICKLY! SIGN ME UP FOR THE TOURNAMENT!
SHOES FOR RENT
YOU'RE KIDDING? YOUR PUNY 140 AVERAGE AGAINST MY 210? HAH!
I MIGHT GET LUCKY!
2

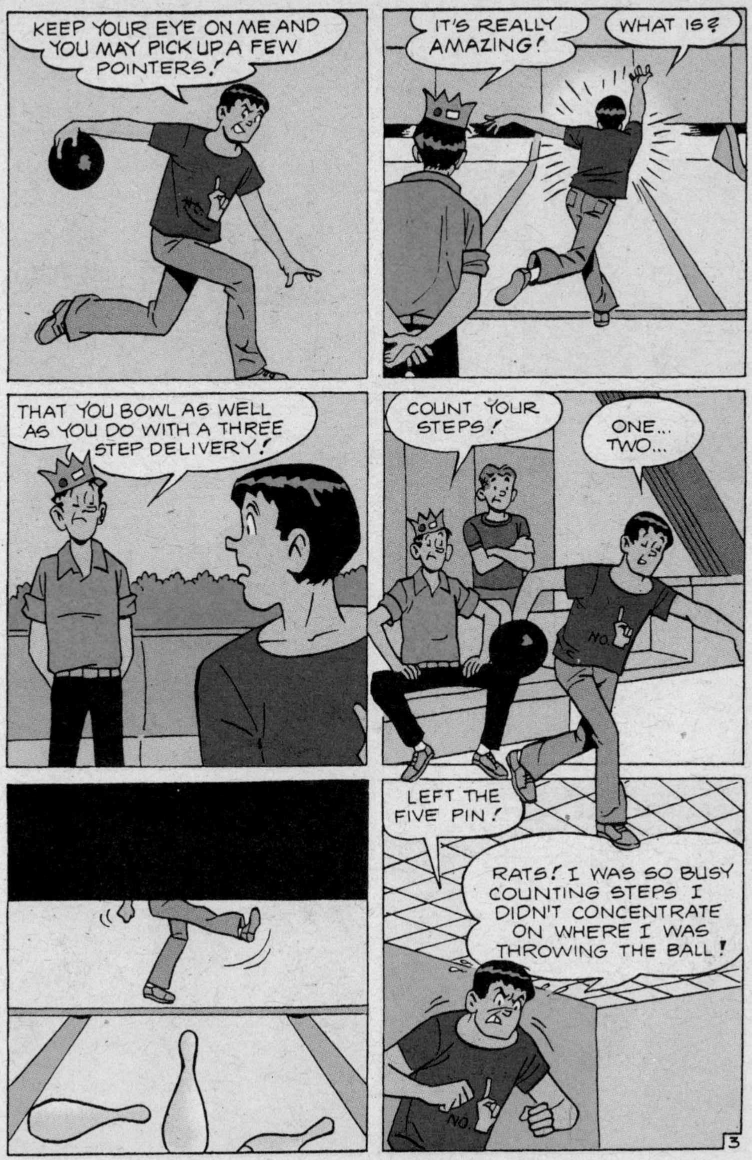
KEEP YOUR EYE ON ME AND YOU MAY PICK UP A FEW POINTERS!
IT'S REALLY AMAZING!
WHAT IS?
THAT YOU BOWL AS WELL AS YOU DO WITH A THREE STEP DELIVERY!
COUNT YOUR STEPS!
ONE... TWO...
NO.
LEFT THE FIVE PIN!
RATS! I WAS SO BUSY COUNTING STEPS I DIDN'T CONCENTRATE ON WHERE I WAS THROWING THE BALL!
NO.
3

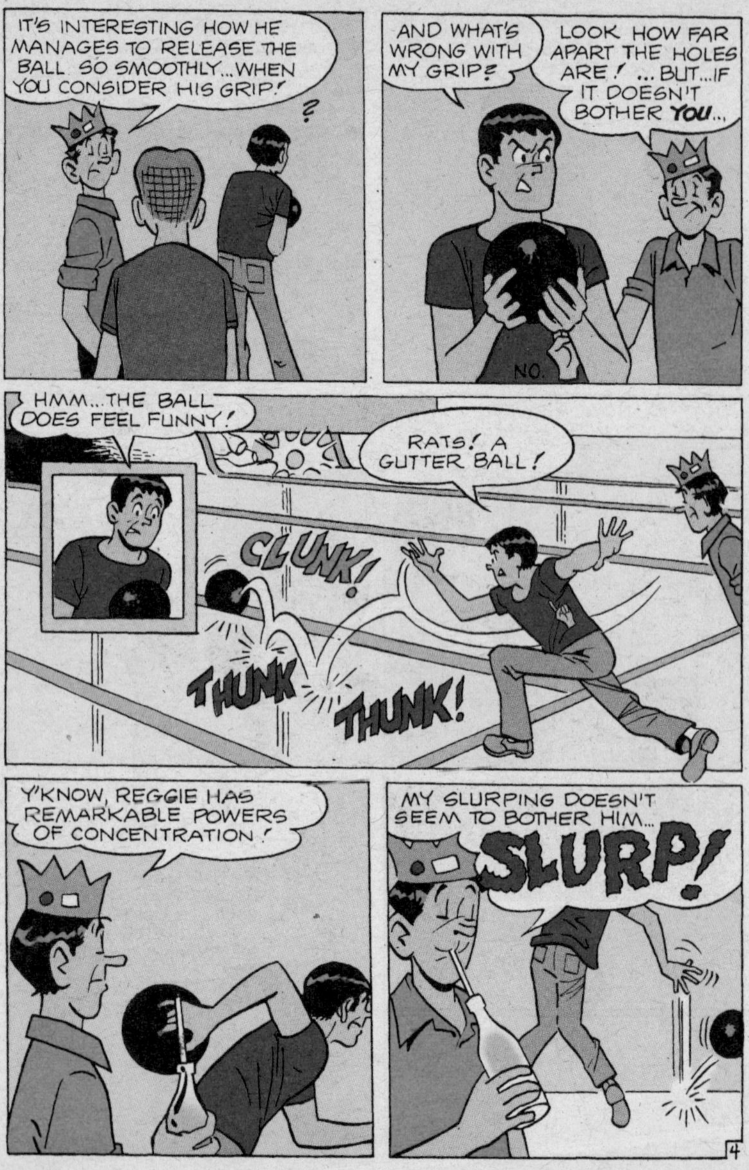

IT'S INTERESTING HOW HE MANAGES TO RELEASE THE BALL SO SMOOTHLY... WHEN YOU CONSIDER HIS GRIP!
?
AND WHAT'S WRONG WITH MY GRIP?
LOOK HOW FAR APART THE HOLES ARE! ... BUT... IF IT DOESN'T BOTHER **YOU**...
NO.
HMM... THE BALL DOES FEEL FUNNY!
RATS! A GUTTER BALL!
CLUNK!
THUNK
THUNK!
Y'KNOW, REGGIE HAS REMARKABLE POWERS OF CONCENTRATION!
MY SLURPING DOESN'T SEEM TO BOTHER HIM...
SLURP!

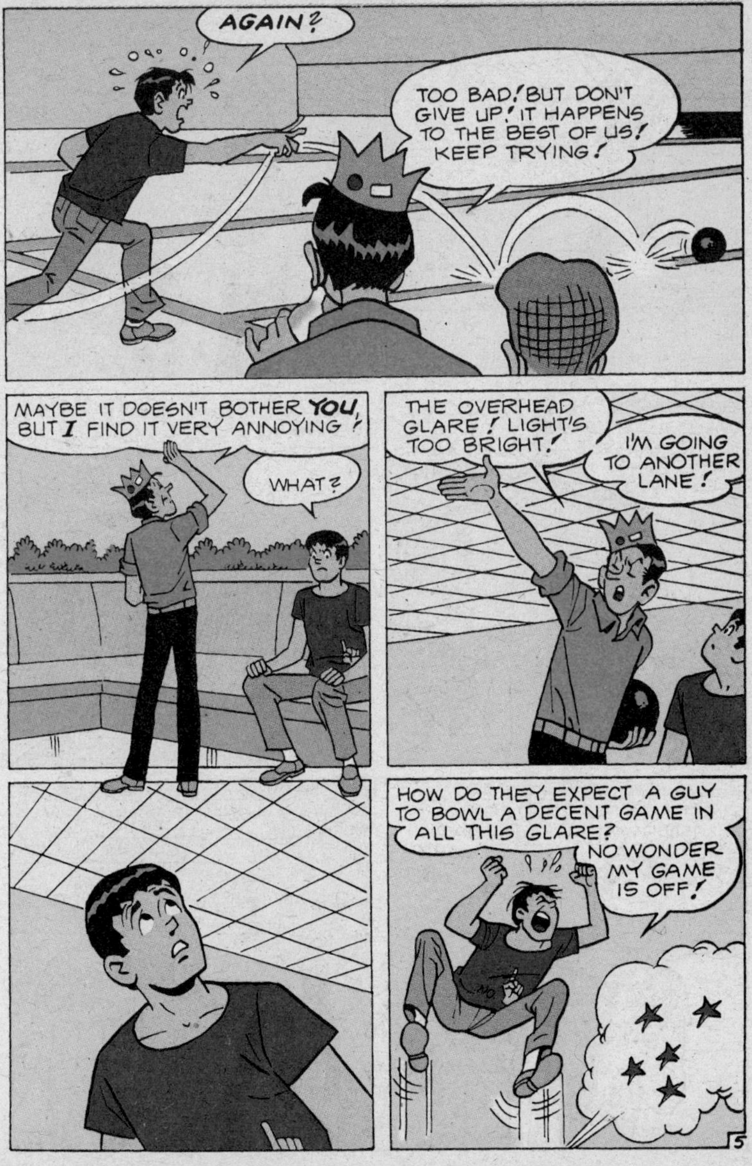
AGAIN?
TOO BAD! BUT DON'T GIVE UP! IT HAPPENS TO THE BEST OF US! KEEP TRYING!
MAYBE IT DOESN'T BOTHER YOU, BUT I FIND IT VERY ANNOYING!
WHAT?
THE OVERHEAD GLARE! LIGHT'S TOO BRIGHT!
I'M GOING TO ANOTHER LANE!
HOW DO THEY EXPECT A GUY TO BOWL A DECENT GAME IN ALL THIS GLARE?
NO WONDER MY GAME IS OFF!
5

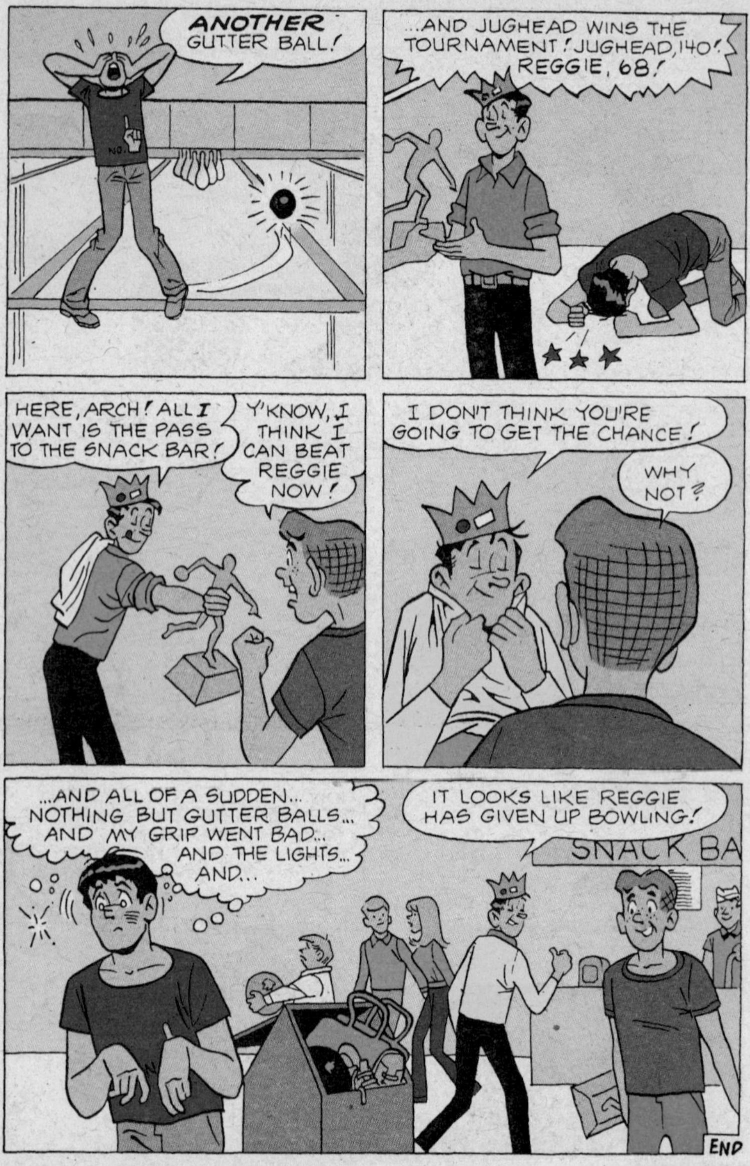
ANOTHER GUTTER BALL!
NO.
...AND JUGHEAD WINS THE TOURNAMENT! JUGHEAD, 140! REGGIE, 68!
HERE, ARCH! ALL I WANT IS THE PASS TO THE SNACK BAR!
Y'KNOW, I THINK I CAN BEAT REGGIE NOW!
I DON'T THINK YOU'RE GOING TO GET THE CHANCE!
WHY NOT?
...AND ALL OF A SUDDEN... NOTHING BUT GUTTER BALLS... AND MY GRIP WENT BAD... AND THE LIGHTS... AND...
IT LOOKS LIKE REGGIE HAS GIVEN UP BOWLING!
SNACK BA
END

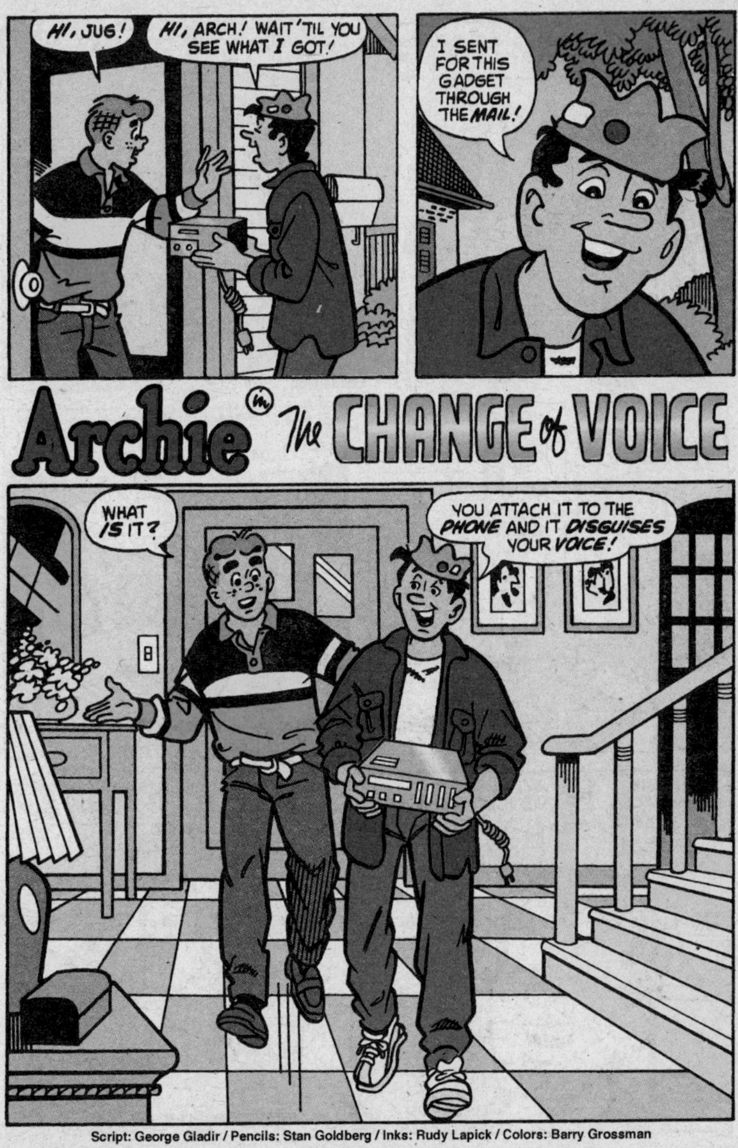
HI, JUG!
HI, ARCH! WAIT 'TIL YOU SEE WHAT I GOT!
I SENT FOR THIS GADGET THROUGH THE MAIL!
Archie in The CHANGE of VOICE
WHAT IS IT?
YOU ATTACH IT TO THE PHONE AND IT DISGUISES YOUR VOICE!

Script: George Gladir / Pencils: Stan Goldberg / Inks: Rudy Lapick / Colors: Barry Grossman

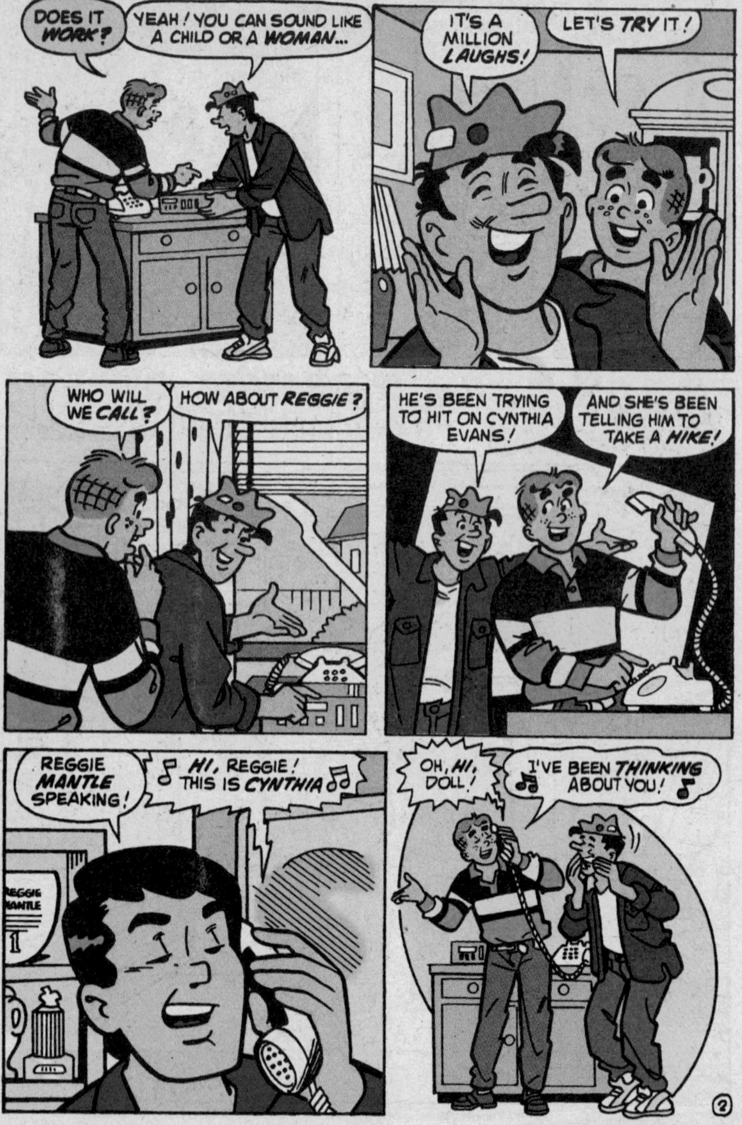
DOES IT WORK?
YEAH! YOU CAN SOUND LIKE A CHILD OR A WOMAN...
IT'S A MILLION LAUGHS!
LET'S TRY IT!
WHO WILL WE CALL?
HOW ABOUT REGGIE?
HE'S BEEN TRYING TO HIT ON CYNTHIA EVANS!
AND SHE'S BEEN TELLING HIM TO TAKE A HIKE!
REGGIE MANTLE SPEAKING!
HI, REGGIE! THIS IS CYNTHIA
REGGIE MANTLE
OH, HI, DOLL!
I'VE BEEN THINKING ABOUT YOU!
2

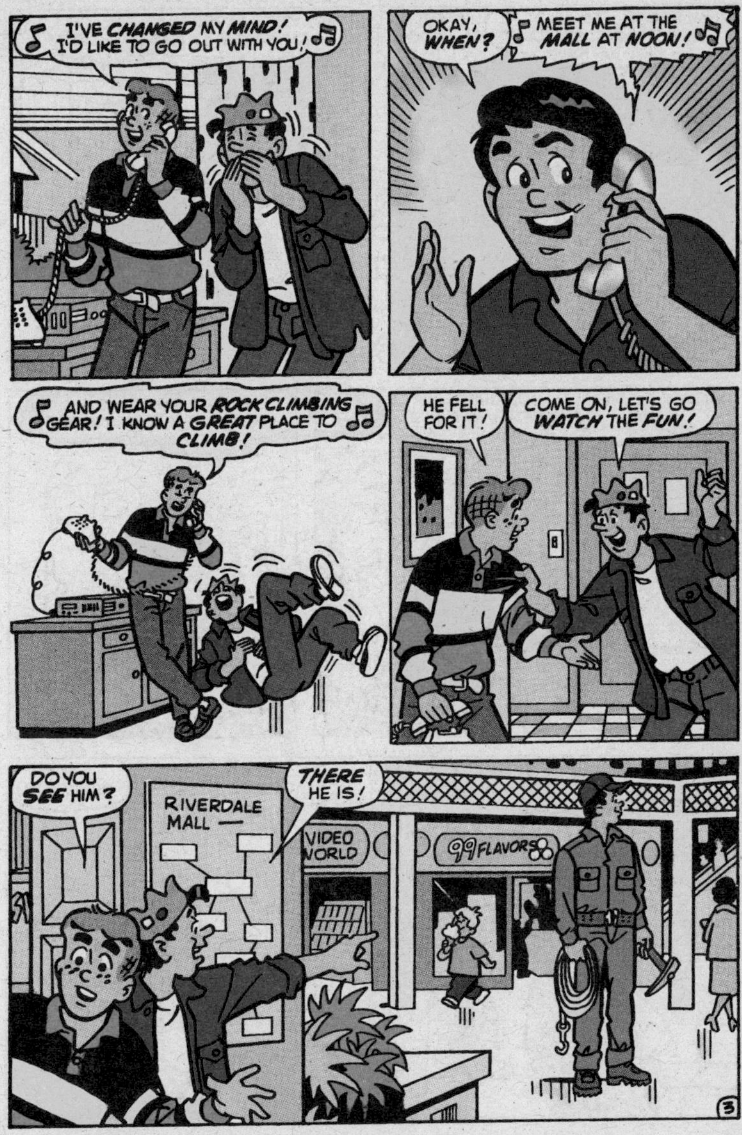
I'VE CHANGED MY MIND! I'D LIKE TO GO OUT WITH YOU!
OKAY, WHEN?
MEET ME AT THE MALL AT NOON!
AND WEAR YOUR ROCK CLIMBING GEAR! I KNOW A GREAT PLACE TO CLIMB!
HE FELL FOR IT!
COME ON, LET'S GO WATCH THE FUN!
DO YOU SEE HIM?
RIVERDALE MALL —
THERE HE IS!
VIDEO WORLD
99 FLAVORS
3

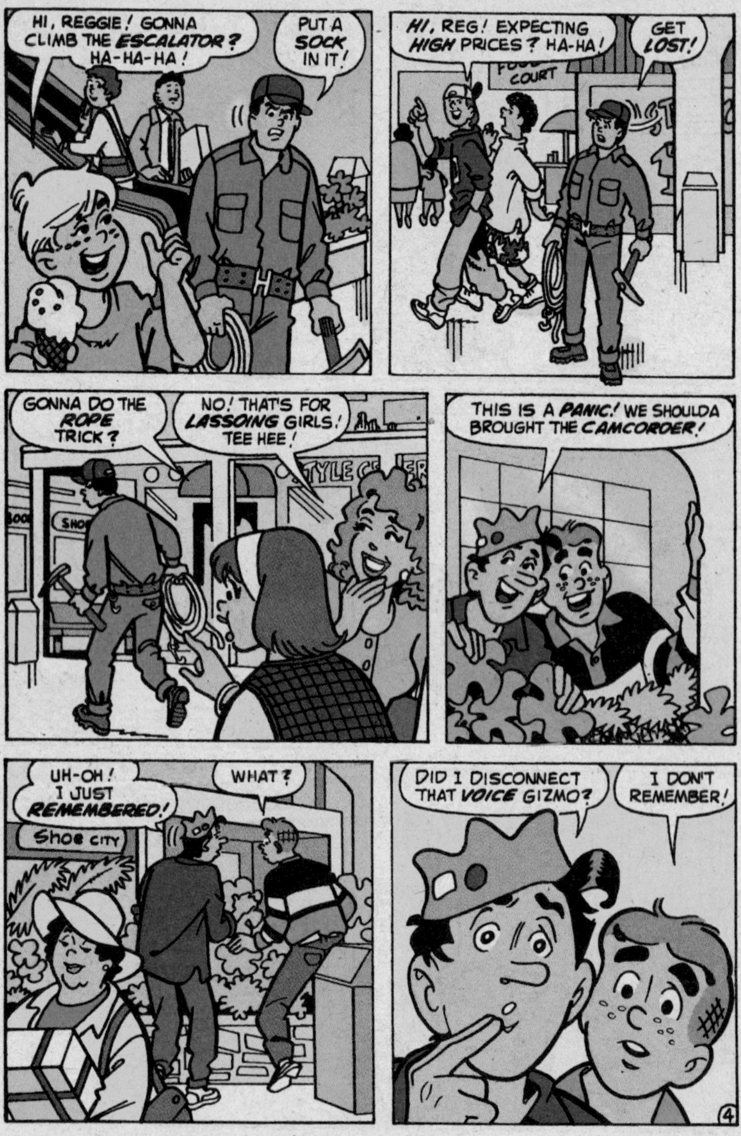
HI, REGGIE! GONNA CLIMB THE ESCALATOR? HA-HA-HA!
PUT A SOCK IN IT!
HI, REG! EXPECTING HIGH PRICES? HA-HA!
GET LOST!
FOOD COURT
GONNA DO THE ROPE TRICK?
NO! THAT'S FOR LASSOING GIRLS! TEE HEE!
THIS IS A PANIC! WE SHOULDA BROUGHT THE CAMCORDER!
UH-OH! I JUST REMEMBERED!
WHAT?
Shoe CITY
DID I DISCONNECT THAT VOICE GIZMO?
I DON'T REMEMBER!

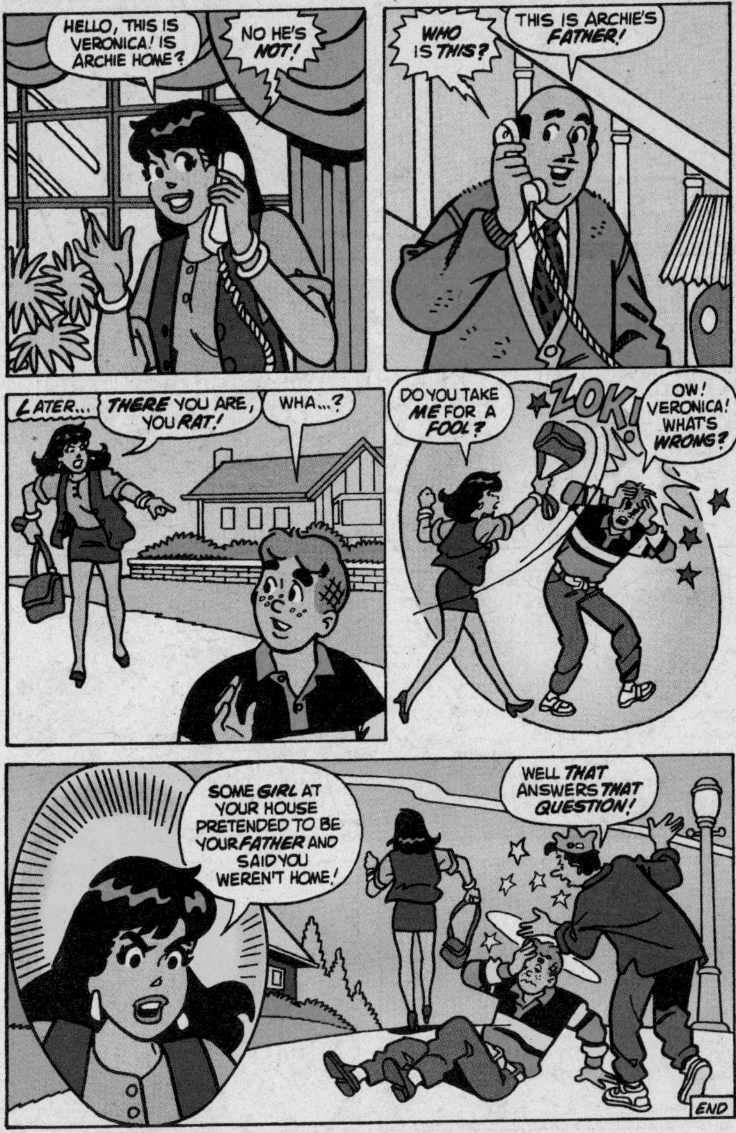
HELLO, THIS IS VERONICA! IS ARCHIE HOME?
NO HE'S NOT!
WHO IS THIS?
THIS IS ARCHIE'S FATHER!
LATER...
THERE YOU ARE, YOU RAT!
WHA...?
DO YOU TAKE ME FOR A FOOL?
ZOK!
OW! VERONICA! WHAT'S WRONG?
SOME GIRL AT YOUR HOUSE PRETENDED TO BE YOUR FATHER AND SAID YOU WEREN'T HOME!
WELL THAT ANSWERS THAT QUESTION!
END

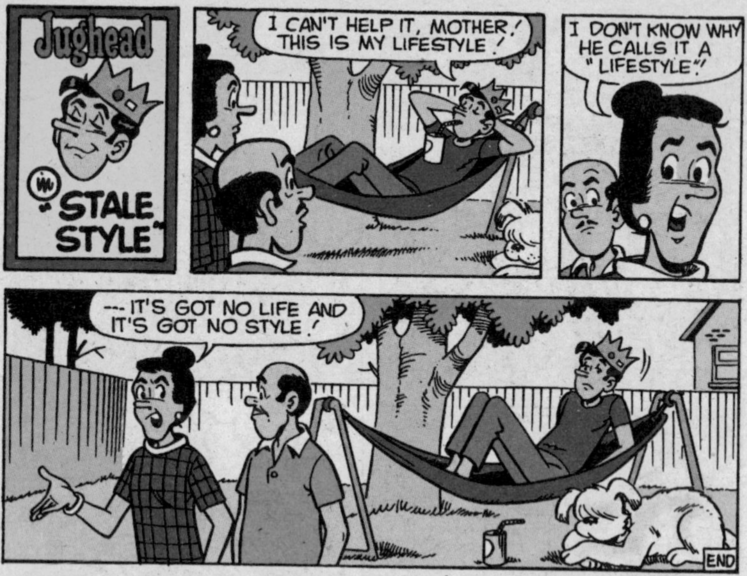
Jughead
in
"STALE STYLE"
I CAN'T HELP IT, MOTHER! THIS IS MY LIFESTYLE!
I DON'T KNOW WHY HE CALLS IT A "LIFESTYLE"!
--- IT'S GOT NO LIFE AND IT'S GOT NO STYLE!
END

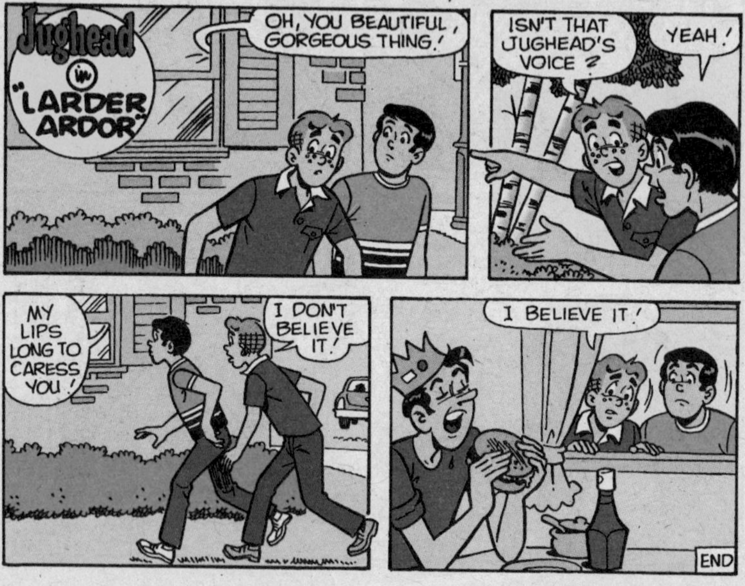
Jughead
in
"LARDER ARDOR"
OH, YOU BEAUTIFUL, GORGEOUS THING!
ISN'T THAT JUGHEAD'S VOICE?
YEAH!
MY LIPS LONG TO CARESS YOU!
I DON'T BELIEVE IT!
I BELIEVE IT!
END

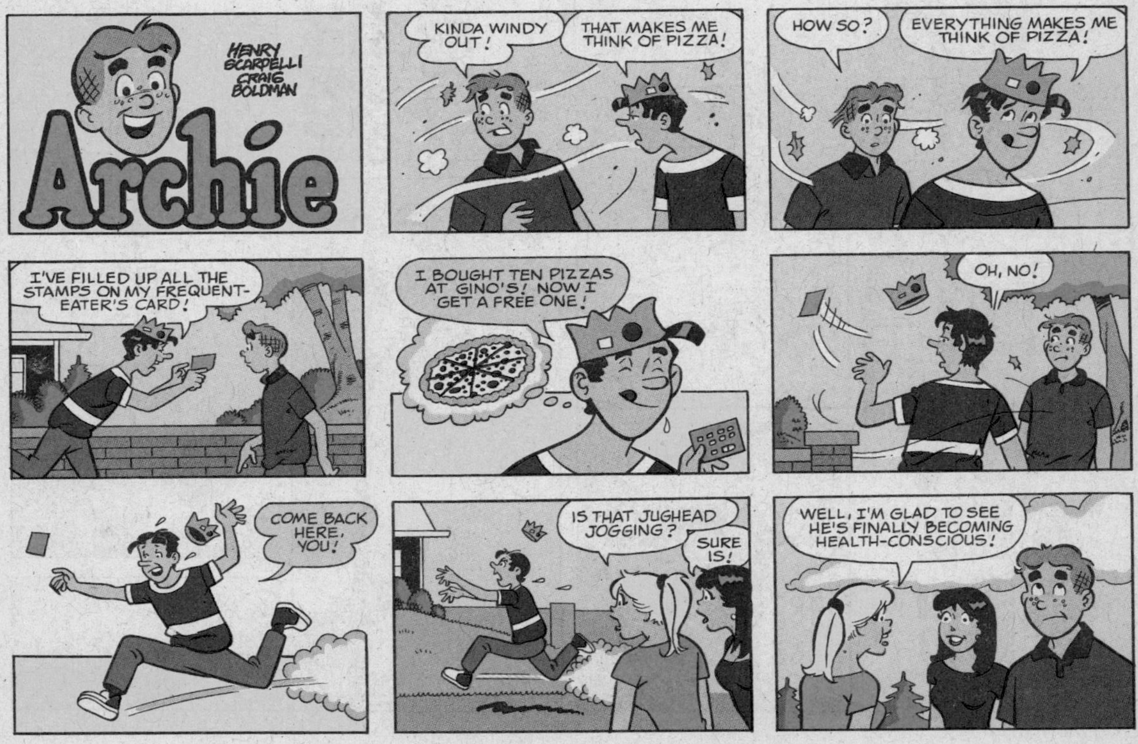
Archie
HENRY SCARPELLI
CRAIG BOLDMAN
KINDA WINDY OUT!
THAT MAKES ME THINK OF PIZZA!
HOW SO?
EVERYTHING MAKES ME THINK OF PIZZA!
I'VE FILLED UP ALL THE STAMPS ON MY FREQUENT-EATER'S CARD!
I BOUGHT TEN PIZZAS AT GINO'S! NOW I GET A FREE ONE!
OH, NO!
COME BACK HERE, YOU!
IS THAT JUGHEAD JOGGING?
SURE IS!
WELL, I'M GLAD TO SEE HE'S FINALLY BECOMING HEALTH-CONSCIOUS!

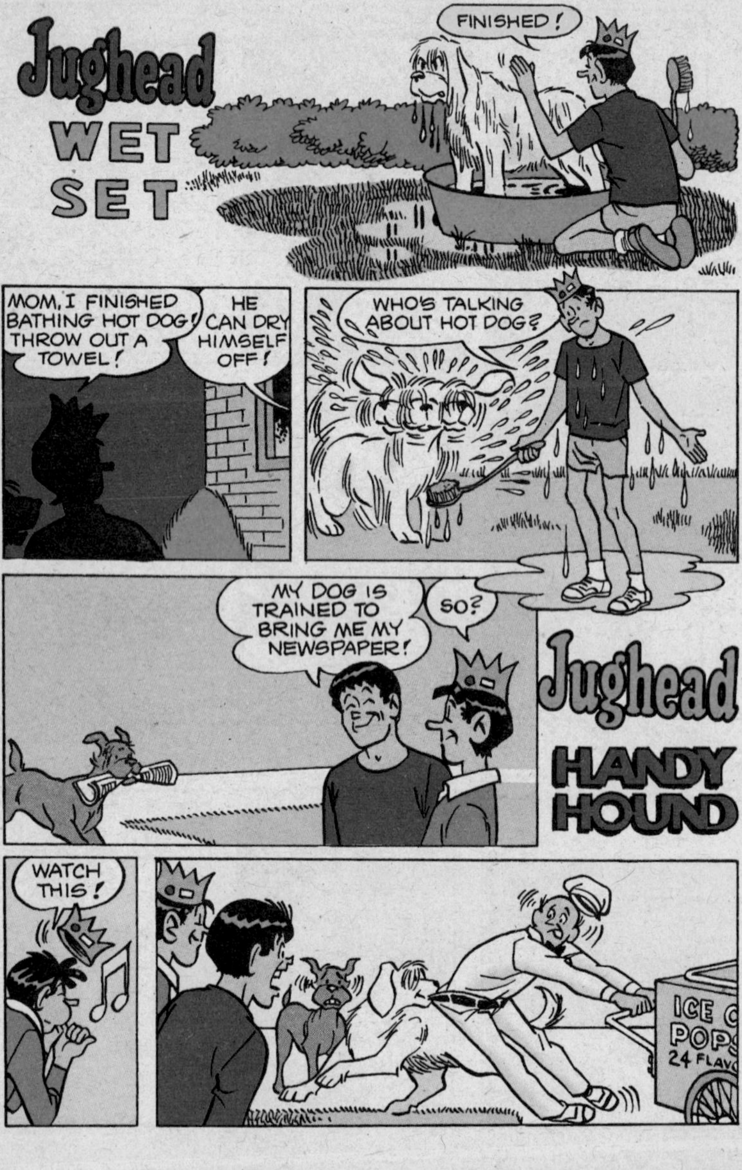

Jughead
WET SET
FINISHED!
MOM, I FINISHED BATHING HOT DOG! THROW OUT A TOWEL!
HE CAN DRY HIMSELF OFF!
WHO'S TALKING ABOUT HOT DOG?
Jughead
HANDY HOUND
MY DOG IS TRAINED TO BRING ME MY NEWSPAPER!
SO?
WATCH THIS!
ICE C
POPS
24 FLAVO

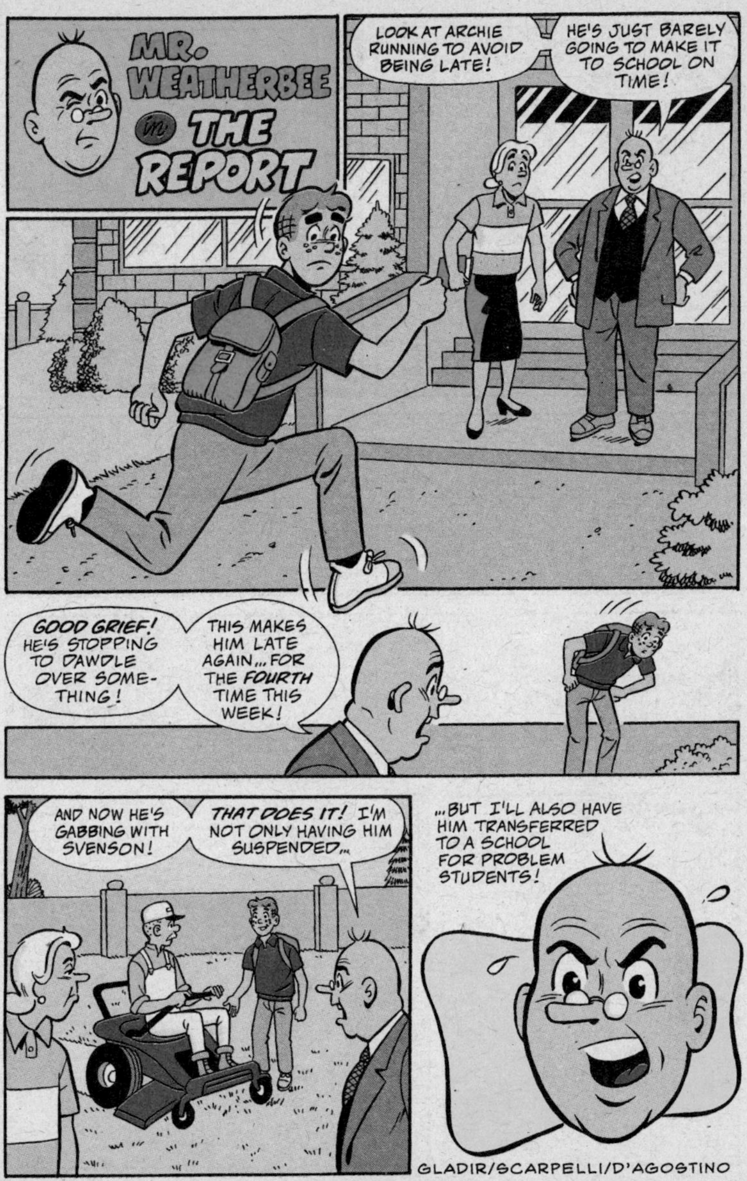
MR. WEATHERBEE in THE REPORT
LOOK AT ARCHIE RUNNING TO AVOID BEING LATE!
HE'S JUST BARELY GOING TO MAKE IT TO SCHOOL ON TIME!
GOOD GRIEF! HE'S STOPPING TO DAWDLE OVER SOMETHING!
THIS MAKES HIM LATE AGAIN... FOR THE FOURTH TIME THIS WEEK!
AND NOW HE'S GABBING WITH SVENSON!
THAT DOES IT! I'M NOT ONLY HAVING HIM SUSPENDED...
...BUT I'LL ALSO HAVE HIM TRANSFERRED TO A SCHOOL FOR PROBLEM STUDENTS!
GLADIR/SCARPELLI/D'AGOSTINO

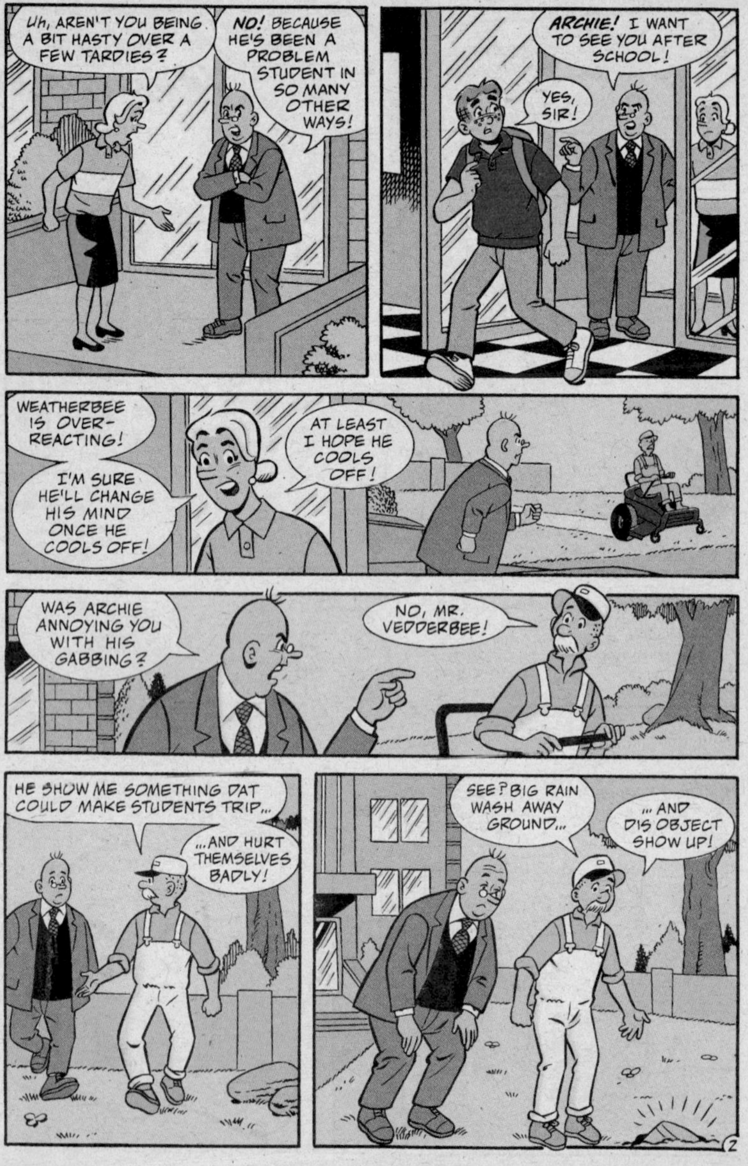
UH, AREN'T YOU BEING A BIT HASTY OVER A FEW TARDIES?
NO! BECAUSE HE'S BEEN A PROBLEM STUDENT IN SO MANY OTHER WAYS!
ARCHIE! I WANT TO SEE YOU AFTER SCHOOL!
YES, SIR!
WEATHERBEE IS OVER-REACTING!
I'M SURE HE'LL CHANGE HIS MIND ONCE HE COOLS OFF!
AT LEAST I HOPE HE COOLS OFF!
WAS ARCHIE ANNOYING YOU WITH HIS GABBING?
NO, MR. VEDDERBEE!
HE SHOW ME SOMETHING DAT COULD MAKE STUDENTS TRIP...
...AND HURT THEMSELVES BADLY!
SEE? BIG RAIN WASH AWAY GROUND...
...AND DIS OBJECT SHOW UP!
2

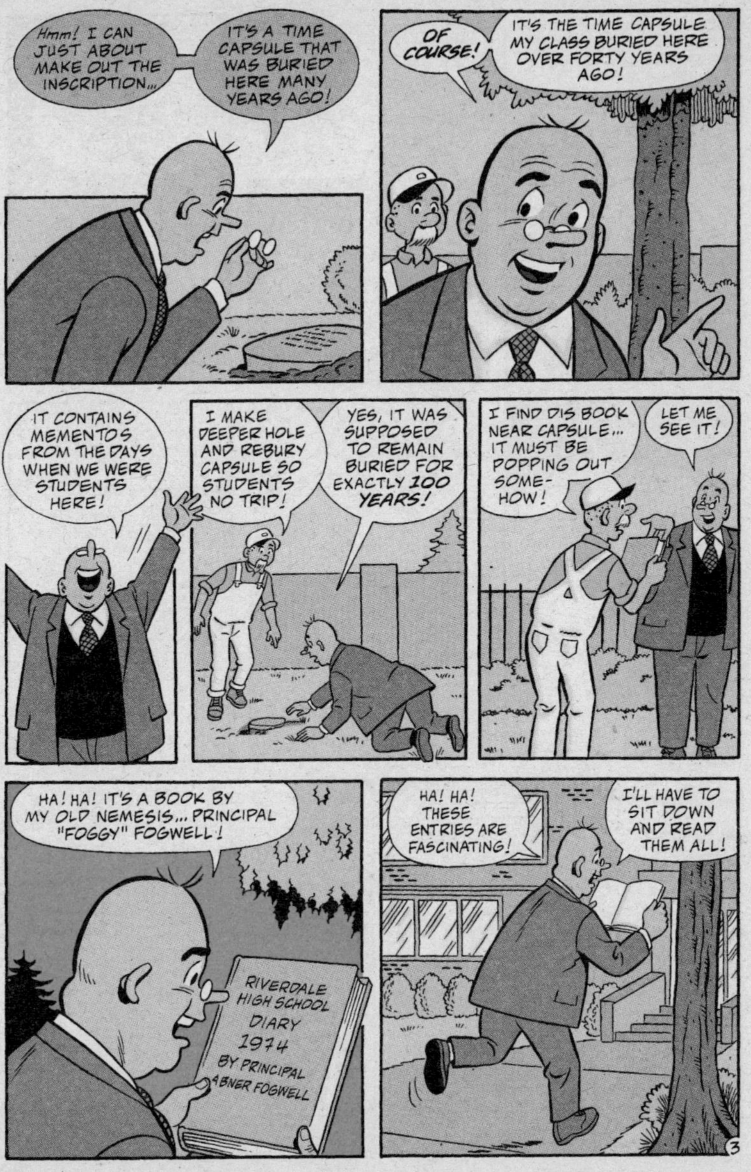
Hmm! I CAN JUST ABOUT MAKE OUT THE INSCRIPTION...
IT'S A TIME CAPSULE THAT WAS BURIED HERE MANY YEARS AGO!
OF COURSE!
IT'S THE TIME CAPSULE MY CLASS BURIED HERE OVER FORTY YEARS AGO!
IT CONTAINS MEMENTOS FROM THE DAYS WHEN WE WERE STUDENTS HERE!
I MAKE DEEPER HOLE AND REBURY CAPSULE SO STUDENTS NO TRIP!
YES, IT WAS SUPPOSED TO REMAIN BURIED FOR EXACTLY 100 YEARS!
I FIND DIS BOOK NEAR CAPSULE... IT MUST BE POPPING OUT SOME-HOW!
LET ME SEE IT!
HA! HA! IT'S A BOOK BY MY OLD NEMESIS... PRINCIPAL "FOGGY" FOGWELL!
RIVERDALE HIGH SCHOOL DIARY 1974 BY PRINCIPAL ABNER FOGWELL
HA! HA! THESE ENTRIES ARE FASCINATING!
I'LL HAVE TO SIT DOWN AND READ THEM ALL!
3

HERE'S AN ENTRY ABOUT ME AND MY DISRUPTIVE BEHAVIOR AT OUR HOMECOMING GAME!

"DISRUPTIVE BEHAVIOR" INDEED... ALL I DID THAT DAY WAS PLAY SOME HARMLESS SCHOOLBOY PRANK!

RIVERDALE HIGH SCHOOL DIARY 1974 BY PRINCIPAL ABNER FOGWELL

WHAT'S THIS...? GOOD GRIEF!

PRINCIPAL FOGWELL GOES ON TO COMPLAIN ABOUT MY "CHRONIC LATENESS"!

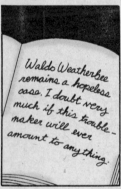

Waldo Weatherbee remains a hopeless case. I doubt very much if this trouble-maker will ever amount to anything.

Hmpf! I MANAGED TO BECOME THE PRINCIPAL OF OUR SCHOOL... I GUESS I SHOWED "FOGGY" FOGWELL!

I JUST WANTED TO REPORT ON OUR UPCOMING BAKE SALE!

Ahh! MS. HAGGLY! COME ON IN!

THE SALE PROMISES TO BE A HUGE SUCCESS...

...THANKS TO THE EFFORTS OF STUDENTS LIKE ARCHIE ANDREWS!

ARCHIE?

YES, THE POOR LAD HAS BEEN WORKING FOR US EVERY NIGHT THIS WEEK...

...DON'T THINK HE WAS ABLE TO GET VERY MUCH SLEEP!

Hmmm!

4

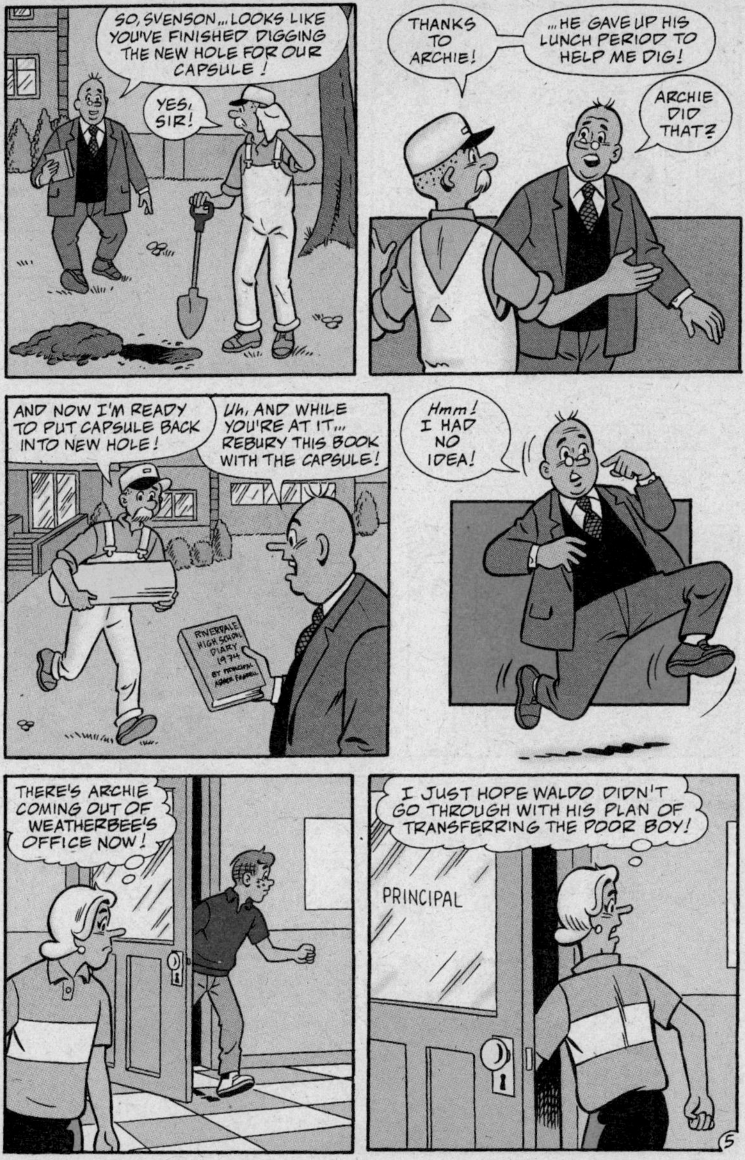
SO, SVENSON... LOOKS LIKE YOU'VE FINISHED DIGGING THE NEW HOLE FOR OUR CAPSULE!
YES, SIR!
THANKS TO ARCHIE!
...HE GAVE UP HIS LUNCH PERIOD TO HELP ME DIG!
ARCHIE DID THAT?
AND NOW I'M READY TO PUT CAPSULE BACK INTO NEW HOLE!
Uh, AND WHILE YOU'RE AT IT... REBURY THIS BOOK WITH THE CAPSULE!
RIVERDALE HIGH SCHOOL DIARY 1974
Hmm! I HAD NO IDEA!
THERE'S ARCHIE COMING OUT OF WEATHERBEE'S OFFICE NOW!
I JUST HOPE WALDO DIDN'T GO THROUGH WITH HIS PLAN OF TRANSFERRING THE POOR BOY!
PRINCIPAL
5

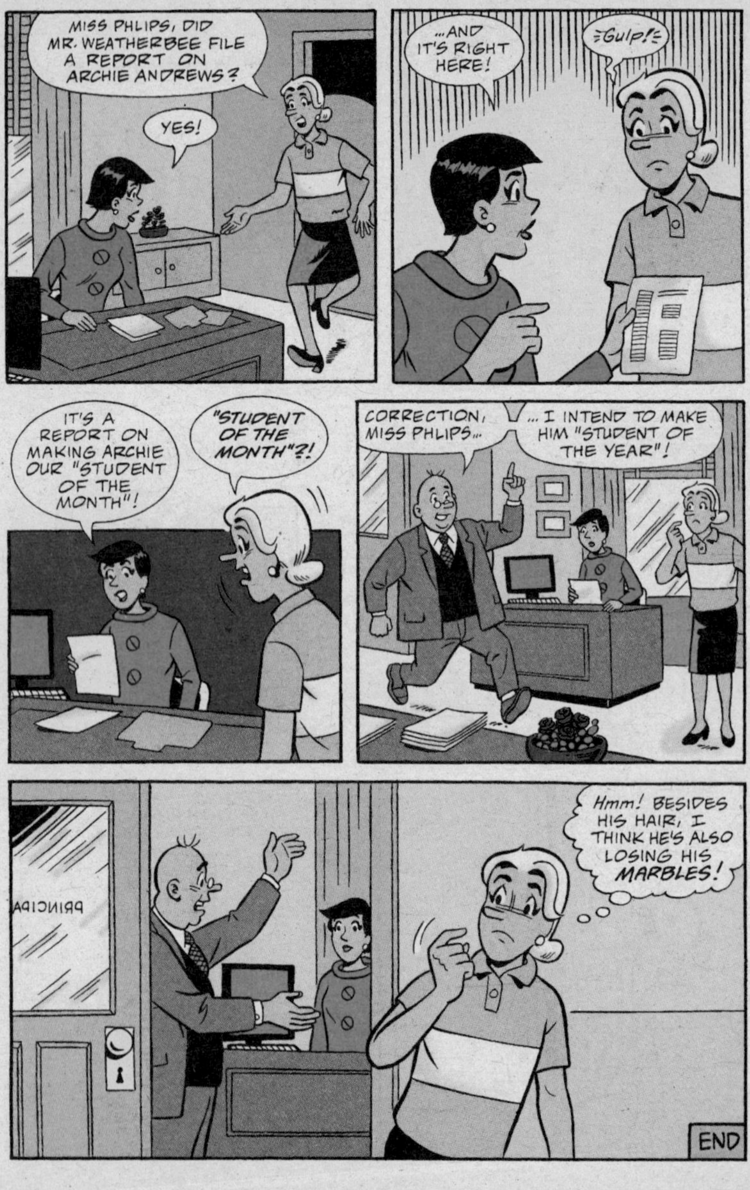

MISS PHLIPS, DID MR. WEATHERBEE FILE A REPORT ON ARCHIE ANDREWS?
YES!
...AND IT'S RIGHT HERE!
Gulp!
IT'S A REPORT ON MAKING ARCHIE OUR "STUDENT OF THE MONTH"!
"STUDENT OF THE MONTH"?!
CORRECTION, MISS PHLIPS...
...I INTEND TO MAKE HIM "STUDENT OF THE YEAR"!
PRINCIPA
Hmm! BESIDES HIS HAIR, I THINK HE'S ALSO LOSING HIS MARBLES!
END

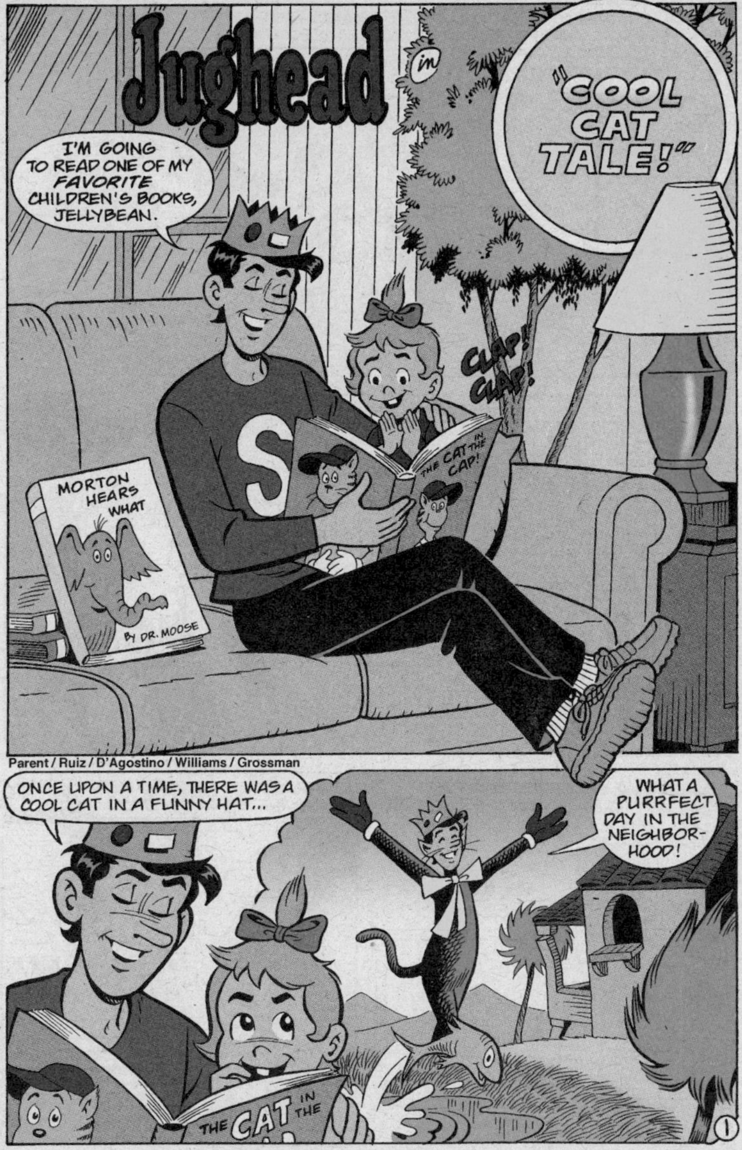
Jughead in
"COOL CAT TALE!"
I'M GOING TO READ ONE OF MY FAVORITE CHILDREN'S BOOKS, JELLYBEAN.
CLAP! CLAP!
THE CAT IN THE CAP!
MORTON HEARS WHAT
BY DR. MOOSE
Parent / Ruiz / D'Agostino / Williams / Grossman
ONCE UPON A TIME, THERE WAS A COOL CAT IN A FUNNY HAT...
WHAT A PURRFECT DAY IN THE NEIGHBOR-HOOD!
THE CAT IN THE
1

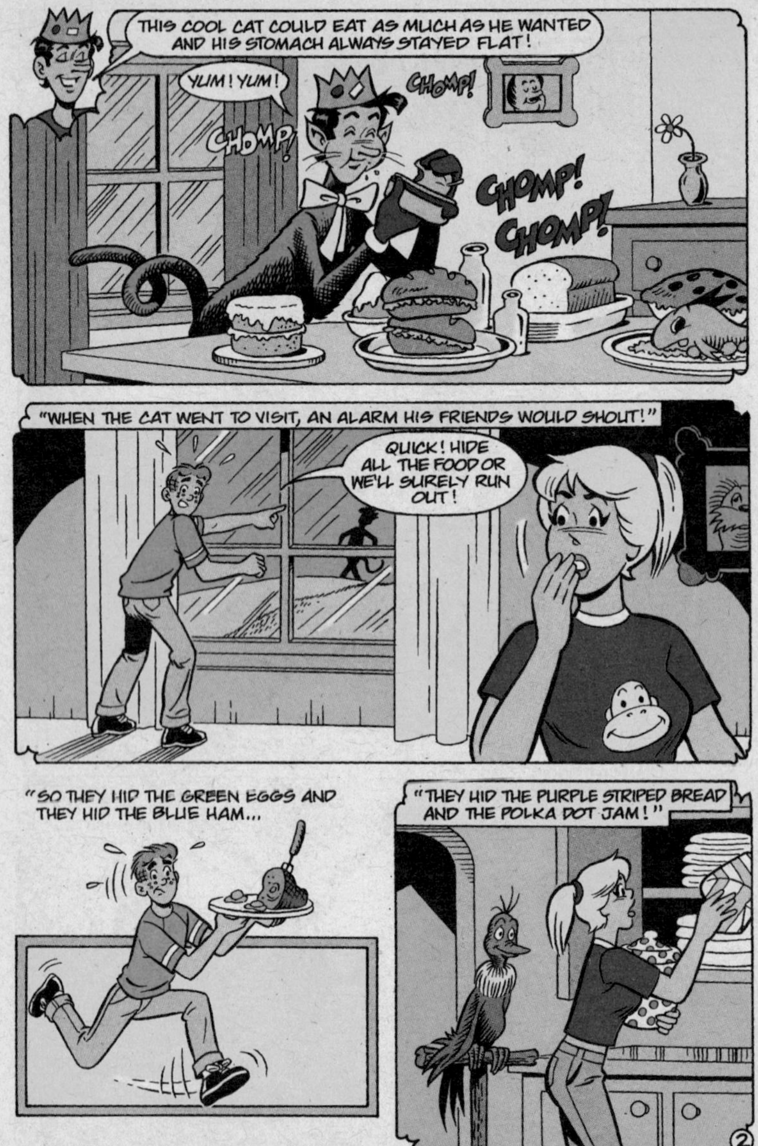
THIS COOL CAT COULD EAT AS MUCH AS HE WANTED AND HIS STOMACH ALWAYS STAYED FLAT!
YUM! YUM!
CHOMP!
CHOMP!
CHOMP!
CHOMP!
"WHEN THE CAT WENT TO VISIT, AN ALARM HIS FRIENDS WOULD SHOUT!"
QUICK! HIDE ALL THE FOOD OR WE'LL SURELY RUN OUT!
"SO THEY HID THE GREEN EGGS AND THEY HID THE BLUE HAM...
"THEY HID THE PURPLE STRIPED BREAD AND THE POLKA DOT JAM!"

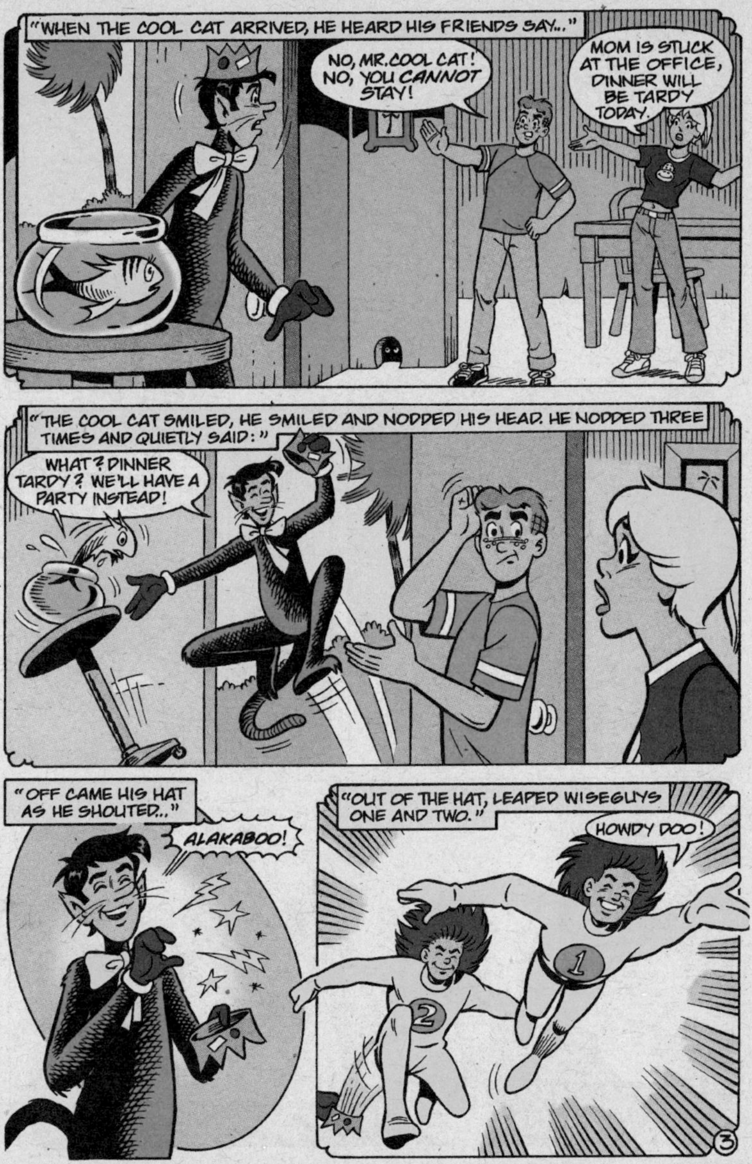
"WHEN THE COOL CAT ARRIVED, HE HEARD HIS FRIENDS SAY..."
NO, MR. COOL CAT! NO, YOU CANNOT STAY!
MOM IS STUCK AT THE OFFICE, DINNER WILL BE TARDY TODAY.
"THE COOL CAT SMILED, HE SMILED AND NODDED HIS HEAD. HE NODDED THREE TIMES AND QUIETLY SAID:"
WHAT? DINNER TARDY? WE'LL HAVE A PARTY INSTEAD!
"OFF CAME HIS HAT AS HE SHOUTED..."
ALAKABOO!
"OUT OF THE HAT, LEAPED WISEGUYS ONE AND TWO."
HOWDY DOO!
1
2
3

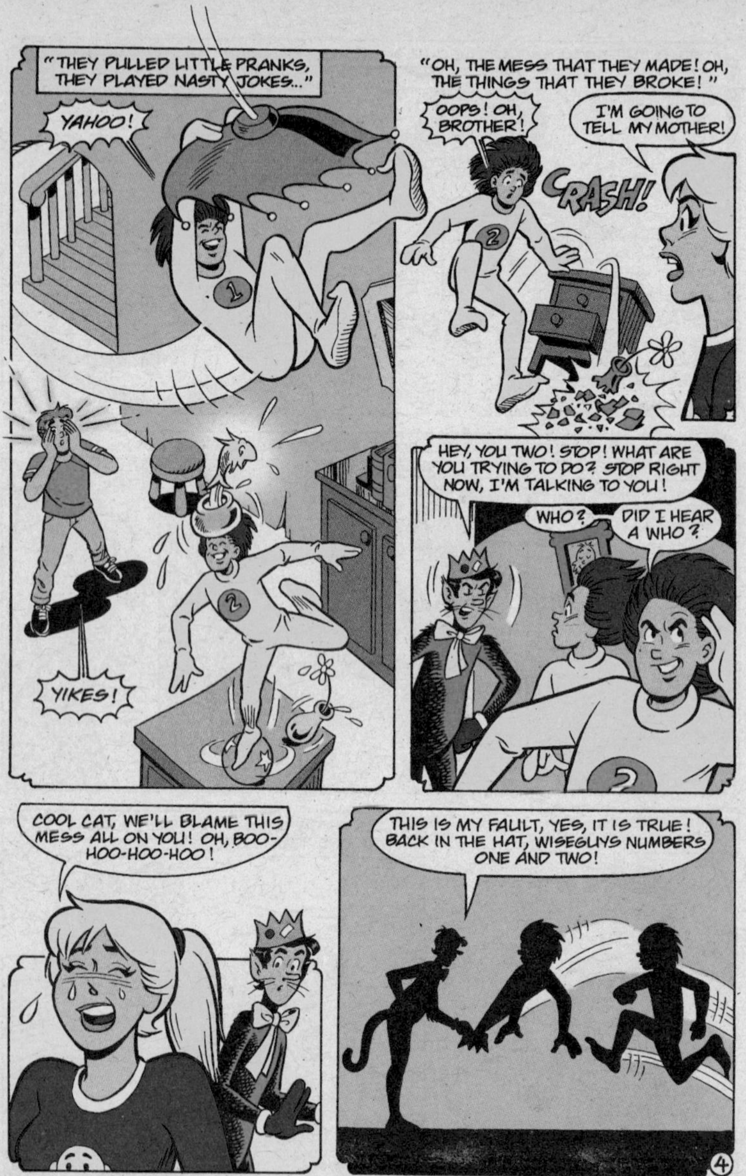
"THEY PULLED LITTLE PRANKS, THEY PLAYED NASTY JOKES..."
YAHOO!
YIKES!
"OH, THE MESS THAT THEY MADE! OH, THE THINGS THAT THEY BROKE!"
OOPS! OH, BROTHER!
I'M GOING TO TELL MY MOTHER!
CRASH!
HEY, YOU TWO! STOP! WHAT ARE YOU TRYING TO DO? STOP RIGHT NOW, I'M TALKING TO YOU!
WHO?
DID I HEAR A WHO?
COOL CAT, WE'LL BLAME THIS MESS ALL ON YOU! OH, BOO-HOO-HOO-HOO!
THIS IS MY FAULT, YES, IT IS TRUE! BACK IN THE HAT, WISEGUYS NUMBERS ONE AND TWO!
4

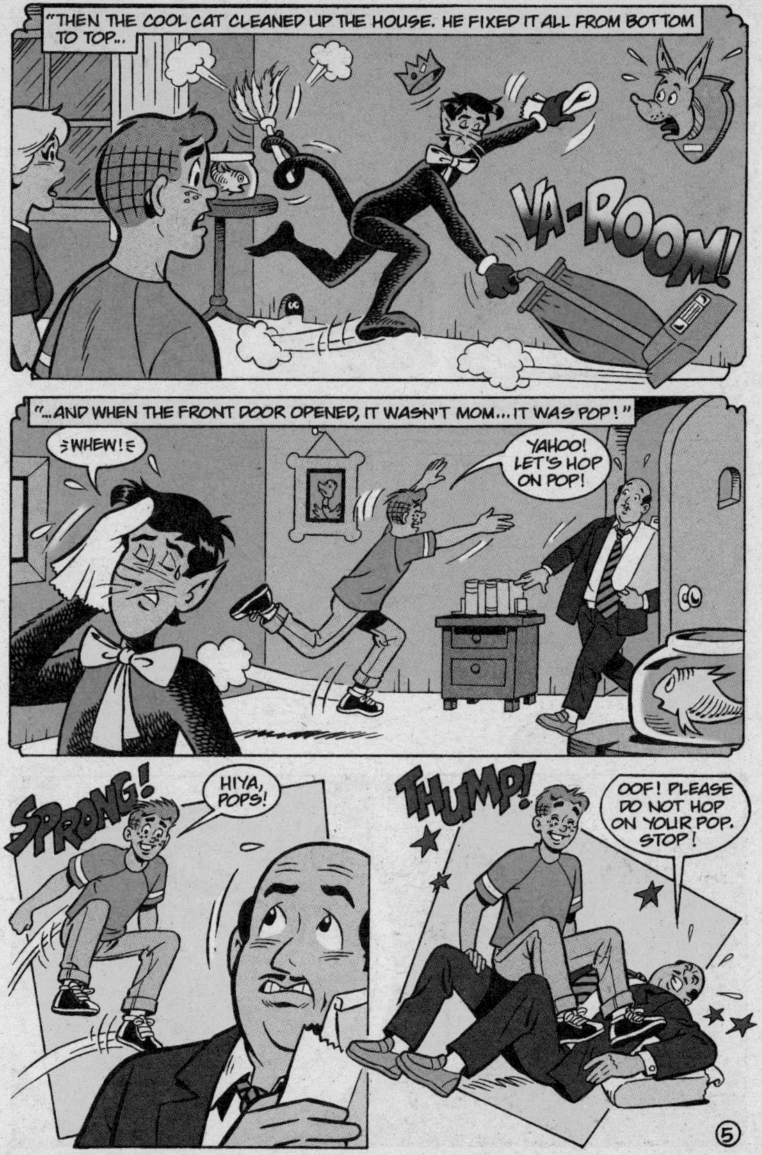
"THEN THE COOL CAT CLEANED UP THE HOUSE. HE FIXED IT ALL FROM BOTTOM TO TOP...
VA-ROOM!
"...AND WHEN THE FRONT DOOR OPENED, IT WASN'T MOM... IT WAS POP!"
WHEW!
YAHOO! LET'S HOP ON POP!
SPRONG!
HIYA, POPS!
THUMP!
OOF! PLEASE DO NOT HOP ON YOUR POP. STOP!

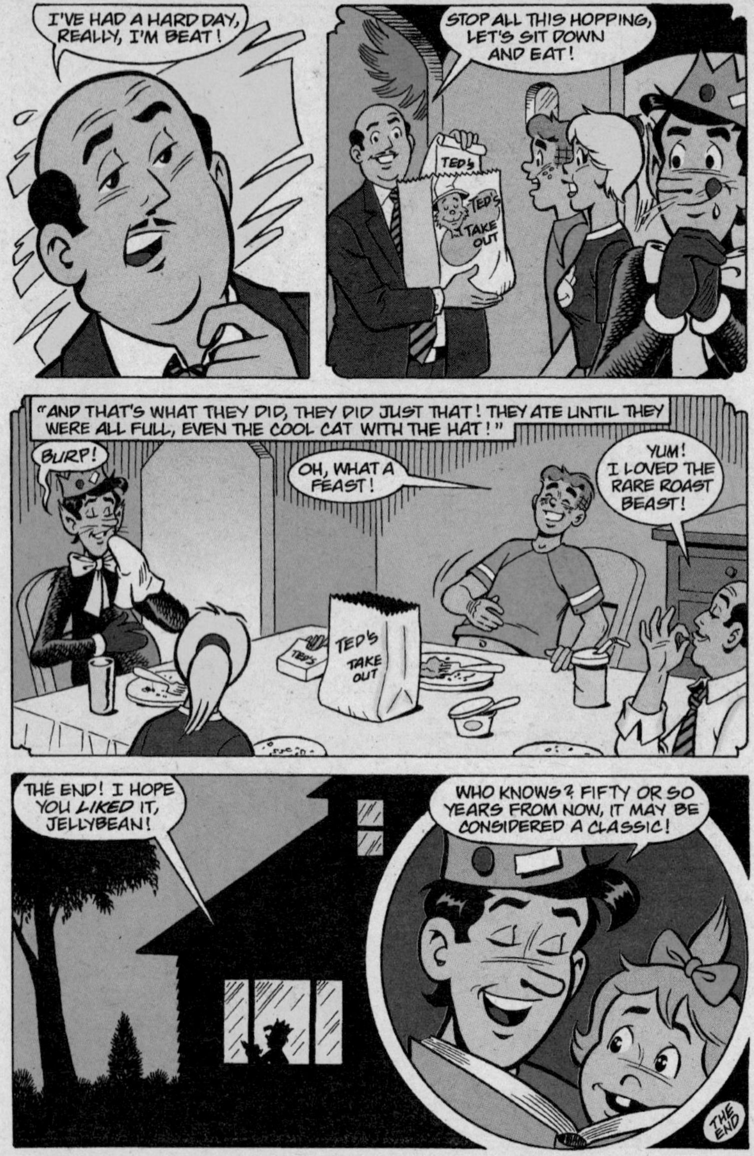
I'VE HAD A HARD DAY, REALLY, I'M BEAT!
STOP ALL THIS HOPPING, LET'S SIT DOWN AND EAT!
TED'S
TED'S TAKE OUT
"AND THAT'S WHAT THEY DID, THEY DID JUST THAT! THEY ATE UNTIL THEY WERE ALL FULL, EVEN THE COOL CAT WITH THE HAT!"
BURP!
OH, WHAT A FEAST!
YUM! I LOVED THE RARE ROAST BEAST!
TED'S TAKE OUT
THE END! I HOPE YOU LIKED IT, JELLYBEAN!
WHO KNOWS? FIFTY OR SO YEARS FROM NOW, IT MAY BE CONSIDERED A CLASSIC!
THE END

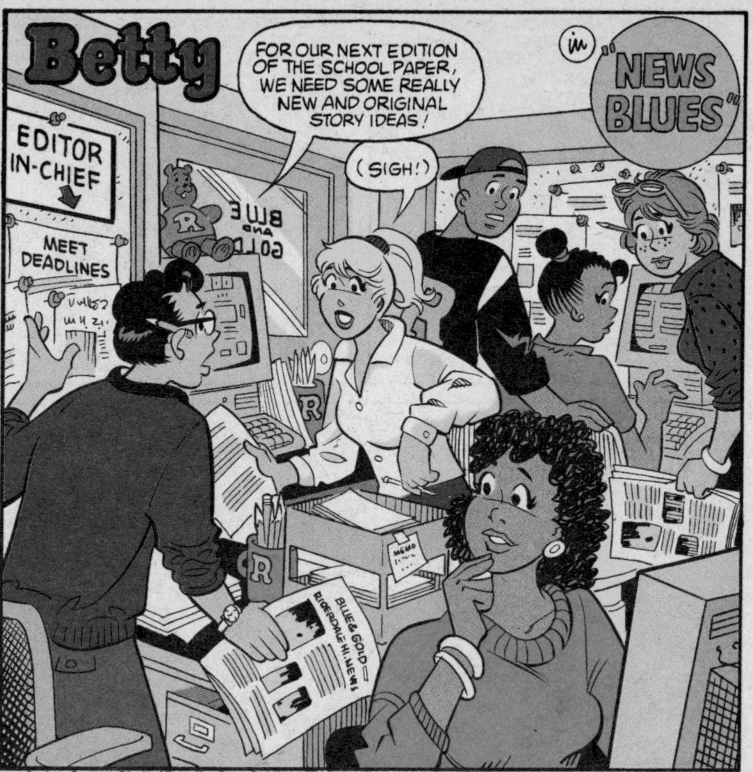
Betty
in "NEWS BLUES"
FOR OUR NEXT EDITION OF THE SCHOOL PAPER, WE NEED SOME REALLY NEW AND ORIGINAL STORY IDEAS!
(SIGH!)
EDITOR IN-CHIEF
MEET DEADLINES
BLUE & GOLD
RIVERDALE HI. NEWS

Script: George Gladir / Pencils: Stan Goldberg / Inks: John Lowe / Letters: Bill Yoshida / Colors: Barry Grossman

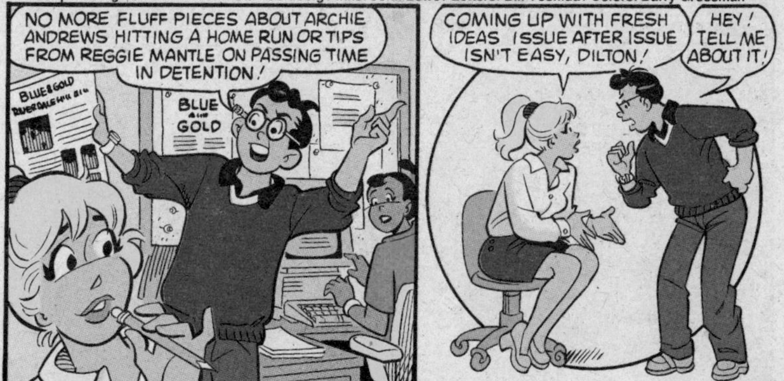
NO MORE FLUFF PIECES ABOUT ARCHIE ANDREWS HITTING A HOME RUN OR TIPS FROM REGGIE MANTLE ON PASSING TIME IN DETENTION!
BLUE AND GOLD
COMING UP WITH FRESH IDEAS ISSUE AFTER ISSUE ISN'T EASY, DILTON!
HEY! TELL ME ABOUT IT!

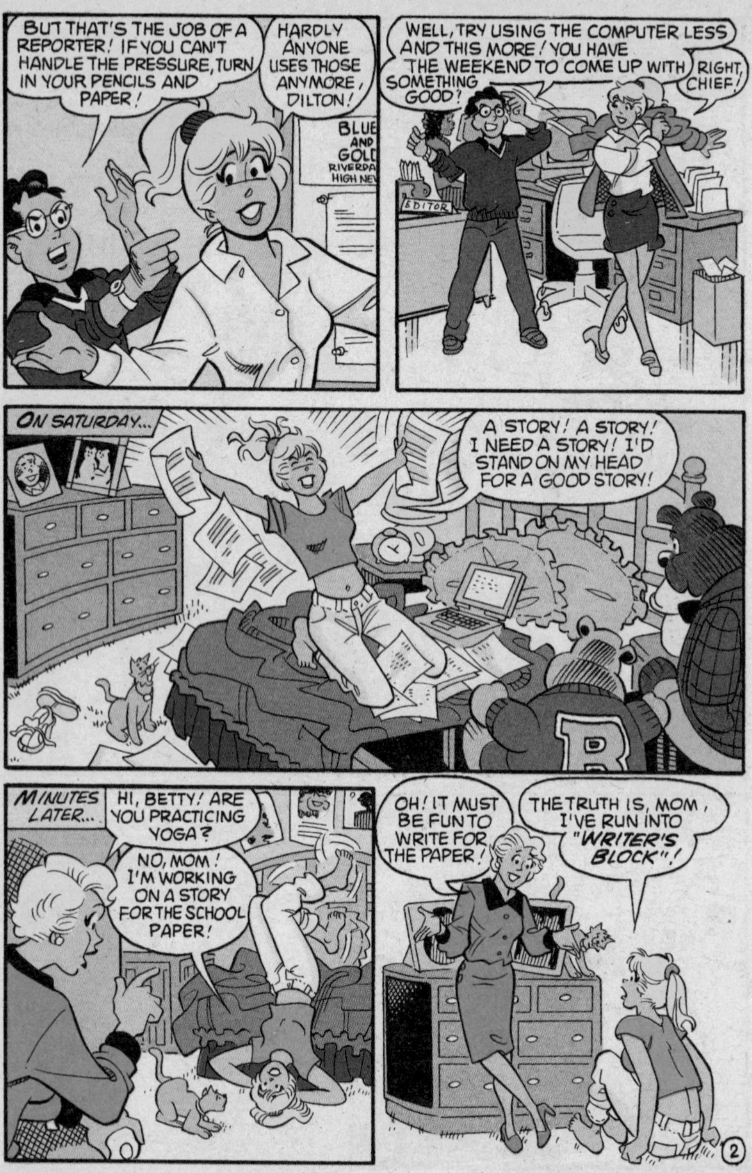
BUT THAT'S THE JOB OF A REPORTER! IF YOU CAN'T HANDLE THE PRESSURE, TURN IN YOUR PENCILS AND PAPER!
HARDLY ANYONE USES THOSE ANYMORE, DILTON!
BLUE AND GOLD RIVERDA HIGH NEW
WELL, TRY USING THE COMPUTER LESS AND THIS MORE! YOU HAVE THE WEEKEND TO COME UP WITH SOMETHING GOOD!
RIGHT, CHIEF!
EDITOR
ON SATURDAY...
A STORY! A STORY! I NEED A STORY! I'D STAND ON MY HEAD FOR A GOOD STORY!
MINUTES LATER...
HI, BETTY! ARE YOU PRACTICING YOGA?
NO, MOM! I'M WORKING ON A STORY FOR THE SCHOOL PAPER!
OH! IT MUST BE FUN TO WRITE FOR THE PAPER!
THE TRUTH IS, MOM, I'VE RUN INTO "WRITER'S BLOCK"!
2

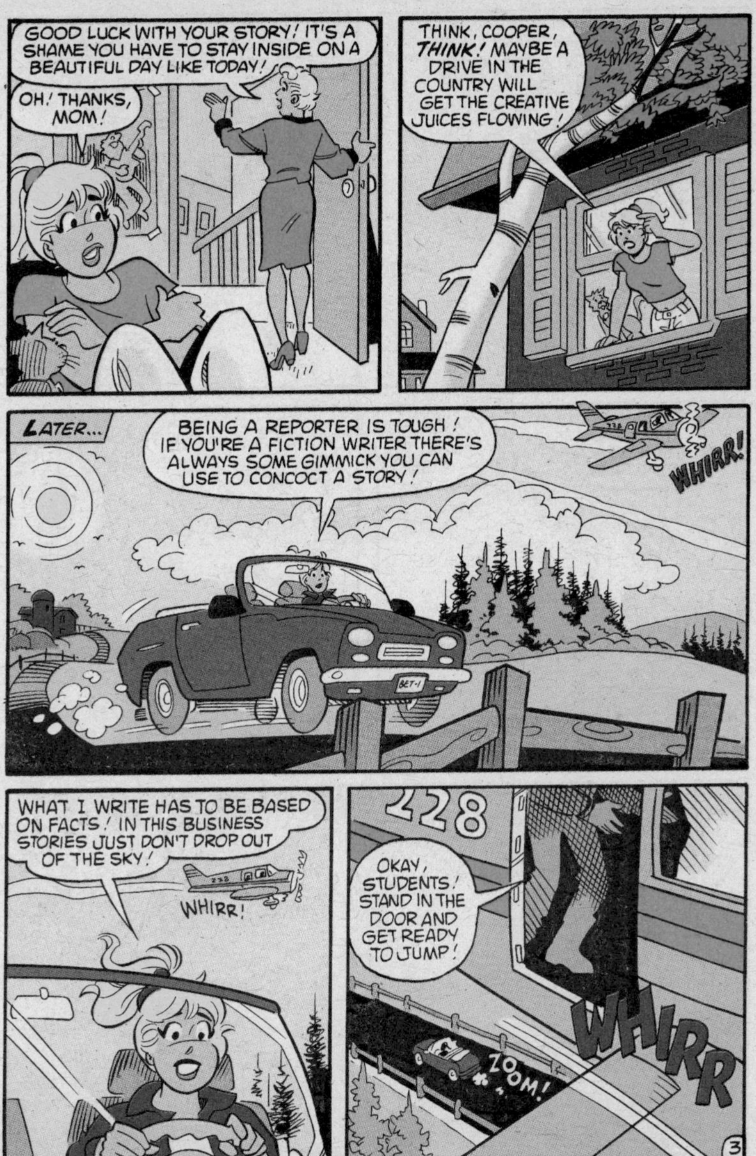
GOOD LUCK WITH YOUR STORY! IT'S A SHAME YOU HAVE TO STAY INSIDE ON A BEAUTIFUL DAY LIKE TODAY!
OH! THANKS, MOM!
THINK, COOPER, THINK! MAYBE A DRIVE IN THE COUNTRY WILL GET THE CREATIVE JUICES FLOWING!
LATER...
BEING A REPORTER IS TOUGH! IF YOU'RE A FICTION WRITER THERE'S ALWAYS SOME GIMMICK YOU CAN USE TO CONCOCT A STORY!
WHIRR!
BET-1
WHAT I WRITE HAS TO BE BASED ON FACTS! IN THIS BUSINESS STORIES JUST DON'T DROP OUT OF THE SKY!
WHIRR!
228
OKAY, STUDENTS! STAND IN THE DOOR AND GET READY TO JUMP!
WHIRR
ZOOM!
3

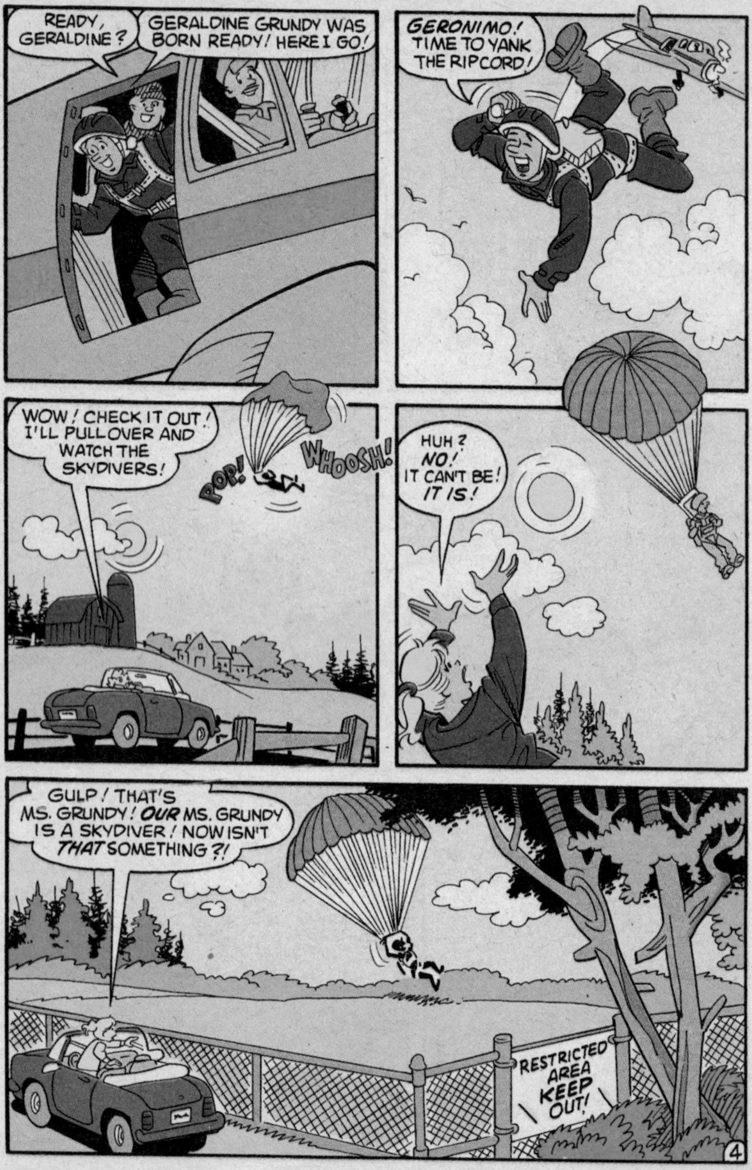

READY, GERALDINE?
GERALDINE GRUNDY WAS BORN READY! HERE I GO!
GERONIMO! TIME TO YANK THE RIPCORD!
WOW! CHECK IT OUT! I'LL PULL OVER AND WATCH THE SKYDIVERS!
POP!
WHOOSH!
HUH? NO! IT CAN'T BE! IT IS!
GULP! THAT'S MS. GRUNDY! OUR MS. GRUNDY IS A SKYDIVER! NOW ISN'T THAT SOMETHING?!
RESTRICTED AREA KEEP OUT!

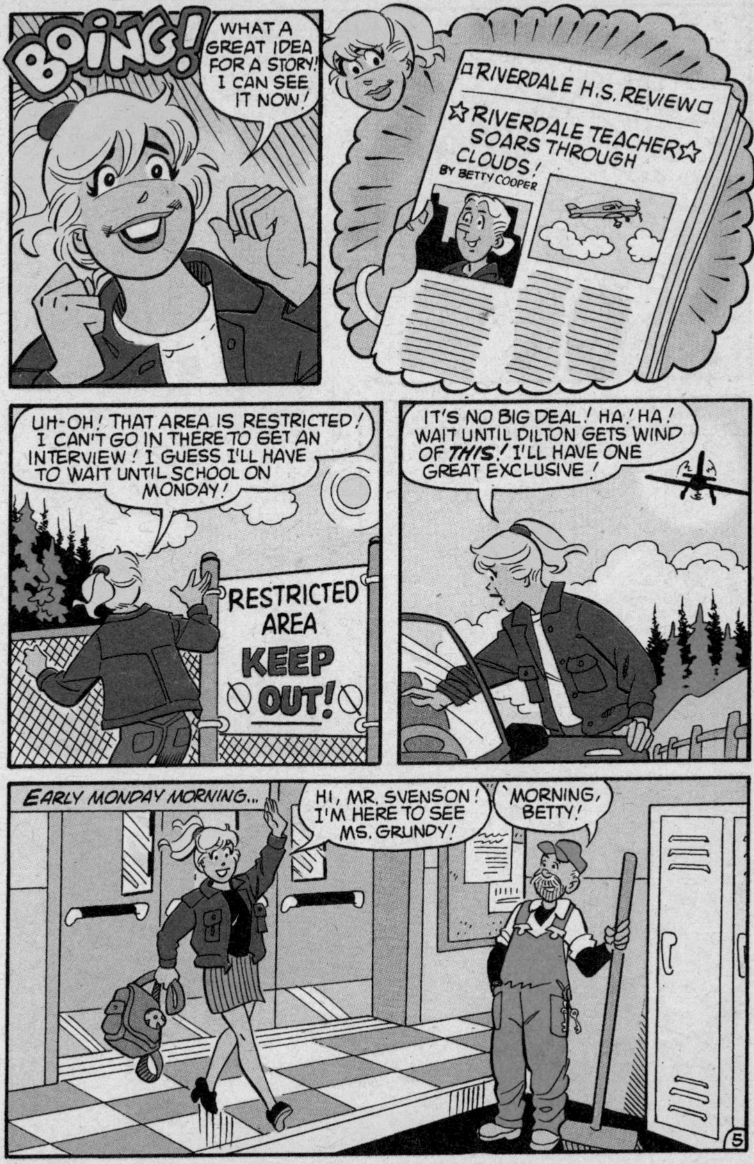
BOING!
WHAT A GREAT IDEA FOR A STORY! I CAN SEE IT NOW!
RIVERDALE H.S. REVIEW
RIVERDALE TEACHER SOARS THROUGH CLOUDS!
BY BETTY COOPER
UH-OH! THAT AREA IS RESTRICTED! I CAN'T GO IN THERE TO GET AN INTERVIEW! I GUESS I'LL HAVE TO WAIT UNTIL SCHOOL ON MONDAY!
RESTRICTED AREA KEEP OUT!
IT'S NO BIG DEAL! HA! HA! WAIT UNTIL DILTON GETS WIND OF THIS! I'LL HAVE ONE GREAT EXCLUSIVE!
EARLY MONDAY MORNING...
HI, MR. SVENSON! I'M HERE TO SEE MS. GRUNDY!
`MORNING, BETTY!
5

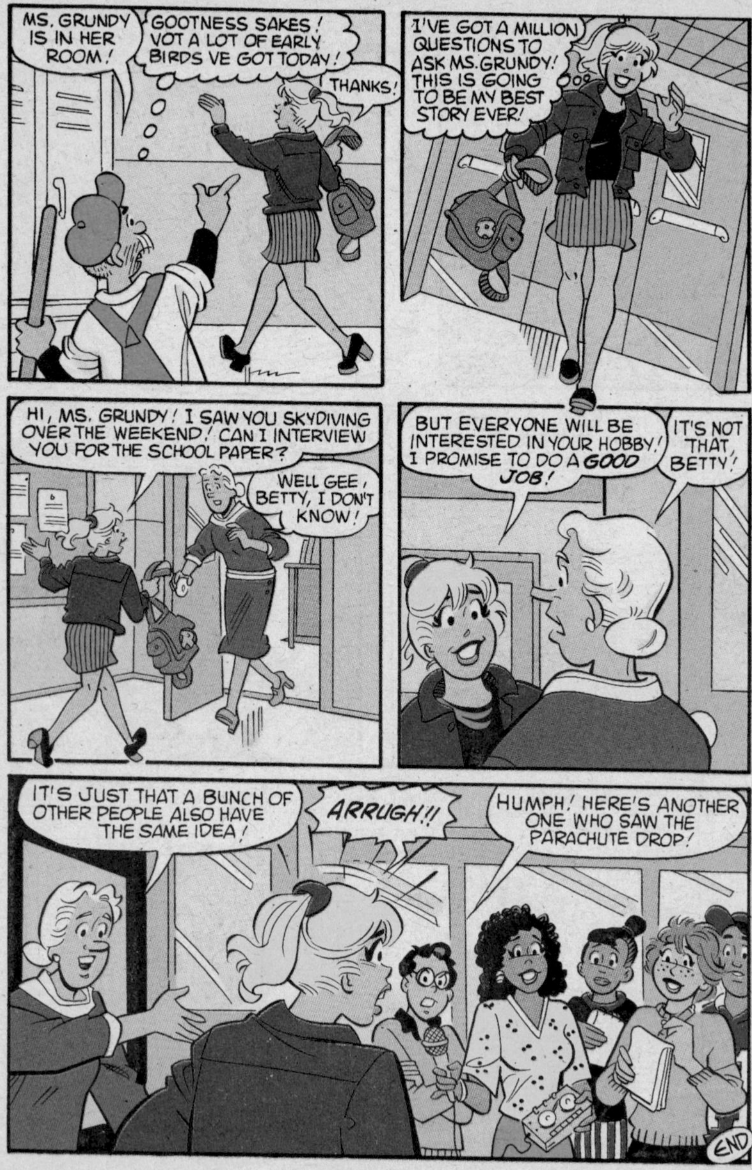
MS. GRUNDY IS IN HER ROOM!
GOOTNESS SAKES! VOT A LOT OF EARLY BIRDS VE GOT TODAY!
THANKS!
I'VE GOT A MILLION QUESTIONS TO ASK MS. GRUNDY! THIS IS GOING TO BE MY BEST STORY EVER!
HI, MS. GRUNDY! I SAW YOU SKYDIVING OVER THE WEEKEND! CAN I INTERVIEW YOU FOR THE SCHOOL PAPER?
WELL GEE, BETTY, I DON'T KNOW!
BUT EVERYONE WILL BE INTERESTED IN YOUR HOBBY! I PROMISE TO DO A GOOD JOB!
IT'S NOT THAT, BETTY!
IT'S JUST THAT A BUNCH OF OTHER PEOPLE ALSO HAVE THE SAME IDEA!
ARRUGH!!!
HUMPH! HERE'S ANOTHER ONE WHO SAW THE PARACHUTE DROP!
END

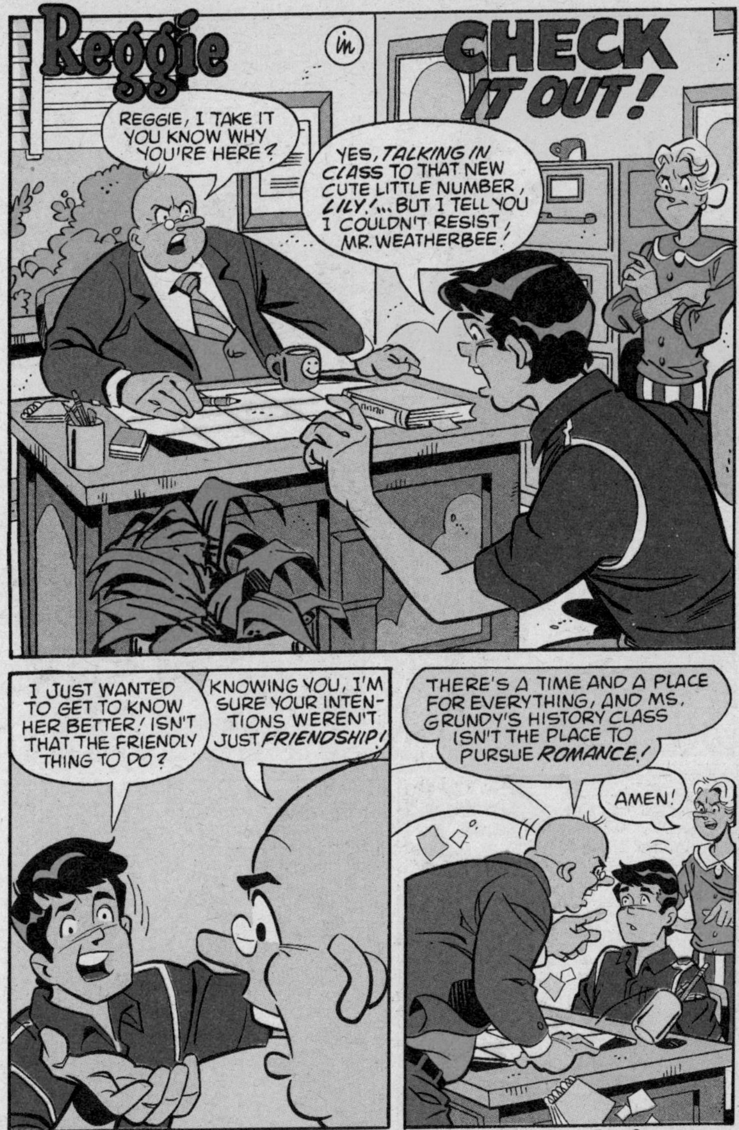
Reggie
in
CHECK IT OUT!
REGGIE, I TAKE IT YOU KNOW WHY YOU'RE HERE?
YES, TALKING IN CLASS TO THAT NEW CUTE LITTLE NUMBER, LILY!... BUT I TELL YOU I COULDN'T RESIST, MR. WEATHERBEE!
I JUST WANTED TO GET TO KNOW HER BETTER! ISN'T THAT THE FRIENDLY THING TO DO?
KNOWING YOU, I'M SURE YOUR INTENTIONS WEREN'T JUST FRIENDSHIP!
THERE'S A TIME AND A PLACE FOR EVERYTHING, AND MS. GRUNDY'S HISTORY CLASS ISN'T THE PLACE TO PURSUE ROMANCE!
AMEN!

Script: Mike Pellowski / Pencils: Al Bigley / Inks: Bob Smith / Letters: Bill Yoshida / Colors: Barry Grossman

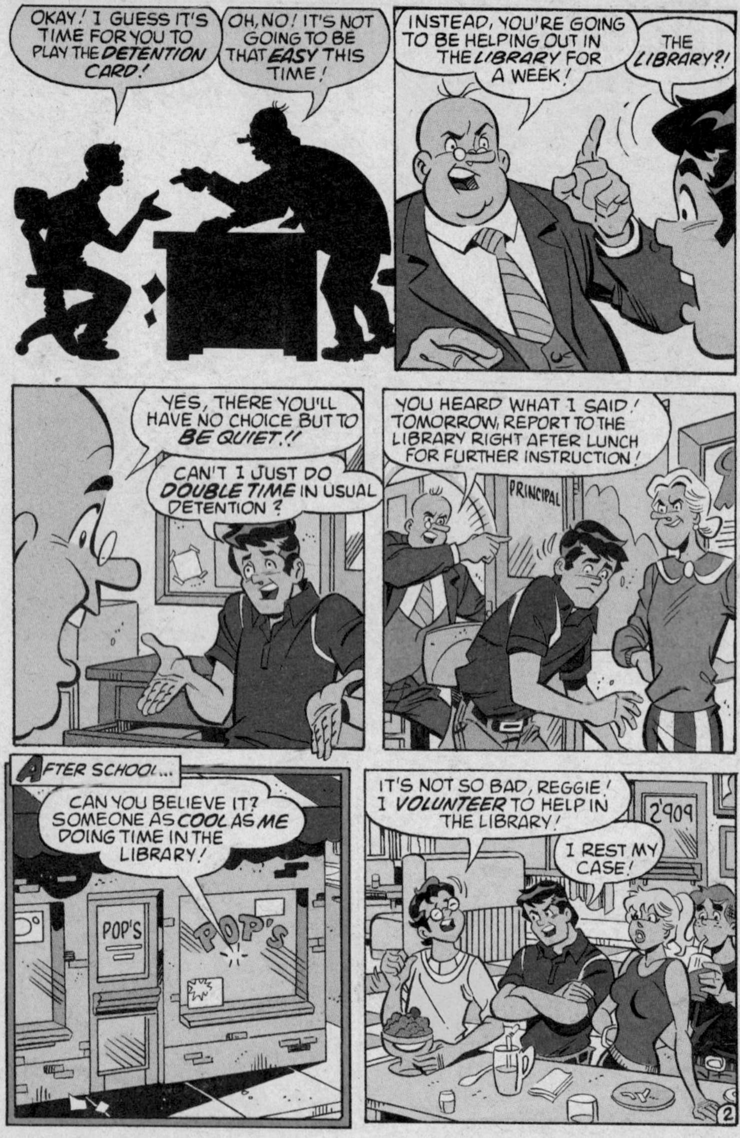
OKAY! I GUESS IT'S TIME FOR YOU TO PLAY THE DETENTION CARD!
OH, NO! IT'S NOT GOING TO BE THAT EASY THIS TIME!
INSTEAD, YOU'RE GOING TO BE HELPING OUT IN THE LIBRARY FOR A WEEK!
THE LIBRARY?!
YES, THERE YOU'LL HAVE NO CHOICE BUT TO BE QUIET!!
CAN'T I JUST DO DOUBLE TIME IN USUAL DETENTION?
YOU HEARD WHAT I SAID! TOMORROW, REPORT TO THE LIBRARY RIGHT AFTER LUNCH FOR FURTHER INSTRUCTION!
PRINCIPAL
AFTER SCHOOL...
CAN YOU BELIEVE IT? SOMEONE AS COOL AS ME DOING TIME IN THE LIBRARY!
POP'S
POP'S
IT'S NOT SO BAD, REGGIE! I VOLUNTEER TO HELP IN THE LIBRARY!
I REST MY CASE!
POP'S
2

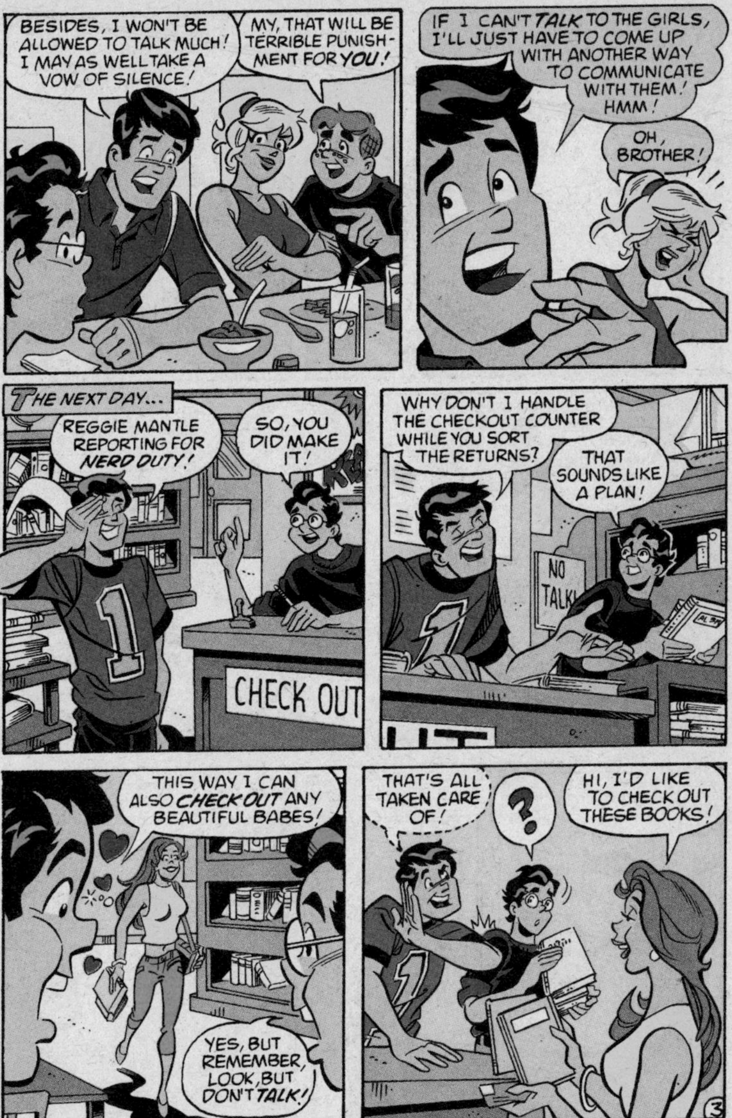

BESIDES, I WON'T BE ALLOWED TO TALK MUCH! I MAY AS WELL TAKE A VOW OF SILENCE!
MY, THAT WILL BE TERRIBLE PUNISHMENT FOR YOU!
IF I CAN'T TALK TO THE GIRLS, I'LL JUST HAVE TO COME UP WITH ANOTHER WAY TO COMMUNICATE WITH THEM! HMM!
OH, BROTHER!
THE NEXT DAY...
REGGIE MANTLE REPORTING FOR NERD DUTY!
SO, YOU DID MAKE IT!
CHECK OUT
WHY DON'T I HANDLE THE CHECKOUT COUNTER WHILE YOU SORT THE RETURNS?
THAT SOUNDS LIKE A PLAN!
NO TALK
THIS WAY I CAN ALSO CHECK OUT ANY BEAUTIFUL BABES!
YES, BUT REMEMBER, LOOK, BUT DON'T TALK!
THAT'S ALL TAKEN CARE OF!
?
HI, I'D LIKE TO CHECK OUT THESE BOOKS!

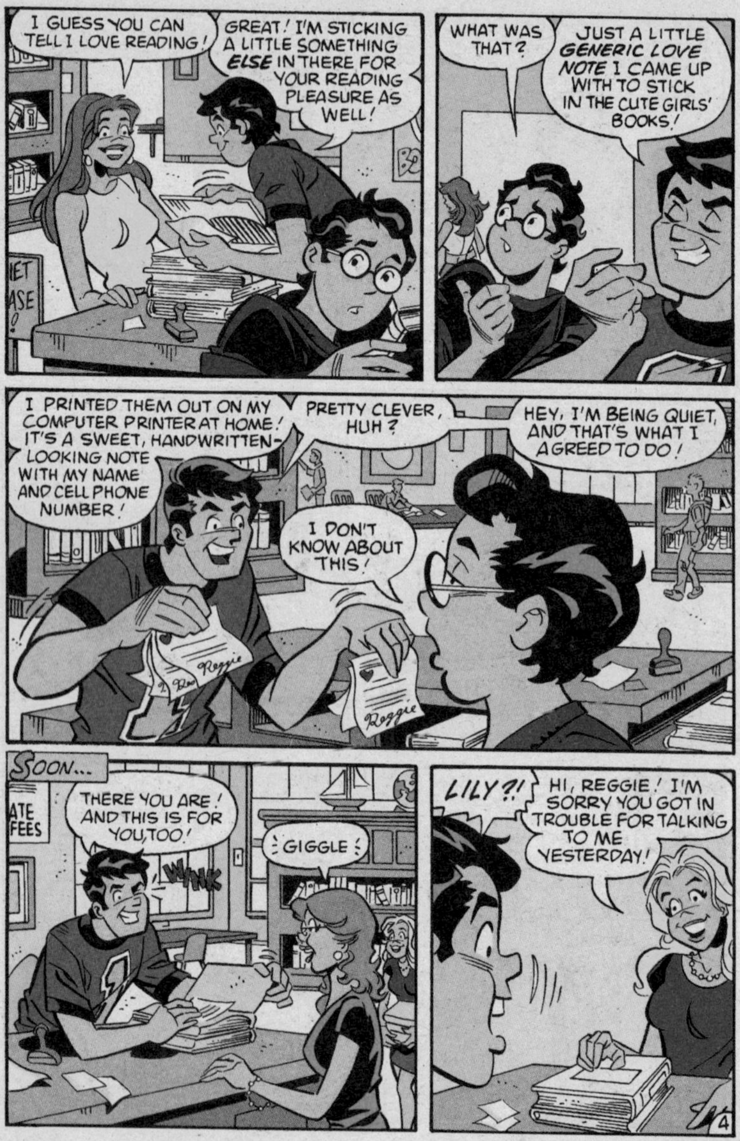
I GUESS YOU CAN TELL I LOVE READING!
GREAT! I'M STICKING A LITTLE SOMETHING *ELSE* IN THERE FOR YOUR READING PLEASURE AS WELL!
WHAT WAS THAT?
JUST A LITTLE *GENERIC LOVE NOTE* I CAME UP WITH TO STICK IN THE CUTE GIRLS' BOOKS!
I PRINTED THEM OUT ON MY COMPUTER PRINTER AT HOME! IT'S A SWEET, HANDWRITTEN-LOOKING NOTE WITH MY NAME AND CELL PHONE NUMBER!
PRETTY CLEVER, HUH?
HEY, I'M BEING QUIET, AND THAT'S WHAT I AGREED TO DO!
I DON'T KNOW ABOUT THIS!
Reggie
Reggie
SOON...
THERE YOU ARE! AND THIS IS FOR YOU, TOO!
WINK
GIGGLE
LILY?!
HI, REGGIE! I'M SORRY YOU GOT IN TROUBLE FOR TALKING TO ME YESTERDAY!
4

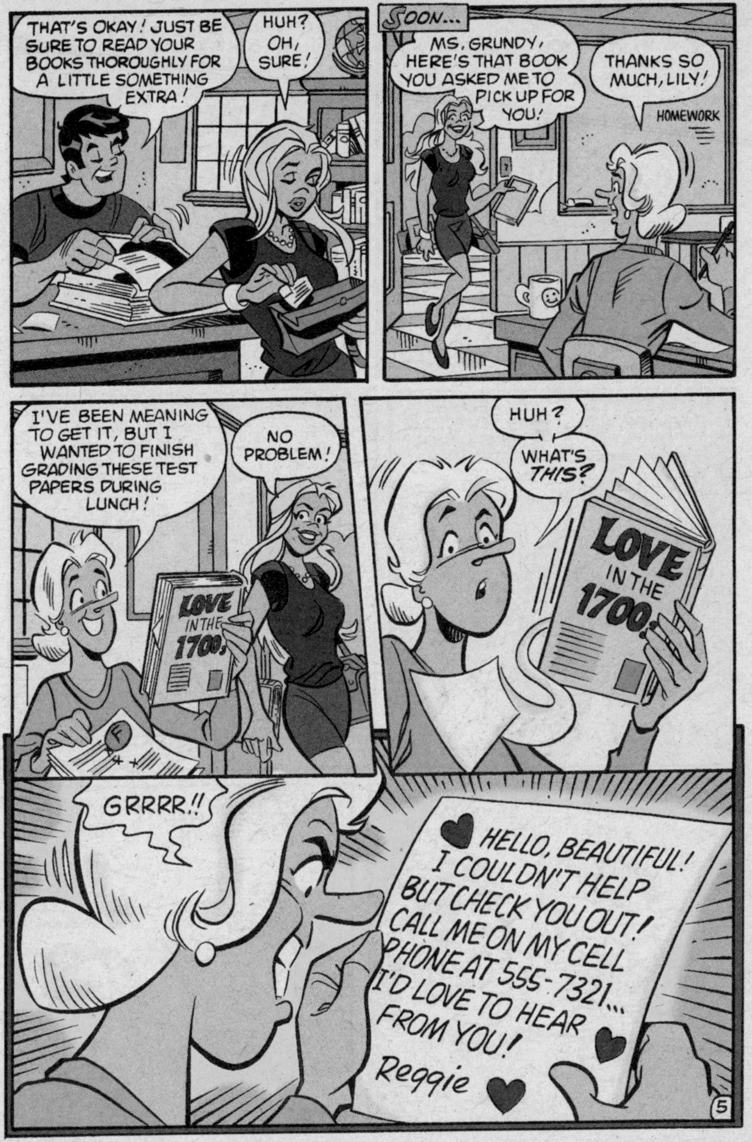
THAT'S OKAY! JUST BE SURE TO READ YOUR BOOKS THOROUGHLY FOR A LITTLE SOMETHING EXTRA!
HUH? OH, SURE!
SOON...
MS. GRUNDY, HERE'S THAT BOOK YOU ASKED ME TO PICK UP FOR YOU!
THANKS SO MUCH, LILY!
HOMEWORK
I'VE BEEN MEANING TO GET IT, BUT I WANTED TO FINISH GRADING THESE TEST PAPERS DURING LUNCH!
NO PROBLEM!
LOVE IN THE 1700s
HUH?
WHAT'S THIS?
LOVE IN THE 1700s
GRRRR!!
HELLO, BEAUTIFUL! I COULDN'T HELP BUT CHECK YOU OUT! CALL ME ON MY CELL PHONE AT 555-7321... I'D LOVE TO HEAR FROM YOU!
Reggie
5

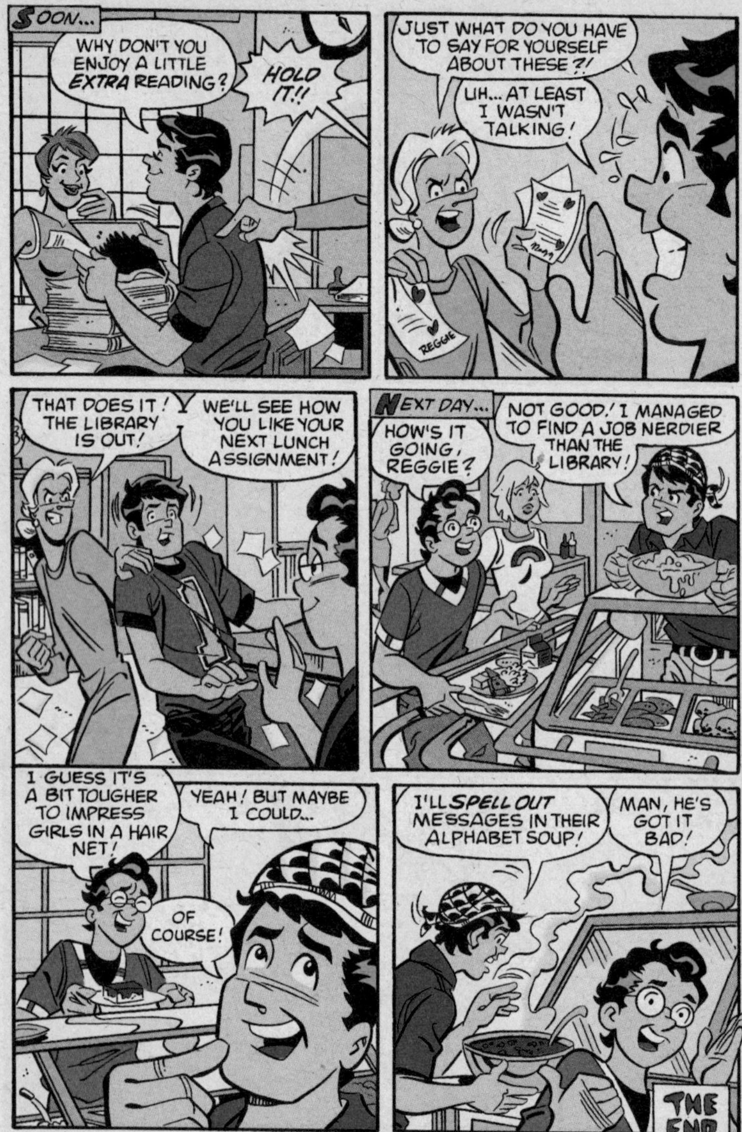
SOON...
WHY DON'T YOU ENJOY A LITTLE EXTRA READING?
HOLD IT!!
JUST WHAT DO YOU HAVE TO SAY FOR YOURSELF ABOUT THESE?!
UH... AT LEAST I WASN'T TALKING!
REGGIE
THAT DOES IT! THE LIBRARY IS OUT!
WE'LL SEE HOW YOU LIKE YOUR NEXT LUNCH ASSIGNMENT!
NEXT DAY...
HOW'S IT GOING, REGGIE?
NOT GOOD! I MANAGED TO FIND A JOB NERDIER THAN THE LIBRARY!
I GUESS IT'S A BIT TOUGHER TO IMPRESS GIRLS IN A HAIR NET!
YEAH! BUT MAYBE I COULD...
OF COURSE!
I'LL SPELL OUT MESSAGES IN THEIR ALPHABET SOUP!
MAN, HE'S GOT IT BAD!
THE END

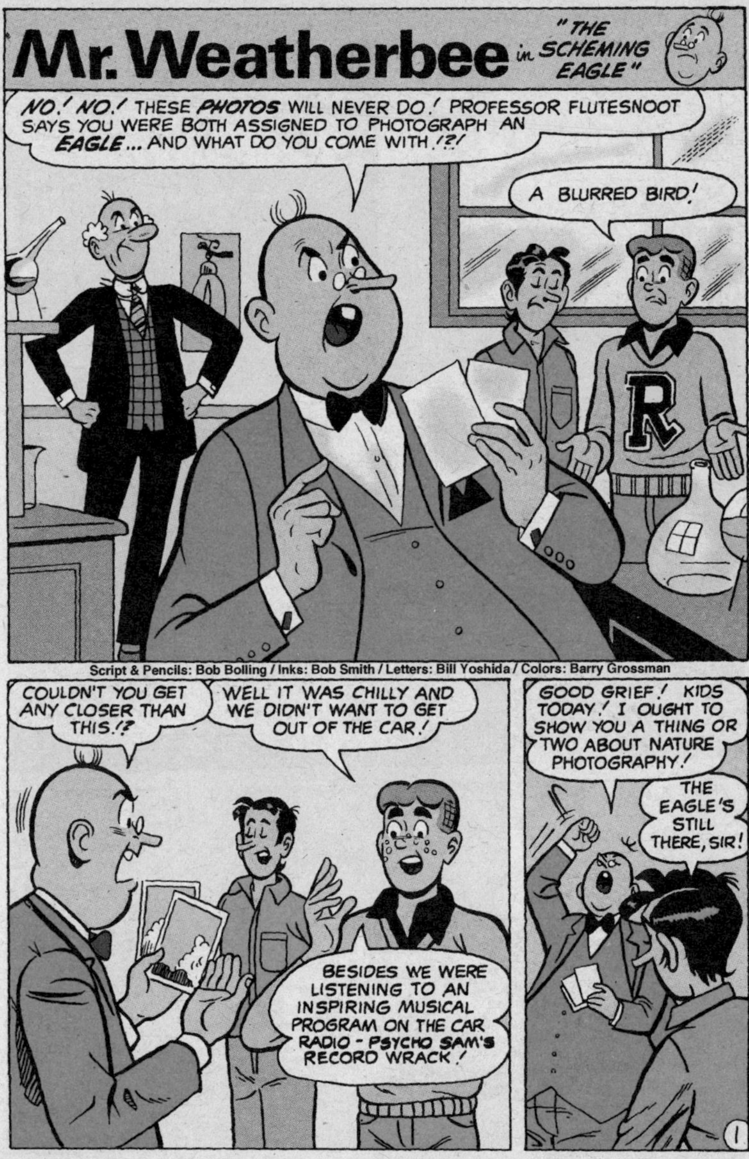
Mr. Weatherbee in "THE SCHEMING EAGLE"
NO! NO! THESE PHOTOS WILL NEVER DO! PROFESSOR FLUTESNOOT SAYS YOU WERE BOTH ASSIGNED TO PHOTOGRAPH AN EAGLE... AND WHAT DO YOU COME WITH!?!
A BLURRED BIRD!
COULDN'T YOU GET ANY CLOSER THAN THIS!?
WELL IT WAS CHILLY AND WE DIDN'T WANT TO GET OUT OF THE CAR!
BESIDES WE WERE LISTENING TO AN INSPIRING MUSICAL PROGRAM ON THE CAR RADIO - PSYCHO SAM'S RECORD WRACK!
GOOD GRIEF! KIDS TODAY! I OUGHT TO SHOW YOU A THING OR TWO ABOUT NATURE PHOTOGRAPHY!
THE EAGLE'S STILL THERE, SIR!
1

Script & Pencils: Bob Bolling / Inks: Bob Smith / Letters: Bill Yoshida / Colors: Barry Grossman

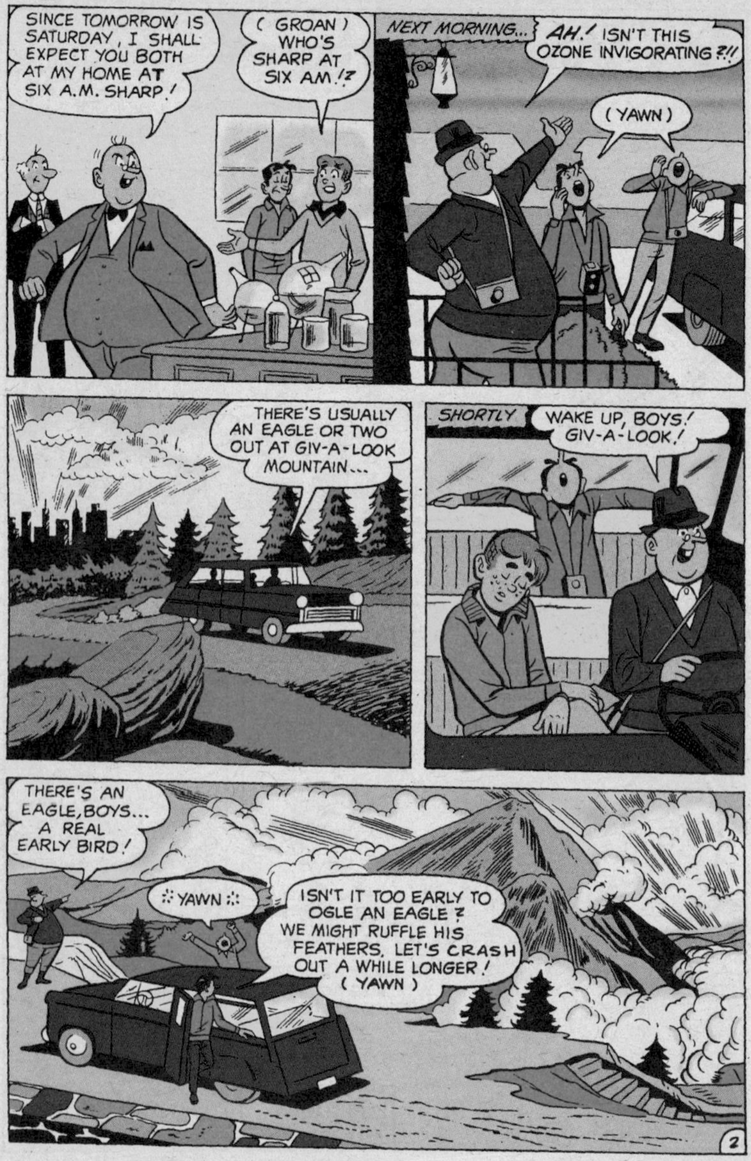
SINCE TOMORROW IS SATURDAY, I SHALL EXPECT YOU BOTH AT MY HOME AT SIX A.M. SHARP!
(GROAN) WHO'S SHARP AT SIX AM!?
NEXT MORNING...
AH! ISN'T THIS OZONE INVIGORATING?!!
(YAWN)
THERE'S USUALLY AN EAGLE OR TWO OUT AT GIV-A-LOOK MOUNTAIN...
SHORTLY
WAKE UP, BOYS! GIV-A-LOOK!
THERE'S AN EAGLE, BOYS... A REAL EARLY BIRD!
YAWN
ISN'T IT TOO EARLY TO OGLE AN EAGLE? WE MIGHT RUFFLE HIS FEATHERS. LET'S CRASH OUT A WHILE LONGER! (YAWN)
2

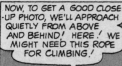

NOW, TO GET A GOOD CLOSE-UP PHOTO, WE'LL APPROACH QUIETLY FROM ABOVE AND BEHIND! HERE! WE MIGHT NEED THIS ROPE FOR CLIMBING!

(PUFF!) (PANT!) (WHEEZE!)

GETTING GUSTY UP HERE!

BLAST! THAT'S THE THIRD, HAT AND TENTH TOUPÉE THIS YEAR!

SOON...

AH! SHE'S ON HER NEST! QUIET NOW! CAMERAS READY!?!

AND NOW LET'S HEAR "WHAT MAKES YOU SO SPOTTY, DOTTY?" BY CHICKEN AND THE FOXES!

GOOD GRIEF! WHAT'S THAT!

I BROUGHT MY TRANSISTOR... I HATE TO MISS PSYCHO SAM!

IMBECILE! TURN IT OFF! NOW THE EAGLES ARE FLYING AROUND MAD!

URK!

YEAH, LIKE, REAL SOAR! THIS IS A REAL FOWL-UP!

ANYWAY, FOR NOW LET'S GET A SHOT OF HER NEST... STRANGE! NO EGGS IN IT! THERE SHOULD BE EGGS THERE THIS TIME OF YEAR!

CAREFUL! IT'S A SHEER DROP OF TWO THOUSAND FEET TO THE BOTTOM OF THE CANYON!

3

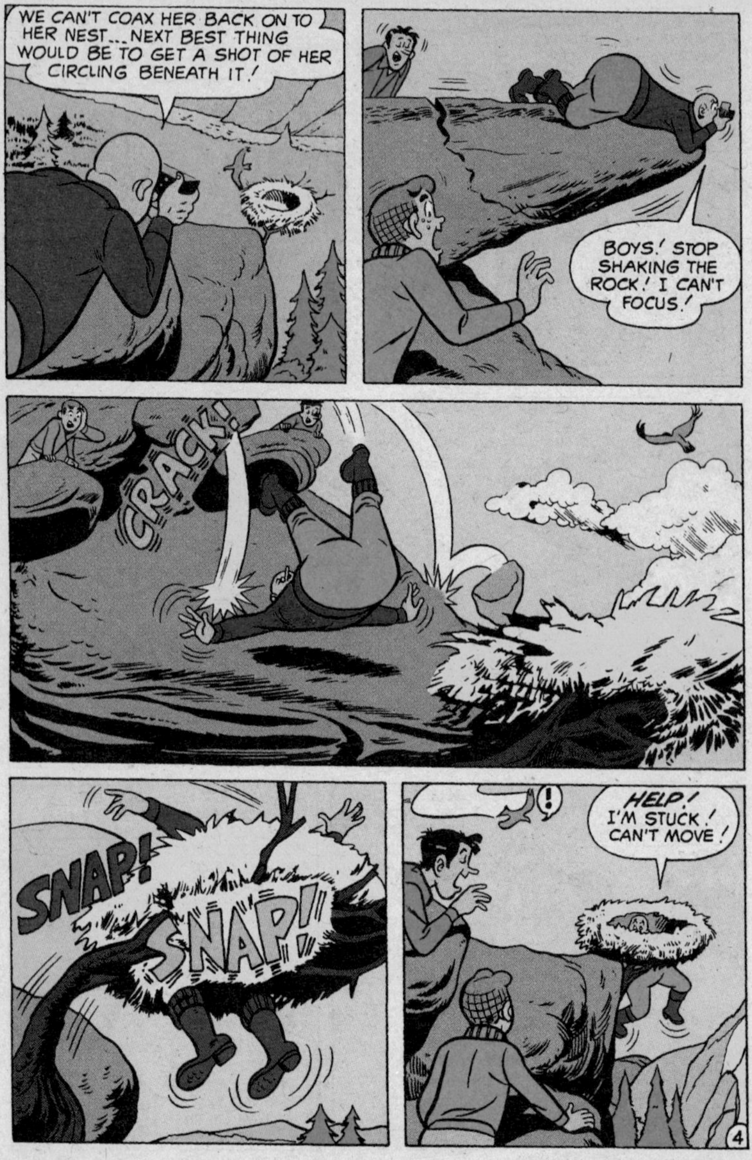
WE CAN'T COAX HER BACK ON TO HER NEST... NEXT BEST THING WOULD BE TO GET A SHOT OF HER CIRCLING BENEATH IT!
BOYS! STOP SHAKING THE ROCK! I CAN'T FOCUS!
CRACK!
SNAP!
SNAP!
!
HELP! I'M STUCK! CAN'T MOVE!
4

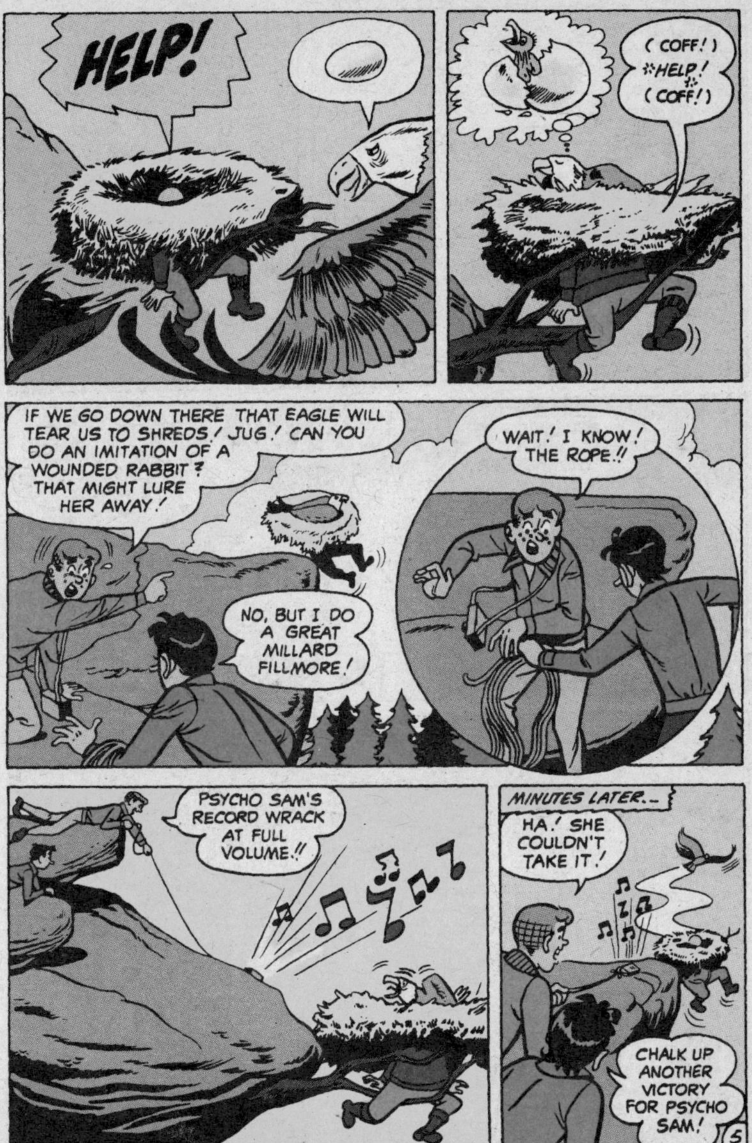
HELP!
(COFF!)
HELP!
(COFF!)
IF WE GO DOWN THERE THAT EAGLE WILL TEAR US TO SHREDS! JUG! CAN YOU DO AN IMITATION OF A WOUNDED RABBIT? THAT MIGHT LURE HER AWAY!
NO, BUT I DO A GREAT MILLARD FILLMORE!
WAIT! I KNOW! THE ROPE!!
PSYCHO SAM'S RECORD WRACK AT FULL VOLUME!!
MINUTES LATER...
HA! SHE COULDN'T TAKE IT!
CHALK UP ANOTHER VICTORY FOR PSYCHO SAM!
5

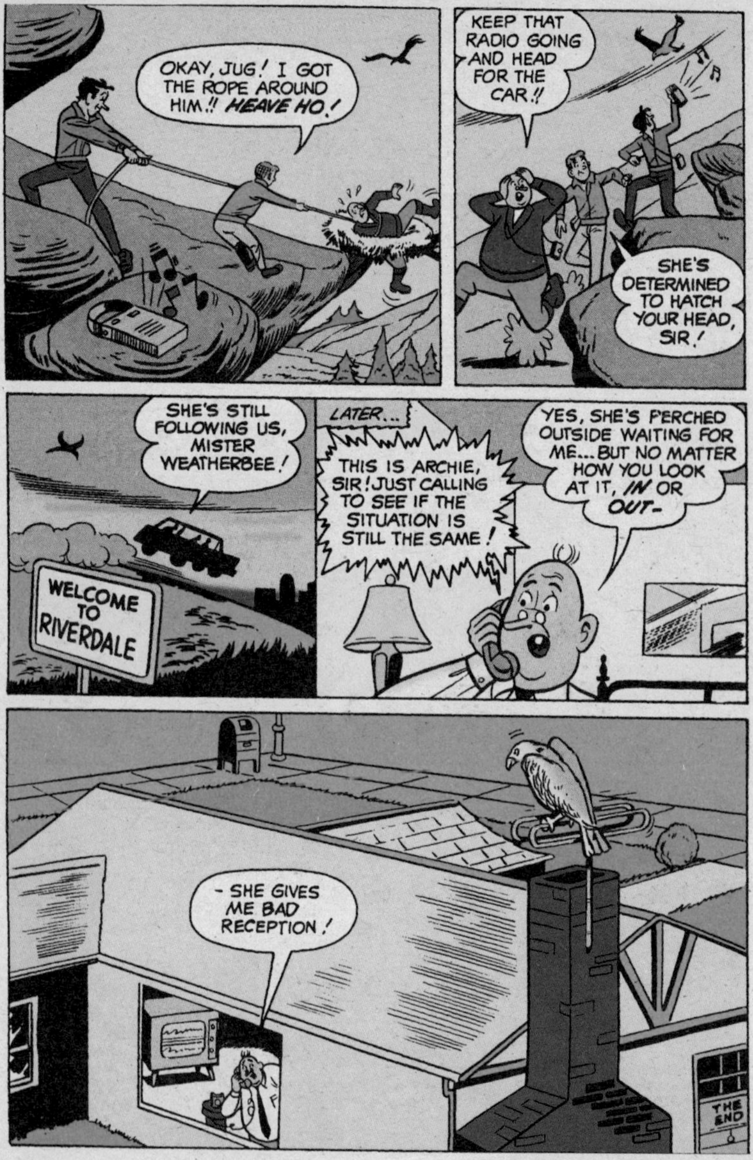
OKAY, JUG! I GOT THE ROPE AROUND HIM.!! HEAVE HO!
KEEP THAT RADIO GOING AND HEAD FOR THE CAR.!!
SHE'S DETERMINED TO HATCH YOUR HEAD, SIR!
SHE'S STILL FOLLOWING US, MISTER WEATHERBEE!
WELCOME TO RIVERDALE
LATER...
THIS IS ARCHIE, SIR! JUST CALLING TO SEE IF THE SITUATION IS STILL THE SAME!
YES, SHE'S PERCHED OUTSIDE WAITING FOR ME... BUT NO MATTER HOW YOU LOOK AT IT, IN OR OUT-
- SHE GIVES ME BAD RECEPTION!
THE END

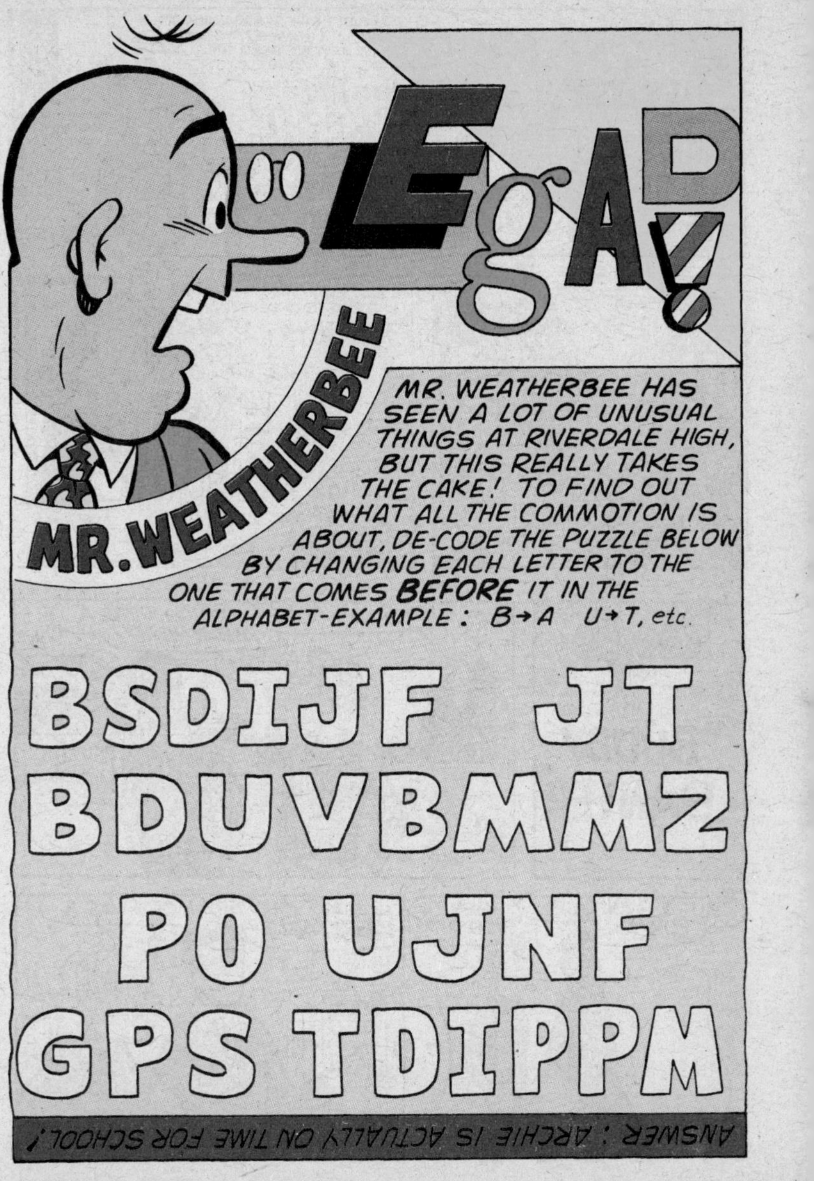
EGAD!
MR. WEATHERBEE
MR. WEATHERBEE HAS SEEN A LOT OF UNUSUAL THINGS AT RIVERDALE HIGH, BUT THIS REALLY TAKES THE CAKE! TO FIND OUT WHAT ALL THE COMMOTION IS ABOUT, DE-CODE THE PUZZLE BELOW BY CHANGING EACH LETTER TO THE ONE THAT COMES BEFORE IT IN THE ALPHABET-EXAMPLE: B→A U→T, etc.
BSDIJF JT
BDUVBMMZ
PO UJNF
GPS TDIPPM
ANSWER: ARCHIE IS ACTUALLY ON TIME FOR SCHOOL!

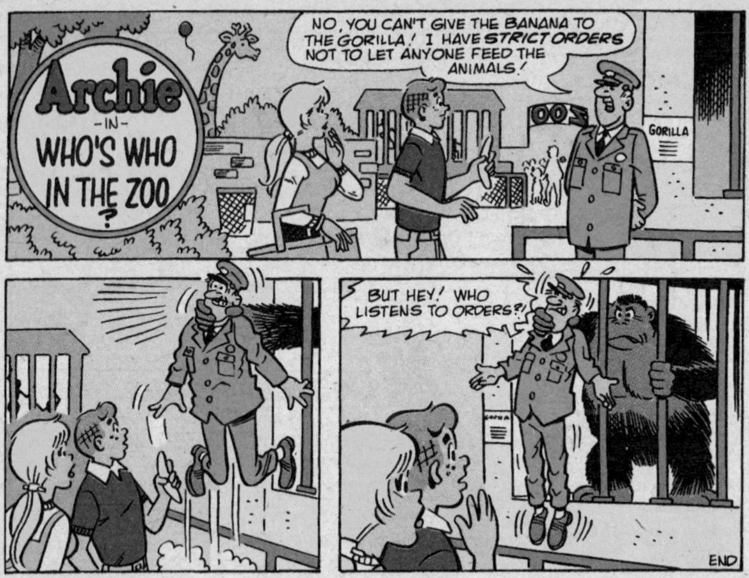
Archie
-IN-
WHO'S WHO IN THE ZOO?
NO, YOU CAN'T GIVE THE BANANA TO THE GORILLA! I HAVE STRICT ORDERS NOT TO LET ANYONE FEED THE ANIMALS!
ZOO
GORILLA
BUT HEY! WHO LISTENS TO ORDERS?!
END

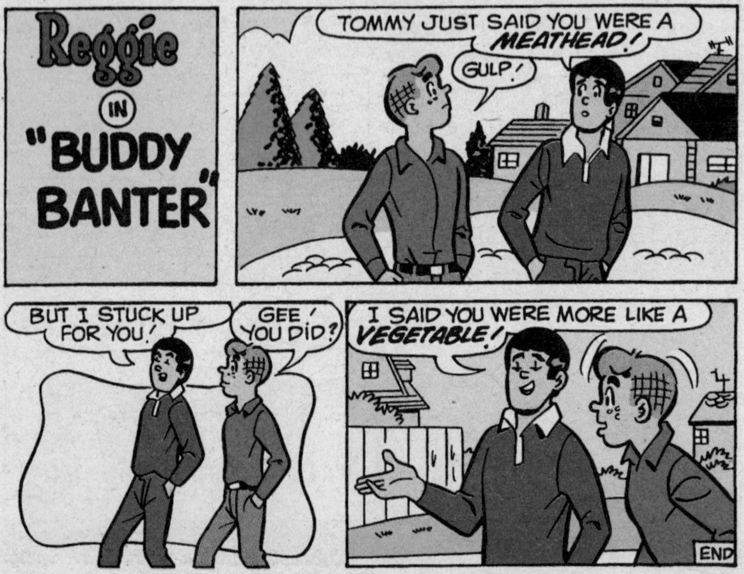
Reggie
IN
"BUDDY BANTER"
TOMMY JUST SAID YOU WERE A MEATHEAD!
GULP!
BUT I STUCK UP FOR YOU!
GEE! YOU DID?
I SAID YOU WERE MORE LIKE A VEGETABLE!
END

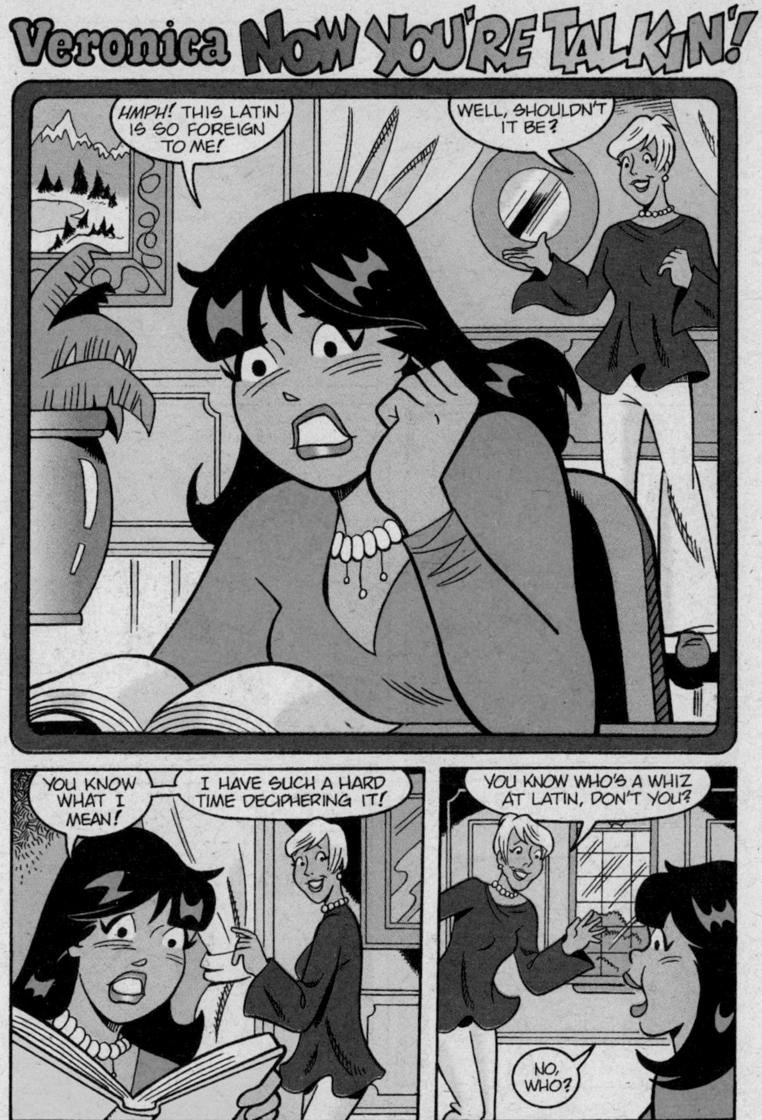
Veronica
NOW YOU'RE TALKIN'!
HMPH! THIS LATIN IS SO FOREIGN TO ME!
WELL, SHOULDN'T IT BE?
YOU KNOW WHAT I MEAN!
I HAVE SUCH A HARD TIME DECIPHERING IT!
YOU KNOW WHO'S A WHIZ AT LATIN, DON'T YOU?
NO, WHO?

Script & Pencils: Dan Parent / Inks: Jim Amash / Letters: Dan Nakrosis / Colors: Barry Grossman

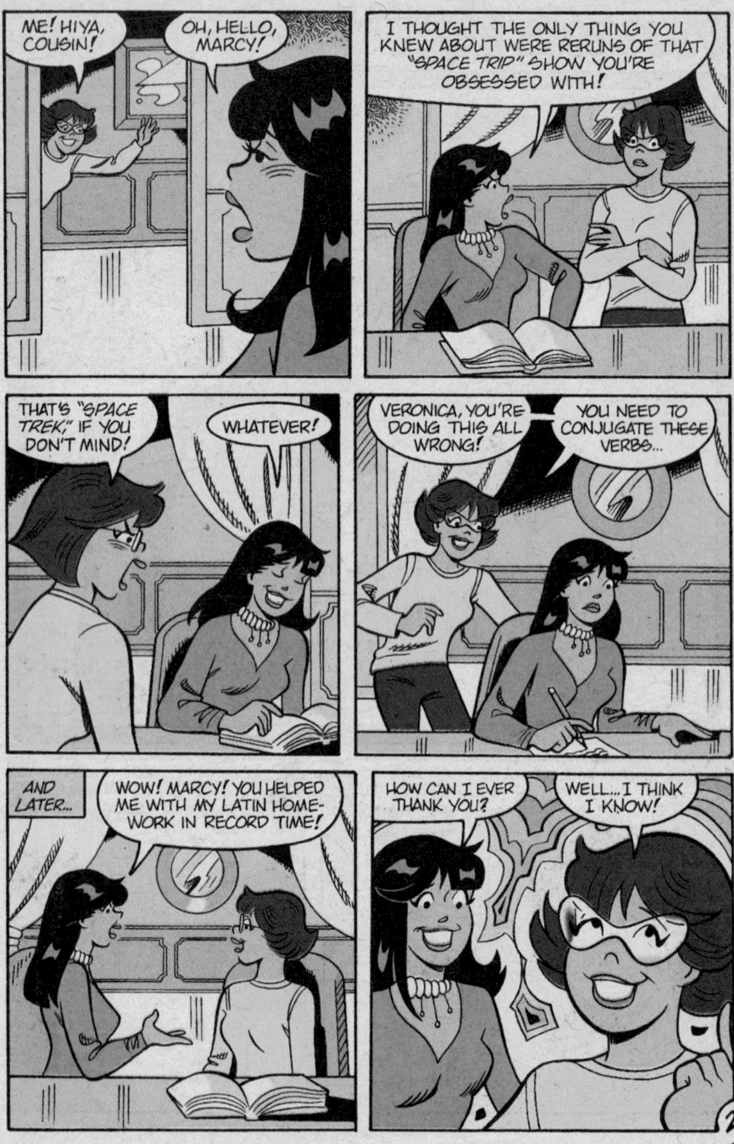
ME! HIYA, COUSIN!
OH, HELLO, MARCY!
I THOUGHT THE ONLY THING YOU KNEW ABOUT WERE RERUNS OF THAT "SPACE TRIP" SHOW YOU'RE OBSESSED WITH!
THAT'S "SPACE TREK," IF YOU DON'T MIND!
WHATEVER!
VERONICA, YOU'RE DOING THIS ALL WRONG!
YOU NEED TO CONJUGATE THESE VERBS...
AND LATER...
WOW! MARCY! YOU HELPED ME WITH MY LATIN HOME-WORK IN RECORD TIME!
HOW CAN I EVER THANK YOU?
WELL...I THINK I KNOW!

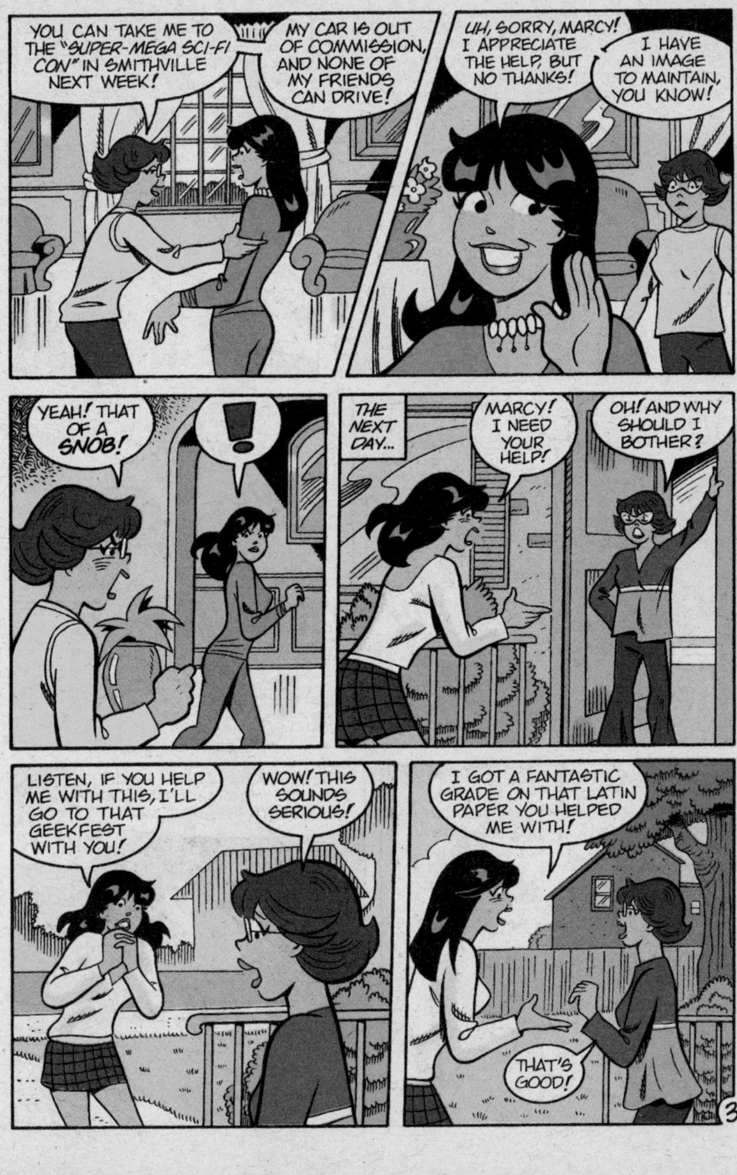
YOU CAN TAKE ME TO THE "SUPER-MEGA SCI-FI CON" IN SMITHVILLE NEXT WEEK!
MY CAR IS OUT OF COMMISSION, AND NONE OF MY FRIENDS CAN DRIVE!
UH, SORRY, MARCY! I APPRECIATE THE HELP, BUT NO THANKS!
I HAVE AN IMAGE TO MAINTAIN, YOU KNOW!
YEAH! THAT OF A SNOB!
!
THE NEXT DAY...
MARCY! I NEED YOUR HELP!
OH! AND WHY SHOULD I BOTHER?
LISTEN, IF YOU HELP ME WITH THIS, I'LL GO TO THAT GEEKFEST WITH YOU!
WOW! THIS SOUNDS SERIOUS!
I GOT A FANTASTIC GRADE ON THAT LATIN PAPER YOU HELPED ME WITH!
THAT'S GOOD!
3

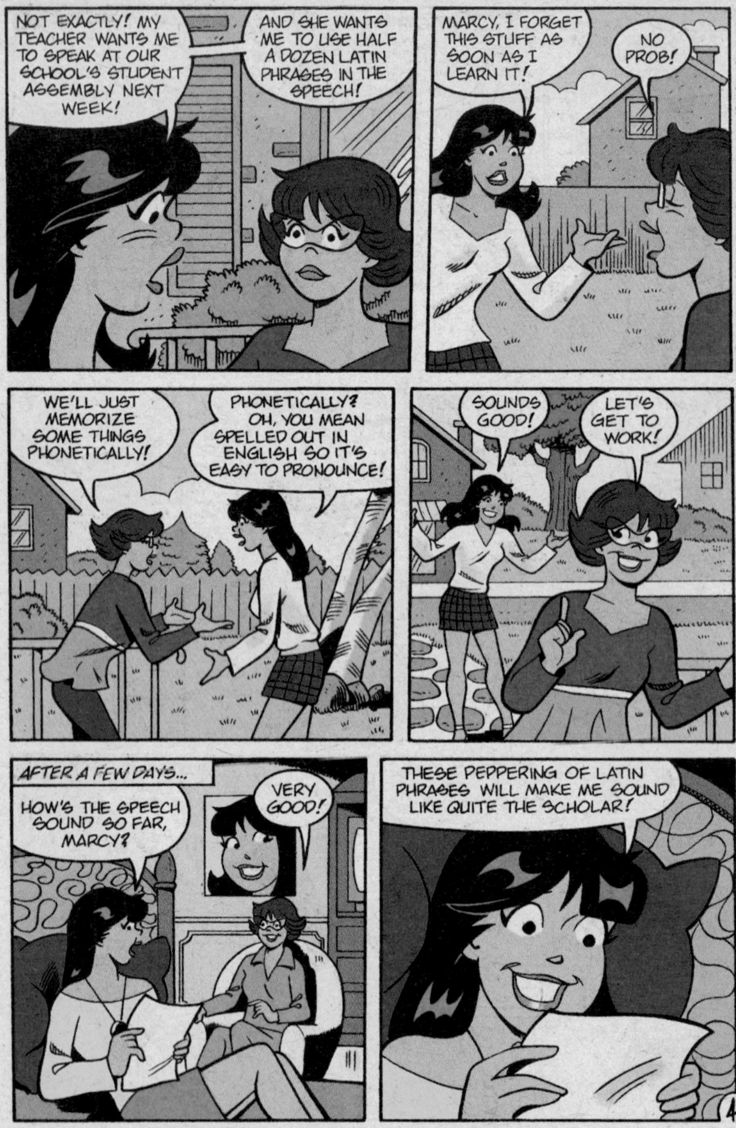
NOT EXACTLY! MY TEACHER WANTS ME TO SPEAK AT OUR SCHOOL'S STUDENT ASSEMBLY NEXT WEEK!
AND SHE WANTS ME TO USE HALF A DOZEN LATIN PHRASES IN THE SPEECH!
MARCY, I FORGET THIS STUFF AS SOON AS I LEARN IT!
NO PROB!
WE'LL JUST MEMORIZE SOME THINGS PHONETICALLY!
PHONETICALLY? OH, YOU MEAN SPELLED OUT IN ENGLISH SO IT'S EASY TO PRONOUNCE!
SOUNDS GOOD!
LET'S GET TO WORK!
AFTER A FEW DAYS...
HOW'S THE SPEECH SOUND SO FAR, MARCY?
VERY GOOD!
THESE PEPPERING OF LATIN PHRASES WILL MAKE ME SOUND LIKE QUITE THE SCHOLAR!

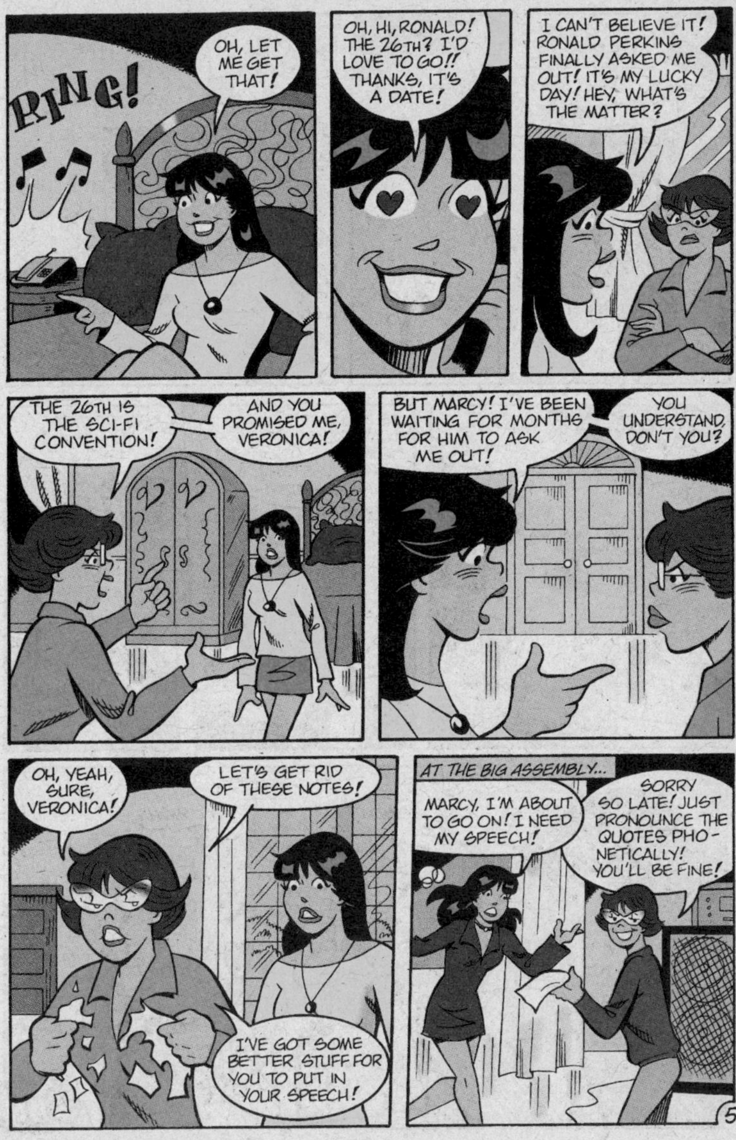
OH, LET ME GET THAT!
RING!
OH, HI, RONALD! THE 26TH? I'D LOVE TO GO!! THANKS, IT'S A DATE!
I CAN'T BELIEVE IT! RONALD PERKINS FINALLY ASKED ME OUT! IT'S MY LUCKY DAY! HEY, WHAT'S THE MATTER?
THE 26TH IS THE SCI-FI CONVENTION!
AND YOU PROMISED ME, VERONICA!
BUT MARCY! I'VE BEEN WAITING FOR MONTHS FOR HIM TO ASK ME OUT!
YOU UNDERSTAND, DON'T YOU?
OH, YEAH, SURE, VERONICA!
LET'S GET RID OF THESE NOTES!
I'VE GOT SOME BETTER STUFF FOR YOU TO PUT IN YOUR SPEECH!
AT THE BIG ASSEMBLY...
MARCY, I'M ABOUT TO GO ON! I NEED MY SPEECH!
SORRY SO LATE! JUST PRONOUNCE THE QUOTES PHO-NETICALLY! YOU'LL BE FINE!

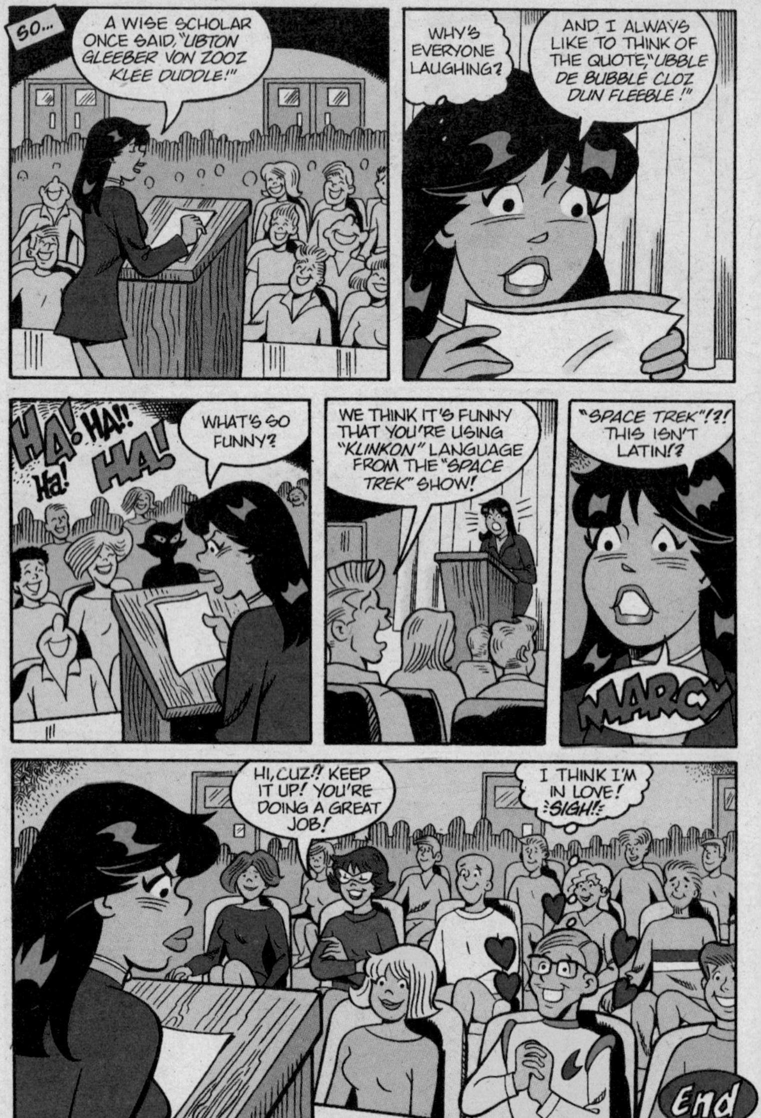
SO...
A WISE SCHOLAR ONCE SAID, "UBTON GLEEBER VON ZOOZ KLEE DUDDLE!"
WHY'S EVERYONE LAUGHING?
AND I ALWAYS LIKE TO THINK OF THE QUOTE, "UBBLE DE BUBBLE CLOZ DUN FLEEBLE!"
HA! HA!! HA! Ha!
WHAT'S SO FUNNY?
WE THINK IT'S FUNNY THAT YOU'RE USING "KLINKON" LANGUAGE FROM THE "SPACE TREK" SHOW!
"SPACE TREK"!?! THIS ISN'T LATIN!?
MARCY
HI, CUZ!! KEEP IT UP! YOU'RE DOING A GREAT JOB!
I THINK I'M IN LOVE! SIGH!
End

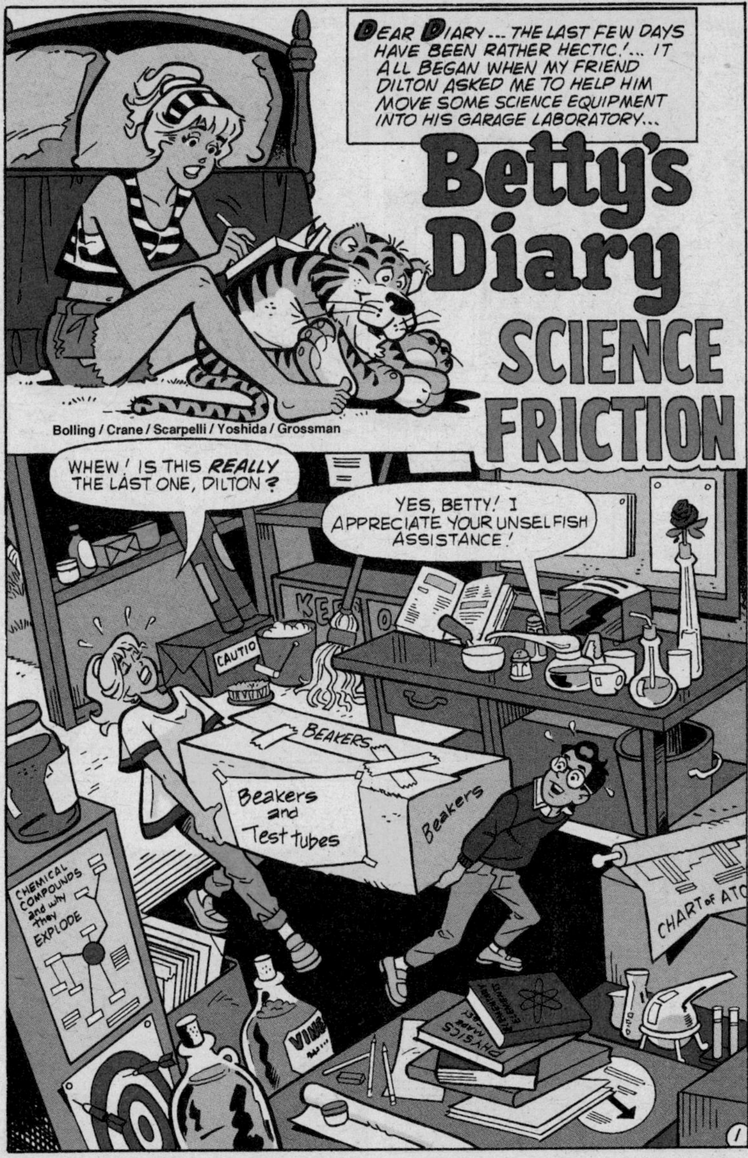

DEAR DIARY ... THE LAST FEW DAYS HAVE BEEN RATHER HECTIC!... IT ALL BEGAN WHEN MY FRIEND DILTON ASKED ME TO HELP HIM MOVE SOME SCIENCE EQUIPMENT INTO HIS GARAGE LABORATORY...
Betty's Diary
SCIENCE FRICTION
Bolling / Crane / Scarpelli / Yoshida / Grossman
WHEW! IS THIS REALLY THE LAST ONE, DILTON?
YES, BETTY! I APPRECIATE YOUR UNSELFISH ASSISTANCE!
CAUTIO
BEAKERS
Beakers and Test tubes
Beakers
CHEMICAL COMPOUNDS and why they EXPLODE
CHART of ATO
PHYSICS MADE EASY
ELEMENTARY ELEMENTS
1

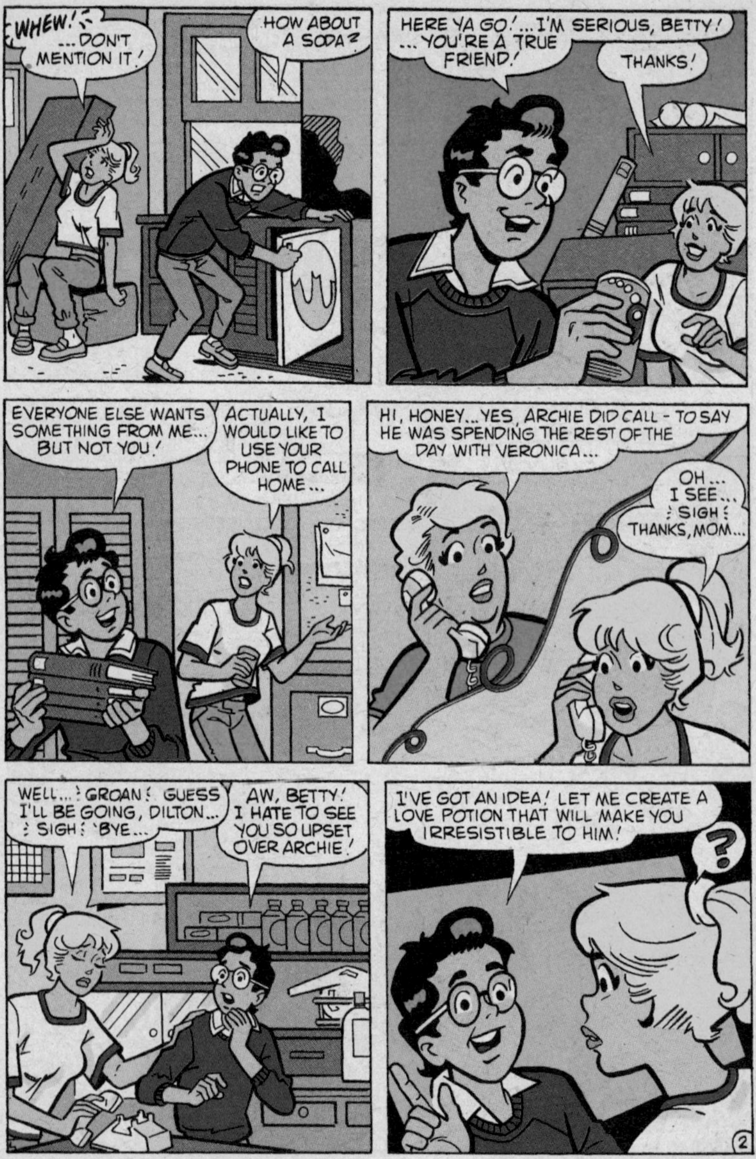
WHEW!
... DON'T MENTION IT!
HOW ABOUT A SODA?
HERE YA GO! ... I'M SERIOUS, BETTY! ... YOU'RE A TRUE FRIEND!
THANKS!
EVERYONE ELSE WANTS SOMETHING FROM ME... BUT NOT YOU!
ACTUALLY, I WOULD LIKE TO USE YOUR PHONE TO CALL HOME...
HI, HONEY... YES, ARCHIE DID CALL - TO SAY HE WAS SPENDING THE REST OF THE DAY WITH VERONICA...
OH... I SEE... SIGH THANKS, MOM...
WELL... GROAN GUESS I'LL BE GOING, DILTON... SIGH 'BYE...
AW, BETTY! I HATE TO SEE YOU SO UPSET OVER ARCHIE!
I'VE GOT AN IDEA! LET ME CREATE A LOVE POTION THAT WILL MAKE YOU IRRESISTIBLE TO HIM!
?

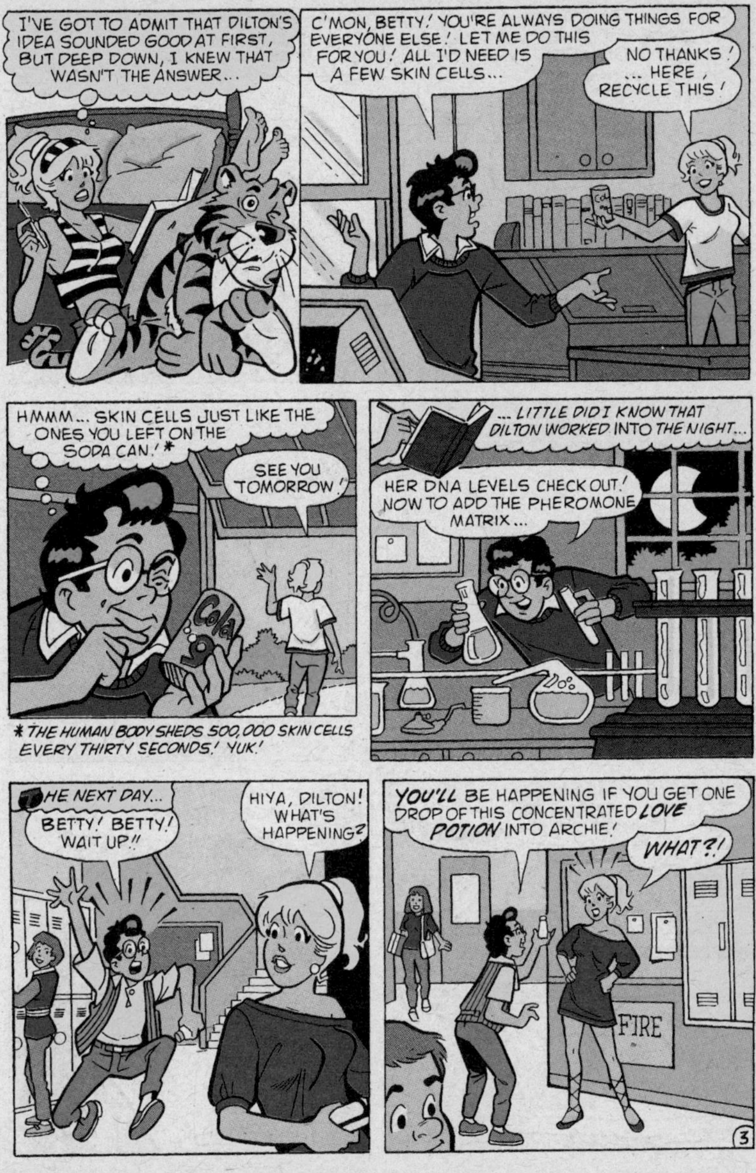
I'VE GOT TO ADMIT THAT DILTON'S IDEA SOUNDED GOOD AT FIRST, BUT DEEP DOWN, I KNEW THAT WASN'T THE ANSWER...
C'MON, BETTY! YOU'RE ALWAYS DOING THINGS FOR EVERYONE ELSE! LET ME DO THIS FOR YOU! ALL I'D NEED IS A FEW SKIN CELLS...
NO THANKS! ... HERE, RECYCLE THIS!
HMMM... SKIN CELLS JUST LIKE THE ONES YOU LEFT ON THE SODA CAN! *
SEE YOU TOMORROW!
Cola 9
* THE HUMAN BODY SHEDS 500,000 SKIN CELLS EVERY THIRTY SECONDS! YUK!
... LITTLE DID I KNOW THAT DILTON WORKED INTO THE NIGHT...
HER DNA LEVELS CHECK OUT! NOW TO ADD THE PHEROMONE MATRIX...
THE NEXT DAY...
BETTY! BETTY! WAIT UP!!
HIYA, DILTON! WHAT'S HAPPENING?
YOU'LL BE HAPPENING IF YOU GET ONE DROP OF THIS CONCENTRATED LOVE POTION INTO ARCHIE!
WHAT?!
FIRE

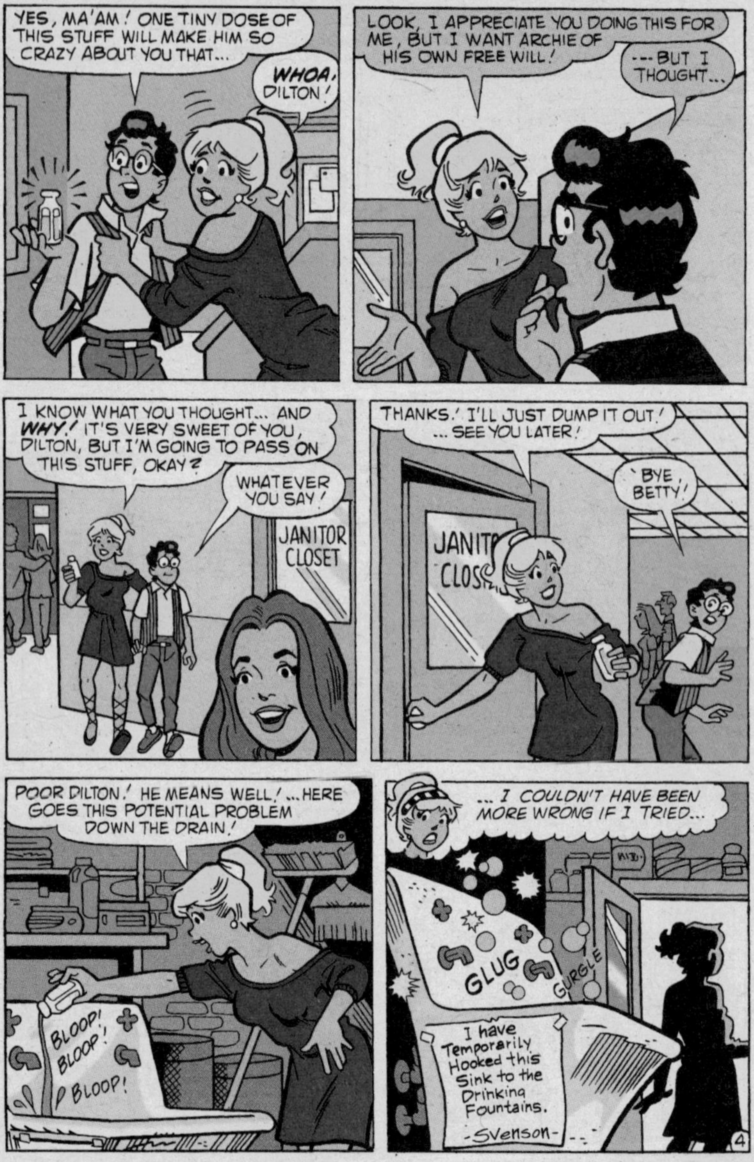

YES, MA'AM! ONE TINY DOSE OF THIS STUFF WILL MAKE HIM SO CRAZY ABOUT YOU THAT...
WHOA, DILTON!
LOOK, I APPRECIATE YOU DOING THIS FOR ME, BUT I WANT ARCHIE OF HIS OWN FREE WILL!
---BUT I THOUGHT...
I KNOW WHAT YOU THOUGHT... AND WHY! IT'S VERY SWEET OF YOU, DILTON, BUT I'M GOING TO PASS ON THIS STUFF, OKAY?
WHATEVER YOU SAY!
JANITOR CLOSET
THANKS! I'LL JUST DUMP IT OUT! ... SEE YOU LATER!
'BYE BETTY!
POOR DILTON! HE MEANS WELL! ...HERE GOES THIS POTENTIAL PROBLEM DOWN THE DRAIN!
BLOOP! BLOOP! BLOOP!
... I COULDN'T HAVE BEEN MORE WRONG IF I TRIED...
GLUG
GURGLE
I have Temporarily Hooked this Sink to the Drinking Fountains. -Svenson-
4

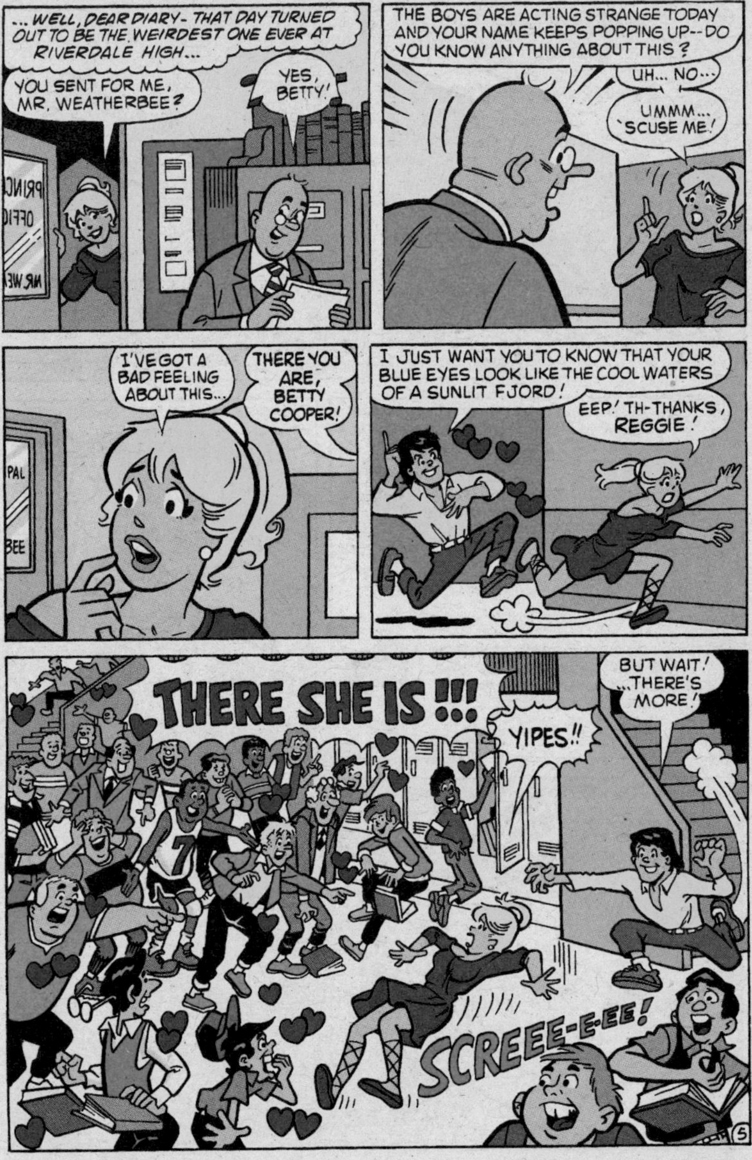
...WELL, DEAR DIARY- THAT DAY TURNED OUT TO BE THE WEIRDEST ONE EVER AT RIVERDALE HIGH...
YOU SENT FOR ME, MR. WEATHERBEE?
YES, BETTY!
THE BOYS ARE ACTING STRANGE TODAY AND YOUR NAME KEEPS POPPING UP--DO YOU KNOW ANYTHING ABOUT THIS?
UH... NO...
UMMM... 'SCUSE ME!
I'VE GOT A BAD FEELING ABOUT THIS...
THERE YOU ARE, BETTY COOPER!
I JUST WANT YOU TO KNOW THAT YOUR BLUE EYES LOOK LIKE THE COOL WATERS OF A SUNLIT FJORD!
EEP! TH-THANKS, REGGIE!
THERE SHE IS!!!
YIPES!!
BUT WAIT! ...THERE'S MORE!
SCREEE-E-EE!
5

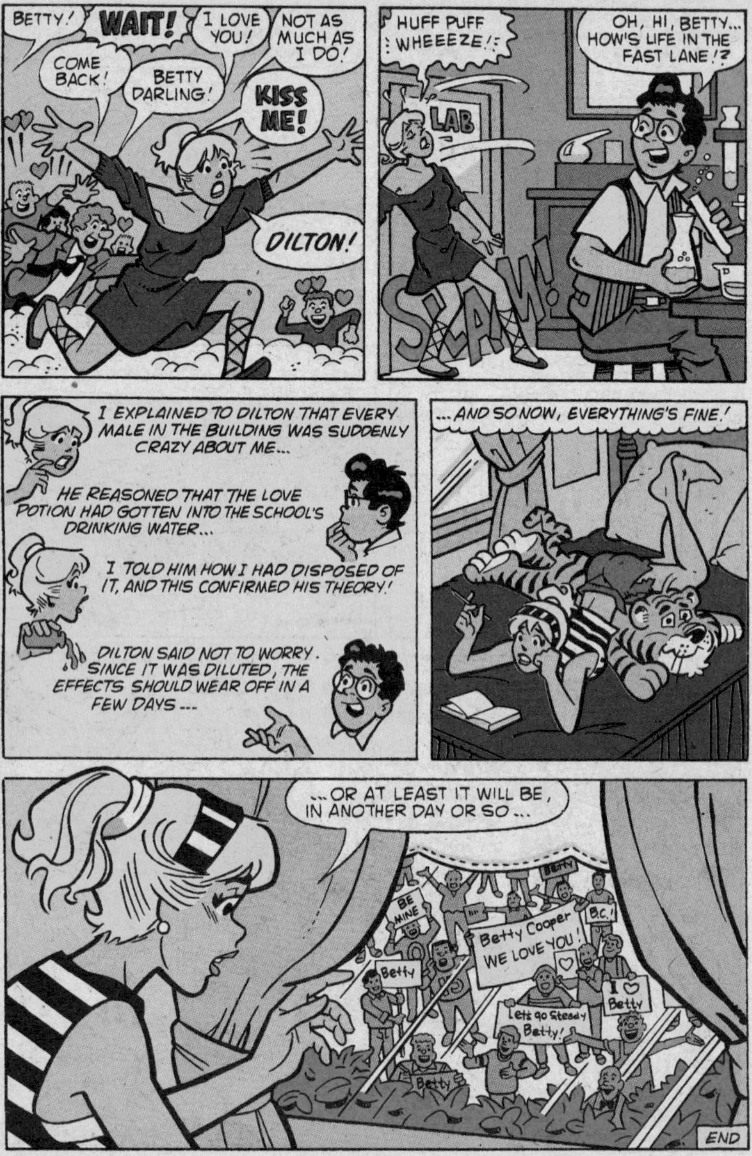
BETTY!
WAIT!
I LOVE YOU!
NOT AS MUCH AS I DO!
COME BACK!
BETTY DARLING!
KISS ME!
DILTON!
HUFF PUFF WHEEEZE!
LAB
OH, HI, BETTY... HOW'S LIFE IN THE FAST LANE!?
SLAM!
I EXPLAINED TO DILTON THAT EVERY MALE IN THE BUILDING WAS SUDDENLY CRAZY ABOUT ME...
HE REASONED THAT THE LOVE POTION HAD GOTTEN INTO THE SCHOOL'S DRINKING WATER...
I TOLD HIM HOW I HAD DISPOSED OF IT, AND THIS CONFIRMED HIS THEORY!
DILTON SAID NOT TO WORRY. SINCE IT WAS DILUTED, THE EFFECTS SHOULD WEAR OFF IN A FEW DAYS...
...AND SO NOW, EVERYTHING'S FINE!
...OR AT LEAST IT WILL BE, IN ANOTHER DAY OR SO...
BE MINE
B.C.!
Betty Cooper WE LOVE YOU!
Betty
I ♡ Betty
Let's go Steady Betty!
Betty
END

Veronica in "YOU'VE GOT CASH"

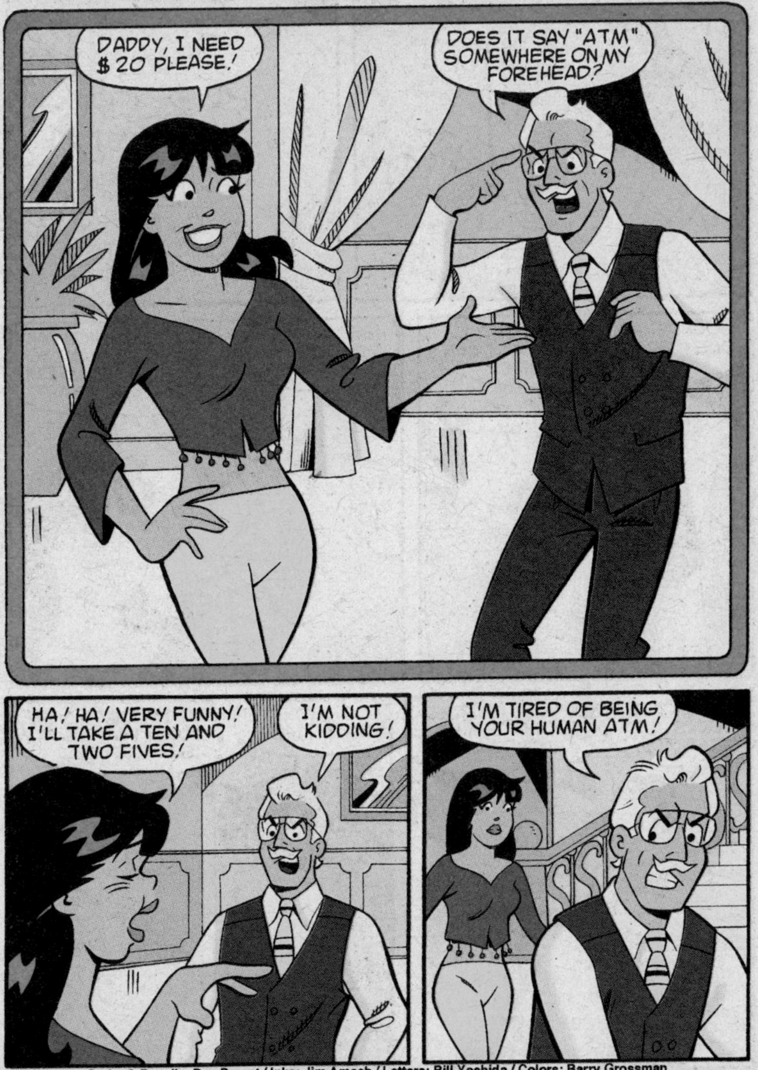
DADDY, I NEED $ 20 PLEASE!
DOES IT SAY "ATM" SOMEWHERE ON MY FOREHEAD?
HA! HA! VERY FUNNY! I'LL TAKE A TEN AND TWO FIVES!
I'M NOT KIDDING!
I'M TIRED OF BEING YOUR HUMAN ATM!

Script & Pencils: Dan Parent / Inks: Jim Amash / Letters: Bill Yoshida / Colors: Barry Grossman

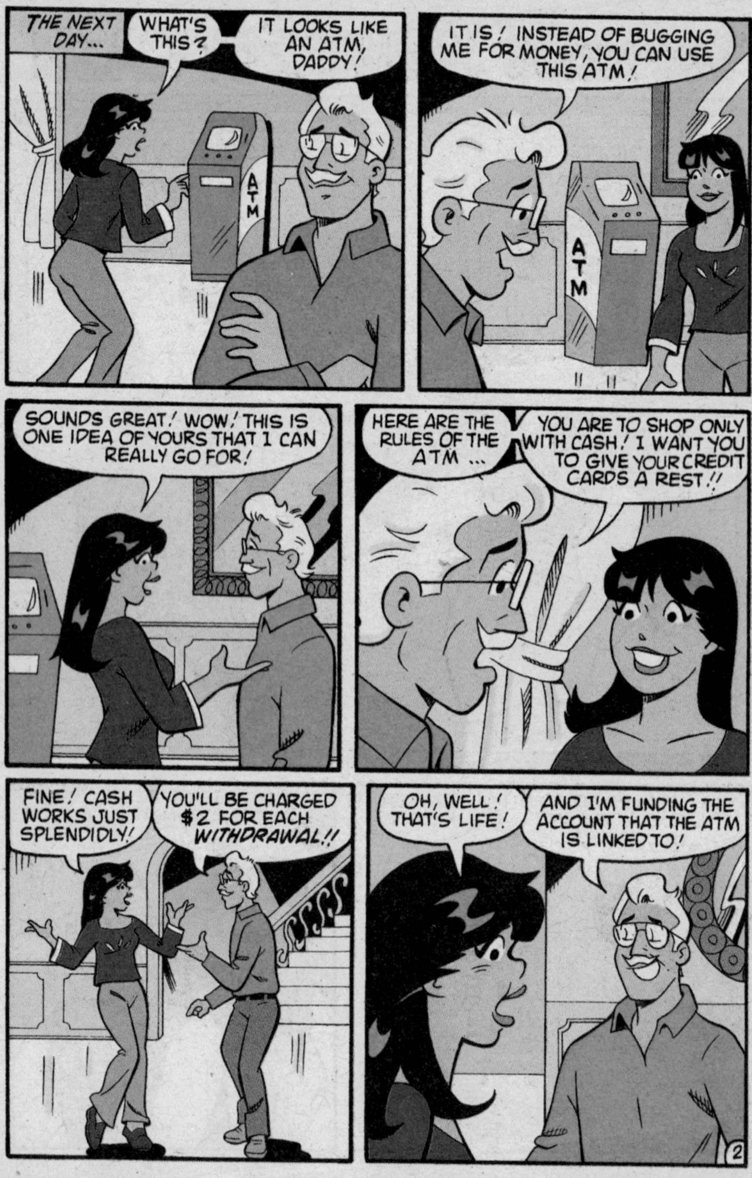
THE NEXT DAY...
WHAT'S THIS?
IT LOOKS LIKE AN ATM, DADDY!
IT IS! INSTEAD OF BUGGING ME FOR MONEY, YOU CAN USE THIS ATM!
ATM
SOUNDS GREAT! WOW! THIS IS ONE IDEA OF YOURS THAT I CAN REALLY GO FOR!
HERE ARE THE RULES OF THE ATM ...
YOU ARE TO SHOP ONLY WITH CASH! I WANT YOU TO GIVE YOUR CREDIT CARDS A REST!!
FINE! CASH WORKS JUST SPLENDIDLY!
YOU'LL BE CHARGED $2 FOR EACH WITHDRAWAL!!
OH, WELL! THAT'S LIFE!
AND I'M FUNDING THE ACCOUNT THAT THE ATM IS LINKED TO!

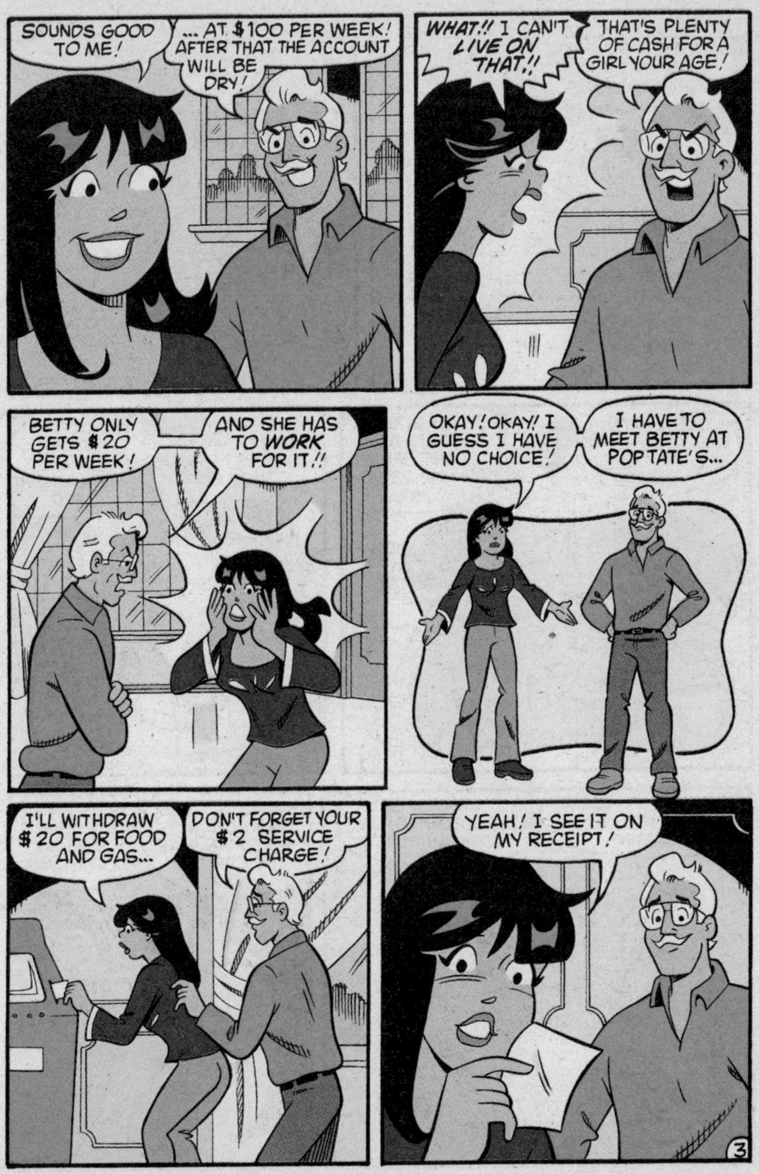
SOUNDS GOOD TO ME!
... AT $100 PER WEEK! AFTER THAT THE ACCOUNT WILL BE DRY!
WHAT!! I CAN'T LIVE ON THAT!!
THAT'S PLENTY OF CASH FOR A GIRL YOUR AGE!
BETTY ONLY GETS $20 PER WEEK!
AND SHE HAS TO WORK FOR IT!!
OKAY! OKAY! I GUESS I HAVE NO CHOICE!
I HAVE TO MEET BETTY AT POP TATE'S...
I'LL WITHDRAW $20 FOR FOOD AND GAS...
DON'T FORGET YOUR $2 SERVICE CHARGE!
YEAH! I SEE IT ON MY RECEIPT!
3

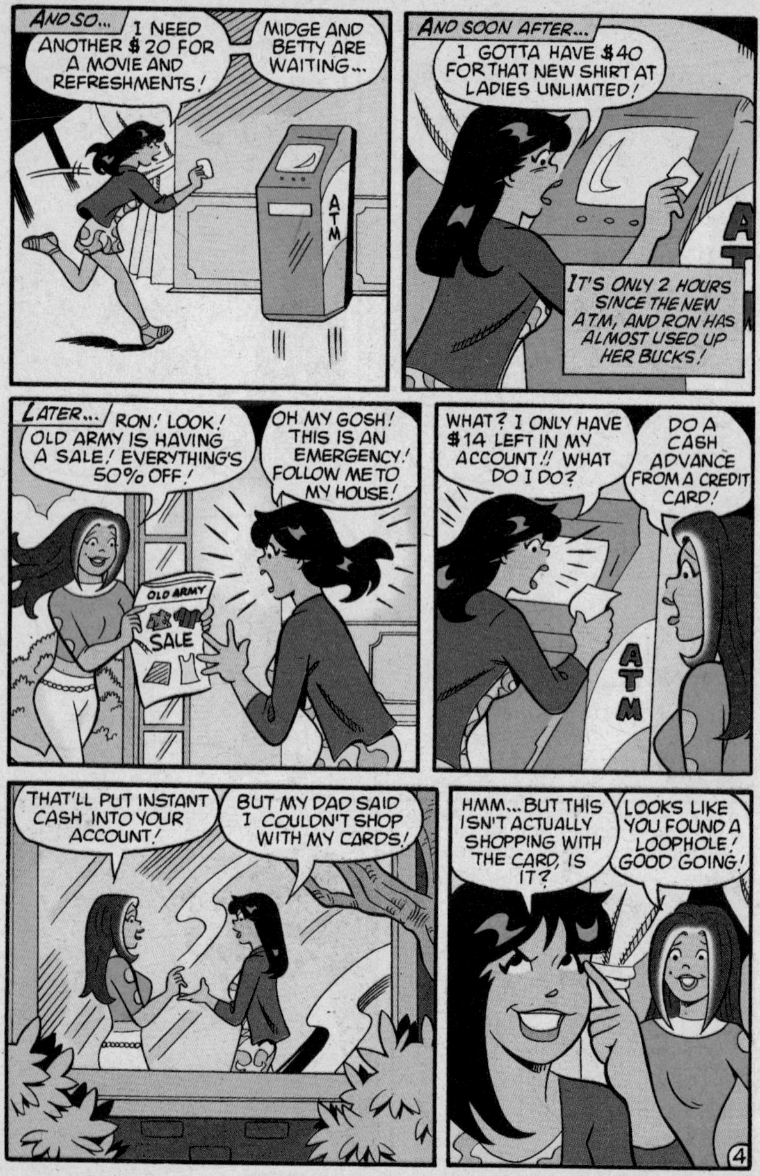
AND SO...
I NEED ANOTHER $20 FOR A MOVIE AND REFRESHMENTS!
MIDGE AND BETTY ARE WAITING...
ATM
AND SOON AFTER...
I GOTTA HAVE $40 FOR THAT NEW SHIRT AT LADIES UNLIMITED!
IT'S ONLY 2 HOURS SINCE THE NEW ATM, AND RON HAS ALMOST USED UP HER BUCKS!
LATER...
RON! LOOK! OLD ARMY IS HAVING A SALE! EVERYTHING'S 50% OFF!
OH MY GOSH! THIS IS AN EMERGENCY! FOLLOW ME TO MY HOUSE!
OLD ARMY
SALE
WHAT? I ONLY HAVE $14 LEFT IN MY ACCOUNT!! WHAT DO I DO?
DO A CASH ADVANCE FROM A CREDIT CARD!
ATM
THAT'LL PUT INSTANT CASH INTO YOUR ACCOUNT!
BUT MY DAD SAID I COULDN'T SHOP WITH MY CARDS!
HMM...BUT THIS ISN'T ACTUALLY SHOPPING WITH THE CARD, IS IT?
LOOKS LIKE YOU FOUND A LOOPHOLE! GOOD GOING!
4

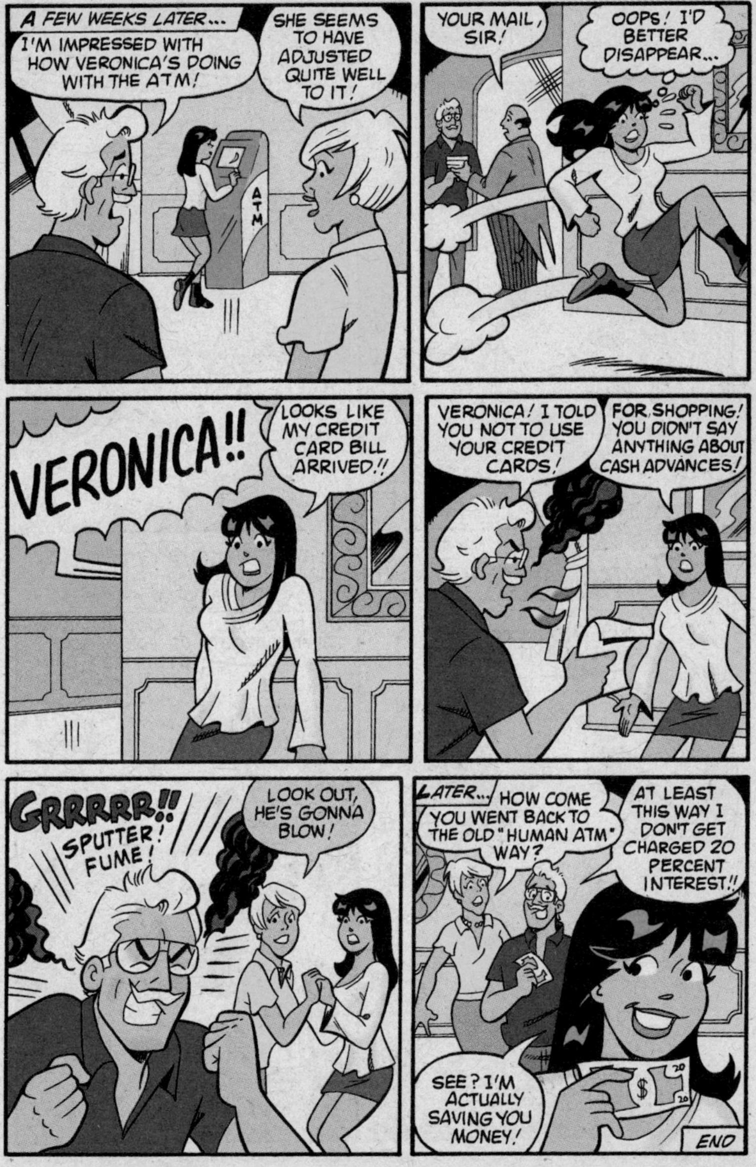
A FEW WEEKS LATER...
I'M IMPRESSED WITH HOW VERONICA'S DOING WITH THE ATM!
SHE SEEMS TO HAVE ADJUSTED QUITE WELL TO IT!
ATM
YOUR MAIL, SIR!
OOPS! I'D BETTER DISAPPEAR...
VERONICA!!
LOOKS LIKE MY CREDIT CARD BILL ARRIVED!!
VERONICA! I TOLD YOU NOT TO USE YOUR CREDIT CARDS!
FOR SHOPPING! YOU DIDN'T SAY ANYTHING ABOUT CASH ADVANCES!
GRRRRR!!
SPUTTER! FUME!
LOOK OUT, HE'S GONNA BLOW!
LATER...
HOW COME YOU WENT BACK TO THE OLD "HUMAN ATM" WAY?
AT LEAST THIS WAY I DON'T GET CHARGED 20 PERCENT INTEREST!!
SEE? I'M ACTUALLY SAVING YOU MONEY!
END

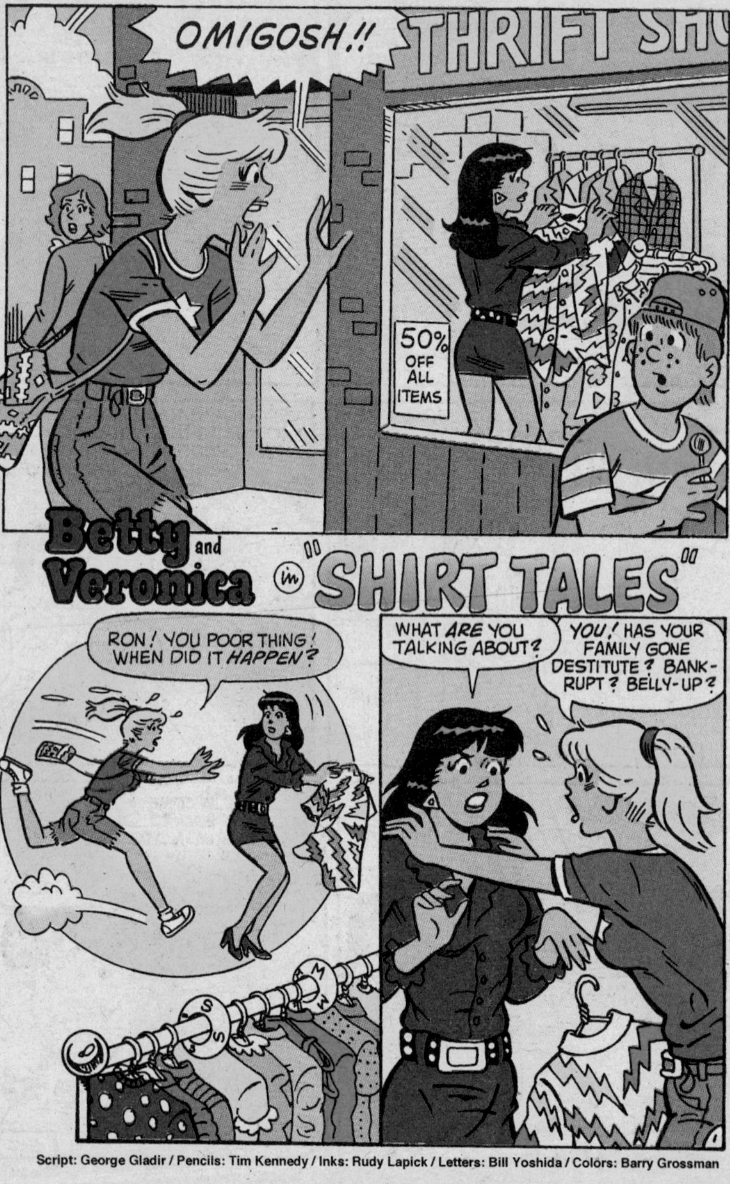
OMIGOSH!!
THRIFT SH
50% OFF ALL ITEMS
Betty and Veronica in "SHIRT TALES"
RON! YOU POOR THING! WHEN DID IT HAPPEN?
WHAT ARE YOU TALKING ABOUT?
YOU! HAS YOUR FAMILY GONE DESTITUTE? BANKRUPT? BELLY-UP?
S
M

Script: George Gladir / Pencils: Tim Kennedy / Inks: Rudy Lapick / Letters: Bill Yoshida / Colors: Barry Grossman

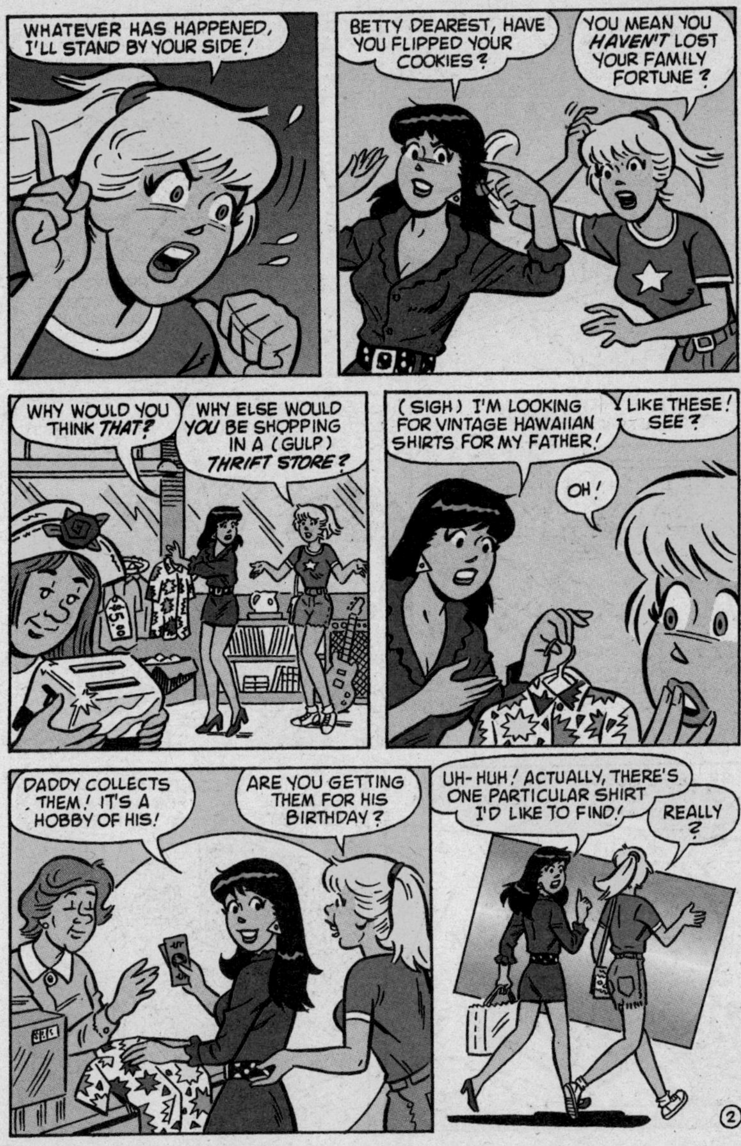
WHATEVER HAS HAPPENED, I'LL STAND BY YOUR SIDE!
BETTY DEAREST, HAVE YOU FLIPPED YOUR COOKIES?
YOU MEAN YOU HAVEN'T LOST YOUR FAMILY FORTUNE?
WHY WOULD YOU THINK THAT?
WHY ELSE WOULD YOU BE SHOPPING IN A (GULP) THRIFT STORE?
$5.00
(SIGH) I'M LOOKING FOR VINTAGE HAWAIIAN SHIRTS FOR MY FATHER!
LIKE THESE! SEE?
OH!
DADDY COLLECTS THEM! IT'S A HOBBY OF HIS!
ARE YOU GETTING THEM FOR HIS BIRTHDAY?
UH-HUH! ACTUALLY, THERE'S ONE PARTICULAR SHIRT I'D LIKE TO FIND!
REALLY?
2

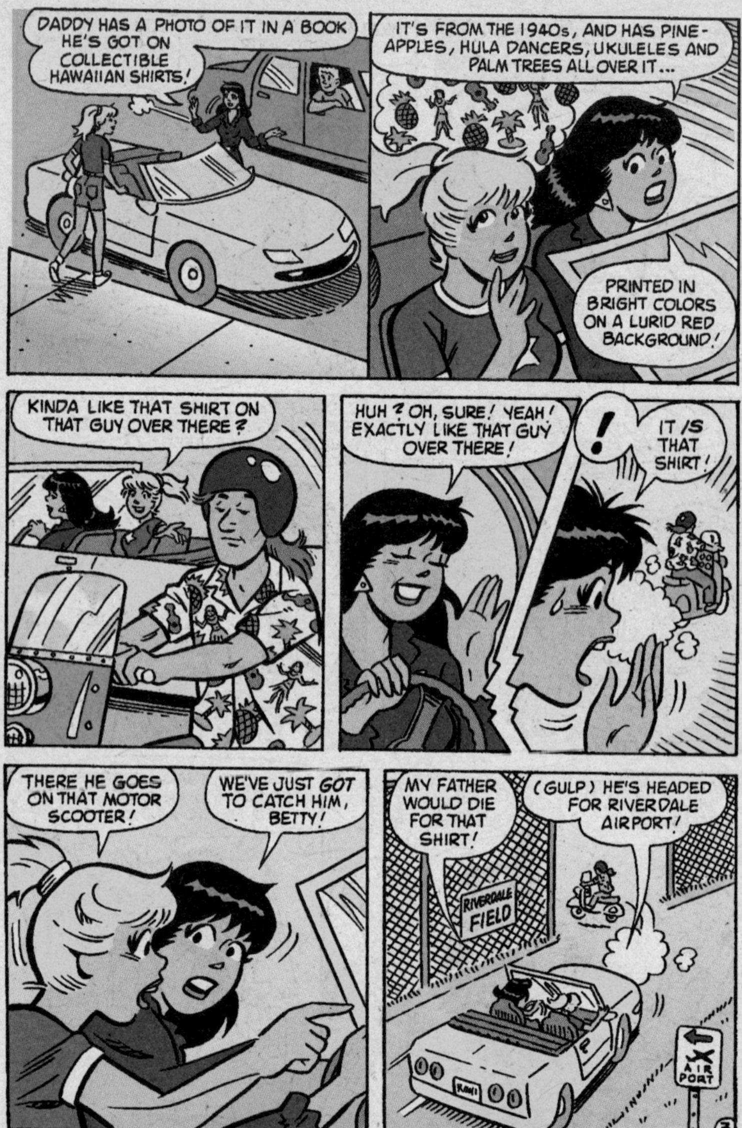
DADDY HAS A PHOTO OF IT IN A BOOK HE'S GOT ON COLLECTIBLE HAWAIIAN SHIRTS!
IT'S FROM THE 1940s, AND HAS PINE-APPLES, HULA DANCERS, UKULELES AND PALM TREES ALL OVER IT...
PRINTED IN BRIGHT COLORS ON A LURID RED BACKGROUND!
KINDA LIKE THAT SHIRT ON THAT GUY OVER THERE?
HUH? OH, SURE! YEAH! EXACTLY LIKE THAT GUY OVER THERE!
!
IT IS THAT SHIRT!
THERE HE GOES ON THAT MOTOR SCOOTER!
WE'VE JUST GOT TO CATCH HIM, BETTY!
MY FATHER WOULD DIE FOR THAT SHIRT!
(GULP) HE'S HEADED FOR RIVERDALE AIRPORT!
RIVERDALE FIELD
AIR PORT
3

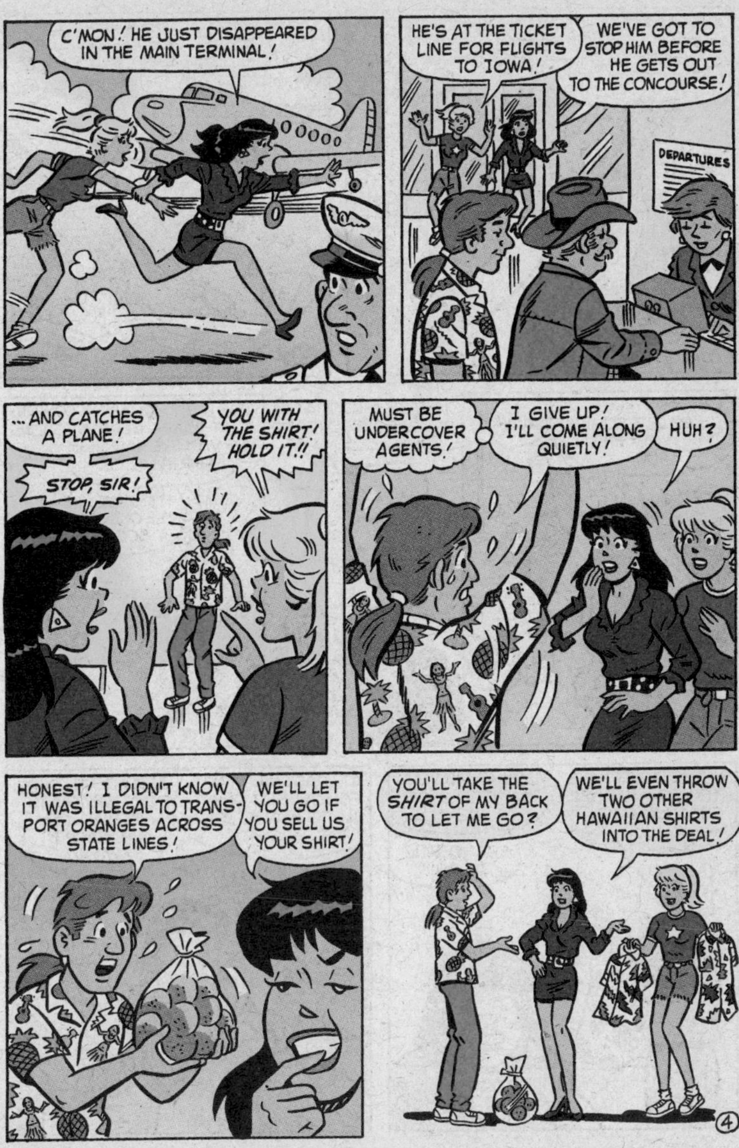

C'MON! HE JUST DISAPPEARED IN THE MAIN TERMINAL!
HE'S AT THE TICKET LINE FOR FLIGHTS TO IOWA!
WE'VE GOT TO STOP HIM BEFORE HE GETS OUT TO THE CONCOURSE!
DEPARTURES
...AND CATCHES A PLANE!
YOU WITH THE SHIRT! HOLD IT!!
STOP, SIR!
MUST BE UNDERCOVER AGENTS!
I GIVE UP! I'LL COME ALONG QUIETLY!
HUH?
HONEST! I DIDN'T KNOW IT WAS ILLEGAL TO TRANS-PORT ORANGES ACROSS STATE LINES!
WE'LL LET YOU GO IF YOU SELL US YOUR SHIRT!
YOU'LL TAKE THE SHIRT OF MY BACK TO LET ME GO?
WE'LL EVEN THROW TWO OTHER HAWAIIAN SHIRTS INTO THE DEAL!
4

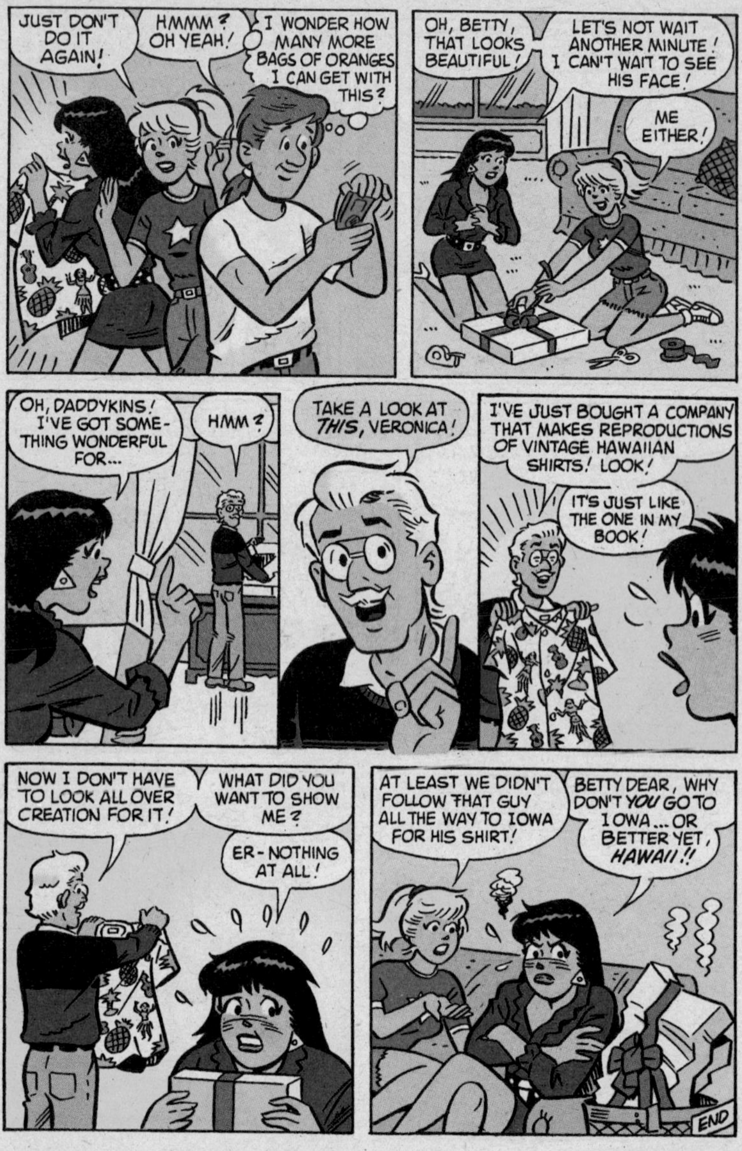
JUST DON'T DO IT AGAIN!
HMMM? OH YEAH!
I WONDER HOW MANY MORE BAGS OF ORANGES I CAN GET WITH THIS?
OH, BETTY, THAT LOOKS BEAUTIFUL!
LET'S NOT WAIT ANOTHER MINUTE! I CAN'T WAIT TO SEE HIS FACE!
ME EITHER!
OH, DADDYKINS! I'VE GOT SOME-THING WONDERFUL FOR...
HMM?
TAKE A LOOK AT *THIS*, VERONICA!
I'VE JUST BOUGHT A COMPANY THAT MAKES REPRODUCTIONS OF VINTAGE HAWAIIAN SHIRTS! LOOK!
IT'S JUST LIKE THE ONE IN MY BOOK!
NOW I DON'T HAVE TO LOOK ALL OVER CREATION FOR IT!
WHAT DID YOU WANT TO SHOW ME?
ER-NOTHING AT ALL!
AT LEAST WE DIDN'T FOLLOW THAT GUY ALL THE WAY TO IOWA FOR HIS SHIRT!
BETTY DEAR, WHY DON'T *YOU* GO TO IOWA... OR BETTER YET, *HAWAII*!!
END

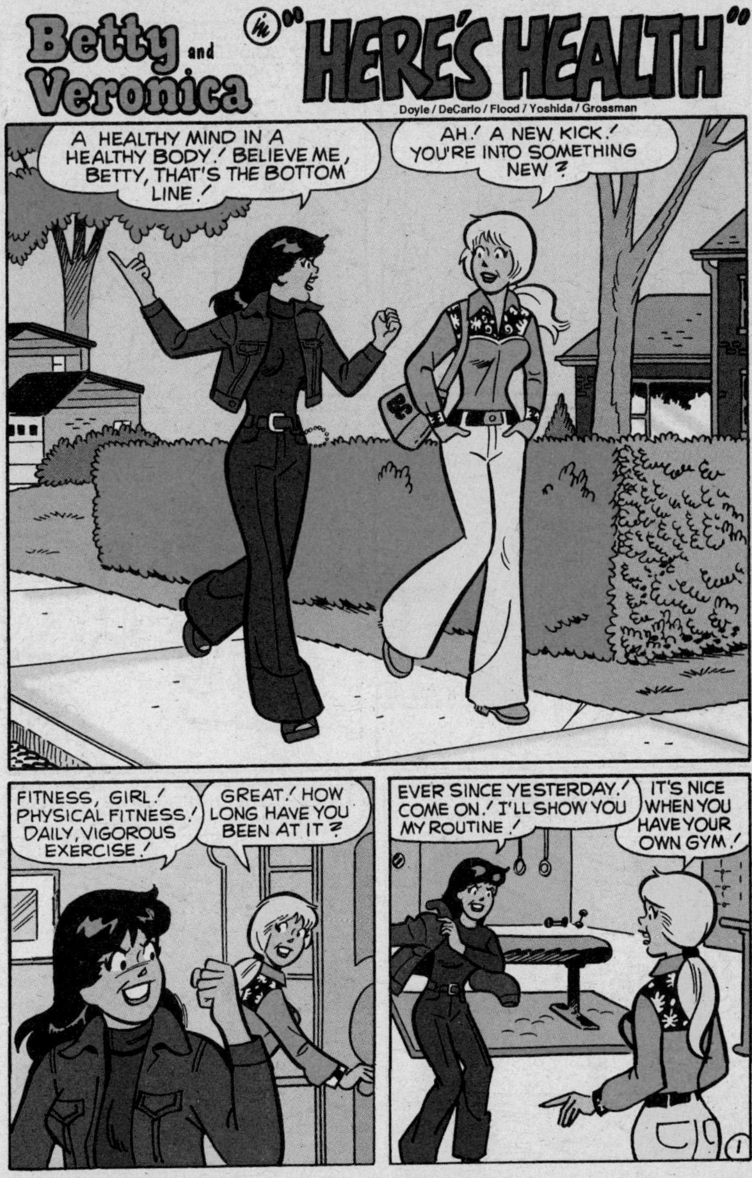

Betty and Veronica
in "HERE'S HEALTH"
Doyle / DeCarlo / Flood / Yoshida / Grossman
A HEALTHY MIND IN A HEALTHY BODY! BELIEVE ME, BETTY, THAT'S THE BOTTOM LINE!
AH! A NEW KICK! YOU'RE INTO SOMETHING NEW?
FITNESS, GIRL! PHYSICAL FITNESS! DAILY, VIGOROUS EXERCISE!
GREAT! HOW LONG HAVE YOU BEEN AT IT?
EVER SINCE YESTERDAY! COME ON! I'LL SHOW YOU MY ROUTINE!
IT'S NICE WHEN YOU HAVE YOUR OWN GYM!
1

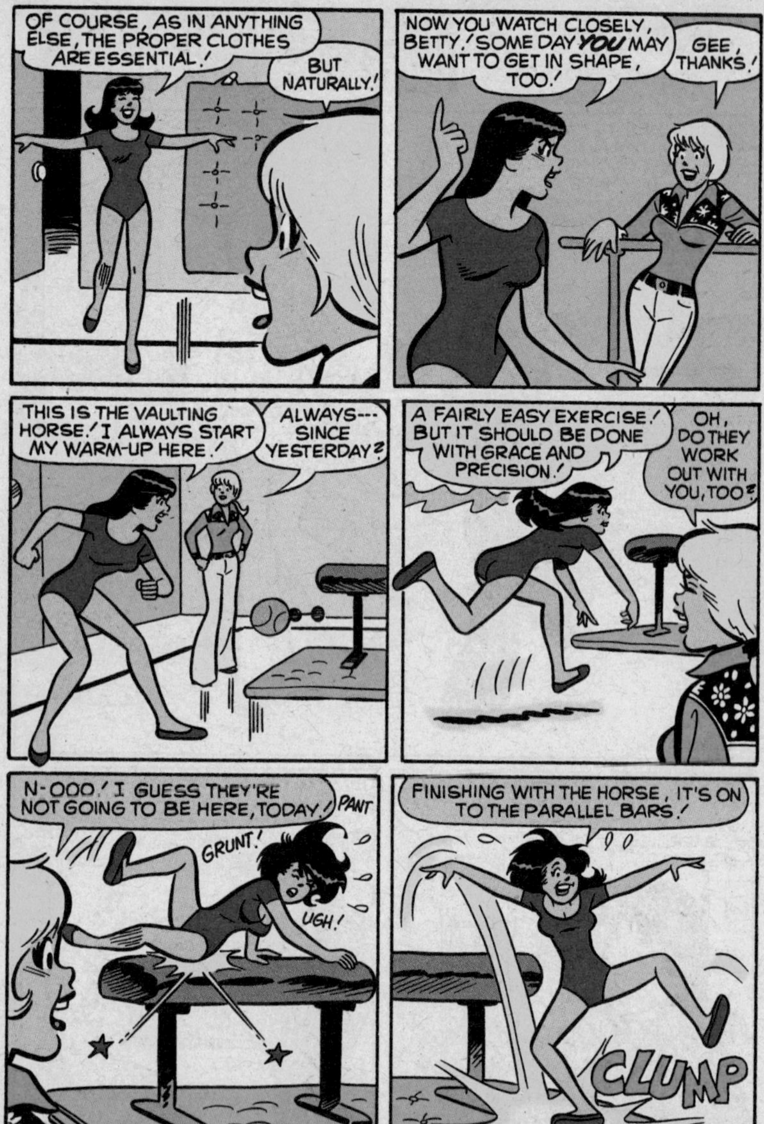
OF COURSE, AS IN ANYTHING ELSE, THE PROPER CLOTHES ARE ESSENTIAL!
BUT NATURALLY!
NOW YOU WATCH CLOSELY, BETTY! SOME DAY YOU MAY WANT TO GET IN SHAPE, TOO!
GEE, THANKS!
THIS IS THE VAULTING HORSE! I ALWAYS START MY WARM-UP HERE!
ALWAYS--- SINCE YESTERDAY?
A FAIRLY EASY EXERCISE! BUT IT SHOULD BE DONE WITH GRACE AND PRECISION!
OH, DO THEY WORK OUT WITH YOU, TOO?
N-OOO! I GUESS THEY'RE NOT GOING TO BE HERE, TODAY!
PANT
GRUNT!
UGH!
FINISHING WITH THE HORSE, IT'S ON TO THE PARALLEL BARS!
CLUMP

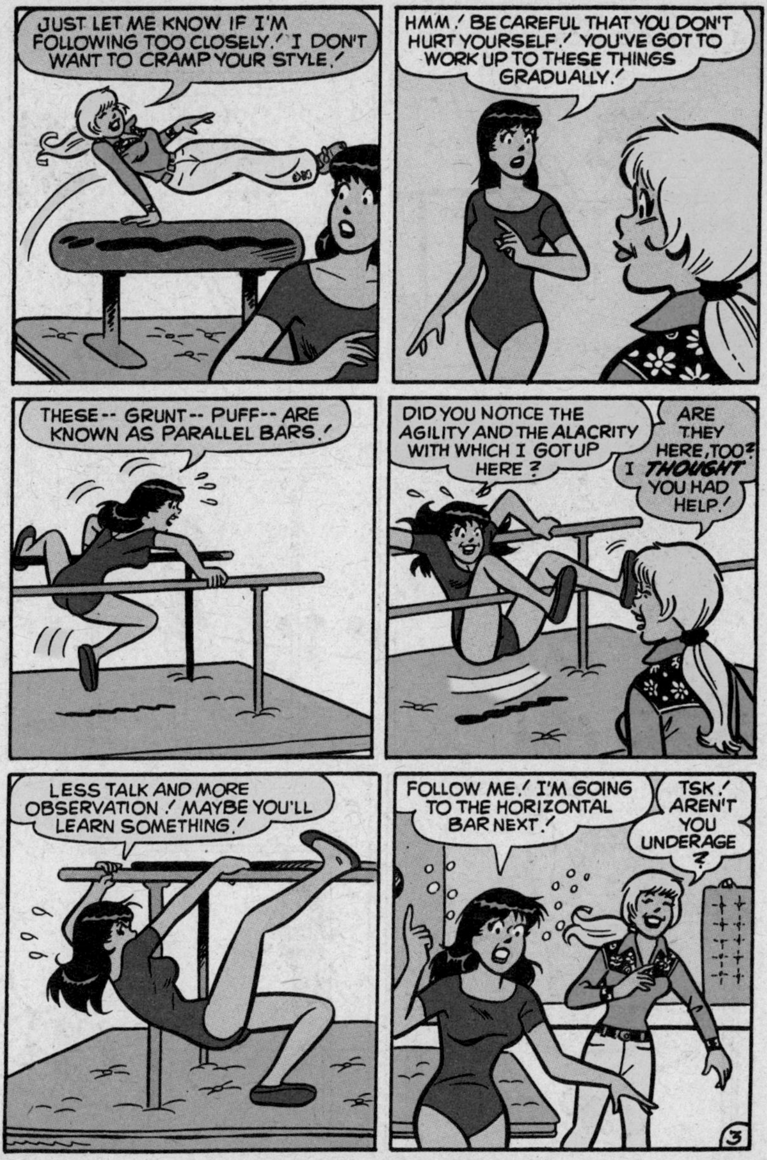
JUST LET ME KNOW IF I'M FOLLOWING TOO CLOSELY! I DON'T WANT TO CRAMP YOUR STYLE!
HMM! BE CAREFUL THAT YOU DON'T HURT YOURSELF! YOU'VE GOT TO WORK UP TO THESE THINGS GRADUALLY!
THESE-- GRUNT-- PUFF-- ARE KNOWN AS PARALLEL BARS!
DID YOU NOTICE THE AGILITY AND THE ALACRITY WITH WHICH I GOT UP HERE?
ARE THEY HERE, TOO? I THOUGHT YOU HAD HELP!
LESS TALK AND MORE OBSERVATION! MAYBE YOU'LL LEARN SOMETHING!
FOLLOW ME! I'M GOING TO THE HORIZONTAL BAR NEXT!
TSK! AREN'T YOU UNDERAGE?
3

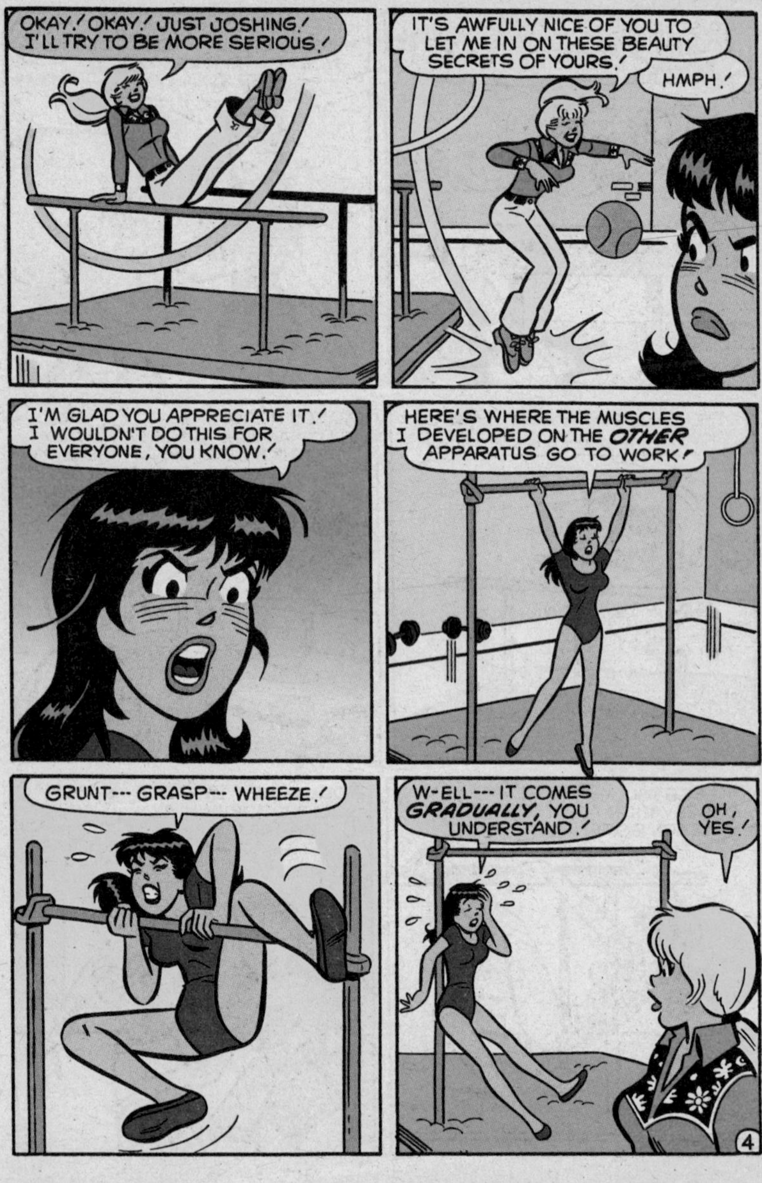

OKAY! OKAY! JUST JOSHING! I'LL TRY TO BE MORE SERIOUS!
IT'S AWFULLY NICE OF YOU TO LET ME IN ON THESE BEAUTY SECRETS OF YOURS!
HMPH!
I'M GLAD YOU APPRECIATE IT! I WOULDN'T DO THIS FOR EVERYONE, YOU KNOW!
HERE'S WHERE THE MUSCLES I DEVELOPED ON THE OTHER APPARATUS GO TO WORK!
GRUNT--- GRASP--- WHEEZE!
W-ELL--- IT COMES GRADUALLY, YOU UNDERSTAND!
OH, YES!
4

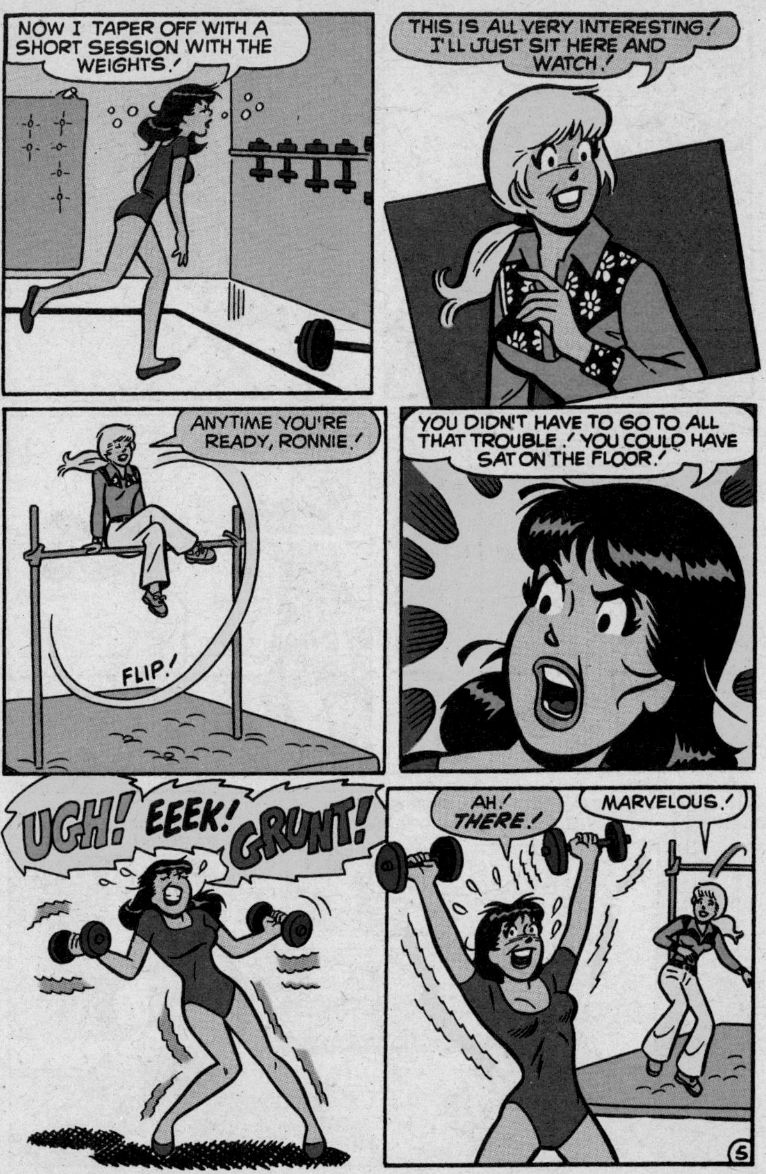
NOW I TAPER OFF WITH A SHORT SESSION WITH THE WEIGHTS.!
THIS IS ALL VERY INTERESTING! I'LL JUST SIT HERE AND WATCH!
ANYTIME YOU'RE READY, RONNIE!
FLIP!
YOU DIDN'T HAVE TO GO TO ALL THAT TROUBLE! YOU COULD HAVE SAT ON THE FLOOR!
UGH! EEEK! GRUNT!
AH! THERE!
MARVELOUS!

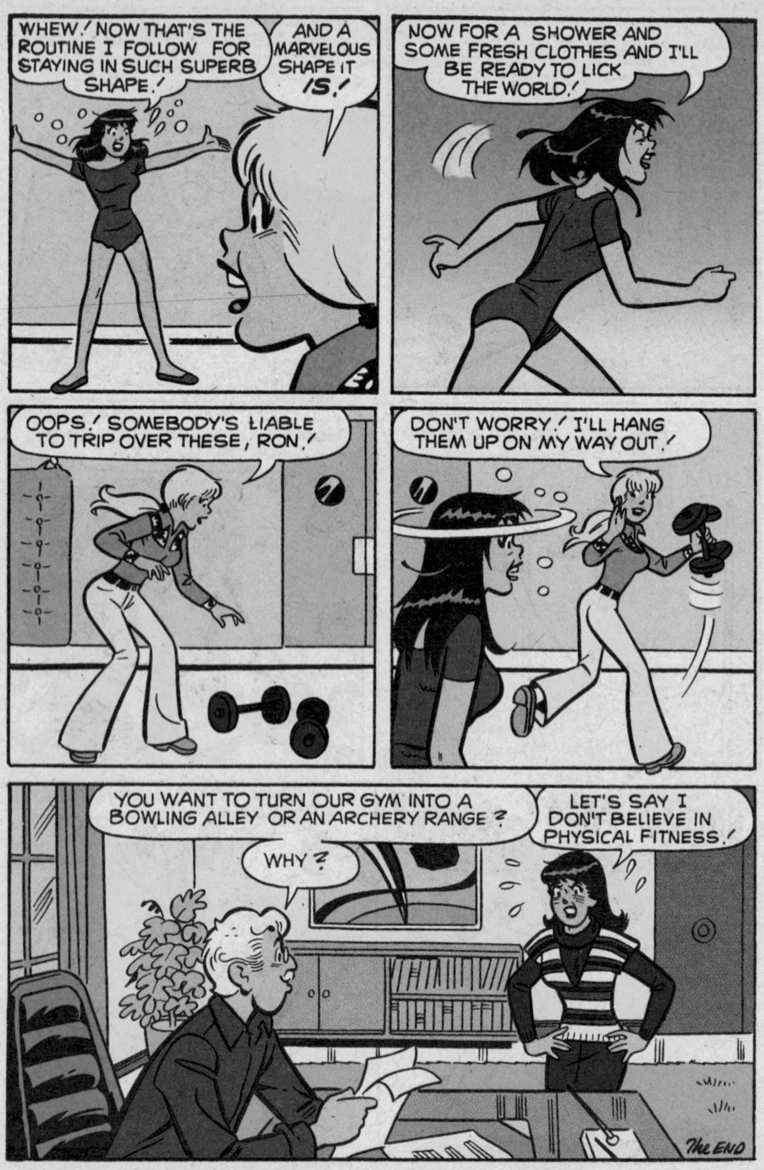
WHEW.! NOW THAT'S THE ROUTINE I FOLLOW FOR STAYING IN SUCH SUPERB SHAPE.!
AND A MARVELOUS SHAPE IT IS.!
NOW FOR A SHOWER AND SOME FRESH CLOTHES AND I'LL BE READY TO LICK THE WORLD.!
OOPS.! SOMEBODY'S LIABLE TO TRIP OVER THESE, RON.!
DON'T WORRY.! I'LL HANG THEM UP ON MY WAY OUT.!
YOU WANT TO TURN OUR GYM INTO A BOWLING ALLEY OR AN ARCHERY RANGE?
WHY?
LET'S SAY I DON'T BELIEVE IN PHYSICAL FITNESS.!
THE END

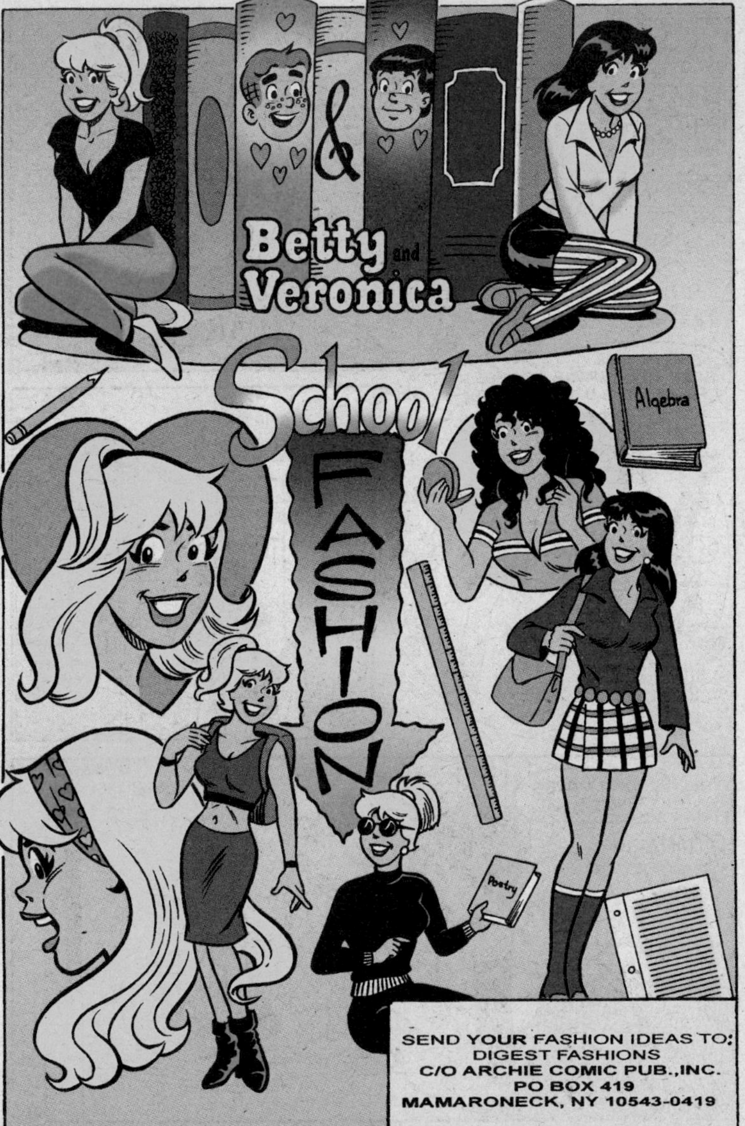
Betty and Veronica
School FASHION
Algebra
Poetry
SEND YOUR FASHION IDEAS TO:
DIGEST FASHIONS
C/O ARCHIE COMIC PUB.,INC.
PO BOX 419
MAMARONECK, NY 10543-0419

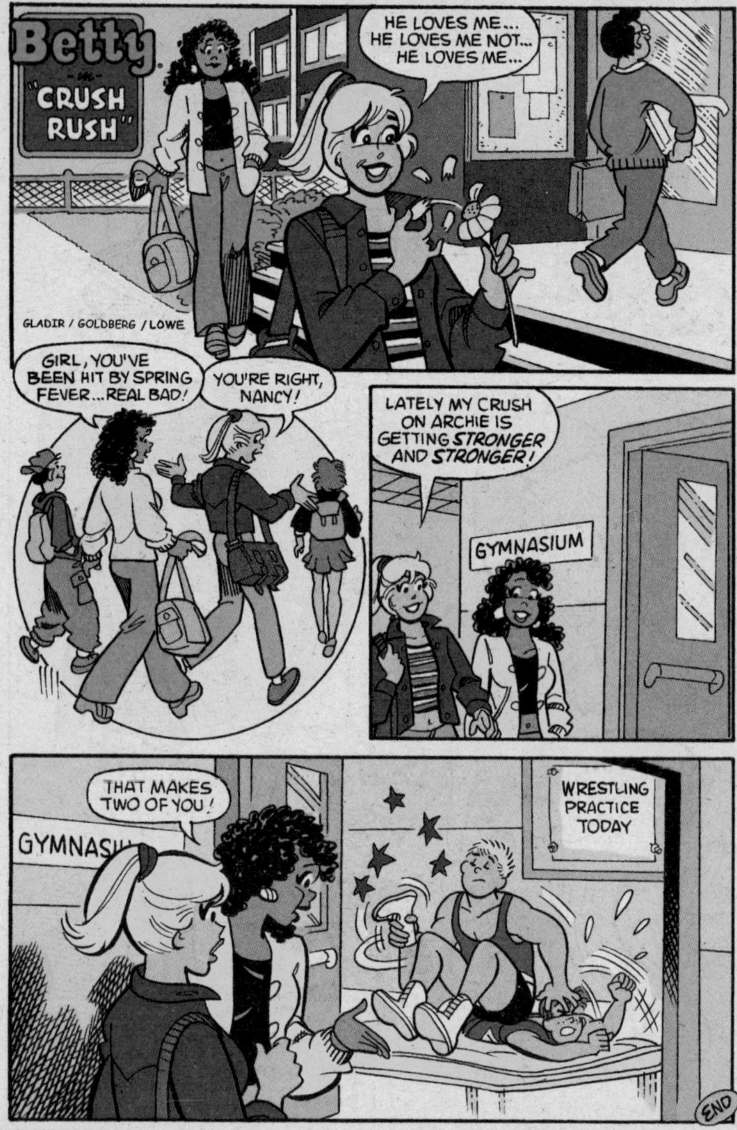
Betty
in
"CRUSH RUSH"
HE LOVES ME... HE LOVES ME NOT... HE LOVES ME...
GLADIR / GOLDBERG / LOWE
GIRL, YOU'VE BEEN HIT BY SPRING FEVER...REAL BAD!
YOU'RE RIGHT, NANCY!
LATELY MY CRUSH ON ARCHIE IS GETTING STRONGER AND STRONGER!
GYMNASIUM
THAT MAKES TWO OF YOU!
GYMNASI
WRESTLING PRACTICE TODAY
END

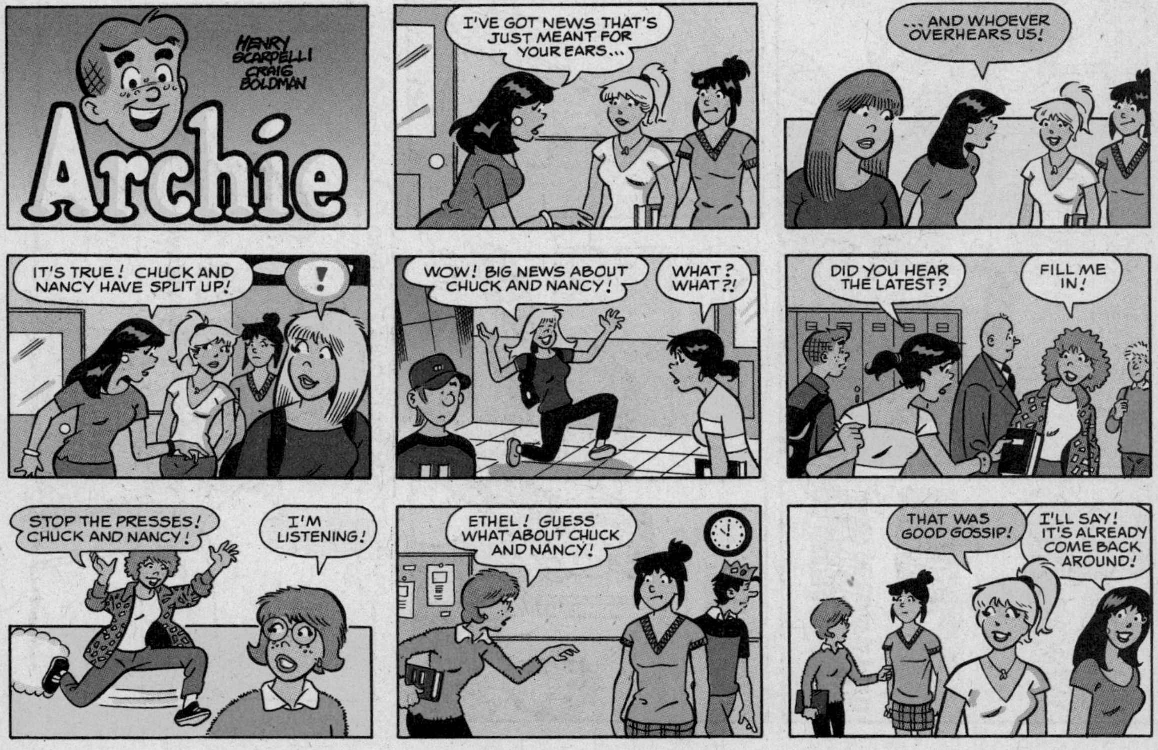
Archie
HENRY SCARPELLI
CRAIG BOLDMAN
I'VE GOT NEWS THAT'S JUST MEANT FOR YOUR EARS...
... AND WHOEVER OVERHEARS US!
IT'S TRUE! CHUCK AND NANCY HAVE SPLIT UP!
!
WOW! BIG NEWS ABOUT CHUCK AND NANCY!
WHAT? WHAT?!
DID YOU HEAR THE LATEST?
FILL ME IN!
STOP THE PRESSES! CHUCK AND NANCY!
I'M LISTENING!
ETHEL! GUESS WHAT ABOUT CHUCK AND NANCY!
THAT WAS GOOD GOSSIP!
I'LL SAY! IT'S ALREADY COME BACK AROUND!

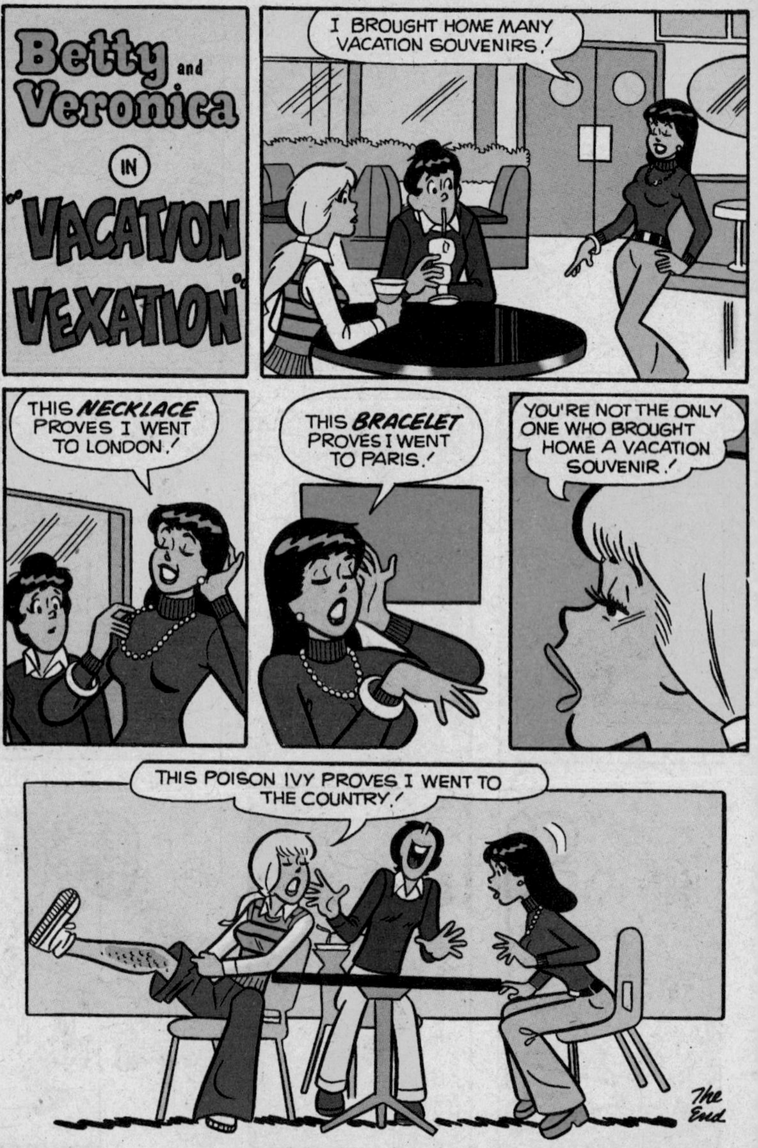
Betty and Veronica
IN
"VACATION VEXATION"
I BROUGHT HOME MANY VACATION SOUVENIRS!
THIS NECKLACE PROVES I WENT TO LONDON!
THIS BRACELET PROVES I WENT TO PARIS!
YOU'RE NOT THE ONLY ONE WHO BROUGHT HOME A VACATION SOUVENIR!
THIS POISON IVY PROVES I WENT TO THE COUNTRY!
The End

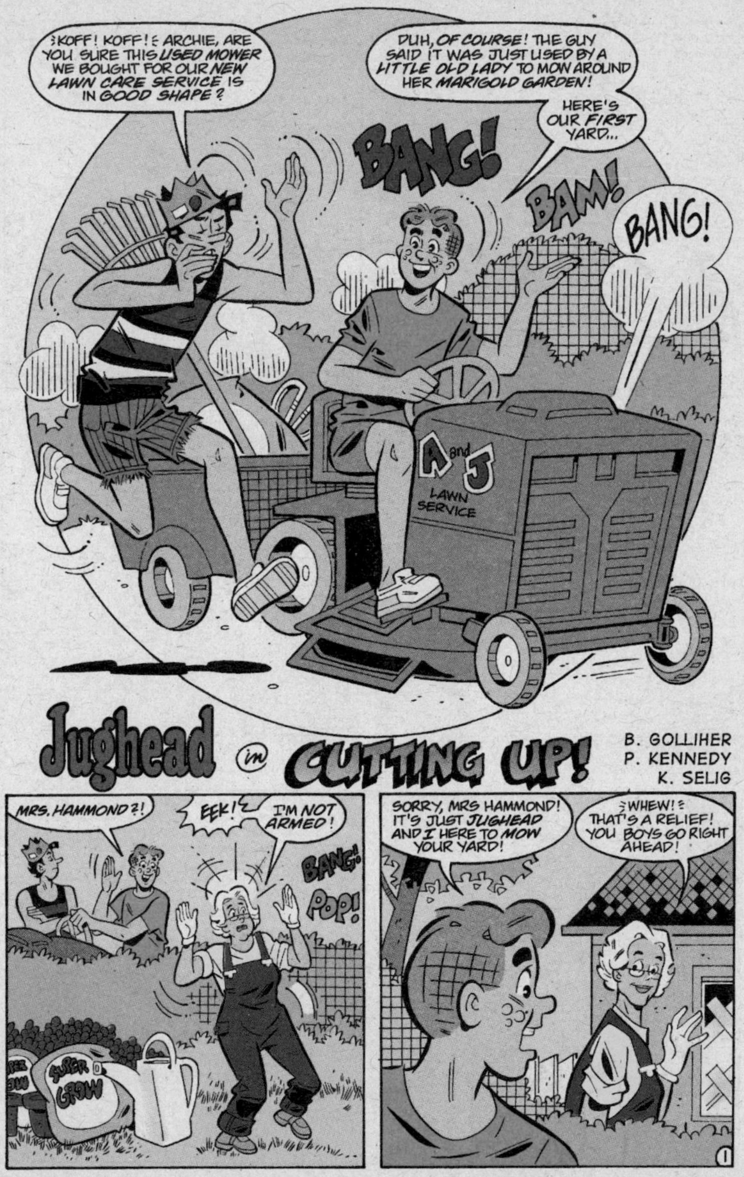

KOFF! KOFF! ARCHIE, ARE YOU SURE THIS USED MOWER WE BOUGHT FOR OUR NEW LAWN CARE SERVICE IS IN GOOD SHAPE?
DUH, OF COURSE! THE GUY SAID IT WAS JUST USED BY A LITTLE OLD LADY TO MOW AROUND HER MARIGOLD GARDEN!
HERE'S OUR FIRST YARD...
BANG!
BAM!
BANG!
A and J LAWN SERVICE
Jughead in CUTTING UP!
B. GOLLIHER
P. KENNEDY
K. SELIG
MRS. HAMMOND?!
EEK!
I'M NOT ARMED!
BANG!
POP!
SUPER GROW
SORRY, MRS HAMMOND! IT'S JUST JUGHEAD AND I HERE TO MOW YOUR YARD!
WHEW! THAT'S A RELIEF! YOU BOYS GO RIGHT AHEAD!

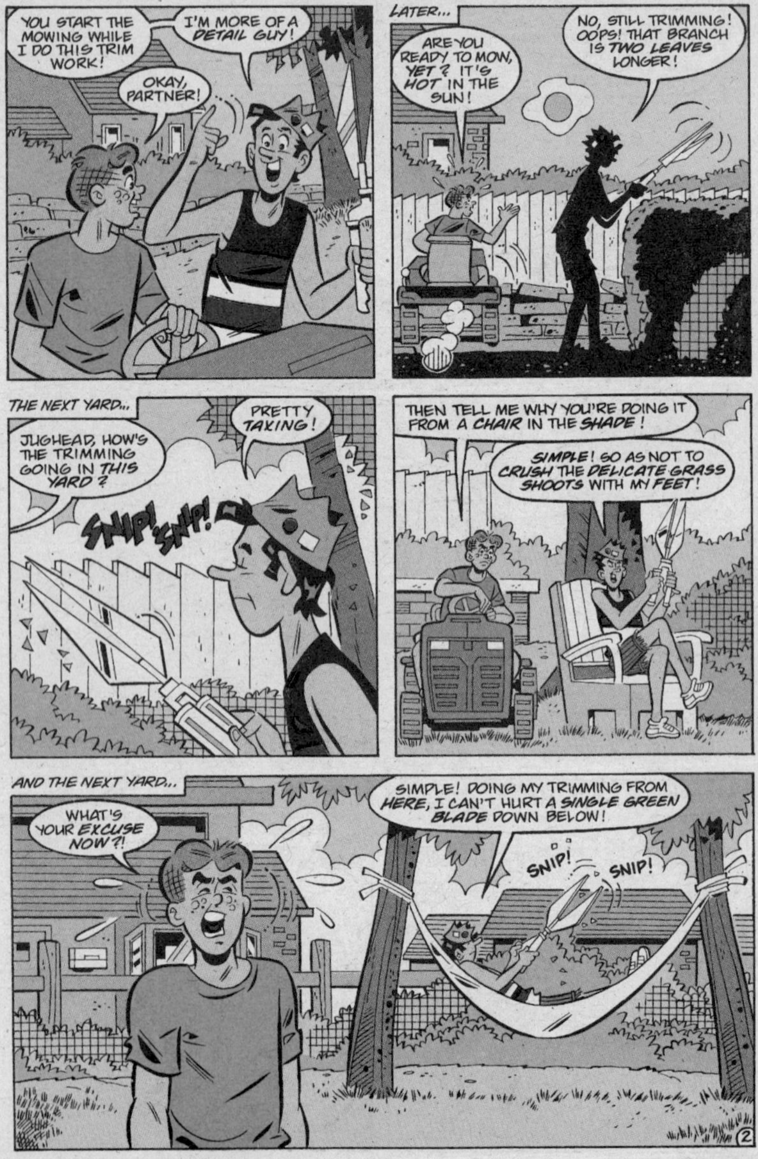
YOU START THE MOWING WHILE I DO THIS TRIM WORK!
I'M MORE OF A DETAIL GUY!
OKAY, PARTNER!
LATER...
ARE YOU READY TO MOW, YET? IT'S HOT IN THE SUN!
NO, STILL TRIMMING! OOPS! THAT BRANCH IS TWO LEAVES LONGER!
THE NEXT YARD...
JUGHEAD, HOW'S THE TRIMMING GOING IN THIS YARD?
PRETTY TAXING!
SNIP! SNIP!
THEN TELL ME WHY YOU'RE DOING IT FROM A CHAIR IN THE SHADE!
SIMPLE! SO AS NOT TO CRUSH THE DELICATE GRASS SHOOTS WITH MY FEET!
AND THE NEXT YARD...
WHAT'S YOUR EXCUSE NOW?!
SIMPLE! DOING MY TRIMMING FROM HERE, I CAN'T HURT A SINGLE GREEN BLADE DOWN BELOW!
SNIP! SNIP!
2

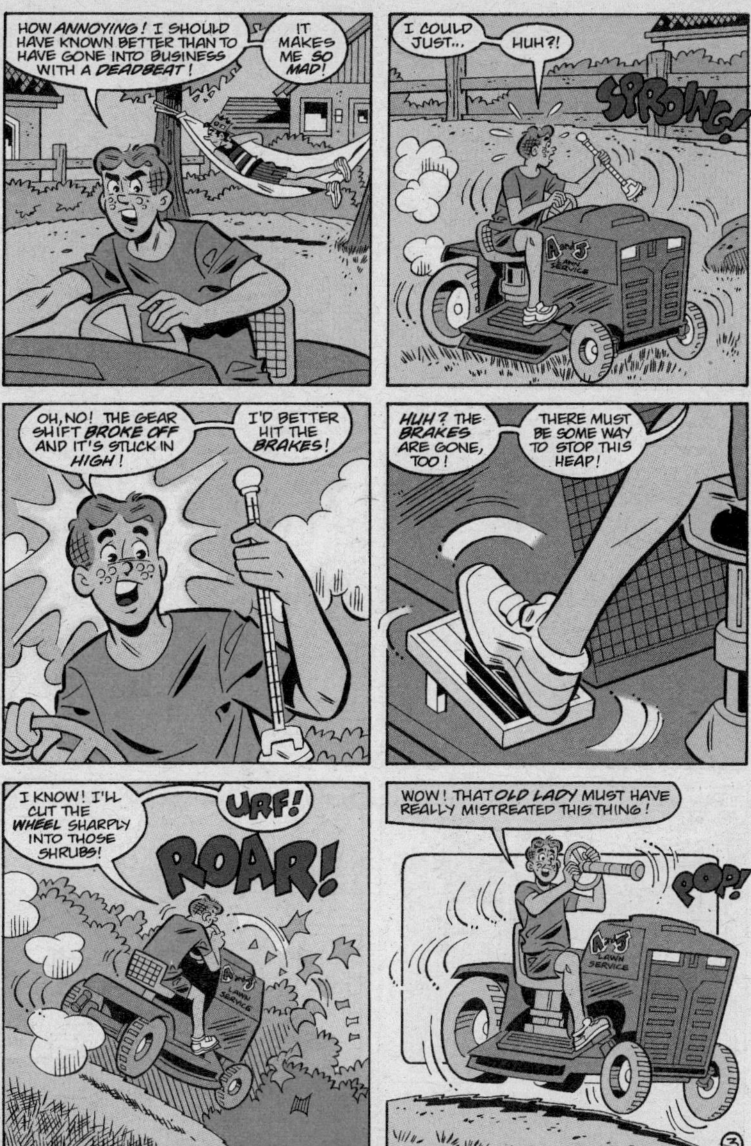
HOW ANNOYING! I SHOULD HAVE KNOWN BETTER THAN TO HAVE GONE INTO BUSINESS WITH A DEADBEAT!
IT MAKES ME SO MAD!
I COULD JUST...
HUH?!
SPROING!
A and J LAWN SERVICE
OH, NO! THE GEAR SHIFT BROKE OFF AND IT'S STUCK IN HIGH!
I'D BETTER HIT THE BRAKES!
HUH? THE BRAKES ARE GONE, TOO!
THERE MUST BE SOME WAY TO STOP THIS HEAP!
I KNOW! I'LL CUT THE WHEEL SHARPLY INTO THOSE SHRUBS!
URF!
ROAR!
WOW! THAT OLD LADY MUST HAVE REALLY MISTREATED THIS THING!
POP!
3

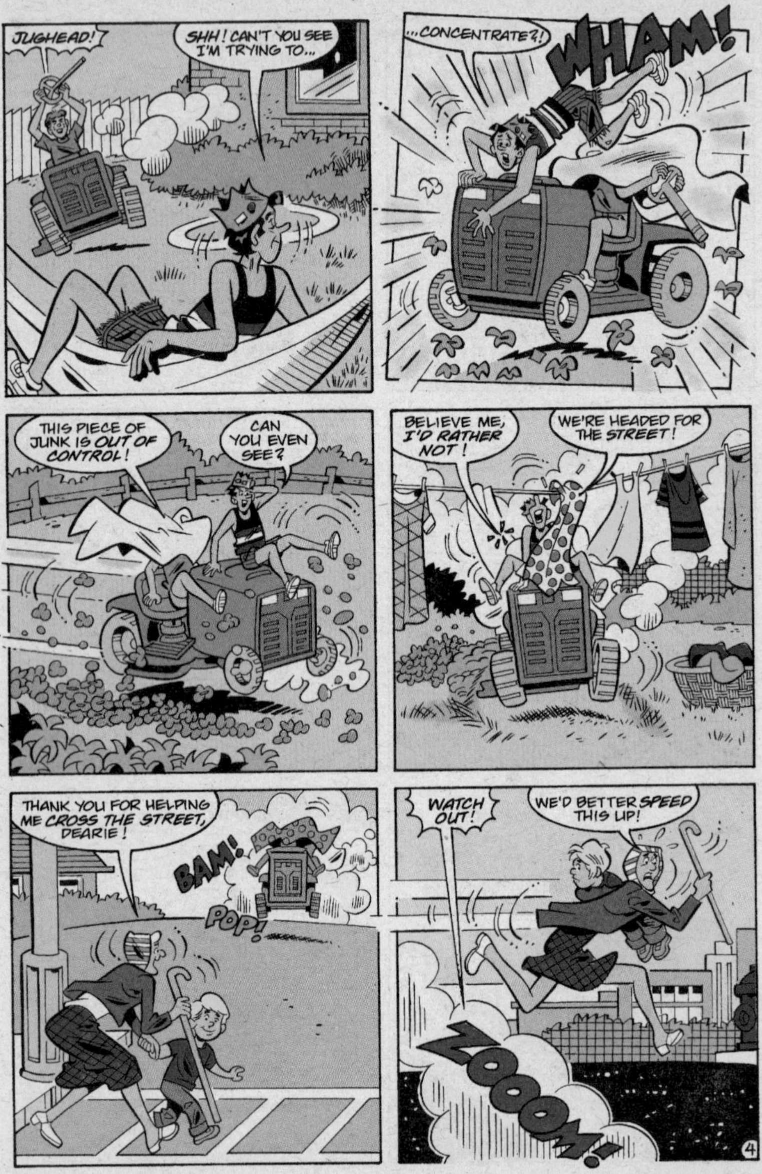

JUGHEAD!
SHH! CAN'T YOU SEE I'M TRYING TO...
...CONCENTRATE?!
WHAM!
THIS PIECE OF JUNK IS OUT OF CONTROL!
CAN YOU EVEN SEE?
BELIEVE ME, I'D RATHER NOT!
WE'RE HEADED FOR THE STREET!
THANK YOU FOR HELPING ME CROSS THE STREET, DEARIE!
BAM!
POP!
WATCH OUT!
WE'D BETTER SPEED THIS UP!
ZOOOOM!
4

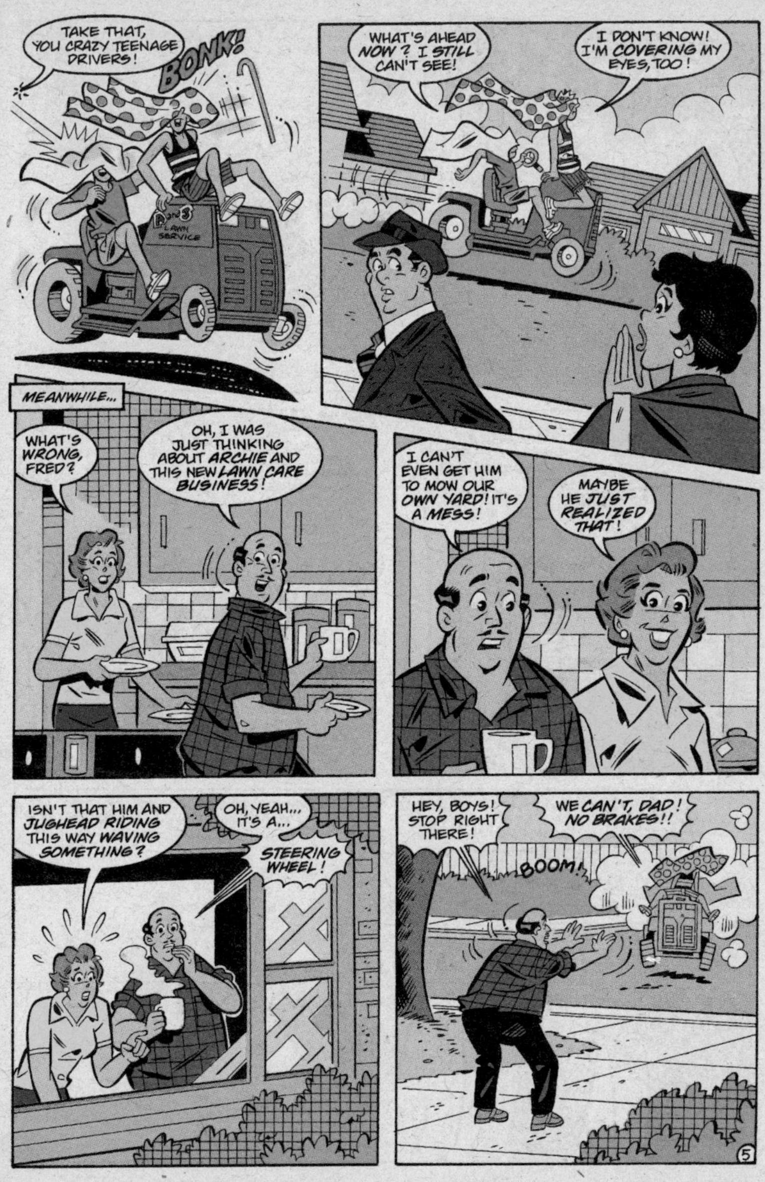

TAKE THAT, YOU CRAZY TEENAGE DRIVERS!
BONK!
A and J LAWN SERVICE
WHAT'S AHEAD NOW? I STILL CAN'T SEE!
I DON'T KNOW! I'M COVERING MY EYES, TOO!
MEANWHILE...
WHAT'S WRONG, FRED?
OH, I WAS JUST THINKING ABOUT ARCHIE AND THIS NEW LAWN CARE BUSINESS!
I CAN'T EVEN GET HIM TO MOW OUR OWN YARD! IT'S A MESS!
MAYBE HE JUST REALIZED THAT!
ISN'T THAT HIM AND JUGHEAD RIDING THIS WAY WAVING SOMETHING?
OH, YEAH... IT'S A...
STEERING WHEEL!
HEY, BOYS! STOP RIGHT THERE!
WE CAN'T, DAD! NO BRAKES!!
BOOM!

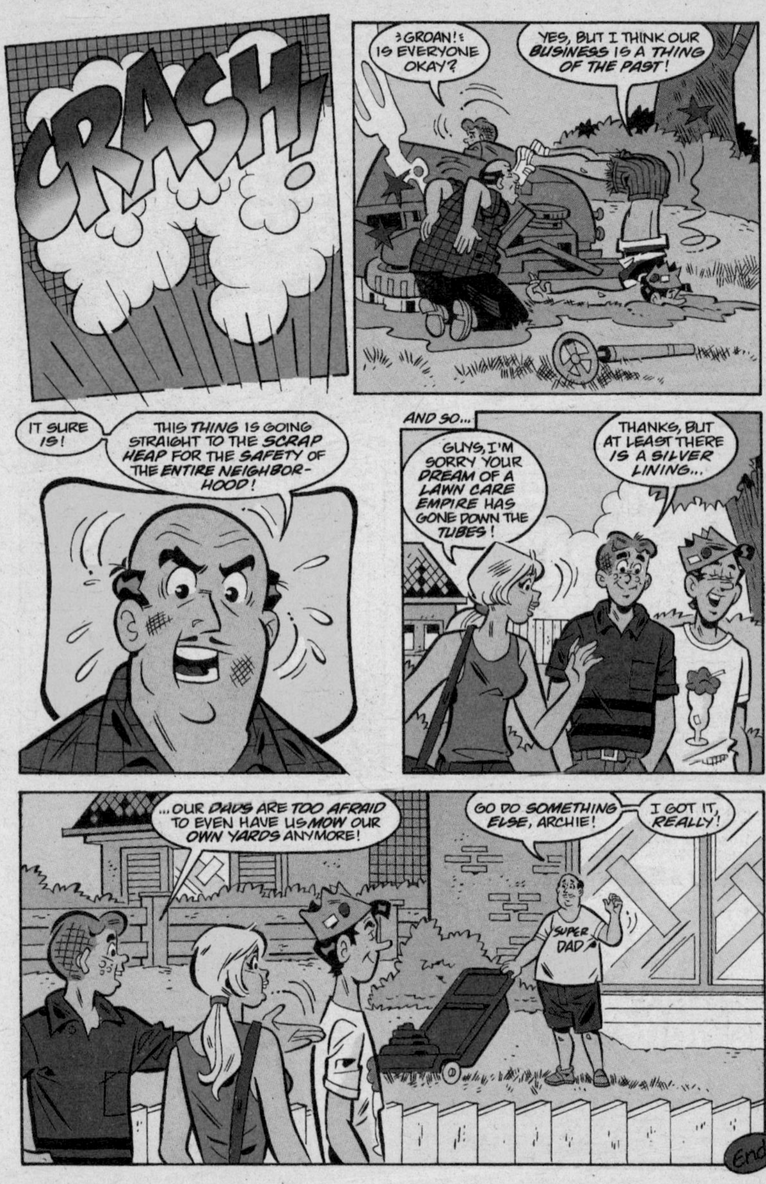
CRASH!
GROAN! IS EVERYONE OKAY?
YES, BUT I THINK OUR BUSINESS IS A THING OF THE PAST!
IT SURE IS!
THIS THING IS GOING STRAIGHT TO THE SCRAP HEAP FOR THE SAFETY OF THE ENTIRE NEIGHBOR-HOOD!
AND SO...
GUYS, I'M SORRY YOUR DREAM OF A LAWN CARE EMPIRE HAS GONE DOWN THE TUBES!
THANKS, BUT AT LEAST THERE IS A SILVER LINING...
...OUR DADS ARE TOO AFRAID TO EVEN HAVE US MOW OUR OWN YARDS ANYMORE!
GO DO SOMETHING ELSE, ARCHIE!
I GOT IT, REALLY!
SUPER DAD
End

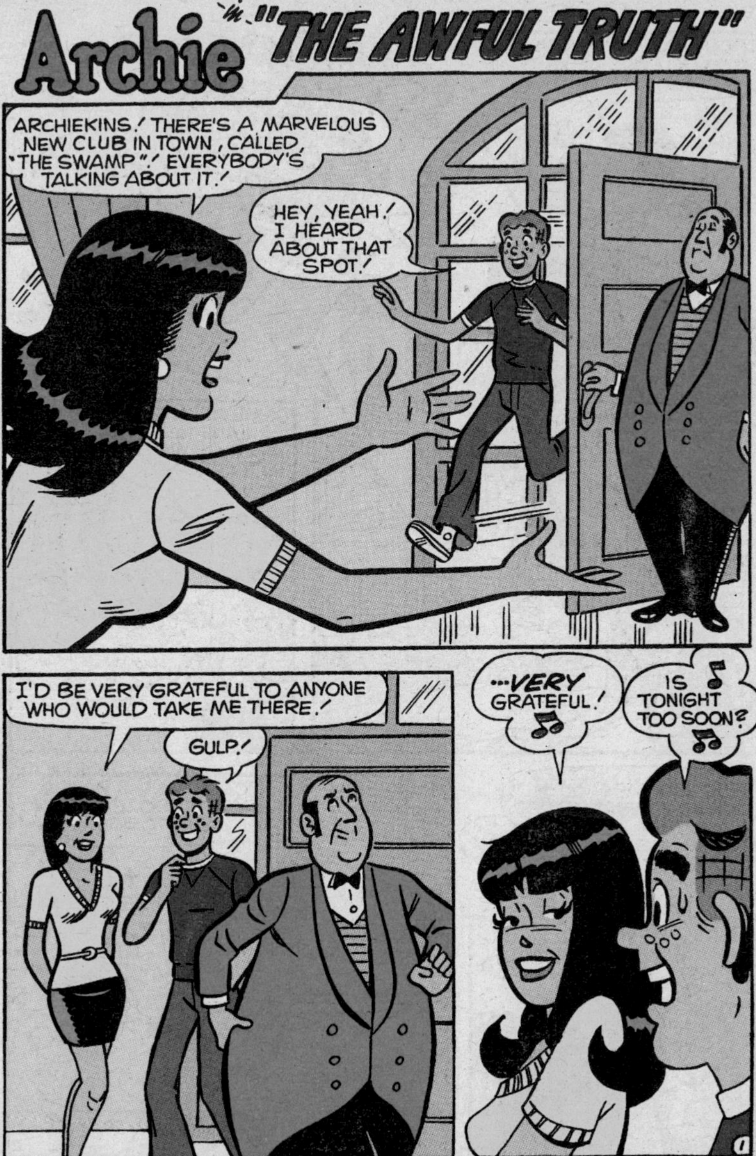
Archie in "THE AWFUL TRUTH"
ARCHIEKINS! THERE'S A MARVELOUS NEW CLUB IN TOWN, CALLED, "THE SWAMP"! EVERYBODY'S TALKING ABOUT IT!
HEY, YEAH! I HEARD ABOUT THAT SPOT!
I'D BE VERY GRATEFUL TO ANYONE WHO WOULD TAKE ME THERE!
GULP!
...VERY GRATEFUL!
IS TONIGHT TOO SOON?
1

Script: Mike Pellowski / Pencils: Bob Bolling / Inks: Rudy Lapick / Letters: Bill Yoshida / Colors: Barry Grossman

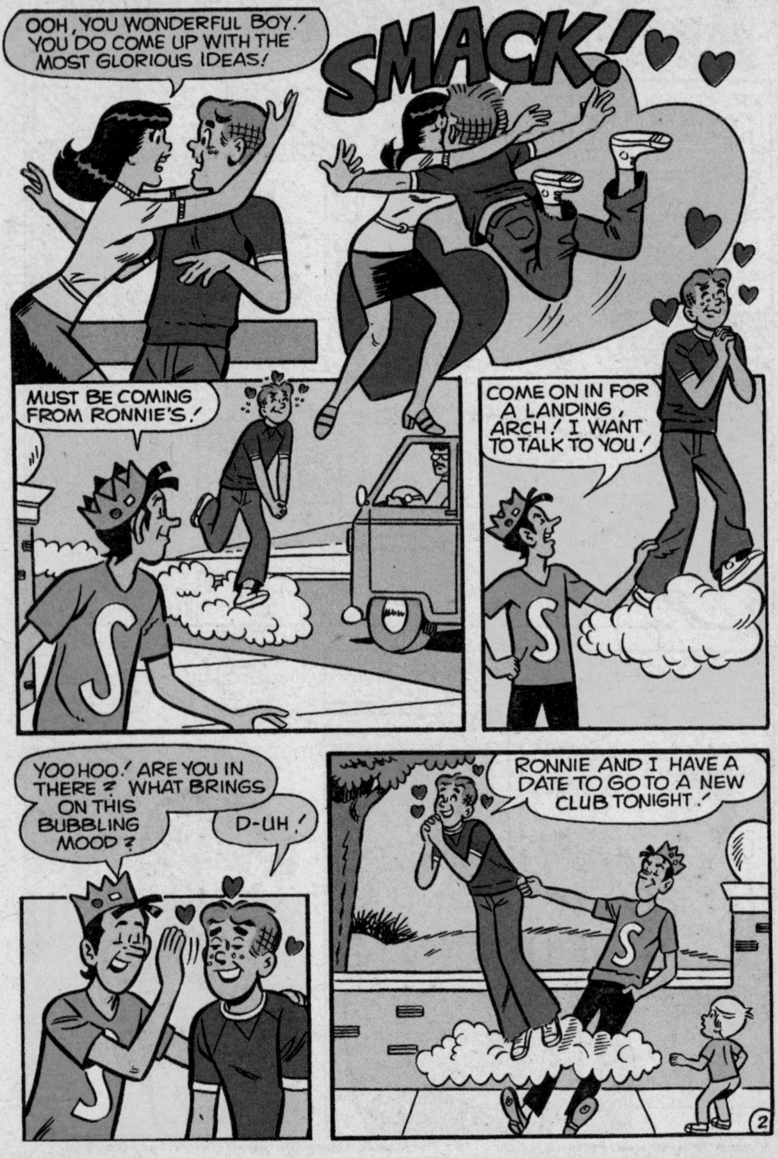
OOH, YOU WONDERFUL BOY! YOU DO COME UP WITH THE MOST GLORIOUS IDEAS!
SMACK!
MUST BE COMING FROM RONNIE'S!
COME ON IN FOR A LANDING, ARCH! I WANT TO TALK TO YOU!
YOO HOO! ARE YOU IN THERE? WHAT BRINGS ON THIS BUBBLING MOOD?
D-UH!
RONNIE AND I HAVE A DATE TO GO TO A NEW CLUB TONIGHT!
2

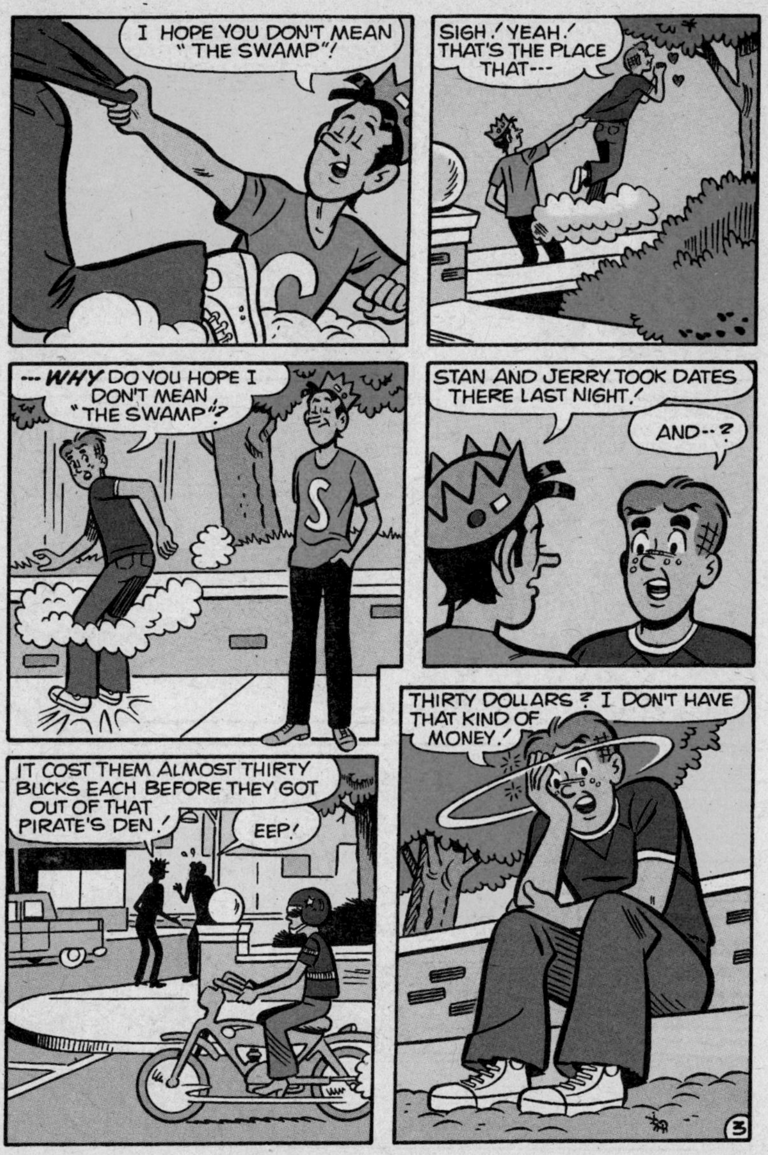
I HOPE YOU DON'T MEAN "THE SWAMP"!
SIGH! YEAH! THAT'S THE PLACE THAT---
---WHY DO YOU HOPE I DON'T MEAN "THE SWAMP"?
STAN AND JERRY TOOK DATES THERE LAST NIGHT!
AND--?
IT COST THEM ALMOST THIRTY BUCKS EACH BEFORE THEY GOT OUT OF THAT PIRATE'S DEN!
EEP!
THIRTY DOLLARS? I DON'T HAVE THAT KIND OF MONEY!
3

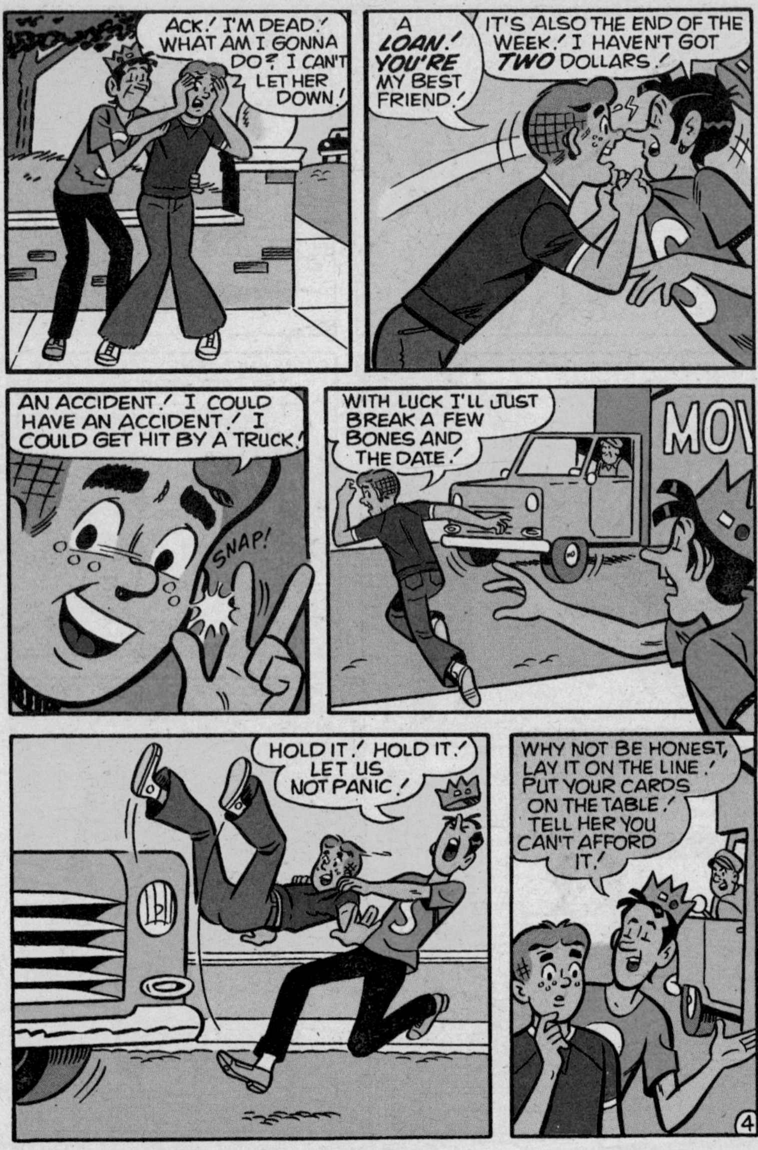
ACK! I'M DEAD! WHAT AM I GONNA DO? I CAN'T LET HER DOWN!
A LOAN! YOU'RE MY BEST FRIEND!
IT'S ALSO THE END OF THE WEEK! I HAVEN'T GOT TWO DOLLARS!
AN ACCIDENT! I COULD HAVE AN ACCIDENT! I COULD GET HIT BY A TRUCK!
SNAP!
WITH LUCK I'LL JUST BREAK A FEW BONES AND THE DATE!
MOV
HOLD IT! HOLD IT! LET US NOT PANIC!
WHY NOT BE HONEST, LAY IT ON THE LINE! PUT YOUR CARDS ON THE TABLE! TELL HER YOU CAN'T AFFORD IT!
4

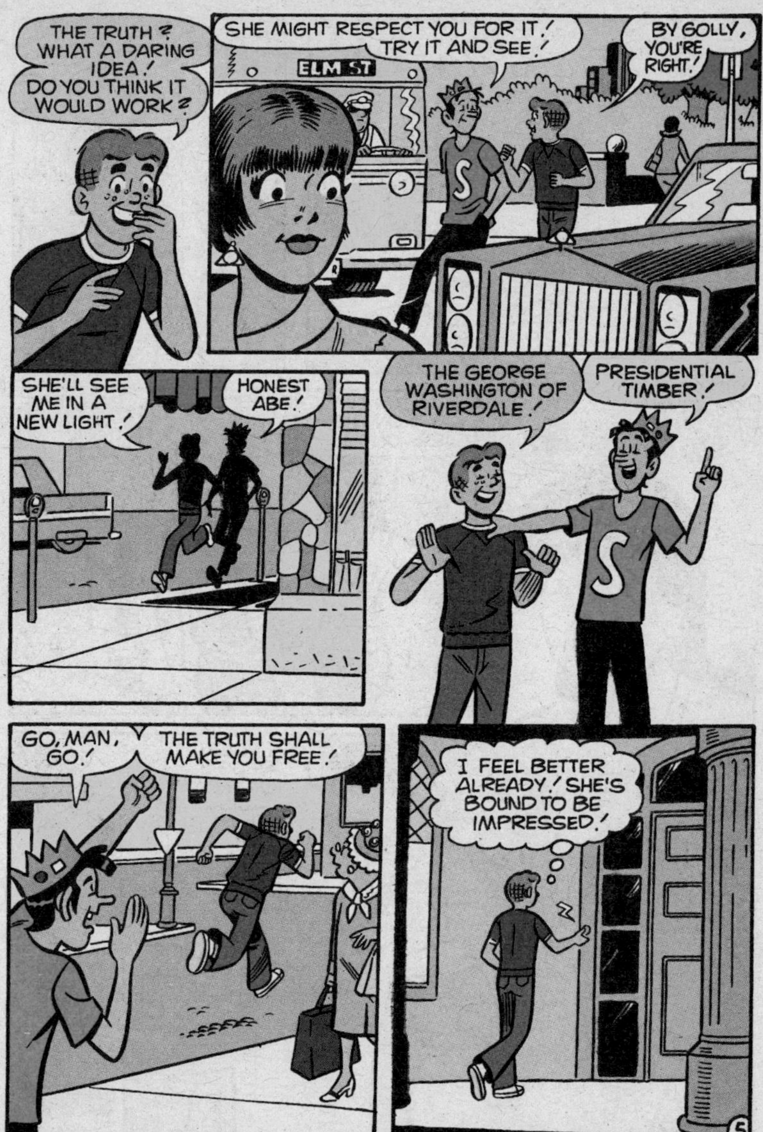
THE TRUTH? WHAT A DARING IDEA! DO YOU THINK IT WOULD WORK?
SHE MIGHT RESPECT YOU FOR IT! TRY IT AND SEE!
ELM ST
BY GOLLY, YOU'RE RIGHT!
SHE'LL SEE ME IN A NEW LIGHT!
HONEST ABE!
THE GEORGE WASHINGTON OF RIVERDALE!
PRESIDENTIAL TIMBER!
GO, MAN, GO!
THE TRUTH SHALL MAKE YOU FREE!
I FEEL BETTER ALREADY! SHE'S BOUND TO BE IMPRESSED!
5

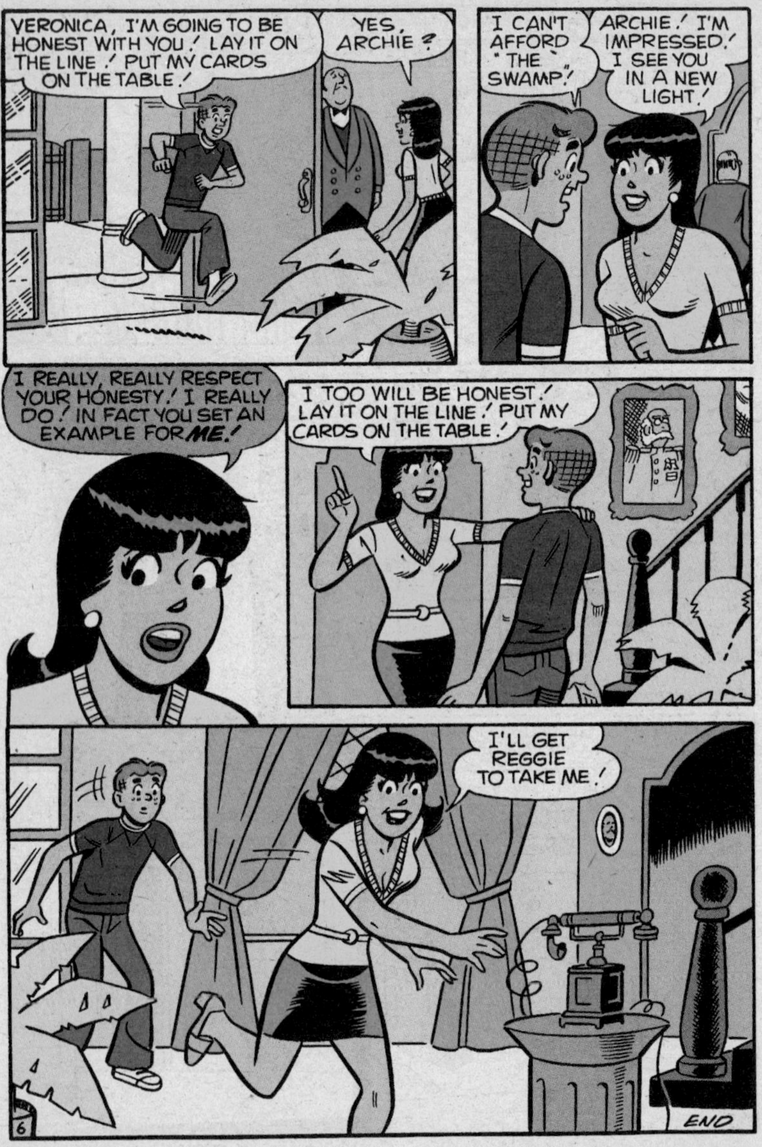
VERONICA, I'M GOING TO BE HONEST WITH YOU! LAY IT ON THE LINE! PUT MY CARDS ON THE TABLE!
YES, ARCHIE?
I CAN'T AFFORD "THE SWAMP"!
ARCHIE! I'M IMPRESSED! I SEE YOU IN A NEW LIGHT!
I REALLY, REALLY RESPECT YOUR HONESTY! I REALLY DO! IN FACT YOU SET AN EXAMPLE FOR ME!
I TOO WILL BE HONEST! LAY IT ON THE LINE! PUT MY CARDS ON THE TABLE!
I'LL GET REGGIE TO TAKE ME!
6
END

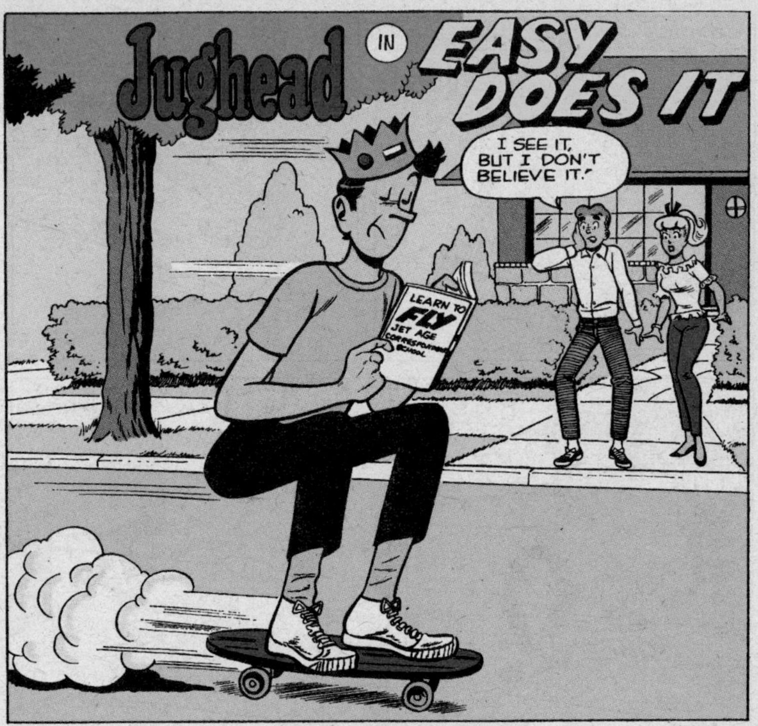
Jughead
IN
EASY DOES IT
I SEE IT, BUT I DON'T BELIEVE IT.
LEARN TO FLY JET AGE CORRESPONDENCE SCHOOL

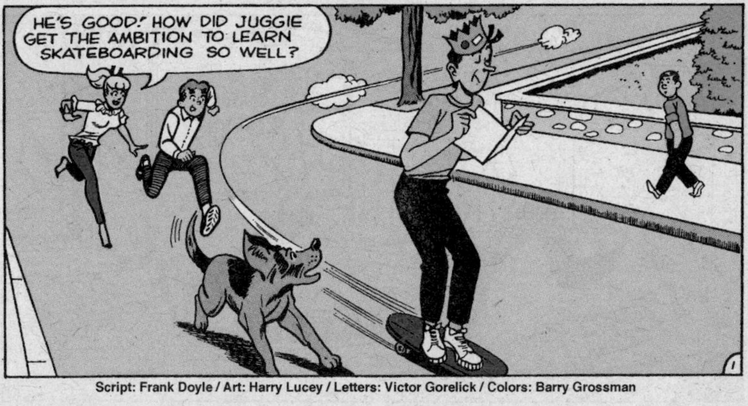
HE'S GOOD! HOW DID JUGGIE GET THE AMBITION TO LEARN SKATEBOARDING SO WELL?
1

Script: Frank Doyle / Art: Harry Lucey / Letters: Victor Gorelick / Colors: Barry Grossman

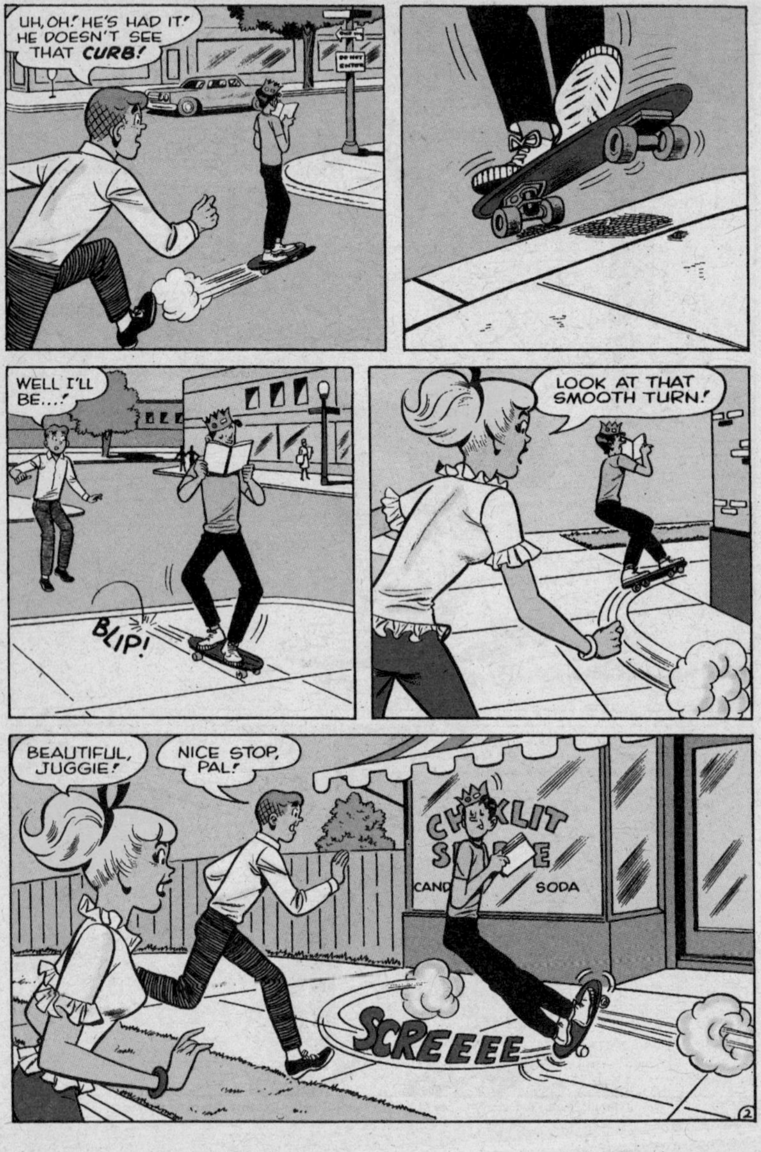

UH, OH! HE'S HAD IT! HE DOESN'T SEE THAT CURB!
WELL I'LL BE...!
BLIP!
LOOK AT THAT SMOOTH TURN!
BEAUTIFUL, JUGGIE!
NICE STOP, PAL!
SCREEEE
SODA
2

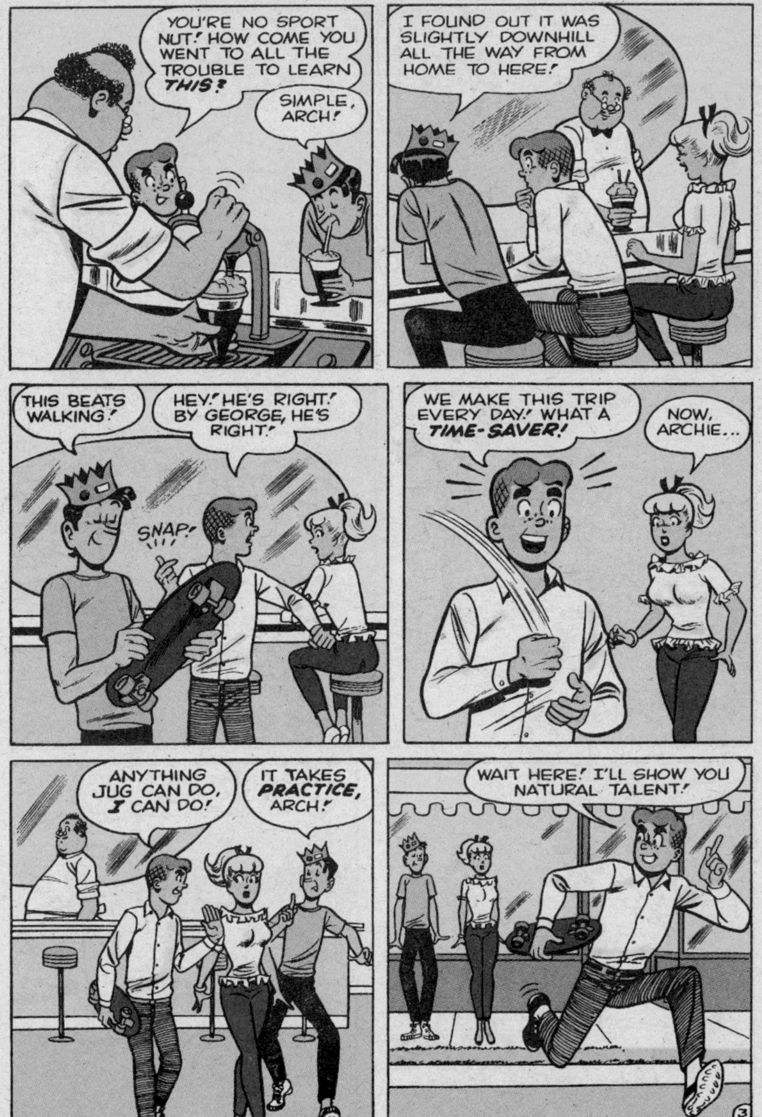
YOU'RE NO SPORT NUT! HOW COME YOU WENT TO ALL THE TROUBLE TO LEARN THIS?
SIMPLE, ARCH!
I FOUND OUT IT WAS SLIGHTLY DOWNHILL ALL THE WAY FROM HOME TO HERE!
THIS BEATS WALKING!
HEY! HE'S RIGHT! BY GEORGE, HE'S RIGHT!
SNAP!
WE MAKE THIS TRIP EVERY DAY! WHAT A TIME-SAVER!
NOW, ARCHIE...
ANYTHING JUG CAN DO, I CAN DO!
IT TAKES PRACTICE, ARCH!
WAIT HERE! I'LL SHOW YOU NATURAL TALENT!
3

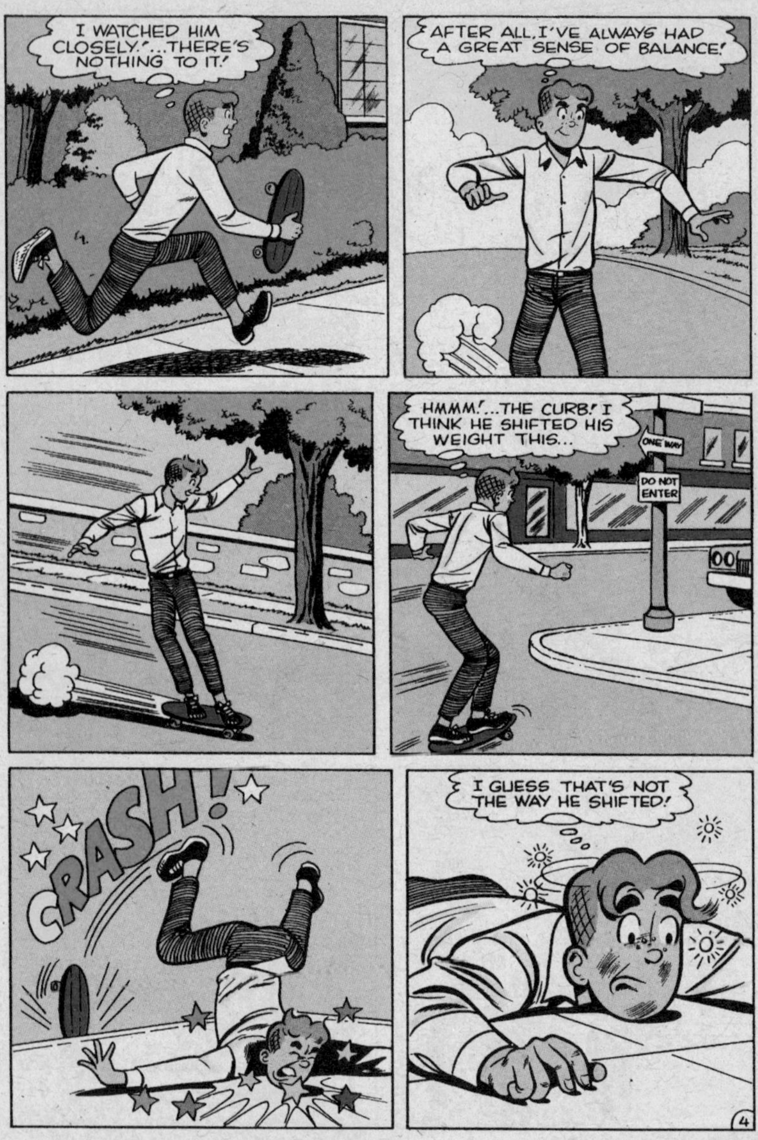

I WATCHED HIM CLOSELY!...THERE'S NOTHING TO IT!
AFTER ALL, I'VE ALWAYS HAD A GREAT SENSE OF BALANCE!
HMMM!...THE CURB! I THINK HE SHIFTED HIS WEIGHT THIS...
ONE WAY
DO NOT ENTER
CRASH!
I GUESS THAT'S NOT THE WAY HE SHIFTED!

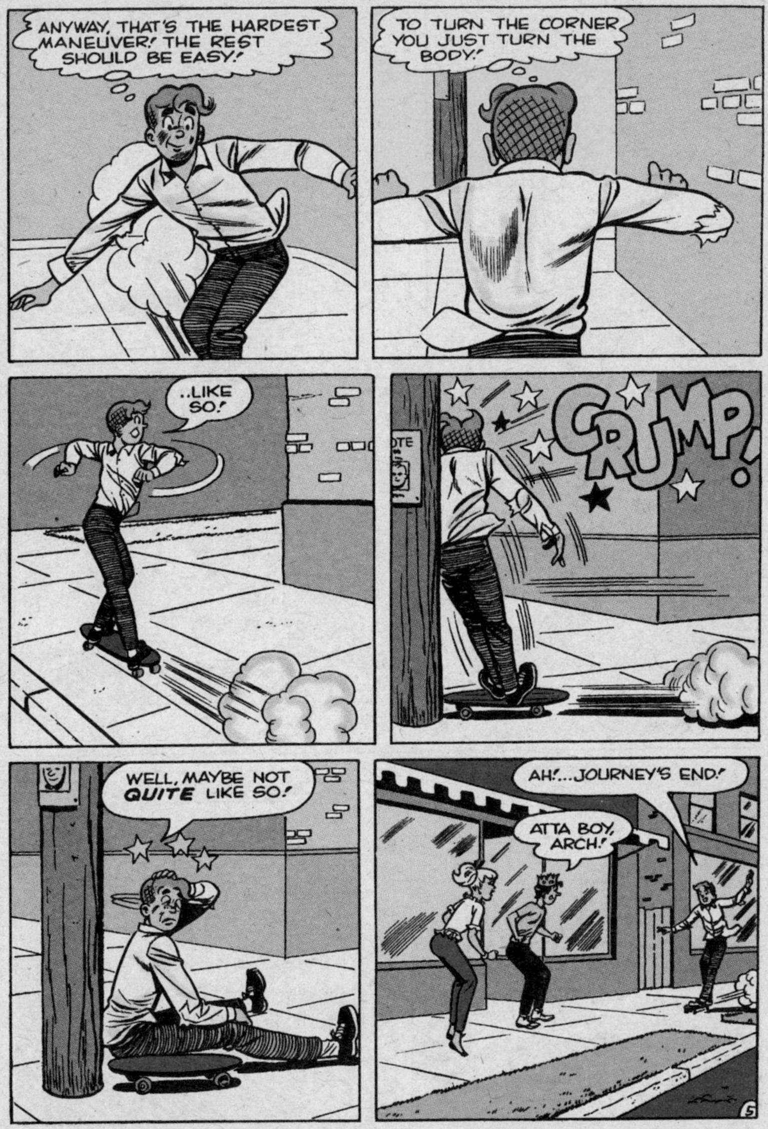
ANYWAY, THAT'S THE HARDEST MANEUVER! THE REST SHOULD BE EASY!
TO TURN THE CORNER YOU JUST TURN THE BODY!
..LIKE SO!
CRUMP!
WELL, MAYBE NOT QUITE LIKE SO!
AH!...JOURNEY'S END!
ATTA BOY, ARCH!
5

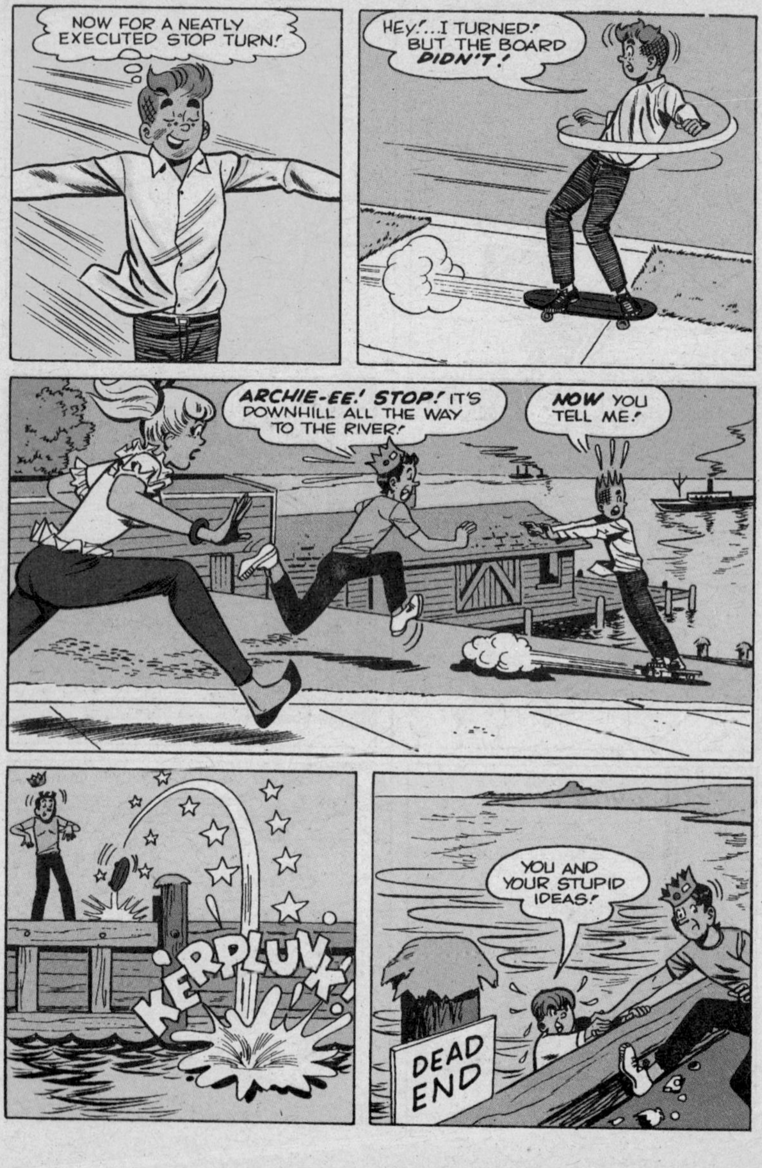
NOW FOR A NEATLY EXECUTED STOP TURN!
HEY!...I TURNED! BUT THE BOARD DIDN'T!
ARCHIE-EE! STOP! IT'S DOWNHILL ALL THE WAY TO THE RIVER!
NOW YOU TELL ME!
KERPLUVK!
YOU AND YOUR STUPID IDEAS!
DEAD END

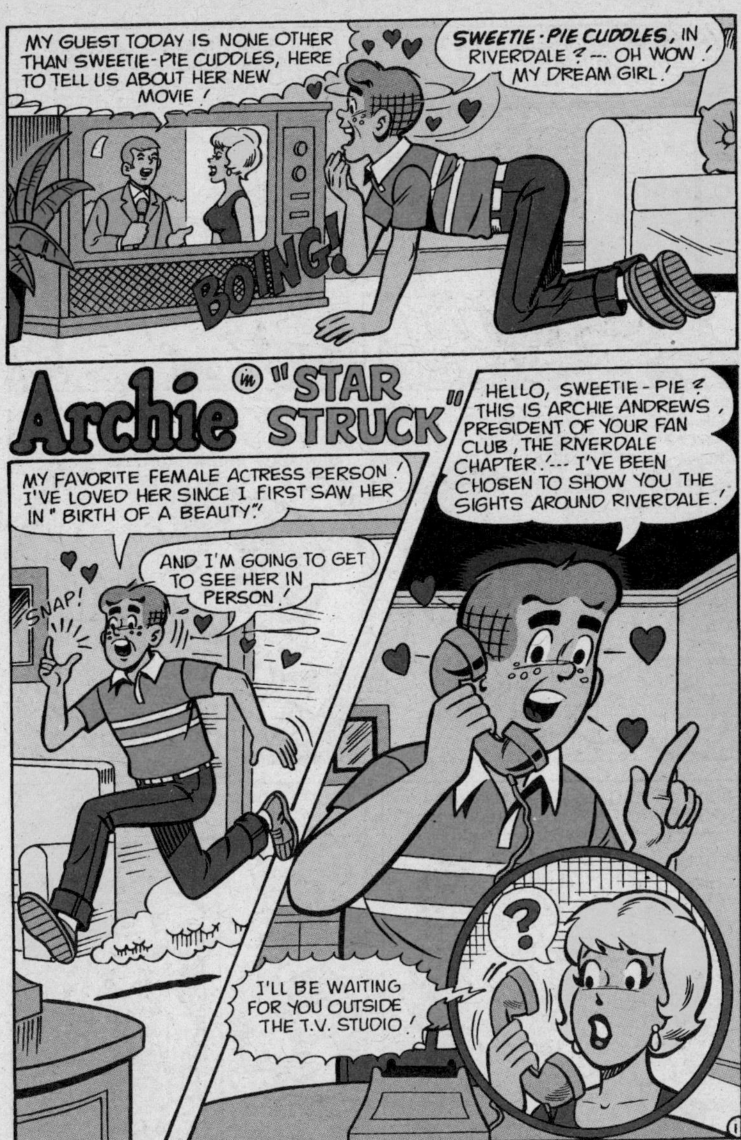
MY GUEST TODAY IS NONE OTHER THAN SWEETIE-PIE CUDDLES, HERE TO TELL US ABOUT HER NEW MOVIE!
SWEETIE-PIE CUDDLES, IN RIVERDALE? -- OH WOW! MY DREAM GIRL!
BOING!
Archie in "STAR STRUCK"
MY FAVORITE FEMALE ACTRESS PERSON! I'VE LOVED HER SINCE I FIRST SAW HER IN "BIRTH OF A BEAUTY"!
SNAP!
AND I'M GOING TO GET TO SEE HER IN PERSON!
HELLO, SWEETIE-PIE? THIS IS ARCHIE ANDREWS, PRESIDENT OF YOUR FAN CLUB, THE RIVERDALE CHAPTER! -- I'VE BEEN CHOSEN TO SHOW YOU THE SIGHTS AROUND RIVERDALE!
?
I'LL BE WAITING FOR YOU OUTSIDE THE T.V. STUDIO!
1

Script & Pencils: Dick Malmgren / Inks: Jon D'Agostino / Letters: Bill Yoshida / Colors: Barry Grossman

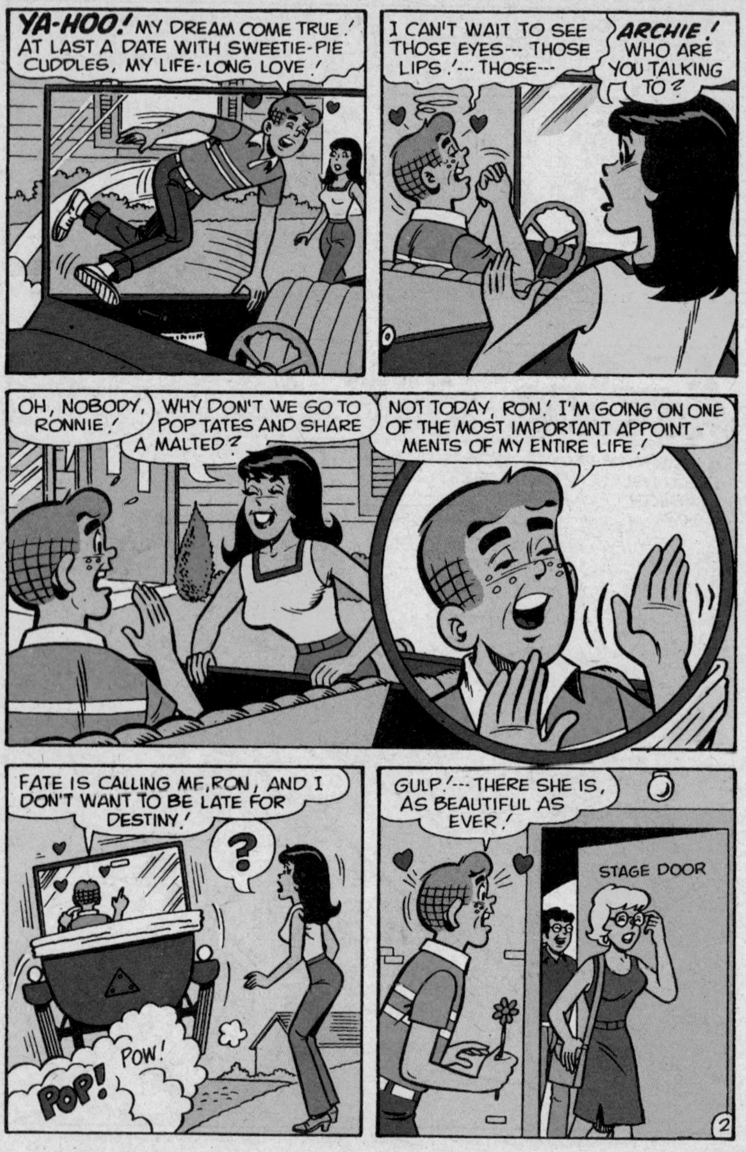
YA-HOO! MY DREAM COME TRUE! AT LAST A DATE WITH SWEETIE-PIE CUDDLES, MY LIFE-LONG LOVE!
I CAN'T WAIT TO SEE THOSE EYES--- THOSE LIPS!--- THOSE---
ARCHIE! WHO ARE YOU TALKING TO?
OH, NOBODY, RONNIE!
WHY DON'T WE GO TO POP TATES AND SHARE A MALTED?
NOT TODAY, RON! I'M GOING ON ONE OF THE MOST IMPORTANT APPOINT-MENTS OF MY ENTIRE LIFE!
FATE IS CALLING ME, RON, AND I DON'T WANT TO BE LATE FOR DESTINY!
?
POW!
POP!
GULP!--- THERE SHE IS, AS BEAUTIFUL AS EVER!
STAGE DOOR
2

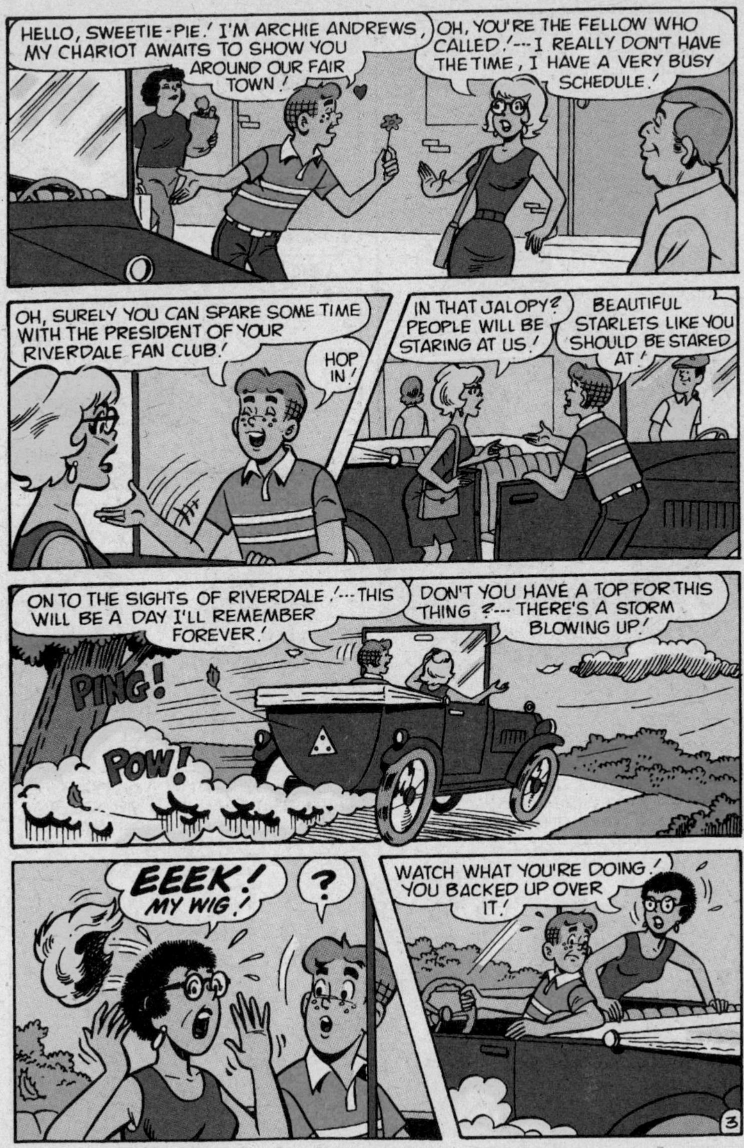
HELLO, SWEETIE-PIE! I'M ARCHIE ANDREWS, MY CHARIOT AWAITS TO SHOW YOU AROUND OUR FAIR TOWN!
OH, YOU'RE THE FELLOW WHO CALLED!--- I REALLY DON'T HAVE THE TIME, I HAVE A VERY BUSY SCHEDULE!
OH, SURELY YOU CAN SPARE SOME TIME WITH THE PRESIDENT OF YOUR RIVERDALE FAN CLUB!
HOP IN!
IN THAT JALOPY? PEOPLE WILL BE STARING AT US!
BEAUTIFUL STARLETS LIKE YOU SHOULD BE STARED AT!
ON TO THE SIGHTS OF RIVERDALE!--- THIS WILL BE A DAY I'LL REMEMBER FOREVER!
DON'T YOU HAVE A TOP FOR THIS THING ?--- THERE'S A STORM BLOWING UP!
PING!
POW!
EEEK! MY WIG!
?
WATCH WHAT YOU'RE DOING! YOU BACKED UP OVER IT!
3

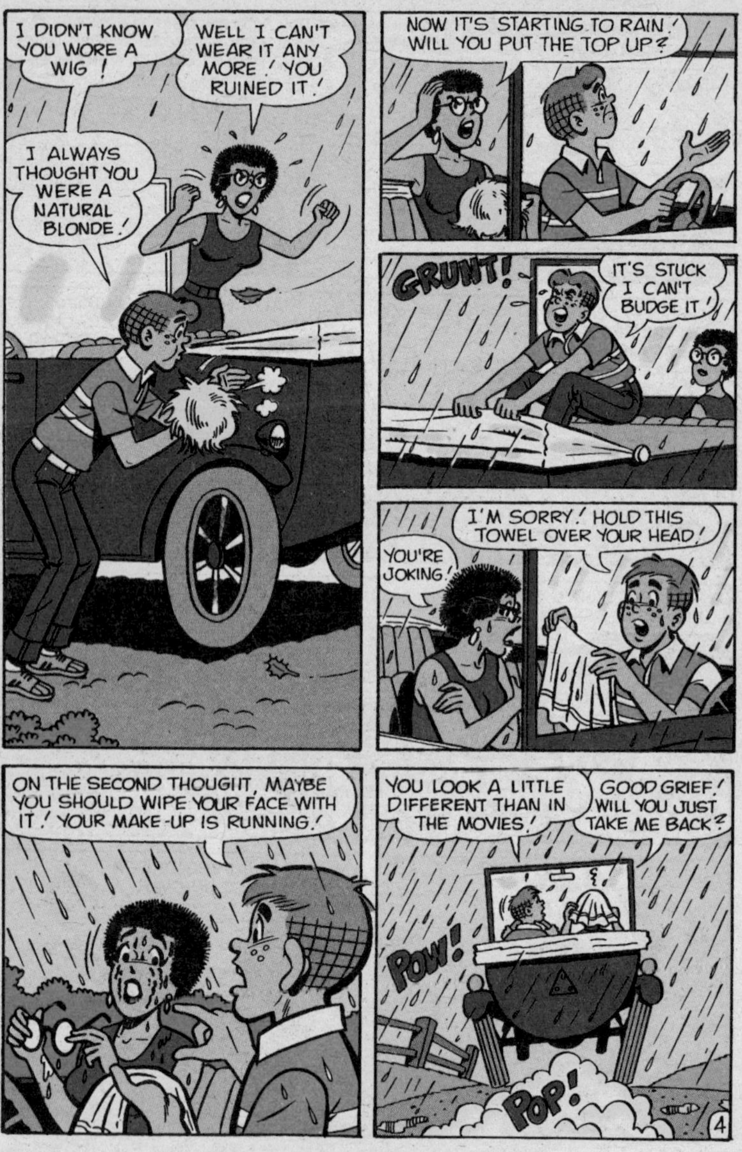
I DIDN'T KNOW YOU WORE A WIG!
WELL I CAN'T WEAR IT ANY MORE! YOU RUINED IT!
I ALWAYS THOUGHT YOU WERE A NATURAL BLONDE!
NOW IT'S STARTING TO RAIN! WILL YOU PUT THE TOP UP?
GRUNT!
IT'S STUCK I CAN'T BUDGE IT!
I'M SORRY! HOLD THIS TOWEL OVER YOUR HEAD!
YOU'RE JOKING!
ON THE SECOND THOUGHT, MAYBE YOU SHOULD WIPE YOUR FACE WITH IT! YOUR MAKE-UP IS RUNNING!
YOU LOOK A LITTLE DIFFERENT THAN IN THE MOVIES!
GOOD GRIEF! WILL YOU JUST TAKE ME BACK?
POW!
POP!

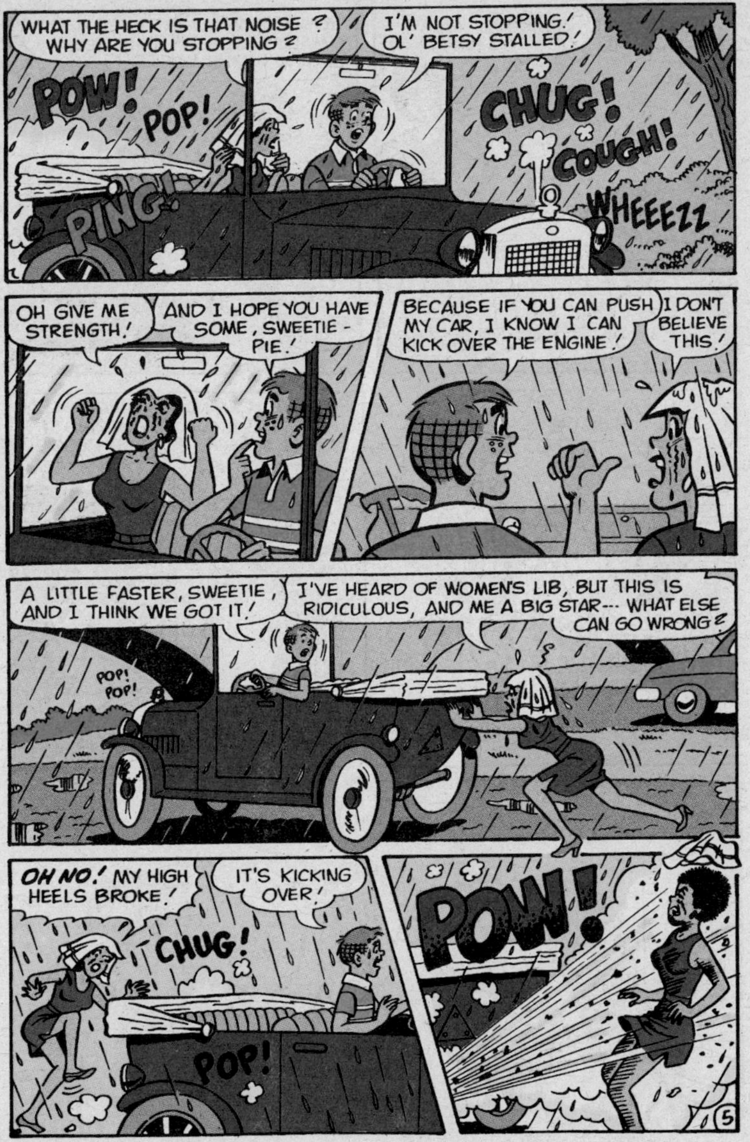
WHAT THE HECK IS THAT NOISE ? WHY ARE YOU STOPPING ?
I'M NOT STOPPING! OL' BETSY STALLED!
POW! POP!
PING!
CHUG!
COUGH!
WHEEEZZ
OH GIVE ME STRENGTH!
AND I HOPE YOU HAVE SOME, SWEETIE-PIE!
BECAUSE IF YOU CAN PUSH MY CAR, I KNOW I CAN KICK OVER THE ENGINE!
I DON'T BELIEVE THIS!
A LITTLE FASTER, SWEETIE, AND I THINK WE GOT IT!
I'VE HEARD OF WOMEN'S LIB, BUT THIS IS RIDICULOUS, AND ME A BIG STAR--- WHAT ELSE CAN GO WRONG?
POP! POP!
OH NO! MY HIGH HEELS BROKE!
IT'S KICKING OVER!
CHUG!
POP!
POW!
5

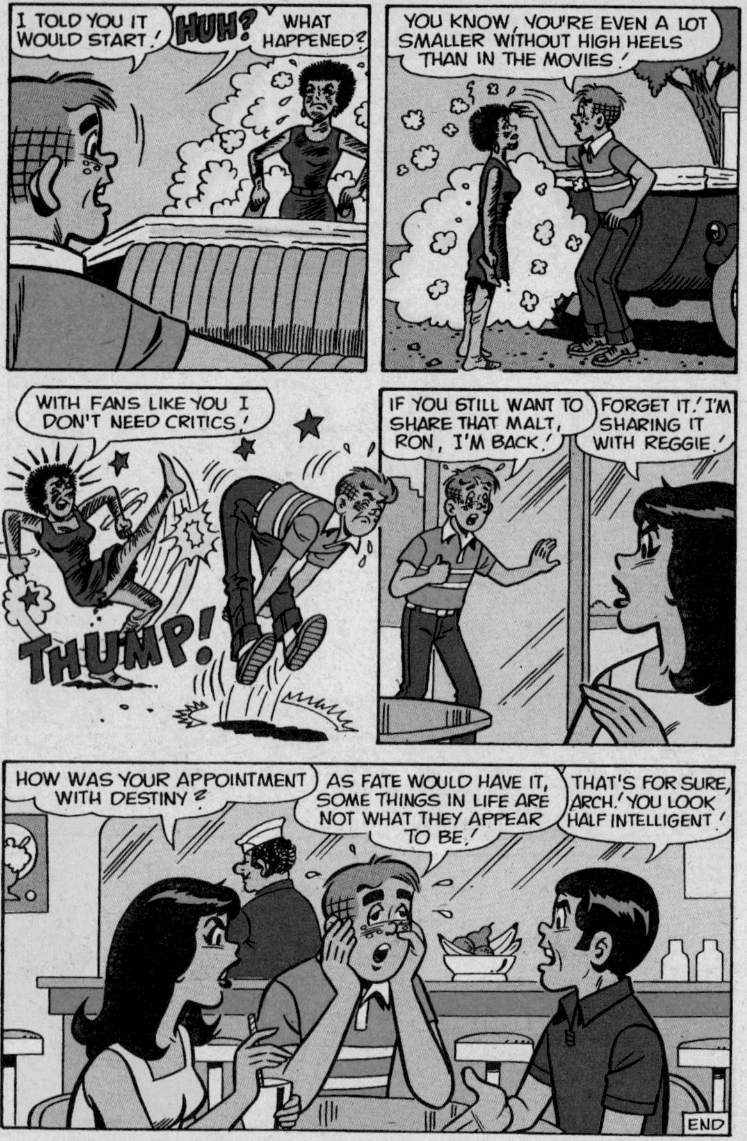
I TOLD YOU IT WOULD START!
HUH? WHAT HAPPENED?
YOU KNOW, YOU'RE EVEN A LOT SMALLER WITHOUT HIGH HEELS THAN IN THE MOVIES!
WITH FANS LIKE YOU I DON'T NEED CRITICS!
THUMP!
IF YOU STILL WANT TO SHARE THAT MALT, RON, I'M BACK!
FORGET IT! I'M SHARING IT WITH REGGIE!
HOW WAS YOUR APPOINTMENT WITH DESTINY?
AS FATE WOULD HAVE IT, SOME THINGS IN LIFE ARE NOT WHAT THEY APPEAR TO BE!
THAT'S FOR SURE, ARCH! YOU LOOK HALF INTELLIGENT!
END

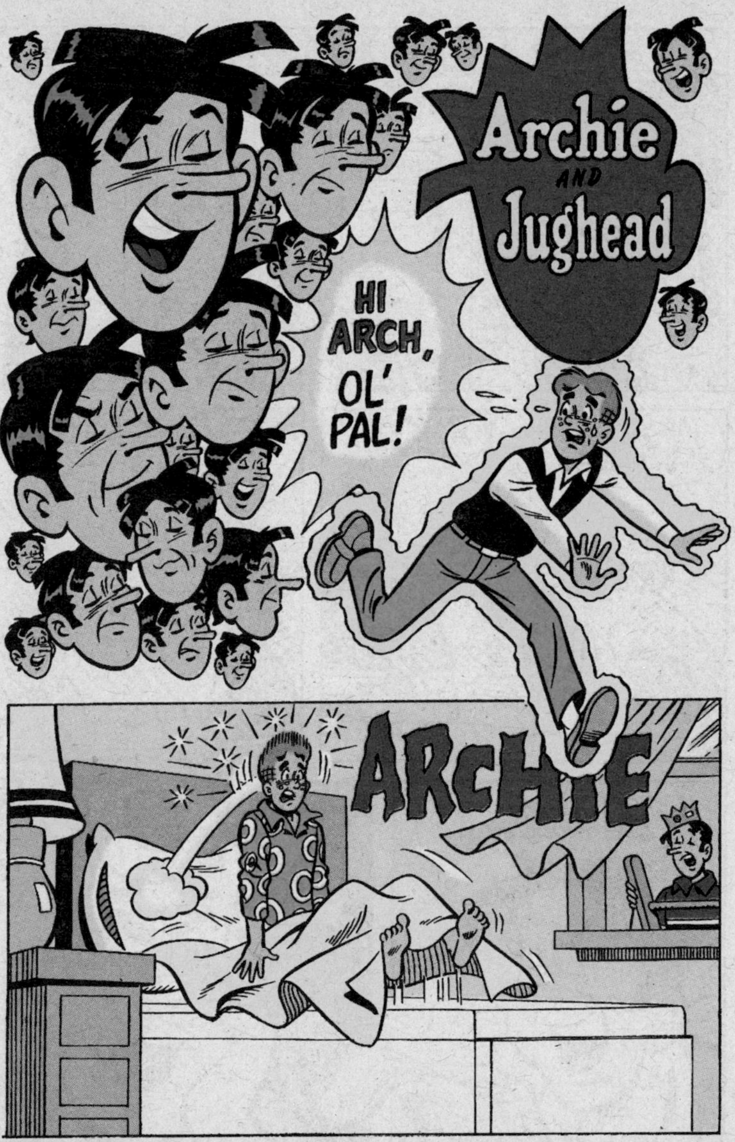
Archie
AND
Jughead
HI ARCH, OL' PAL!
ARCHIE

Script & Pencils: Joe Edwards / Inks: Jon D'Agostino / Letters: Bill Yoshida / Colors: Barry Grossman

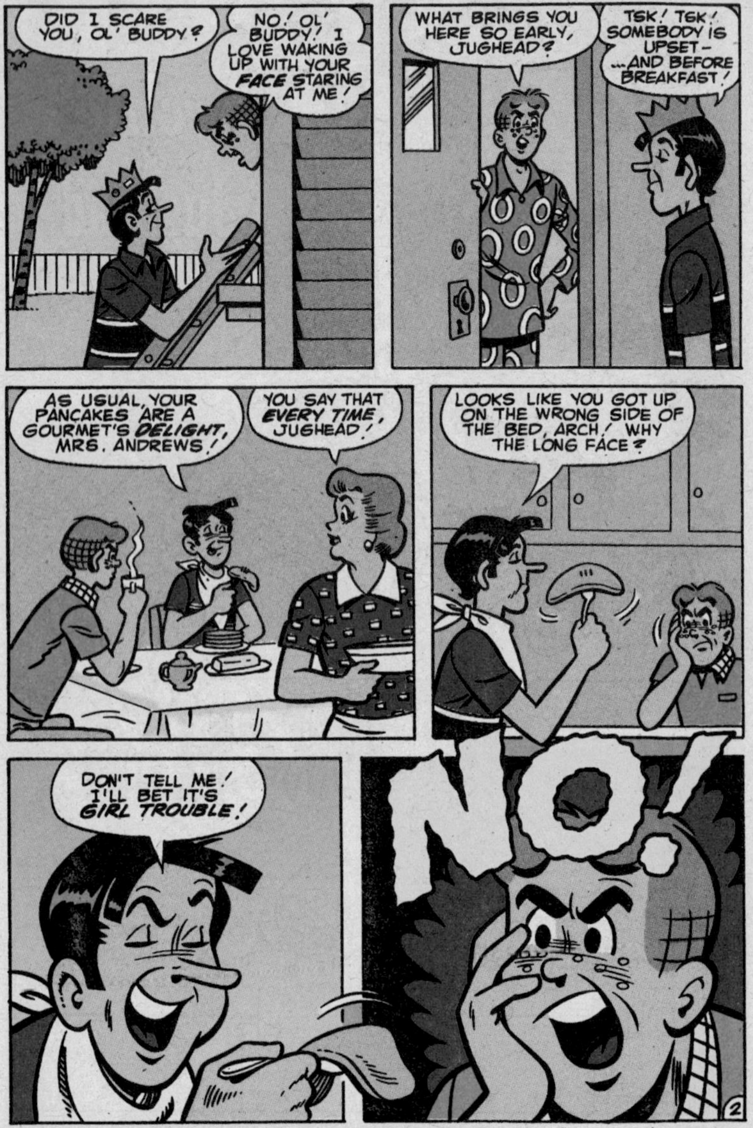
DID I SCARE YOU, OL' BUDDY?
NO! OL' BUDDY! I LOVE WAKING UP WITH YOUR FACE STARING AT ME!
WHAT BRINGS YOU HERE SO EARLY, JUGHEAD?
TSK! TSK! SOMEBODY IS UPSET-- ...AND BEFORE BREAKFAST!
AS USUAL, YOUR PANCAKES ARE A GOURMET'S DELIGHT, MRS. ANDREWS!
YOU SAY THAT EVERY TIME, JUGHEAD!
LOOKS LIKE YOU GOT UP ON THE WRONG SIDE OF THE BED, ARCH! WHY THE LONG FACE?
DON'T TELL ME! I'LL BET IT'S GIRL TROUBLE!
NO!
2

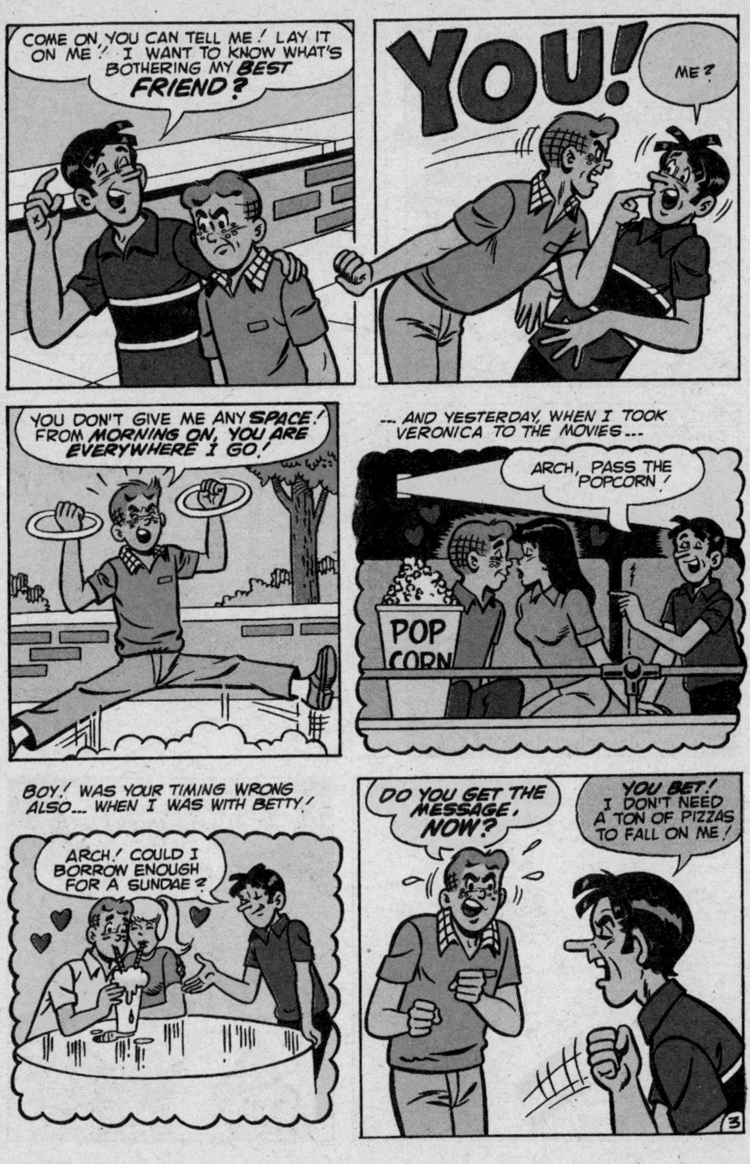
COME ON, YOU CAN TELL ME! LAY IT ON ME!! I WANT TO KNOW WHAT'S BOTHERING MY BEST FRIEND?
YOU!
ME?
YOU DON'T GIVE ME ANY SPACE! FROM MORNING ON, YOU ARE EVERYWHERE I GO!
... AND YESTERDAY, WHEN I TOOK VERONICA TO THE MOVIES...
ARCH, PASS THE POPCORN!
POP CORN
BOY! WAS YOUR TIMING WRONG ALSO... WHEN I WAS WITH BETTY!
ARCH! COULD I BORROW ENOUGH FOR A SUNDAE?
DO YOU GET THE MESSAGE, NOW?
YOU BET! I DON'T NEED A TON OF PIZZAS TO FALL ON ME!
3

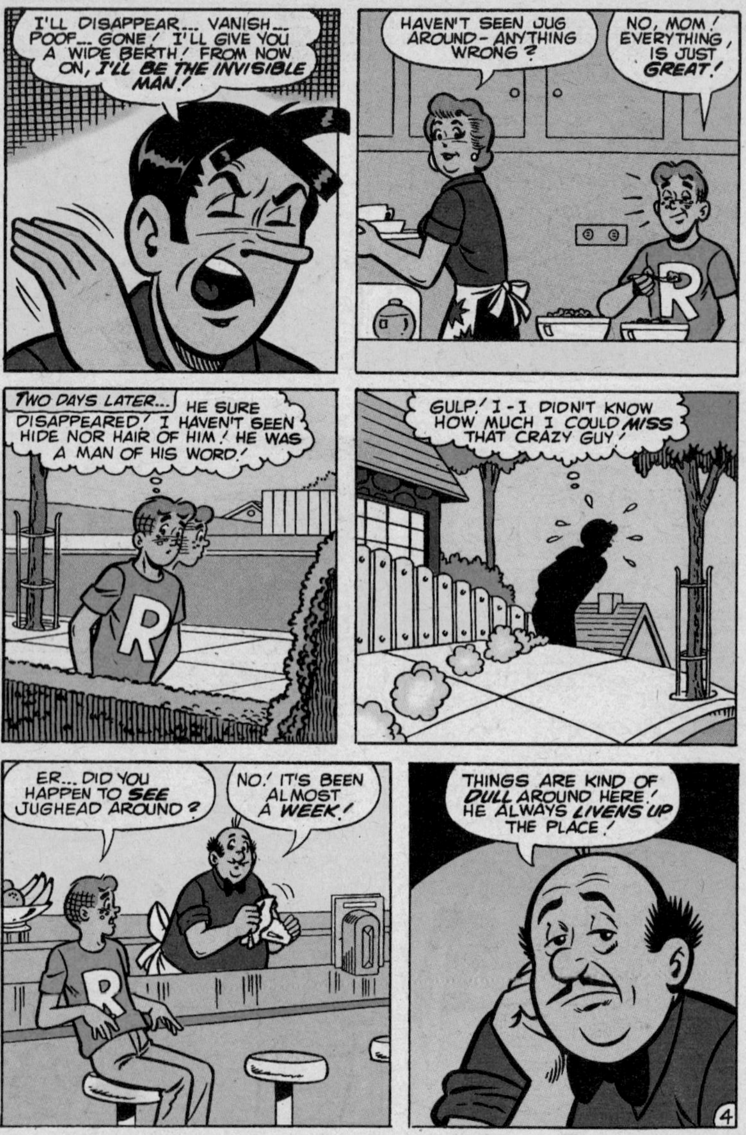
I'LL DISAPPEAR... VANISH... POOF... GONE! I'LL GIVE YOU A WIDE BERTH! FROM NOW ON, I'LL BE THE INVISIBLE MAN!
HAVEN'T SEEN JUG AROUND - ANYTHING WRONG?
NO, MOM! EVERYTHING, IS JUST GREAT!
TWO DAYS LATER...
HE SURE DISAPPEARED! I HAVEN'T SEEN HIDE NOR HAIR OF HIM! HE WAS A MAN OF HIS WORD!
GULP! I-I DIDN'T KNOW HOW MUCH I COULD MISS THAT CRAZY GUY!
ER... DID YOU HAPPEN TO SEE JUGHEAD AROUND?
NO! IT'S BEEN ALMOST A WEEK!
THINGS ARE KIND OF DULL AROUND HERE! HE ALWAYS LIVENS UP THE PLACE!
4

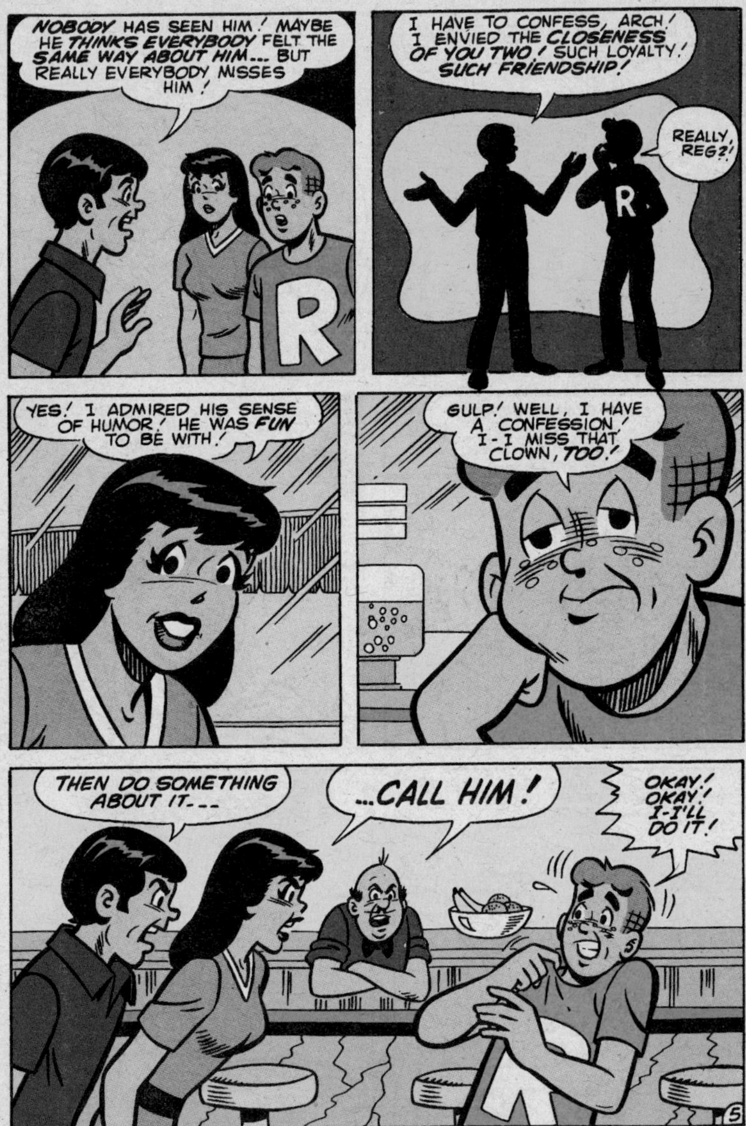
NOBODY HAS SEEN HIM! MAYBE HE THINKS EVERYBODY FELT THE SAME WAY ABOUT HIM... BUT REALLY EVERYBODY MISSES HIM!
I HAVE TO CONFESS, ARCH! I ENVIED THE CLOSENESS OF YOU TWO! SUCH LOYALTY! SUCH FRIENDSHIP!
REALLY, REG?!
YES! I ADMIRED HIS SENSE OF HUMOR! HE WAS FUN TO BE WITH!
GULP! WELL, I HAVE A CONFESSION! I-I MISS THAT CLOWN, TOO!
THEN DO SOMETHING ABOUT IT---
...CALL HIM!
OKAY! OKAY! I-I'LL DO IT!
5

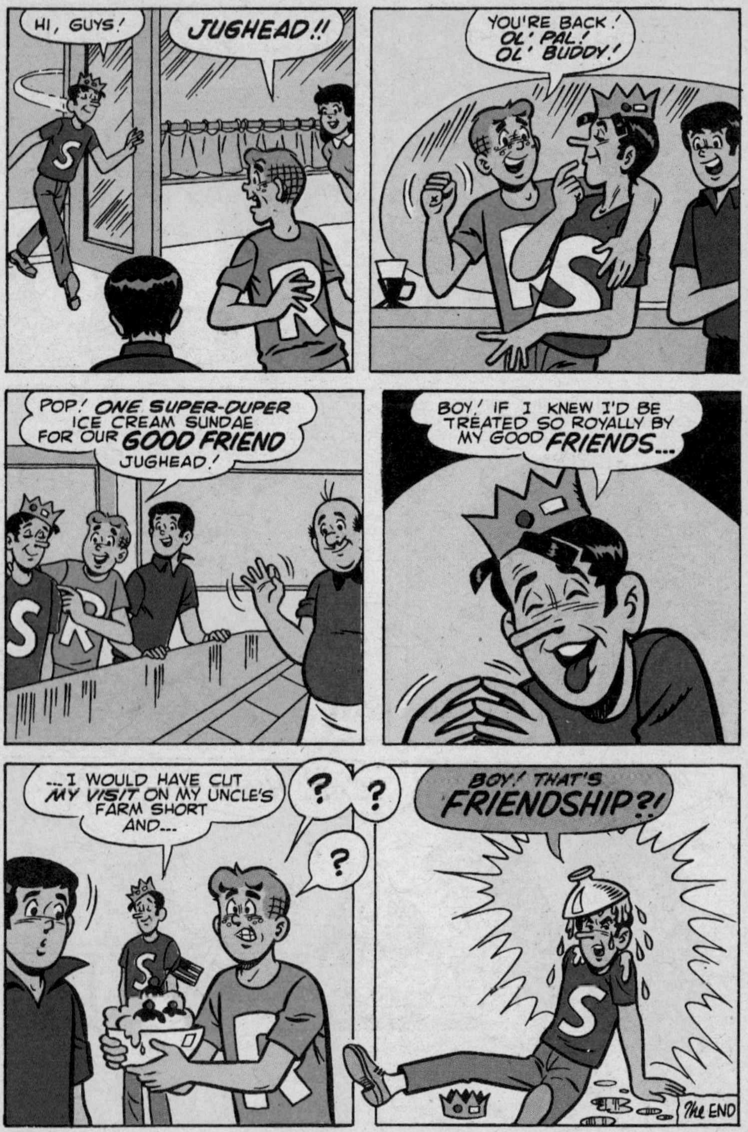
HI, GUYS!
JUGHEAD!!
YOU'RE BACK! OL' PAL! OL' BUDDY!
POP! ONE SUPER-DUPER ICE CREAM SUNDAE FOR OUR GOOD FRIEND JUGHEAD!
BOY! IF I KNEW I'D BE TREATED SO ROYALLY BY MY GOOD FRIENDS...
...I WOULD HAVE CUT MY VISIT ON MY UNCLE'S FARM SHORT AND...
?
?
?
BOY! THAT'S FRIENDSHIP?!
The END

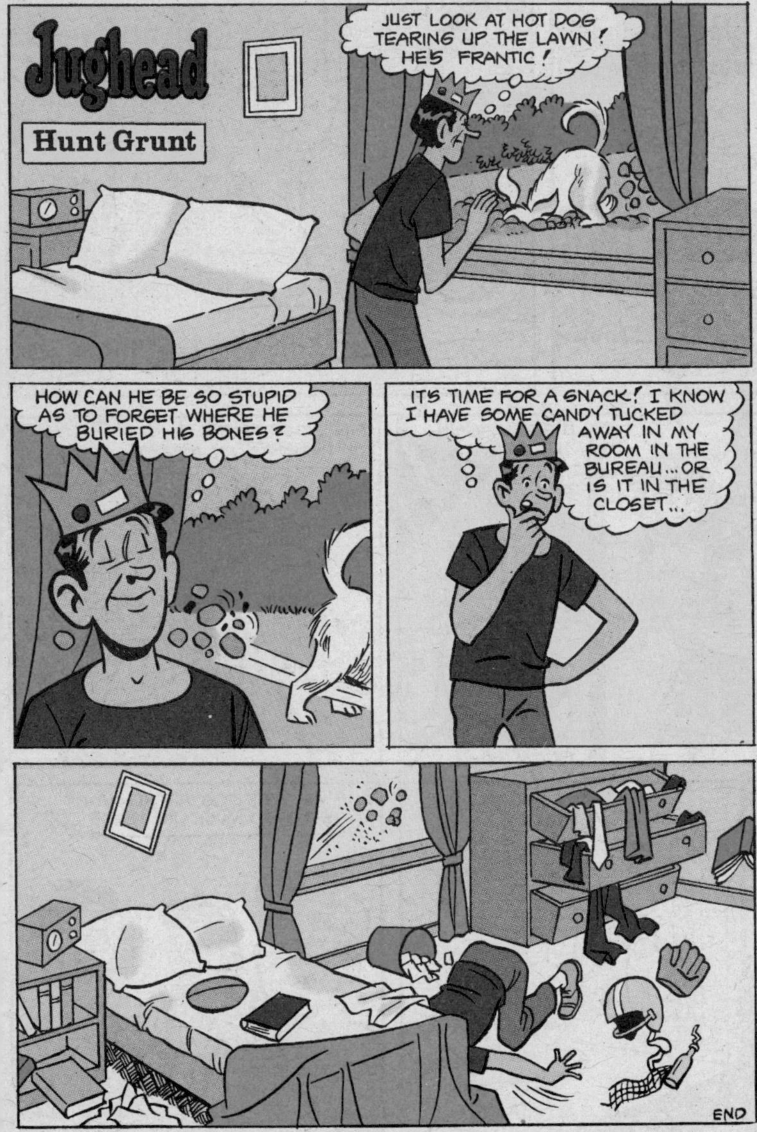
Jughead
Hunt Grunt
JUST LOOK AT HOT DOG TEARING UP THE LAWN! HE'S FRANTIC!
HOW CAN HE BE SO STUPID AS TO FORGET WHERE HE BURIED HIS BONES?
IT'S TIME FOR A SNACK! I KNOW I HAVE SOME CANDY TUCKED AWAY IN MY ROOM IN THE BUREAU...OR IS IT IN THE CLOSET...
END

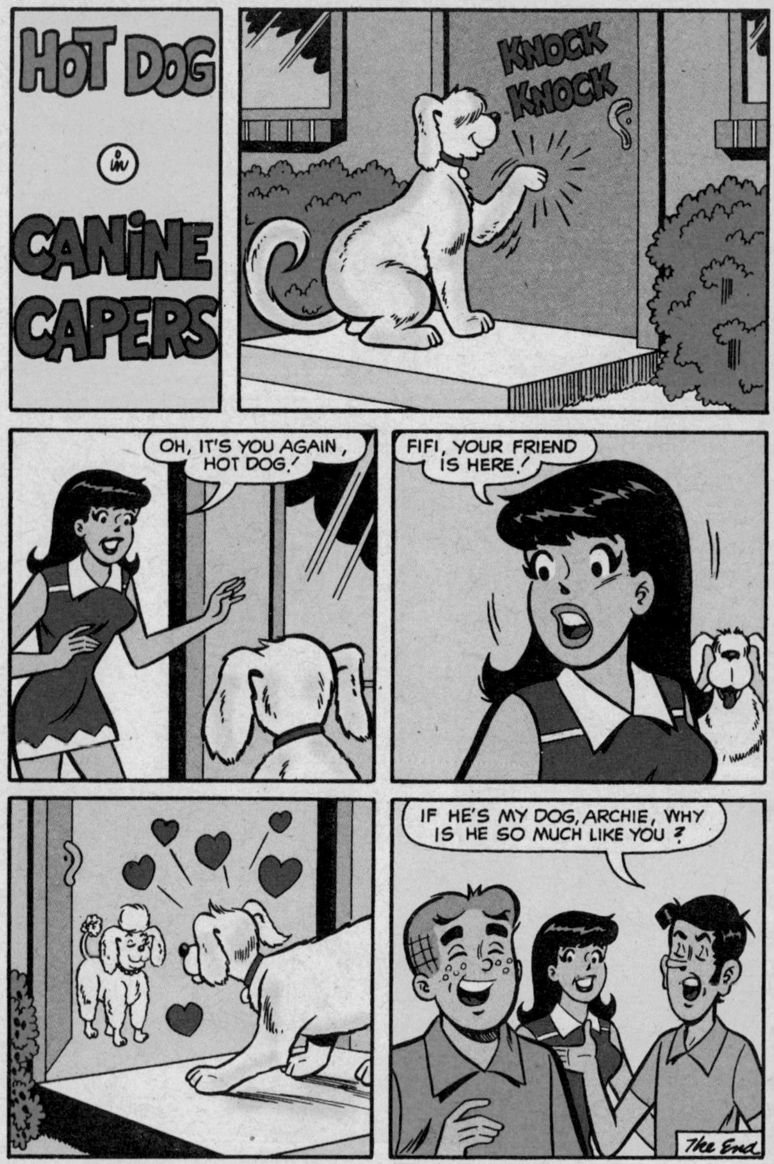
HOT DOG
in
CANINE CAPERS
KNOCK KNOCK
OH, IT'S YOU AGAIN, HOT DOG!
FIFI, YOUR FRIEND IS HERE!
IF HE'S MY DOG, ARCHIE, WHY IS HE SO MUCH LIKE YOU?
The End